DARON'S GUITAR CHRONICLES

Volume 3

Also by Cecilia Tan

Short Story collections:
White Flames
Black Feathers
Edge Plays
Telepaths Don't Need Safewords

The *Magic University* Series:
The Siren and the Sword
The Tower and the Tears
The Incubus and the Angel
The Poet and the Prophecy
Spellbinding: Tales from Magic University

The *Struck by Lightning* Series:
Slow Surrender
Slow Seduction
Slow Satisfaction

Erotic romances:
The Prince's Boy
The Hot Streak
Mind Games
The Velderet
Royal Treatment

The *Secrets of a Rock Star* Series:
Taking the Lead
Wild Licks
Hard Rhythm

The Vanished Chronicles:
Initiates of the Blood

DARON'S GUITAR CHRONICLES

Volume 3

A story of rock and roll, coming out,
and coming of age in the 1980s and '90s

by Cecilia Tan

Daron's Guitar Chronicles Omnibus 3

ISBN 978-153318426-9

Contents of this ebook were serialized online at Daron's Guitar Chronicles (http://daron.ceciliatan.com) between November 11, 2011 and May 28, 2013. There may be slight variations in the text between the serialized version and the book.

Cover and interior design by Gilly Rosenthol
Copyediting by Jennifer Levine

Published by Cecilia Tan
with the help of Kickstarter backers
39 Hurlbut Street
Cambridge, MA 02138

http://daron.ceciliatan.com

CONTENTS

PART TEN: AUGUST 1989

PART ELEVEN: DECEMBER 1989

ZIGGY'S DIARY

PART TWELVE: JANUARY 1990

PART THIRTEEN: AUGUST 1990

THE Hollywood REPORTER

Spotted Around Town: Funnyman **Robin Williams** is rumored to be mentoring **Ethan Hawke** after Hawke's sensational breakout performance in *Dead Poet's Society*...the two of them were spotted lunching at Rubio's with **Robert Hart**, the latter's agent... Cheerleader-choreographer-turned-chart-topper **Paula Abdul**'s birthday celebration at The Hunt Club was supposed to be low key but with her album still spawning No. 1 hits the gathering brought out the likes of **Keanu Reeves**, director **Oliver Stone**, **Emilio Estevez**, and rockers **Susanna Hoffs** (The Bangles) and **Jane Wiedlin** (The GoGos)....Overnight sensation **Sarah Rogue** has been seen about town numerous times with soulful music man **Daron Marks** (Moondog Three)... **Harrison Ford** and his *Last Crusade* co-star **John Rhys-Davies** were saved from the breakdown of their Jeep north of Malibu by a passing minivan, driven by none other than **Thomas F. Wilson** (recently re-signed to reprise his role of Biff Tannen in the third *Back to the Future* film).

Daron Moondog has been lying low since Moondog Three lead singer Ziggy's rehab stint and subsequent departure for India. We caught up with the rocker at last month's gala fundraiser to benefit the Good Shepherd Shelter.

US: I'll come right out and ask, anything you can tell us about Ziggy or when Moondog Three might return to the studio?

DM: You guys probably know more than I do about Ziggy's whereabouts right now.

US: Have you relocated to Hollywood permanently?

DM: I'm keeping busy. There's a lot of work here. But I wouldn't say it's permanent, no.

US: We heard you played on a Battleaxe record and a Garth Brooks record in the same week.

DM: It wasn't Garth Brooks but I've done a lot of sessions, yeah. So you'll be hearing a lot of me even if there's nothing new from Moondog Three.

US: How'd you get involved with Lacey Montaigne's domestic violence campaign?

DM: Well, I know her through Christian [Moondog Three drummer -ed.] and it just seemed like a good idea. I'm glad to be able to do something good for the world.

Remo Cutler's Nomad are here to do a series of sold out shows before heading to Australia, but an injury to Cutler has prompted the veteran rocker to call in reinforcements. Daron Marks, Cutler's protegé, has been tapped to fill in on guitar and join a beefed-up Nomad lineup that includes not only the core players of Alex and Alan Mazel and Martin Jansen, but a collection of backing musicians highlighting Nomad's American folk and blues roots. "No harmonica player, yet, though," Cutler jokes, "and I never could get the hang of that thing."

The set is constructed of crowd-pleasers from the band's ever-growing catalog of hits, any of which could turn into a long jam. Their opening night concert had a few glitches but otherwise was a welcome taste of home for the few Americans in the audience. Nomad's popularity in Japan has matched their US growth and this is their third such tour. When asked if they change their set for Japanese audiences, Cutler replied, "We change our set for every tour. We added Cray on pedal steel this time around to give folks a little different sound."

A jet-lagged Marks seems to be taking his first trip to Tokyo in stride. When asked how he's enjoying his trip so far, he says, "It's nice. The food's good." When a reporter expresses surprise that Marks had previously eaten Japanese food, he replies, "In America poor musicians and students pretty much live on ramen noodles, you know." When asked what he's enjoyed about the country so far, that would appear to be a visit to Tokyo's musical instrument district.

Nomad's biggest hit in Japan is the song "Widowmaker" from their now-classic album Gary's Garage. When asked about the subject of the song, Cutler explains, "It's an expression in English with a couple of meanings. In a rodeo it's the name you'd give to a bull so difficult to ride you might die. It's also the word for a dead branch on a tree that could fall and kill you, and in medicine it's the vein in your heart that'll kill you instantly if it gets blocked. But, you know, the whole thing's a metaphor about being driven to do self-destructive things to yourself in the name of honor or whatever." He then looks at the cast on his arm and laughs wryly.

Nomad will perform three more shows at Budokan before moving on to stops in Nagoya, Yokohama, Osaka, Kanazawa, Hiroshima, and Fukuoka.

Three Best Albums of the 1980s
by Kristof Harber

I swear I didn't pick these selections because they're so eclectic. If you've been reading my column for a while you know I don't write it to impress other critics. I tell you what I really think is worth listening to and why. So when my editor asked me to make my top picks for the decade in review, I decided instead of trying to make some grand statement about the future of music I would just look at what albums were so good that they were what I listen to for pleasure. These are the ones I actually bring with me on planes to listen to when I'm trapped next to an unconscious, drooling stock broker.

GONE TO EARTH, David Sylvian, 1986
I'll confess I used to think of David Sylvian as one of the most pretentious men on Earth, but when you can make music as complex, varied, and grand as one finds on this double album—his first solo effort—you should be allowed some pretenses. Sylvian picks canny collaborators like Robert Fripp but every texture, every timbre only serves to frame Sylvian's honeydripping baritone in music so gorgeous the lyrics don't even matter. Except 'round about the tenth or eleventh listen when the lyrics break through you realize how good they are. It's time to give the most pretentious crown to Sting, anyway.

LIVE! YOU GODDAMNED SON OF A BITCH, The Revolting Cocks, 1988
On the other end of the mood spectrum is a concert album from The Revolting Cocks (video also available). If you still can't figure out what industrial is all about and the neatly packaged version served up by Nine Inch Nails seems alienating, I recommend this live album. Revco's singles and studio work has never moved me—too many beeps and buzzsaws—but live they are a juggernaut that grabs you by the brainstem. These songs are good. They're solid pop craft driven with an intensity and energy that comes from not giving a fuck what the critics think. Utterly fresh. Best track: "Attack Ships (On Fire)."

1989, Moondog Three, 1989
Moondog Three's *1989* lets me have my cake and eat it, too. It's got both musicality and freshness and just doesn't sound like anything else out there. The word chameleon gets thrown around a lot but what else can you call the voice of a lead singer like Ziggy that can go from operatic to a pained whisper to a seductive croon all within a single song? Meanwhile the music sometimes seems deceptively simple, no more than a catchy riff to back up the vocal fireworks. But it's only when I listen with headphones and no distractions—on cross-country flights for example—that I clue in to how much is going on. The guitar is in constant conversation with the other instruments, Ziggy's voice included, and that conversation extends from song to song. If you only know the hits from this band, here's a plea to put the "long play" on, lie down in the dark, and listen.

PART TEN

August 1989

Where Is My Mind

I have a small confession to make. I had to reconstruct some of the sequence of events of these upcoming chapters with the help of dates in Jonathan's diary. I never realized before how handy it might be to have someone writing things down all the time. Honestly. Because thinking back on it later I would have gotten things all out of order and made them seem like they went slower than they did. Or faster. As it was, I had pretty much convinced myself that I had moped around at home for a month or two before we went to Mexico, but no, they'd actually whipped me down there pretty quick. And of course Ziggy's Betty Ford stint was supposed to be a month long, but it felt like six months to me.

And Jonathan didn't have notes on all the times I talked to Digger, or when Digger talked to Mills. I feel like everything in that quarter—with BNC, I mean—was sliding backward that whole time. Or at least our momentum was stalled so it *felt* like we were going backward. Of course we did. Our singer was in limbo. That meant we were all in limbo.

Time doesn't pass in limbo. Or it goes too slowly. Except when things are moving really fast, like with Jonathan's agent and all that. Okay, I guess I should get to that. So let's talk more about Mexico.

I had a really vivid dream the third or fourth night we were down there. In the dream I was playing bass in a Motown group, with these two lead singers who would trade off singing and dancing and doing James Brown kind of vocal riffs, and they really, really needed a tight rhythm section because they would go off improvising and need something to anchor the beat. I didn't know the drummer—I didn't know any of them—and it's unclear to me now how I got roped into the gig in the first place, given that I don't even play bass. But there I was just faking my way through, thinking, *Wait, how did I end up here?* The audience looked like they were having a great time, though, all dancing with each other, many of them with drinks in hand. I remember thinking, *Wait, if this is a dream, can I just put myself in the audience where it looks like a lot more fun?*

And then I woke up thinking, *What?* Since when was it more fun to be in the audience than on the stage?

"I don't even play the bass," I said out loud.

Jonathan rolled over and looked at me. "What?"

"Nothing. Wacky dream."

"Aha."

We could hear the waves on the sand through the open window. A breeze fluttered the white gauze curtains like something from a music video. I yawned and wondered what time it was. The sun was so bright, it always seemed like noon.

"What do you want to do today?" Jonathan asked.

"Well, that's the beautiful thing, isn't it? We don't have to do anything. Well, except eat. We have to do that at some point."

The day before, we'd gone into the town to see the sights. Carynne and Courtney had taken to the beach to sun themselves, and we'd gone wandering. We saw the church of Our Lady of Guadalupe and walked along the beach to where the ruins of some arches were standing in the sand. My legs were tired by that time, but I didn't really care.

It was the first time Jonathan and I had spent such a long time together. A week in New York, but where every hour of the day was devoted to tour business, really did not count. And that weekend we'd spent in Boston was nothing compared to this: no agenda, just be together, talk, and eat, and drink, and goof off, and look at buildings and art, and play random guitars being sold in the corners of shops here and there and everywhere. I got the feeling many of the guitars were meant as souvenirs, not serious instruments, but some of them sounded really nice, the humid air keeping the wood supple and the strings fat.

In Mexico there are guitars everywhere. I hadn't known that when I'd suggested it.

It's kind of hard to describe what doing nothing with Jonathan was like. I mean, the whole point is that we weren't doing anything important, so there isn't a lot to say. He worked an hour or two on his novel every day while I either took a nap or played backgammon with Courtney or whatever. Carynne and Courtney seemed to be having a grand time together. Carynne was an only child, and she later told me that Court was like the little sister she always wanted. I think that was good for Court, too, since at some point she had started feeling like the little sister no one wanted, which I admit was at least one-third my fault while we were growing up.

Anyway, suffice to say, we had a good time in Mexico. J and I had sex every day, sometimes twice a day, because why not? We ate a lot of mangos. We drank a lot of tequila. I jotted down a few song ideas but otherwise did not work on anything. My brain was very content to do nothing for a while.

Two nights before we were due to leave, we were all eating together in the hotel restaurant. This restaurant, by the way, had sand for a floor and no walls, kind of like there was no firm delineation where the hotel ended and the beach began. We were sipping margaritas and watching the moon set over Banderas Bay when a manager came looking for us to say there was an important phone call. My heart lodged in my throat as the first thing that came to mind was Ziggy.

But the call wasn't for me. It was for Jonathan. He went to take the call, looking puzzled.

When he came back, he looked shell-shocked, and I wondered what terrible thing had happened. But when he sat back down, he said, "Um, should we get champagne?"

"Why, honeycakes?" Carynne asked.

"Because apparently my agent's agent got a deal for my script treatment."

"Does that mean you sold it?" I asked, a little confused.

"Uh, yeah, I'd say that means they sold it," he said, sounding a little confused himself. "Hot damn."

"Hot damn!" Carynne repeated, waving down a waiter and ordering a bottle. "That's great, J."

"Haha, yeah, kind of a big shock, though," he said, though he looked up and smiled. "I just hope they don't find out I don't actually know how to write a screenplay."

Thus ensued a raucous round of razzing him about it, and the champagne arrived and the waiter popped it, accidentally losing the cork when it shot out over the beach.

Later, though, when we were lying in bed, sweat cooling on the night breeze off the ocean, Jonathan told me he really *didn't* know how to write a screenplay.

I tried to wrap my head around that. "Okay, so... is that like you're writing a symphony and you know how to write a symphony... but now someone wants you to write a musical instead?"

"Hmmm." He mulled it over a bit. "When you put it that way, yeah, I guess. That makes it sound not so hard."

"Well, you tell me. Writing a novel already sounds impossible to me. Could a screenplay be harder?"

"With a novel you have more freedom, I guess. A screenplay has to be an exact length, for one thing. Sure, you hear stories all the time of directors who film a four-hour movie and have to trim it down and all that. But those are the exceptions. You're supposed to turn in exactly sixty pages, at two minutes per page, to make a two-hour movie. It has to be structured into three acts. The first act has to be a half-hour long, the middle act is an hour long, and the third act is a half-hour again."

"Okay, that's sounding pretty similar to a symphony."

"Well, and now that I think about it, a novel is supposed to have three acts also, but I'm not really sure if mine does. When I first started writing I thought it did, but it's kind of strayed from the original plan..." He trailed off without going into what the novel was about. I hadn't asked because I figured if he wanted to tell me about it, he would.

We lay there in silence for a while and I thought maybe he had drifted off to sleep. But then he spoke again. "You're right."

"I'm right? What am I right about?"

"I should approach it like a symphony. It's good that a screenplay has this kind of structure. It makes it clear what I have to do. I just have to get over being afraid that I'll suck at doing it."

"You're not going to suck at doing it," I said.

"Are you saying that because you really think that, or because you're my boyfriend and you think you should make me feel better?"

"Both, Jonathan. Both, duh."

Promised Land

The next day I was asleep under a thatched shade thingie on the beach when Jonathan got another phone call. I was just waking up and looking at the spot on my arm where the skin was still darker than the rest—where the pyrotechnic had burned me, I mean—and thinking how different my body felt than it had while we were on the road. I was less tense, less high-strung, I guess. I wasn't convinced that was a good thing because I also felt unstrung, if you know what I mean. But, if I'm going to use the string example, I guess I know as well as anybody that you can crack the neck of a guitar if you wind too tight for too long. But the thing is... it sounds best when all the strings are tight. Whatever. Maybe that analogy doesn't work for people. Or maybe it does. Anyway. Jonathan sat down on the lounge chair next to mine and I said, "I don't think I've ever been so relaxed. Physically, I mean."

"Maybe you haven't been." His eyes were hidden behind sunglasses, but he had that curious tilt to his head. "You aren't worried about Zig?"

"I am. But I don't feel it in my gut like I did before we left."

He patted my arm. "Maybe some part of you knows he's doing okay."

"You think?" That idea had never occurred to me. I wasn't a believer in *woo-woo* kind of stuff, and I don't think Jonathan was, either. But whatever. Jonathan had something to tell me.

"So I just got another call. They want me to fly to LA for a meeting with the development team."

"When?"

"Straight from here. Carynne's got the hotel washing my laundry right now so I'll have something to wear when I get there."

"Wow, this is really serious." I sat up so I could look at him without craning my neck. "Wait, why is Carynne doing your laundry?"

"She's not, she has the hotel doing it. And, um, I think once a manager always a manager...? She was on the phone before I could stop her." He shrugged. "Anyway, so first there's this meeting, and then it sounds like I might have to stick around Hollywood for a week or two."

"That's good, though, right?" In my mind, thinking like a musician, the longer a gig lasted, the better. But I wasn't sure how it worked for writers, so I asked, "Are they paying you while you're there?"

"Well, that's the thing. I'm not getting anything by the hour or by the day. I'm getting a payment for the rights and I'll get royalties and stuff if the film makes money, but... this is sort of like the part where you go into the studio. You don't get paid for the hours you spend in there."

"Ah, gotcha."

"In fact, you spend money doing it." He ran his fingers through his hair, which had gotten even blonder in the sun. "On the other hand, it's an incredible opportunity to be involved in the process. All the horror stories you hear are about them taking a book and ruining it. That they want me to be involved... it's great." His look went from dreamy to slightly panicked again. "I'd better look into finding somewhere cheap to stay."

"You want me to come with you?" I asked suddenly.

"Daron," he said. "This won't be like a vacation."

"I'm not expecting it to be," I said. "I'm not saying let's stay at the Ritz on my dime, either, if that's what you're thinking. I have another idea. Remo asked me if I could house-sit."

J's eyebrows went up. "Oh? Where's he live?"

"Um, one of the hilly parts. Laurel Canyon, I think?" I pulled my sunglasses down to see him better. "It'd be free. He's got like five bedrooms in that place. He sounded really disappointed when I didn't say yes to his invitation."

"Why'd you say no?"

"I didn't say no. I said I'd think about it. And you just gave me something else to think about."

It took more phone calls and such, but the upshot is, that's the story of how Jonathan and I ended up going directly to LA from Mexico. There's nothing left to tell you about Mexico, anyway. Beach, tequila, repeat.

Carynne and Courtney went back to Boston, Courtney with ideas to redo my room. At first she was reluctant, claiming she didn't know what I liked.

I explained that what I liked was not having to make any decisions about furniture.

Remo picked us up himself—insisted on it, in fact—and since Jonathan hadn't been there before, Remo gave us a tour of the house when we got in. "All the rooms have queen-size beds, so pick any one you want," he said, then tried to correct himself, "I mean, ones—I mean... oh, hell."

We just laughed. "I'll take one for a writing office," J suggested with a smile.

Remo was red-faced but good-natured about it.

He grilled steaks and burgers and vegetables on a propane grill in the back and warned us to check what the fire threat was before we fired it up in the future—I guess because sometimes the conditions could get so dry that a stray spark could send the whole neighborhood up in flames. We sat on the deck watching the sunset and catching him up a little more about Matthew's photography show.

When Remo and I cracked open fresh beers, Jonathan excused himself to do what he called his "daily typing." So then Remo and I sat drinking in silence and watching the sky turn to purple.

"You want to know what I got out of your old man?" he asked, casual-like.

"Fuck yes." I took a pull on my beer.

He turned his own bottle in his fingers, like he was looking for cold spots. "You were right. They thought he was suicidal." Ziggy, he meant, but even Remo knew, I guess, that in my world "he" always meant Ziggy unless otherwise specified.

"I told you that had to be it. But *was* he?"

"Well, remember that this was Digger talking, so I actually have no idea, but I'll tell you what he said. First off, whatever had happened or was said was all before Digger even got there. At first I thought, yeah right, that's the kind of thing he always says to make it sound like it's not his fault. But later he told me the doctor said it started all the way back in the ambulance."

"What started?"

"Them being freaked out and thinking they had to restrain him."

"Restrain? Physically?" I jerked upright in alarm. All this time I'd been imagining that Ziggy, woozy from his performance high and maybe from hitting his head, had said something crazy-sounding, or maybe even got misinterpreted, just like I was hoping I had been wrong about thinking what I thought when he climbed up the stack. I suddenly wondered if he'd tried to do something extreme in the ambulance.

Remo made a "calm down" kind of motion with his hand. "I don't mean like with a straitjacket or anything. I meant *retain* more than restrain, sorry."

"But what did he say?"

"Digger wanted to know that, too. Best guess is he was describing what happened with the fall to the paramedics and either they suspected or he flat out told them it was a suicide attempt."

"Fuck." That made sense but also didn't make sense. "Did that mean he wanted to kill himself, still? Or that he regretted trying but they kept him under watch anyway?"

"No idea. The important thing is it's out in the open now and they're dealing with it. Along with the drug thing."

I leaned back again and looked at the sky, which was growing dark, but there were no stars. "I don't even know how to deal with this. Maybe because right now I don't even know what to do."

Remo got up and closed the lid of the grill and then sat back down. "I've had two girlfriends who were suicidal."

"No shit, really?"

"Yep. One was the kind who would threaten to kill herself, but who as far as I know only tried it once, a year or two before she met me, and after a while I started to doubt even that was true."

I kept my mouth shut, but I was thinking I knew what it was like to be with someone whose word you questioned all the time. But Ziggy had never used suicide as a threat. "Why'd she make the threat, then?"

"She wanted me to get as worked up over her as she got over me."

"You're really not the type to get worked up over anything, Reem."

"I know. And I guess for her that was a problem. Once she figured that out, she moved on. Anyway, the other one never said anything, never gave a hint anything was wrong until I found her passed out after she tried to OD on sleeping pills. That's when I threw away all the drugs in the house."

"Wait, did she live?"

"She did. And after living through it, she was really changed. Changed enough that she was ready to move on, too." He gave a little "what can you do?" sort of shrug, but he looked pained. "Anyway, there are lots and lots of reasons people attempt suicide. The main piece of advice I have is listen. Listen real hard to what he's got to say about it."

"I'd love to," I said. "But from what I understand, there will be another ten days of radio silence before there's even a chance."

"Not that you're counting the days or anything," Remo ribbed gently.

"Yeah." I finished the last of my beer, upending the bottle in my mouth. Then I glanced back at the house.

Remo glanced back, too. Then he said, "So how's it work, exactly?"

"How's what...? Oh. You mean with Jonathan and Ziggy? I don't know. It's new. I have no idea."

"Aren't you kind of playing with fire there?"

My hackles rose a little, but before I could say something stupid or defensive or both he went on.

"I'm the last person in the world who'll tell you what to do, Daron. And I know things can get really complicated. Here's the simple part. I don't like to see you heartbroken. That's the only reason I'm nervous about... anything. Or anybody."

"Thanks, Reem." I really didn't want him worrying. I had enough of that myself. "I'll figure it out. Somehow. Right now, I'm just taking it one day at a time."

Girl(s) on Film

The next day, Jonathan went to his meeting and Remo and I spent all afternoon in his home studio, with Remo teaching me various parts and me overdubbing a bunch of soundtrack stuff. I had completely forgotten he'd told me months ago about a soundtrack he had been working on, and I thought it was funny that he didn't bring it up sooner. Maybe he just didn't want to pressure me, or maybe he'd known I was going to show up on his doorstep at some point anyway. That led to an engineer coming over for dinner and us spending the evening working on it some more while Jonathan dove into reading two books he had bought about how to write screenplays.

The concept that he could learn to do it from a book was fascinating to me. You can't learn to play an instrument from a book. But he wasn't learning to play an instrument, he was learning to do something similar to what he already knew, which was using words, and so yeah, learning about words from a book makes perfect sense.

The next two days, we fell into a routine where Jonathan would read his books and work on his stuff in the afternoon while Remo and I worked in the studio. But then it was time for Remo to leave town. He hit the hay early after dinner, and Jonathan and I stayed up watching movies from Remo's LaserDisc collection. (Well, that is to say we got through one before we conked out.)

The fact that I called having two days in a row that were the same a "routine" probably tells you something. Whether it says how unusual it was for me to have two days the same or how quickly I fall into ruts, I'm not sure. Both? Both. Why do we always try to split things into two options when in reality both are valid?

The first morning we woke up alone in the house, we didn't get out of bed until noon—and not because we were asleep. I guess I felt we had a few days of not having sex to make up for. After getting used to it every day in Mexico, it's like it built up while we were holding back. We hadn't actually talked about not doing it while Remo was around, but I guess we both felt self-conscious about it enough that we were hands-off until he left.

That weekend I took J to a Hollywood function of some sort that Digger got us invited to. It was at some swanky restaurant that had been taken over for the night, and the crowd was more movie-industry people than music-industry people. This forced me to deal with the fact that I had a suitcase full of beach clothes and not much appropriate for going out in public. J's mother had mailed him his clothes, so he was basically set, and he took me shopping. We ended up with something that looked basically like my usual "rock star" stuff, only more expensive. New jeans, new shirt, new low boots. I wore the BNC leather jacket I had stashed in my bag for the over-air-conditioned plane flights, the one that Ziggy had added a few little studs and rhinestones to. He'd also drawn a rocket on the shoulder in silver marker. The goal was to look "respectably disreputable," at least in the words of the woman we ran into while shopping who handed J a business card that labeled her a "fashion consultant." I think she assumed J was my manager or handler. J told her he was fairly sure that was the look I'd in fact already established but thanked her and put the card in his pocket.

I'm pretty sure everyone in Hollywood, whether they realize it or not, is putting everyone into a big list of casting credits rolling through their minds. *The part of the rock star in today's episode is played by Daron Marks.*

At the party I got to play the part of "rock auteur," possibly. The engineer who had come over to Remo's the other day was there, and he introduced me to some other people. At one point I ended up in a conversation in a corner booth after having drunk too much of a purple champagne cocktail—the purple had something to do with the movie, but I don't remember what, since I don't remember what movie the party was connected to. Pretend it was a *Grapes of Wrath* movie and the drink was a clever pun. It was probably a lot stupider than that. But anyway, the conversation was about guitar sounds and emotional response to music, and I basically talked out my ass, but the guy I was talking to kept nodding and encouraging me to go on. I forgot his name, but later I would find out it was Michael Chernwick. I'll tell you more about him later when he becomes important. At the time, in my mind, he was Mr. Cap-and-Mustache, because he was wearing one of those beanies like you see on paper boys in old films and had a black mustache so tiny it almost looked drawn on with eyeliner.

I talked to a lot of people that night. So did Jonathan. At the time, I thought he was networking, so I was just keeping myself busy. Apparently the level of fame I'd achieved ensured that I was never without a drink in my hand and someone to talk to.

Digger did actually rescue me from one guy who had been going on and on for a while about the concept album he wanted to make as a new soundtrack to *Citizen Kane*. I had never seen the movie and still hadn't ascertained if this guy played an instrument, and I didn't want to ask him any questions because that might make it seem like I was interested in his idea. I wasn't completely sure he even knew anything about music beyond what you might learn from reading magazines, honestly.

So I didn't protest when Digger steered me away from the guy with a "Pardon me, I need him for a minute," and cornered me at the end of the bar.

"Jeez, kiddo, you're popular. Hard to get a word in edgewise."

"I've actually talked to so many people my throat's getting sore," I said. "What's up?"

"You're staying in town for a while?"

"Couple of weeks? Not sure, really."

"Okay. I'll make sure you get on the list for a couple more of these things." He looked around. "It's good business, you know?"

"Sure," I said automatically.

"I'm getting a lot of static from Mills," he said, then, as if it was a related topic. "But I'm not going to push until we know what's going on with your singer."

Your singer. Like Ziggy was my problem? Or maybe he just didn't want to say his name. I nodded noncommittally.

"You want to do something that's good for business?" Digger said then, leaning closer to me.

"Sure, what?"

"I'm going to introduce you to Sarah Rogue."

"How about you tell me who that is first?"

He cracked a "gotcha" smile. "She's about to be the next big thing."

"Okayyy." I assumed that meant she was a client of his. "How about clue me in. Model? Actress? Dancer?"

"All of the above, but let's go with singer for now. Come on. You can talk music." He pushed away from the bar and tugged his jacket sleeves down, trying to smooth the wrinkles at his elbows.

I followed him over to an indoor fountain, where a towering blond girl was standing in a pale yellow sleeveless dress that showed off her very long legs, clutching a tiny purse with both hands in front of her stomach. I didn't hear the introduction Digger gave me, but her fingers were long and slender when she shook my hand gently.

"I'm Sarah," she said, like I didn't already know. "Oh, thank goodness!"

I wasn't sure what she meant by that, but she reached down and took one shoe off her foot and threw it into the fountain, then took off the other one and threw it in, too. The two shoes circled each other in an eddy of water like a pair of yellow fish. She grinned. Now she was only an inch or two taller than me, which made her a lot easier to talk to.

"Digger tells me you're a singer?"

"Yeah, I've got a demo making the rounds right now." She reached up like she was going to touch her hair, then stopped herself with a sigh. "A couple of companies are interested, and, well, you know."

"Yeah, I know. So, I hate to ask this because I'm kind of down on the concept of categories, but what kind of music is it?"

Her smile suddenly got more real. "It's pop because I'm a woman. And because I play the piano."

"Aha, yeah, I know exactly what you mean."

"Yeah. The songs are rock as far as I'm concerned, but you know, the furthest they can stretch their tiny brains is to label me 'Billy Joel with tits.'"

It's a good thing I didn't have a drink in my hand, because I might have spurted it with laughter. "And how do you label yourself?"

"I thought you didn't like labels?" She gave me a skeptical eyebrow almost exactly like Carynne's.

"I don't, but I figured I'd ask."

"How do you label *your*self?"

"I'm just a guitar player," I said with a shrug.

"And your music?"

"Like you said, it's rock. But apparently to the industry it's... let me see if I can get all the labels in the right order: alternative guitar-driven album rock."

"Huh. What's alternative about it? I mean, I'm not trying to be judgey about it, I'm trying to figure out what that means."

"Um, as far as I can tell, all it means is we're too weird to not get the label." Something clicked for me then. That was something Mills had said, or tried to say, about not getting lumped in with the alternative crowd. "Wait, I think I just figured it out," I said aloud. "You'd think, you know, that alternative would be the pinnacle, the top, of the rock and roll heap, right? What's alternative is the most 'out there,' and the whole point of rock and roll is it's too much sex and drugs and itself for the mainstream, right? So from a creative point of view, of course we're like, hey, cool, we're alternative. We're cooler than cool. But within the industry it means we're second-class citizens."

"Whoa. Digger said you were cynical."

"I don't think I'm being cynical here. It just suddenly became obvious. At least at BNC, alternative is a dirty word."

"They're one of the companies we're talking with."

Of course they are, I thought. Digger had a ton of contacts there. I was sure her demo tape was on Mills's desk. "Well, the good thing about them is their goal is to sell a ton of records, which is hard to argue with."

She nodded. "Okay, so explain 'album rock,' then."

"You know, I think it's a nice way of saying we're not built around hit singles. Which now that I think about it is also a second-class thing." No wonder Mills was so cranky.

"Don't be so down on yourself," she said. "The only time I take *1989* out of my car's tape player is to put *Prone to Relapse* in."

"Really?" I noticed she had started blushing. Fortunately, by then I'd had a lot of experience with blushing girl fans so I didn't get all bashful back at her. "Which one do you like better?"

"Oh, be serious, that's an impossible choice. I do have a favorite song, though."

"Which one?"

"'Fire and Ice.'"

"Really! I don't think anyone's ever told me that."

"Well, I'm not just anyone," she said with a flash of her teeth, getting her "star" mojo back. "Hey, it's been super awesome talking to you. I think I'm supposed to leave now, though."

"Are you? Is there, like, a time limit on how long we're supposed to talk?"

"Well, actually it's that if I have to wear this stupid dress five more minutes I'm going to scream," she said, though her smile and facial expression were perfectly mild. "But I am so happy you turned out to be cool."

"Oh. Um, likewise. Digger's always trying to get me to talk to models and things, and most of them the conversation peters out after we discuss the weather."

"Of which there isn't any in LA," she said, "so the conversation is dead before it even starts. I was expecting you to make a pass."

"Huh. Oh, wait, are we supposed to be making it look like we're getting together? Or was just being seen together enough? I'm unclear on how this whole fame thing works."

She laughed and touched my forearm, and I realized that when she did there were a few flashes and shutter clicks. "I suppose it wouldn't hurt for you to walk me to my car."

"Are you parked far?"

She snorted. "I meant the limo waiting outside."

"Oh. Hey, I told you I'm unclear on how it works. I drove an SUV I borrowed from a friend."

"You're cute." She held out her arm and I took it, steering her toward the door. I guess it didn't matter that she wasn't wearing shoes if she was going home.

At the door of the limo she reached into her tiny purse and took out a business card. "Hey, do you have email?"

"I do."

"Excellent! Email me! Nice meeting you, Daron!" She disappeared into the car and the driver shut the door.

I put the card into the inside pocket of my leather jacket and went to find Digger and grill him on what her deal was.

Looking for Clues

I learned a couple of really important things that night, which I guess just goes to show you never know what good leaving the house might do you. Here they are in chronological order.

The first is that the expression "counting the days" to me didn't mean counting the actual days, because I didn't know when exactly the clock had started and I didn't assume that a trip to Betty Ford was like a vacation condo with an exact checkout date. I figured there was easily a day or two of grace period or slop in the system, so my idea of when Ziggy's "thirty days" were up was a general one. (In fact, as it turned out "thirty days" wasn't even accurate: the real time for a stay was twenty-eight days on the dot.) My worldview and Digger's were vastly different, though, you know? Digger's idea of counting the days was, well, counting them.

"Eight days to go," he said, when I told him I was going to call it a night.

And maybe our minds aren't that different, since I knew exactly what, and who, he was talking about. "Then what?"

"Dunno. If we're not lucky, they keep him for another stint, but they told me that's rare. If we're lucky, they spring him and he goes back to normal. Or at least back to work."

What work? I wanted to say. But I couldn't really jump down his throat about how we didn't know what we were doing next. The festival dates were off the table, and we didn't have a commitment on when we could start the next album, either. Were either of those things Digger's fault? Well, maybe I could hint at it: "You know Jordan Travers wants to work with us again."

"One thing at a time, kiddo. Your chicken has to hatch, first, and better hope he's not fried."

In that moment I saw how anxious Digger was. His fingers shook a little as he took the cigarette out of his mouth. He flicked the ash into the glass tray on the bar. So that was the second thing.

I wondered when a good moment was going to come to fire him. This wasn't it, anyway. And I had decided to leave, if Jonathan was ready to. I went to find him.

He was sitting at a small, round table talking very intently with an older man, but when he saw me coming he stood up, shook hands with the guy, and practically ran away.

"You want to go?" I asked.

"Good idea," he said, moving me toward the door.

"What was that all about? You seem like you got up in a hurry."

"Just didn't want to overstay my welcome. But oh my god, I got some fantastic advice from that guy."

"Who was he?"

"Here's the embarrassing part: I didn't get his name. But he's a screenwriter. Really gave me some good tips."

"I can ask Digger who he was. He might know."

"That would be fantastic! That would save my bacon. Thank you, Daron."

I drove us back to Remo's. If Jonathan seemed a little more effusive than usual, it's because he'd had a few too many of the purple cocktail. Not enough to make him ill, but enough that he was still tipsy when we got home. J was usually careful with what he drank, especially in a professional context. I'd never seen him quite like that. I learned that alcohol could make him not only horny but also even more direct than usual.

"Fuck me until I'm sober enough to get back to work," he said, jamming his hands into the pockets of my jeans and pulling my groin against his leg.

So I did, but by the time we were done he decided to sleep instead of burning the midnight oil.

I was the one who went back into the studio in the wee hours, though I didn't actually make any music. I sat there making a list of the songs we had close to ready for a new album. Eight days until Ziggy might be free. I'll admit that by then I was thinking of it like he was in jail, not rehab. I'd convinced myself that by now he was probably just fine and climbing the walls.

I had images and sounds burned into my brain from that set we'd done, just the two of us, before it had all gone wrong.

Here's the list I made:

Infernal Medicine (D)
Mano a Mano (Z)
Blue Skies (D)
Moving Parts (D)
Face Value (D)
I Have No Idea (Z)
(Needs) A Bridge (D)
Do No Wrong (D)
Thin Ice (D)
Yes or No (Z)

"Blue Skies" was the sappy love song I'd written the weekend Jonathan had come to Boston.

That was ten songs right there, and I knew Ziggy had a ton of stuff in his notebook we could work on. I was sure if we sat down with Trav some of my songs would get bumped, but that was all right. Hadn't Trav said that Ziggy had more the ear for hits, anyway? That'd make Mills happy, wouldn't it? I just wanted it to be a kick-ass record. I wanted it to be better than *1989*, a new step. Ziggy was right: when we trusted each other, we made great songs. Some of them, like "Moving Parts," were as much Ziggy's as mine now.

I sat there looking at the list in the light on a gooseneck attached to the mixing board. I hadn't bothered to turn on the full lights in the studio. It was a single room in an addition that had been built onto the back of the house. Unlike a pro studio, it wasn't divided by a window partition, but it didn't have to be. Remo had a DX7 II in there, and a lot of guitars, including an Ovation almost identical to mine, which was why mine was still in Massachusetts. (Both of mine, I should say, to be accurate. Or all three, if you count the twelve-string, which I don't.)

I did not fall asleep in the studio, though I came close. I did climb into bed still half dressed, though.

Pop Song '89

In the morning, it was seven days until Ziggy's release. Jonathan had a meeting, so he got up, somewhat bleary from a hangover, and I got up with him, somewhat bleary from staying up too late. But I wanted to do some shopping and so I drove him to the meeting and dropped him off, then took the SUV to run errands.

I bought a computer like the one I had at home, so I could hook it up to Remo's DX7 and get my email. I didn't go crazy with spending money, but I figured Remo could use the computer and it was the least I could do for letting us stay.

I did some record shopping after that, after getting some recommendations from the guy in the computer store on where to go, and bought a bunch of CDs at some smaller shops before ending up in Tower. I couldn't bring myself to buy anything in Tower, but it was kind of fun to look around. I even found Sarah Rogue's indie album in the "folk" section. Absolutely no one acted like they recognized me, but I didn't actually interact with anyone in there. I imagined a parallel universe where this was the Tower where I had worked.

Imagine if Remo had taken me with him all those years ago. And I had... I dunno... lied about my age and gotten a job there. I would've learned to drive a lot sooner, that's for sure. Remo probably would've been charged with kidnapping, though. Well, maybe not. Who was going to complain, my mother? Doubtful.

I hadn't thought about that in a long time. There was no realistic way it could have worked. I knew that. But it was one of those scabs I used to pick at when I felt like I was going nowhere.

And where are you going now? said that ugly little voice of doubt in the back of my head. *Your career is dead in the water without Ziggy...*

I reminded myself I hadn't eaten since the half of an English muffin I'd had in the car on the way into town. I took that as a cue to go to the deli where I was supposed to meet Jonathan.

He wasn't there yet, but it was the sort of place that wouldn't care if I took up a table for a while, or so J had surmised when we had picked it as our rendezvous point. "If you get there first, it's fine, because you're famous."

"What if you get there first?" I asked.

"I've got my laptop, I'll get some work done, and if they give me a hard time I'll explain I'm waiting for someone famous."

"Oh."

I got into a discussion with a waitress that went sort of like this:

Me: Okay, so I'm kind of craving roast beef because I'm hungry, but isn't roast beef kind of bland?

Her: Put mustard on it?

Me: Not a huge fan of mustard.

Her: What about corned beef instead? Or pastrami?

Me: What's pastrami? I mean, I know it's a sandwich thing, I just never thought about it before.

Her: It's kind of like corned beef. Only spicier. Sounds like just the thing, doesn't it?

Me: Huh, it does. Can I get it with cheese?

Her: What kind of cheese do you like? We've got Swiss, Cheddar, Provolone...

Me: I've never really liked Swiss, Cheddar eh, Provolone doesn't really taste like anything, does it?

Her: American, then?

Me: No. I feel like I've outgrown American.

Her: What, you want, like, goat cheese or something? We've got the spreadable kind. It's like cream cheese.

Me: Heyyyy. What about cream cheese?

Her: You know, I never thought of having cream cheese and pastrami, but now that I think about it, it sounds kind of good.

Me: It does?

Her: Yeah. Lettuce and tomato?

Me: Um, good question.

Her: You know, to give it some crunch.

Me: I've never been a big lettuce fan.

Her: How about cucumber?

Me: Will that work?

Her: Cucumber sandwiches are an English thing. But it should work.

Me: Okay, sure.

Her: What kind of bread?

Me: Isn't it supposed to be pastrami on rye?

Her: Rye it is. You want that grilled?

Me: Uh...

Her: Grilled it is.

So that's how I ended up with a grilled sandwich of pastrami, cream cheese, and cucumber—and damn, it was good.

I was licking hot cream cheese off my face when J came in. "What are you eating?"

"Don't ask," I said. "How was your meeting?"

"Long." He waved down the waitress, ordered a cheeseburger, and then looked at me again. "No really, what are you eating?"

So I explained that I had started out trying to order roast beef and had ended up with pastrami, cream cheese, and cucumber, grilled, and that it was good enough that I was considering ordering a second one. "But seriously, how was the meeting?"

He sighed. "Good, I guess. Every day they don't throw me out for being a fraud I consider a moral victory, at least."

He didn't seem inclined to say much more about it. I figured if he wanted to talk about the details, he would. He switched the subject to my day, and I showed him the CDs I'd bought.

"Hey, which reminds me to ask you," I said, "what's the story with Sarah Rogue?"

"She was at the party last night, right?"

"She's a client of Digger's now, apparently."

"Ah, interesting. She got some college radio play last year but I don't really know more than that."

"I found her record in the folk bin today, but I'm pretty sure that's just industry-speak for 'acoustic.' She didn't look much like a folk artist last night. I get the feeling they're trying to jazz up her image."

"And she isn't jazz, either," Jonathan joked.

After we ate, we drove home, which meant that we sat in a bunch of traffic, but that's just how it is around there. After we got in, J went to do his daily typing while I went into the studio to set up the Mac. I ended up having to go back out to a RadioShack to get a phone cord long enough to run from the main part of the house to the modem, since there wasn't a phone jack in the studio. Fortunately, there are malls open until nine. Insert obligatory "Valley Girl" reference here.

I didn't know very many people with email, so once I had caught up on that, I played around with music until I got hungry. Sometime around midnight Jonathan and I met in the kitchen and split a big can of Dinty Moore Beef Stew I found in the cabinets, and then we were going to watch a movie but ended up having sex instead.

Of Course I'm Lying

When there were only six days left before Ziggy's time was up, Remo's phone rang and I answered it, figuring it was the pool cleaning crew or something. But no, it was Michael Chernwick asking me if I could "show my face" at a meeting that afternoon. It took me a minute to remember that Chernwick was the producer at the party from the other night. I agreed because it wasn't like I had something better to do.

I took a shower and got dressed in rock star standard and told J I was going to a meeting.

"What kind of a meeting?"

"I'm not sure, really. Chernwick wants me to meet someone to talk about music," I said.

"That's vague."

"Yeah, I guess."

If it's sounding to you like I was really underprepared for an actual meeting, that's because I was. It turned out that Chernwick was consulting on a documentary project where the music direction had gone off the rails some time earlier, and they essentially needed a rescue job. They needed someone who could write and record incidental music for the scene changes ASAP. At first I figured they were trying to hire Chernwick to compose, and he wanted me to play on it. But the more I nodded my head and said yes, the more it dawned on me that no, they were trying to hire me to *do the whole thing*. People kept coming into the meeting and sitting down, and each time it was someone more important than the previous one. It was like being at the highest-pressure job interview ever. All that bullshit I'd said the other night about creating emotional states with different kinds of guitar playing and musical modes? It came back to haunt me here. I basically said it all again with an extra layer of bullshit, and they bought it. Except who was fooling whom, here?

Looking back on it now, it's clear to me they figured they had a rube on their hands. They were offering me almost no money to do something in almost no time. I probably should have said no, or at least asked for more, or to keep the copyright or something. But they also needed something almost impossible, and the only way to get it was to hire someone who didn't know any better, who didn't know it was impossible. I figured what the fuck, why not give it a try? "There's no money in documentaries, of course," they said, but it wasn't like *no* money. It was a couple thousand dollars, kind of just enough to justify saying yes. I mean, why not? What else was I doing with myself right then? And besides, the deadline was so soon, I figured it would be out of the way soon enough, so no matter how much it sucked at least it would be over with.

I got the shakes on the drive home, though, and had to pull over and get a drink. Not an alcoholic drink, I'm not that dumb. I went through a drive-thru and got a milkshake and sat there in the parking lot drinking it, thinking, *What the fuck have I gotten myself into? I don't know the first thing about what I'm supposed to do. Who am I kidding?*

I went to a pay phone and used my calling card to call Remo's answering service, and then I felt better. Then I called J at the house and asked him if I should bring home take-out. And then I got back in the truck and drove back around the restaurant for a second trip through the drive-thru, which prompted a double-take from the cashier.

I loaded up with burgers and fries and took them home to my lover, who appreciated my panic. "They're doing the same thing to you that they're doing to me," he said with a laugh. "Movie people. They're all crazy."

It occurred to me to call Digger and tell him what I was doing. I left a message. When he called back, he didn't even sound put out that I hadn't had him negotiate for me. "Sounds like a great foot in the door, kiddo," he said, and then told me about another party I should be at in a couple of days.

Remo called a little later, and I told him what I'd gotten myself into. He laughed and said not to worry and gave me the number of the producer who'd been here the other day, whose name I'd forgotten, but this time I wrote it down: Cadmon Molina. Then he walked me through the steps of what I was going to need to do, pointed out that the reason there was a TV and a VCR in the studio was for just such gigs like this, and explained that there was no way they expected me to be involved in the post-production. "Just give them sixty-second chunks, maybe one or two that are two minutes, and make them easy to fade in and out, and they'll do the rest."

"You make it sound like it's not that hard."

"Not if what you're doing is some new-age-y guitar stuff that you can lay down yourself. Did they tell you how many transitions they need?"

"About two dozen. Oh, by the way, I bought you a computer."

"What? Did you say you're commuting?"

"No, no. I'm using your studio here. I said I bought you a computer. It talks to the DX7."

"What does it say?"

"Beep, don't beep? No seriously, with the Yamaha sound library I can probably make it sound like I have a whole orchestra if I really want to."

"Sounds like a lot of work."

"Which is why I'm probably going to stick with mostly new-age-y guitar. They want the roughs in three days."

"Well, what the hell are you doing talking to me on the phone, then? Get to work," Remo said, although we stayed on the phone a little bit after that, shooting the breeze about Germany and international touring and stuff. I didn't get around to mentioning Ziggy—not that there was anything more to say since the last time we talked, anyway.

I dove into it, playing around with bits of songs, making composer's notes, and sticking snippets on tape but not laying down anything formal yet. I cooked up three different themes and a few possible motifs. I cribbed some riffs from my warm-up routines. It felt good to be working.

At two in the morning J stuck his head into the studio, looking tired and rough around the edges. "Hey."

"Hey." I yawned.

"This is your... uh... what's the opposite of a wake-up call?" He ran his hand through his hair, which was all standing up like he'd been pulling on it.

"A booty call?" I said hopefully.

He laughed in surprise. "Why didn't I think of that?"

"Because you're thinking about your book. Screenplay. Whatever." I stood up and kissed him. "Come on.

If you're really tired we can make it quick."

"I'm suddenly feeling more awake," he said. "But we probably should make it quick."

So Alive

Five days to go on Ziggy, three days to go on the scoring gig. J and I had some breakfast together in the kitchen and then went to our respective work rooms.

It's hard to describe what it was like working alone. I mean, I was used to sketching out tracks and writing lyrics and practicing alone. But this was being completely on my own, both to make the music and to decide what it was going to sound like.

There were moments when it was weird, like I'd gotten so used to taking everyone else into account during the creative process that I forgot what it was like to just... fly. *Float.* Me and my strings and my riffs and my ideas. It was almost scary, but I got used to it again real fast. I didn't even have to teach it to anyone else. This must be what it's like to be a painter, I thought. Standing there in front of the canvas with everything in your control and doing whatever pleased you.

I might have talked some shit to Chernwick at that party about emotional states and guitar sounds, but it wasn't *all* bullshit. I really felt that way.

I stumbled out some hours later because I paused in my track-laying to check email, but then I got bounced offline by the phone ringing. I answered it and was surprised to hear Cadmon Molina's voice.

"How's it going?" he wanted to know.

He must've heard from Remo, because it didn't sound like a casual question. "Um, okay, I guess. I'm getting hung up on some technical things, but—"

"But nothing. I hear you haven't got time to get stuck."

"Well, that's true but—"

"Come down to the Front 242 show tonight and I can answer all your questions. I'll guest you."

"Uh, plus one?"

"Sure. No problem. See you later."

"Um—"

He hung up before I could ask him anything. Okay. I went and stuck my head into Jonathan's writing room.

He looked up, but he wasn't really focused on me.

"Hey, how much work do you have to get done today to go to see a show tonight?"

He blinked at me. "Might depend on which show."

"Front 242."

He looked skeptical. "Let me call an editor I know."

"I already got us on the guest list."

"Not for that," he said with a smile that finally snapped him out of his work daze. "To see if I can turn it into a writing gig."

"Ohhh. Smart. Let me know. I'm going back to it." I went back to it.

By dinnertime I had five or six pretty solid snippets of music laid down, I thought, using just some instrumental washes on the synthesizer and playing the rest double-tracked with acoustic guitar. I still wasn't happy with my own performance on two of them, but for background music no one but me would hear what I didn't like. I was trying to do a thing with a hammer on; maybe I needed to try it with a Takamine instead of an Ovation. Or maybe I needed to give myself more time for acoustic takes and spend less time programming the computer.

We hit a drive-thru and then ate in traffic but still made it to the club in a reasonable amount of time. I should mention that a reasonable amount of time in a car in LA is equal to the amount of time it takes to drive clear across most New England states. Anything under two hours was considered "good time" in SoCal, or so I was repeatedly told by people there. Jonathan had his reporter notepad, the kind with the spiral binding on the top, tucked into his back pocket. I was in rock star standard.

As promised, we were on the list. The place was dark and a little dingy inside and smelled like fake fog. Have I talked about fake fog? A fog machine is not something I ever want to have in our stage setup. For one thing, there's no way it's good for you. It's not smoke, it's some kind of chemical that the machine turns into mist. I'm really not fond of how they smell, but it could be worse. If you look in the stage equipment catalogs, when you buy the liquid that goes in the fog machine, they sell regular and scented. And the scents are stuff like piña colada scent. I have never smelled piña colada-scented fake fog, and I hope I never do. Just thinking about it makes me a little queasy.

Our timing was good: the opening band was just starting. I put my earplugs in and waded into the crowd at the front of the stage. Biggest advantage by far to being my height is that almost no one gives a fuck if I end up in front of them in a general admission crowd. Jonathan hung back. The opening band was loud and industrial and not much to look at, so I didn't pay attention so much as I merely soaked in the noise the way you stick your feet in a pool but don't go swimming. They were only on for a half hour, anyway, and then I meandered back to the bar to get a drink and see what Jonathan thought.

We ended up discussing Einsturzende Neubaten. Here's the funny thing about the conversation: he was surprised that I knew of them, and I was surprised that he knew of them. If you don't know Einsturzende Neubaten, I'm not sure what to tell you about them.

"But what do you like about industrial music?" J asked me. "It just doesn't seem like it would be your thing."

"My thing?"

"I mean, it's not very musical."

I made the losing-buzzer noise. "Wrong. It's not very *melodic*, but it's intensely musical. It's all the energy and aggression of punk and the angst of goth but presented in waves of mathematical structures."

"Huh. Was it Eno who said all music is math?"

"I don't know, but it's true. We're not conscious of it usually, but there are physical, mathematical realities to why notes sound how they do and why we respond to sounds the way we do. I had a class on this. I can't remember any of the details, but I don't have to. Just knowing the equations exist is enough. Music is sound, sound is waves, wavelengths are a mathematical measure... that's all you really need to know. That DX7 I've been using? The big breakthrough in sound synthesis was in figuring out the math of wavelengths to recreate realistic sound. Yamaha got there first, which is why the DX7 is what everyone has."

"Huh. It's funny I didn't know that. I guess I never thought about that side of it." J pulled on his beer. "So who's your favorite industrial band?"

"Honestly, it's probably the Revolting Cocks. KMFDM a close second."

"You know, I heard KMFDM were supposed to tour this year, but it keeps getting put off for some reason. But really? Revco? Not Nine Inch Nails?"

"Nine Inch Nails are..." I paused to think about it. "I think they're the next step. I hesitate to call them industrial when I feel like they're beyond that. Besides, *Pretty Hate Machine* is their only record so far—I reserve judgement until there's a larger body of work."

At that point Cadmon found us. He took me upstairs where it was quieter and let me pin him to a wall with a steady stream of questions about fades and breaks and tempo and dynamic range, answered them, and then told me he'd really have to hear some of what I'd done to know if I nailed it or fucked it up.

"I have to turn in roughs day after tomorrow," I told him. "Can you come up to the house tomorrow? Remo's house, I mean."

He shook his head. "I'm pretty much booked solid."

"Are you going to be at the thing tomorrow?" I tried to remember what Digger had told me about the party. "Something at the Bonaventure?"

"Yes, perfect," he said. "Bring a tape and a Walkman, and don't be late, because if they get into doing blow I might not be in any shape to hear it."

"All right."

By then the band was onstage and had played a couple of songs. I waded back into the crowd and let myself get knocked around a bunch at the edge of the pit. I wasn't in the mood to get right in the middle of it, but that way I got right up close. I got hot and sweaty and forgot who I was. That's probably the best thing that ever happens to me at concerts, where the music somehow takes me right out of myself. For me that's the sign of a really good show. And that was true before I got "famous." (It was also probably why I liked industrial even though it wasn't a style I played myself.)

When it was over I stumbled into the men's room to splash my face, feeling every bit as wrung out and horny as I often did when coming off the stage myself.

Only, here I didn't have a dressing room or a shower or a bus to go back to.

I had an SUV and Jonathan, though. He got in the driver's seat and took us down an industrial side street and parked. I kissed him until my lips felt as bruised as my shins. He sucked me off for a while, then, but didn't finish, and made me wait until we got home. I suppose that was a lot safer from all perspectives. LA had a lot of random carjacking and stuff going on then, plus who knew who might see, yeah yeah. No one at that show had given a fuck who I was, and that was great. But that didn't mean someone walking down the street might not recognize me in the car.

Somehow I just wasn't able to muster up my usual paranoia. When we were done and lying there in bed together, I actually felt okay. Like for once my life wasn't on the brink of disaster. Then I remembered I had 48 hours to finish this soundtrack and four days until Ziggy, but even thinking about those things wasn't enough to make me panic.

I attributed it to Jonathan. "You're really solid," I told him.

"Does that mean I should lose weight?" he joked.

"No. I mean, it's like you're like a big piece of ballast and it keeps me on an even keel."

"That's a very nautical metaphor."

"But it works, doesn't it?"

"The metaphor? Or me being your emotional ballast."

"Both, J. Both."

Putting on the Ritz

I only slept four or five hours, and then I was up prowling the kitchen and then the studio in the dark, too restless to sleep when there was work to be done.

Four days until Ziggy, and one day until I had to turn in roughs.

And a matter of hours before I was going to tape what I had and carry it on a cassette with me to an industry party. And my head was full of music and thoughts and criticisms of my playing and how today it was going to sound better because I'd do a better take. Right?

Why did I take this gig again? I asked myself. I checked my email while waiting for an old tube amp to warm up. There was one from Sarah Rogue saying she'd be at the party, too. Okay, good, that was one person I knew I could talk to without going insane. She'd gotten onto a couple of the email lists that Colin had gotten me interested in, too, one for "new music" and one for electronic music. Would it be weird to talk about something we'd kind of already "discussed," but in email? I'd find out.

It was a frustrating morning. My playing was, frankly, not as good as I wanted it to be. I hadn't been playing acoustic very much, and almost none of the Moondog Three set was finger style, but that's the sound I wanted for this. I was rusty. My fingernails weren't grown out. Thank goodness for all those lessons I taught Colin, because that was the only time I had played that style in the past several months.

I finally gave up, took a break from the music I was trying to record, and practiced a couple of my old classical guitar pieces. I didn't have the sheet music in front of me, but I had large swaths memorized.

Maybe it helped. I at least convinced myself I didn't completely suck. I ended up re-recording almost everything I'd put in the can the previous day, and a couple more things, and it came out better, sounded better. It still wasn't as polished as I wanted, but that was why they called it roughs, right? So I could still redo it if they wanted?

Jonathan snuck in sometime in the afternoon and handed me a tuna salad sandwich he must have made himself. After I inhaled it, I looked up and said, "Um, thanks. Why do you look so amused?"

He was standing by the studio door, his back against the wall, his arms and ankles crossed. "Do you always record without pants on?"

"Oh, um, I didn't want to wake you by banging the dresser drawers this morning," I said. "So I just wandered straight in here." I was in my underwear and a T-shirt.

He only looked even more amused. "How's it going? Or should I not ask?"

"I have no freakin' idea. How about you?"

"Same." He stretched and yawned. It didn't look like he'd showered either, but he at least was wearing clothes. "This thing tonight, would you mind going alone?"

I stood up, intending to go put some shorts on, at least. "No. If you need to stay in and work, I'll be okay."

"If you're sure."

"J. It's not like we talk to each other much at these things anyway."

He cocked his head like he hadn't realized that before. "Huh. I suppose so."

"You know, we don't power schmooze each other. Besides, you can talk to me anytime."

"True." He stretched and shook himself one more time. "Okay. I'm going to try to push through. If I get a lot done I might come with you after all. What time are you going to go?"

"I should try not to be too fashionably late. I actually want Cadmon to hear what I've got and tell me what I'm doing wrong."

"So, leave by six?"

"Which'll mean at least an hour in traffic, but so be it." I could have used that hour in the studio. But that wasn't how it was going to be.

In the end J did come along, which made the sitting in traffic a lot more bearable. We handed off the SUV to valet parking at the Bonaventure and headed up to the party. I had a cassette in one pocket and a Walkman in the other.

I don't remember much of how we got up or in to the party because on the walk from the car I went into nervous obsession mode, thinking, what if what I've done is *completely* wrong? I don't really get nervous about musical things. I had that block going on during the warm-up tour, yeah, but that wasn't like I was afraid to get on the stage. This, though, my neck was sweating and I wondered: *What if he hates it? What if it just sucks?*

I was still thinking that, standing by a window, staring but not really seeing the view, when Cadmon came up and clinked my glass with his. I am guessing Jonathan put the glass in my hand. Cadmon was a fairly tall guy, thin mustache and wisps of unruly black hair escaping from under a black hat.

"How's it going?" he asked.

"You tell me?" I said faintly, putting the drink down and fishing in my pocket for the cassette.

He grinned. "You look green around the gills. Come on."

We went out into the hallway where it wasn't as noisy, and I put the tape into the player and handed it to him. "So it starts off with—"

He cut me of with a "stop" gesture of his hand. "Let me listen." He took off the hat, put on the headphones, and closed his eyes.

So I stood there sweating, with my hands in my pockets. If he hated it, I decided, at least I'd know not to take a gig like this again. Maybe it'd be a good lesson.

I have no idea how long he listened. He fast-forwarded at one point. There was about a half hour of music on the tape, total.

When he pulled the headphones off his ears, he said, "Chernwick heard this yet?"

I shook my head.

"He's going to shit his pants."

"That bad?"

"Fuck no." He looked around. "I'm half of a mind to just tell you it's fine, because it is, and quit worrying about it, and I half want to take you somewhere and give you advice until you can't stand it anymore."

"Um..."

"Follow me."

I followed him back into the party, where he got on the suite's phone and talked animatedly to someone. It sounded kind of like he was telling them off, though he looked pretty happy about it. I had two content-free "hi how are you" kind of non-conversations during the phone call, and then he rescued me. We went into the bathroom then, and he shut the door. I was still too paralyzed to make a joke about how compromising that looked.

"Okay, the advice part. Tell me honestly. Is this some of your best stuff? Is this all instrumental stuff you've been saving up your entire life?"

"Um, a little. I mean, some of those riffs are things I've never done anything with before."

He put the lid down and sat on the toilet. "What I'm saying is, this is way too good to waste on a crappy work-for-hire job that your name isn't even going to be on. And if it's that you're just that good, okay fine, but don't throw away your best stuff on this."

"I don't have time to start over," I pointed out. "But no, this isn't my best stuff. There's plenty more where that came from. I improvised half of what you heard, anyway."

"Good. Perfect. My only question is, how closely did you stick to their cues?"

"They didn't really give me any cues. They gave me some general footage without transitions, and a list of about how many tracks they wanted of about how long each."

"Are they loopable?"

"Um, I haven't tried."

He put the headphones on again, rewound, and listened with his eyes open this time. Then he handed it all back to me. "You're good. You left them plenty of places where they can fade out, or where they can loop if they decide they need to make it longer. You'd think you were a pro or something."

"I just gave it my best guess. I listened to a lot of soundtracks when I was a kid."

"Did you? Like what?"

"Like the John Carpenter/Alan Howarth soundtracks to *Escape from New York* and *The Fog*. Giorgio Moroder. Maurice Jarre—"

"Okay, okay. Anyway. You're golden. I should've known—Remo doesn't throw around the word 'prodigy' lightly. Get a check when you deliver the master tape. That's the only other advice I can think to give you. Now." He cracked his knuckles. "Everyone thinks we came in here to do a line. You want to?"

I assumed he meant cocaine. "No, thanks, I'm trying to cut down," I joked—but you know how I'm deadpan, so I think he thought I was serious.

"Good for you. Me too, but, you know." He shrugged and took a container out of his pocket. It was about the size of a cigarette case, but I guess it was some kind of custom-made cocaine dispenser. I didn't watch, fussing with the headphone cord and tucking it back into my jacket pocket. In LA it seemed like it was always leather-jacket weather, at night anyway: low humidity and cool.

He didn't seem much different when he was done snorting. Maybe a little brighter-eyed, I don't know. "Chernwick's on his way, by the way. I told him to get his ass down here to hear this. So don't leave until after he gets here."

"Oh, you know him, too?"

He laughed. "Digger, everyone knows everyone in this town."

"Daron," I said automatically. "Digger's my... manager."

"Right. Sorry. Wow. Both start with a D, you know. Come on." Okay, maybe he was high. He opened the door and we went back into the schmoozefest.

And then I got a drink I actually wanted and let myself smile a little inside. He liked it. It was good. I did good. I wondered when the last time was that I felt like I had gotten an "A."

I got into a conversation then with a random guy who had been to the Robert Fripp Guitar Craft School in Virginia, and we bonded over how the Ovation semi-acoustics were basically the most perfect guitars ever made. I didn't get his name, but it was a fun conversation anyway. I got another drink and sat down.

"Hey kiddo, how's it hangin'?" Digger sat down next to me.

"A little to the left. Where's Sarah? Didn't you say she was going to be here?"

"I just saw her. Hang on, I'll find her." And he got back up and went away. Huh. If only it was always so easy to get rid of him.

She practically fell onto the leather sectional sofa next to me. "Hey! I was hoping I'd see you."

"Likewise. Hey, I picked up *Eve and the Odds* the other day."

"No way! Now I'm embarrassed."

I pulled her leg. "I didn't say I *listened* to it..."

She slapped me on the arm. "Jerk."

"No, seriously. I liked it. But no way did it belong in the folk section."

"That's the section where they always stick any woman singer-songwriter with a political conscience," she said. She crossed her legs. She was wearing a dress that came to mid-thigh, but she had tights on under it that were patterned to look like blue jeans. She had kicked off her shoes again. I wondered if they were hidden in a potted plant or something. "But, really, you liked it?"

"I did. I don't think I appreciate the piano as much as I should, you know? I'm crap at playing it so I just don't think about it."

"It doesn't get much respect," she said. "It's like you have Jerry Lee Lewis, Elton John, and Billy Joel, and they're held up as some kind of exception that proves the rule. Everyone else has to be some kind of balladeer or jazz crossover."

"Heard anything new about how your demo is doing?"

"Latest rumor is that Mills is on his way to LA to meet me."

"That what Digger said?"

"Yeah."

"Nervous?"

"Yeah. It'd be one thing if I was playing a showcase or something, but I'm not. Sounds like I'm just going to meet him."

I was a little confused by this. "But how is he going to tell if you're any good?"

"Well." She uncrossed and re-crossed her legs. "I am under the impression that what they're looking for most is a woman with 'it.'"

"I've heard about this 'it' before." From Mills, in fact.

"Yeah, and if you're you, your 'it' includes what you're like with a guitar in your hands. I think in my case, being female, they mostly want to see if my tits are big enough." She shrugged, which emphasized the fact that actually her tits weren't particularly big, so far as I could tell. I wasn't really the best judge of that sort of thing.

"Well, good luck with it," I said, and I meant it.

"Not that I wouldn't play a cabaret gig for him if he wanted. Girl and a piano, not that hard to set up." She emptied her glass and set it on the side table. "Though I'm betting the first thing he'll say is *lose the piano*. If I'm lucky, in concert they'll let me stand at a synthesizer for one song."

"Do you—"

"Oh, who am I kidding. If I even reach that stage I'll be lucky to begin with." She patted me on the arm. "But you were saying."

"Um, I was going to say something about synthesizers. I saw Front 242 last night."

"No kidding? I'm more of a KMFDM gal myself."

I must have looked surprised. "You've heard KMFDM?"

"Daron. Don't ruin my impression of you by being sexist. You think a woman can't like industrial music?"

"Hang on, who said it has anything to do with you being a woman and not with them being an obscure industrial band? Almost no one I know likes industrial, male or female." Except Colin. "How'd you get into them?"

"Worked for a little while in an indie record store," she said. "You?"

"Listening to college radio. Then I worked at Tower and discovered the whole Wax Trax catalog."

"You worked at Tower? Oh wait, I knew that. From the video." She accepted a glass of champagne from a caterer, and I did, too. I guess the room was about to toast something. I'd already forgotten who or what this party was for. "But anyway, what were you going to say about synthesizers?"

"Oh, I don't know. Insert the usual gear talk here. I'm partial to the DX7, but that might be because it's what I know best."

"Korg has the best key feel, but I like some of the other piano patches better. I know, I know, I use the Korg as a MIDI controller for something else, get the best of both worlds, but you know, that's one more piece of equipment that can break. On the other hand, it's nearly impossible to tour with an actual piano. Can you imagine? Tuning that motherfucker every day? Not until you're someone like Elton John. Can't just put it in the back of a van."

"Kind of tricky to busk with, too." I said. "What if it rains?"

"A bitch to get down to the subway platform," she replied, perfectly matching my deadpan tone. She looked around then. "I'm trying to figure out if we can drink the champagne yet or if we're supposed to wait."

"No one else seems to be drinking yet. Oh wait, that guy over there."

She followed my line of sight to where an older man wearing a T-shirt under his suit jacket was swaying to the music in the background and sipping from his glass.

"He's in his own world," Sarah said, and raised her glass in his general direction.

"Hey, you want to come up to the house and jam sometime?" I asked then. "I mean, if you can stand the DX7."

"Wait, what? What house?"

"I'm house-sitting for Remo Cutler. He's got a home studio fancier than some of the pro setups I've been in. It's awesome."

"Huh, cool."

At that point the music quieted down and everyone began looking the same direction, and someone whose voice didn't carry at all made some kind of a speech from the far side of the room. We really couldn't hear any of it, but when we saw other people raising their glasses we did the same, clinked with each other, and drank.

Then Chernwick found me. Sarah moved on with a little wave, and I got an earful from Chernwick about how he got an earful from Cadmon Molina, and where the fuck was this tape he needed to hear so desperately. I handed him the player without saying anything.

"Hang out," he said, which I took to mean "wait here," and then he walked away with the player in his hand.

He came back maybe five minutes later and tossed me everything, which I caught. "Good job," he said. "They'll love it. Exactly what they wanted."

"Well, I did do it based on what we talked about in that meeting," I said.

"Yeah, you might be surprised how many artists don't absorb anything we say, though." He was wearing a navy blue blazer over a polo shirt. "And some can't work to spec no matter what we say. And some don't have the chops to get it done."

"What would you have done if what I turned in sucked?"

"Well, they would have paid you anyway."

"No, I mean as far as music for the documentary?"

"Eh. Might've tried to license something from some B film in an emergency. But this is way better. I knew you could do it."

"Great. Get me more money and more time next time," I said, as a joke—but just like with Cadmon, he took it seriously.

"You bet. You get a reputation for being good, reliable, and fast, there'll be no shortage of people who want you." Then he looked at me. "Of course, you lose people if you're on tour too much, you fall off their radar. Price of fame, I guess. Do some artsy solo albums."

I wasn't sure if that was advice or some kind of given in Chernwick's world. "Yeah," I said, figuring I was in general agreement with his sentiment, regardless.

After that, J and I got ready to leave. I saw Digger on the way out. "Hey, old man, I hear Mills may be coming to town."

"Yeah, probably day after tomorrow. Don't get your panties in a bunch. I'll work him about the next record. So far so good from the docs. So, you know, three days to go, I figure I can talk to him like Z's as good as back."

"Yeah. Okay." Technically I guess it was three days, now, since it was after midnight.

I left then, but the words "Z's as good as back" rattled around in my head. Say that out loud. It's got a kind of rhythm to it. I wrote it down when we got in the car. A little piece that could fit in a song somewhere.

"How'd it go?" J asked, once we were on the road.

"Molina loved it, Chernwick loved it. Let's celebrate."

"When we get home, okay?"

"Okayyyy."

Strangelove

Three days to go. I spent a couple of hours cleaning up my recordings and making a backup tape, and then I drove over to the production office in Santa Monica to deliver it. The delivery tape was on a reel, but I'd made a dub onto a cassette also, which I handed them in case they needed to check it. I sat down in an office with two production guys who listened to about five minutes of it and then shook my hand and said it was exactly like what Chernwick had described. I took that to mean they had talked to him on the phone that morning. I asked what they wanted me to do with it. They said nothing, consider it done.

I felt a little weird asking for payment on the spot, but Cadmon had said to. They gave me a bit of a weird look, too, but had no problem writing the check and handing it to me. I'd later learn that that *was* kind of weird, but given what a weird emergency job it was in the first place, a small production company like theirs was happy to just pay me and get on with things.

I wasn't sure if I could deposit the check here in LA anywhere, what with my bank being back in Boston. I didn't think putting money in through the ATM was quite the same as getting it out. Well, I supposed I could probably mail it in somehow. Then I realized, duh, Digger must have some way of putting money into my account. I'd ask him later.

I guess because I felt good about having money, even in the form of a check, in my pocket, I stopped to buy bourbon and ice cream on the way home. I also stocked up some other things I knew we'd eaten out of Remo's pantry: canned tuna, Campbell's soup, eggs.

When I got home, I put the groceries away in the kitchen and was about to go look for J in his writing room when I noticed he was sitting on the edge of the pool with his feet in the water. He was wearing cargo shorts, not swim trunks, so I guessed he was just cooling off. Then he put his face in his hands and I wondered what was wrong.

I hurried out the back door. "Hey, you okay?"

He looked up. His face was red, and I didn't think it was from sunburn. "It's hopeless."

I crouched down next to him. "What's hopeless?"

His answer was a heavy sigh.

I recalled something Carynne and several other people had said to me in the past, about how I needed to eat to maintain any faith in the world. "Want to tell me about it over some ice cream? Or a tuna sandwich?"

He blinked at me a little. "That... sounds sensible."

"I learned it from you. And Carynne. Come on."

So we went inside and I attempted to make tuna salad. Fortunately for me, the recipe is on the side of the can, and there was mayo and celery in the fridge. Unfortunately for me, I had neglected to buy bread, so what J actually got was a half sandwich on the last piece of bread, and the rest on Ritz crackers. Then I kind of tiptoed around on tenterhooks. He was sitting at the counter in the kitchen while I put the things away and washed the knife.

When he was done, he wiped his mouth on a napkin, said, "Thank you," and then burst into tears.

Okay. I just hugged him then, because I didn't know what else to do. He was still on the stool and I was standing there with my arms around him, trying to think of what to try next. I figured he was like me, and if I waited long enough, he'd eventually come up with the words to tell me what was going on. I had no idea at that point what had upset him so. If I had to guess, though, I would have guessed it was something to do with the screenplay and not something like... his cat at home. He buried his face in my neck.

Confession: I thought about Ziggy when he did that. I thought about Ziggy collapsing in my arms after the MSG show, exhausted and unable to carry himself even as far as the green room, unable to even hold his composure one more second.

J didn't cry anywhere near as hard, or as long. But I figured if he needed to let go that badly, he must've also been really wound up and at the end of his rope. I racked my brain for suggestions of what to try to make him feel better.

"You want to go lie down?" I tried, figuring that could mean sex or rest, but leaving the interpretation up to him.

He shook his head. "I'll be fine," he said, his forehead against my collarbone.

"You don't feel fine," I pointed out.

"No, really."

I kissed him on the ear to be sure, and he lifted his head, so I kissed him on the cheek, and he turned his head and caught my mouth with his then. But just when I thought I was sure—*okay, sex*—he pulled back. He got off the stool and splashed his face with water from the sink. I followed him to the living room. He was ready to talk.

Remo's living room looked like it didn't get a lot of use. He had white-beige leather sectional sofas on three sides around a round, glass coffee table, a couple of knick-knacks on the table, and a stereo cabinet against one wall. J pulled me down beside him.

"I know what happens in the end of my book," he said, sounding miserable.

"The book you've been working on for years?"

"Yes. The same book that my agent sold the dramatic production rights to, the same one that I've been working on the screenplay for, the screenplay that I've been faking my way through."

"Okay." I had been under the impression that finding out what was going to happen in the end was the thing J had been working on all this time. So the fact that it was upsetting him this much was confusing. "So, what happens?"

"He dies," J said, and squeezed his eyes shut again as they began to leak. I put my arm around him and he leaned his head on my shoulder.

"And that's a problem," I said, after what I hoped was a respectful length of silence.

"That's a problem," J said, nodding his head. "See, if I see things through to their natural conclusion, so that the book has literary integrity, that pretty much kills the entire Hollywood deal."

"It does?"

"It does. You're not allowed to kill off a main character in Hollywood. For one thing, it messes up the possibility of sequels."

"Ah."

"Plus, no one wants to go see a downer of a movie. And this is actually kind of a miniseries now that we're working on, and that's even worse. I mean, I know they say the secret to a happy ending is to end the story at the right place, right? But now that they're trying to make a series? Who's going to invest night after night of their time in a show if it doesn't have a happy ending? Not the studio who's making it, certainly." He let out a long breath. "My career as a screenwriter would be over before it even began."

I had something to say to that, but I decided to hold it until he wasn't so upset.

"It's the ultimate artistic catch-22, isn't it? The classic one. In order to keep the gravy train rolling, I have to betray my art. Betray my principles."

"Um, but don't lots of books have different endings from their movie or TV versions?"

He made a dismissive noise. "I hate the thought it would be one of *those*," he said. "This would be worse, though. I mean, usually the novelist doesn't get any say in what they do with the adaptation. If they chop the head off and stick Ronald Reagan in it, there's nothing you can do. But this would be me chopping the head off of my own baby."

"Oh." Yeah, that sounded bad, all right. I decided to try to say what I was going to before. "How much do you want to be a screenwriter, though? You've got a great career as a journalist, and novelist on top of that wouldn't be so bad...?"

"It isn't enough," he said. "The money, I mean. There isn't much more upward I can go in rock journalism, and I still barely make ends meet. My parents cover my rent whenever I can't. But I don't want to mooch off them forever. I don't... I don't know if this writing thing is really going to ever work out." He started to shake again, drawing a ragged breath. "Even if this gig works out, then it's over and who knows if there'll be another one? Even if I don't kill off my main character... what's the likelihood the show does well and the book sells well enough to put me on the map? Pretty slim. I don't know why I'm even trying and putting myself through this much grief."

That was the point where I understood this wasn't about the industry or the actual thing he was writing—it was a total collapse of artistic self-confidence. I'd seen it before. At school. The night before a big recital, the most talented oboe player or singer or whatever on the hall would have a massive meltdown, as if they were totally unaware that they were the best singer out of anyone there. Thing is, they *are* unaware of it. They can't see their own talent. The ones who don't make it are the ones who let that collapse of confidence cripple them. The ones who do make it are the ones who act like they're the best, even if they suck. They're the ones who think they're the best, even if they're not. And it becomes a self-fulfilling prophecy because they're the ones who survive.

The only way I got through without it happening to myself was two things. One, I never took conservatory that seriously because I knew being a classical musician was not going to be my thing. Two, I didn't finish.

Jonathan, on the other hand, how did he know how good a writer he was? Writers didn't get standing ovations. I supposed until they were famous, writers didn't get fan mail or really any kind of feedback other than paychecks and maybe rewrite advice from editors or agents. Right? "What did your agent say about it?"

"I haven't told her yet. I'm afraid she's going to chew

me out."

"And if she does? You'll quit writing, or what?"

"Um..."

"Serious question, J. Is she the right agent for you if you're afraid to tell her what your artistic aims are?"

"Um." He shifted. "Why are you so short? I've got the worst crick in my neck."

"Lie down, then." I squished him between me and the back of the couch as we lay side by side. "And don't dodge the question."

"I guess maybe I'm afraid... that she'll hate the idea, it'll put a rift between us, and I'll be back to square one, looking for a new agent *and* a new writing gig. Do you have any idea how hard it is to get a literary agent?"

"No. I'll assume it's hard, though."

"She's a good one. She makes deals. She goes out and finds money. I like her."

"But you're afraid she's going to say you're nuts for killing this character."

"Maybe I *am* nuts for killing this character. Maybe this is all an elaborate form of self-sabotage."

"Maybe you don't really want to be a Hollywood screenwriter and that's why you're sabotaging it."

"Hm." He appeared to be seriously considering this as a possibility.

The tearful kiss in the kitchen and now being pressed up against him had my libido rearing its head again. But I refrained from doing anything, waiting for him to say something. When he didn't, I went with a truism. "You have to be true to yourself, J. But only you can figure out what you really want."

He ran his hand up my leg. "Feels like you know what you want."

For some reason, that made me blush. "Yeah, well."

He pulled me into a kiss then. It wasn't long before he was under me. I was more than willing to talk more, but it seemed like talking time was over. We didn't even go back to the bedroom. I took him right there *au natural*, using just spit and patience. I felt his pain and I wanted to take it into myself, and if I couldn't do that, I wanted to at least make it better for a while.

He was gorgeous and wanton under me, never more beautiful than in those moments, and I'd never felt closer to him. I'd never felt more like I might want to say something like "I love you" while I waited for us both to catch our breath afterward in the afterglow.

I didn't say it, but I thought everything was going to be okay, then.

But J himself had said it: you have to stop at the right point to get a happy ending.

Debaser

Everyone hates being wrong. I'm no exception. I really thought Jonathan's attack of angst was over with. Maybe I was having post-sex rose-colored glasses, though. We took a shower together and everything seemed rosy, like a sunset after a rainstorm.

But I was wrong. I had just pulled my jeans on while we were getting dressed when I asked, "Do you want to do anything tonight?" In my mind I was asking him to say whether we were staying in or going out, whether he needed to work or he wanted to punt until he'd worked out what to do, or what.

Jonathan apparently heard it as something else. "Stop pressuring me to go out," he said.

I basically froze with my hands on the sides of my suitcase, which had all my shirts folded in it. I tried to recall what my exact words were and what I'd said wrong, while at the same time my brain was scrambling to come up with the words to fix it. "I... No pressure... I..." I felt my skin flash hot and cold, and then a surge of anger. "That's why I'm asking. If you don't want to go out, just say so."

"Of course you want to go out," he said, pulling on his jeans. His tone of voice was fairly reasonable. "You finished your project. You're ready to celebrate. Why not?"

"Why not?" I forced myself to straighten up and face him. "Because I've barely slept for three days and because if you don't want to go out—"

"You could go out without me," he pointed out.

"Yeah, I could, but I don't... wait, are you trying to get me to leave the house?" I kept trying to put myself in his position. "If you need some time alone—"

"No, I don't need some time alone!" He sat on the bed and pulled a shirt over his head, his wet hair sticking in all directions. "I need you to stop acting like I'm a twenty-four-hour sex dispenser and I need to stop thinking about how unfair it is that you just aced the gig that fell in your lap while I'm drowning over here."

We stared at each other, then, my eyes and mouth wide, and then his slowly growing to match mine. My mind was racing. Jonathan felt that way? Was I treating him like a groupie and not realizing it? And since when did he feel *competitive* with me?

He was apparently coming to his senses now that he had vented and was realizing what he'd said. He even put his fingers over his mouth.

"Let's start over," I whispered. I still hadn't moved a muscle since I'd stood up, like I was afraid to spook him. I cleared my throat and tried to say a little louder, "You... you've had a tough day. What... do you want to do tonight?"

He ran his hands through his wet hair, trying to get it to lie down. "I should call my agent."

"Okay. That's a good idea." In fact, before we'd had sex, hadn't I been the one telling him to call her, and hadn't he been the one arguing against it? Had he been lying there the whole time thinking *I'll just let Daron have his way and then I'll go call her? Because that's what's really important?* Maybe I didn't want to know. "I'll... I'll go in the studio so you can talk in private, all right? I'll... I'll be right in there if you need me for anything."

"All right," he said, staring at the carpet and looking miserable.

I really wanted to do something to ease that miserable look. But right then I was worried I'd make it even worse.

I grabbed a shirt on my way out and put it on as I crossed the house. I went into the studio, picked up the Ovation, and sat down with it in the far corner behind an amp, on the floor, my back to the wall and the guitar in my lap.

And then I just sat there thinking. How did I fuck this up? He kissed *me*. He touched me first. Didn't he? Had he felt pressured to do it? Had I been... ignoring his signs of reluctance or something? The way Ziggy used to willfully ignore mine?

I didn't think so. But I was suddenly really not sure what to think. Jonathan had never been a drama queen with me before. He was always the voice of reason.

But this was the first time I'd been there for an artistic setback. I knew perfectly well how a creative block could fuck up my perspective on life and the people around me. Why should J be any different?

I wanted to cut him some slack. But what I didn't trust now were my own reactions. I'd thought I was helping. I'd thought I was being a good boyfriend. In fact, I'd say that up until the point where it all took a left turn when he'd accused me of pressuring him, today had been the most like his boyfriend I'd ever felt.

I played the moment over in my mind again and again. Eventually I realized something. My reaction, freezing like that, trying to fix it... that was the same reaction I used to have as a kid when Digger would suddenly take a left turn on me. Those nights when he'd go from being the cool dad I looked up to to the god of caprice. And that was why I got so angry. I was done with that shit. It was not my job to tiptoe around him anymore.

Which didn't mean I didn't care about Jonathan's feelings. I did. Was it something about me that kept me from reading Digger's moods and kept me from reading Jonathan's mind? I don't think it's reasonable to expect me to be a mind reader. In fact, I thought Ziggy had said that to me once, or me to him, I couldn't remember. Or maybe it was Carynne. At any rate, I was pretty sure mind reading was not actually on the list of things that were required to be a decent boyfriend.

Which didn't mean it wasn't my fault somehow, but I didn't think it was that.

Two hours later I was still sitting there. I heard the hinge on the studio door as Jonathan pushed it open. It was meant to be a silent hinge, but when there was no other sound at all, I could hear it clearly.

"Daron?"

I scrambled to my feet, suddenly not wanting him to see that I'd been literally hiding. I don't think until that moment I had realized that's what I was doing. It had seemed perfectly reasonable when I'd walked in to stuff myself in the back of the room behind a piece of equipment.

"Over here," I said, holding the guitar by the neck in one hand. "Um, just checking out the cables back here." I put on that false bravado that had helped me fake through so many tough situations in the past. I didn't feel anywhere near as brave or chipper as I sounded when I said, "Hey, how are you feeling?"

There was no falseness in his reply. "I am so sorry." He stepped closer, and I put the guitar into a stand and let him take my hands. "I said some things I really didn't mean. I don't know what got into me."

I do, I thought, but figured it wouldn't be a good thing to say. "I'm not good at telling what people mean other than what they say."

"I know."

"And I'm even worse at telling what they want to say but don't."

"I know. I'm sorry. I don't usually suck quite so badly at expressing my needs." He looked me in the eye, which meant he was looking down at me, but you know, it wasn't like he was looking down *on* me. He was just taller.

I made a preemptive guess. "If you want to have less sex, just say so."

"That isn't it, Daron. I have no idea why I said that. If we're anything, first and foremost, it's lovers. I was just being hurt and angry and stupid. I was feeling like I'm losing control of my life and my stupid reaction was to try to grab it from you."

"Control?"

"You don't feel like you're the one who dictates when we have sex?"

"Not as such, no. I was under the impression it was more of a mutual thing...? Am I wrong?"

He seemed to be thinking it over.

"Tonight, for example," I said, "I really *really* thought was your idea."

His eyes unfocused. "It's kind of fuzzy to me now how it started. I guess it was a bad idea, though. I didn't realize how I was going to feel, I guess. I mean, I feel like I'm on the verge of whoring myself to Hollywood for the money, but I didn't realize that having actual sex when I feel like that was going to make me feel like a cheap piece of ass."

"Why don't you get on top when you feel like that?"

He laughed a little, then realized I was serious. "You wouldn't mind?"

"No. I don't care which of us does what. I wouldn't want it to always be the same in either direction."

"I can't believe I never asked you that before."

"We're still new, J," I said. I think he actually *had* asked me that once before, but I guess the answer didn't stick. "Look. I don't know how long it usually takes people to get to know each other, but really, our relationship as lovers can still be counted in days, not months. I don't count the time we're apart unless we talk on the phone. By my count that gives us... a couple of days in Boston, two days in Georgia, a week in New York, a week in Mexico, and what, a little over a week here in LA?"

"I suppose you're right. I've been thinking of you as someone I've known for years..."

"But not *known*."

"In the Biblical sense."

"Yeah." I squeezed his fingers but didn't want to make a false move toward ending the conversation if he still had more to say.

But no, he was done. This time, his face and voice were as clear as the sky after a storm. "Well, I'm really sorry. For saying totally uncalled-for things."

"Apology accepted. And I knew you must really be having trouble," I said with a grin. "Normally you can't lay on the bullshit so thick!"

"God, I know! *Save it for the manuscript, Jonathan!* Say that to me next time, okay?"

"Okay. Now, tell me seriously, what do you want to do tonight? Order a pizza? Work? Drive to Mexico and pretend we were never here? Totally up to you."

"Well, my agent said sleep on it, don't make any decisions until after that. She wants me to meet with the team tomorrow. So she basically said don't touch it, don't work tonight."

"All right. We could watch movies? Or go see one?"

He made a dismissive noise. "Let's go see a show. I'm sure there's something. Come on. It's not too late."

So that's how we ended up going to see some local bands at the Whiskey after all.

The Art of Noise

The next morning there were two days left until Ziggy's program ended, and breakfast turned into a pep talk for Jonathan. We had his agent on speakerphone.

"Honestly, Jonathan," she said. "If anything, your problem in Hollywood is that you'll always be the smartest guy in the room. I've seen the pages you faxed. You're doing great. They love you. They think it's novel and interesting that you're invested in the character development arcs."

"But how am I going to tell them that we're going to kill off one of the main characters?"

"You have to sell it as literature. The whole concept here is that we're bringing the Great American Novel to television, right? I mean, tell me about this death, is it a huge downer?"

"Well, the thing is, it's a moral triumph, and it's the right thing for the character and the world. I think it's earned. I really do. It's not cheap."

"Okay, you know what they say to baseball pitchers when the manager goes to the mound? Trust your stuff. You have great stuff, Jonathan. Go in there and knock them out. If you hit resistance, you have them call me and we'll conference in. Something will work out. I promise."

"What if they laugh me out of the room as a fraud?"

"Then you can forever hold your head up high saying you were too good for Hollywood. But that's not going to happen. Look, I set the meeting for noon your time, that'll be three o'clock here, so if it goes south just call me. If it all goes well, you'll end up going out to lunch with those guys and I'll go off to have cocktails here. Be goal oriented. Positive visualization. I'm visualizing a cosmo. Let's get there, all right?"

"All right."

After she hung up, I picked up the ball. "She's right, you know. They didn't bring you into the development team out of pity for you as a poor novelist. They need you. Without you, it doesn't work. And you have to keep reminding them of that. You're indispensable."

He looked like he was about to argue, but he didn't. "Okay. I better hit the road, though, in case I hit traffic."

And then we had this moment where neither of us moved, where I wasn't sure if it was okay to give him a goodbye kiss and I guess he wasn't sure if he still wanted one? Or had the right to ask for one?

He finally leaned in and gave me a quick peck on the cheek and we both laughed. "Sorry I'm so ridiculous. I'll be sane again once this screenplay is done."

"We're both ridiculous. Now go." I shooed him out.

After he left I put on my swim trunks and actually swam in the pool, which I didn't do anywhere near as often as I would have thought, what with the pool right there in the back. Then I dried off and went into the studio out of habit.

There was email from Sarah Rogue with her phone number saying she wanted to know when she could come and jam. I called her back, and an hour or so later I was giving her a tour of the house. She was in jeans and a batik-print shirt, carrying a western-type jacket with fringe on it. She looked the most comfortable I'd seen her, though the first thing she did once we got inside was take her shoes off.

"So what's the story with you and Remo again?" she asked while we drank some soda in the kitchen. She was sitting on a stool while I leaned against the stone countertop.

"Long story short: when I was a kid, he and Digger were friends, and I used to play with Nomad sometimes when I was twelve, thirteen, fourteen. Then they got discovered and Remo moved out here and I didn't see him for a couple of years."

"Did he teach you to play the guitar?"

"He got me started, anyway." I drained my glass and put it in the sink. "What about you? Did you have a cool uncle-type?"

"My mother tells the story that when I was two or three, I would climb up to the piano, push it open, and push the keys. At first she didn't think anything of it. Toddlers will bang on anything. But then she realized I was playing along with TV commercials."

"Wow. That's young."

"Well, she swept me straight into a special arts program, and by the time I was seven I was in the Julliard pre-college program."

"Julliard!" I made bowing motions in her direction. "You went there for undergrad, too?"

She snorted. "I quit before I could finish."

"Huh. Me, too. RIMCon."

"No kidding. Why'd you quit?"

"Ran out of money. How about you?"

"Ran out of patience." She came toward me and set her glass next to mine in the sink. "Come on. Let's play."

Okay, Julliard, do I have to explain that? I mean, my school was a good one, but Julliard is to other music schools what Harvard is to other universities. It's the household name. It's the best. It's also supposedly the toughest. Bart once told me he didn't want to go there because he didn't want to have to work that hard, but that his father wanted him to apply anyway—presumably so that if he got in, his father could say he had a son who got into Julliard.

What was great about Sarah having gone to Julliard was that I didn't worry for one second that she couldn't keep up with me. Didn't even enter my mind. In fact, there was a half-second when we were warming up where I wondered if I was going to be able to keep up with her. But the moment passed, and the rest was just fun.

We jammed a bit, using some jazz improv chord progressions first, but then she played me a thing of hers and we played with that, passing the solo back and forth. Then we had a little break, and then I played her one of the things I had cooked up for the soundtrack but that I hadn't really developed. And the next thing you know, we were writing a song, planning out a bridge and parts and all that kind of thing. It wasn't even like we intended to, it was more like a reflex we couldn't stop. We ended up recording it, and I dubbed us cassettes of it. Then, for total hilarity, I sat down at the keyboard and she picked up the guitar, and we ended up with a kind of halting country-ish thing—country because she knew pretty much just folk chords and the Ovation easily leans that way and because all I really knew to do with the piano as an accompanist was when to hit the seven. So we ended up with something that sounded like Johnny Cash's backing band had gotten into the wrong drugs.

I had no idea how much time had passed, but my thumb was starting to hurt a little. I looked up from the keyboard, which I had to look at most of the time as I played, and saw Jonathan in the doorway. I stopped playing and Sarah looked up from her fingers, too, and said, "Oh, hey!"

"Hey," Jonathan said, looking a little surprised but mostly bemused. "I thought that didn't sound like you." Meaning me on the guitar.

"Heh, yeah. You guys met at one of those parties, right? Sarah, Jonathan, Jonathan, Sarah." I stood up from the keyboard and my stomach growled. "Did you have lunch?"

Jonathan nodded. "And it's getting closer to dinner, you guys."

"Wait." I blinked at him. "So does that mean he lives or he dies?"

"He dies!" Jonathan said exultantly.

"Yeah!" We high fived. Then I turned to Sarah. "Um, long story. And, dinner?"

Jonathan looked chagrined. "I didn't know we'd have a guest, so I only bought for two."

"Oh, don't worry about me," she said. "I should probably get going." She looked at her watch.

"But if you leave now, you'll be in traffic for two hours. Or more. It's Friday, and everyone and their brother is out there." Jonathan waved his hands. "I'll make it tomorrow. And I'm still full from lunch anyway. Why don't you guys have a snack and then let's go out."

"Are you sure?" I asked.

"I would love to hang out more with you guys," Sarah said. "I just don't want to impose."

My stomach growled again.

"Snack," Jonathan said, pointing at my belly button. "That's the first priority."

"Okay." So we followed him to the kitchen, where he looked like he was in the middle of putting away groceries. There was now a bowl of fruit on the counter that hadn't been there before, a handful of avocados on the windowsill, and a vase of flowers on the breakfast table.

J felt up the avocados, picked two, pitted and skinned them, then mashed them up in a bowl with onion salt. He handed us the bowl and a bag of tortilla chips and stood back.

Okay, we were slightly more civilized than that

might lead you to believe. We sat down on the stools at the eating counter, and while Sarah and I methodically devoured every morsel of guacamole, J told us about the meeting and subsequent champagne lunch.

"I would have been home sooner, but I had to sober up before I could drive," he said. "Those guys can drink."

"So what did you tell them?"

"In the end I approached it just like pitching a feature story to a major magazine. In other words, hey, I got this absolutely brilliant idea, here's why it's brilliant, here's why it's perfect for *you*, and here's why I am the perfect one to write it. While I was driving in I realized of course that's how I should approach it. I kept thinking of it in terms of relationship, you know? Like I'm nothing, just a pimple on the ass of the industry, but hey, when you're a writer, there's always someone who thinks that. When you're a freelance journalist, you're a dime a dozen. But someone has to write the cover story for *Rolling Stone*, for *SPIN*. That's been me. Why shouldn't this also be me? It's my novel, my story. I basically had to convince them that I'm a genius."

"But you are a genius," I said.

"Sounds like you had to convince yourself you're a genius," Sarah put in.

"Exactly, my dear, exactly. And so they listened to me, decided I was right about where the story should go, and off we went to have champagne and caviar."

"Is caviar good?" Sarah asked.

"Well, they give you such a teensy amount on a cracker with some other stuff... I guess it was okay. It tasted mostly like cream cheese on a cracker with a little something salty." He got up and poured us all ice water. "If it were a bigger production company, maybe we would have gotten more. Hollywood. Who knows how it works."

Sarah was nodding like she was listening to a song in her head but agreeing at the same time. "Well, wish me luck. Tomorrow I meet Mills."

"Mister Magic Pen," I said. "So it's tomorrow?"

"Yep."

"We had champagne when he signed us, but no caviar. Of course, we were in the green room of some hockey arena in Seattle at the time..." Which wasn't exactly true, but it was a good story.

"And you played hard to get," Jonathan said.

Her eyes got wide. "You did?"

"Not really." I explained the circumstances of our contract with Charles River, and how in the end we broke that one with their blessing and signed a brand new one with BNC and got a chunky cash advance.

"And Digger negotiated it for you?" She was all ears. I would've been too, at that stage.

"No. I negotiated it myself. We were still self-managing at that point. It was when dealing with Mills became too much for me to handle that we brought Digger in."

"And he's your dad, right?"

"Yeah." I bit my lip. "I'm going to fire him, though."

"Why? Because it's too weird having your dad as a manager?"

"Uh, it's complicated, but yeah, it boils down to that."

"The funny thing is," she said, "the reason I got him is because I didn't want my mother trying to manage me. And for some weird reason he's the only one she'll listen to. First we were with a big agency in New York, but the guy there and my mother, it was like oil and water. Or like oil and fire, BOOM, every time they talked something blew up. He introduced us to Digger and here we are."

"Whatever works," I said, trying to stay really neutral. "I haven't told him I plan to fire him. I guess I'm waiting for the right moment."

Jonathan looked at me with concern. "What kind of moment?"

"Oh, you know, when he really pisses me off and I want to kick him in the nuts, I'll fire him instead...?" I suggested. "Bad idea?"

"Well, I'm thinking if you want to make sure all the finances transfer properly, it might be better not to do it when you're having a fight, you know? Don't get him all pissed off at you."

"Oh, he'll be pissed off from being fired no matter what," I said.

"Is Ziggy going to stay with him?" J asked.

"I assume so. They've been really chummy lately." I didn't explain about the whole Betty Ford family-orientation thing.

"He introduced me to Galani Gilliman," Sarah said. "She seems pretty happy with him. But yeah, parent as manager? I'd go nuts. I go nuts as it is."

Jonathan went into friendly reporter mode. "How old are you, Sarah?"

"Twenty-three."

"No way!" I burst out. "I could swear you were younger than me."

"That's because I look like I'm fourteen in the stupid dresses they make me wear." She sighed. "How old are you?"

"Twenty-two. What are you going to wear to the meeting?"

"Oh, fuck if I know. What does this guy Mills like?"

"No idea."

"Well, I'll leave my outfit to the fashion consultant. She probably planned it weeks ago."

"Long way from Julliard," I said.

"Hang on, Julliard?" Jonathan did not do an actual double-take, but he came close. "I thought you were mostly a fashion model."

"That's exactly what they want you to think," she said. "I wouldn't put it past them to decide to lie and say I'm younger, too."

"Oh, right, and you had that indie album. Daron told me about it." Jonathan shook his head. "Well, good luck tomorrow."

"Huh, wish me luck, too," I said. "I think Digger and I are going to try to pin him down on making the commitment to the next record. If not tomorrow, before he leaves town. You first, though."

She gave me a little bow across the table.

The three of us went out to dinner shortly after that. We got stalked by a paparazzo in the parking lot, but Sarah said she was used to it.

Lay Your Hands on Me

We had taken separate cars to the restaurant, and I drove on the way home. That helped me keep my mind off wondering whether things were going to be good or weird when Jonathan and I were alone again.

Was it better to be proactive about it? Ask him about whether it was my imagination that he looked a little jealous when he came home and found her there? Or was it better to let it drop, don't embarrass him with it and work harder to make him happy? But my way of making him happy, or making it up to him, would have been sex. And obviously I had questions about that.

I should let him make the first move, I thought. Except he thought I was the one who dictated when we did or didn't have sex. That was the thing. If it were up to me, the answer would always be yes, let's have sex. It was hard for me to imagine not wanting to, unless we were really having a terrible fight. I mean, even when Ziggy and I were at our absolute worst, I never stopped wanting him.

So much for keeping my mind off wondering. Having to drive kept it to a dull roar, though.

Once we got into the house I found myself going through the motions of pouring a glass of ice water. "Want some?"

"Sure."

I poured two glasses and handed him one. My fingers touched his and I blurted out, "Does it have to be complicated?"

"Which 'it'?"

"Figuring out whether to have sex or not. I mean, just tell me if you're too tired or too wrapped up or... or you know what? You don't have to give me a reason. I don't want to take it for granted. I get it now. I did really make the assumption that... that we're..." Ah, damn words, why is it so hard to make them sound the way you want?

He sipped. "We're lovers, Daron. It was a reasonable assumption to make."

"Okay. But there's a difference, maybe, between a vacation to Mexico and... and... whatever this is we've got going on here."

He gave me that "you're being adorable again" smile, put down the water glass, and kissed me. I put mine down without looking and miraculously did not spill it. The kiss was very tender. I think that made me even hornier than a rough one would've. Quite possibly.

And what went through my head at that point was this: *Please don't say no just to make a point. Please say yes, please say yes. Please Jonathan please.*

Part of me wanted to prove that I didn't need to have sex every single day to survive. Part of me wanted to prove that rational, mature human beings weren't ruled by their dicks.

That part of me was completely drowned out by need. What would I do if he said no? At that moment I wasn't rational enough to cook up good answers like, oh, jerk off in the bathroom.

He didn't say no. Thank god. He slid down the front of me and pulled open my jeans and worshiped what stuck out using his tongue. Reminded me so very much of a caterer at a hotel not that far from here.

I pulled free of him before I could come, trying to ask him what he wanted, trying to ask what he was thinking since I didn't know, trying to figure it all out, but I couldn't get any words out, and so I let him coax me back into his mouth and finish me off.

When I finally got words back, we were in bed, cuddling. "Are you sure?"

He nuzzled me. "I'm sure."

Except I wasn't sure he'd known what I meant. "I mean, was that enough for you?"

"I'll make love to you in the morning, when I'm recharged," he said. "All right?"

"Only if you want to..."

"Daron. I want to. In the morning."

"Okay. I don't understand it, but I don't have to. I'll just accept it."

"There's this thing called delayed gratification," he said.

"Oh. Is that what it is?"

"It's a luxury to know that I can wait and that you'll still be here in the morning."

"I suppose I can imagine that feeling." I was drowsy with post-orgasmic haze.

He was drowsy with just being tired. "I'm going to wake up next to you and be thrilled all over again that it's you lying here next to me, and then I'm going to roll over and have my way with you."

"Sounds nice."

And it was.

The End of Innocence

So it began to dawn on me that Jonathan was a morning person, no pun intended.

That particular morning he confessed how much he loved penetrating with his morning wood and told me that the only reason he hadn't done it to me more often was that he knew how much I liked to sleep in. (He didn't bring up the fact that half the time lately insomnia had been sending me into the studio before dawn, but whatever, point taken.) I told him he could basically do me anytime of day or night and I'd tell him if it became a problem. We basically had to make a mutual promise to tell each other when to back off. That we made this promise while he was balls deep in me didn't detract from the significance of it.

Maybe it added to it.

We were lying there and I was contemplating going back to sleep when the phone rang. He answered it, but I was assuming it was for me, probably Digger to tell me when and if we were meeting with Mills.

But no, it was for Jonathan. I yawned, decided to take a shower, then decided to take a swim right from getting freshly showered without bothering to put on trunks. What was the point of a private pool and a sheltered backyard if you couldn't skinny dip?

When I was done doing my half-assed laps I climbed out and got back into the shower to get the chlorine off. I was just getting out of the shower when J got in it, and when he got out I was still in the bathroom, Q-tipping my ears and combing out my hair, which was getting long.

"So, that was the production company on the phone," he said as he toweled his torso. "Looks like things are really shaping up into... some kind of shape."

"Oh yeah, what shape is that?"

"Very definitely mini-series. Backing's come through. They want me to commit to being here to work with them three days a week for at least three months." He wrapped the towel around his head. "But probably more like six."

"That's great! Your mom won't mind feeding the cat?"

"Well, I'm thinking of giving up my place in Jersey. Lease is about to run out anyway. That way I can pay for a place here." His eyes looked very blue in the bathroom light as he drew me slowly into a damp half-hug, our hips touching. "Remo will want his house back eventually, I assume."

"Um, probably, though I'm under the impression we could stay right through Christmas if we wanted. That way you could save your money."

"It'd be weird if you weren't here, though," J said. "He's your mentor."

"He's your friend," I replied. "At this point, you *are*, you know."

"It'd still be weird. I think I should look for a place." His gaze bore into mine, and I knew he was trying to say something important. "Want to move in with me?"

I did not say "what?" though I thought it, because it took my brain a moment to believe that's what he had asked. "In LA?" I asked stupidly, because I was still trying to work out if that was all he had asked. I mean, wait, *move in*? He had used the words "move in." Move in doesn't just mean, you know, move in. Does it?

"Maybe West Hollywood," he said. "A little less traffic between there and the office."

The gay neighborhood. I tried to keep the discussion to logistics, since I had no idea what I was feeling. "I don't even know if I'll be here, though. What if we end up with overseas dates after all? What if Jordan Travers wants us in New York to record?"

And then what I was feeling hit me like a fire hose. *What about Ziggy?*

"Don't make me any promises," J said. "You don't have to. But if I'm going to be here, and you don't have to be anywhere else, I'd rather have more mornings like this one than not. I don't exactly feel like you're rushing to get back to Boston."

Boston and my homophobic-but-trying-to-get-over-it housemate, plus the housemate that I really liked sex with but probably shouldn't tempt myself with, and my little sister. He was right. I wasn't rushing back to that.

Then the phone rang. This time it was Digger, and he was telling me when to be at the BNC offices. I felt weird talking to him with no clothes on. I got dressed somewhat hurriedly after I got off the phone.

"Look," I told Jonathan. "I'll probably know more about what my next few months will look like by tonight."

"The subject is wide open," J said, combing out his hair. He'd gotten dressed in his work clothes while I'd been on the phone. "But there you have it. I'd like you to move in. Or for the two of us to keep staying here. Whatever. Now you know how I feel." He turned to face me. "I want more mornings like today."

I gave him a quick kiss. "I can't complain about that. Now come on, I'm dropping you off and then taking the truck to BNC. I'll pick you up after? Or should we meet at the deli?"

"The deli," he said, putting his laptop into his bag.

So I drove him to the production office, and then I got into traffic even though it wasn't rush hour. I flipped the channels on the radio, but I wasn't really listening to what songs I was finding.

I was thinking about Ziggy. Would I see him tomorrow? Would he come out of the clinic and head into LA? Would Digger put him up? Would he be surprised to see me?

Under other circumstances I would've told him there were guest beds at Remo's. Something told me that putting the three of us under one roof right now was a recipe for disaster bigger than an earthquake, mudslide, and fire combined.

I'd have to ask Digger. For all I knew, Ziggy could be flying straight back to Boston. I remembered there was also a small chance they might decide at the last minute to keep him for another 28 days. But I was pretty sure they would have already told Digger if it looked like that was what was going to happen. Of course, that didn't mean that Digger had bothered to tell me, but I was reasonably sure Digger was operating under the same assumption I was, that Ziggy was getting out tomorrow.

The only reason I wasn't a nervous wreck thinking about that, or about meeting with Mills, was because the sex that morning had been so good. My entire body felt as good as I'd ever felt. I opened the window, and as the traffic broke up I let the wind blow my hair around. Yeah, that's how I got that carefree, wind-blown look. I swaggered up to the BNC offices looking and feeling like a rock star, all right.

Paper in Fire

The secretaries were not as fawny as the last time I had been here, but then, that time had been preceded by a lot of hype and there was the little matter of the unveiling of the gold record. Or maybe it was just that Ziggy wasn't here this time.

Some junior publicist sat me in a conference room with a can of Pepsi. Doesn't anyone drink Coke anymore? I wondered. Or was it that BNC had so many artists with Pepsi endorsement deals? Mills and Digger were both late. I wondered if Mills had met Sarah yet and what he thought of her. I wondered if I could put in a good word for her or what.

The meeting room had a windowsill that ran the length of the room and was pretty much covered with music trade magazines. I thumbed through *Cashbox*.

About 45 minutes later, they came in. They were together, and it dawned on me that maybe the meeting with Sarah had happened somewhere else—Digger's office?—and then the two of them came here together. I still hadn't been to Digger's office. It was in the same building where Nomad had their rehearsal space, but I only had a vague memory of where that was.

Mills shook my hand and then excused himself to "get something." Digger sat down across the table from me, leaving the head seat for Mills.

"How's it hanging, kiddo?"

It was high time for a new answer to that question. "Loose as a goose, old man."

He cracked a little smile at that. "You get that background music work done?"

"Yeah. In fact, they paid me by check."

"I can put it in your account for you if you're not heading back East anytime soon. Are you?"

"That probably depends on what happens tomorrow."

"Oh, you mean with Ziggy? Yeah, they're springing him. I'm supposed to pick him up."

"Where are you taking him?"

Digger snorted. "You sound like something out of a B-movie thriller. Like I'm kidnapping him or something. 'Where are you taking him...' Calm down, kiddo."

"I am calm," I said, but you know, whenever you have to say that...

Mills came in and handed a couple of pages of something to Digger and sat down with his own pages at the seat we'd left for him. Digger examined the sheet on top.

"What's that?" I asked.

Mills was wearing a beige leisure jacket over a salmon polo shirt and had a pair of sunglasses still perched on his head. His voice was serious. "Latest sales numbers. Let me tell you, they don't look good."

I blinked at him for a couple of seconds, then rose partway out of my chair to snag the paper he had in front of himself and pull it across the table to me. Did he think I couldn't read? Or was the artist not supposed to look at numbers? It seemed pretty stupid to me that he hadn't copied it for me to see, too.

Of course, when confronted with the columns of numbers, I didn't know what I was seeing.

Digger acted like he didn't either, but I had the feeling maybe that was his way of saving face for me. Nicest thing he ever did for me, really. "This one here, is that how many units shipped? And this column is the breakdown to each market?"

Mills took a pen out of his pocket and went into detail, then. "Yeah. This here..." He circled a number on Digger's paper and I found it on my own. "That's the net. And here are the sell-through percentages."

The names on the rows were familiar enough. "So you're saying Tower is selling the shit out of it, but Sam Goody isn't."

"That is one takeaway from these numbers, yeah. It's baffling. Tower's presence is heaviest on the West Coast, but you just played many more and many bigger venues in the east. The carryover into eastern and midwestern retail just isn't there."

"That's because the initial inventory was way too low," Digger said. "Looks like Newbury did all right."

"They do a lot with Boston-local bands." Mills shrugged like it didn't matter. Maybe it didn't. "We have a problem. A really big problem."

"I've been telling you that since the pre-release buy," Digger said.

"It's not the pre-release buy that's the problem. The problem is that you just did one of the biggest, highest-profile tours of the summer, and the record is still selling for shit. That means one of two things. Either the record is shit—which, I will say before you get me wrong, that it most certainly is *not*—or you've got some other PR problem bedeviling you. And like I said, the record's good. So that isn't it."

"What kind of PR problem?" I asked. "Is this back to that stuff about category? The whole question of do they even have an 'alternative rock' shelf, and if they don't, are we buried between Metallica and Motörhead?"

"But the radio play's been so strong," Digger added, "across all categories. That has to have an impact."

Mills was stony-faced. "Radio play doesn't always translate to sales. Maybe radio guys like it better than the general public does. Wouldn't be the first time. And sometimes people like something on the radio, but they lose interest for some other reason." He tapped his pen against the fake wood grain of the table. "A PR reason."

So it was back to that. "Some other PR reason," I repeated. "You mean... like Ziggy being in rehab?" His picture hadn't been on the cover of any of the tabloids in the supermarket the other day, but I hadn't been watching TV, hadn't been reading the news or magazines lately, so maybe there was some train wreck going on that I missed.

"That is the sort of thing that can have this sort of effect, yes," Mills said somewhat vaguely.

Digger shook his head. "You know how many celebs he's up there with right now? A ton. I don't see most of them tanking their careers."

Mills shrugged. "With actors, it's all about convincing a director to take you on despite the drugs. Actors can do that. Music's different. This is the American consumer we're talking about. They're a much more Puritanical bunch than the people who run the industry, you know."

The back of my neck began to prickle. "You still haven't said what you think the problem is with Moondog Three," I said.

"The problem is that you're under water," Mills replied, looking me straight in the eye. "You haven't earned back the advance we paid the band, and frankly, I don't think there's more we can do to boost album sales at this point. Maybe, just maybe, we're going to see a bump when this movie with Ziggy comes out, but I'm skeptical about that. If sales keep up at the low rate they're at, then maybe we'll see it recoup in another year to eighteen months."

Under water. I was suddenly really glad Carynne had run the tour on an absolute shoestring, meaning we actually made money on the road instead of blowing it all in the service of boosting album sales. My hackles rose as shock and panic flashed across my skin. Being labeled "unrecoupable" was far worse than anything else I could think of, including being called gay, honestly. And that's what he had just said, though he hadn't used the word yet. He'd said "under water" and "recoup" and that was what he meant. "Unrecoupable" was the record-company equivalent of "unredeemable failure."

"We can hit the road again," I said, trying to scrape whatever I could to salvage things.

"Can you? You weren't even out eight full weeks and your singer landed in the loony bin," Mills snapped. "Shed-and-festival season's over. You'd be back to smaller venues, and you wouldn't have the publicity push of a new record anymore. The videos are falling out of heavy rotation."

"I thought we were going to make another one. Another single."

Mills shook his head. "Throwing good money after bad. If the band wants to spend the dough to do something, we can talk about it. But at this point BNC won't be putting you any deeper in the hole than you already are. Moondog Three is officially unrecoupable."

There it was. He said it. Rage and fear now battled each other, turning my stomach to knots and my face red. The loony bin comment made me want to slap him. I felt, basically, like he'd kicked me in the balls already, and he knew it, which made the loony bin comment totally uncalled for.

Digger, the useless sack of shit, had clammed up. He'd left me to be the one to get in the ring. Fine. I didn't have a comeback at this point. "Unrecoupable," I said, forcing myself to say the word.

Mills nodded, leaned over, and flipped the paper in front of me over so I could see the next page. He pointed at the number at the bottom. "That's how much you owe us."

Just kick me in the balls again, why don't you.

I put my hand over my eyes like I couldn't stand looking at it anymore. Digger finally said something.

"What about the re-release of *Prone*? Where are those numbers?"

"That includes those," Mills said.

"Oh." That's all Digger said. "Oh."

It filtered through my brain what that meant. If Digger wasn't going to do this, then I had to. "Are you saying that even when you factor in what *Prone* made, the combined amount still isn't enough?"

Mills nodded and cleared his throat. "You got a single advance that included both records."

"No, we didn't. You made a payment to Charles River for the rights to *Prone to Relapse*, and they paid it through to us. The deal for *1989* was a separate contract."

Mills shrugged. "We can move the money around like a shell game, but then all it will mean is the unrecoupable amount is even higher."

If he could be stone cold about it, so could I. "But it might mean a royalty check on the sales of *Prone* and 'Candlelight,' unrelated to the sales, or lack thereof, on *1989*."

"That's not how we do things here," Mills said, his voice rising a little. "Your product nets are ganged together. That's just how it is."

There was too much static in my head,—worrying over whether I was really that stupid to have signed something that said that—for me to clearly remember what the entertainment lawyer Watt had referred me to had said about that. I decided I was better off bluffing than showing fear. "That's not my interpretation of what I signed."

"That's certainly what's in our standard boilerplate."

"I didn't sign the standard boilerplate," *like a chump*, I silently added. "We made a lot of changes."

Mills sat back in his chair, which I took as a sign that I'd made a wrong move. He gave a nonchalant sniff. "The contract's back in the New York office or I'd show you what you signed."

I'd have Carynne look at my copy as soon as I could. "You know there's no way I'm accepting these numbers as fact without an audit," I said. I definitely remembered our lawyer putting in something about that. One audit per year, I think.

Mills shook his head. "You'll just be wasting your money on the auditor."

"I'll be wasting even more if it turns out you underreported the net on 'Candlelight' singles," I shot back.

Mills then gave Digger a look. "You better tell your boy here what reality is."

Digger, to his... credit?... tried to weasel out. "That contract is from before me. I don't know what it says."

"I mean, this audit business." A chummy laugh escaped Mills. "Seriously."

Digger now gave me a look, and it was one of the most pathetic expressions I'd ever seen on his face. Like he was trying to tell me not to shoot the messenger. "Oh, yeah, total waste of time and money if you ask me," he said weakly.

Of course he was going along with Mills, I realized. He had either just signed Sarah that morning for big money or he was still in negotiations trying to. He had to play nice with Mr. Magic Pen.

I didn't. Mills had basically already taken the gloves off and told me my band was less than worthless to him at this point. I had nothing to lose. I stood up. "Expect a call from my lawyer. And my new manager."

Digger sat upright then liked I'd just kicked *him* in the balls. Which I suppose I had. "Are you kidding me?"

Mills gave a dismissive snort. "Not that you're going to need much managing anytime soon." He leaned back further in the chair, pressing the pen between his two index fingers. "Another company can't touch you now. May I remind you of the exclusivity and option clauses, my friend."

Ever notice the only people who call you "my friend" are the ones who are not your friends? Exclusivity, that was the clause that said I couldn't start another band and sign somewhere else. Whatever. I had no intention of starting another band when I had put so much into this one. The option clause, on the other hand, was the thing in the contract that said BNC had dibs on the next Moondog Three record. It had seemed like a good thing to sign at the time. "Are you saying we should do another album?"

"No. I'm saying we won't commit to another album." Mills gave me a little smile, like he was trying to be nice, like maybe if I sat down and worked with him instead of against him, he'd come up with an answer.

I wasn't buying it. He went on. "But if you make one on your own, contractually it's ours. Its sales will go toward recouping the old advance, of course. But you're wasting your time and money if you don't solve your PR problem."

Wait, back to that again? I took a step back from the table, backtracking in my mind as well. He'd never come out and said what the PR problem was.

By now, I knew whenever there was something that no one would talk about, whenever there was something making people act weird, or suddenly turn into jerks...? Well, I knew what that thing was.

Which only made me more determined in that moment to make him say it. "What. PR. Problem."

Mills made another one of those condescending snorts and put both his feet on the floor. "This is really the wrong time for it. AIDS hysteria is only going to get worse. In a couple of years, don't be surprised if you don't see internment camps."

I played dumb. "For AIDS victims? I don't have AIDS, Mills."

"You don't have to. You know what the public calls it, right?"

"What they call what?"

"The Gay Plague." There. He finally said it.

I was surprised to hear myself say, "So the fuck what."

At that point he shook his head sadly, like I was a cancer patient arguing with my diagnosis, and reached into his inside jacket pocket and took out an envelope. He stood up to look at me eye-to-eye. "I paid a paparazzo for these this morning to keep them from going to *Us* or *People*. His negatives, too. Your auditor will find a line item for it."

He tossed the envelope onto the table and walked out. A handful of photos spilled partway out. I pulled them free of the envelope and looked at the small stack.

Me and Jonathan getting into the truck together in the parking garage of the Bonaventure. Me and Jonathan walking into the Whiskey. Me and Jonathan at the Front 242 show. Me and Jonathan getting into the truck together in some other random parking lot, probably outside the party where we'd met Sarah for the first time.

The next one was me and Jonathan holding hands... outside the doorway of the gallery where Matthew's photo exhibition was in New York. Who the fuck was this photographer? I half wondered if the next one was going to be us in a full lip lock on a loading dock in Atlanta.

It was worse. It was me and Ziggy at the Palladium, Ziggy with his arms around my neck. I nearly sat back down because my legs didn't want to hold me. But I didn't. Instead I looked at the next photo, the last one in the stack.

Another one from New York. From an odd angle, but zoomed in and clear as day. Ziggy lying on top of me—half naked and between my legs, for chrissake!—on the floor backstage at Madison Square Garden. His back was glistening with sweat, and my hand was planted between his shoulder blades. My face was visible over his shoulder.

I hadn't noticed that Digger had come around to my side of the table so he could look at the photos in my hands.

"I tried to tell you," he said.

I really, really wanted to belt him right then, but I didn't. Knowing that I had just fired him felt like armor. His "I told you so" didn't get under my skin. "Tried to tell me what?"

"This is your fault," he went on. "You didn't think someone was going to notice? What the hell were you thinking catting around Hollywood with your boytoy every night?"

I nearly smacked him then, too, right in the mouth, because insulting me was one thing, but insulting Jonathan I wasn't going to stand for. "Jonathan's done more for the success of Moondog Three than you ever did," I said.

"Oh, so that means he can flaunt planting his flag in your ass every night?"

Was I justified in hitting him that time? Was I? I don't know. It was like at that point the only thing I could do to fight back against vile words was to smack the mouth that spoke them. *Bam.* I used my open hand, right on his lips, and from the way he reached up quickly and grabbed his own chin, I would guess I loosened his jaw. Even a slap can make your head spin, you know.

Digger didn't hit back. He just stared in shock.

"Are you going to tell Ziggy the good news or should I?" I snapped.

"I… I don't know," he said, blinking.

"Give him Remo's number. That's where I'll be." I didn't wait around for Digger to get his head together. I didn't wait around for anything. I got in the car and did what everyone in LA seems to do all the fucking time. I drove.

I Need to Know

I ended up in the parking lot of a Circle K, on the pay phone on the outside of the building, to Carynne.

"Are you crying?"

"No, I'm not crying. What the hell makes you ask that?"

"Well, you sound upset."

"I am upset." I was not crying. This wasn't a "cry over it" kind of problem. This was a "fuck the world because the world is fucking me" kind of problem. "Mills has declared the album unrecoupable because I'm gay."

"What!"

"You heard me. You want it in more detail?"

"You bet I do."

"Okay, let me see if I can do it justice. First he shows me and Digger some numbers…"

"Wait, you had a meeting with him?"

"Yeah. At the BNC office out here. Oh, by the way, I fired Digger."

"What!"

"Let me tell the story in order and maybe it'll make sense. Okay, so he shows us these spreadsheets…"

"Did you keep a copy?"

"I did. Will you stop interrupting me? This shit is complicated."

"All right, all right."

"Anyway. He shows us how much money we owe them, then tells me the contract I signed not only lets them gang the payments they owe us for the re-release into the debt, he rubs my nose in it, reminding me we can't record with anyone else and we're dead in the water. And he says the reason the album isn't selling as well as it should, especially given the great publicity and the sellouts on the tour, is *not* that they fucked up and didn't get enough stock into the stores—"

"Wait, not? I thought they were saying the laydown was low because of genre confusion."

"They were, before, but we've moved on from that now, apparently, to the album isn't selling because I've been seen all over Los Angeles with Jonathan."

"Wait. That makes no sense."

When she said it like that, it hit me that it really *didn't* make sense. I mean, when Mills had first said it, I had been in denial, but I had half-believed what he'd said. Maybe because this was the sort of thing I was afraid of all along? Right? Wasn't that the reason everyone stayed in the closet? Because everyone knew it would hurt your career if you didn't?

But no one had ever come right out and explained *how* it would hurt a career. This wasn't like a group of concerned mothers was leading a campaign against stores carrying the album or picketing outside the stadiums. This wasn't like venues refusing to book us. This wasn't even like actual bad press had been appearing… yet.

"You're joking. I mean, you *aren't* joking, but I mean, he can't be serious about that."

"Serious enough that he paid some tabloid photographer for photos and negatives of me and J and Ziggy."

"When did you have a threesome with—"

"Dude! I'm on the phone here." I waved off a guy who kept approaching the phone with a handful of loose change and a hopeful expression. He had the grimy look of someone who had slept in his car and hadn't showered in a week. You see a lot of that in LA. "Come back later."

"Are you on a pay phone?"

"Yes. Anyway. I have the photos. I don't have the negatives."

"Are they bad?" She sounded like she was cringing.

"Pretty bad, I guess. Especially when you see them all together. The bitch of it is the most incriminating one is totally innocent. Not that that matters. Anyway. Digger said 'I told you so,' and I said 'You're fired.' That's the short version, anyway."

"Jeez, Daron."

"In the meantime, did I tell you I did a soundtrack for a documentary?"

"Did you just say you're going to do the soundtrack for a documentary?"

"Already did it. Turned it in and got paid. Which reminds me, I have the check. No way in hell I'm handing it to Digger now. We need to make sure he can't get at our accounts anymore."

"I can handle that. But, reminder: you're part owner of his company."

"Yeah, I know. And he's still Ziggy's personal manager. I know, Car'. I know firing him isn't like putting a genie back in the bottle. I won't get to pretend he doesn't exist. Alas. The point is, don't let him make off with anything if he gets pissed off enough to be that stupid."

"Okay. When are you coming back? When does Zig get out?"

"Zig's supposed to be out tomorrow. Digger's supposed to go pick him up."

"I'm supposing you didn't volunteer to ride in the car."

"Yeah, no."

She made that tick-tick sound with her mouth she sometimes made when she was thinking about things. "Dar'. You have to get there first."

"What?"

"If he hears this entire thing from Digger it's going to sound like... like..."

Like I'd been catting all over Hollywood with my boytoy. Fuck.

"Like it's your fault. You have to get there first. I'll get you directions to Betty Ford. Does Remo have a fax machine at the house?"

"I think so, but I don't know the number off the top of my head. Call me there later and we can figure it out. There's a line forming for the phone here."

"Okay. Shit, I wish I was there. Daron, listen to me, don't do anything drastic."

"You're the one telling me to kidnap Ziggy!"

"I didn't say kidnap! Just talk to him first. Jeez. Don't be so dramatic."

"You either. The most drastic thing I'm going to do tonight is... eat a sandwich and vent to Jonathan."

"Okay. I'll call you later. Remember that people love you, though, Daron. I love you."

"I love you, too, Carynne."

At which point the grimy guy with the loose change in his hands made smoochy kissy noises at me and I thought about punching him in the face. I decided he wasn't worth the trouble. There was no way smacking anyone was ever going to be as satisfying as smacking Digger had been. Maybe now was the time to dedicate myself to nonviolence for real. No, really. Quit while I was ahead.

Blasphemous Rumors

I got back in the truck and drove to the deli.

Jonathan was already there. He stood up when I approached the table, which I took to mean I had an alarming expression on my face.

And say what you want about what he did or didn't mean to me and what our relationship was or wasn't at that point, but I basically grabbed onto him with a death-grip kind of hug and then stood there like that for I have no idea how long. My mind went blank, thought ceased, and I felt... I have no idea what I felt.

That's not true. I just have to think about it for a while. Here goes:

What I felt was like my world was crumbling around me, like it was all just painted backdrops and they were peeling away to show the grungy backlot they had been hiding. When I'd been on the phone with Carynne, I'd tamped it down. We'd talked strategy. I'd vented.

But with Jonathan, two things were happening. One was that, just seeing him, I couldn't keep up the bullshit bravado. I'm not wired that way. Once I've let someone under my skin, they can always get in. They always *do* get in, even if they're not trying. My armor unzips like a Godzilla suit the second I'm with them.

The other thing is that I grabbed on to the one thing I could see that maybe wasn't crumbling as fast as my career.

I'm sure we stood there way too long. I'm sure people were staring. I didn't have the brain cells to think about it right then, and Jonathan didn't have the heart to push me away.

When I came to my senses, I sat down and ordered a pastrami sandwich with cream cheese and cucumber on rye, grilled, and a malted milkshake, even though I wasn't sure I was going to have the stomach to eat any of it.

I proceeded to give Jonathan pretty much the same story as Carynne, only more quietly, and with fewer interruptions. When I was done I put my head on my arms on the table and stared into the darkness behind my eyelids for a while.

I stayed that way until the food arrived. After a couple of sips of milkshake I discovered I did have the stomach for it after all, and I ate. J didn't say anything until I was finished, but he looked like he was thinking a lot.

He ordered a piece of chocolate cream pie when the waitress came to take my plate away. Then he spoke. I wondered if he was going to say something soothing, or something that was going to wreck me.

It was neither. He had gone into reporter fact-finding mode.

"Have you talked to Sarah yet?"

"No. The only person I've talked to is Carynne. Called her from a pay phone."

"Do you think Mills would give you the name of the photographer?"

"Doubtful. Mayyyybe Digger would have been able to get it, but I'm not sure I'm speaking to either of them right now."

"What's Carynne's relationship with Mills like?"

"Mills has always been Digger's job. I'd say Mills has a good impression of her, but that's about it."

"Are you sure about the contract?"

"No. Well, I'm pretty sure we didn't sign something that gangs all our profits into the same bucket, but until I see it, I can't be sure. He's right about the option clause, though. We're pretty much obligated to deliver them another album, but if they won't pay for it, we don't have the money to record something ourselves, and even if we do, they can still say it's not good enough and make us go back to square one. And we can't go anywhere else."

"How much of this has something to do with the merger, I wonder," Jonathan said, taking a bite of pie. "New legal department decides on their take on certain clauses, next thing you know when they want to clean house...? I'll make some calls tomorrow, find out more during business hours."

"Okay." Now I just felt drained. Some gigantic corporation was gobbling up the already huge corporation that owned me. I didn't even know how to feel about that. "I think this milkshake made my head hurt."

Jonathan gave me a look like he thought it probably wasn't the milkshake. He put his hand on mine instead of contradicting me, though. I wondered if some bullshit photographer hiding in the bushes outside was photographing it, but I didn't have the heart to pull away. At some point you have to say "stop" to the people who want to force you to be a certain way.

"Let's go home," Jonathan said. "We need to be near a phone."

"Okay." I had that black-cloud voice in my head saying it wouldn't do any good and why were we even putting any more effort into it because it was a done deal. Usually eating makes that voice go away, so the fact that it didn't? Well, this was some serious shit.

Jonathan drove while I sat in the passenger seat with my hands over my eyes. It was starting to sink in, I guess. My career was over...? That motherfucker Mills, had he actually gloated over it, or was that my imagination? Money. I was going to have to worry about money. The mortgage on the house. Ziggy paying for his mother's medical care. How was I going to keep Carynne as a manager if we didn't have money coming in to pay her, too? We couldn't tour year round—we barely made it through one summer. In fact, how was I going to keep the band together if we had no record deal? Ziggy could go into acting. Chris didn't have much incentive to stay...

Jonathan cleared his throat. "I'm sorry."

I looked at him. "For what?"

"We should have been more careful. I shouldn't have been—"

"Stop. Stop stop stop." I gripped my own thighs with my fingers because I needed to hold on to something. "It's not your fault."

"But without the photos you could have... played it straight."

I thought about that. Could I have fixed it all by groveling or telling Mills he was mistaken, J and I were just friends, and really I had a thing going with Sarah Rogue? It felt to me like the sort of thing you heard in the press all the time. Now I knew why.

Could I have done that? *Should* I have done that? No. Don't think so. "That wouldn't have helped. Mills was looking for an excuse to kill the next record. That had to be it. If not this, he would have come up with something else. This isn't your fault, J."

Which didn't mean it wasn't mine. "Wonderland" came on the car stereo, and I hit the off button so hard I almost broke it. Almost.

At the house, I found the fax machine in a corner of the room Jonathan used for writing. Helpfully, there was a phone number written in Sharpie on the front. That meant we had two phones. Jonathan took over the fax handset to make some calls. I went and got on the one in the living room.

I called Remo first. That is, I called his answering service and left a message.

Then I called Charles River Records, whose number I still had memorized, and got their answering machine. "Watt, whenever you get this, it's Daron. Marks. Moondog." Yeah, like he wouldn't remember me. "Just got some shitty news from BNC and I need your advice. Seriously. Here's the number where I'm staying in LA. I might need to talk to that lawyer you sent me to again, too. I'm pretty sure Carynne has his number, but in case she doesn't, I should get it."

Then I went and got my notebook and looked through the numbers in it to see if there was anyone else I should call. There were not a lot of numbers in it, and most of the ones there weren't for people who could help with this. Jay. Tread. Fans.

Courtney. Wow. Where was my brain? Of course Courtney needed to know what was going on with me and Digger, at the very least. Kicking Dear Ol' Dad to the curb was being kind of overshadowed in my mind by the other issues.

I knew I had to call Bart and Christian, too. But I wanted to have a chance to maybe know a little more about the contract and be sure what I was telling them before I got them all upset. I tried Carynne again, got her machine, and told her I was at Remo's.

Then I had the choice of waiting around for people to call me back or calling the house.

I called the house.

Colin picked up the phone and heard my voice. "Daron! How are you, man?"

"Shitty. Some serious music-industry bullshit is going down."

"Like what?"

"I should probably tell Chris before I tell you. No offense, but it's that kind of stuff."

"He's out right now, but I'll tell him to call you. Um, how's LA otherwise?"

"Otherwise, I hate the people and the traffic and the smog. But I did a kind of cool gig." I told him about how I basically pulled a soundtrack out of my ass in three days. "Couldn't have done it if I didn't have a studio right here at my fingertips, though. The Mac helped a little, too. Quick and dirty, and I got paid."

"Like a musician temp gig."

"Yeah. Although, when you think about it, every gig is a temp gig when you're a musician."

"This industry bullshit that's happening must be really bad for you to say that," Colin said.

Which made me think about what I'd said. "You know, that isn't how I meant it? But maybe it is. I really didn't think Moondog Three was going to... Wait a second. You haven't heard the story yet."

"Nope."

"Okay, I'll tell you, but don't let on to Christian that I didn't tell him first."

"Sure thing, boss."

So I recounted the whole meeting with Mills, including the bit about not giving me a copy of the spreadsheets, and Digger being a wimp, and Mills being a dick, me firing Digger, and how I walked out with the papers and photos in my hand.

"That is fucked up," Colin said, which was about as validating a thing as he could say. "The world is not supposed to work that way."

"At least I'm not blindsiding Carynne with it. I've been telling her for years that I want her to take over."

"She can handle it."

"Assuming there'll be anything to handle. She keeps telling me she can't do everything Digger can do. I keep telling her that just means it's her job to hire someone who can."

"What can't she do?"

"I think she can handle the negotiations and ball-busting part of the job just fine. She knows booking and live-show stuff like the back of her hand. But she doesn't know the recording company side or stuff like taxes."

Colin started laughing.

"What's so funny?"

"Carynne needs someone to do the band's financials?"

"Yeah, why is that funny?"

"Daron. I'm a CPA. Did you forget?"

So then I started laughing. "Yes. Yes, I did forget. Let's face it, Col'. You don't look like anybody's idea of an accountant."

"I know. I know. But this is who I am. Accountant is not who I am, it's just what I do. Who cares if your accountant has blue hair if he gets the numbers right, right? But people judge. I know they do. And I say fuck them, but they say fuck you right back. Because I chose to be this way, I chose not to fit their conception of what they think I should be like. And that's kind of the point, isn't it? I know when I've met someone who accepts me for who I am. I did choose to be this way."

"Your hair is blue now?"

"Uh, yeah. Midnight blue, so it actually doesn't look that different from the black until I go in the sun. Which I try to avoid. But my point is, Daron, I know that's how the world works, and I choose to do it anyway, and if the world fucks with me, at least I'm ready for that. What kills me is that you're going through the same stupid-ass shit as me, except in an industry that really, really, *really* should not care who the fuck you sleep with, and they're judging you and saying that's not what they want or expect from you when holy fuck, *come on*, you're a rock star and should (A) be able to fuck anything that moves, and (B), see (A)."

"Yeah."

"The other possibility is that this isn't casual unconscious homophobia floating around, boss. This could be that someone has it in for you and the gay is the excuse."

"That's what I told Jonathan. I don't know what I did to piss Mills off so much, though."

"This Mills character, is it his fuck-up that led to low sales? Maybe he's trying to deflect blame off of himself onto you."

I hadn't thought of that possibility. "I don't think he has that much to do with sales, personally. But maybe he's trying to deflect the blame from BNC as a whole. Hm. Especially if they're getting bought by another company."

"Hey, your sister's here, you want to talk to her, too?"

"Yes. Definitely. Thanks, Col'. You've given me a lot to think about." The really ironic thing, of course, was that Colin was in a profession where the way he looked was a problem, but if he had been in mine, no one would have given a flying fuck how many piercings he had or if his hair was Day-Glo green.

"No problem. Call whenever you want to vent. See you in email."

He handed the phone to Courtney, and I heard him say to her as he did, "Big brother has some news."

"Hey, what's up?" She sat in a chair; I could hear it scrape on the kitchen floor.

"Will you still love me if I'm broke and fired our father?"

"What the hell kind of question is that? Of course. What did he do this time?"

"Weaseled out of defending me when a record company exec was tearing me a new one. And then blamed me for bringing it on myself."

"Sounds like Dad. Is this something me and Carynne can fix?"

"Whoa, wait, you and Carynne?"

"Come on, she shouldn't have to do everything by herself. Is it?"

"No. I don't think there's anything we can do. It's technical, and it involves contracts, and I'm not even sure what the details are going to be, but the main thing is that BNC has totally turned on us. I'm thinking we're looking at lawsuits."

"That ugly, huh?"

"That ugly. And I swear I'm not being condescending by not explaining more to you, Court'. In fact, back up a second, though. What about you and Carynne? She's the one who can explain it. But I thought you were going to try to get into Mass Art."

"I changed my mind. I'm applying to Emerson. They've got rolling admissions and an amazing media program. I'm serious. Walk into any radio station, TV station, movie set, you name it, throw a rock and you'll hit someone from Emerson."

"And Digger'll foot the bill?"

"He said he would. Hey, if you're hard up, I have a great idea. I'll live here and he'll have to pay you rent."

"Court', I'd rather have less to do with him than more."

"I know. But just think how much it'll singe his nut hairs to have to write you a check every month."

That made me laugh. "I am so glad we're on the same page about this."

"Come home soon, will you? I miss you."

"That's kind of funny, given that you didn't even see me for years."

"Yeah, but on tour I got used to being around you all the time."

"You know, you don't have to get some kind of entertainment business degree to spend more time around me..."

"Daron, the world does not revolve around you. I want to do this."

"Okay, fine, just checking. But are you sure you don't want to go to art school?"

"I talked to Ziggy about that. I think I agree with him. The problem with art school isn't the art. It's all the artists. I'll still have plenty of chances to be my crazy, creative self, don't you worry."

"I just—"

"You're the only person who thinks it would be a better idea to study art than business."

"Of course I think that. I'm a musician."

"When are you coming back?"

"I don't know. Ziggy's supposed to get out tomorrow. I'll figure it out after I know what's up with him, I guess."

"Is that the real reason you're out there?"

"What, my cover story about house-sitting for Remo wasn't good enough?"

"Nooooope. You're busted."

"I confess. Carynne thinks I should go get him myself. What do you think?"

"I think Carynne's usually right."

Another Day in Paradise

By midnight Carynne had faxed me a copy of our contract along with directions to Betty Ford. She also told me she had filled Bart and Chris in, which flipped me out a little. But she said it was really fine. She was the manager now, she said, and she took it as her job to tell them. She told them she was in charge first, then went into the explanation of how it happened, I guess. That set me on another round of worrying that there wouldn't be a career to be managed soon, and she basically told me to shut up and let her do the worrying for a little while.

Bart called to say hey and check on me. We didn't talk a lot. I think we kind of figured we'd see each other soon enough one way or the other. So I hung up with him after a pretty short conversation and looked at what Carynne had faxed.

I re-read the contract with a sinking feeling in my stomach. Clauses that had seemed innocuous, or ones we'd decided not to fight for in order to pick different battles, now seemed fraught with doom.

Good name for a band. Fraught with Doom. Goth, probably.

Jonathan rubbed the tense spot between my shoulders as I sat there at the dining table with my forehead on the fax, unable to actually keep reading after a certain point.

I looked up. "Shoe's on the other foot, now, I guess."

"How's that?" he asked. "Which shoe are we talking about?"

"So much for me acing my gig and you drowning at yours," I clarified.

He paused for a moment, maybe thinking over having said that. "It'll work out somehow," he said gently, and kissed the side of my head.

I sighed. "I'm fucked if they get nasty about exclusivity." I pushed the fax toward him and pointed at the section I was talking about. "If they get really strict about it... I won't be able to work at all."

Jonathan leaned over the table and looked at it. His back looked long and straight as he leaned on his hand as he pored over the words. "It doesn't say anything about playing live, at least. And you kept your publishing rights?"

"I did." Not a dime of the "Candlelight" ASCAP or BMI money would be going to BNC, thank goodness. "So I'm not going to starve, I don't think." But just the thought that I might be hamstrung musically was winding up that tense spot between my shoulders again.

"If they get really strict... yeah." He was still staring at the words when he said, "But I thought it was the option clause that worried you more?"

"That's here." I showed him the other section Mills had invoked.

J read it silently. "This is pretty tough. I know why companies put these clauses in, but... you don't have a pay-for-play out?"

"We do. But that would only apply if we delivered an album they decided not to release. In this case, they're saying they won't even let us get to that point. Why that doesn't just release us entirely... I'm not clear on."

He nodded. "There have been a lot of bands caught in this limbo, you know."

"I know. Everyone said when we were first sending our demo tape around that four out of five bands who signed with a major label ended up in hock." I looked up at him. "I really didn't think we were one of them. The sold-out shows? The radio play? The gold fucking record?"

"That was the 'Candlelight' single, though, not *1989*?"

"Yep."

J shook his head. "I smell a rat. Then again, that's the scent of the whole industry."

"I know. Doesn't make it suck any less. I threatened an auditor already. Now we have to find one. How much is that going to cost, I wonder?"

"Let Carynne worry about that."

"Good plan." I took a deep breath. Absolute backup plan was what? Go back to busking in the park? I used to spend $500 a month to sublet that place in the Fenway. I spent about $250 a month on food, not counting when Bart paid for meals, about $50 for utilities, $50 for a monthly T pass... In the days when I first moved in with Chris I could live on about $12,000 a year. If I had to, I could do it again.

Doing math in my head made my eyes glaze over.

Jonathan brought me back to the room by closing his fingers around mine, warm and firm.

He led me out of my chair with a steady pull on my hand, then pulled me into a hug.

I figured he was going to say something comforting. What he said was, "Do you want to be on top?"

Don't get me wrong—that *was* comforting. But it took me a second to shift my brain out of math and legalese into sex. "Um... sure."

"Or would you rather lie back and let me take care of you?"

"You make it hard to choose," I said, and meant it, warming to both ideas. "Wait, how do you know I'm interested?"

"I'm still waiting for the day you say you're not," Jonathan pointed out. "I promised I'd handle it with grace when you do."

I wasn't on fire like I often was, but I didn't see any reason to say no, and I didn't want to disappoint him. "This isn't that day," I said. "And yeah, I do want to be on top. We shouldn't stay up too late, though."

"It's already after midnight."

"I know." With all the other things hanging over me, I hadn't told him yet about my plan to talk to Ziggy. "I need to get up early."

"Oh?"

"Yeah. Carynne's advice, and I've decided I agree, is that what with firing Digger and all... I should try to get to Betty Ford first. Before Digger."

"Oh." J sounded slightly alarmed, and I wondered if he imagined the same thing I had when imagining Digger explaining everything to Ziggy. He seemed to think it through. "I suppose it would be a good idea."

"It's a two-hour drive. I'm going to try to get on the road by seven... oh but rush hour, fuck me, I better try to be on the road by six."

"Daron, we could wait..."

I pulled his hips against mine. "Uh-uh. I'll never get to sleep at all at this point if we don't get rid of the tension that's built up."

"Just now?"

"Just now. You know I always sleep better after sex."

"Okay, then. You convinced me. Come on, lover."

We went right to the bedroom at that point and had fantastic, uncomplicated sex. Can't really call it "quick and dirty." More like quick and clean. I really needed that.

We fell asleep together and I slept about two hours, which meant it was around four in the morning when I woke up. I'd slept really deeply, but I couldn't get back to sleep, so I took a shower and ate some breakfast and was on the road by five.

Mountain Song

I took I-10 east and was amazed to find the mountains coming into view as I cleared the city and the sky lightened. It was impossible to tell how far away the mountains were or how big. For once I encountered no traffic, and I sped along. As the sun was rising, I stared at something I could not make sense of until I got closer: an expanse of huge white wind turbines that I eventually drove straight through. They made me feel like I was in a science fiction movie.

I drove through San Bernadino and wondered if I'd be hitting any of the other places mentioned in that song about Route 66. But no, Barstow (which I always heard as "Barstool") and the old track of Route 66 went north from there, while I-10 went more directly east, toward Joshua Tree National Park. There's a U2 reference there. (I don't know why they called the album *The Joshua Tree*. Maybe someday I'll find out.)

I think I've been remiss in telling you about Remo's SUV, which he called a "truck" and Jonathan called a "Jeep." Technically it was made by Jeep, but I thought of Jeeps as looking a certain way, and this was something else. Which was probably why Remo called it a truck. It was a thing called a Wagoneer, and I call it an SUV now, but at the time that term wasn't really in vogue yet except among car manufacturers. Anyway, the important thing about it was that it was taller than a regular car, so when you were sitting in traffic you could see further ahead and when you were driving through the desert you could imagine you were on some kind of a safari adventure.

Yeah, I admit, I had fantasies of kidnapping him and disappearing into Mexico together. Blame the truck.

The other thing about the truck, Jeep, whatever, was that it had a huge gas tank. I was getting close to the place when I happened to glance down at the gas gauge. Not a moment too soon, as the needle was lagging below the E. I pulled off the highway, and as I saw a gas station a few hundred yards ahead, the engine died. Apparently I really should have looked at that gauge sooner. I rolled the truck as far as it would go until I came to a stop at the curb.

I walked the rest of the way under blazing morning sun. I-10 basically runs along a wide, flat valley between mountains. It's not Death Valley, but it makes you think of it if, like me, you're from the East Coast and never walked anywhere in 100-degree heat. This was hotter than that day in Arizona when Marty and I had walked to find breakfast. That was like a balmy spring day compared to this. By the time I got to the gas station I was wearing my denim jacket over my head because, although that was hot, it hurt less than the intensity of the direct sun. The sun made the sunglasses on my face so hot they felt like they were burning the bridge of my nose.

The inside of the gas station was like a little oasis. I stood there relieved to be out of the heat. The clerk looked to be about my age, tall and skinny, unruly blond hair shoved under a baseball cap.

"I ran out of gas up the road," I told him, pointing.

"Oh. Um. I guess you can buy some," he said, looking kind of unsure of himself.

I was expecting him to be a little more helpful than that. "Uh, sure." We stood there facing each other. "How?" My brain started to work a little now that I was in a temperature I could stand. "Can I borrow a gas can or something?"

"Hang on." The kid went and stuck his head through a doorway into the garage portion of the station and talked to someone I couldn't see. He pulled the door shut behind himself as he came back to talk to me. "Uh, I don't have a can you can borrow. You can buy a gallon of washer fluid, though, and dump it out, and then put some gas in that."

"Seriously? You don't have, like, an empty jar or something I could just carry a little gas in, enough to drive it up here?"

"Um." He made a furtive "one second" gesture and opened the door again and stuck his head through. Then he backed up suddenly as an old man came barreling through. He was bent over, which made him shorter than me.

"Okay, let me see him!" He got about two feet from me and squinted, like he still couldn't really make out my face. "You Indian?" he demanded.

"Uh, no..."

"Mexican?"

"He's fine, Grandpa," the kid said.

"You thirsty?" Grandpa asked in the same demanding tone.

"A little?" I answered, not sure why he was asking.

"Sell him a Coke, Jimmy. He can put some gas in there after he drinks it." Then he went back into the garage, a bit more slowly than he'd come, feeling for the knob on the door.

When it was shut, the kid, who looked terrified about the whole thing now, stammered, "Sorry about that. Being almost blind's made him kind of bitter."

Was being blind what made him crazy? I thought, but I didn't say anything. At that point I was just trying to get out of there. I bought a can of Coke from the fridge, drank it in more or less one go, which proved how thirsty I was, and then bought something like 27 cents of gas to put in the can, including what I spilled on the ground trying to pump into the can. I carried it in one of the paper windshield-wipe towels they had in a dispenser by the pump.

The walk back to the car seemed even longer. The whole way there I was playing the weird scene over again in my mind, and it sank in that the old guy was trying to figure out if I was white or not. "He's fine" must've meant yes, right? I didn't look like some kind of criminal trying to rip them off? That just made me even angrier. I spilled half the gas down the side of the vehicle trying to get it into the tank and hoped that wasn't a hazard of some kind. Getting in the car, I could still smell the gasoline on my hands.

The engine started, hallelujah, and then I realized there was a gas station down a little ways and across the street from the place I'd been. I decided to go there. It couldn't be worse, right?

It wasn't. Inside were two guys who might have been of Mexican descent, or maybe Indian, with black hair and wide smiles. I think they were brothers. They told me I was lucky I hadn't run out of gas out on the highway somewhere. I told them about the weird guy at the gas station across the street.

"Shit, man, you shoulda come in here first. We woulda just pushed you over here," one of them said.

"Or lent you a gas can. Crazy."

They filled up the tank and wiped up the spill and let me wash my hands in their restroom. I washed my face, too, and tossed my hair back, and for the first time it occurred to me to wonder whether I should have played the rock star card back at the other place. Except, no, I didn't actually want to give them my business even if they did magically start kissing my ass or something. Bleah.

Meanwhile, I wouldn't have minded if the guys on this side of the street knew, except why make things weird? They were perfectly nice to me without knowing who I was, or without caring. I liked it better that way. They even gave me some lemonade to drink when I came out. I sucked it down and still felt thirsty, but I figured it would take a while for it and the Coke to soak in. I thanked them.

I got on the road again. I probably had thirty miles or so still to go. The gas shenanigans had cost me a good half hour to forty-five minutes.

I spent the rest of the drive trying to come up with the words I was going to say to Ziggy. At first I was trying to figure out how to boil down what had happened with BNC. But after I turned off the highway and was making my way there through the streets of Rancho Mirage, I switched to trying to figure out how to get him to come with me. I didn't know where I'd take him. Maybe he'd want to be dropped off at Digger's office. Maybe he'd come back with me to Remo's and then I'd figure out something. I mean, things with me and Jonathan had definitely changed in the past few weeks, but one thing I was sure hadn't changed was that Jonathan knew how fucking important Ziggy was to me.

I really hadn't come up with anything that sounded all that good in my own ears by the time I pulled up to the place. There were signs to it from the highway. I parked in a parking lot near what looked a lot like the lobby entrance of a hotel but was actually the entrance to the center.

The one thing I had not expected to see upon walking in the door was Digger. His face was flushed, and he was shouting at a blond woman who had the expression of someone who was unfazed by being shouted at, her lips curled in a professional smile but her eyes stony.

What stopped me in my tracks was what he was shouting.

"What do you mean 'left'? How could he leave?"

"As I've been trying to explain, sir, he checked out already this morning. He had been cleared to leave."

"Well, where the fuck did he go?"

"I do not know that, sir."

"I mean, I've been here since last night! Someone could have told me! How could you just let him walk like that?"

"Sir, I've been trying to explain, we had no orders to keep him. He was cleared to leave under his own—"

Digger cut her off with a frustrated gesture. "Let me borrow a phone. I've got to call my answering service."

"Of course, sir." Every time she said "sir" it sounded more and more ironic to me. I'm sure in her mind she was replacing "sir" with "asshole."

She eyed me like I'd better not start up next. I folded my hands and tried to look like I wasn't trouble. She had handed a phone handset to Digger, who punched in a series of numbers and listened. He still hadn't seen me. I gestured to the clerk that I was going to wait outside. She gave me a friendlier smile and a shrug while Digger started haranguing the operator at his service.

I ducked out. When I looked back a minute or two later, I didn't see him, but he hadn't come out the door. Well, now was my chance.

I went up to the woman. Her nametag read "Sheeri."

"Can I help you?" she asked.

"Sheeri, you probably can," I said.

"Hey, you got my name right, that's amazing. Most people call me Sherri."

"I've got a friend named She-REE," I said, thinking of Louis's ex-wife. "People are always getting hers wrong, too. I'm Daron."

Her eyebrow went up in recognition. "And what can I do for you?"

"Sounds like there's been a little confusion about Ziggy's discharge. Do you happen to know what time he left?"

"Had to be at like six in the morning," she said.

"He couldn't have just... walked out, though?" I asked. "My worry is he's sitting at a Circle K somewhere, dehydrated and in need of a ride. That sun is brutal. I ran out of gas on the way here and had to walk to get some. Or I would have been here earlier."

I did not outright lie, but I let her think that maybe I was supposed to be here to pick him up.

She appeared to be considering something. Her lips pursed.

"Don't tell me anything that would, you know, break confidentiality rules or anything," I said. "I just need to figure out what to do. And I'm worried."

She came to a decision. "He got in a cab," she told me. "So you don't have to worry that he's expired of heat stroke somewhere down the road."

A cab. "Was he alone?"

She hesitated. "I can't tell you that."

I took that to mean he wasn't. "Thank you very much for your help. Last question. Where'd the guy you were just talking to go?"

"I believe he's in the men's room." She pointed to a door across the foyer.

"Thank you. Really."

Her smile was real. "Good luck."

I Hate Myself for Loving You

So I used up all my luck running out of gas only a few hundred yards from a gas station, and I used up all my *nice* getting the information out of the nice woman at the desk. I took my frustration out on Digger, and he took his out on me.

We didn't have the argument in the men's room at the Betty Ford Center, though. We had it in the parking lot, where the temperature was hitting 104.

I followed him as he stalked out of the building. He turned when he heard my footsteps and startled a little when he saw me.

"What the fuck are you doing here?" He sounded really angry to see me. Or maybe just angry. Then he smiled suddenly. It was disconcerting. "Tell me you're putting one over on me. You've got him, right? You've got him."

"No, I don't got him." I shook my head slowly.

He looked at me over the tops of his Ray Bans. "Oh. Well *la dee da*, then I guess you're here to say you're sorry and you want me to fix this BNC mess."

Maybe it was because it was 104, but my temper was already close to boiling. "Did you think I didn't mean it when I fired you?"

"I thought maybe you'd come to your senses. It's not like you to have a big emotional outburst like that, kiddo."

"I didn't—"

"You think I'm not concerned? I'm very concerned. You didn't used to be so weak."

"*Weak*—?"

"I guess that's what happens, though. I told you not to take it up the ass."

Okay, so I boiled over then so much I couldn't even get words out. There were so many things wrong with *everything* he'd said I couldn't even *argue*, really. Do you know what I mean? When words finally did come out they were, "What the fuck is wrong with you! What drugs are you on! What planet are you from!"

He amazed me by shouting questions right back. "Is that where your priorities are? Where the fuck is Ziggy! What do you know about this? What kind of crazy-ass shit are you trying to pull!"

"I'm not crazy, you're the one who's crazy!"

"Oh yeah? You gonna hit me again? Is that where this is going?"

"Is that what you want? Sorry you didn't slug me back in front of your buddy Mills, *Dad*?"

"See what I mean? No sense, no sense at all!" He moved like he was going to poke me in the chest with his accusatory finger.

In an instant I went from epic shouting-match mode to something else. Something much quieter but no less forceful. "Touch me and I'll bury you." I had never heard my voice so hard or cold.

Neither had he. He froze. Then his mouth moved like he was chewing on the insides of his lips, probably trying to keep from saying what he really wanted to say. Apparently he either believed me or decided not to test how serious I was, because he stuck his hands in the pockets of his Bermuda shorts. He muttered, "I don't care how much you love cock. I don't. I don't. But stay the fuck away from Ziggy. You want to toss your career down the john, you go right ahead, but I'm not letting it happen to him."

I twitched, that's how much of a double-take I did there. "What? A couple of weeks ago you were begging me to 'throw him a bone.'"

"That was before he snapped. None of this would've happened if you'd listened to me then. None of it!" He whipped his sunglasses off dramatically. "Listen to me now, cocksucker. I'm not letting anything get in his way, you hear me? Not even you."

Yeah, I know, he called me the c-word. (Well, the *other* c-word.) It struck me as the most honest thing he said, actually, and kind of funny. In fact, I almost laughed, but I didn't. I felt a lot calmer all of a sudden, though. Maybe just knowing I could make him show his true colors made me feel better. Maybe seeing how low he could sink, and how pathetic he was... I don't know. I shrugged and spread my hands. "I'm not stopping you. Good luck finding him."

I turned to walk to the truck.

"Wait. Wait! What do you know about where he went?"

"I don't know shit, Digger," I said as I kept walking. I heard him following me. "I don't know shit other than he thought it was a good idea to fly the coop before you got here. Did he know you were coming?"

"Don't try to pin this on me! Yeah, he knew I was coming." Digger ran around in front of me. "Did he know *you* were coming?" He pointed at me so violently his sunglasses slipped down his nose.

I couldn't stop baiting him. "He had no idea. So it wasn't me he was trying to get away from by skipping out early." I stepped around him and unlocked the door of the truck.

"Fuck you. This ain't my fault."

"Fuck you, too," I said mildly, with a little salute as I got into the driver's seat, "and have a nice day."

I slammed the door and started the engine. He took that as his cue to walk away.

If there was a winner in that fight, I think it was me. But given what happened next, you'd think I'd not only lost, I'd been beaten black and blue. Nope.

You ever cry so hard you puke?

I made it to a convenience store a couple of miles away before the shakes set in, and I had to park the truck and pull my jacket over my head and just cry and cry and cry.

Twist and Crawl

It took me a long time to get back to Remo's. I think maybe there's some chance that heat stroke may have had something to do with that.

Or maybe I just felt like shit.

The crying jag ended when I got out of the truck and puked into a garbage can outside the convenience store. I wasn't really thinking at that point. I was on autopilot. I remembered puking backstage in Austin, Texas, and I remembered Christian introducing me to Gatorade. Remember that? Not just for jocks—who knew?

So I went into the store and bought some Gatorade, and then I went back to the truck and turned the engine and the AC on and sat there really cautiously sipping the stuff. I don't actually remember now, but it's possible that I had sat there with it off all the time I had been crying. At the time I was pretty sure I was the stupidest human being on earth anyway, so I wouldn't have put it past me. My brain was in that mode where it replayed a montage of horrible moments from the last several days but didn't think useful thoughts of any kind, and the coherent ones were mostly me blaming myself for everything.

The problem is you're underwater.

A PR reason.

Tell your boy what reality is.

Weak.

That's what happens when...

It took me an hour to make my way through the bottle of Gatorade—it was one of the big bottles—and then I went in and bought two more of them and tried to drive.

I only went a couple of blocks before I decided I wasn't ready for that, and I parked in the shade, kept the AC cranked, and drank another bottle. This one went down quicker.

I started to feel a little better then, and I decided to just try to get back on the highway and make it to the next exit, and I'd pull over again there. I am at my stupidest when I'm sick or injured, I think. All I could think was that I wanted to get back, and somehow that turned into this plan to take it one exit at a time. Never once did doing something intelligent like driving to the hospital occur to me. (Despite the fact there was a hospital pretty much right there.)

So I made it to the next exit and parked again. And I switched from Gatorade to water. And I began to worry that maybe sitting in the car with the engine running wasn't that good an idea because maybe I was carbon monoxide-poisoning myself. That's how terrible I felt. Horrible. So I drove to the next exit—yeah, I know and found an actual groccry store and walked up and down all the aisles, pushing a cart, because at least the cart held me up when I felt somewhat weak and at least I looked like I was a shopper rather than a derelict.

Let's face it. I *was* a derelict. I thought, well,at least they can't get me for vagrancy—because I had probably a hundred dollars in my pocket, but then again, knowing the "war on drugs," maybe I had too much cash on me and they would get me for suspicion of dealing or intent to buy or some dumb shit...?

So, add paranoia to the list of things I was suffering. I broke down again in the dairy section. Actually, I didn't cry. I just covered my face with my hands and stood there holding it in until I thought maybe I was going to puke again. Amazingly, no one challenged me or said anything. Maybe they were afraid of the crazy person.

When I got myself back together I put a gallon jug of water into the cart, along with some more Gatorade.

I went to the checkout stand being worked by the person who looked the most like a responsible adult to me: a woman even shorter than me, with her black hair in a net and very chubby arms. She looked at what I was buying and said, "That's it?"

"Um, yeah. Hey, do I look like I have heat stroke?"

She looked me up and down. She was probably fifty. "You look okay to me. If you're sweating, you're okay. If you stop sweating, that's when your brain boils."

I accepted this diagnosis at face value. "Thanks."

Thus reassured that my temperature probably wasn't going to be fatal, and feeling somewhat more coherent after spending half an hour wandering around in the air conditioning, I went to the pay phone to call Jonathan. The line was busy. I tried calling the fax number, but it was busy, too. Jonathan must have been on both lines at once.

I ended up dumping half the gallon of water over myself in the parking lot and then getting back in the truck.

I limped the rest of the way back to Laurel Canyon, sticking with my plan to stop at every exit to make sure I wasn't about to pass out. I know, I know, that doesn't make any sense when I think about it now. But at the time it seemed like the best thing I could come up with. I did not pass out, and I made it, though it took five or six hours.

To this day I don't know if I was actually in physical distress or if it was entirely emotional. Maybe when emotional pain is bad enough there's no difference.

Anyway, I made it to the house. I didn't crawl in, but I felt almost like I did. Instead I carried in the two bottles of Gatorade I hadn't yet opened, put them in the fridge, and then sank down and sat at the foot of the refrigerator. It blew hot air onto my butt. No rest for the wicked. I didn't care. I didn't move. I could hear Jonathan's voice from the writing room, where he must've been on the phone, but I couldn't make out the words.

A few minutes later he came out and looked around, I guess because he had heard the garage door but couldn't figure out where I was. When he finally realized I was on the floor behind the counter island, he said, "Oh!" and rushed over and knelt down. "Are you all right?"

"I'm fine," I said. But I just could not say anything more. I couldn't even begin.

He held my hand for a bit and brushed my hair out of my face. He eventually stood, still holding my hand, and encouraged me without saying a word to move from the floor to the couch. I guess my silence was contagious. I ended up lying on the couch with my head in his lap, and he stroked my hair soothingly while I tried to untangle my distress enough to explain.

I failed. I failed to say anything, and I had failed to talk to Ziggy, and I had failed to keep Ziggy's interest once he was separated from me, and I had failed as a professional musician.

And I was pretty sure I was going to fail at this relationship with Jonathan, too, if I couldn't even make some words come out of my mouth, at least some simple ones.

I think an hour or two went by. The phone rang at one point and we ignored it. The machine picked up, but no one left a message. I would quit trying to say anything for a while, and then every 20 or 30 minutes I would try again, and the most I managed was a kind of choked sound.

Then I finally thought of some actual words to say. *He was already gone.* But it took several minutes of repeating it over and over in my head before I finally said it out loud.

"He was already gone."

The last thing I expected J to say in return was, "I know."

That was a jolt. You know how in old movies they slap people across the face to "snap out of it"? This was like that; I sat up suddenly, nearly banging my head on his chin. "What?"

"I said, *I know*. I've been on the phone all day. Ziggy's on his way to India with a woman who hasn't been positively identified yet but is probably his *Star Baby* co-star."

"Jennifer Garner?"

"Jennifer Connelly. No, wait, Jennifer Carstens. Too

many actresses named Jennifer, sorry."

I honestly had never been sure, even when I heard her name, which one she was. "And... India? How do you know that?"

"I didn't expect to find out anything about him, you know. I was trying to find out who took the photographs of you, of us, and one thing led to another. I have a very crappy fax of a photo taken as he was leaving Betty Ford at dawn if you'd like to see it."

I blinked at him. "That's... wow. That's amazing."

"This is what I do, Daron. It's not all fluff pieces in the record trades."

"I... I didn't say it was. I mean, I had no idea investigative journalism was... was so investigative."

He smiled and went to get the fax. In it I recognized the lobby entrance of the clinic, where I had been some hours before. Ziggy was clearly recognizable, holding hands with a woman wearing dark sunglasses and her hair under a scarf.

"There's also one of them getting into a cab, but you can't make out their faces at all in that one."

"Oh."

"You *can* make out the cab's license plate and the company name and phone number, though. I called them and managed to find out where he took them, which was Burbank Airport, which only has about forty flights a day..." He paused. "You get the idea."

"I get the idea. Which means you have a scoop. Right?"

"You know, I hadn't really thought of it that way." He made a face. "I don't think I really want to sell this story, Daron. The only reason it matters is because it matters to you."

"Oh. Oh. Then." I wasn't making sense. "And you're sure India?"

"I'm sure."

"Thank you."

He took hold of my hand. "You're scaring me, dear."

"I'm sorry. I... I'm..." I didn't have a word for it.

Jonathan did. "Devastated."

"Yeah." It felt like my heart and soul had been laid to waste by a nuclear bomb. All that was left of me was one of those shadows on the side of a building.

Learning to Fly

So what do you do when you wake up after the apocalypse and find that you're still alive?

If you're me, you jot down notes for a song about the end of the world. I was still too drained and wrecked to actually work on it, though. I hoped the notes would make sense later.

Sometimes I look at pages in my notebook and wonder what the hell I was thinking. Since the purpose of the notes is supposed to be to remind me what I was thinking, it's frustrating when they don't. "Double-knotted shoelaces." That's in the margin of one set of lyrics. It's underlined twice like I thought it was important at the time.

I mentioned this to Bart once, one time when we were working on a song together after I'd moved to Boston. "I mean, I wrote it, shouldn't I know what it means?"

He had shrugged and said, "Maybe you're not the same person you were when you made the note."

I wondered, staring at the ceiling that morning in Remo's house, if Ziggy was ever the same person twice.

I could hear the television from the living room, and also Jonathan's voice, like he was on the phone.

I got myself together. Washed my face. My hair was damp. I barely remembered taking a shower before I'd gotten in bed. I still had that feeling like there was nothing left of me. No energy, no emotions, no thoughts, no ideas.

Well, okay, I had that one idea. I looked at the notebook again and jotted down a few more words. I put clean clothes on. It was going to be time to do laundry soon. It was very hard to care about that, but at least I noticed, right?

Out in the living room Jonathan was facing the TV with the cordless phone on his shoulder. "I'm letting him sleep as late as possible. He was in bad shape last night."

I had a feeling he was talking to Carynne. How did I know that? Something about the tone of his voice.

"This whole thing has just wrecked him. I mean,

what a one-two punch, right? First the BNC bullshit and now this?" He nodded, listening to the reply. "Who, me? I'm doing fine. It's hard to see him like this, but at least I'm here where I can help. Has there been any other news? Okay. I'll tell him to call you when he gets up. Yeah, I'll tell him."

He clicked off the phone and then turned the volume back up on the television. The MTV news was just coming on. Their slogan was, "You hear it first." I was half expecting them to mention Ziggy. But no, they were talking about something else and I quit paying attention partway through. J changed the channel. CNN.

They were reporting that ten people had been killed, mostly teenagers studying music at the Royal Marine Academy in Kent, in an IRA bombing. The bomb blast had been so strong that an entire three-story building, the barracks rec center, was destroyed. Most of those killed had been rehearsing at the time.

I wondered what piece they were rehearsing. Like it mattered.

"Holy fuck. Kind of puts my problems in perspective, doesn't it?"

Jonathan whipped around. "You're awake."

"For the moment, anyway."

"Carynne's desperate to talk to you." He muted the TV.

"I bet she is."

"She heard from Ziggy."

That gave me a jolt. "Oh yeah?"

"Yeah. He sent a statement, anyway. Looks like it went to her and to Digger—a fax, from London, during the flight's stopover in Heathrow."

"Statement?"

"It's less of a letter and more of a PR statement. Call her and she'll read it to you." He handed me the phone.

I walked out by the pool where at least I could enjoy what was considered "beautiful weather" everywhere I had ever lived, sunny and dry and not too hot. Remo had a few lounge chairs by the poolside. I lounged in one.

Carynne picked up on the first ring.

"J said to call you."

"Yeah. Did he tell you I got a message from Ziggy?"

"Yeah."

She launched right into it. "Okay, here it is. *Dear fans and friends, I'm sorry I'm not there to be with you right now. If there's one thing that recent challenges have taught me, it's that I need to be true to myself. I always heard those stories about people going into spiritual retreat to 'find themselves' as cliché and stupid. Why would you need to find yourself when you're always with yourself? But having lost my way, I now realize how crucial it is for me to find it. Otherwise the 'me' you love couldn't keep existing. Drugs were very definitely blinding me, but now that my eyesight is clear, I can look for the missing piece. I tried to find what was missing, in drugs, onstage, in other people, but I know now it must be inside me. Please wish me the best on my journey.*"

"That's it?"

"That's it. You know, if this is what he said to the guys in the ER, that's probably why they nabbed him for suicide watch. The bit about how he couldn't keep existing, I mean."

"Yeah." I wondered if any of the message was actually aimed at me, or if he had moved on completely from trying to get my attention. "What should I do next, Car'?"

"I would like you to come home and take care of some stuff here, honestly, and meet with that lawyer you told me about. I talked to him yesterday, and I think he has some good ideas. There's some stuff with the house I know Christian wants to talk to you about, too."

"Why doesn't Christian just call me?"

"Because he thinks you're mad at him and it would be better to talk face to face."

"Oh. Why does he think...?" I realized it didn't matter why he thought I was mad at him. Maybe because it seemed like I was avoiding him? "Okay, you're right. I should come home for a little while. What do you think, a week?"

"Two at the most. If you want to go back to LA with Jonathan after that, I don't see why you can't. Maybe then you can get some more soundtrack work."

"Assuming BNC doesn't sue the fuck out of whoever because I broke my exclusivity clause?"

"I told you, this lawyer, he has some ideas."

"Okay. Book me a flight and let me know when to be at the airport. And which airport. And, you know the drill."

"I'll check the prices. I've got a travel agent who often has cheap last-minute seats, especially if you can go from one of the dinky airports."

"Okay, cool. Hey, have you heard from Remo?"

"No, why?"

"He's the one person I feel like I've been leaving messages for who hasn't called back. But then again, he's on the road and in a drastically different time zone."

"Everything okay there?"

"Other than me feeling like the survivor of a bombing or something, everything's fine."

"J said you were wrecked."

"Good word for it. I'm... just..." I trailed off, lost for words. Or maybe just lost.

Maybe Carynne knew that. "Come home for a little while, okay?" she reiterated.

"Okay. Call me with the details."

"I'm calling the travel agent the second I hang up with you."

"Thanks. Love you, Car'."

"Love you, too, D."

I went back in the house. Jonathan was making macaroni and cheese in the microwave. He was watching it go around and around. I joined him. There were two of them in there.

"Is one of those for me?"

"Yeah. I figure if it turns out you're not hungry I'll eat both." He snuck a glance at me sideways.

"I'm okay, you know. I'm not a suicide risk."

"Suicide isn't the only thing that worries me."

"I want you to stop worrying." I took a deep breath. "I'm afraid if I become too much of a drag, it'll hurt you. And make things suck."

"So... let me get this straight. You want me to stop worrying..."

"Yeah."

"And what I want is for you to stop worrying about hurting me." He put his arm around my shoulder and kissed me on the hair. "So how about this. You try to stop worrying about me, and I'll try to stop worrying about you, and we can just help each other instead."

"I'll try. Carynne wants me to come home to meet a lawyer and deal with Christian." And I really needed to see Bart, I realized. I needed to know what was going through his mind. "Will you be okay for like a week or maybe two without me?"

"Of course. I'm used to being a solitary workaholic, you know."

Two days later I was on a plane to Boston. I kissed Jonathan goodbye at the airport and didn't give a fuck who saw.

State of Mind

Carynne picked me up at the airport and took me straight to a Vietnamese restaurant in Chinatown. I went through the motions of talking to her, telling her about some of the parties in LA and about Remo's house—though she'd been there before, she reminded me. More times than me, in fact. I forget how long everyone's known each other. I almost forget sometimes that it was through Remo I met her in the first place. I almost forget sometimes that once upon a time I was scared to death of being alone in a room with her.

Anyway, like I said, I went through the motions of talking while we ate. Then I looked around. "We've been here before, haven't we?"

"Yeah. This is where I took you the night of the Jingle Bell show."

"Ahhh." I rubbed my face. "I seem to recall I felt pretty crappy that night."

"I think you felt a little better after eating here."

"I think I felt a little better after talking to you."

"Did you? I think that was the night you told me about you and Ziggy."

"That was the night I convinced you to be our road manager." It felt a lot longer ago than it actually was. People are like used cars. It's not the time that matters. It's the mileage.

"Yeah, it was." She pushed what was left of the thick, white rice soup around in the bottom of her bowl. "So. He's in India."

"At least, that's what we've been told." I scraped the last of my own soup onto the ceramic spoon and licked it clean. "He might as well have said 'I'm going to Mars,' as far as I'm concerned." I dropped the empty spoon into the bowl and felt my brain trying to shut off. Click, click, click, but my eyes stayed open, staring at the velvet Buddha on the wall. *Hey, Buddha, can you spare a dime? No? How about you watch over Ziggy, then, hm? He's in your world now, instead of mine, right? Is there some special way I'm supposed to pray to you, or is this good enough?*

"Daron."

I blinked. "Uh, sorry. I was just, um, never mind..."

"You're sure you don't need drug rehab yourself?"

"I'm sure. I'm not on anything. Those painkillers he got to liking so much? By the end I was giving him mine. Shit, does that mean it's my fault?"

She shook her head. "You know what? I think you keep trying to blame this on yourself, but I really think this is an extreme case of Ziggy really, really, really needing to slip the leash for a while. I mean, that's his nature already. The worst part of touring, far as he's concerned, is that someone else dictates what the hell you do every minute of the day."

"He told you this?"

"Not in so many words, but come on, think about him."

"Yeah, I see what you mean."

"The more pinned down and constrained he is, the more desperate he gets to express himself creatively or stretch his wings. So he writes, he draws, he decorates your clothes..."

"And stuffed animals."

"Yeah. And now he's just been through a month of the most intense controlled environment you can get, short of prison. I can't say I'm totally surprised at him doing something like this."

"Huh, when you say that, I can almost believe maybe it had nothing to do with me."

"Would it hurt you if it didn't?"

I froze, trying not to think that, but of course that was one of the thoughts that had been swallowing me like a shark from the deep every time I considered it. I closed my eyes, but I'm sure she saw the depths of the pain before I did.

Her voice was soft. "I admit... I thought... I thought you guys were starting to get along again, by the end of the tour there."

My voice was so soft maybe I didn't even speak. Maybe I just nodded. But I think I said, "I thought so, too," or at least tried to.

She did that thing where she sat silently, making me want to fill the silence with words.

"It's like time hasn't moved forward for me since just after Madison Square Garden, really," I said. I put the heels of my hands over my eyes and I could still see him, in a spotlight at center stage, both arms raised...

"From the moment he fell?"

"No. No, just..." I took a long, slow breath, trying to be as Zen as I could about it. It didn't work. I looked at her. "I fell in love with him all over again in New York. I mean, okay, that sounds so stupid I'm probably lying to myself with it. Maybe I never stopped. But between MSG and soundcheck the next day, I just... I just..."

It was sheer force of will that kept me from breaking down and sobbing at the table. That and the memory of how sore and in pain I'd been after all the crying I'd done while driving from Betty Ford back to Laurel Canyon. Let's not do that again.

It helped that I'd just eaten a good meal and that Carynne was there. She was looking at me with pretty much the expression she would have if I bawled my eyes out, so I knew she knew what was going on inside me. She put a hand on mine, and my forearm was so tense it shook.

Buddha. Zen. Take a deep breath, Daron. Let it out slowly. "Whatever. I finally quit fooling myself and went head over heels that night, and before I could tell him, bam, he's in the psych ward, and time hasn't moved forward for me since that day, Car'. It's like the farther away from that moment we get, the less of a grip on reality I've got. It's like a science fiction movie where the farther I get as a time traveler from my own time the weaker I am or something."

She squeezed my fingers. "You know, a lot of guys feel like they lose their purpose in life when they get off the road. Try to remember that."

"Yeah, okay."

"But yeah, it makes sense you feel that way. But it won't be forever, Daron. I know it feels like it, but he's going to come back. You'll get your say eventually."

"If that's true, then maybe for once I ought to figure out what I want to say."

"What do you want to say?"

"I don't know. That's why I have to figure it out." I sighed. "In other news, Jonathan wants me to move in with him."

"What?"

"He wants to get a place in West Hollywood and... and shack up. He keeps saying no strings attached, but you know, that's kind of a serious thing, isn't it? I mean, I'd hate to go through the guilt trip of leaving him there with double rent if I couldn't hack it, but I don't know. The whole thing sounds intimidating to me."

"Well, I am the last person to ask for advice about co-habitation. I've ended up hating all my roommates and each of the boyfriends I've tried to live with."

"Hate, really?"

"Really. The guys I broke up with who I didn't live with? Still friends. I dunno. When you live with people you really find out what you hate about them."

"You just lived with me and the guys for two months," I pointed out.

"And I learned I didn't hate any of you," she said. "Match made in heaven, by music industry standards, eh?"

That made me chuckle a little. "Okay, then I guess you can't give me advice about Christian, then?"

"Oh, sure I can, because that's band stuff as much as roommate stuff. Come on. I'll drive you home and we can talk about it on the way."

It Ain't What You Do, It's the Way that You Do It

Carynne, it turned out, had been talking to Christian a lot. And Lacey. After her collapse in LA, Lacey had gone through a rehab almost as intense at Ziggy's, but at a less-famous place, because—get this—her mother didn't like how many paparazzi photos she saw in the tabloids of other celebrities leaving Betty Ford. Apparently it was a thing. I suppose if I had ever read a tabloid paper, maybe I might've known. I wondered if someone out there had photos of me and Digger arguing.

Chris, meanwhile, had started therapy and long-term drug abuse counseling at a center nearby. At the time I didn't understand the difference between the crash-course type of rehab and getting into a longer-term relationship with a counselor, because at the time I didn't have to. All that mattered to me was that he was taking care of himself. He met with his guy every week, Carynne said, and had him on call in case of emergency.

"Emergency?" I asked as we parked in front of the house.

"You know, like someone offers him drugs at a party and he needs the moral support to say no."

"Ahh, I see." I climbed out of the car. I didn't even have a suitcase with me, since I had a ton of clothes here. As I walked up the driveway I noticed the bushes had been trimmed and that someone had put planter boxes of flowers on the stairs. My money was on Courtney or Lacey. "Is Lacey here?"

"She might be. I've lost track of when she's here and when she's not. She's got a lot of gigs she flies off to, and then she shows up again." Carynne shrugged. "She's redecorated the living room, you know."

"Yeah, we talked about her doing that." It had been one of the halfway normal conversations Christian and I had in recent months. I put my key in the lock and opened the door, not sure what to expect.

Okay, yes, there was new furniture that didn't look like it had been trash-picked or come from Goodwill like our old stuff. But what looked different to me was how large the room looked. I had forgotten the ceiling was so high. The walls had been painted, and the crappy carpets were gone. The hardwood floor looked shiny like something from a TV commercial for floor wax. The former junk room that Chris had turned into a workout room had plants in the windowsills.

Plants are one of those things, like pets, that are hard to take care of when you may be gone for months at a time.

Anyway, the fireplace had been re-pointed and the mantelpiece polished and refurbished, and someone had framed a set of photos taken on the tour and set them up there. The TV was the same—it was the humongous one Chris had bought back when we bought the house in the first place. The furniture around it was new, though, and there was an actual coffee table now. A magazine with our photo on it sat atop a small stack, and I had a feeling they were all ones that had a band article or something in them.

The stairwell had been refurbished at the same time they did the floors, so now the treads were shiny rather than grimy-looking, and the banister gleamed.

I was taking all of this in when Lacey came stomping halfway down the stairs. "Daron Moondog Marks, don't you dare lay a hand on him."

"What, me? Who?" I glanced at Carynne, who just gave a microshrug. "Nice to see you, too, Lacey. Care to let me in on what you're talking about?"

She came down the rest of the way and then stalked past me to the kitchen. I followed her. The kitchen hadn't changed at all, really. Same appliances, cabinets, etc. The linoleum had been scrubbed so clean it looked like a new floor and countertops, but I knew it wasn't. Only the table and chairs were new. She pulled a bottle of club soda out of the fridge, then poured herself some and drank it before she went on. "He's in a state, knowing you're coming home."

"I do live here," I said, trying not to sound annoyed.

"He's convinced you're going to kick the living shit out of him," she said, pointing at me with the water glass like that proved something.

"Why the hell would I do that?"

"Maybe you should be asking yourself that!" Lacey was still one of the prettiest faces you can imagine, so when she looked angry it was honestly kind of difficult to take her seriously. Well, especially when she wasn't making any sense.

"No, I mean, what the hell makes Christian think I would do that? When have I ever kicked the shit out of anybody, for that matter?"

"But you—"

"Nobody is kicking any shit out of *any*body, you get me? I'm not even mad at him."

"Liar."

"I'm lying? How about you tell me why I'm mad at him, then?"

"I don't know. You just are. Look how upset you are."

"I'm upset because you're not talking sense, Lacey!"

She didn't answer because instead she looked behind me toward the living room.

I turned and saw Christian. You know how the ceiling looked higher? Chris looked taller. Maybe I'd just forgotten how tall he was.

He looked good. Just... surprised. "Daron, man, you look like crap." He put his hand on the side of my shoulder. To translate for those of you who see things the way Lacey does, that was as good as a hug.

"I feel like it, too. How are you, though, man?"

"Doing all right. Doing all right. You want to go grab a beer or something?"

I know, I just ate, but let me explain something. When guys who don't talk or express their feelings are trying to make up, when that type of guy asks another guy who doesn't talk or express his feelings to go grab a beer, well, if you're the guy getting asked you have a choice. Say yes, and admit that you're okay with talking, or say no, in which case you're not okay with it. Of course, there's two kinds of not-okay. One is that you don't want to talk but you don't have to because really everything's okay, or at least you're hoping it's going to be if you just don't talk about it. You know that's the kind of guy I used to be. Then there's the not-okay where everything is messed up but you're refusing to talk about it. Now that I think about it, maybe in reality those last two things are actually the same.

Doesn't matter anyway, because I said, "Sure. You driving?"

"If we're both drinking, let's walk."

"Good plan."

"I'll grab my wallet." He ducked out of the kitchen to get his jacket, and I looked back at Lacey, who said nothing but kind of stared at me with her special brand of skeptical ire.

"Call me tomorrow," Carynne said, and gave me a peck on the cheek. "I'll call that lawyer."

"Okay. Bye." I checked that my own wallet was still in my pocket. It was. Christian said goodbye to Lacey, and the two of us went out the door before we could lose momentum.

Don't Let Me Down

We walked toward the Sunset, though if it was really crowded there we might keep going until we found somewhere quieter. The Sunset had many, many beers to offer, and the result was usually many, many people trying to get in.

"You hungry?" he asked. His feathered hair fluttered as he walked.

"Carynne took me through Chinatown on the way from Logan," I said. "But you know me. I can always eat."

"I'm trying to be really cognizant of my dependence on everyday crutches," he said, and I knew he'd been in therapy because normally you wouldn't hear Christian use a word like "cognizant."

"Food's a crutch?" I asked, trying to understand.

"What? No. Well, not for me. I was thinking of the beer. Like, you know, do I *really* want a beer? Or am I thinking it's necessary to use it as a crutch to give me permission to say what I gotta say?" He shrugged. "Thing is, I don't know."

"Is it bad to use it as a crutch if at least you say what you wanted to?"

"See, that's the thing, it isn't necessarily bad, but I'm suppose to be *aware* of it, at least." With Christian's accent, the word "aware" was more like *awehh.*

"Well, for what it's worth, I don't feel like I need a beer to hear it, whatever it is. But I totally wouldn't mind having one."

"Okay, cool. Yeah, what the hell. Let's get a beer because we like beer, not because we have to."

"Now you're talking."

We ended up at a sports bar a few more blocks down where things were pretty quiet. It wasn't a game night, I guess. We sat at one end of the bar next to some kind of a lottery machine and got Sam Adams on draft, and then Christian said, "You want to start or should I start?"

"I think you should start," I said.

"See, thing is... I'm not sure where to start."

I reminded myself I was the boss. "Okay, well, how about we start with what was up with Lacey there? She was convinced I was coming home to beat your brains in, which frankly is pretty baffling. Do I come across as a really violent person? Plus there's the fact I'm half your size, and also the fact that I'm not angry at you in the first place."

"Yeah, I heard some of that when I was coming down the stairs. I did not send her down there, by the way. She got that wild hair across her ass all on her own." He took a gulp of the beer. "Let me back up a little and see if I can figure out where she's getting that from. I've been working with my therapist on a lot of shit, you know, not just drug dependency. Crap about my father and... oh, maybe that's it."

"What?"

"Just the other day I told her a whole thing that I figured out in my last appointment about how when I lived at home I was always worried my father was going to come home and beat the shit out of me."

"Why?"

"Well, either he was drunk so he had some drunken reason, or I'd done something bad like dented the car, failed English, knocked down somebody's mailbox, joined a band... the usual."

"Oh." I'd meant *why did you worry that*, not *why did your old man beat you multiple times*. It was a big reminder that Christian's reality and mine were different.

"And I think she decided that meant I was trying to tell her without telling her that this was what I was worried about with you. What I actually said about you is that I had no idea how you were doing or what you were feeling. Which is maybe a parallel to my dad, in that I never had any clue what he was thinking, but jeezus girl, that's a leap." He shook his head. "Anyway. Therapy's grueling. It absolutely sucks. But it's necessary. And I think it's helping."

"That's good." I sipped my own beer, which was the "seasonal" Sam Adams so it tasted different from the usual but, you know, still tasted like beer.

"And it's weird, because what I'm about to tell you is what a moron I am, and you're going to ask how the hell can therapy help your self-esteem if it makes you realize what a moron you are? But, you know, it helps you not make that mistake again."

"What are you a moron about?"

"About you. I let a lot of shit get in the way of what I know to be true, what I know in my heart." Or as Christian put it, *hahht*. "I let a lot of bullshit about gays—which all came straight from my father's bullshit mouth, so I should have known better—get all blocked up in my head and get in the way of reality. Which is that, Daron, I really feel like..." He paused for a quick sip. *It's okay man, crutches are for leaning on. Just keep going.* "I really feel like you're the brother I never had."

Wow. Yeah. No wonder he was scared to death to say it. He was clearly scared I was about to tell him to fuck off.

I didn't. "Thanks, man."

"And believe me," he continued, his shoulders slumping in relief, "I know it isn't like I'm not *awehh* that family stuff is messy and complicated and not always good for you, or me. But, you know, after all we've been through... you know."

"I do. I understand exactly what you mean." My own shoulders relaxed, too. Being in a band was a lot like being in a complicated family business, even if your actual family wasn't involved. "I hope... I hope you understand now why there's no way in hell I was kicking you out and replacing you unless I had no other choice. And why I was so... ripshit that you seemed like you were taking the side of the actual morons."

"I know. I'm sorry. I was a total idiot about the whole thing, about Megaton, about... all of it. Thank fucking god, though, I had the balls to tell Dave to stuff it." He took a larger gulp of his beer and wiped his lip. "Understand that I don't think drugs are any excuse. But when you're on drugs, you don't think straight. Wait, I said that wrong. When *I'm* on drugs, I can't see reality for what it is. I was convinced you were all out to get me, for one thing. And the thing with the explosion? I was convinced I was next. No wonder I couldn't play. I was looking under the riser for a bomb before every set."

"Wow."

"I know, it sounds so crazy, doesn't it? But that's how bent the mind can get. I... I wouldn't blame you for getting rid of somebody that crazy. I mean, even if you're family, sometimes you just have to show somebody the door."

Like I'd just done to Digger? But we weren't talking about him right now. "But you're not crazy. You were on drugs. Right? I mean, I don't know the technical definitions of these things, obviously..."

"Well, one thing I wanted to ask you about was if you and Carynne would go to this orientation thing at the center. They can explain a lot better than I can. I mean, I'm clean now, but there can be long-term withdrawal crap that can come up."

"What kind of crap?"

"Depends on the person. Depression, panic attacks, suicidal thoughts, that kind of thing." He didn't sound too worried about it, though. "So far so good, I think, but still."

"Have you ever had a panic attack?"

"You know? I don't think so. I've gotten a little spazzed out here or there, but not the full-blown hyperventilating and stuff people talk about."

"I've had that."

He looked at me from under his bangs. "Seriously?"

"Yeah, without drugs. Only a couple of times in my life." I shrugged. "Not a big deal. You'll know if you're having one, anyway."

"Hopefully I'll never find out."

We sat drinking in silence for a little while. Then I said, "But yeah, I'd love to go to an orientation. Sounds like a useful thing for me to know. Occupational hazard and all."

"I know. Knowing what I do now, part of me says, shit, every touring band should be forced to sit through drug education before going on the road."

"Or dating a supermodel with a coke habit."

"Oh, for sure. For sure." He picked up his glass and clinked it against mine. "She's been awesome, though. I thought for sure she'd be outta here the second I told her we were having problems, you know? And no, Daron. You don't strike me as a violent person. You're like a cat. The claws only come out when you're cornered." Then he looked at me with a slightly panicked look. "Oh shit, that didn't come out sounding right."

"Um...?" I wasn't offended by what he'd said, and I couldn't quite figure out why he was worried about it.

"I mean, I wouldn't want you thinking that I was implying that you were some kind of pussy because of—well yeah, never mind *I'lljustshutupnow*."

I snorted. "It's really okay. I knew that wasn't what you meant."

"But that's just it, isn't it? It's like I say shit without even realizing that maybe I really am brainwashed. Lacey's reading me the riot act about that. Your sister, too. And Carynne. It's like I can't even open my mouth without somebody telling me what a dumb shit I am."

"My sister called you a dumb shit?"

"No no. She just points out when I say something sexist or insensitive. Which makes me feel like a dumb shit." He dragged his hands through his hair. "You know, I'm thirty, and I feel like I should have this shit figured out by now."

"Well, it's not like you had good role models for it."

"That's true. But I feel like that's no excuse. Still. Sometimes I feel ganged up on."

I chuckled a little. "You mean, it went from being everyone was gay to everyone's a girl?"

"Kinda, yeah! I guess... I guess I've never lived with so many women around." He laughed. "Your sister is actually pretty cool, you know. We've been swapping stories about what happens when the people in your life suddenly turn into religious nuts." But then he gave me a chagrined look. "Man, did I really say that?"

"Say what?"

"That everyone around me was turning gay?"

"I don't remember your exact words now. It was something like that. But you know, I can sympathize. Because it felt kind of like that to me, too. I mean, I am gay, but I got used to thinking that the world was basically mostly straight people. I'm starting to rethink that assumption. It's like every time I turn around, someone else I assumed was straight... isn't."

"Yeah, well, but what's the thing they say, if you're not part of the solution you're part of the problem? I want to be part of the solution, Daron. I'm like... man. I just want to stop feeling like a total heel all the time, though. You know, like am I ever going to get over how dumb I was?"

"You will, man, you will." I took a couple of bigger swigs of my beer, since it was starting to get a little warm. "But tell me seriously. If a gig came along that was three straight guys looking for a drummer, would you, you know, be more comfortable with them?"

He shrugged. "I doubt it. I mean, there are a helluva lot more important things that would affect a decision like that. Besides, all the guys in Miracle are straight."

I was about to agree when I suddenly had an idea. "Are you sure?"

"Of course I'm—" He stopped. "Wait. You think they could be closet cases?"

"Probably not all of them, but you know, they've decided the only way to stay clean is to give up everything the Bible is against, right?"

"Right."

"So they're against homosexuality because of that, even though technically it doesn't have anything to do with drugs."

"Right."

"So what are the chances that one of them was already in the closet and now is even deeper in it?"

"Man."

"I'm not saying it's true. But it could be true. And maybe we'll never know."

We were both out of beer. Funny how that happens. Christian signaled for two more.

"Must be miserable," Chris said, when we had fresh glasses in front of us.

"Which thing, now?"

"Being in the closet. Having to hide all the time."

"Well, you know, there's a weird way that you were right."

"What was I right about?"

"About how you and me were alike. Stay with me here." I hadn't drunk enough to be actually drunk, but I was at that state where everything seemed logical but where putting together a logical argument might have some unforeseen gaps in it. Booze is like that. "Here's how I'm starting to see it. Liking drugs or being gay, neither one is inherently bad, unless you believe like Dave and those guys."

"And those guys are nuts, so, no. Okay, I'm with you."

"But when drugs are a problem is when they start to totally rule your life and make other things suck, right? Like if somebody can't do their job or take care of their kids, right? When that happens, obviously, everyone disapproves of it, and so the drug use has to be kept hidden. It has to be illicit."

"Well, and remember, drugs are illegal."

"True. But even alcohol."

"Oh, I get you. Yeah, even though booze is legal there are alcoholics who hide the bottle under their bed and only drink in the bathroom and stuff."

"Right. Exactly. Because they know that people in society are going to give them the hairy eyeball if they see it. Being gay is like that, too, if you have to sneak around and hide it because you know people are going to disapprove." Which brought me to my point. "So actually, you know exactly what it's like to be in the closet, Chris."

"Huh! I guess I do. I bet there's a lot of paranoia that goes along with it, too."

"Yes. Yes, exactly. So you know what? I have to apologize to you."

"Wait, why do *you* have to apologize to *me*?"

"Because you said my vice and yours were the same and I bit your head off for it. But you were actually right. So I'm sorry I bit your head off."

"Yeah, well, I deserved it because I was being a dick, even if I was right. But apology accepted." Chris looked at me. "Is it better for you now, though? I mean, I could get off drugs. I can't imagine getting off sex, though."

"Well, that's a decent question, really, and one I ask myself a lot. I tried quitting it a couple of times, actually, and it doesn't really work."

"D, that's like trying to give up food, I think. And people who do that are seriously messed up. I'm dating a model. I should know."

"Yeah. So, but here's one of the things I'm trying to say. What made it like that was me trying to hide it, was me being obsessed with people giving me the hairy eyeball about it. But if being gay doesn't hurt the job I do or the people around me, then nobody should judge me for it. And if no one is judging me, then I don't have any reason to sneak around or act like it's a dirty habit. And you know what? I like the sex a lot better when it's not in sketchy circumstances."

"Sounds like you and that writer have a thing going, Carynne said."

"Yeah. A thing." I took a deep breath and realized I was almost halfway through my second beer already. "So, there it is. I think I've finally got it figured out, I should treat sex like something I need as much as food and that is... as much a part of me as..."

"As music?"

"Yeah. But of course, just when I think I've got that figured out, *bam*." I whacked the bar for effect, and the bartender glanced over. I looked away. "Did Carynne actually tell you the whole story of what went down at BNC?"

"She told me it was gay bullshit, if that's what you mean. I mean, anti-gay. You know what I mean."

"Yeah."

"I get it." Christian put on his righteous face. "I can totally see where this guy gets off on that, but at the same time, dude, wake up and smell the cappuccino, the entertainment biz is full of gays. Right?"

"I think his point was that of course there are a ton of gays, but we're supposed to stay quiet and in the closet to get anywhere. I used to buy that line. I really did. But after everything that's happened... I don't know. I just can't swallow it when there are too many other things they obviously did wrong. It's mismanagement at their end that scuttled the sales, not the fact that I'm gay, or that Ziggy's flamboyant, or whatever."

Chris's glass was empty. "Okay. So where do we stand?"

"I'm meeting this lawyer, I guess. Carynne says it's not time to go look for day jobs yet, but if we don't get this worked out, then I don't know."

"No no. I mean you and me."

"I think we're cool, Chris."

"Are you sure?"

"We're just two guys trying to make it all work. You're not perfect, but neither am I. I'm... I guess I'm still a little sore, but you know, having seen what some of my real enemies look like? I'm a lot more forgiving of anyone who's sticking by me."

"I'm sticking by you, D." We shook hands, not the business style, the arm-wrestling style, with a half hug for good measure. "Tell me when you need me and where, and I'll be there."

I had a feeling that resolve was going to be tested. But it was nice to hear.

Don't Lose My Number

I don't know which were the more exhausting conversations I had that week, the ones with the lawyer or the ones with Lacey. They were equally difficult to understand, but sometimes you just have to go along with things and hope you figure them out later.

The lawyer's name was Harold Feinbaum, and the first time I'd contacted him had been when Watt had given me his number back when BNC had first put a contract on the table. I'd met him at a swanky Boston office where the carpeting was plush and even the secretaries wore suits.

This time, he came to us. He met us at the house in the afternoon, in jeans and a polo shirt, carrying his briefcase in one hand and a six-pack of bottled beer in the other, and I wondered if maybe Watt had been a good influence on him. I found myself feeling pleased that the living room was so cleaned up, though.

"Thank goodness you talked to me before you signed the thing in the first place," he said as he plopped his file copy of the contract onto the brand new coffee table. On Feinbaum's advice, I'd pushed hard on a couple of points back when, though I was honestly unsure which things I ended up winning outright and which we had compromised on. Master recordings, exclusivity, publishing rights, I knew we'd negotiated on them... Feinbaum was in the big arm chair. Carynne and I were on the loveseat next to him, and Chris, Bart, and Courtney sat on the couch. Courtney was taking notes. Feinbaum was a little on the chubby side, and his face had sort of bulldoggy jowls where his cheeks had sagged. "That's the good news."

I pretty much burst out with, "Tell it to me straight, doc. Am I going to live?"

Feinbaum chuckled and did a reverse Star Trek: "I'm a lawyer, not a doctor."

"I know. But they're throwing the word *unrecoupable* around and I'm trying to figure out if we can keep the lights on, you know what I'm saying?"

"I do, I do. You're saying we should stay focused on your revenue-generating power and the ways this contract infringes or limits that."

"Yes." I'm pretty sure I understood what he said. "I mean, I'm not interested in suing them just to prove a point."

"You're wise. Carynne can give the details on your operating income and expenses better than I can, but here's what I know. You want to talk earning potential? Because Watt's a mensch, you already kept all the publishing rights on 'Candlelight,' so first of all, every penny from radio play and incidental use is coming straight to you. That could dry up any time without warning, when stations finally quit playing the song, but for right now, it's probably just enough to 'keep the lights on,' as you put it."

"Okay, that's good." The beers were twist-offs, and I opened one. Pretty soon everyone had opened one except Court. Not that I would have said anything if she wanted one, but her hands were full.

"Next, you already of course keep anything the band makes performing live. They can't touch you there, obviously."

"Right." Though I didn't see us hitting the road again soon, especially with Ziggy on another continent.

"We lost on master recordings. They own them on *1989*, but of course they don't own the publishing rights. So that's good because you've had high air play, supposedly. So I'd be expecting BMI and ASCAP checks there, too. But I know, that's all dwarfed by how much you might be making from album sales, which I'm getting to. You absolutely do have the right to the accounting review you mentioned, and it sounds to me like the fact that they put up any resistance at all that makes it a one-hundred-percent guarantee you should audit their finances. A forensic accountant isn't going to come cheap, but if you find anything, there are a couple of ways it could pay off. One, you get the money they under-calculated. Two, you prove some kind of misconduct that gets them to dissolve the contract."

Bart piped up. "Wait, how does dissolving the contract help us?"

"Because then the band can sign with another company. Which brings me to my final point, about exclusivity."

"I know we talked about that a bunch," I said. "But

Mills made it sound like they own me."

"As I recall, even the other company you had bidding—Wenco, wasn't it?—didn't want to budge on the exclusivity issue, but you at least got BNC to replace their standard exclusivity clause with the one I gave you." He had a smug smile on his face, the lawyer that ate the canary. "They might squawk about it, but they really have no case. The way it's written, you can perform, record, write, and be credited on any other gig you want, so long as you're not using your stage names."

Bart's eyes lit up. "Yes! I knew that was a good idea!"

"Wait," I said, trying not to get too excited yet. "But as individuals or as a band?"

"As individuals," he said, looking at me. "BNC owns the recording rights to Moondog Three and to Daron Moondog. Daron Marks, on the other hand, can do what he wants. So could Mergatroid Hershenbloom if you want to pick up another name, but something tells me Daron Marks will have better cachet." He shrugged.

Courtney looked at her notes. "Okay, does that mean the band could also just change names?"

"Unfortunately, as a group it's a little more complicated. You'd have to make significant changes of some kind besides just a name change or they'll nail you. If the four of you started playing Romanian folk music, or acid house techno, maybe, and called yourselves something else, Starcat Quartet or something, they might still try to get you but chances are that would be a tough sell to a judge since it's less obviously a stealth attempt to subvert the contract or to exploit company property. But it could still be frowned upon. There have been bands who did that who were sued because they were dawdling from delivering an album. That's supposedly why the exclusivity clause exists, so itinerant musicians don't wander off and do other things."

"But we're not dawdling. We'd like to do another album," Bart pointed out.

"I know." Feinbaum took a swig from his bottle, then coughed a little before he went on. "But the precedent is still there. Let me explain something else, too. No one wants to actually end up in court. The only people who win in court cases are the people like me who get paid to argue them. Everyone else loses, pretty much. They've got a bunch of lawyers like me whose job it is isn't to sue people, it's to make the risk assessment of whether it's worth it to potentially get sued, or to sue and lose. If they feel like the law's on their side, they're more aggressive. If they feel like maybe you have some points that are really strong or like they don't want to chance being decided in your favor, then they're more likely to just ignore you, or to settle somehow."

"Okay, so, if they tried to come after us for taking other recording gigs—"

"Which many companies would," he pointed out.

"—then with the wording of this clause, that's much less likely."

"Exactly. And I feel confident we'd win. They know that. Which is why I predict they're going to let it go rather than take the risk."

"Okay, wow. Well, that's the best news I've had in a while." I still had the image of Mills's face looking smug stuck in my mind, though. I wondered what he would look like when he found out he was wrong, or if he'd even care. Maybe for him it was all about winning the argument in the moment.

"Now, you'd think the big prize at the end of the day would be for them to roll over, say they were sorry and wrong, and cough up the dough for another record and then actually sell and promote it properly to make amends. But justice is a pipe dream, guys. I don't see any way for that to happen. Would you actually trust them with another record? Would you take that chance even if they handed you more money, after this experience? They could sink your careers. In fact, they think you're sunk already. I think we're much better off doing the audit and then trying to get them to let you walk away with no penalty."

"Would they still own the sales on *Prone* and *1989*?" I asked.

"They would. But at least you'd be free to start again somewhere else. Like Wenco, maybe?"

"Artie's a nice guy, but I don't recall their offer being any better."

"Sometimes it's not about the offer." Feinbaum shrugged. "And sometimes it's about leverage. Anyway, that's my take. Another lawyer or a judge might see it differently, of course, but that's my advice."

"Do we have to hire a forensic accountant?" I asked.

"Well, ideally you need someone who knows the music industry or it would be too easy to hide things from him."

"What about Watt?" Bart asked. "He'd know what to look for."

"Not a bad idea," Feinbaum said. "But Watt, for all his genius, isn't always the best with the tiny details like numbers."

"What about Watt and Colin together?" I suggested. "Colin's a CPA."

Bart made a skeptical noise. "My father has forensic accountants working for him."

Feinbaum put his beer down. "Sounds like you have options. Let me know as soon as you're ready and I'll serve the letter saying you want to look at their books. And we'll go from there."

Confession: I used Courtney's notes to reconstruct the conversation above. There were a lot more twists and confusions in the real thing, I think, but since it was my head that was twisted and confused it's hard to remember what it is I couldn't figure out. Feinbaum explained it all pretty well by the end, though, and hopefully I've done the same.

He hung out for a little bit after the official meeting, and Watt came over as planned and hung out, and there was a barbecue. Autumn was pretty much in full swing, which mean sitting around the driveway with the grill going was a good way to spend an evening. Throw some kielbasa on there and I'm happy.

Bart and I gravitated together. Even with all the changes we'd been through, whenever we were together it was like we hadn't been apart. For me, that was the definition of a true friend. And we talked about everything. Serious things. Not-serious things. Band stuff. Other stuff. His parents were on a cruise to Greece, and he and Michelle were thinking about going to their house down the Cape for a week or so. They had invited whoever wanted to come for the weekend, but no one had made up their minds yet.

I said I'd go. Next thing you know, everyone was going.

Bart and I ended up in my room, where I played him the Sarah Rogue CD and wondered why she hadn't called me. Then I realized she probably didn't have my number in Massachusetts and also that I hadn't checked email in days.

We talked about the industry. Bart wasn't fazed so much by what was happening to us as he was by the unwillingness of the industry as a whole to care what people actually wanted to listen to. "The whole point is that something new and different is always coming along," he said. We were lying on my bed with our heads between the speakers, because that's how my room was set up. The best place to hear it was like that. "So it's weird. They say they're always looking for the new hot thing, but really they aren't. The companies and stores and systems are built to keep doing the same thing again and again, and they can't accommodate big changes."

"No kidding."

"I mean, look at how huge acid house is in the UK. It'd be just as huge here, or huger, if there were radio stations that could play it without it violating their precious formats and if there were stores that could sell it because they thought people would like it, not because they had a bin marked for it."

"What's different in the UK?"

"I think it's just a smaller country, first of all, so the distribution networks are less vast and they have more small stores and not so many chains. And they aren't as rigid about format or genre."

"But all it takes sometimes is one hit to break through, right?"

"Sometimes. Or sometimes that's just seen as one weird outlier. Look at what's happening with Technotronic right now."

"Which band is that?"

"That's 'Pump Up the Jam.' That's as close to a house crossover hit as we've seen so far. But there's so much going on in the dance realm."

"But record companies still act like no one wants to buy it but deejays and no one would want to listen to it on the radio or at home, only in clubs."

"Yeah. Weird, isn't it?"

"When you put it like that, yeah."

Someone knocked on the door, and the two of us both yelled "Come in!" at the same time.

Michelle looked in. "I figured you were in here. I'm going to head home. If you want to hang out more you can, but..." She looked behind her, then back at us.

Bart sat up. "Nah, I'll come home with you. See you on the Cape, Daron."

"You bet."

Out they went. That left me alone in the room staring at Ziggy's travel bag, which was still sitting there.

I tuned the radio to WZBC, the Boston College radio station that played weird music all night, and lay there looking at the ceiling for a while. Then I remembered I meant to check my email. I went down to the basement where the Mac and everything was still set up, just like I'd left it.

There was an email from Sarah, all right, saying she'd signed with BNC, a major multi-year, multi-album deal, but she really wanted to talk to me on the phone and could I please call her? The email was almost a week old. I shot her back one quickly apologizing for being out of touch and giving her the Allston number, but I was about to leave for the Cape. Whatever. I'd catch up with her eventually.

I went back upstairs to pack stuff to bring to the Cape. I eventually got caught up in trying to decide what to do with Ziggy's stuff, though. Carynne had a key to his apartment, so I could go and leave it all there if I wanted to. But that felt a little weird. I didn't know if he'd appreciate feeling like I'd been there while he was gone. On the other hand, if I held onto it, he'd eventually have to come get it, and I felt like I was holding the stuff hostage. Or maybe he would forget about it entirely, and I'd feel stupid waiting for him to remember. Or I'd remind him and then it would really come off like I was keeping the stuff hostage to get him to come talk to me...?

The phone rang and I jumped, forgetting I'd turned the ringer on in my room again and wondering who was calling so late. Maybe somebody realized they forgot their wallet here or something.

I picked up. It was Jonathan.

"Hey, stranger," he said. "You busy?"

I lay down on the bed and turned down the radio. "Oh my god, we had the meeting with the lawyer today and it's mostly good news but wow I really hate this side of the business."

"No kidding. Fill me in."

"No, wait, tell me first how you've been doing." It was good to hear his voice, I realized. Very calming. "Because once I start recapping the whole lawyer thing, you know, it's a rabbit hole."

"Things are going great. I'm really pleased with how it's shaping up. I talked to my parents, though. They're taking my cat. I found a place here."

So much for calming. But I kept it light, even if I was thinking about his asking me to move in. "Oh yeah?"

"Yeah. Surprisingly affordable and really nice. Not as nice as Remo's but you know, not much is. Speaking of which, he called here trying to reach you. I told him you were back East for a bit and he said he'd try you there when he next had a chance."

"I've been wondering. He and Sarah both owe me calls."

"She called here, too. She's out of town for the next week or so, though. Doing the same thing I am."

"Which is?"

"Flying home, packing up, and then driving it all back here."

"Wow, really? You're going to drive cross-country?"

"Well, actually, I don't think I have time to do that, so I'm flying home, packing up, and then movers are going to drive it all while I fly back. I'd have to take a whole week off work, and right now I can't leave for that long."

"When are you doing it?"

"I'm flying tomorrow, packing over the weekend, and then flying back Monday morning."

"Wow."

"Yeah, quick turnaround. My mother's already collecting boxes from all the grocery stores. I should probably think about selling off a lot of my books. I'll probably end up putting them in her basement, though. I'll be packing like a fiend to get it all done in time to fly back on Monday. How about you? Not that I'm trying to pressure you to hurry back here or anything."

"Miss me?" I said it like a joke, like a toss-off, without thinking about it.

"Terribly," he said, and it didn't sound like a joke. He sounded nervous. "It's... exactly like that Police song, about the bed being too big without you."

"Oh." I had a pile of immediate thoughts which all boiled down to "oh no."

But Jonathan had gotten good at reading my mind. "I know. It's not like you wouldn't be on tour a lot. Tour widow I could handle, I think. It's not knowing when I'm seeing you again that makes it rough."

And I was thinking, *What happened to "let's see each other a couple times a year?"* I couldn't ask that, though—it was obvious things had changed. We had changed. I had a flash of hot and cold, like even my skin couldn't decide what to feel.

"I know," I said, because I had to say something or he'd start trying to interpret my long silence as something else. "There's a lot uncertain right now. I'm sorry about that."

"So how's everybody? How's your sister?"

And just like that, he had moved us on to normal stuff. I rolled with it. "Carynne and Courtney have a plan that on Monday we're going to buy me some actual furniture, now while we have the income, because they don't think I should live out of milk crates anymore. Bunch of us are going to Bart's house on the Cape for the weekend first, though. Next week, I've got a couple more things to do and then I can head back, I guess. Carynne's in charge."

"You could wait until I get moved in, and then—"

"J. I really have to think about it."

He was silent a moment.

"I don't mean it like that," I said. "If I get another soundtrack gig, I'm going to want to stay at Remo's. I can work there in the studio. I won't have to rent something."

"You could try going up there during working hours and coming back into town at night," Jonathan pointed out. "I know, I'm usually the one who writes at all hours, but this working regular office hours or some semblance anyway is really working for me."

"You have a point," I conceded. "Let me see what's going to happen, I guess." I'm not even sure what I was asking there, only that it sounded like I wasn't really committing myself to anything, still.

He didn't press. "Okay."

Trouble Me

I had been to Bart's parents' Cape house before, when they weren't there. What's funny is that I had forgotten what it looked like. I had convinced myself it was a split-level, with a large deck in the back. I later figured out that in my head I had transposed some other rich family's Cape house where we'd gone to a party around the same time, three or four years ago. There was a while when that was sort of a thing we did, going to parties of mostly college-aged people Bart kind of knew. I don't think it's a coincidence that after he and Michelle hooked up we went to a lot fewer of them. Not that Bart only went to them to cruise (is that even the right word? does it apply to straight people, too?). I mean, if he was only there to pick up girls, you wouldn't think he'd drag me along? Whatever. It was a thing we did. I didn't think too much about it at the time.

Beach houses are inherently relaxing. Even the beach houses of rich people. I had forgotten what it was like to be with a bunch of people and to have no agenda of my own. I didn't have to be the center of attention. I didn't have to be anything. I could just hang around. Other people had various agendas: food, drink, swimming, walking somewhere, that kind of thing. Amusingly enough, not only did I have no agenda, but Ms. Agenda herself didn't. Carynne, like me, let other people pick the music on the stereo. Someone else picked the beer, the food, the topic of conversation.

It was nice. We were sitting together on the couch one night, drinking whatever someone else had opened, when she commented on it: "I forgot what it's like to not be in charge."

"And I forgot what it's like to be in the background," I added. "I used to be in the background all the time."

"You're funny," she said. "Because when you want to light up a room, you can."

"I guess. Nobody here gives a shit if sunlight comes out my butt, though. Thank goodness."

"We know you too well." She gave me a smug smile. "So Jonathan's really moving to LA?"

"Yeah. He signed a month-to-month lease, he said,

though, so if he's done in six months and he has opportunities, he can move on." I shrugged. "I don't think he likes LA that much."

"I don't think *you* like LA that much."

"Got that right. I like Remo's. Not so much the traffic, earthquakes, and surgically-plastic population." I yawned. "The clubs are okay. But we've got better here."

Colin sat down across from us. "Check it out. I found a set of Hollywood Trivial Pursuit cards." He began pulling out a game board.

So we got sucked into playing the game. And by the time we were done with that, it was time to eat again. And that was just how things went. Bart and I wrote a song on the beach. Just because.

Over the course of the weekend, I had a couple of conversation with Lacey, and it became clear to me after a bit that she was trying really hard to figure me out. Like she'd taken it on herself to shrink my head since I was the only one there who wasn't currently in or who hadn't previously been to therapy.

No, I'm not kidding. Bart, Michelle, Carynne, Chris, Lacey, Colin, Courtney, they'd all had something.

Lacey's way of starting one of these conversations would be to say something like, "So it's really a problem that you let your daddy issues get in the way of effective leadership."

We'd be sunning ourselves by the water, or peeling carrots, or whatever, and I'd have to say, "Excuse me?" And then a kind of non-argument would ensue where I'd have to pick apart whatever the theory was—meaning she had to explain to me what she meant by "daddy issues," or "passive-aggression," or whatever jargon she was throwing around, and I'd then have to debunk whatever conclusion she'd come to about me, which always seemed three or four steps too far in the wrong direction. She wasn't what I would call confrontational about it, not like she was the night I'd come home and she'd accused me of wanting to bash Chris's brains in, but she wasn't exactly what I'd call sympathetic and understanding, either.

Mostly no one talked about our problems, I guess because we all felt that the point of going to the Cape was to leave troubles behind.

The one time I took the tack of questioning Lacey as a form of self-defense, it went something like this.

Lacey: Your sexual repression is the source of all your anger, you know.

Me: Okay, I've about had it with the generalizations. Yeah, I'm pissed off about the way the world has pissed on me for being gay, but you know what? I've got plenty of other things to be angry about, too. Life isn't that simple, Lacey. There's not one magic single thing that explains it all.

Lacey: Sure there is. And you can find it through Transcendental Meditation.

Me: What?

Lacey: If you close your eyes and repeat your mantra for twenty minutes, twice a day, you'll figure it all out.

Me: Is that how you figure it all out? Meditating on everyone else's problems?

Lacey: No, silly. When you meditate, you try not to think.

Me: I'm great at not thinking already, thanks. Pass me another beer. But seriously, you meditate?

Lacey: I don't have time. I'm too busy. Chris does, though. I'm trying to do it with him, but it's so boring.

Me: Chris meditates?

Lacey: Every day. I think he does it instead of praying, since he doesn't believe in God. Dave sort of ruined that for him.

Me: Do you believe in God?

Lacey: Yes. Yes, I do. I believe God is testing me every day.

Me: Really?

Lacey: Yes. And you know, I thought it would be difficult to stay with someone godless, but Chris isn't like other godless people.

Me: Because of the meditation thing?

Lacey: Yeah. I think he really is communing with God, he just can't bring himself to call it that. I figure he'll come around in good time, if he can just stay clean.

Me: What about you? What do you do to stay clean? Pray?

Lacey: I'm just over it now. I learned my lesson. I'm so young, I wasn't addicted that long, so it's not as bad for me.

Me: Is that how it works?

Lacey: Sure is. Anyway, what about you? Do you believe in God?

Me: I don't know. I think there probably is a god, but I think as puny humans we can't even comprehend. So I don't think about it much.

Lacey: You think of yourself as puny because you have crippling self-esteem issues.

Yeah, yeah.

Actually, you know what? I don't think I have crippling self-esteem issues. I've got issues, yeah, but if I really had an esteem problem, do you think I could get up in front of ten thousand people each night and do what I do? Do you think I would have gotten this far? Would I even still be alive now if I thought myself that worthless? I don't think I would. One of the reasons suicide has never entered my mind except as a subject of momentary morbid curiosity is that taking myself out of the equation would never occur to me as an option. Now, you could argue that someone with really incredible talent can make it on luck while still fighting "crippling self-esteem issues," but if that's the case with me, well shit, I guess that means I've got incredible talent. And if I believe I've got incredible talent... then Q.E.D. I don't have self-esteem issues.

I decided, for the third or fourth time, that I should look into therapy, though. So at least I'd know what the fuck I was fooling myself about.

Sick of It

Okay, here's a question for the guys in the audience who have sisters, especially little sisters. Pop quiz. What's the right thing do when you accidentally walk in on her crying?

To be more specific, when you've climbed an outcropping of rock near the beach because you're kind of feeling like you want to get away from everyone for a while, and it sure looks like she beat you to it? Everyone else was on the beach. I took a walk. On the other side of the rocks, the sound of the waves was a lot quieter. I heard her before I quite realized what I was walking into.

She was sitting on a rock with her hands over her eyes. I had a moment where I thought I should just sneak away. I mean, if that had been me sitting there, I wouldn't have wanted anyone to see me like that. And I thought Courtney was probably the same.

But at the same time, there's a level on which you aren't thinking logically. You just feel: *crap, my sister's crying I have to do something about it.*

At least, that's how I felt. I don't know why. I'd never been particularly protective of her, you know?

Just because I felt that way didn't mean I knew what to say, though. So I stood there, paralyzed, trying to figure out what I should say or if I should sneak away and try to figure out later if there was something bothering her. She looked up before I could move, and since that meant sneaking off was definitely only an option if I was a total heel, I went and patted her shoulder and said, "What's wrong?"

"Oh, nothing." She snorted loudly and blew her nose into a tissue.

"It doesn't look like nothing..."

"I know. It's not as bad as it looks, though. Hormones. I'm just lonely, that's all."

I sat down on the rock next to her.

"And I got myself all upset, thinking *how can you be lonely when you're here with all these awesome people?* And so then I was mad at myself for being lonely, and that was the last straw." She blotted her eyes with the back of her hand. "It's okay now. I feel better."

"I'm sorry," I said.

"It's not your fault."

"Well, it kind of is, isn't it? I mean, without me you wouldn't have dragged yourself out here."

"Daron. While that is true, it's also true that I basically invited myself along on your tour bus. You're not the only one responsible for me being here."

"Okay. Well, I wish I could do something."

"It's not your fault everyone's older than me. Except Lacey. Who is from another planet."

"Oh man, I'm glad I'm not the only one who thinks that."

She gave a little snort-laugh and had to blow her nose again. "She's a trip. I think Michelle's going to kill her if she opens her mouth one more time about her relationship with Bart."

"Wait, Michelle? Michelle gets along with everyone."

"I calls 'em like I sees 'em," Courtney said.

"Hey, does this mean I'm not the only person she over-analyzes?"

"Oh, hell no. We've all had the Lacey treatment this weekend."

"Really. Huh. So what's she think's wrong with you?"

"Where to start? First of all, the reason I'm so lonely is because I don't have a steady boyfriend, and the reason I don't have that is because I have to stop pretending I'm bisexual just because it's cool." She snorted again and ended up coughing before she pulled another tissue from her shorts pocket and blew her nose much harder. "Should I go on?"

"Lacey thinks you're pretending to be bi?"

"I'm pretty sure Lacey thinks all bisexuals are pretending. But how about you? What's wrong with you, according to Doctor Lacey?"

"What *isn't* wrong with me, according to Doctor Lacey? I swear it's something new every day."

"Ha. It's too bad Ziggy isn't here. He'd play with her mind."

She'd said it in an offhand way, and I tried to answer as casually as possible. "Yeah." But I felt his absence keenly right then. "She's off to a shoot on Tuesday anyway," I added. "Isn't she?"

"Something like that." She stood and stretched. "Are we going shopping for your furniture when we get back to town?"

"I guess so." I shrugged.

"Jeez, don't get over-excited about it."

I stood, too. "If you start school soon, I'm sure you'll make some friends your own age."

She waved her hand as we started back in the direction I'd come. "Don't worry about it. I don't really want to be weighed down by a relationship right now anyway."

"Well, but maybe the thing is to find a relationship that doesn't weigh you down. Something that fits. Something that doesn't mean everything has to turn upside down for you to be together."

"That's a nice fantasy," she said. "Well, I dunno. Maybe that works for gay men. With heterosexual relationships, the girl always has to cater to the guy."

"You think so?"

"Yeah. At least with lesbian relationships it's a little more even."

"Is that why you're bisexual?"

"I don't think there's a 'why.' I think it just is."

"Okay. I didn't want to assume that just because I can't get my relationship needs figured out or controlled that no one else could either."

She chuckled. "You're a weirdo, you know that?"

"So I've been told." We were on a path of sand through the sea grass. "I want you to be happy."

"I want us both to be happy," she said.

"What about the rest of the family?"

"Ah, fuck them," she joked as she tossed her damp tissues into a trash can at the end of the path.

We wandered up the next path, though, instead of going straight down to the beach. "I was lonely a lot when I was your age," I said, feeling kind of silly since it wasn't that long ago. "But then again, I was in the closet and I was in denial."

"Well." She shrugged. "Same result, though. I wonder if I at least had a fuckbuddy if that might take the pressure off."

"I'm not supposed to be comfortable hearing my little sister say things like that, am I?"

"Are you comfortable with it?"

"Not in the slightest."

"Damn. And I was about to be proud of you for being so supportive and open-minded."

"Don't get me wrong. I would support you having... whatever kind of thing you wanted to. It's talking about it that I'm not comfortable with."

"Ahhh, okay. I probably better not bring up the fact that Colin would be ideal in some ways."

"Oh, hell no."

"Hey, hey, hey, I know the rules. He's not ideal because (A) you've already slept with him, and (B) we're housemates and that can be too close. Otherwise, though, damn, he's my type, and I like older guys who—"

"La la la can't hear you!"

She giggled. "I'm totally baiting you. Sorry, can't help it. You're so easy."

"Court—"

"No, seriously, if I get a thing going it has to be with someone where I can go to their place. Between you and Chris and Colin it's like I have not one big brother but three in the house." She shook her head. "If I get into Emerson, maybe I should see about getting into the dorm, too."

"I thought you wanted to stay in Allston and get Digger to pay me rent."

"That's a possibility, too, I guess. But one thing at a time."

"Yeah."

The next day, me, Bart, Courtney, and Carynne took a car to the local renaissance faire, which had opened over the weekend. It was run by a concert promoter Carynne's old boss knew, so she had comp passes for us. She told us the guy was good friends with Aerosmith, so we might see Steven Tyler walking around. I don't think they were there that day, but no one really paid any attention to us, either. I guess if they were blasé about Steven Tyler and Joe Perry in those parts, we were small potatoes.

At one point, Bart and I were standing under a tree while the women were in line for food, and we were watching two buskers, one with a guitar and the other with a tin whistle. They were rocking some wild Irish tune that they did faster and faster each round. When they were done, people around clapped, and one or two put a dollar into the hat lying on the ground in front of them. Bart nudged me and said, "There but for the grace."

"Hm?"

"That could totally have been us if just a few things had been different."

"Yeah, I suppose." I went and put a fiver into the hat. That's the thing. Everything could have always been different in life. But it's the things that you can make different in the future that should matter the most.

We ended up stopping at Jordan's Furniture on the way back from the Cape on Labor Day, since it was on the way, and Courtney picked out stuff for me and arranged to have it delivered.

I wondered if picking a therapist was going to be as easy. I decided it would have to wait until after I'd figured out whether I was going to be in LA for the next six months or not.

Listen to Your Heart

Bart came over on Tuesday because we all wanted to play. As the saying goes from when we were kids: just 'cuz. And the funny thing was, I had vague plans of teaching them some stuff, but we ended up learning a large portion of Led Zeppelin's "Black Dog." If you're not familiar with the song, it's kind of polyrhythmic, basically the drums going along in four while the guitar is in three. The guitar and bass are in unison, which is unusual, but that's one of the things that makes that song so interesting.

The way we got started on it was that I was trying to explain to Christian one of the things I liked about his drumming, which led to us discussing when his playing style was behind the beat and when it was ahead, which at first I think he was kind of worried about. Eventually we started speaking the same language, though. Here's the thing. I think Chris felt that a couple of guys like me and Bart, coming out of music school like we did, would be some kind of rhythmic purists, wanting everything on a metronome. You'd think by now he would have realized we didn't, but you know, that's why it's good to talk about these things. Granted, Bart and I are purists about some things, like pitch, but even there it's all relative.

You sometimes hear bands described as "tight." The thing about the really tight bands is not that their tempo never varies. It's that as they vary the tempo they are so tight, so together, that you don't notice the variations.

Interestingly enough, Led Zeppelin I would not describe as tight, but I think that looseness was intentional. Listen to "Black Dog" again. How are the guitar and bass able to play so tightly together given the riffs that Page is ripping? And yet the drums have the most extreme "behind the beat" feel I can remember hearing on the radio.

Anyway. We ended up learning the song, and Christian ended up feeling a lot better about himself, and then my fingers got tired and we went out for pho.

I can't remember if I've explained pho. Pho is Vietnamese noodle soup. I'm not sure why, but the Boston area has a ton of pho restaurants. Like a lot of the other ethnic food restaurants—Indian, Chinese, Thai, Mexican—they were cheap and delicious and filling. There were two pho places walking distance from the house, so we ate it a lot. Courtney came along. Michelle met us.

After dinner we went back to the house, and Bart and Christian got into playing a video game. Court was having fun watching them. Michelle and I sat on the front steps, drinking beer out of bottles.

"Are you glad Lacey's gone for a while?" I asked, remembering something Court had said.

"I hate to admit it, but yes. She was really starting to get to me." Michelle had long black ringlets of hair, hazel eyes, and a face right out of a classical Greek or Roman sculpture. "I feel a little bad, because I don't want to alienate her, you know? Here I am trying to get this design business going, and here's a supermodel who could be really helpful..."

"Yeah."

"And here I am wishing she'd just shut up." Michelle took a swig of her beer. "At first I thought she was trying to be helpful, and then I thought I would cut her some slack because she was working out her stuff with Chris. But then she went off into fantasyland."

"What kind of fantasyland?"

"I knew she was out of touch when—" She had to stifle a laugh. "—she warned me that I better keep a close eye on Bart if I didn't want him sleeping with you."

That made me nearly snort my beer. "Really? Where did that come from?"

"I have no idea. Bart is straighter than a plumb line." She shrugged.

"And even if he wasn't, our relationship just isn't like that."

"I kind of wonder if Chris talked to her about stuff but she only hears what she wants to, you know?" Michelle set her empty bottle down on the brick steps. "She only absorbs a little and she fills in the rest with her imagination or something."

"Or if he didn't really talk to her about us and she's just guessing based on what she sees."

"That could be it. If she thinks she saw you and Ziggy and Colin and Jonathan all in quick succession, maybe she thinks"—a half-giggle—"you're working your way through all the guys."

She was joking, but I wondered if that was actually how it looked. "I do feel kind of like maybe I've slept with too many people I know."

"Would it be better if you slept with a lot of people you don't know?"

"Errr, no. Probably not. I just... worry. When you name people off like that, it's like... I must come off as a nymphomaniac or something."

Michelle turned and looked at me seriously. "I've known you a long time."

"Yeah."

"You know what I've never known you to do?"

"What?"

"Make the first move."

"Um, does that matter?"

"Daron, I'm pretty sure you can't be a serial seducer if you're the one getting seduced. Tell me. What the hell was going on with you and Roger?"

"Roger?"

"Back in Providence, when you lived with him."

"Nothing really. I mean, when you get two horny nineteen-year-olds living in the same apartment, things are going to happen. Roger was a lot more... sure of his sexuality than I was, then."

She accepted my explanation at face value. "Okay, but tell me, are you always the pursued? Are you ever the pursuer?"

"Are those technical terms?"

"You know what I mean, don't you?"

"Yeah, I know what you mean."

"With Bart and me, I think the reason we've lasted so long is that we were each the exception for each other. Bart was always the pursuer of his conquests. Meanwhile, I was a pretty girl. All I ever had to do was sit back and wait to be pursued. But when we met, he was wrapped up in chasing Ruthanne—"

"I never even met Ruthanne. Was she the one who was the Dean of Students' daughter?"

"Dean of Admissions, I think," Michelle said. "He was wrapped up in chasing her, but I couldn't stop thinking about him. I chased him like crazy. And you know Bart. He doesn't usually say no to sex. But it really quickly turned into something more than sex. I was the first woman he really wanted to move in with, and he was the first guy I ever wanted to invite to move in, too. We kept finding things that were against our usual patterns. After three months I usually started trying to find a way out of a relationship. Not this time. And so on."

"So you knew you were really right for each other," I said.

"Yeah."

"For what it's worth, it really looked to me like the instant you got together you bonded like Superglue. I mean, Bart went from being Bart to one-half-of-Bart-and-Michelle pretty much immediately. But because you're so cool, that was okay." My beer bottle was empty, and I picked at the label. "I don't mean to sound so condescending. I mean, you fit in when none of the other girls he slept with or dated did. I really didn't think about it at the time. I just accepted it, I guess." A thought hit me then. "Are you guys going to get married?"

"Maybe? We've talked about it. I've got to decide if I'm getting an MBA first or if I'm going to dive right into this business. I think maybe I can't wait. I have to strike while the iron is hot."

"Yeah."

We sat there a while in silence, watching the cars go by, various splashes of music coming from the open windows. One of the songs stole a riff that had been big when I was in high school, and I spent a few moments racking my brain to remember it. Right. "Super Freak" by Rick James. Whereas the song that was pumping out of car stereos tonight was MC Hammer's "U Can't Touch This."

I thought about what Michelle had said. About the "right" one being the one that wasn't like all the others. About her being pursued all the time, but the one she knew was for her was the one she wanted to pursue. I thought about all the time Ziggy had spent chasing me, catching me, and playing with me like a cat does with its prey.

But I'd wanted him first. I was just too chicken to chase him. I held back and held back until he decided he could use that, until he broke through my resolve.

He admitted he'd been more interested in making sure he had control of the band by controlling me than in a genuine relationship.

He'd admitted it.

He'd admitted it because he was apologizing for it, though. He admitted it because he wanted another chance. A real chance, maybe.

I never gave him that chance. Not really. It had taken the whole tour, the accident, the fights, the drugs, the challenges, the talks, the songs, the performances, for me to finally get myself into a state where my barriers were down and I could see that actually, none of the crap mattered. That *in spite of* or *because of* didn't matter. What mattered was how ridiculously deep my passion for him ran.

Maybe if I still believed that, if I still felt that way, it meant it was finally my turn to be the pursuer...?

"Penny for your thoughts?" Michelle asked.

"Thinking about Ziggy," I said.

"Thinking about going to India?"

I shook my head. "Can you imagine? It's a really large country. Ziggy went there to find himself. I don't think he wants to be found by someone else."

"Could be."

That had given me the idea for a song lyric though, about finding, and foundlings, and foundering, and I hopped up to write it down. I ended up in my room, where the new bed hadn't been delivered yet, working on it.

I worked on it until three in the morning, when I realized what time it was, and decided to try to call Jonathan, since it would only be midnight his time. I dialed Remo's number and J picked it up on the second ring.

"How was your flight?"

"A little bumpy over Colorado, but otherwise fine. My stuff won't be here for another couple of days, though."

"I know. Which is why I'm still calling you at

Remo's."

"Ah, right. When I get a phone hooked up I'll let you know the number, unless you're here by then."

I didn't say anything about it since I hadn't booked a return ticket yet and wasn't sure when I was going to.

He plowed on. "How was the Cape?"

"Capey. We hit King Richard's one day, too. It was nice. I'm having a kind of weird problem, though."

"Oh?"

"Yeah. My jeans here don't fit right. I'm starting to worry I'm gaining weight."

"Go look in the mirror and see if you can see your ribs."

"Hm. Not really."

"You're fine, Daron, I promise."

"What do you mean?"

"I mean, yeah, you've gained weight, but you're far from being chubby. It's that you used to be too skinny. And now that you're not expending as much energy as you did on tour, and you're eating more regularly, you're putting on weight."

"Huh."

"I kind of thought about saying something a few weeks ago, but you know, telling someone they've put on weight is so easily construed as negative."

"Ah. Yeah." I examined myself in the mirror. "I think I look fine, actually. It's just a pain that my old jeans are too tight."

"Argh. Now you have me picturing you looking at yourself in the mirror."

"I'm clothed."

"Not in my imagination, you're not."

I flushed with heat then, turned on and bashful at the same time. "J—"

"I miss you."

"I miss you, too." Especially now that I was horny.

"Let me know when you figure out your schedule, all right?"

"All right. I really will check with Carynne and have her book me a ticket back."

Wouldn't It Be Good

I spent another week in Boston, during which Carynne made me go to the dentist, and I got all my new furniture arranged. My room seemed bigger when it had actual shelves and a sleek chest of drawers instead of all the piled milk crates. Having an actual bed meant that there was room under it for two guitar cases. It was nicer, yeah, but I couldn't help but feel a little bit like I'd made it more like a hotel room. Which wasn't exactly my idea of home, even if I'd slept in a lot of them in the past few months.

Courtney helped me, though, and it was actually kind of fun to go through my stuff with her and arrange it for the first time since I'd moved into the Allston house. I had a lot of magazines piled up. I didn't want to throw them away, but with Court's help I moved a bunch of them to the basement, which is where the computer and stuff was anyway, and was therefore the place I was most likely to want to refer to, say, a back issue of *Musician.*

Court took all the milk crates for herself, amusingly enough. When I said I'd buy furniture for her, too, she reminded me that she might end up in a dorm in a few months anyway, so the milk crates were actually the best thing. They'd certainly served me well in all my many moves, so I couldn't argue.

Chris and I went out to see a show, some local metal. We paid the cover at the door, and apparently this caused some consternation among the club's management. I didn't see anything wrong with paying like normal people instead of calling up to try to get on the guest list or pulling favors. I think the cover was eight bucks, so it wasn't a big deal. But I guess they felt we were trying to "sneak" in? I don't know. People are weird. Carynne told me not to worry about it. The show was nothing special, but it was nice to hang out with Chris like we used to.

I flew through Chicago and Jonathan picked me up at LAX. We went straight to In-N-Out Burger, and I caught him up on what everyone was up to, which was mostly nothing, but you know, that's the thing. Every conversation isn't about some life-changing decision or something. I told him about the furniture and about Courtney trying to figure out what to do school-wise and about Led Zeppelin and Michelle trying to get her design business going.

"I had no idea what was involved, but apparently a lot," I told him, while we sat in the car eating. He had picked me up in his red hatchback, which had come across the country with his stuff. "So she's focusing on accessories, which I guess means handbags mostly."

"That's gutsy. I mean, all the challenges of starting a small business *and* a retail operation *and* a manufacturing operation at the same time? And being creative about it?"

"Apparently Bart's father is totally fascinated by the whole thing and has decided there's a missed opportunity in capital investment in small entrepreneurship and so not only is he fronting a bunch of the money she needs, he's starting some kind of think tank or consultancy or something." I licked grease off my fingers. "Though I think maybe it's also just his way of showing he approves of Michelle."

"Are they getting married?" Jonathan asked.

"Not that I know of. But they bought that condo in the Back Bay together, which as I understand it is halfway there. Pretty sure they're married in their minds, if you know what I mean."

"Committed to each other."

"Yeah."

There's no way to describe the silence that fell then as anything other than awkward. Commitment was the elephant in the hatchback. Or at least in my mind.

Jonathan started the car and turned us toward Laurel Canyon. It took me a moment to orient myself. "Hey, we're not going to West Hollywood?"

"Utilities aren't getting turned on until Friday. My stuff's all there, but once it gets dark it's a bit dull." He gave me a wry smirk.

"Ah, I see."

"Besides, I didn't ever get a real answer on whether you're moving in with me or not."

"I know." I sucked in a breath, suddenly spurred by the need to explain myself. "I figure my failure to muster an objection is a pretty strong indication that I want it to happen."

"What?" His brow wrinkled as he tried to figure out what I said while keeping his eyes on the road.

"I mean, I suck at saying yes."

"Ah, yeah. You do." He was grinning. "So you're saying... you're not saying no, and that leaves only one alternative?"

"Yes. So, yes. There, I said it."

He laughed happily, and a giddy but frightened feeling ran through my veins.

It wasn't until we were at Remo's house and I was getting my stuff together that I realized what I should have said. My stuff was actually pretty well consolidated in and around my suitcase in the bedroom and in one corner of the studio. Something about being on the road a lot had trained me to keep my shit together and not spread it all over, I think. Anyway, what I should have suggested was that I stay at Remo's during the week and then at Jonathan's on the weekends. But having not said that, I felt it would be weird to try to say it now, as it would seem like backing out. I decided maybe I should just tell my inner voice to shut up and enjoy the ride.

Besides, I didn't have a gig at the moment and maybe it would be stupid to sit around alone in the canyon with my thumb up my butt. At least until Remo got back in a couple of weeks.

We watched a Tom Hanks movie out of Remo's collection and got in bed earlyish for us, since J had to be at the office for a meeting in the morning. And because he was eager to get into bed. I mean, yeah, we hadn't seen each other in over ten days, so it should come as no surprise that he was eager. No complaints here.

The next day I finally talked to Remo. He'd managed to miss me in Boston a couple of times. He had pretty much pieced together the whole story for himself by the time he reached me, between talking to Carynne once, Christian once, Digger once, etc. He didn't have a lot of time to talk, and long-distance from Europe to LA has got to be a killer, but he wanted the whole thing from me with the full Arlo Guthrie four-part harmony treatment. So he got it.

And I told him I was moving in with Jonathan for a couple of months in West Hollywood, but I wanted to know if it was okay for me to still come use the studio here if I needed to, and of course he said yes. And never once did he say or imply that it might not be a good idea to move in with my boyfriend immediately after getting dumped from my record label for being too gay. Remo's exact words about the whole BNC situation? "Fuck 'em."

Two days later I officially moved in with Jonathan. I don't know which thing I was more terrified of: that it wouldn't work out, or that it would.

Lost in the Supermarket

When I think "apartment," I think of a cubicle inside a big square box of a building. That's what comes from growing up near New York City. In Boston, of course, an apartment is just as likely to be a couple of rooms in a Victorian house as it is a piece of an "apartment building."

I wasn't sure what to expect from Jonathan's "apartment," but once we got there I realized it looked sort of familiar. It was the same style of building as the one that guy lived in—the guy who picked me up in the bookstore that time I drove myself from LA on the tour. The building was two stories, one apartment upstairs and one downstairs. The front of the house had a walled-in courtyard next to the driveway, and the living room had a faux stone floor. It was a sort-of open plan, where the division between the living room and dining room was delineated by the fact that the dining room was a step up from the living room, and then the kitchen in the back was another step down. A narrow hallway off the kitchen led to the back door, the bedroom, and the small office. I found it weird that none of it was carpeted, but then again, the weather was so warm, maybe carpeting would have just been stupid.

"The upstairs unit has three bedrooms because they have all the space on top of the garage, but they don't have the garage," J explained as he showed me the layout.

"Who lives upstairs?"

"Two older men and their two small dogs."

"Are they a couple?"

"The dogs?" He laughed at his own joke. "Pretty sure they are, though I've only met them once so far."

The first thing we set up in the house was the answering machine. Jonathan recorded the message and kept it simple: "If you need to leave a message for either Jonathan McCabe or Daron Marks, do so after the beep."

Yeah, I know. I had decided to use my real name. I probably should have thought of another one for business purposes, but I didn't.

We spent most of the weekend unpacking. Jonathan didn't have terribly much stuff. He said he'd put almost all the books and LPs into his mother's basement and left most of the CDs behind, too. Most of them were promo freebies anyway. He had a futon couch, an arm chair, a card table and chairs, a couple of bookshelves, and a matching bed, nightstand, and dresser. He didn't have a TV. We debated the merits of putting the stereo in the living room versus the bedroom. For the moment we settled on the stereo in the living room and a boombox in the bedroom.

This necessitated a shopping trip to find the perfect boombox, which in our minds should have both a CD player and two cassette tape slots for dubbing purposes, because you never know when you're going to need to dub something. A backup option would be to get a small portable CD player and a box that had audio inputs, but it would be less ideal. A third plan would be to replace the cassette player in Jonathan's stereo with a dubbing deck, but cost-wise it wasn't the greatest plan.

So we went on the hunt. RadioShack, Sears, a bunch of places in the mall attached to the Sears... we struck out at them all. Several salespeople seemed to think the thing we were describing existed, but it was starting to sound like a mythological beast. It didn't help that neither of us was familiar with West Coast stores, either.

"You know what we need?" I told him, as we sat in the car trying to figure out where to try next. "Crazy Eddie's."

"You're so right. But I think they only had those in New Jersey and New York." Jonathan paged through a freebie newspaper he had picked up, looking for ads.

"Had?"

"Didn't you hear? They went out of business. There

was a huge fraud case, something about overcharging people for warranties. Last I heard they were declaring bankruptcy."

"Wow, no way. That was Digger's favorite place to shop."

Jonathan chuckled. "Think about what you just said."

"Haha, you're right. Hey, once you figure out where we're going next, figure out how we can get Sarah away from Digger. Speaking of frauds and all."

"Sure." He folded back the newspaper. "Well, I don't see anything else to try. I wonder if they have Service Merchandise here? We'll have to check the Yellow Pages at home. Meanwhile, this reminds me that I have to pick up some office supplies."

Amusingly enough, we found just the thing we were looking for while shopping at the "office supply superstore" Staples. I'd ever been in an office supply store the size of a warehouse, and Jonathan, it turned out, had a kind of fetish for office supplies. Okay, maybe fetish is too strong a word. He was a big fan, though. So we ended up walking up and down every aisle and coming out of there with more stuff than I had imagined we would: notebooks and pens and pen holders and desk doohickeys and whatever else he needed. But anyway, yeah, right there in the section with the other small electronic appliances was exactly the boombox we wanted, at the price we wanted.

I felt like we'd won some kind of victory against the vagaries of the retail distribution system that had derailed my career.

Okay, not really, I just wanted to see how it sounded to say something grandiose. Fact is, not everything is about me or my career. But until then I hadn't quite thought about how many middlemen there are between the consumer and the product, whatever it is: hydroponic tomatoes or denim jackets or cameras or albums. Like it or not, I was part of a big, complicated ecosystem. And what's that thing they say when you're facing extinction? Adapt or die?

On Monday I called around to everyone I knew involved with soundtracks and scoring. While I was at it, I called some guys who knew the guys that Bart knew about session playing. That sounds sketchy, I know, but that's the rule, isn't it? It's not what you know, it's who you know.

Word travels fast. By Monday night I was meeting a guy at a show who told me that word had traveled *so* fast he'd not only heard I was looking to pick up session work, he'd heard BNC was being dicky about exclusivity. I told him my lawyer had told BNC to shove it and would happily see them in court and that BNC were bluffing. He was still a little leery, but I'd come with good recommendations, you know?

That gig didn't work out, but by the end of the week I had a couple more leads. Here's the thing. Playing guitar for a living is one of those things a lot of people dream of doing. But out of all those who dream it, how many actually go and do it? Not as many as you'd think. Now look at it from the point of view of someone who needs to record a jingle for a TV commercial. That person needs to hire musicians. Yeah, it's tough and competitive and most people wouldn't make it if they tried, but the plain fact is that Jingle Guy really, really *needs* musicians. And so does Soundtrack Guy. So does Pop Singer trying to fatten up their album sound. And so on. They need someone who can show up on time with the chops to do the job. I was far from the only guitarist in the LA session market, but it was worth a shot.

Carynne called a couple days later. "Hey, what is this I hear about you looking for session work?"

I was sitting in the walled-in courtyard next to the driveway with a guitar, but I had the cordless phone out there with me, hoping for some calls. Jonathan was at work. "Yeah. You knew I was going to."

"We talked about soundtrack stuff. I didn't realize you wanted to do sessions, too. Don't go leaping in all willy-nilly."

"Willy-nilly?"

"I think you should let me handle those bookings for you. Seriously."

"If you want to. I just figured it would be easier for me to do it since I'm here. If you still want a cut, that's fine." I stood up suddenly, as a spider dropped onto the guitar from the vines hanging over the wall. I shook it out and went into the house. "You can do collections?"

"Okay, sure, but you're forgetting one thing."

"Which is?"

"You, mister, are a Famous Musician, and people

feel weird just calling you up directly. So they call me."

"Oh. Is that why you're calling now?"

"Yes. So how about you tell me how much you were planning on charging."

"Um, not sure. I figure it might depend on the budget of who's hiring, you know?" I set the guitar in the stand next to the couch. "Not all the seats on the airplane cost the same."

"True. But seriously, what ballpark are you thinking?"

"I don't know. I guess two-fifty to five hundred a day?"

"So how much would you charge a band going into the studio three to five days, cutting two tracks? Let's say they're pretty well capitalized."

I got a can of Coke out of the fridge, doing the math in my head. "I guess fifteen-hundred to twenty-five hundred then."

"No. You're not walking in there for less than five thousand, minimum."

"Are you serious?"

"Daron! Get it through your head! You're Daron Fucking Moondog—"

"Marks."

"Whatever! You're pretty much a household name among guitar players right now, okay? They're not paying for Joe Schmoe, and you damn well better not charge like that's who you are. I also honestly think you shouldn't take any gig too small."

"Really?"

"Really. Image is worth something, Daron, and it's worth more money. If word gets around that you're cheap, your value goes down. If you look desperate, your value goes down. If, on the other hand, you look like a maverick getting screwed by your record company..."

"You think I'll get 'pity' work?"

She laughed. "I think every band *loves* to stick it to the man. And besides, you already have a sterling reputation as a hired gun."

"I do?"

"Yeah. Because of Nomad."

"Right. I hadn't even thought of that."

"Which is why you have me. Look, anything under two days or under a grand, do it yourself if you want, but if you can be a little patient I'm sure I can get you some better sessions than that."

"Okay, fine. So who is it who was afraid to call me?"

"He's not afraid, he'd just rather speak to someone who speaks his language. Anyway, it's Herbie Herbert."

"Is that a band?"

"He's the manager of Journey. He's putting together a project with one of the guys from David Lee Roth's band and some guys from Racer X. They're not ready to record an album yet, but he's got two soundtrack theme songs already sold for them so, boom. They need to cut two radio-ready singles ASAP and figure out who's in the actual band later."

"I can do that."

"I know you can do that. That's the point. They're at Sound City on Monday."

"What time?"

"I'll find out."

"I'll bring the Fender."

Change

I'm not going to tell you the name of the band. It doesn't matter anyway.

I showed up at Sound City driving Remo's truck. The place was in Van Nuys, in yet another one of those low, flat-roofed industrial buildings that are everywhere in Southern California.

No one from the band was there yet, but I introduced myself to the woman who seemed to be the secretary in charge, and she introduced me to an engineer named Pike. We got to talking shop immediately, and the next thing you know we're crawling under the board where he's showing me the circuits. It was the biggest Neve I'd ever seen, but then again the studios where I had worked, like the Aquarium, had been smaller than this place, and the loft where we'd recorded *1989* had been more of a jerry-rigged setup. Not all twenty-four-track setups are created equal is all I can say.

Primo desk or no, though, the rest of the place was a dump. Pike saw me looking at the suspicious-looking stains on the couch and said, "It's always been like this."

"Like what?"

"Grody as hell. Shivaun will tell you, business has been dropping off for a while now. Everyone's moving to drum machines and stuff. If you've got a machine, you don't need a room like this to record in." He shrugged.

I took some time to examine the gold and platinum records on the wall. Fleetwood Mac, Rick Springfield, Pat Benatar, Tom Petty and the Heartbreakers, REO Speedwagon, Dio... Okay, there were a lot of them.

Next to appear was the manager-slash-producer: the impresario who was putting this "project" together, meaning he'd be the manager of the band and produce the songs, apparently.

We shook hands and sat on the least stained-looking of the couches. "You come highly recommended," he said.

I didn't ask by whom. "I can play a lot of styles."

"I'm looking for straight-up pop rock here, something in the style of that Kenny Loggins song from that Tom Cruise movie."

I was pretty sure I knew which song he was talking about. "'Danger Zone.'"

"That's the one. So here's the thing. I want to get this out of the way early. I'd appreciate it if you wouldn't push the issue of credits."

"Um, sorry?" My brain scrambled to figure out what he was talking about. "If you mean which name to use for me—?"

"That's the thing. We'd like you to go uncredited. Things are a little sensitive with this thing so close to getting off the ground, you know? We don't want any rumors going around that you might be 'joining' the band."

"I'd be happy to avoid those rumors, too. Honestly, I don't care if my name is on it. Or call me Scrooge McDuck if you want. I have no problem with it."

He was obviously relieved. He shook my hand again as he rocked back and forth on the couch. "Whew! Great. Come on, let's get set up."

So he had apparently written some lyrics and had an idea for the riff, which he threw out the window once he heard what I cooked up, and while we were working on it the other band members drifted in and out. Honestly, I was never totally sure who were the members and who were other hired guns like me.

The bass player, I'm pretty sure, was the main musician involved. Once he got there, things got more focused, and he took over a lot of the discussions on the musician side of the glass while Mr. Impresario went to work the board.

By the end of the day we had a pretty workable three-minute song, and we laid down one solid take of it with a guitar solo in the middle. I had thought that was probably just going to be filler and that they'd cut that out and put another take in there, or put in whoever got the lead-guitar gig later. But I would later realize that was the take they ended up going with. Kind of funny.

I got back to the apartment around nine or so. Jonathan was in his office, a pair of Walkman headphones on his ears, typing away. I could make out the tinny sound of Elvis Costello leaking from the headphones. I knocked on the door frame, and he jumped and looked over his shoulder. "Startled me!" He slid the 'phones off and came to give me a hug and a kiss. "How was work, dear?" he joked with a wide grin.

"Not bad, how about you, dear?"

"Not bad. But I am starved."

"Me too. Let's go grab something? Falafel?"

"Eh. The food's good, but that place is so grungy."

"You should hear about where I was today." We ended up walking to a taco shop and bringing the food back with us, eating half of it along the way while I told him about Sound City.

Jonathan knew about it. Of course. "Yeah, one of the owners was at one of the parties we went to a couple of weeks back. Joe Gottlieb. Managed Rick Springfield."

"You are like a walking Rolodex. You never cease to amaze me."

We finished eating while sitting in the living room. The windows were the kind we put on porches back East, with slats of glass on metal crank louvers, and a breeze brought the scent of some kind of night-blooming flower into the room. Don't get me wrong, LA mostly smells like car exhaust. But that was nice.

J threw out the wrappers and napkins and stuff and then paced back and forth like he was getting ready to say something. Which, apparently, he was.

"I have to get up early and be in for a meeting," he said.

"Okay." His car was in the garage. Mine was on the street. I wasn't parking him in. I tried to figure out what else about morning logistics I needed to know.

"I guess what I'm trying to figure out is, do you want to have a quickie now, or can it wait until tomorrow?"

Oh. God, I'm so dense sometimes. "I think we're both a little full from dinner for a quickie right this minute."

"Eh, yeah, you're probably right. I'm probably too full to go to sleep right away, too." He stretched. "I think I'll get in bed and read and hopefully get sleepy."

"Okay."

He came and kissed me goodnight "in case" he was asleep when I got in bed, and then off he went.

I got out the Fender and played around with some things. No amp, just the strings, just enough to get my brain working. My thumb was a little sore from playing so much earlier, though, so I didn't do that for very long. I could hear the TV of our upstairs neighbors. Sounded like they were watching a movie, since I didn't hear any commercial breaks.

J was asleep with the light on and his book on his chest when I looked into the bedroom. I got ready for bed myself, and by the time I was done with that he hadn't moved. I plucked the book carefully out from under his fingers and put it on the nightstand, and then I turned out the light.

J had picked the left side of the bed to be his. I climbed in on the right, then set my alarm clock so I'd remember to get up and drive back to Sound City. It was only around fifteen miles, but with traffic that could easily be an hour.

I wondered what the likelihood was that I'd be able to get five grand for a gig each month. In my mind I tried out the math. Five grand a month for a year was $60,000. Of course, a big chunk went to taxes, plus a percentage to Carynne. But I could live really easily on half that. Well, okay, it might get tight keeping up the mortgage payments and actual renovations that might be needed on the Allston house. But there would be some residuals coming from "Candlelight," through BMI and ASCAP, separate from album sales. And I still had a little money in the bank. So I wasn't in any danger of money stress, was I?

The real question was whether Carynne could live off of what we could afford to pay her.

No. The real question was whether there would still be a band when Ziggy returned to this continent.

I fell asleep while having a complicated daydream, trying to imagine for myself what he was doing in India and what it must be like, and my daydream involved elephants and singing and women in saris, because I didn't know anything about India beyond seeing the movie *Gandhi* in a history class in high school. Once I fell asleep, it became a dream that had something to do with a beetle crawling across the back of his hand while he was meditating, and I couldn't decide whether I should disturb him or not. I had a vague notion that we shouldn't go around killing beetles at a monastery or wherever this dream was, but I didn't know for sure. So I watched it, shiny black and green, as it crawled up his arm.

I woke myself with a start before it could crawl into his sleeve. *Oh, I get it,* I thought. A beetle. The Beatles. Rock stars who went to India. Good one, subconscious.

Stand and Deliver

I went back to Sound City the next day and cut the other track they wanted.

This time, the producer-manager-guy had nothing. I mean, okay, he had a cliché for a chorus, which the bass-player-slash-band-leader put the kibosh on, and when I got sick of them fighting, I just piped up with, "Hey, how about this?" and played them a riff and pulled some string of words out that scanned. I don't actually remember what the words were now. Something that made sense with the theme. We cut the track in a couple of hours and we were done. They were going to do vocal overdubs the next day, but the rest of us were free to go. I made sure they had my number in case something cropped up and they needed me to drive over to do one more, but they seemed to really feel we'd nailed it. I suppose that's the point of using guys who are good session players. There's nowhere near as much fussing around as when you're a regular band and everyone's trying to have creative input and learn their parts and stuff keeps changing.

Yeah, we nailed it. They were so ecstatic about getting everything done in such a short time that they offered me partial songwriting credit. That was interesting for a couple of reasons. One, it meant my name got attached to the project anyway, just not as obviously as it would if I were listed as a musician. Two, it meant that if the song got air play, I'd get paid some more.

I went out for a beer with Pike after the recording was done, and we bonded over engineer stuff. If Moondog Three hadn't taken off when we did, I might be doing exactly what he was doing right now, working as an engineer and hoping to get a crack at producing.

I told him about what a struggle I'd had with that soundtrack thing I did, using the MIDI sequencing software as well as multitracking, and the next thing you know we drove up to Remo's so I could show him the studio there. And then we had another beer there and played around with the equipment.

When we were tired of playing around in the studio, we ended up sitting on the side of the pool with our feet in the water, and I asked him how much he thought Remo had spent on the home studio. He said he couldn't really guess. So I asked him instead how much he thought it would cost to build something like that starting from scratch, and his guess was about half what Chris and I had paid for the Allston house.

"If you're thinking about doing it, though, man," he said, "Don't. Wait another two years. By then we'll know if tape is even going to survive, or if everything will be DAT."

"I thought DAT was dead in the water."

"For home consumers, maybe, but not for commercial recording. Seriously. Sit tight. I should bring you over to Keith's place, though."

"Keith's place?"

"Right there by Sound City. It's a digital studio called Goodnight LA. And you'll like Keith." He proceeded to rattle off a list of acts and albums equally impressive as the platinum records on the wall at Sound City. I would later piece together that Keith had been the engineer at Sound City until he built the place next door because he wanted to do more with digital.

See, it's not just me and my band and management who are incestuous and intertwined. That's just the way the business is.

Okay, here's where I have the urge to say that Jonathan and I had some idyllic weeks together before the next big trouble arrived, because I realize a lot of heavy shit has been in the story recently and it would be nice to think that I had it easy for a while. But it wasn't that easy.

I got home that night to find him in a bit of a state. Let me see if I can get it right.

It was probably eleven o'clock by the time I walked in. He was sitting in the raised "dining room" at the card table with a bowl of Campbell's Soup and some crackers. He looked sort of stressed out, though, with circles under his eyes and a drawn mouth. I tossed my jacket onto the couch and went over to kiss him hello.

"Everything okay at work?" I asked, wondering if this was another writer's block situation or what.

He looked at me. "I had no idea you were going to be so late."

Huh. "I had no idea I was going to be so late, either. Did something happen?"

He gave me an "oh come on" sort of look, which really didn't seem like Jonathan and switched me instantly into walking-on-eggshells mode.

I racked my brain for something to say that wouldn't come off as too defensive or inflammatory. "I'm sorry, I must be forgetting something...?"

"What happened is you didn't come home." He winced at his own accusatory tone. He picked up his spoon, then put it down again like he wasn't hungry, and tried again: "I thought we had a plan for tonight."

For a second I thought he meant we'd accepted an invitation to some party or something. "We did?"

"I certainly thought we did." He pushed the soup around in the bowl with the spoon.

Okay, I told myself. He was working hard to stay calm. I didn't have to pretend he was some kind of bomb that could go off if I didn't handle it right. Be honest. That'll get you through.

How's this for honest? "You were expecting me home, and so you didn't eat anything earlier. No wonder you're cranky."

"I am not cranky!" Jonathan put his hand on his face then, like he could hear perfectly well how cranky he sounded.

"Can I suggest you eat your soup before we try talking about it?"

He put a finger into it; it had clearly gone cold.

"Here. I'll warm it up for you." I carried it to the built-in microwave under the cabinets and nuked it for a minute. While it hummed and spun around I stood next to it, trying not to let my anxiety build up. I brought him the soup and then sat down in the chair across from him, hoping that would encourage him to eat it.

I ate a cracker while I watched him eat. When he was done, he looked less wan and a lot calmer.

"I just didn't think you'd be so late," he said, trying again. "Did the recording go late?"

"Pretty late, but it was better to go a few extra hours today than have to go back tomorrow," I said. "And then I schmoozed with the engineer. And you know how that goes."

"You could have... called...?" He sounded tentative even bringing it up.

"I didn't realize you... needed me to...?" I replied, sounding just as tentative.

He looked disappointed.

My instinct was to brush it under the rug and just try to make it up to him, but if I did that, this would keep happening. I reminded myself that this was Jonathan, and not Ziggy the cipher or Digger the mercurial. "Can we back up? I'm really feeling like you're having a different conversation from me."

"Me too," he said, and I got the feeling the disconnect itself was why he was so disappointed. I'd missed something here. "Which conversation did you think we were having?"

"Well, I don't really want to come out and say that you're a grown man and I kind of expected that if you needed to eat you would, without me having to be here or call you to remind you...?"

"Ah." He blinked at me. "Yeah. That's not the conversation I thought we were having."

"Okay, clue me in, then?"

"Remember last night? When I went to bed early?"

"Yeah." I pictured the scene in my mind. "You offered me a quickie and I said no thanks. I thought that was pretty mature and sensible of us."

"What I actually said was that you had a choice between a quickie last night or not-so-quick tonight."

"I don't remember anything about 'not so quick.'" And I didn't have to remind him that my memory was auditory.

"Maybe I didn't use those exact words..."

"So, wait, this is about you feeling like I blew you off when we were supposed to have sex?" Funny, I know, I had thought the conversation was about dinner but it was actually about sex. So much for my one-track mind, eh?

"Well, I wouldn't have put it quite that way," J said, "but I guess that's what it boils down to."

Fuck. "Okay. I'm sorry. I didn't even realize you were expecting it." It was impossible to stay calm when my heart was hammering and my anxiety spiked as I wondered what kind of hell there would be to pay for fucking this up. Because that's what would happen with Digger or with Ziggy, wouldn't it?

But here's what he said: "Am I setting my expectations too high?"

"I don't know, J. Didn't we agree a couple of weeks ago that we'd just tell each other when we were horny and that we'd tell each other when it was time to back off?"

"You're right; we did." He sat back, pondering.

"Because if you're all wound up because you think I don't actually want you or something, that's not the case. I'm just a dumbass and I didn't realize what you meant last night."

"Just because you're a 'dumbass' shouldn't mean I have to do all the work," he said. "That's no excuse."

That stung. "It's not an excuse! If you wanted to have sex tonight, why didn't you just say so?"

"I did!"

"You didn't, J. I swear you didn't. Not in a way that it sank in, anyway."

He frowned a little. "Yeah, okay. I suppose that's possible. I'll try to be clearer next time."

"It's very sexy when you're clear, you know." It sounded like a line, but I meant it. It was such a turn-on for me not to have to guess whether he wanted me or not. "Here. You pick the time. The next time. Whenever it is. I'll be there. You want morning sex? Go for it. Saturday morning? No problem, either."

I was trying to be sincere. I was trying to make it up to him and be solid, make him a promise I could keep. But looking back on it now, don't I sound like a bullshitter? Don't I sound like I'm promising my ass to soothe the savage beast? Jonathan is about as far from "savage beast" as you can get. Really. And yet I hear this sort of victimy tone in my voice. Which means it all comes from me.

I don't think he heard it that way, either, or he would've called me on it. Instead he said, "Saturday morning's a good idea. But I have an even better one."

"You do?"

"Yeah. I think we should try it right now. Talking about Saturday morning... got me wound up."

"Okay, sure. And of course you're wound up if you thought all day that we were doing it tonight."

"Hm, that and I think if we do it now, we'll feel better, whereas if we wait we'll both sort of brood over it," he added.

"You're probably right about that." I stood up and pulled my T-shirt over my head. "In fact, I know you're right about that."

He smiled. "C'mere." He stayed in his chair, pulling me between his knees and nibbling on one of my nipples.

Click. My arousal had been simmering as soon as the subject of sex had come up, but once he put his mouth on me it was like flipping a switch. Two days of pent up energy from fucking the back of a guitar in the studio suddenly came online. I unzipped my fly and his mouth worked its way down, and pretty soon we had to go to the bedroom because the faux stone floor was a killer on J's knees.

While we were fucking I was sure we had figured it out. We were in synch. Things would be smoother now. But, you know, while I'm fucking I always think that.

Lovely Money

Friday night we went to a party and Pike introduced me to Keith, who it turned out had heard about me from Chernwick. And that led to another gig. This band was partway through cutting their album when one of their guitarists broke his wrist in a swimming pool accident. The story was that he had been trying to clean the pool while on drugs, and he fell in. I guess that wouldn't have been so bad if he hadn't been right at the stairs and railing of the pool at the time, which also explained the broken ribs and a couple of other things wrong with him, too, though it was the wrist that kept him from playing. They were running out of studio money and running out of time to deliver a product, and they had more than half the tracks in the can already, so they were desperate. Keith was their producer and, I think, more than a little paternal toward them. I later heard rumors they'd already run through their budget and that Keith stuck with them anyway.

No, I'm not going to say which band it was. Keith was a genuinely nice guy who cared about what he did. They weren't the only band he helped out.

So I went to Van Nuys every day. At first everything was pretty straightforward. Play this part. Play that part. No problem.

Things got hot and heavy after I'd been recording with them for two weeks, I think because Keith got more and more in love with the way I played. He also loved that he could bring in sheet music and I could play from it. To me that's no big deal, but I know, I know: most rock musicians don't read music, and of those who do, most can't *sight* read.

Let me confess something, though. Sight reading is a party trick. Seriously. I don't think being able to do it makes you a "better" musician than someone who can't. I know that's not what is preached in the music schools, where you're lower than dirt if you can't do it. But music school is all about them finding things to make you feel lower than dirt. Now that I think about it, that's really what music school is for. It's to make you want to quit. It's a weed-out machine. Those who aren't culled are the ones who get shots at those tip-of-the-iceberg gigs. And all pro gigs are tip-of-the-iceberg. Sessions included.

In other words, I'm motherfucking lucky to have survived this long, but that's because, fucked up as I am about other things, my playing isn't one of the things I let myself doubt.

Of course, music school isn't the only mechanism that is set up to make you think you're lower than dirt. The industry as a whole has two modes: top of the world, or not. There's really not a lot of middle ground. If the album sells a million copies, that's a hit. If it sells "only" 100,000, it's a flop. "Only" 200,000, still a flop. Maybe it's all about expectations.

We'll come back to that subject—expectations—at a later time. Because right now I'm talking about this band, and Keith, and how that all unfolded. So the basic gist is, Keith kept rearranging stuff to feature my playing more and more, and then—so that the new tracks would mesh with the previously recorded ones—he started having me overdub parts on the songs that were already done. That led to him wanting to re-record some of those tracks...

Recall what I said about them running out of money. So Keith was doing this not for money, but because he really thought it sounded better. Eventually the band put their collective foot down and said no, they couldn't keep rearranging stuff because of how I sounded or how I played. This turned into a huge fight between Keith and them until I finally butted in and said what I should have said in the very *very* beginning, which was that I could play exactly like the injured motherfucker if that was what they wanted. Once I understood the issue, I realized that I should listen to the band more and Keith less, even though Keith was the one paying me (and stroking my ego). Keith was a smart guy, though, and didn't have so much of his own ego invested that he couldn't see how to make it work.

Among the things we did then was I put my own guitars away and just played the ones they had already used on the record, and I went to school studying the guy. I listened to the previous album in the car everywhere I went, and at home I sat there with my headphones on, picking away at recreating his solos, the way I would've when I was fourteen. It took a couple more weeks to get everything done to everyone's satisfaction.

Bottom line: we got it done. And most people can't tell it's me on the record.

Note that I haven't said a word about Jonathan. We didn't have any fights during those three or four weeks. I also made sure my ass was at home by nine PM at the latest, and that meant no issues about either dinner or sex. We had plenty of both.

But to get back to the story about the guitarist who broke his wrist in his swimming pool. Chris and Lacey arrived shortly after the gig ended, and we got together with them for dinner at some swanky place Lacey picked. That was fine, though I always felt whenever I had a moderately fancy dinner that Bart should have been there. Afterward we went to a celebrity hot spot for some kind of schmoozefest. I don't remember what it was now—someone's birthday, or the release party for their self-help tape, or announcement of their new deal with William Morris? It doesn't matter who or what. If it had been someone I knew maybe it would have stuck, but it was someone Lacey's agent knew.

Apparently Chris and I were still considered A-list. I wasn't surprised about that. I mean, the videos were still getting played, and our pictures were still appearing in magazines. It wasn't like anyone but us knew we were on our record company's shit list.

So the hot spot was a kind of night club room in the back of a restaurant. It had a dance floor and lots of alcovey booths. It was supposedly hard to get into normally, but there was this party, and I was never clear on whether everyone there was there for the party or if it was only some people. I don't suppose it matters.

What matters is that at one point Lacey grabbed me, literally, and placed me in front of her so her back was to the wall and my back was to the room.

"Lacey, what the hell?"

"Act like you're talking to me until that creep goes away."

"What creep?"

"Don't turn around! He'll give up and go away if I look busy. Normally this is Chris's job, but he's in the men's room." She seemed really anxious.

"Um, okay. Does this happen a lot?"

"Depends." She took a deep breath and smoothed

her hair. "There's always some guy who can't control himself when he gets this close to a ten."

"A ten? Oh, I get it." Ten as in that Bo Derek movie. "Should I try to get Jonathan over here, too?"

"No! If he thinks I'm talking to a group he'll try to horn in. Trust me, just stand where you are."

"Okay, anything to help a woman in need."

She frowned at me then, giving me one of those sour-fruit faces. "Oh, yeah, right."

"Wait, what did I do now? You asked me to stand here, I'm standing here."

"Didn't you just make an album for (insert name of guitar player here)?"

"Yeah, what about it?"

"Oh, come on, you don't actually believe that 'I fell in the pool' story, do you?" She crossed her arms and glared at me.

"I heard he was high as a kite when it happened. Why, is there more to the story?"

"You could say that. Like why his falling into the pool landed his girlfriend in the hospital."

"I didn't even know he had a—"

"Mandy Killington. Why the hell do you think I'm here?"

It was kind of loud in there, between the music and everyone trying to out-schmooze each other, and I thought, *Did I miss something?* "Lacey, slow down. I have no idea what the hell you're talking about."

"That's always your excuse, isn't it? Listen to how often you say that to me."

That's because you're batshit crazy, I thought, but didn't say. "Nonetheless, who is Andy Kingston and why are you here?"

"Mandy Killington. She's a model. She was supposed to do a shoot this week but she can't because her face is disfigured."

I started to get that sinking feeling. Don't get me wrong. I'm a realist when it comes to how badly people can treat each other. But sometimes you get the feeling something is going to be really ugly. "From something that happened a month ago?"

"Yes, that's how bad it is."

"What did he do?"

"He beat her, you dummy."

"Okay, no, I get that! I mean... never mind." I tried to get back to the logical thread of the conversation. "So you're here to do the shoot in her place?"

"That's right. And if you think it's right that a guy can wreck a woman's career by wrecking her face, you're wrong, mister."

"Whoa whoa whoa, wait a second, when did I say that?"

"You're an enabler! Without you, *his* career would be in the toilet!"

"What? Lacey, I don't even know this guy. A producer hired me to—"

"Excuses! You're one excuse after another! No wonder Carynne is fed up with you."

"Carynne is what? Listen to me, you're not talking sense. If I don't do it, the producer just hires Steve Vai or some other guitar player to fill in. It's not like I took the job because I have any personal connection whatsoever. I'd never even met the guy."

"Is he nice?" she demanded. "Was he nice to you?"

"Not particularly, no. He didn't come to the studio most of the time, and I only met him a couple of times." It dawned on me finally that probably none of the injuries had anything to do with a swimming pool. "He had a black eye, too."

"See?"

"So they had a fight. Lacey, lots of lovers have fights."

"You are *soooo* trying to justify the actions of your friend."

"We're not friends. I'm just saying that's all I know. How do you know he battered her? Does he have a record?"

"See, no one ever believes the victim. You took that guy's money to save his ass when he deserves to burn in hell for what he did. You're not part of the solution. You're part of the problem."

Okay, I had had it by then with her pat therapist sayings and her constant digs at me and my lack of psychological savvy. In other words, she was pissing me off. "Oh, is this about money? Is this about money, Lacey?"

She thrust her chin at me, which I took to mean yes.

"If I've got blood money on my hands, so do you. You're taking her gig. When are you going to donate that money to a battered women's shelter, huh?"

"Hey, don't you tell me how to run my career. You don't know anything about it."

"No shit. But here, how's this, you pick the charity and I'll donate every cent I made from this gig to it *if you do the same.* How's that for putting my money where my mouth is? Huh? If you really believe everything you're saying, you'll do it."

"You're infuriating! You're only saying that so you can say you were the one who won the argument!"

"You're the one who picked the fight in the first place! What's it going to be, Lacey? Put up or shut up!"

That was when she went bonkers and attacked me. Her fists were small but hard. Remember that in her heels she was probably almost a foot taller than me. She got me once in the face before I grabbed her by the arm, and then Chris came to the rescue and grabbed her from behind, and then someone who was adept at celebrity wrangling hurried me out of public view. A club security guy.

They had a backroom production office or something. I had them grab Jonathan and bring him to me while they gave me an ice pack to put on my cheekbone where she'd really whacked me. The club security guy here was more like a member of the Secret Service than like Antonio and his crew. Suit and collared shirt. He was white.

The conversation went something like this:

Security guy: How are you feeling, Mister Marks?
Me: I'm fine, really. I don't think I need the ice.
Security guy: Are you in need of medical attention? Or any other form of official attention?
Me: Uh, I don't need a doctor, if that's what you mean.
Security guy: We'd just like to know if you'll be reporting this to any other official... officials.
Me: (blank)
Jonathan: You mean do we need to involve the police?
Security guy: For obvious reasons, we'd like to maintain discretion...
Me: Oh, for fuck's sake, so would we. And you've got to be kidding me, like I'm going to charge Lacey Montaigne with assault? I'm fine. Really.
Security guy: May I take an official statement from you to that effect?
Me: Uh, sure?
Jonathan: I think he means repeat yourself to prove you really mean it.
Me: Aha.

So I promised them I wasn't pressing any charges or anything like that. We snuck out and went home.

I got a phone call from Chris about an hour later.

"I have to ask you a favor," he said, sounding pretty shaky.

"Anything. What is it?"

"One, can you come pick me up. Two, can I stay on your couch."

"Yes and yes, where are you?"

He gave me the address, and I told Jonathan where I was going. J then had the bright idea that if Chris was going to stay over that we go to Remo's, where there were more beds. Right. So we went and retrieved Chris from a bar in Hollywood, and then we took him through In-N-Out Burger, and *then* we drove up to Laurel Canyon. It was in the car on the way up there that Chris finally told us what was going on.

"Lacey's on drugs," he said.

"No kidding," I answered automatically, then realized he meant it for real, not as an expression for "bonkers." "Wait, which drugs?"

"She scored some coke in the girls' room there. Just a little, she said. Can you believe it?"

"Man. She seemed really high-strung when we started talking, kind of sweaty and nervous, but it didn't occur to me it was that. She told me some guy was stalking her and so she wanted to talk to me to keep him away. And that turned into her accusing me of practically battering Candy Millington myself and saying my gig money was blood money. So I said fine, if my gig money is blood money, so is yours. And then she went postal and tried to beat my face in." I was driving, so I paused to check the mirrors. "Did what I just said make any sense?"

"Yeah." Chris heaved a sigh. "Yeah, unfortunately, I understood every word."

"In the end, I challenged her. I said, fine, you donate your gig money and I'll donate mine, to whatever battered women's shelter you want."

Jonathan spoke up from the back seat. "That's a brilliant idea. What did she say to that?"

"That was, literally, when she attacked me." I shrugged. "I have no idea how much money she makes on one of these shoots. Maybe I was out of line."

"Or maybe she was on drugs," Chris said. "That's it." He gestured over his shoulder with his thumb like a hitchhiker. "I can't be around her."

"You're serious? I thought you were just coming to stay the night. Is this breakup a permanent thing?"

"I don't know. I think it has to be, though. If she's going to fall off the wagon that easily? Our first night in Hollywood, she goes into the restroom and scores some blow? When she's been through rehab, and she knows what I'm going through, too? What the fuck. So wrong. I thought she understood. I thought she was stronger than that."

"Okay, all that," I said, "but if I remember what they told me and Carynne at the orientation thing, we shouldn't judge you as strong or weak. Right?"

"Well, okay, that's true. But... I don't know. I'm... I don't know what to think."

"I think you should sleep on it before making any big promises or pronouncement," I said.

"Shit. When did you get so mature and wise?"

Haha, yeah, that's me.

Karma Chameleon

The next day I drove Chris to meet Lacey at her mom's house in Beverly Hills. We got lost twice on the way there because neither of us knew our way around and the roads are curvy and confusing, and at least once on the way I told Chris I felt like we were back in the days of driving lessons. Except this time neither of us knew where we were going.

We pulled up at the house about forty-five minutes late. Chris had been there before but had never driven himself there, so I would have cut him some slack, especially since going on Lacey's directions wasn't the most straightforward thing ever. But Lacey tore him a new one right out there on the front patio.

I had planned to stay there, in the car, until I heard for sure whether he was staying with her or giving a goodbye speech and leaving. I had figured they would do their talking in the house while I waited outside.

No such luck. With her lighting into him right on the front stoop, amid the artfully sculpted topiary bushes, I got to hear the whole thing.

I was trying not to listen. But that was impossible, since she started out at the top of her lungs. "Where the hell have you been?"

Christian tried to be real soft and contrite. "Driving around trying to find this place. Lacey, I'm sorry."

"You bet you're sorry. Sorry excuse for a man."

"Excuse me? Look, if all you want to do is dish out verbal abuse—"

"I can't believe you left me alone there last night! Do you know what could've happened to me? I had to take a cab here!"

"If you want me to pay for the cab—"

"No, I don't want you to pay for the fucking cab! I make ten times what you make, fuck face, and don't you forget it! I had to spend the night here all alone! My mother's in Cancun!" Now she sounded on the verge of tears.

"Hey, I'm sorry, but I told you, I can't be around drugs. I can't be around you when you're on drugs—"

"Because you're a wimp and a loser! I know the real reason you want to get off coke, because you can't afford it."

"Lacey—"

"Loser!"

"Lacey! We got off coke because you almost died from it."

"No, I didn't. I turned out fine. My only mistake was picking you, you fuck-faced loser. What the hell was I thinking? The drummer! Who the hell dates a drummer?" Suddenly she was banging on the window of the passenger door. "This is your fault! It's always supposed to be a lead singer or a guitar player, but you're both *gay*." She repeated it like a five-year-old, in a petulant, nasal sing-song. "Gay gay gay!"

I think Chris would have gotten back in the car then, except now she was between him and the passenger door. "Lacey—"

"They're going to turn you gay, too. You watch. You've already got no balls. Next thing you know, you'll be putting on a dress and lipstick. Loser. Loser loser loser."

I started the engine, and that spooked her away from the door. If Chris had been my size, I would've seriously considered rolling down the back windows and gesturing for him to dive into the back seat and just peel out of there. But Chris was too big for that.

Her rant from there broke down into more name-calling, and once she started stomping around, he made a quick dash for the car and slammed the door behind himself, and I wasted no time in speeding out of that circular driveway. She chased after us, screaming, "Noooo! Don't leave me alone here! Noooo!"

I waited until we got out of sight of the house. "Should we go back?"

"No way, man," he said.

"Should we call the police?"

"On ourselves?"

"No. To tell them she's distraught about being left alone."

"And have them bust her for being high as a kite? I'm not feeling that great about her right now, Daron, but that doesn't mean I think we should get her busted."

"Ah. Sorry, it hadn't occurred to me." I pulled us onto a busier road.

"You remember how I turned into a paranoid jerkoff who didn't even seem all that much like me when I was using?"

"Yeah. I get it. That's not the real Lacey."

"Except if she's going to insist on doing drugs, that *is* the real Lacey. That's the Lacey she chooses to be." He made a hand gesture like he was flicking something away with both hands. "Well, she made it easy to dump her, I guess, given that it sounded a lot more like she was dumping me, didn't it?"

"Jeez, man. She... jeez." I didn't know what to say.

"Fuck. I can't believe she stooped so low."

"I know. It's like she hit you below the belt with everything she could think of."

"And where does she get off? Okay, money, big fucking deal, if she wants a guy with a wallet larger than hers she's narrowing her dating choices drastically, but come on. All the stuff about you and Ziggy? Like she'd have left me in a heartbeat for one of you guys if you hadn't been doing each other?"

"She was just making digs at everybody. And what's wrong with drummers? Heather Locklear married Tommy Lee, didn't she? And Barbara Bach married Ringo."

"Okay, but maybe being a Beatle trumped being a drummer."

"Are you saying you agree with her?" My head spun a little.

"No. No no," he was saying, but I could tell the whole thing had been a massive blow to his confidence.

"Okay, so, I'm going to make a suggestion now and you should totally shoot it down if you think it would be a bad thing mentally or rehab-wise or whatever. But I could really use a drink."

He exhaled heavily. "Yeah, me too."

"Is it too much of a crutch?"

"I don't know."

"If it were nighttime I'd take you to a bar with incredibly loud live music. But something tells me if I take you record shopping or something all you'll do is brood and hear her voice in your head over and over. At least a strong drink will shut that right up."

"Yeah, all right. It's only, what, two o'clock, though? Where are we going to go?"

"I have an idea." I had to figure out in my head where I thought the place was, but I was pretty sure it wasn't too far from where we were.

I was right. I pulled up at the front of the hotel where we had stayed in June, gave Remo's truck to the valet, and took Chris into the lobby bar.

The place was pretty much deserted. We took seats at the bar. I wondered if there was any chance in hell that the bartender who had been so nice to me when I'd been so freaked out the night of Lacey's overdose was there. I figured the chance was pretty slim.

Maybe I was lucky. Crystal came out from the back and I gave her a big smile and a hug across the bar like we were old friends, which surprised me because I honestly hadn't been sure she'd even remember me.

"So... this is my friend Christian," I said, introducing them, "and my drummer, though I don't think you met last time we were here."

"Nope, didn't have the pleasure," Chris said.

"Chris just got dumped by his girlfriend in no uncertain terms," I added.

Crystal made a frowny face. "Not the same girlfriend who had the problem at the party?"

Chris looked a little red-faced at that. "Uh, yeah, same one."

"Well, it sounds like maybe you're better off without her," Crystal said, "but you know, who am I to judge? I'm just the bartender. What can I get you?"

"Something mind-numbing," Chris said.

"Mind-numbing because it'll mule-kick you in the teeth with how alcoholic it is, like a martini, or mind-numbing because you'll suck it down so fast you won't realize how strong it was until you try to stand up? Like... a margarita."

Chris thought it over. "I'm trying to be really mindful of what I put into me, you know? So something where it doesn't hide it. I've never been much of a martini drinker, though."

"Well, I want a View Car A," I said.

"Vieux Carré," she corrected with a bit of a laugh.

"Yeah, that. Sorry, never learned French. Chris, you want to try it? This is the drink that convinced me I actually like mixed drinks."

"Okay, sure." He watched her mix it and then took a sip of mine. "Huh, kinda good. Not sure about the cherry, though."

She mulled it over. "How about absinthe?"

"You have absinthe?"

"Well, I have Pernod. I wasn't meaning as a straight-up drink. I'm thinking you might like a Sazerac. It's a lot like what he's drinking, only no cherry, and the glass gets a Pernod rinse."

"Sure, what the hell."

She mixed him something that looked and smelled a lot like what I had—heavy on the American whiskey—only with a twist of lemon peel. We clinked glasses.

Eventually we ordered some food, too, and after our second drink I borrowed the phone and told Jonathan where we were and that we'd be there a while.

I don't actually remember a lot of what she and Chris talked about. I drank too much for that. But I do remember that she really made him feel at ease, and flirted a little, which made him feel like less of a loser, I think. She'd had a lot of friends go through AA or Narcotics Anonymous and sympathized with both his rehab and the fact that his old friends had gone so far into "God Squad"-land that he couldn't even be around them, either.

At one point when Chris went off to the men's room, though, she asked me how I was doing.

"I'm actually living here, in West Hollywood," I told her. "At least, for a little while."

"You don't sound too sure about that." She was shaking my next cocktail and had to step back from the bar for a moment to shake it vigorously. Then she stepped close again to pour it. "You don't like it here?"

"Well, I'm living with a friend who got a gig that's supposed to last six months, and I said okay, I'll move in with you, and gee, when I say it like that it all does sound kind of sketchy, doesn't it?"

"Does it?"

"You're right. I don't really like it here. But there's work for me as a session player here, so that's good?"

"True. But you really sound to me like you don't want to be here."

"LA's nice to visit...?" I tried.

"You're a sweetheart. I'm not offended if you don't like my town."

Chris came back then. "You badmouthing LA?"

"Maybe," I said. "So here's a question. When are you going to go back?"

"To Boston? I was supposed to be here until Friday. I guess I have to see if I should change my ticket or what."

"Or what," I said. "Let's stay at Remo's in the canyon until then. Another friend of ours," I explained to Crystal.

"Oh, I know who you mean," she said. "If you see him, tell him I said hello."

At that point Jonathan came in, and we moved to a table with fresh drinks so we could tell him the whole saga of Lacey's Jekyll-and-Hyde act, and he ordered dinner, and eventually we were full and ready to go home, and I wasn't in any shape to drive. So Chris drove me back to Remo's while J said he was going to stop at home to get clean clothes for tomorrow.

At the house we sat with our feet in the pool, and eventually Chris took the rest of his clothes off and dove in. "What's the point of staying at a house with a pool if you don't swim in the pool?" he asked.

"You know, that's what I say every time I bother to get in," I said, swishing my feet back and forth.

"Hey," he said, from the deep end, where he was treading water, his hair floating around his shoulders like dark seaweed. "I want you to know, what Lacey said? I was really not okay with."

"She sure was spouting a load of crap."

"No no, I mean specifically the stuff about you and Ziggy. Honestly. Where does she get off saying something like that? Like all men are nothing but potential dates for her? I knew she lived in a world of self-delusion, but that takes the cake." He shrugged. "I'm over being fucked up about you being gay, I guess. Her saying that to you made me madder than anything she said to me directly."

"She's crazy."

"She is. Really. It's like we never had a relationship. It's like she was going through the motions because she wanted to have a rock star boyfriend and that was it. What I don't get, though, is that she spent all that time in Allston, decorating the house and going to my rehab with me and all that, way beyond what you'd expect from somebody just dating you for the fame."

"Well, but it's like you said, the drugs undermine it all. They warp the reality around you. That bit about how the reason you got off coke was you couldn't afford it? It's like the drug itself makes her think of that shit."

He nodded. "I know. Crazy shit. But it's over. I'm not even going to think about her anymore."

And that was it... for the next couple of days. The morning he was due to leave, she called from a rehab center and begged him to forgive her. She said she had been so high she didn't even know what she was saying. She said she'd understand if he couldn't be with her, but she begged for another chance. He told her he'd think about it, and talk with his therapist back in Boston, and call her next week. And then he hung up on her before she could repeat her tearful confession.

As I dropped him off at the airport, I asked, "So, are you going to give her another chance?"

"I don't know. Maybe if she'll sit down with me and my therapist, so the therapist can translate for us, and see what comes out of that. Then maybe."

When I got back to the West Hollywood house, there was a message on the answering machine from Lacey's manager wanting to confirm the details of the donation I'd be making. And then a second one, from Carynne saying that she'd already talked to the donation people and they were working it out. So after all that, we were far from done with Lacey Montaigne.

Don't Worry Be Happy

Jonathan. I'm doing a terrible job of explaining what was going on between him and me because it's so much easier to tell the dramatic stuff, like getting assaulted by a drug-crazed supermodel.

It's a lot more difficult to figure out what's important to say about a relationship. Maybe that's the problem. At the time I still didn't know what a relationship was, and so a huge part of the development of our relationship was him schooling me on what a relationship was supposed to be.

Those words, "supposed to," came up a lot—well, maybe they came up in my head more than out loud. How is a boyfriend supposed to act? For that matter, what is a boyfriend supposed to look like?

By the time Chris and Lacey visited, I thought I had figured out how a boyfriend was supposed to act. If I wasn't stupid and didn't, for example, stay out too late without warning after playing a session, everything was pretty smooth. If I waited until the weekend to ask for sex, we had some of our best sex ever. (It was still a luxury to me to have sex with the same person multiple times.) One really tricky puzzle was this: what was the right thing to do when neither of us could figure out what we wanted to eat? I quickly learned that if I let that get out of hand, a meltdown was imminent, so it was better not to let it get out of hand. I wrote a list of restaurants we liked onto the back of a business card, and when I got desperate I would peek at it. I'd make suggestions, hoping he would jump on one and that would solve it.

Eventually I figured out that sometimes what Jonathan really wanted was not tacos or falafel or Italian food. What he wanted was for *me to decide what we were eating*. Far as I was concerned, I would have just made us a schedule of places and we'd rotate through them, but somehow I knew that wouldn't work. And then I figured out that Jonathan wanted me to decide what we were eating, but he wanted me to make that decision by *figuring out what we would actually both enjoy most.* And if only I could figure *that* out, I could beat the level and move up.

But I'm not so good at mind-reading, you know? When it came to actual relationship stuff, Jonathan was all for getting it out in the open and talking about it. I mean stuff like how we felt about each other and what boundaries we were going to set and sex. How come we could get that stuff worked out and yet somehow falafel versus tacos was a life-or-death decision? What's a good boyfriend supposed to do?

Jonathan idolized the couple upstairs, Jerry and Robert. We got to know them a little, he better than I. Jonathan called them the Queens of West Hollywood, and at first I thought, okay, "queens" is a term and it's okay for gay men to use it for each other. But as time went on I realized how appropriate a term it was. The two of them went around with their noses in the air as if they were some kind of benevolent monarchs, and they treated everyone else like their subjects. Plus we saw them being treated like elder statesmen from time to time. They also went everywhere together. Jonathan often ran into them at the bookstore or the cafe when he would get up on weekend mornings to grab coffee and do some writing while I slept in. (A few times, with Jonathan's blessing, I went out to shows after dinner when he went to bed. Generally speaking, he always had to be up earlier than I did.) Overall, I didn't spend as much time in the neighborhood as J did; between driving around to different studios to do sessions and sometimes spending a day or two at Remo's, I just wasn't there as much. So it's no wonder that J got to know our upstairs neighbors much better than I did.

I'm saying a lot about them now, but at the time I hadn't given them that much thought. I didn't interact with them all that often and wasn't even sure which one was which. They were two fifty-something white guys who dressed alike and talked alike. One was slightly taller, but they both had the same amount of gray, similar haircuts, and they were almost always together. So I never heard one mentioned without the other, either, as if "Jerry and Robert" was their collective name.

One Saturday afternoon, Jonathan and I had sex after lunch and then were lying in bed listening to music.

"Let's see a movie," Jonathan said.

"What movie do you want to see?"

"I don't know. I've never seen a movie at Mann's, though, and I feel like I should."

"Mann's?"

"Mann's Chinese Theater?"

"Oh, right." There was a photo shoot of us standing in front of it from that long-ago time when we'd done that warm-up tour for MNB. Wasn't that the day after Ziggy and me...? Yeah. It was. "I think there are photos of the band there. Were you in that entourage?"

"I was," Jonathan said.

I wondered if it felt as long ago to him as it did to me. Almost a year and a half. "So is seeing a movie there kind of like actually going up in the Statue of Liberty instead of just walking around it?"

"I guess. I just feel like here we are in movie-land and we've hardly seen any movies."

"We've seen a ton of movies. *Beetlejuice*, *Heathers*, *A Fish Called Wanda*..."

"I mean in a theater, not video rental." He gestured at the plain white ceiling above us. "On the big screen."

"Okay, sure."

He had perfected the mind-reading thing of knowing when I actually meant "okay, sure" versus when I was saying that because I wanted to say no but couldn't actually think of a reasonable objection. "What's wrong?"

"Nothing. It's a great idea."

"You're all tense."

I wasn't about to tell him that it was because it reminded me of me and Ziggy's first time. And I don't even know if that was why I had tensed up. Maybe that wasn't it. "Isn't that kind of Paparazzi Central?"

"I thought you decided not to worry about that."

"Me *deciding* to stop worrying and actually stopping are two different things." I rolled onto my side to face him. We were buck-naked still, and under only a sheet. "Although it has been pretty quiet."

"Yeah."

"I mean, not that it's good that nobody gives a fuck about us—the band, I mean—but..."

"I know what you mean." His hair was blonder than usual from all the sun he was getting. I played with the sex-tousled wisps of it. He'd let it grow a little.

"Why would going to Mann's be all that different from us seeing a show at the Whiskey?" he asked.

"Good question." We had been out plenty of times to see shows and live music all over the area. "I think it's two things. One, at a movie theater you're trapped in one place, whereas at a show you can move all over."

"Well, that's true, but in the actual theater it's dark, and no one's going to be taking photos in there. What was the second thing?"

"Crap, I don't remember. I guess you're right, though." I reminded myself that most of the photos were from cocktail parties where we could walk around freely, and most of them were taken in parking lots. "Would it be stupid to take separate cars?"

"This is really bothering you, isn't it?"

"I guess so. I keep trying to talk myself out of it, but I keep thinking of other things." I lay flat on my back and stared at the ceiling. "Am I being nuts?"

"I wasn't trying to turn it into a whole big deal—"

"No, no, it's okay, I mean, let me get over myself and then I'll be fine." I'm pretty sure that if there was a video game called Good Boyfriend, that line just lost me half my points.

Jonathan was pretty smart, you know. He caressed a squiggle on my chest with his fingertip. "Is it because it's a date? Going to a movie is really like a 'date' thing."

I thought about it for a second. "That might be it. It seems kind of obvious if we go together, doesn't it? It's not like a party, where maybe we happened to show up—" I sat up suddenly. "Wait. Wait-wait-wait. Did you suggest it because you want to have a date kind of thing?"

"No. It was more the movies-equals-Hollywood thing."

"Are you sure? Because I'm sorry and I suck if that was what you wanted and here I am worrying about bullshit."

"Daron, you know, a date would be nice, but seriously, that isn't what this is about. If you want to romance me, a candlelight dinner works just as well. But seriously, I don't need candles and flowers when you're here with me every day."

He pulled me down to snuggle with him side by side, and I relaxed. He was warm and his skin smelled comfortingly familiar, and that was worth something, you know?

But that was how a simple question like "What do you want to do tonight?" could turn into a whole bout of relationship processing and introspection. I started to understand how Lacey could go down the rabbit hole of figuring out what was wrong with people. I don't think you ever get to the bottom of it. At some point you have to decide you've gone deep enough and it's time to stop.

We didn't go to the movie. Does that mean I won?

Pop Singer

Then there was the day Sarah Rogue called me up in tears.

Good thing I was home and not at a session. I had actually turned out to be pretty busy, and some of the gigs were actually fun. But that day I was home. "Hey, hey, are you okay?"

"I'm totally totally *totally* fucked," she said, punctuating it with a wet-sounding snort.

"Yeah, but aside from that, how are you?" I joked.

She let out a very snot-heavy laugh. "Ah, you bastard. Hang on." She blew her nose. "Okay. Seriously. I need help."

"Okay, which kind of help? I've got connections in drug rehab and digital audio processing. If it's either of those two things, I'm there. Otherwise, you're out of luck."

"It's neither of those things."

"Thank god. The number of people in my phone

book who are hooked on coke is larger than the number who aren't. Okay, let me guess again. Shoulder to cry on?"

"Wrong again. I need help with a song."

"Aha! Why didn't you say so? Want to meet me at Remo's?"

"Desperately."

"Great. I've already got clothes on, so I can be there lickety-split."

"You're my hero. Be there in an hour."

I got the company voice mailbox when I called to try to tell Jonathan where I was going, but I didn't leave a message. He didn't have a direct line himself at the production office. So I left a note for him in case we didn't connect by phone later and he got home first.

I got to Remo's before Sarah, and I figured the one person I may as well call while there was Remo himself. I mean, I couldn't call him directly, but I called his answering service to see if they had a number where he could be reached today. They didn't, but they took a message, and they knew the answer to one of the questions I had, which was what date he was coming back. He'd be back in about ten days, actually, but only for two weeks for Thanksgiving, and then it was off to Japan for Christmas. I wondered if they celebrated Christmas in Japan. The Young Adults had a song about that, didn't they?

Sarah showed up soon after, and we went into the studio, where it was easier to talk about music because she could sit behind a keyboard and I could sit behind a guitar and we could communicate more that way.

"Okay, so what's the problem? Is it really a song or is it that my old man is making you cry?"

"Your old man is a shyster and an ass, but I'm starting to think those are necessary traits in a manager," she said. "But seriously, let's not talk about him. It's Mills who's the problem."

"What's the problem?"

"Oh, just that he's hated everything we've sent. Everything. To the point where he fired the producer, stuck us with another, and the new guy is hiring songwriters and writing songs himself, and I'm like what the fuck do you even need me for if I don't have a shred of input? For fuck's sake, with the production job they're doing on my voice it may as well not even be me singing, either."

"Can I ask you who the new guy is?"

"Jellybean Benitez."

"Huh." The guy who had produced megahits for both Madonna and Whitney Houston. "They sent you to New York to work with him?"

"Yeah. And now I'm here because I had a meltdown and they said everyone take a week off. So I decided to get as far away as possible."

"Shit. It's too bad we're not in Boston, because we could totally put you up, take you to all the good live music, and make you forget it all." I shrugged. "Here, it's like we're still figuring it out. But anyway. Go on."

"Yeah, well, I'm supposed to be taking it easy this week, but of course what I'm actually doing is trying to make demo tapes like crazy so I can bring them something good, something they'll grab and run with."

I nodded and silently thanked the stars in the sky that my experience making *1989* hadn't been like that. My heart and soul was in that album. So was Ziggy's. Jordan hadn't made us compromise on much—mostly only with each other, not our artistic principles.

"The problem, of course, is that they think everything I do sucks. And I'm starting to believe that everything I do *does* suck."

"Which it doesn't, so shut up about that. What do you need, though?"

"At minimum I need two things: a power ballad with some kick and a love song that I won't barf while singing."

As soon as she said "love song" I thought of the silly love song I'd written for Jonathan back in Boston, the day after we'd had a date. Remember that? I could never picture either me or Ziggy singing it. I mean, come on, a silly love song? But a girl singer, now that could work...

So of course we worked on the power ballad instead. "Okay. Show me what you've got. Let's pick something and work on it. Got a riff? A lyric?"

She cracked her knuckles and played a scale to warm up her fingers. "How about a riff. Here."

She laid down a chord progression. With the piano you didn't really get a "riff" in the same way as with the guitar. I picked up the progression and turned it into something. I gave it texture. I made it rock. She had some bits of lyrics.

I'm not going to describe everything we did, because it's a lot more boring to describe than it was to do. I will say that we were doing it until almost nine, though, when hunger forced us both to stop, and I tried calling Jonathan. I got the group voice mail at his office again and got the machine at the apartment.

"Hey, I'm still in the canyon but about to knock off and head home, I think? Okay if I bring Sarah Rogue with me? Or do you want to meet us somewhere? Wait, I know, meet us at the deli if you want to have dinner. We're going to go there right now."

Sarah and I took separate cars to the deli, ate like absolute pigs, lingered over cheesecake and coffee, and then made a plan to meet again the next day. I drove back to West Hollywood with my windows down, singing on the highway.

When I got in, J was just stumbling in the door, too. He collapsed on the couch with his car keys still in his hand. "Oh my god, my eyes are crossing. It's amazing I was able to get home."

At first I thought he meant from drinking too much, and I was about to scold him for that, when I realized as he went on that he meant cross-eyed from working too much. Apparently there had been some kind of deadline that day, and they had cranked until late in order to meet it. That was why no one was picking up the phone either, I guess.

"I'm taking the day off tomorrow," he declared. "You know what that means."

"You get to sleep late?" I guessed.

"Mm. Or at least stay in bed until later." He gave me one of those smiles that still warmed me down to my toes when they were aimed at me.

I smiled back. "Okay. But I actually have a gig tomorrow."

"A session?"

"Sort of." I explained Sarah's problem while we got ready for bed.

J was nothing if not knowledgeable about the industry. "See, that's one thing I don't understand. They'd never do that to a male artist. Jellybean Benitez? She's a folkie at heart, and they're trying to make her into the next Paula Abdul? How does that make sense? It doesn't. But they think they'll make a lot of money or they wouldn't do it."

"She said it to me herself, the main things she has going for her are a fantastic voice and that she's thin, white, and pretty. She knew what she was getting into. It's just a grind for her to realize how little of Sarah herself is going to wind up in the end product."

"So tell me, how much of Sarah ended up in the song you wrote with her today?"

"Oh, um, probably forty-five percent?"

"You don't sound so sure."

"Well, you know, it was a collaboration."

"Daron, you wrote a song for her."

"I didn't. I did the same thing a producer like Keith would do. I took her raw materials and worked with her to make it into something."

"That's the line you can give to me when I'm in reporter-mode," he said. "What's the truth?"

"The truth is that even if I did hardly anything, this is an industry that is going to believe that I wrote it and not her, anyway."

"Hm, that's true."

"So that's my story and I'm sticking to it. It's Sarah's song." But I was right. A week later when she went back to New York, she had two whole songs that we'd worked on together. They both made it onto her album. The power ballad would become one of the highlights of her live show. The love song would eventually be a Top 40 hit. But if you mentioned that song at an industry cocktail party, you know what you were likely to hear? "Oh, you mean that song Daron Marks wrote for her?"

The really ironic thing being, of course, that was the song I wrote for Jonathan.

I Didn't Mean to Turn You On

Bart came to visit. Michelle had come to town for some convention or something and he went with her, then she flew back East and he stayed to hang out with me.

We went out to hear live music every night for four

nights in a row, just him and me, and then we took a night off to let our ears rest. Jonathan curled up in bed with me that night wanting to know all about the show the night before.

"I'm so envious," he said, his voice low. Bart was asleep on the couch out in the front room. "Working like I am now, it's the one thing I miss."

"The sleeping late?"

"Going to see a lot of shows. I feel like I'm falling behind like crazy here, there must be so much going on that I'm missing." He had his head on my shoulder.

"You always love bands most when they're still unknowns."

He looked up at me and said in a meaningful voice, "You never know when you're going to see one that's really special."

I took it as a cue to kiss him. He kissed back. I did a really small thing then: I slid my hand down his rib cage. At least, it seemed like a small thing to me. I wasn't even thinking about it.

He caught my hand in a death grip, though, stopping me. And that felt like a sudden stab through my ribs, before he even said anything. I was too stricken by the moment to say anything at first.

"Not with your best friend out there," he said.

"You know Bart wouldn't care in the slightest."

"Yes, but I care."

"He's not even awake."

I think he was trying to be glib when he said, "Hey. This is our house, not a tour bus."

Glib or no, that one really stung. I don't think he meant it to. But I remembered the "sex dispenser" comment from back when he was really upset, and it felt like a slap in the face. I sat up. I tried to get off the bed, but I guess that made it obvious to him that I was offended.

He caught me by the arm. "I'm sorry. That didn't come out right."

"It sure didn't." I got up anyway, suddenly restless, and J let go. I wasn't the least bit concerned about waking Bart up with the sound of sex, but I sure as hell didn't want to wake him up with the sound of arguing. In my mind, my plan was to go into the kitchen. Because if we weren't in the same room, we couldn't fight. I know that doesn't make any sense now, but at the time it did.

And you can't argue when you don't know what to say, anyway. I got as far as the dresser.

"I'm sorry," he repeated, but I wasn't sure if he was sorry about what he said or if he was saying he was sorry he couldn't have sex with me right now. "Don't go."

I sat back down on the corner of the bed, which creaked. I think he thought I was planning to go a lot farther than the kitchen. Something about his tone of voice. "Where would I go?"

He threw up his hands. "Wherever horny men go? I'm being stupid. I'm sorry. I'm... that didn't come out right either."

Did he really think I'd go out cruising because he'd said no? Did he think sex was that important to me? Maybe "important" wasn't the right word. Did he think I needed it that much?

Did I need it that much?

This wasn't the time to try to figure that out. I tried to take a step back. I didn't know if I was taking a step in the right direction, but I had to give it a try. It was better than freaking out, anyway. "Are you feeling stressed out about work right now?"

"What makes you say that?"

"Well, remember the last time we had a fight where you had a big flip-out and stopped making sense? It was because you were having issues with work. I'm trying to figure out if this is more of the same." *Or if the work issues last time were an excuse for the real problem...?* I didn't say that last part out loud. "It's been a while since you've said anything."

"Not that you've been around to talk about it with very much this week," he said, then added quickly, "Not that I resent you spending time with Bart... I'm just pointing it out."

"I didn't really mean this week only, anyway." I edged back to my spot in the bed and slid under the sheet. "You've been kind of clammed up about it for a couple of weeks. I figured that meant there wasn't much to talk about. Was I wrong?"

We got close again, sitting up against the pillows, but arm in arm. "You know, not everything is about my writing."

I didn't argue.

"I mean, maybe with you, everything in your life revolves around music, but that isn't true with me." He sighed.

"If you say so. But you sound a lot like a person trying to convince themselves of what they're saying."

"Do I?"

"Yeah. And what's wrong with everything in your life revolving around your writing? I mean, of course everything in my life revolves around music. It's not just a job, J. It's what I was put on Earth to do. Without that, there isn't anything else."

"Writing is different," he said, but in the dim light through the curtainless windows I could see that he was giving himself a skeptical frown. "Writing shouldn't be the only thing that defines me."

"Why?"

He seemed at a loss for an answer.

"Just because the world doesn't value art doesn't mean that art doesn't have value," I said.

"That isn't it."

"Isn't it? It's like you're saying writing isn't good enough to be the thing that defines you."

"Well, it's true, the world doesn't value writers or writing, everyone always wants you to do something else with your time. My parents used to think it was a phase I was going through."

I held in a laugh.

"I know, isn't it funny? They had no problems with me being gay. They were 'very concerned about my life choices,' though, when I said I wanted to be a writer. My dad wanted me to be an engineer. But then in college I fell in with the music industry crowd and... well, you know the rest."

"You've been making it work. Are you afraid it's going to stop working? That one of these days you'll have to leave it behind and become an engineer after all? Because I don't think I could."

"Are you saying you wouldn't find something else to do if you couldn't play?"

"I'd find some other way to play. I'd compose. I'd use the computer. I don't know. If I lost an arm in a shark attack, I'd come up with a way. Are you saying if you *couldn't* write you'd find something else?"

"Well, I wouldn't want to, but..." He paused to think. One of J's best qualities is that he would stop and think, no matter how emotional the issue. Come to think of it, that's how I learned to stop and think, from his example. "Any way I try to imagine it, I imagine getting a day job and still figuring out a way to write a novel at night. I imagine dictating to someone if I couldn't type."

"See? Writing isn't something you do, J. It's part of who you are."

He nodded. "But that doesn't mean that every problem I have is because of something in my writing."

"Okay, then, so how is the novel going, anyway?"

I took his total silence to be the worst possible answer.

"I see." I pulled him close and petted his hair. "That bad, huh?"

He nodded. I held him close.

I had always thought that the expression "just be there" for someone was kind of dumb, just a bunch of words that didn't really mean anything. But right then I thought I understood what they meant, because that was what I was doing. Literally. All I was doing was lying there, "being there" for him. And it didn't feel dumb at all. It felt like the right thing to do. It felt like maybe part of the point of having a relationship was so that there was someone there for this. Because, yeah, either of us could have gone out and found someone for sex. But not for this.

A Little Respect

Bart and I went and played a session together before he left. I had actually turned down a job knowing he was going to be there, something Chernwick wanted done really quickly, but I guess things didn't happen as quickly as he thought, or maybe they got someone they didn't like. I don't know. Guitar session players, even really good ones, weren't exactly in short supply in Los Angeles.

Chernwick called again, though, a week later, and said they were really hot to trot about me in particular, which probably wasn't true so much as it was him stroking my ego thinking that would work. The thing about playing sessions, though, is that you have to leave ego at the door. He told me they'd up my fee. I told him it was only a deal if they'd put that additional money toward hiring Bart, too. Oh, and renting a vintage Rickenbacker for him to play. Honestly, I did it just to yank Chernwick's chain a little, but he agreed, so the next thing you know, Bart and I were on our way to a studio instead of to comb some used record store or whatever else we might have done that day.

When I told him his reaction was, "Wait, you got us a gig?"

"Yeah."

"You mean we're playing a session tomorrow."

"Yeah. What, did I speak in tongues or something?"

"No, it's just unexpected is all."

"If you don't want to do it, I'll call back and say forget it."

"I didn't say that! I'd love to go play a session! Hot diggety. Although you know I don't have a bass with me."

That's when I told him about the Rickenbacker and also, hey, it was about time I paid him back for all the times he'd talked guys in Boston into pulling me into sessions. Everything I know about session playing I learned from Bart, pretty much.

That was how we ended up playing a session in the bottom of an empty swimming pool in the backyard of some executive, for a girl singer who was so strung out on drugs we never made eye contact the whole day. Nice voice, though. They were trying to make something really experimental and sixties throwback, I think. Bart and I both wore earplugs to do the playing, which had us each with pretty large amps in the bottom of the pool, and multiple microphones set all over the place, some close to the amps, some far.

Why the hell not, right? Maybe it would be a stroke of genius. Maybe it would just be a mess. It wasn't my place to judge.

On the way home we had the windows rolled up against the smog, which was bad that day, and the radio on, though not very loud. Our ears had taken enough of a beating.

"Convenience store," Bart said.

"Sure. You want the kind that sells Slurpee, ICEE, or Slush Puppie?"

"See, the thing is, Frozen Coke is so superior to anything Slush Puppie could ever do," he said. "But that's not why I want to stop."

"I don't know if they sell Yoo-hoo out here."

"It's not that either."

I glanced away from the traffic to see what his facial expression was. Halfway between bemused and serious. He held up something small and white.

"What is that?"

He squinted at it. "Supposedly it's cocaine."

"What!"

"Producer gave it to me. Like a tip, I guess." He shook the baggie and frowned at it.

"Um, okay," I said, trying to figure out where the convenience store came into the picture. I gave up trying to figure it out. "So where's the convenience store come into the picture?"

"I figure there's no way in hell you or Jonathan want it, and I sure as hell am not getting on a plane while carrying it."

"I have zero desire to try cocaine. You don't either?"

"Tried it. I've decided it's really not a good idea."

"Wait, when did you try it?"

"Don't you remember that party we had after filming the 'Wonderland' video? That whole crew was cokeheads."

"Right. I left early." In fact, Ziggy and I had left together. "But... you still haven't explained the convenience store."

"I don't even want to bring it into your house. I'm thinking I'll just toss it in a trashcan. I suppose I could give it to some bum, make his night...?"

"But what if it's bad or he overdoses and dies or something?" I felt like Nancy Reagan was sitting on my shoulder shaking her wicked-witch fingernail at me.

"Yeah, wouldn't want to be responsible for that. I'll just toss it."

"OK. I'll get off the highway. There's always something. Should we go in and buy something? Like, will it look too suspicious if we just pull up and you throw something away and then we drive away?"

"I don't think anyone's going to be paying that much attention to us." Bart sighed. "I should've just waited to tell you after I tossed it."

"Why bother to tell me at all, then?"

"Just relax, Daron. There's a Circle K up there." He rummaged around in the footwell of the car and came up with some other garbage to toss out: a bag from In-N-Out Burger, some candy wrappers, etc. "See. Perfectly plausible that we wanted to dump our garbage."

I pulled up next to the dumpster on the side of the building. Bart got out and tossed the stuff in, looking perfectly casual about it. He got back in and I drove away.

"You still seem really nervous," Bart said, as I looked for a place to turn around to go back to the highway.

"I'm fine. Drugs just make me antsy. I mean, come on. Look at what's going on with the other half of the band."

"I totally agree. It's just... it's okay, you know. I only took it to be polite. He was handing it to me like it was no big deal, like it was totally expected."

"It is totally expected, which is why so many people in this damn industry are hooked."

The next place we came to with Frozen Coke, I stopped and went in and got one, because I'd been craving one ever since he mentioned it. So had he. Cokeheads, haha.

You Got It

I turned out to be much busier as a session player than I expected to be. And despite all Carynne's best intentions to manage it for me, guys like Chernwick couldn't resist calling me directly, which meant I would then have to call her to make sure she hadn't already booked something else. It's funny. When you're a kid growing up playing guitar, you learn to play like all the big players. You imitate everything. Eddie Van Halen, ZZ Top, Carlos Santana, Neil Young, you name it. Okay, maybe I shouldn't generalize, but that's what I did. At the time, I didn't expect it to come in handy; it was just something you did. I did. Whatever.

But that inadvertent training came in very handy. I'd brought the Strat with me when I returned from Boston, and it saw a lot of use. More than half the jobs were of the "can you play something like so-and-so?" variety. Fill in name of big name guitarist here. For me, the answer was always yes.

Chernwick summed it up in a conversation at a party he took me and Jonathan to at a mansion somewhere. Sorry to sound so vague about it but I have no memory now of where the place was since I didn't drive, and I don't think I ever knew whose house it was. Some movie producer's, probably, since it was more of a film-industry party than a music-industry one. I could invent something, sure, for the sake of making myself sound like a genius, but honestly, it doesn't matter where the hell it was.

I ended up in a bathroom bigger than my old Fenway apartment with all the music-industry people doing coke. That came out wrong. They were doing coke, I wasn't. Yeah, I was back to that old routine. The entire bathroom was done in black and gray marble and had flower arrangements the size of ostriches and a Jacuzzi tub. No one was in the tub.

Chernwick had lost his hat somewhere during the night, and the top of his head was disturbingly shiny. I think cocaine makes people sweat. Anyway, how he could think about business while coked up I don't know, but he turned to me and said, "Do you play anything else?"

"What? You mean genre-wise? Or instrument-wise?"

"Don't use such big words when I'm high, Moony." He had started calling me Moony a while back, but no one else had. "I mean besides the guitar."

"Eh, you know, I can get by with the mandolin, ukulele, that kind of thing, but if you're talking about for sessions, you don't want me trying to figure out how to play something while the clock is ticking."

"See, that's what I like about you. So focused."

It was easy to be more focused than everyone else when you were the only one not on coke. But anyway. "Why, you have a gig you need something else for?"

"Naw. Just seeing if you were even more outta sight than I thought."

Chernwick talked like he was from the sixties a lot. Far as I could tell, "outta sight" translated to "awesome." I just shrugged.

He went on. "No, seriously, you show up on time,

not hung over, you can play anything anyone asks for, you work hard, you can fucking sight read, you do good work, and you leave it all out there. No one feels like you're saving the good stuff for someone else."

"It's not like I'm going to run out of notes," I said.

"Tell that to some of these assholes who act like they're using up their mother's inheritance every time they play." He mopped his forehead with a hand towel. "And you never say no."

"That's not true. I told you no two weeks ago."

"Until you said yes."

"Uh, true."

"And that was the first time. Which is okay. And you should, you know."

"I should what?" Talking with people on drugs can be confusing.

"You shouldn't say no to me, except when you have to, but you know, overall, it's important to know when."

"Chern, you're not making any sense."

"I know. That's all right. Hey, I know any day you're probably going to hit the road and I'll have to find someone else to do what you do."

Which gave me pause. Who was doing it before I started doing it, and was that guy out of a job? Or was he on the road himself right now? Or was it that Steve Lukather was next in the Rolodex?

Then there were the gigs where they wanted me to sound like me. The Ovation came out a lot more often on those. I was starting to feel like the hip color of the month, like everyone wanted mauve accents in the decor, except it was Moondog accents in their mix.

I was surprised to find Jonathan said something similar to Cherwick, though, one night when I came home with my thumb aching from playing too much.

"Let's eat in," he said. "I'll cook, and you can soak your hand and keep me company while I'm doing it."

"Soak my hand?"

"You've never soaked in Epsom salts?" He was giving me a surprised look, like I'd just told him I didn't know how to tie my own shoes.

"Um, no?"

"Sit down. There's some in the bathroom." He retrieved a white cardboard box from under the bathroom sink. "I used to get cramps in my hand from writing in longhand," he explained. "This helps."

So the next thing you know, I was sitting there with my hand in a Tupperware container of warm water with Epsom salts in it while Jonathan decided to make pizza.

"You're going to make pizza?"

"Yes," he said, pulling out a block of mozzarella from the refrigerator. I didn't remember him buying it, so he must have gone to the store when I hadn't noticed.

"From scratch?"

"What else would I make it from?" He started the oven heating.

"Have you done this before?"

"You sound skeptical."

It was just I had never heard of anyone making their own pizza. Which didn't mean I wasn't game to try it. "It couldn't be worse than the pizza they sell around here."

"This is true." Both being from New Jersey, we agreed that the pizza in LA was atrocious.

He had bought flour and other things that were necessary for making dough, and we had a jar of Prego sauce in the cabinet, and while the dough was rising I got bored of sitting there with my hand in the bowl, so I shredded the cheese. And while I shredded the cheese, he cut up mushrooms, and we sang along with the radio and danced in the kitchen.

This is notable because I might have previously given the impression that it was some kind of angst-fest every minute of the day living with him. And it totally wasn't. In fact, I may have danced a little too energetically and gotten some cheese on the floor. Only a little, though. There was still plenty for the pizza.

Anyway, while it was in the oven I was stretching my fingers and thumb, and Jonathan said, "It's not worth hurting yourself for some session, is it?"

"I'm not hurt. This just happens sometimes."

He pulled me into a hug. The song playing then was a slower one, and we slow-danced around the kitchen floor. "But do you ever worry that you're sort of using yourself up for all these other people's songs and albums?"

"Chernwick asked me that, too. Honestly, it's not like fossil fuel and I'm going to run out. How can you run out of music?"

"I guess."

"I might get tired like my hand today, but that's not the same thing. My mind is still full of ideas."

"Okay." He was taller, and he liked to kiss me on the hair when we were close like this.

By the way, the pizza was not anything like New York-area pizza, but you know, when you make it yourself it's flavored with satisfaction.

Bad English

Remo called from Paris and caught me at home one night. "Hey, how's things?"

"Things are good. Well, depending on what things, but you didn't call to check up on me, did you?" I was doing the math in my head. It had to be, what, nine hours later for him? "What are you doing calling me at the crack of dawn?"

"I'm in the Paris airport, making a last transfer to London. I'll be home day after tomorrow. Everything all right at the house?"

"It was on Monday." I'd gone there to record some sample tracks to give to Chernwick for a gig that didn't pan out. "Want me to swing by there tomorrow? The pool cleaners should have come today, if I remember your schedule right."

"I'm sure everything's fine. So, have you and your boy made plans for Thanksgiving yet?"

"You know, we haven't even talked about it."

"Well, if you're in town and don't have other plans, I'm thinking of having some people over at the house and would love if you would come."

"For Thanksgiving?"

"Isn't that what I just said?"

"Yeah yeah, just checking. The connection's fuzzy." It wasn't actually, it was that I was somehow surprised by the offer, or by the thought that Remo cooked Thanksgiving dinner. Having lived in his house for a couple of weeks, I wasn't certain he did much in that kitchen other than make coffee and heat up canned soup. "I'll ask Jonathan."

"You don't think he'll want to?"

"I'm sure he'll want to. He loves parties and talking to people. But, you know. I don't want to assume."

"Sure, sure." He made one of those uncomfortable coughs. "While you're asking him, see if he wants to have dinner this Friday. Or come stay for the weekend and we can catch up."

"I'll ask." I figured we'd be a yes for dinner, but I didn't want to stay the weekend because I knew that would mean no sex. We'd fallen into a reliable pattern—that is to say, I relied on it. Any Saturday afternoon when we didn't have other plans was completely safe territory. So was Saturday night, but we more often went out to see bands or sometimes to a party. Sunday was pretty good, too, but not as reliable, so I considered Sunday sex a bonus. "So how was the tour?"

"I'll tell you everything when I get in."

"Crap, I guess this means you need your truck back."

"I suppose it does. I'm only back for two weeks, though, before we leave for Asia. I can rent something."

"Or I can rent something, which would make more sense."

"Yeah, you're right. Where is my head?"

"Paris."

"Right. See you when I get in."

"You want me to pick you up?"

"I can take a limo."

"I'll pick you up and you can give me the fifty bucks you would have given the limo."

"For picking me up in my own car?"

"Yeah."

He laughed. "Will you carry my bags, too?"

"Naw. That costs extra."

He was still chuckling a little. "It'll be good to see you. Got a pen? Write down my flight info."

I wrote it down, and for good measure I wrote *Friday? Thanksgiving?* so I'd remember to ask Jonathan. He was at a work thing—they'd hit some benchmark or something and were all going out to dinner together, and I wasn't that interested in tagging along on that. It wasn't like other people were bringing their boyfriends or girlfriends, as far as I knew.

I had some microwave mac and cheese and amused myself by sitting on the terrace to work on a song with the Ovation. But during my warm-ups I started playing some old stuff, and I ended up just sitting there playing whatever I felt like, going from song to song, like I used to when I busked in the subway, when it didn't actually matter whether anyone listened or not, so I played whatever my fingers felt like. Snippets of songs I had never written, snippets of songs that were yet to be written, and bits of songs I knew, some original, some not. I just let it flow.

He hadn't returned yet by the time I felt done, which was just as well, because then I wouldn't feel compelled to play for him, and I got in bed with a book.

He came in quite tipsy around midnight and crawled into bed with me and whispered, as if someone might be listening, "I would really like you to make love to me right now."

"I would be happy to," I said, and kissed him.

"You don't mind?"

"Shut up and lie back so I can get your shirt unbuttoned."

He was drunk enough that I wondered how he'd gotten home. I found out later that a coworker had dropped him off, but at the time I didn't think about it too much. I was much more concerned with how excellently warm his skin was, how his belly tasted when I licked a stripe down from his navel, how fantastic it felt to have him flow under my hands the way the notes had an hour before.

When we were done I felt like I'd picked up some of his buzz, the room spinning a little as if the bed were on a giant turntable, as we lay there, damp and limp and content, my arm across his chest.

"That was nice," he said, as if mildly surprised.

"All you have to do is ask," I answered, without really thinking about it.

"Do you really mean that?"

"What do you mean?"

"I mean, do you mean that all I would have to do is ask?"

I thought over what we'd said and then got into thinking over what we'd said before, and before long I was trying to recap every conversation about sex we'd had and that took way too long, so I simply said, "Yes." Then I decided to check myself. "Haven't you asked me that before?"

"Kind of. I guess it still hasn't sunk in."

I made a guess. "Did some previous boyfriend hold out on you a lot?"

"Not really." He sighed. "I'm sorry. It's that I feel like I'm being unfair to you."

"Unfair?"

"Because I don't always say yes to you. I can't make you that same promise."

"It's not a promise, J. It's just a fact. And I said a while ago that if I wasn't willing for whatever reason, I'd tell you."

"But you never have."

"So maybe it would be a rare thing." I shrugged and wiggled around so I could see him. "I like sex. I like sex with you. I haven't ever had a reason to say no. You've had plenty of reasons to say no. It's okay, J." In the back of my mind, I was thinking: since when did I become the guy who figured it all out and explained it and J become the guy who was insecure about sex?

"You wish we did it more often."

"Once a week is perfectly adequate to my needs." *Oh jeez, I sound like Lacey*, I thought.

"But twice a week would be better."

"If you wanted twice a week, I'd say yes in a heartbeat." Which was true. And I admit I got really hopeful that was what he was offering, and I admit that I think I showed that hope way too much, and that made me feel like I was pressuring him, so before he could say something else, I tried to fix the hurt I might have made: "But really, every Saturday afternoon is fine."

Which just goes to show that I didn't know shit after all, because that was when he got that hurt look. "Is it really every Saturday afternoon?"

"Regular as a metronome," I said.

"Ouch. I didn't realize we were in such a rut."

"We're not in a rut," I said, even though I pretty much thought we were. "That's like saying because we eat every day we're in a rut. Isn't it?"

"Did you like the sex better tonight than you did on Saturday?"

"No. I liked it plenty both times. This was nice because it was unexpected, and Saturday was nice because it was expected. Do you get what I mean?" I nuzzled his neck and licked the sweat that had dried.

"I think so." He sighed and ran his hand down my bare back. "Would you do me again right now, if I asked you to?"

"Absolutely. Well, it might take another fifteen or twenty minutes for me to recharge, but there's plenty we can do to stay busy until then. I mean, if you're leading up to actually asking."

"Would it be weird if I said I wanted to see you come again and I didn't care if I did?"

"I have no idea if that's weird or not. If what you're really asking is would I mind, though, the answer is no."

He kissed me then and said he wanted to use his hand so he could watch my face, and he used lube, and I felt the orgasm really intensely even though not a lot came out.

"Thank you," he said, and kissed me when I was done.

"No, thank you," I insisted. "I think we just had another conversation where I saw everything backwards from you."

"What's backwards? I asked you for something, you said yes, so I thanked you."

"Okay, I guess I still felt like you did more for me than I did for you."

"Because you're the one who came?"

"I guess? Doesn't that make sense?"

"I guess it depends on how you look at it. What I get out of sex with you, Daron, is a lot more than an orgasm. It's an extension of being with you, of living with you, of everything that you are, everything that I get to enjoy about having you here, under the same roof with me. You're not like anyone else I've ever been with. You're... God, I hate clichés, but it's so true: you're special. You're really special."

When a guy gives you a speech like that while his hand is still coated in your jizz, you're supposed to hear violins in the background, you know the ones, with the sun setting and the crashing waves and little hearts floating up like soap bubbles. Thing is... I hate clichés, too. I'll play them all day long in the studio if that's what they're paying for, but when something's mine? That's different. I didn't like the sound of those violins. Did I feel special? I did, but not in a way I liked. It would take me a couple more weeks to figure out why. Yeah, I felt special, the way a leopard in a zoo is special, exotic, different. I didn't much like that feeling.

But I did feel loved. Confusing as that sounds. I did. So I stuck with that as the take-away from the conversation.

What's on Your Mind

I went to pick up Remo in his own truck. I was surprised he didn't have much with him, but apparently most of it was being taken care of by the road crew. "It means they'll dump off a load of my dirty laundry after everything's unpacked, but at least I didn't have to carry it," he explained as he buckled himself into the passenger seat. "Now let's get Mexican food. It's the one thing you can't get in Europe."

I drove, and he directed me to a taco stand in Silver Lake, where we stuffed our faces for about five bucks while sitting on the back bumper of the truck. And Remo talked about how touring in Europe was different from the States, and it took more support and more coordination, but the album sales bump was huge. And I told him what he'd already heard, but with more detail, about how our US tour hadn't bumped sales much at all, seemingly because of lack of inventory in the right places.

We drove to the deli then for dessert, and I bemoaned the lack of good ice cream places in Los Angeles. I told him about doing session work over an ice cream sundae while he had a cup of coffee.

"Do you like the work?"

"Yeah, I like it. Sometimes it can be a bit dull, but come on, I'm getting paid to play the guitar."

"Better than playing in a cover band, though?"

"Oh, way better. It's apples and oranges, can't compare. I'd rather be doing my own thing, but that's all in limbo right now." With a spoon, I dug into the hard ice cream where the hot fudge had weakened it.

"Last time we talked, you said a lawyer was gearing up. Anything happening with that?"

"Here's how he explained it to me. 'Lawyers are like

gorillas. We go in there and beat our chests at each other and usually that's all you need before someone backs down and there's no actual fight.' Far as I can tell, the chest beating is still in the firing-letters-back-and-forth stage."

"In other words, nothing."

"Yeah."

"Heard from Digger?"

"Not a peep. And nothing from Ziggy, either."

"How long's he been gone?"

I winced like I was having brain freeze, but really it was that I had avoided actually calculating how long it had been. And now I couldn't avoid it anymore. "Three months since we heard he went to India." Which meant I'd been living with Jonathan for almost as long.

Remo whistled appreciatively. "I can't believe I've been gone that long."

"That's because the weather hardly changes here. So it seems the same as when you left."

"Smartass. Europe's a big continent, and you end up with days off between shows. We did summer festivals first in August, then some in the Mediterranean in September, and then back through the cold countries for regular shows before winter comes."

"And why Japan in the winter?"

"The winters aren't too bad there, I hear, and it's summer in Australia. It's only a nineteen-day tour anyway. Done by Christmas." He had creases by his eyes, and the wrinkles in his forehead were starting to show, but that was a good look on Remo. It went with his sort of cowboy-ish image. His sandy hair hid the gray that was salted all over his head. "Speaking of holidays, you ask about Thanksgiving?"

Shit, I hadn't. But I was really sure J would say yes. "We're in. Should we bring anything?"

"How about a bottle of wine?"

"Okay, but, you know, you don't have to do all the cooking."

He chuckled and took a sip of his coffee. "I'm not doing any of the cooking. I hired caterers."

That was a relief. I wasn't sure I was actually up to candying yams or whatever. I couldn't help needling him a little, though. "Caterers? Isn't that cheating?"

"You'd rather eat undercooked turkey and burnt potatoes?"

"Bottle of wine it is. So is this going to be fancy? What should I wear?"

"Hell no, not fancy. Well, you know, the Mazel wives might get prettied up, but the rest of us, no."

"So who else is going to be there?"

"Well, Alan and Alex and their wives, and Martin wasn't going to come but then he had some plan fall through so he is, and I invited Carynne and Waldo and her mother, but they said no."

"Carynne is on the other side of the country, and she can't stand her mother," I said.

"I know, but I figured I could at least ask." Remo shrugged. "Alan's kid is four now, I think?"

I hadn't even realized Alan had a kid. Then again, Alan was the quiet type who didn't say much about himself. Alex was pretty much the same. When we'd gone on that short tour three years earlier, I'd spent a lot of time hanging around with them but not really saying much. Then I remembered that Alan had a photo of a baby taped inside one of his road cases, and there was only one logical reason for that. Duh. "Yeah, four, I would guess."

Remo dropped me off at the apartment then and drove himself home from there. Jonathan got home a few minutes later.

He kissed me. "How's Remo?"

"On the verge of collapsing from jet lag, but he won't admit it," I said. "How was your day?"

"Exhausting. What do you want for dinner?"

"Want to go to a really awesome taco stand in Silver Lake?"

"How did you find out about a really awesome taco stand in Silver Lake?"

"That's where Remo and I went to re-acclimate him to Southern California. I'm sure I can find it again."

"But didn't you just eat there?"

"I didn't get to try the fish. Come on, you love the little authentic places, you said."

"That is true..." He paused to think about it. "Let me change and then let's go."

I stayed in the living room, fussing around with the Ovation, figuring that following him into the bedroom while he was getting undressed might seem too much like a come-on for a weeknight. He re-emerged in ratty jeans and a T-shirt.

I drove and figured out how to get back there, and had fish tacos while Jonathan had the tongue. I had a bite of his and was immediately envious they were so good. Sadly, when I went back to the window I was told they were out of tongue then, so I couldn't get any. It was probably just as well, since three full orders of tacos (plus an ice cream sundae) was getting to be a lot of food for one night, even for me. We debated whether we were actually in Silver Lake or Los Feliz and determined that neither of us knew well enough where the border was to speak knowledgeably about it.

On the drive home, Jonathan said, "Thanks for taking me there."

"Here you go with the baffling thanking again."

He was driving. "You were just there. You could have said you already ate and told me to fend for myself."

"Could I? Wouldn't it make you feel like shit if I did?" I rolled up the passenger side window so I could hear him better.

"Well, maybe."

"I'm pretty sure it would, and I'm pretty sure it's my job as your boyfriend not to make you feel like shit unless absolutely necessary."

I'd said it half as a joke, but it came out sounding really serious. And, well, I took being Jonathan's boyfriend really seriously.

He took his eyes off the road to look at me for a moment before he had to concentrate on driving again. "I... appreciate that."

A sort of heavy silence fell in the car then, though, and I couldn't tell what it was about... other than our relationship as a whole, which I knew at that point was broken, but I didn't know how we'd broken it or how to fix it. Maybe all relationships were inherently difficult to reconcile.

Or maybe they were for anyone who thought that. Like me.

I stared out the window at the hills and lights and buildings going by and ended up staring at my reflection. *Why am I so bad at this? Is it me or is it everyone? It's not everyone. Bart and Michelle are happy. Alan and his wife are happy. Maybe it is me. Hey, didn't you have therapy on your to-do list? Crap.*

Maybe it was time to have a discussion with Jonathan about therapy. But that would be a discussion about whether our relationship was ready for therapy. Which would be the discussion about our relationship that I was terrified to have in the first place, much less in the course of therapy. If he brought it up, I would have gone along with it. But I couldn't bring myself to be the one. Too afraid of messing up. Too afraid of the expectations that would set.

"How was work?" I asked then, striving for casual and failing.

"You asked me that already."

"And you gave a one-word answer. I thought maybe with some food in you you'd feel like telling me more."

"Eh. It's pretty boring to talk about."

"J. You don't have to worry about boring me."

"Okay. I hear you. But you know, I've been trying to figure out what to tell you about my exes. Since you feel in the dark about that."

I made what I hoped was an encouraging noise and didn't say anything because I didn't want to derail him.

"I haven't had that many steadies. In college it was one or two fuck buddies who weren't serious, and two summer relationships, one of which I knew was a summer affair, the other I thought was going to turn into more but then it fell apart after two months anyway."

"How did you know the difference between the summer affair and the other one?"

"Well, the summer affair we stated up front. We knew we couldn't continue once the school year started again."

"Why?" I was thinking it was because they would be too busy studying for a relationship.

"Because he was a professor and I was a student," J said casually.

"Oh." I wasn't sure what to say about that, good or bad.

"Don't look so worried. I wasn't one of his students. He was at the conservatory, actually."

"Really? Who?"

Jonathan clucked his tongue. "I promised I'd never say. It was a very nice summer, very good for both of us, and then we moved on. He lived a very private life, as you might imagine."

"Ah, okay. What about the other one?"

"First really serious one," J said, so quietly I leaned toward him to hear better. "Gregory. I thought we were perfect for each other. He was a literature major, would be graduating at the same time as me, lived off campus. We moved in together the summer before my senior year, and I thought, this is it, this is the one, we're going to be together for years and years. Well, it was months."

"Can I ask what went wrong?"

"Plain and simple, he lost interest. He was one of those absence-makes-the-heart-grow-fonder types, while familiarity bred contempt. During the semester we'd had to work hard to see enough of each other, you know? But after we moved in together..." J let out a long sigh. "He was downright cruel about it by the end, saying things like 'I'm sick of seeing your face.' I tried to understand it at first, tried to fix things, turn him back into the man I fell in love with, but he very clearly was trying to get me to move out. Then I stayed for a little while out of spite—after all, he'd promised me a place to live for the summer at least... but it was miserable, we couldn't even be friends anymore, and I went to live with my parents until the semester started again."

"Wow."

"I half-suspected he was cheating on me, but I never found evidence. No one moved in with him, as far as I could tell, and around Christmas I heard he'd taken up with a friend of a friend, but it sounded recent."

"So he held out on you emotionally more than sexually."

"I guess." He pulled the car into the driveway. "Let's continue this inside."

Once we were in the apartment, though, J didn't seem to know what to say next, and I didn't really know what to ask.

When we got ready for bed, J did say something, though. "Can I jerk you off again tonight?"

"Haha, twist my arm. Of course you can."

"Good."

In the end he got excited, too, though, and ended up jerking us both off together, his slick hand around both, making for an extra copious mess. Not that I minded.

Fragile

Carynne called. Jonathan had left for work already, and I was taking my time with my morning. There were days when he left and my "morning" essentially dragged on all day until he called and said he was on the way home, which gave me about forty-five minutes to shower and get dressed. There were lots of days like that, where I put a Pop-Tart into the toaster and started writing a song and the next thing I knew it was three in the afternoon and what I had to show for it was a cold Pop-Tart, greasy hair, and a song. I considered that a net gain.

This was one of the days when I didn't chance putting the Pop-Tart in and just ate it cold out of the package while I listened to the answering machine pick up the call.

"Daron, it's me, pick up if you're there."

"Hey, C." I wiped crumbs off my chin as I answered, as if she might hear them.

"You're not planning to go to this shindig of Lacey's are you?"

"Given that I don't know what you're talking about, that would be a no."

"I figured as much. I've been getting calls from her publicist. It's the annual awards dinner for the shelter where the donations went."

"Ah, now I know what you're talking about. If it's all the same to you, I'd rather not go. Giving the money was the point, not the publicity."

"That's what I told him, but he convinced Lacey that she could do a lot more for them by speaking at the dinner, which is true, to be honest, but then he decided to see if he could drum up something more with you. I told him you're busy."

"What's the latest with Lacey and Chris?"

"You'll have to ask him for the latest. As of last week they were still quits, though she talked with his counselor. So maybe."

"I'm mostly asking because if he's going to come out here for the dinner, I should be prepared."

"Prepared?"

"To take him in stray if she goes off again." I considered eating the second Pop-Tart in the envelope but put it back in the box. I could always eat it in an hour or two… if I remembered it was there. "I suppose I should try to make sure I don't show up there by accident, too. When is it?"

"Here. Put it on your calendar with a big NOT next to it."

I jotted down the information. "Do you think I should be worrying about her?"

"I don't think worrying is productive in most cases, but were you thinking of something specific?"

"I keep coming back to the shit she said about how she would have taken up with Ziggy if only he and I hadn't been… together." It was unexpectedly painful to try to come up with the words. "As if it was my fault she didn't get a shot at him."

"She wasn't watching very carefully if she thought she didn't have a shot," Carynne pointed out. "It's not like Ziggy was ever exclusive, much less exclusively gay."

"True," I agreed, though it didn't make me feel any better. "I just worry that one of these days she's going to do a line of coke and then talk to the media, and that will be how we end up tabloid news, no matter what we do."

"Maybe that's the silver lining of Zig being out of sight, out of mind." Carynne said it gently, like she knew I was hurting. "And as much as I want to support Christian in his relationships… maybe that's just one more reason why we'd all be better off without her around."

"Okay, but now I really feel like chickenshit."

"Why?"

"It just feels wrong for me to invalidate all the hard work he's done on his relationship just to shore up my closet."

She was silent, and I couldn't tell if it was because she was thinking or stunned.

"Right?" I asked. "That's chickenshit, right?"

"I'm trying to figure out if I ever heard you talk about the closet so blatantly before."

"Jonathan's rubbing off on me. We have a lot of talks about identity politics. I never even knew what identity politics *was* until him."

"Understood. But here's what I'm getting at, Daron. The so-called closet, you're talking about a social construction based on your own fear and perceived public image. We need to separate things out a little more now."

"We do?"

"Yeah. You being afraid is one thing. You're feeling chickenshit because you feel like you're putting your feelings in front of Chris's feelings, selfishly. But it's a separate issue from your feelings because issues that affect your public image actually could have a negative impact on your career and the band. Do you see what I'm saying?"

"You're saying that even if I weren't afraid of the consequences, there could be consequences?"

"That's one way of putting it."

"I still don't feel right trying to break them up just to cover my ass."

"Don't take on guilt that doesn't belong to you. You didn't break them up, and neither did I. They did that all on their own."

"Okay. Sorry. Anyway, I'll call him later and get the latest." I emailed with Colin almost every day, but Chris was harder to stay in touch with without some effort on both our parts.

Then Carynne asked, quite innocently, "So how's Jonathan?"

"Good," I said automatically, then immediately retracted it. "Actually, I think he's really having a rough time, but he's such a good soldier he just keeps plowing through no matter what. I keep asking him if everything at work is okay, and he says yes, but I feel like something's wrong anyway."

"You think he's in denial?"

"I don't know what to think. I feel like he went from being a really sensible, confident person to a chronic second-guesser. And the only two possible causes are either me or the job, and I guess I'm in denial that it's me."

"Hah. Wait, you're serious."

"Yeah. I mean, if it's me, what can I do about it? Beyond what I'm already doing?"

"Which is…?"

"Try to be a good boyfriend."

"Which means what?"

"Be home on time for dinner and don't fuck anyone else, far as I can tell," I said, and I wished I was joking.

"Oh, and be a good listener."

"Daron, I hate to tell you this, but if you were my boyfriend, and that was what you brought to the table? I'd have to break it to you that you're scraping by with the bare minimum. Maybe Jonathan's different, but for me? That is the minimum requirements you're meeting right there."

"I suck at relationships."

"Hush. This isn't so you can beat yourself up about something else. Hang on, I have another call coming in."

She picked up call waiting, and I decided to eat the other Pop-Tart while I had nothing better to do. I broke it in half and was finishing one of the pieces when she came back.

"That was Skyline. Looking for more filler music for documentaries. Interested?"

"Absolutely, assuming the pay rate's similar, but it'd be nice if I have a little more lead time."

"Sounds like it. I'll call you back with more details."

"Okay."

I took the cordless phone with me to the living room and left it on the coffee table while I fussed with a song. Gee, do you think this one is about Jonathan? No wait, maybe it's about Ziggy, too.

The words - the words - the words
Stuck inside my mouth
I keep them to myself
I never let them out

The words - the words - the words
I'll never say
Because of how they'd cut you
Because you'd never stay

The words - the words - the words
I know by heart
Won't bring us together
They'll tear us apart

The words - the words - the words
I want to say
But only if I mean them
Not to make you stay

The words - the words - the words
Trapped behind my lips
A special kind of poison
I take instead of give

Words are broken
my heart unspoken

Temptation

So I decided to cook dinner for J that night. Whether that had anything to do with what Carynne said is... Okay, I admit, it had everything to do with what she said about me doing the bare minimum.

I still didn't have a car—I figured I'd rent one whenever the next gig was that required me to drive somewhere—so I walked to the convenience store. The one nearest our house was better than a gas station quickie mart, with a modicum of actual food in it. And, as it turned out, it was a place where I could get most of the things I was actually good at cooking, anyway. I knew I could make a decent garlic bread, and pasta wasn't something I screwed up often. I wondered if I should try to make a salad, too, but there was the problem that a head of lettuce was too much for the two of us, and half of it would end up going rusty in the drawer. I came home with various things: ziti, sauce, et cetera. And a candle for the table.

The weather had warmed up again, by which I mean after two days in the seventies it was back in the mid-eighties like usual. I put the table in the courtyard, and while rooting around in the closet I even found a red-and-white checkered tablecloth. That sent me back out to buy a bottle of Italian red wine, as I realized, of course, that was what was needed to complete the picture.

I was putting the folding chairs out when a voice from the driveway interrupted me. It was one of our upstairs neighbors, but I didn't know if it was Jerry or Robert. "Special occasion?"

"Oh, um. Not really. Just a change of pace," I said.

"Since I didn't have a gig today."

"That's nice of you. Jonathan seems like he's working very hard these days."

"He is," I agreed.

"May I be nosy and inquire as to what's on the menu?"

"Oh. Sure. Ziti with meat sauce, grated cheese, and garlic bread. And wine." Saying it aloud, I felt the list sounded a bit thin. "I'm still deciding whether to try to add a salad or not. Salad for two is hard to manage."

"Have you considered a tomato basil salad? We grow fresh basil in a window box. Chop the tomato and basil, sprinkle with oil and vinegar, and voila. Or if you want to get fancy, slice it in thin wedges and place the basil leaves between each one."

"That's a good idea..."

"I'll bring you some." He gave me a quick smile and then went upstairs to get the basil. Until that moment, it hadn't dawned on me that he was suggesting it because he intended to actually give me some. I was still thinking that over when he came back down.

"Thanks." I must have seemed a little bewildered as I took the sprigs of basil from him.

"Something wrong?" he asked.

"No, just... thanks." I couldn't very well say that what was puzzling me was that up until then I'd had the impression that they didn't really like me.

I got artistic with the basil, as suggested.

That left the only thing to dither about whether I should call J to warn him I was cooking or whether I should keep it a complete surprise. The main thing was I didn't want us to run into a situation where he worked late and turned the whole thing into a tragedy. I decided I could maintain an element of surprise if I didn't tell him what I was making. I called the office. Fortunately a human answered, and they put me through to him.

"Hey, what's up? Everything okay?"

"Everything's great. I'm cooking dinner, okay?"

"Okay."

"And I realized I should ask what time you thought you'd be home so I can try to time it right."

"Well, since I know you're cooking, I'll try to be home right at six. But rush hour being what it is here, better say six-thirty. How about I call you before I leave here?"

"Perfect. See you later." I hung up before he could pry into what or why.

Then I had a couple of hours to kill before the actual cooking would have to take place, so I sat in the living room with a portable cassette recorder and worked on themes for documentary soundtracks until J called to say he was on the way. Then, zoom, I took a quick shower, put the water on to boil, browned the meat while the water was heating up, got the bread into the oven... and managed not to burn or undercook any of it.

I almost forgot to get the tomato salad out of the fridge, but I didn't. I lit the candle while he was pulling into the driveway.

The smile on his face was worth the effort. He was pleased, tickled, bemused, and touched all at once. Say what you want about the flaws in our relationship, but it was something to be able to affect a person so directly.

He kissed me and said, "You have sauce on your forehead."

"Oh." I swiped my hand across my brow and licked my fingers. "Hm, needs cheese. Go sit. And open the wine."

He sat in one of the chairs outside and picked up the wine bottle while I went back into the house to get the last few things. And to point the speakers of the boombox out the front window, volume turned low on some Tangerine Dream.

We had a nice meal sitting out there, watching the candle burn down and talking about all the things we usually talked about: pop culture and politics and people. Then, when the wine ran out we took it as our cue to move back inside. I carried the things in while J started the washing up.

I know I can be oblivious. But I didn't live with him for almost four months without learning some of his cues. The way he glanced at me while I loaded the dishwasher signaled desire. The way he fussed his hair out of his face and breathed, though, that was tension.

I figured I had about five minutes—the amount of time it would take to wipe down the counters and put the table back in place—to figure out how to defuse, deflect, or deal with whatever was brewing.

Sometimes honesty and openness isn't a relationship

style or a strategy. Sometimes it's just that you can't think of anything else.

I waited until he dried his hands to ask. "You doing okay? You seem tense."

He took my hands in his. "And sex would be a great way to relieve tension?"

Here we go again, I thought. That was not what I was asking. Or implying. It took me a few seconds to get on track. "Um, well, it usually is..." A light bulb went on in my head. "Unless it's the source of the tension."

J wasn't the type who burst into tears. He was too WASPy for that, he said, no matter how hard he tried to shed his upbringing. So when hugged me, sagging from the sudden release, I knew I'd hit a nerve. Hard.

The couch was too far and was up and over the raised section of the first floor, but the bedroom, which was right there, seemed too charged. I leaned him against the counter, counting his breaths.

When he spoke, he had already figured out a bunch of the stuff I thought I was going to have to say. "You didn't make us a romantic, candlelight dinner because you're trying to get me into bed."

"No. Not on purpose, anyway."

"I'm such a dick for assuming you did."

"You're not a dick—you've got something going on, J." I loosened his grip on me and looked into his face. His eyes were red-rimmed. "Let's sit, okay?"

We moved to the couch as if we were sensible people. I sat cross-legged facing him. He made himself take a long breath.

"Okay, wow, sorry," he said. "I've gotten kind of into this spiral of worrying about it, and assuming... just plain assuming too much."

"You don't have to assume anything with me, J. You know I want you, but you have to believe that I'm okay with rationing."

"I hate that you think of it as rationing, though," he said.

"All right, maybe that's a bad word for it, but trust me, I don't feel like I'm starved." I wasn't sure I could convey the world of scarcity I was used to. I don't think Jonathan ever lived through the kind of dry spells I used to have. Before I was out to anyone in my life.

Which got me wondering why I still thought like that when that was in the past. But right now I was focused on figuring Jonathan out. "Do you feel pressured to put out? Honestly. Am I pressuring you and I don't realize it?"

He shook his head. "No. No, you've been great, actually. But somehow I get sensitive about it. I worry I'm not holding up my end of the deal."

"And I worry I'm not holding up my end, which is why I made dinner!" I grabbed him by the hand then, trying to make him see how that fit together.

He chuckled. "We're like something from an O. Henry story. So if we just worry less, everything will work out?"

"I don't know, but worrying less seems like a really good policy, doesn't it?"

"When you put it that way, yes. But seriously, thinking about it that way... maybe the problem is that my worry level is just... too high. I'm too—too—" He stared at the corner of the ceiling while he searched for the right word. When he didn't find it, his gaze dropped to the floor. "I haven't wanted to burden you with it. You already gave me the best advice there is."

"Burden me with what?"

His voice was small. "I don't know what the hell I'm doing at work."

I refrained from saying *I knew it!* or *I told you so.* "It's been a really long time since I heard you talk about the ending of the novel." Which, as far as I knew, he still hadn't actually written.

And maybe he wasn't going to. He rubbed his face. "I think... I think what we're going to end up with is going to be a very good TV series. And I can be proud of a lot of it."

"That sounds a lot like a disclaimer, though, J."

He nodded. "I know. I'm proud of it, but... it isn't the story I wanted to tell." He had that tight sound to his voice, like he was totally crushed but was trying really hard not to sound like he was. "It isn't my novel."

"I'm sorry."

"It isn't the thing I dreamed of. It isn't ever going to be the great American literary statement I imagined it would be."

I wondered if now would be a good time to give him a supportive hug, but it seemed like once he got started confessing he gesticulated and waved his hands, and I figured I should not get in the way of him getting it all off his chest.

"The book I wanted to write will never be written. The show cannibalizes too much of it. And the show, okay, it's going to be good, but do I want to be doing this the rest of my life? I don't like or trust any of the people I work with. None of them care about the story or characters like I do. Most of what they care about is impressing the higher-ups so they can move on to the next job and the next. They depend on me for the creative drive on the project, but then they do the stupidest shit to it and I have to be the one to fight and scream, and then when I do they tell me I don't know anything about writing for television, and what if they're right and the entire thing is going to fail because I don't know what I'm doing?" His voice rose and he drew a shaky breath, staring into the middle of the room. "And none of them appreciate that I gutted my baby to give them this idea, not a one. Their attitude is, so the fuck what? Write another book the next time you go to Puerto Vallarta. Oh, by the way, we made this character twenty years younger so this hot actress can play her. Rewrite her to be a next-door neighbor instead of his mother."

I couldn't help but hear Sarah Rogue's voice in what he was saying. So much of it sounded the same. "They want you, but at the same time they make you wonder why you're even involved in the first place."

"Exactly. And then you're supposed to be grateful for having the gig! You're supposed to thank your lucky stars you're one of the few, the blessed, who has a gig at all!" He rubbed his eyes. "Aaagh!"

"And you've been keeping this all bottled up?"

"What good does complaining do? I dug this hole for myself. I can't change it. You can't change it. I just... I try to concentrate on the good things."

"Which are?"

"Like that this gig gave me a chance to have this relationship with you, for example," he said, focusing on me at last.

Oh. "You mean the relationship that has you tiptoeing around on eggshells because you're afraid I'm not getting enough?" That's right. I called him out about it.

Long sigh. "Yes. I mean, now that we're talking about it, it's obvious to me that it's not you. It's the fact that all day long I feel like people with hidden agendas are asking me to put out, put out, put out, making me feel like a whore, and when I get home all I want to do is curl up in a ball in a corner."

"Well, speaking as a person who actually *does* curl up in a ball in the corner sometimes, I sympathize with that feeling."

"Oh, Daron." He scooted closer and put his arms around me. "I'm sorry. I'm so sorry. Thank you for making me see the light of day. I promise I'll leave my work problems at work from now on. It'll be better now."

Remember what Carynne said about the bare minimum? I knew at that moment full well that what a real boyfriend should have said was this: *No no no, Jonathan, that's the problem. If we're going to have a real relationship, you have to talk to me about this stuff and work it out and stop trying to keep it from me in the first place.*

But I also knew better than ever that I wasn't there for real. I was playing house with him. It was nice, in its way. It was good, by a lot of measures. So I didn't say that. What I said was a cop-out. "I'm sure it will."

"God. I feel so relieved realizing that."

"Do I get to say I told you so now?"

"Hah. Well, you did keep asking me if something was wrong at work, and I kept saying no. Did you know I was lying to myself so much?"

"No. But I'm getting good at realizing that denial is not just a river in Egypt."

He held me close, and with the night air turning chilly by the uninsulated windows that felt really nice. "So now I'm really relieved about you, but I'm dreading going to the office tomorrow. How am I going to put that face on again?"

I didn't have anything I could say to that.

"Maybe I'll go in late tomorrow."

"I don't have to be anywhere until Friday."

He nuzzled me then. "You didn't mean that as a hint. But what if I took it as one?"

"You mean, what if I was hinting that we'd have plenty of time to have sex in the morning?"

"Or now, and sleep in."

"How about this: no hints. J, you want to? You tell me when."

"How about now."

"Now's good."

Now's good. Just keep thinking that.

Heart of Gold

So what I haven't said about my conversations with Jonathan is what I haven't said. I mean, what I wasn't saying at the time. Which is to say that every time we talked about anything, I meant to bring up the question of Thanksgiving, but every time we got sidetracked into something else—usually some other relationship talk. So I finally brought it up one night when I couldn't sleep because it felt like it had gotten to the point that it was hanging over me so much that it was keeping me from sleeping.

I poked Jonathan in the arm. "Hey."

"Hey," he said back, but I don't think he was awake yet.

"Hey, can I ask you something?"

He blinked and squinted at me. "What? Is something wrong?"

That was a loaded question if ever I heard one. I didn't answer it. Not directly, anyway. "I don't want you to think I'm the crazy sort who wakes you up to talk about trivial things, but at the same time what I need to ask you is one of those things that I've been trying not to make a big deal out of, except that now I'm waking you up in the middle of the night..." That sounded crazy, even to me, and I tried to take it back. "Never mind, go back to sleep. I'll ask you in the morning."

He sat up. "Waitasec. You want to ask me something, but you don't want to make a big deal out of it. Except that you woke me up in the middle of the night about it?"

"Forget it. I promise I'll ask you in the morning."

"I'm awake now, Daron, and too curious to go back to sleep." He turned his little bedside reading lamp on. J liked to sleep in a plain white undershirt, one that was so soft and worn that it was nearly see-through, and the whiteness was bright in the cone of light. "Is this about that phone call from Carynne?"

While living with him I'd gotten into the habit of changing shirts before going to sleep. Before that I had usually fallen asleep in whatever clothes I was wearing. I rubbed my face and sat up, too.

Best just to blurt it out, I thought, now that my preamble to it was so messed up and before he got me sidetracked into talking about BNC. "Remo invited us to his house for Thanksgiving."

"That's nice of him. Does he want us to bring anything?"

"Um, wait. I told him I'd ask you if it was okay."

"Why wouldn't it be okay?"

"Uh..." I tried to remember what my rationale was. "I didn't want to make the assumption that I could speak for both of us. And at the time I thought you might want to visit your folks or something."

"Well, honestly, my mother did ask if I was coming home and if I was bringing you, but I told her I didn't want to have to fly all the way across the country just for a three-day visit. And I can't spare more time than that. So she asked if you'd come for Christmas."

"What did you tell her?"

"I told her I'd ask you."

"Aha." We both laughed a little at that. Apparently, for once, we'd both thought along the same lines. "I know we won't be invited to Remo's for Christmas, since he'll be on tour."

He seemed to me to be holding very still. "Well, then? Will you come meet my family?"

I thought I was pretty smooth about it. "I should head East to see Carynne and the guys anyway...."

"You'd be only the second guy I brought home to meet them."

"You're kidding."

"I'm not. I've had lots of relationships, Daron, lots of boyfriends, but very few serious enough to bring home."

"Okay, okay, can we talk about that? This, I mean?" Yes, that's right, I was demanding that we talk about the thing I'd been refusing to talk about for months.

"Of course we can," Jonathan said, though I don't think he knew yet that I was intending to talk about our relationship as a whole.

"What does it mean to meet your folks? To you, I mean? If you didn't bring other guys home before." I couldn't figure out what I was trying to ask. "I mean, what's different about me?"

"Maybe I feel more strongly about you," he said, which made my heart sink. "Maybe it's just that now I'm older and more sure of myself. And I think my parents will like you."

"You're kidding, right?"

"No, I think you'll get along great with them."

"Why? I have a terrible relationship with my own parents, and your parents are surely going to see me as a bad influence." This conversation wasn't going the direction I intended at all, but I felt I had to say this. "I mean, think about it, J. I don't have a college education. I'm a rock musician. I'm most parents' idea of a disreputable character."

"Well, sure, at first they were really worried when I said I was getting involved with a celebrity I wrote about, but now I'm not on that beat anymore, and you're..." He stopped himself before he could say what he meant.

"I'm what, not on the A list anymore?"

"No no, you're... you don't come across like some kind of Satanist metalhead or something, do you know what I mean? You're not pretentious. You're a nice, hardworking guy, Daron. I'm sure you'd give a perfectly good impression. Especially lately."

"What? Especially lately?" There it was again, that feeling like we were having two different conversations. "You mean, now that I'm not on the road?"

"Partly, yes." He was looking at me earnestly.

This conversation wasn't going remotely the way I had intended, and now I couldn't even remember where I had been trying to steer it.

He saw how lost I was. He took my hand. "I know it isn't really what either of us expected..."

I was thinking: *Wait, what isn't what we expected? Are we talking about the same "it"?*

"...but don't you kind of think we have a good thing going here?"

That sinking feeling for me hit bottom with a clank. I'd definitely let this go way too long without saying something. But what would I have said? Thanks for letting me play house? For that matter, what was I going to say now? Anything I could think of to say was going to burst his bubble. And I didn't want to hurt him. I didn't want to be cruel. "J—"

"I'm not saying it's going to last forever. When this gig runs its course for me, I don't know what I'm going to do. But look at you. You've really settled into session work—"

I jerked. It didn't matter what I was thinking or what I was trying to make myself think—my nerves rebelled and the result was I twitched—I cringed.

He backtracked before I could come up with any words. "I know it's not the peak of fame. I know it's not everything you could dream of. But isn't it...? At least a little? *Some* of what you wished for in life?"

I swallowed the lump in my throat then, trying to swallow my pride and my objections. Because he was right. Could I have imagined a life this good, with a man who loved me, and steady work in music, and everything else, three or four years ago when I was still in the closet, desperately lonely, and wondering if I'd be out on the street in a month? What the fuck kind of ungrateful sonofabitch was I to be thinking this wasn't enough?

But the plain truth was that no matter how good it could be, it had always felt like a plateau, a waystation, a way to fill the time until either my career took off again or until Ziggy came home. It always, always felt that way to me, and I didn't go a day without thinking it. I'd just never said it. And I'd never said it because it would have been a shitty, hurtful thing to say. It would have sapped this of whatever sweetness it might have had.

And then the bottom dropped out again, *whoom*, when I thought I had already hit the bottom. Because... what if I was full of shit? What if this *was* the best my career could do? What if Ziggy never came home? What if Moondog Three was in the past, and if I threw all this with Jonathan away to chase after a past that was already gone, I was a fool? What if?

I choked suddenly, because I had gone so deep down the rabbit hole of my doubts that I hadn't realized I was crying.

And Jonathan, being the deep, caring sort of boyfriend he was, pulled me close and let me cry on his shoulder, even though he was half of what I was crying about. Could he tell I was grieving? It felt like grieving to me. My idealism about how the relationship should have been was dying.

Or maybe I just felt sorry for myself, for putting

myself into such a deep bind to begin with. Jonathan being so good to me made it even harder to tell him what I was thinking.

I was thinking that it had been fun playing house with him, but that's all it was ever going to be for me until I knew for sure Ziggy wasn't waltzing back into my life. Ziggy was the elephant in the room. Didn't Jonathan know that? Jonathan knew that. I was sure he did. And yet...

And yet maybe he was trying to show me how much better it could be. How much saner a relationship could be. How nice and stable. Or even just how nice. Yes, that's what he's said a few minutes before. "A good thing going," he had said.

I finally found my voice. I was pressing one of his hands against my damp cheek with both of mine when I said, "I don't know if I'm cut out for this."

"For what?" he whispered.

"Being happy."

"Don't think like that."

"You've worked so hard to make me happy, and here I am crying."

"Shhh. It's okay."

"It's not okay. Do I make you happy, J?"

"You do. Even if you get like this sometimes. It's okay, D. I'm here."

That just made it worse. I dug down to an even lower low than before. I dug down to the level where I felt like the problem was that I couldn't be happy no matter what. Something was seriously wrong with me. How could I not appreciate what I had right in front of me? I was really fucked up.

But J seemed okay with that. He seemed to expect it. He knew how messed up my childhood had been. He knew how screwed by the industry I was. He knew everything. How could I leave someone who knew me so well? Who knew me that well but stuck by me anyway?

"I don't want to hurt you," I said.

"You're not hurting me. Even if you tell me you won't meet my parents."

"I didn't say I wouldn't meet your parents."

"We can figure that out later. Maybe I'll just bring you for dinner. A couple of hours. Nothing too lengthy. Christmas Eve dinner is when we do the big turkey and all that, and there's lots of singing around the piano."

"Oh."

"Something tells me if you're having trouble holding your own in conversations, you'll have no trouble holding up your end of a Christmas carol."

"Yeah." Somehow talking about concrete things like turkey and singing yanked me out of the deepest depths of the mire. "Um, you're probably right."

"Let's not decide now. Talk to Carynne and Bart about what they want to do, too. But if it works out, I'd love to bring you home with me, okay?"

Wasn't that how he'd convinced me to move in with him in the first place? The whole "if it works out, I'd love to..." strategy? I went along with it before; I was probably going to go along with it again. But I said: "Why don't we see how Thanksgiving goes? Maybe that'll boost my confidence."

"Okay." He kissed me on the temple.

Jonathan was the path of least resistance, I realized. He made it easy to say yes. I wondered if that was why I didn't appreciate him enough. Did I imagine that Ziggy was worth more to me because of how much work I'd put in trying to understand him?

That was the sort of thing Lacey would say. Time to put it out of my mind before I went around in a complete circle again. "We better go back to sleep. You have to get up in the morning. I'm sorry I woke you." *With my stupid angst.*

"I'm not," he said. "I'd much rather talk about something important than have you lie there stewing."

"You are too good to me."

"I understand your needs. Now come on, if we're actually going to get to sleep now, we both need to shut off our brains. I only know one thing that works for you."

He was talking about jerking me off. "Are you sure?"

"I'm sure. And then we'll both be asleep in under five minutes. Roll over."

He reached for the bottle of lube. As he took hold of me, I realized how different this was from the way I imagined relationships would be. I never imagined that something as charged as someone's hand on my private parts could become so common and comfortable between me and another person. It was as simple and yet as intimate as something like the way I drank the milk out of J's cereal bowl when we had breakfast together.

He was right. We were both unconscious shortly thereafter.

Hounds of Love

In the morning I examined whether my *idealism* about the relationship being dead was actually the same thing as the *relationship* being dead. In the morning I felt less fatalistic about it, anyway. Maybe a good cry does that.

These are the thoughts I had in the shower after Jonathan left for work: *Maybe I shouldn't give up. Maybe I should try to work some stuff out. I should at least try to figure some things out for the benefit of understanding. Too much about the future is uncertain. At least this you know is here and is real on Jonathan's part, even if you're a basket case right now.*

With that in mind, I called Bart. "I need a reality check."

"Okay, sure."

"You've been with Michelle a long time. Do you do your laundry together? If you do, is it like... a thing?"

"A thing?"

"Like a thing you do together. Like you're happy about doing the laundry because it's something you do together? As a couple?"

"Well..." I heard rustling in the background, like he was tearing opening a package. "Before we bought a place with our own laundry machines, I paid someone to do the laundry."

"Really? I had no idea. That explains why your shirts were never as wrinkly as mine."

"Yeah, I didn't exactly advertise the fact. It was my stepmother's idea. Wanted me to concentrate on my schoolwork and all that, so she paid for it. When we moved here, I kept up the habit. Anyway, now that we have our own machines, you know, whoever needs clothes just tosses them in when necessary. So, no, it's not a thing. But I get the feeling the question you're asking me isn't really about laundry."

"Jonathan acts like us going to the laundromat together is the equivalent of a sunset walk on the beach. While I agree that it's somewhat nicer to have help doing it than to drag the stuff there by myself, I'm just there to get it done, you know?"

"Daron."

"Yeah?"

"I didn't say anything when I was in LA visiting. Because you seemed okay. But it's hard to tell with you."

"Didn't say anything about what?"

"About Jonathan domesticating you."

I sort-of argued. "I think my roommates had me pretty well trained already, don't you think? Christian's the one who taught me to separate darks and lights, and Lars was the one who was big on kitchen cleaning and fridge etiquette."

"I don't just mean household chores. I mean like a stray cat."

"I never tomcatted around that much."

"I don't mean in the bedroom sense. Well, okay, maybe I do. He's tamed you a lot. Have you noticed how much weight you've put on?"

"I haven't put on weight."

"Are you sure?"

"Well, no, since I haven't weighed myself." The last time I weighed myself was at the doctor's office in the spring. But I had gone up a waist size in jeans, I remembered. Hm.

"I'm not saying this is a bad thing, because when a tomcat gets socialized, you know, they can make great pets. Sleek, beautiful, happy, devoted pets who never want to set paw outside again once they have it made. Tell me honestly: is that how you feel? Or do you feel caged?"

I felt like a sledgehammer was crushing my chest, honestly. "Why do you have to put it that way?" It came out a little whiny.

"Because with every other relationship, that's how I felt. Caged. Like no matter how much fun it was, I couldn't wait to find a way out. Then Michelle happened, and it took me a while to realize, holy shit, that urge to break free was completely absent."

A beep sounded in my ear: call waiting. I ignored it. "And what if I tell you I feel like an indoor-outdoor cat? I can go out all I like as long as I'm home by dinnertime."

"Does that work for you? Be honest, Dar'. You wouldn't be calling me if everything was smooth."

I had the urge to hang up and write a song about it, but maybe talking it through was actually the smarter choice. "It drives me crazy that he's so hung up on domestic things, like doing laundry together. Cooking and eating... okay, I get it that no one really likes to eat alone, but for fuck's sake, would it kill him to have a sandwich without me once in a while? For that matter, laundry..." Another beep. I wondered if it was Carynne trying to call. She was probably wondering why the answering machine wasn't picking up. "I'd almost rather we took turns doing it. At least only one of us would have to waste a weekend afternoon instead of both of us. Hey, wait, I have an idea. I'm going to go do it now while he's at work!"

"Danger, Will Robinson. Don't get yourself into the housewife role or the next thing you know, you'll be stuck with it."

"You think so?"

"I'm sure of it. Seriously. Pay someone to do the damn laundry and do something fun on the weekend. If you can't do something fun together and the whole relationship is about maintaining the household, then you're not in a relationship. You're lords of the manor and that's it."

I heard a click, like maybe now Bart was getting call-waited. "Do your parents have fun?"

"My parents think being lord and lady of the manor is fun."

"Ah." I realized I was standing in the front courtyard on the cordless phone. I didn't remember going outside. I had been in the kitchen when I'd called Bart. "There has to be something more to relationships than being extra-special roommates and just the antidote to loneliness."

"There is, Dar'." He sounded amused.

"What? Oh, wait..."

"Ninety percent of pop songs are written about it, you know."

"Yeah, yeah, *love.* I get it." I gave a heavy sigh, trying to dislodge the sledgehammer.

"Fuck, let me get this call, be right back." He clicked off, and I listened to silence for a few moments. Then he came back. "That was Carynne. She said you should call her when we hang up."

"How did she know I was talking to you?"

"I told her. Oh, you mean how did she know to call me to tell you. She didn't. She was going to call me next. But since I'm talking to you anyway, yeah. Call her and then she'll fill me in on whatever afterward."

"Okay, I guess I should—"

"Wait wait wait. Not until we're done here. Daron, listen to me, just because you're not in love with Jonathan doesn't mean you're a bad person."

Oh jeez. "Is it *that* obvious?"

"No. Like I said, it's hard to tell with you. From the outside you two seem perfectly happy together. I'm not judging you. I don't care if you were in love and you fell out, or if you never got there but it seemed like a good idea to give it a try, or what. None of that matters. What matters is how you feel now."

"I feel like I don't know what to do. I mean... is it that I don't love him enough?"

"Have you told him you love him?"

"No." I hurried to add: "But here's why! Because when he says it to me I feel like it means more to him somehow. So if I say it back, he's going to assume I mean the same thing."

"Maybe that's your real problem with the laundry, you know."

"What do you mean?"

"What bugs you about it is that he's got so much more invested in it than you do. For you, it's about getting the clothes clean. For him, it's about your partnership and his investment in your partnership."

"So I'm a bad boyfriend if I do the laundry when he's not home?"

He made a frustrated noise. "Yes, you're horrible. How dare you deprive him of the laundromat."

"Okay, okay, I was being ridiculous. But seriously, what should I do?"

"As long as you separate the whites from the darks, you're probably fine."

"About the relationship, asshole."

"Oh. Honestly, Dar', I think you could both benefit from couples therapy. I think you're making a lot of assumptions about him, and he's probably making a lot of assumptions about you. If you got past all that, you could find out if you actually have something there or if all you have is... is..."

"Playing house?"

"Exactly."

I went in the house then and tried to write a song about it, because the idea of what was going on between me and Jonathan at least seemed to have crystallized in my mind into something clear. But the song didn't make sense and there was too much there, and I worried too much about how he'd feel if he heard it. So I went for a walk.

I ended up in the drug store, which was a mile from the house at least, but I had a lot to think about so a long walk was a good idea. And once I was in there I walked up and down the aisles not really looking for anything, just sort of enjoying the air conditioning and the brightly colored stuff all arranged, even if I didn't need any of it at the moment. There was something sort of comforting about it.

And then I realized I was in front of the nail polish, and I thought about the time Ziggy had shoplifted some. I still didn't know what to think about that, but for the first time in a week or two the feeling of missing him hit me like an ocean wave, one of those sudden ones that knocks you over and fills your head with salt water.

I coughed and tried to focus on reality. My eyes were drawn to a bottle of clear nail cover. Hm. It had been a while since I'd really grown my nails out for playing finger style. Maybe now was a good time to try it again. I picked up the bottle and had a moment where I considered slipping it into my pocket and walking out. Just to see what that felt like? To see if I learned anything about how Ziggy's mind worked? That seemed like a flimsy reason to do wrong. I paid cash and walked home.

Halfway home I remembered I hadn't called Carynne yet.

Disappointed

When I got home, there was a message from Carynne saying she was on her way to my house to bring Chris up to speed and hang out a little. "I usually like you to be the first to know things, but after you didn't call back, I called Bart and talked to him. Call me at your place, though, and we'll put you on speaker, okay?"

Carynne didn't sound that different from usual, but somehow I could tell there was an edge in her voice. It couldn't be good news, no matter what.

I suddenly feared she was quitting. I dialed the number before I even got some 7 Up poured. It had been seventy outside two days ago and eighty yesterday, whereas today it was ninety, so of course today was the day I decided to walk two miles. Perfect timing.

Courtney picked up. "County morgue, you bag 'em we tag 'em."

"Living with Chris has really rubbed off on you, hasn't it," I said.

"Hey, speak of the devil. We were just talking about you. Hang on." She put me on hold. My guess was she was moving the phone console into the living room. Or maybe they were coming into the kitchen.

I could hear it was the kitchen when Carynne clicked on the line and the echo was kind of tinny. "Okay, gang's all here. Me, Court, Chris, and Bart's here, too, as it turns out."

"I heard you were coming over to hang out so I dropped by," Bart said. "Plus Chris has some new video game to show me."

"Okay," I said. "So what's the news? Please don't say you're quitting, Car', or I'll have a heart attack."

She sighed. "No, though I am taking on another management client. Female punk trio. But I'll tell you about them later. Right now, we've got bigger issues."

"Such as?"

"The lawyer chest-beating isn't going so well. We've gotten a couple of dire-sounding letters from their legal department, and the latest came with a bill from their accounting department."

"What!"

"Near as I can tell, it's for tour support that was not supposed to come out of us, but I don't know what deal Digger cut, exactly. The contract I've seen doesn't specify one way or the other, which might mean it was a Digger handshake special. Feinbaum is ripshit."

"About Digger not getting it in writing?"

"No, no, about them sending a bill. He's sure it's just a scare tactic, that they've got no leg to stand on to actually try to collect this money, but it's scary, all right."

"Okay, but what are they trying to scare us into doing?"

"I don't know that yet. I need answers out of Digger that I'm not getting, and I need for BNC to play a little more of their hand. And I need Feinbaum to take a chill pill. I'm not convinced this 'my dick's bigger than yours' game is actually going to work."

Christian spoke up. "No offense, C, but that's because you don't have one. So of course you think that."

"Yeah yeah. Anyway, Feinbaum keeps saying *don't panic*, but Digger's not returning my calls."

I couldn't say I was surprised by that, but I had very low expectations. "You want me to go over to his office?"

"Or ask Remo to ask him to fucking call me. Something."

"That's an idea. Reem's in town right now."

"Okay. That's a plan then." She blew out a long breath. "When are you coming home?"

I hesitated too long before answering. "I don't know. After Thanksgiving, maybe? Christmas?"

I imagined them all exchanging looks about me.

"Call me later," Carynne finally said, and hung up.

I drank the 7 Up and then sat there at the table thinking, *What the hell am I doing in LA, again?*

Then I called Remo and told him what Carynne had said. And told him that yes, we were coming for Thanksgiving. And then I got out the nail polish and coated my nails on my right hand. Best part about using clear nail polish, if you spill a little you really can't tell.

And then I sorted the laundry. It was going to be really difficult to take it to the laundromat with no car, though. So I looked up car rental places in the phone book and called around and found one that seemed like a decent weekly rate if I was willing to go to Santa Monica to pick it up. So I called Jonathan at work, he skipped out a little early, and yeah we were in terrible traffic for a while, but we made it there before they closed. We saw the sunset over the Pacific Ocean and walked up and down the beach, and I gave five dollars to a busker on the boardwalk who was playing and singing solo reggae on a guitar that only had five strings. By the water it wasn't as hot, and it cooled off as the sky darkened.

There was a nice bookstore, and Jonathan and I each bought a book, and we ended up eating in a Japanese restaurant a block from the beach. We sat in a high-sided wooden booth and I let him hold my hand, and it was such a nice evening I forgot to be angst-ridden about the relationship. I also did not tell him about the lawyer stuff, figuring that could wait. Why ruin a nice time?

By the way, if it isn't obvious, Santa Monica is pretty much the only part of Southern California I actually like.

We had a nice dinner. We resolved that we should come to Santa Monica for dinner and to hang out more often. We also resolved to go see some bands over the weekend. Everything seemed smooth for a little while.

Then we had to get into separate cars to drive home, and while listening to the radio on the way, my mood plummeted. It all sounded like crap. While stopped at a red light not far from the house, I realized that the fade and balance controls on the rental car stereo were all messed up, though, so maybe it was just that there was no bass. But that didn't change the fact that all the songs sounded like worthless pabulum to me right then.

I know I'm opinionated, but normally I don't hate *everything*. So maybe it wasn't the music. Maybe it was that the freeways of Los Angeles are a demonic tangle of soul-sucking concrete that leave you feeling like an alienated misanthrope.

I decided that maybe the best thing to do was sleep. We got ready for bed. Jonathan started reading the book he had bought, and I curled up next to him and tried to recapture the balanced, smooth feeling I'd had when we were walking along the beach. But when I closed my eyes I drifted into thinking about Ziggy.

Half asleep, my guard down, I imagined I'd traveled back in time, to a featureless room backstage where a worn-out couch sat, another stop on the tour, and yet it was still today, I'd just bought the nail polish and started thinking about practicing my finger style again. And pretty soon I was dreaming, and in the dream I was trying to work up the nerve to ask him if he'd paint my nails for me. I was trying and trying, but I never did.

Kiss Them for Me

I ended up having to go to that fundraiser after all. Here's how the conversation went down, when Carynne broke the news to me.

Her: Do you think there's anything in this business that is worth breaking down in tears over?
Me: What? Who's in tears?
Her: Some publicist whose life is going to end if you don't show up to Lacey's thing.
Me: Sounds like Lacey's contagious.
Her: Maybe you're right. But wait, I take it back.
Me: Take what back?
Her: This job wouldn't be worth doing if it wasn't worth blood, sweat, and tears. You know that, right? But honestly. She could have just asked instead of having hysterics. And if you're going to have hysterics, for Pete's sake, make sure you're in a job where it's worth it.
Me: Maybe she feels really strongly about the women's shelter.
Her: Oh, honey. I'm not even sure she knows what the event is.
Me: I can tell you're not impressed.
Her: How much you want to bet she's some poor kid Lacey's mother hired and is terrorizing. When I call her back to tell her you're doing it, I'll give her some career advice.
Me: I'm doing it?
Her: I'm a sucker for a woman in tears, what can I say.
Me: Am I going to need a suit for this?
Her: Hell no. Leather jacket, jeans, and sunglasses. Your appearance will be brief and consist mostly of photographs and autographs.
Me: Thank goodness. I think I'd skip the country before I'd give a speech.
Her: Don't joke about that.

Jonathan and I debated whether he should go with me or not. In the end we decided not. A limo picked me up to take me to the thing, which was silly, I thought, when I could have driven myself, and if the whole thing was a fundraiser, shouldn't they be spending the money on the charity and not on limos?

Maybe I don't know how it works. Maybe the limos were donated, too. I didn't ask.

My biggest fear about the whole thing, of course, was that Lacey and I were going to be trapped at a podium together with a million photographers and she was going to go off on me. I felt better when I arrived there and realized that actually her people had lined up a small slew of celebrity supporters. I also realized why the limo was necessary, which was that there was a pseudo-red carpet situation going on. As a hotel doorman opened the door for me, flashbulbs popped from behind velvet ropes. I was glad Jonathan wasn't with me, then.

A reporter snared me just before the revolving doors into the lobby. She towered over me, probably a former model herself, plus she was wearing heels. Her cameraman, I noticed, was my height. She had to hunch down to hold the microphone in front of my face and still be in the shot herself.

"I'm here with Daron from Moondog Three. So how did you get involved with today's festivities?"

I like to think I picked up a modicum of publicity savvy from Jonathan. So I knew not to say something like *after Lacey tried to beat me up, I got serious about battering as an issue.* Ha. "Oh, well, it's all thanks to Lacey Montaigne. I got to know her a bit through the drummer in my band, you know?" Tricky, I had to avoid saying whether they were still an item or not. "And when I heard about what happened with..." I hesitated a moment, trying to remember the name of the model whose boyfriend's gig I had taken.

The reporter was good. "Mandy Killington," she provided without blinking.

"...right, Mandy... I told Lacey right away I wanted to do something." I nearly said it was my idea, but that might have put too much spotlight on me, and I did not want that right now.

"Do you think we'll be seeing Lacey Montaigne today?"

The way she said it made me wonder if something had happened to her. What to say, what to say? Time to say something super bland and boring that they would never bother to air? Oh, I know, a little profanity and then something dull. "Shit, man, I have no idea what the schedule is here. I just go where they tell me."

She gave me a "you're cute but clueless" smile and stepped back, pouncing on the next person before I was even through the revolving doors.

I never got her name or what cable network she was from.

As it turned out, the schedule I didn't know much about included a cocktail meet-and-greet. Silly me, I would have thought that who we were supposed to be meeting would have been some of the women who were helped by this charity, but no, duh, Daron, it was for the biggest money donors. Okay, I guess that made some sense. That meant they were mostly well-dressed men with Rolexes, mostly interested in talking to the fashion models who were at least half of the "celebrity" population at the event. I latched onto the one person I recognized, an owner of one of the studios where I'd been working, a guy I knew also managed talent, figuring he was there shepherding one of his clients.

No, actually, he was a donor. Hollywood is confusing.

The meet-and-greet was fairly short, maybe forty-five minutes, and then they ushered us into a ballroom, where I found myself sitting at one of the head tables, on a dais, between two more statuesque peers of Lacey's, though at least they weren't quite so towering when we were sitting down. By the way, not all supermodels are super tall. As one of them explained to me, it was all about proportion: what the designers wanted was someone who looked really leggy with a slim waist and shoulders in comparison to how tall she was. So some of them were actually quite elfin up close.

The best part about being seated between two models was that I didn't have to do anything to hold up my end of the conversation. They kept the whole table entertained.

I was told by an organizer—identifiable by her clipboard—that I could leave after the main course. I felt weird about it, though. Wouldn't it look kind of dicky if I got up and left before dessert? Various speeches were made while the caterers were pouring coffee and serving mousse cake. It felt really rude to me to get up and leave during that, too.

Not that I paid attention to the speeches, either. In fact, I started writing a song on the back of the program.

Writing you a letter that I'll never send
Thinking the thoughts that I've never penned
Picking at a wound that'll never mend
Waking from a dream that'll never end

I had started it as a song about Ziggy, but as I thought about it, I realized it could apply to Jonathan, too.

That was when I decided I had to plan an exit strategy. There had to be a way to bring this relationship to an end that didn't leave us both in bloody tatters. I still wanted to be friends with him. Not because he was a well-placed writer in the music business, either. Because I still liked him, I still respected his talents and his qualities, and I didn't want to hurt him.

But it had to end. There had to be a way to disengage, even though he was clearly still really into me and being in a relationship with me. There had to be a way. There had to. I didn't know what it would be, but at least having convinced myself that I would think of something, I felt better.

Lacey never showed up to the shindig, by the way.

She Sells Sanctuary

I called Chris after the limo dropped me off at home. Jonathan had gone out to the coffee shop to write and wasn't back yet. I put some music on and lay down in the middle of the bed with the cordless phone to talk.

"How'd it go?" Chris asked.

"Boring, which is just fine with me. Exciting would have meant trouble—speaking of which, Lacey never deigned to make an appearance."

"I was wondering about that. She tried to call here like six times last night, I can tell from the hangups on the machine. But she never left a message, and when I tried to call her back, I got *her* machine. Man, I hope she's okay."

"Me too." And then the silence got kind of awkward as I tried to imagine what I would do after I broke up with Jonathan if he called me six times a night and didn't leave a message, and then didn't show up to things. It was kind of hard to imagine Jonathan acting like that, but it was easy to imagine how guilt-ridden I'd feel about it. So then I cleared my throat and said, "It's not your fault, you know. You can't make her act different or feel different."

"I know. I still wonder if there was more I could've done."

"You've got your own problems to worry about."

"Well, yeah, and maybe if I hadn't let myself get so messed up I could've helped her... except she's the one who got me back into drugs in the first place... and my therapist says don't play the blame game but there you go, I just played it to a draw."

"You'll find a winner next time."

"You think so?"

"You should've been there today. I sat between these two gorgeous women. You would've easily gone home with both of their numbers. Me, I was pretending I wasn't there."

"With my luck, Lacey would've shown up at just the wrong moment and had a cat-fight with one or both of them." He chuckled, then sobered suddenly. "No one's heard from her?"

"No. Have you tried calling her again?"

"No, I've been afraid to. If I make it seem like I'm pursuing her, it'll just get complicated again."

"Ah, I see."

"But I'm worried about her anyway."

"Because you still like her, even if you can't be in a relationship with her?"

"Pretty much. I mean, come on, we shared some meaningful times together, and I loved her until I realized what an insane, toxic influence she was. And also that either she didn't give an actual damn about me or she'd changed so much that she could pretend she didn't."

"Hmm." I could see that I was setting myself up for a painful time after breaking up with Jonathan if Chris still felt that way about someone who'd been as terrible to him as she had been. I lapsed into silence, trying again to come up with the perfect plan for separation.

"You could call her," Chris suggested.

"Lacey?" For a moment I had forgotten why Lacey was relevant.

"You could call to say *hey, sorry you didn't make it to the thing, I had a good time*, and at least find out if she's alive?"

"Oh. Since you can't."

"Yeah. I mean, would you do that? For me?"

"Of course. It's not like she can hit me through the phone."

"You're a true friend, Daron."

"Even though I punched you in the neck that one time?"

"Especially because of that."

"All right. I'll call her. If I get her voice mail, though, I'll leave a message and that's it."

"Yeah. If you call twice or leave two messages she'll know I put you up to it. One's fine. If that's all we can do, that's all we can do. I appreciate it."

"OK, I'll call you back and let you know what happens."

I had to get out of bed to look up Lacey's number, but sure enough, I had it, handwritten in my notebook.

It rang four times. I was about to hang up when someone picked up. "Hello?" said a tentative female voice, very low, into the phone.

"Lacey?" It didn't sound like her, but I wasn't sure. "It's Daron. I went to the fundraiser today. I figured I'd call and tell you about it, you know?"

"Lacey can't talk right now," the woman said, sounding furtive, and I wondered, *was this her mother?* She sounded too young. "She's kind of busy right now."

"Um, all right." *At least I know she's alive*, I thought. But then the tentative, suspicious way the woman was talking made me wonder. "When she didn't show up today I thought maybe she was sick. Were you there?"

"No. I... don't make those kind of public appearances anymore." She cleared her throat.

I knew who it was suddenly. "Mandy Killington?"

"Formerly. I don't need the stage name now that I'm out of a job. Daron Moondog?"

"Formerly," I said. "Ditto."

Her reserved caution broke suddenly, and she sounded real. "Wait, what? Really?"

"Uh, yeah. My record company apparently owns my name. So if I want to work, I need another one."

"That... sounds pretty messed up." Now that her guard was down, I could hear the "Valley" lilt in her voice.

"It is, which is why I've been doing gigs like the one Lacey read me the riot act over. I'm sorry about that, you know. It wasn't like I was trying to be empowering to your batterer or anything. I didn't even know."

"*Don't* waste your *breath* on that piece of *trash*," she said. "He's such a, you know, spiritually empty shell, which makes him an easy tool of the devil."

"Uh, yeah," I said, wondering how many more weird twists there were going to be in the conversation. "Um, so what name are you going by now?"

"I'm trying to come up with one, actually, that works the whole reluctant prophet thing I have going on. So instead of Jeremiah maybe I should be Jereh-MEE-ah, you know?"

"Are you a reluctant prophet?"

"Well, I'm not reluctant *anymore*."

"Um...?"

"Since I can't get work as a model now, I realized it was totally God's way of recruiting me to his army, to be the one to speak out against the... the... spiritual *emptiness* of our vapid, celebrity culture. Are you an empty vessel, Daron?"

"I don't think so."

"If your heart isn't full of love, full of God, the devil moves right in. Notice that?"

"Well—"

"Seriously. Think about it. You know a ton of people, I bet, right? Rockers and actors and models and millionaires! They have everything, right? Money and fame and stuff. So why are they addicted to drugs? What else could they possibly need? Love. *God's* love. That's what's missing. They try to fill that spiritual void with a high, and you know how that goes."

"I've tried to stay away from drugs, actually."

"They'll get you eventually, unless you accept Jesus Christ as your personal savior."

"Wait, does it have to be Jesus? What about Buddha or whoever?"

"Well, okay, it's possible that some other religions might be just our same God reaching out to people in other ways, and eventually one day we'll all be the same. I don't know. I'm going to stick with what I know, which is Jesus."

"Okay, that's fair, I guess. Um, so anyway, is Lacey doing okay?"

She heaved a dramatic sigh. "To tell you the truth, I'm here to minister to her, but I'm not doing such a hot job of it."

"No? I thought Lacey was into Jesus, too."

"Well, she is, but she's pretty deep in the devil's grip right now."

"Is that a euphemism for 'she's high'?"

"Um, I wish. She locked herself in the bathroom a while ago, threatening to kill herself."

"Jeezus, Mandy! How long ago? What if she hurt herself in there!"

"Hang on, hang on, you're the one who called on the frickin' phone! Here, I'll go check."

I heard a clatter as she put the phone down somewhere. I guess it wasn't cordless? I don't know. I hung there, paralyzed, sure that I was going to hear a scream or something. I waited a long time, I think. I'm not sure.

Then another clatter as she picked up the phone again. "Okay, she's out now. She was ransacking it to see if there was anything left. Apparently her mom took the sleeping pills with her to Tahoe. She didn't find a damn thing and now she's crying, but at least she's listening to me."

"But is she suicidal?"

"No, no, I think she was just being a drama queen earlier."

"You're sure?"

"I'm sure. I'm going to make a frozen pizza and put on a movie, and I'm sure she'll be fine. She's fine as long as someone's here."

"And you're going to stay with her?"

"Yeah. Yeah, ministering, like I said. What do you think, Jeremeah? Does it work? Too new-agey?"

"I think it makes you sound like a rap star."

"I'm worried if it sounds too weird people will think I'm just one of these woo-woo weirdos who thinks they see angels and really what they need is to get on Prozac or something, you know? I want to sound trustworthy."

"Then you ought to pick something that sounds more like a gospel singer or a country music star."

"Like Amy Grant! You're a genius. You're so right. You know, Christian rock is starting to get really big now. Okay, who were the female prophets? Miriam? Anna?"

"Can you use saint names, like the Pope does?"

"Probably. Well, I'm going to go read some Bible passages to Lacey while the pizza's in the oven. Maybe I'll come across something."

"Maybe a flash of inspiration will hit you."

"Of course. Duh. I'll feel the holy spirit when I come up with the right thing. Thanks, Daron. You've been a big help."

"Um, no problem. Tell Lacey I'm glad we did the fundraiser and I hope she feels better."

"I will. Bye now."

I was still lying there staring at the ceiling trying to figure out what that conversation had actually been about when Jonathan came in. "You all right?" he asked.

"Hang on, I have to tell Chris something. Listen in and you'll know why I'm in such a daze."

I dialed my home number. Chris picked it up right away.

"You must've talked to her if it took you this long to call back," he said.

"Close. Mandy Killington was there. She answered the phone and then went on about how now that she's quitting modeling she's becoming an evangelist. I got warned that if I don't accept Jesus Christ as my personal savior then drugs are going to get me, too."

"Well, my program says 'higher power' is okay. It doesn't have to be Jesus."

"That's what I thought, but anyway..." I had a sudden thought. Ziggy had gone to India. We kind of supposed it was a spiritual quest, but I hadn't really thought about it before, not in those terms. Ziggy had been borderline molested by a church choir director and talked about how his mother had shopped for churches. If Ziggy was looking to fill that gap with spirituality, I didn't see Jesus being his choice, either. "Anyway, she's trying to re-brand herself as a reluctant prophet, trying to pick a new stage name, and in the meantime Lacey tried to find any last scrap of drugs in the house, but apparently her mother took them all with her to Lake Tahoe or something. So now they're having frozen pizza and Bible readings."

"Wow."

"Yeah, my head is spinning a little."

"Well, thanks for checking in. I guess she's okay. I mean, she's still incredibly fucked up. But at least she's not OD'ing next to the pool or something."

"Yeah."

"Hey Daron. When are you coming home? We miss you around here, you know."

I met Jonathan's gaze. "I know. I've gotta go."

I tried to pretend I was saying it to J. It didn't work.

Put a Little Love in Your Heart

Another week went by. I was very, very good all week. You know what I mean. I didn't stay out too late. I got up in the morning to have some breakfast with J before he left. Well, okay, I got up to watch J have breakfast since I usually didn't feel like eating until I'd been awake for an hour, by which time he was gone. I made dinner twice.

The second time I did the thing with the table outside and a candle and a bottle of wine. In fact, I got two bottles, thinking that maybe if we had a good enough time we'd drink more and when our defenses were down I'd get the guts to tell him what I really felt.

And then I sat there at the table staring at the two bottles and thinking: *This is the worst idea ever. You're going to wait until his defenses are down to tell him? Stupid.*

Which started a downward spiral in my mind. *You wouldn't even be in this position if you were a better person to begin with. If you weren't so messed up, you'd probably be with Ziggy right now. Maybe if you'd gotten along better with him in the first place the album would have come out better and BNC would be happier.*

Wait, that's bullshit. Stop that right now.

It wasn't lost on me, though, that I was setting up a romantic, candlelight dinner so that I could break up with him. That was definitely messed up.

I was considering whether to take the table back inside when one of our upstairs neighbors cleared his throat at the gate from the driveway. The same one who gave me the basil last time.

"Oh, hey," I said, and went and opened it. "You need something?"

"Just my curiosity satisfied," he said with a slight smile. "Jonathan's a nice boy, isn't he?"

I didn't know what to say to that. "Um, I think so?"

"New Jersey, was it? Are both his parents alive?"

"Yeah. We're both from New Jersey, originally anyway. His parents just moved to Princeton. His father's some kind of engineer? Inventor? He's a Bell Labs guy."

"Oh? So interesting." His look sobered. "And they're the approving sort?"

It took me a second to figure out what he meant. "Oh, about Jonathan? Yeah. They're very approving. Of his writing. His, you know, lifestyle, everything."

"That's wonderful. That's so wonderful to hear. Smart people, I guess. Have you met them?"

"Not yet. Maybe at Christmas. We're so far from them here."

"That's nice. That's very nice. You know. So many of us here on the Left Coast, we came here to get away from judgmental parents and things. Well, and for jobs in the biz." He raised his eyebrows at me.

"Um, yeah. That would be me, I guess." I hedged. That wasn't quite true, and it showed. "I mean, really, the only reason I'm here is because he's here. He's really the one here for a gig. I'm just kind of in between."

He nodded like he agreed with that. He gestured at the table. "So what's on the menu for tonight?"

"Steak. With mashed potatoes and gravy."

"And for a vegetable?"

"Peas." Jonathan liked to pick up his peas using the mashed potatoes on his fork. I thought it was weird but cute.

"I thought maybe it was your anniversary or something last time," he said, giving me an inquisitive look.

"No, just... I wanted to do something nice. Thanks for the basil, again, by the way. That was really good."

"And now you want to do something nice again?"

"Shouldn't I? I mean, we're living in paradise here, shouldn't we act like it?" Okay, maybe my dislike of LA came through a little strong there in the form of unsuppressed sarcasm. But I actually meant it. "Back home they've already had frost."

He smiled. It was a kind of condescending-but-fond smile, like it was cute that I was trying so hard. "Well," he said. "It's good to appreciate what you have when you have it."

"Yeah. Yeah, it is."

He waved goodbye to me then and went upstairs, and I sat back down and thought for a bit. He was right. No breaking up tonight. We should just enjoy what we had for now. When the time was right, I'd know. Besides, Thanksgiving was imminent, and if I suddenly showed up without Jonathan, I'd have to spend the entire holiday explaining that we'd broken up. That would be even more excruciating than explaining that we were together.

Dinner that night went very nicely, I thought. I decided that the fact that I still found it cute rather than weird that he ate his peas that way was a sign that I wasn't totally done with him.

The one difference between this romantic dinner and the previous one was that for this one I didn't warn him to come home on time. So he was really pleasantly surprised when he saw it.

Surprised enough that it gave him a kind of rush, I guess, and so did the wine, and so he was the one who initiated sex that night, which surprised me.

And so there was a moment after we were done, lying side by side with the night air coming in through the cracked-open windows, when I thought, *Maybe that's what it takes. You both pour a lot into the relationship. I poured in a lot of effort this week and I got bonus sex.* Is that right, though? I mean, I see a way in which overall it should work, and yet there's a kind of cynical "transaction" mindset under it. Let me be clear: I did not make dinner so that J would put out. That was not on my mind at all.

But what if he thought it was? Then did he think he was giving in to my unspoken demands tonight? Or was it that he was just swept off his feet?

I decided that in the afterglow I would believe in that last one. Romance. Sometimes it works.

And sometimes it doesn't. I wasn't the only one lying there thinking too much. J said, "Was that okay?"

"What do you mean? That was fantastic."

"Just checking."

"Why? Do I seem less than satisfied?"

"No." He turned and kissed me on the cheek. "I think I just went down a whole gender-roles rabbit hole in my head, which is especially dumb considering we're both men."

"Because I cooked dinner and then you were on top?"

"Yeah."

"For what it's worth, J, I didn't cook because I was trying to coerce you into putting out."

"I know. I have trouble imagining you coercing anyone, D. There's some stupid stuff that's really ingrained though. I wouldn't want it to go unexamined—I mean, do we inherit certain patterns from our parents and then unconsciously recreate them? If we do, would becoming conscious of them be enough to stop us from recreating damaging inequities or behaviors?"

"Your parents are pretty happy, though, aren't they?"

"Well, yeah."

"So why wouldn't you want to emulate them? I mean, where it applies."

"I suppose. But your parents..."

"Yeah, not so much."

"Do you think that's why I'm so much more comfortable with us being domestic, Daron? Because I grew up in a happy domestic situation and you didn't?"

Well, that hit me like a ton of bricks. It felt like they fell out of the sky and crushed me into the bed right there. "I never thought of that." It came out half a whisper because my throat had tightened up. "I'm trying, J. I'm trying."

"You do better than try, Daron. You succeed."

I closed my eyes. Somehow that wasn't what I wanted to hear right then. Was that the real reason I wanted out of this relationship? Was it just that I, deep down, didn't believe that domestic relationships could ever work? And was I turning that into a self-fulfilling prophecy?

"Hey, it's okay..." He put his arm over me.

"Let's not talk about my parents."

"I'm sorry I brought it up."

"Not your fault. I've got to get over it. I know. Shitty childhood, so what? It's over." I buried my face in his shoulder, the familiar scent of his sweat comforting me. I shivered as a realization came over me: J was the first person who loved me who didn't want to hurt me.

Then I thought, that's ridiculous. What about Remo and Courtney? And Carynne? But there was something different about my parents and Ziggy and Jonathan, like they belonged in a different category.

He didn't want to hurt me. And I didn't want to hurt him. That seemed like it should be a better starting place for a relationship than some I'd had, anyway. But was that still as true at the end as it was at the beginning?

Don't Stop the Dance

On the Tuesday before Thanksgiving, the production company where Jonathan was working had a party. I didn't think of Jonathan's company as very large, but apparently they were part of a group of affiliated companies, and each one of those companies had various successful (and not-so-successful) shows and films to their credit, which meant that the party was large and had a lot of A-list and B-list types. I pictured it as if Charles River Records and all the other small record companies that BNC distributed got together to throw a party.

J and I went together. The party was being held at a big ballroom at a resorty hotel. The ballroom itself had two levels, with balconies to overlook the dance floor, and wide arched doors onto an outdoor patio where there was a swimming pool. They had a forty-piece big band playing live. It being a Hollywood party, though, only a few people were dancing, while the rest were schmoozing, most of them by the pool where the music was quietest.

We got somewhat dressed up. That is, Jonathan put on a tie and tails, and he put me in a tuxedo shirt. It was a little ridiculous that black jeans, boots, and a leather jacket dressed up so much just from a change of shirt. But so be it. I even conditioned and blow-dried my hair and put on a little eyeliner for the occasion.

First thing J introduced me to a guy who was in music production for the company, and we got talking about advances in carbon fiber instruments. The guy was apparently ecstatic to have someone to talk to who knew what he was talking about. Then one of the guys I knew from the recording studios in Van Nuys came over and I introduced them. And then that guy introduced me to someone else... I didn't even have to move. Caterers kept passing by with food on sticks and on trays, making us pause to take some and look around. And at some point a waiter came by with champagne in flutes on a tray, which was good since my first drink was long since empty.

Things went like that for I don't know how long. I heard the band take a break, and the music switched to a DJ. At the time, I was talking to a guy who introduced himself to me and I wasn't even sure who he was at first. Then I caught on to what he said. His name was David, and he was some kind of regional muckety-muck at Tower. He looked kind of like he could be cast as one of Jesus's apostles in a movie, a skinny dude with kind of wild black hair. He was in a tux but had no tie, his top button undone fashion-model style.

"You know I used to work at Tower, right?" I said.

"Oh yeah, it's, like, company lore now. Especially after that video. That was practically like a Tower promo piece."

"You mean 'Wonderland'?"

"Yeah. Well, there were those docu bits they put on MTV, too, but the video itself has those shots of you, the logo is everywhere."

"I hardly even noticed." That filming had happened so long ago I'd almost forgotten about it. When was that, April? "Hey, I just thought of something. Was that part of why Tower's sales were so strong on *1989* when every other chain was shit?"

His eyes widened in surprise. "Your other chain sales were shit?"

"Yeah, yeah, you wouldn't believe the load of bullshit they put on it, telling us there was too much genre confusion. Like no one knew where to shelve it, so buyers didn't know where to find it."

He frowned, got a canapé, and then looked back at me. "More like if they didn't know where to shelve it, maybe it never made it into the bins in some places at all, or more likely they didn't order sufficient quantity."

"True. That was what we were trying to say, that there was insufficient stock in the stores. It's frustrating. If we sell out a fifteen-thousand-seat arena in a city, don't you think the record stores in that city might take that as a sign, though?"

He spread his hands. "You'd think? I know we stocked it and sold it well everywhere you went. You do know what's happening here, don't you?"

"No, what?"

"It's the alternative revolution. The chains like Sam Goody? When you think Sam Goody, do you think alternative? Do you think rock and roll? No. You think Captain and Tenille."

"Okay, there's a name I haven't heard in a while."

"Okay, okay, these days you think Debbie Gibson and Cher. You don't think rock and roll. This is what no one in this entire industry seems to get. Alternative *is* rock and roll! Rock and roll is rebellion and what your parents are afraid of and what they should be telling you to turn down. Tower is the only chain that has an alternative rather than mainstream image. Sam Goody may as well be Sears, man."

"You make a lot of sense. Do I have your card?"

He handed me one and went on. "So that's what I'm saying. It makes no sense that the real rock these days, punk, goth, new wave, speed metal, industrial, the stuff that is actually rock music and not some overproduced prepackaged bullshit, why is that stuff struggling an uphill battle in radio play and in big labels and in sales?"

"Why?" I really wanted to know. "*Why?*"

"Because of The Man, Daron, of course!"

"Of course!" I may have had a little too much champagne. "Wait, who?"

"Not a man, *the* man. The system. The entrenched

companies don't like change. They don't want change. It's much better for them if everything stays the same and the artists that are at the top stay at the top. Obviously, right?"

"Right."

"Which means anything that actually challenges the status quo, they don't like. But the purpose of actual rock and roll is to piss off parents and challenge the status quo."

"You know, I think Ziggy said that in an interview on MuchMusic."

"I bet he did. Hey, how is he doing, anyway?"

"Uh, actually, we haven't heard from him since he got out of rehab and went to India."

"India, huh? Finding himself?"

"Yeah, I guess." I made a face. "Such a cliché, I know."

He laughed. "Don't worry. Some clichés you have to live with. Pick your battles with the status quo."

"I will, man. I will," I said while he patted me on the shoulder. "Hey, do you know Chernwick? He says stuff like that, too."

"I do. He here?"

"Haven't seen him, but I wouldn't be surprised. Probably wherever the blow is."

"True, true. He never does too much, but he always does some."

"Seems that way. Speaking of which..."

"Men's room's that way," he said, pointing toward the far end of the ballroom.

"Thanks." I shook his hand and made my way in that direction. Jonathan was nowhere in sight, but that wasn't a surprise. He had a ton of coworkers to talk to.

The bathrooms were huge, with a large lounge area outside the entrances that was full of schmoozing people, too.

I had just finished recycling a bunch of the champagne I'd drunk and was washing my hands when I heard a voice I'd know anywhere.

Digger.

And maybe it was that I had drunk too much or that champagne in particular makes me lose my head or that we were just talking about the stupid, stupid fact that the album didn't sell. Or maybe it was the fact that I had a lot of unprocessed aggression lately. But the sudden urge that seized me then was to turn around and belt him. I gripped the edge of the fancy sink basin instead, but I really wanted him to know, at that moment, what it was like to have someone you thought you knew knee you in the balls seemingly out of the blue.

Hey, that rhymes, someone you knew, out of the blue—I'd have to write it down for a song later.

Rage like that physically hurts. I mean, it's painful, like some kind of poison eating your veins from the inside. Or maybe I was gripping the edge of the sink way too hard.

I didn't even take in a word he was saying. Didn't matter, I guess, since it was schmoozing. Meaningless.

I forced myself to let go and turn around, still not sure what I was going to do or say, thinking that maybe I would try to walk out and pretend I hadn't seen him.

But when I turned around, he was right there, talking to a much bigger man whose face I didn't even see. I was too focused on Digger himself. My aggression bubble popped the second I took in how terrible he looked. His face was haggard and drawn, his skin waxy and yellow-green. It had been almost four months since I last saw him. Was that enough time for him to get hooked on smack and decline this much? I would have thought Digger would be a cocaine guy, not a heroin guy, but this looked more like heroin to me.

Then again, what did I know.

What I *didn't* know was what to do. I stood there frozen.

But Digger knew. He gave me a crooked smile and a wave, like *hey how you doin',* and then went on talking. I gave him the same wave back, like a time-delay mirror, and then pushed my way out.

I made it back to the pool and sat down at a table on the far fringe of the action, where I could look at everybody and wait for my head to stop spinning. A caterer tried to give me more champagne, and I asked if he could bring me some water. I was kind of amazed that he did.

I saw Chernwick's hat on the far side of the pool, but I didn't get up. I was talked out.

It was a party. I thought, *Hey, if Jonathan was a girl, the thing to do would be to dance, which would require no talking to anyone and would be fun.* But I didn't think it would go over so well for me to find him and drag him onto the dance floor. Can you imagine?

I felt very sorry for myself at that moment. It wasn't that I didn't deserve to be happy. It wasn't even that I felt like it would take all that much. But knowing that even some simple things were impossible in the world I lived in, that was pretty depressing.

Jonathan found me some time later, still sitting there. He pulled up a chair and flopped down tiredly. "You don't have to tell me now."

"I don't have to tell you what?"

"Why you're sitting here with a Do Not Approach sign over your head. Had enough? Want to go home?"

"God, yes."

"Here's the valet ticket for the car. I'll just say bye to one or two people and meet you out front."

"Perfect. Thank you." I took the ticket and squeezed his fingers a little.

I told him everything on the drive home. He drove while I talked. It took a lot less time to tell than it had taken to happen. I told him about the Tower guy, and about my sudden urge to do something violent to Digger in the men's room.

"What the hell is wrong with me?" I finally asked.

"I think that's a pretty normal reaction to encountering, especially without warning, someone you've got a lot of resentment and anger built up about," he said.

"Oh." It hadn't occurred to me that suddenly wanting to beat someone's face in could be considered normal. "And did I really have a Do Not Approach sign over me?"

"Well, you had some kind of 'aura of brooding rock star' going on, which was why no one but caterers would approach you."

"And here I thought it was that I was way out on the edge where no one wanted to go. Was that bad?"

"No, dear. A little rock star mystique never hurt anyone. But anyway, about your dad. Hooked on smack, you think?"

"What else could it be? It was shocking how sick he looked."

"Gray, though?"

"Green, I thought. But you know, the lights in there, I don't know. He definitely didn't look well."

"Call Sarah Rogue. Maybe she knows something."

"Maybe I can convince her now to leave him, too."

"Maybe." He stretched and yawned as he drove. "You want to grab something to eat? Or did you get enough?"

"I had more than enough. You don't realize how much you're eating when they keep handing it to you one bite at a time."

"I know. I think I ate enough of those coconut-crusted shrimp to last me a week. Home, then."

"Please."

The good thing about the company having a big holiday party on a weeknight was that they were closed the rest of the week. So we got in bed that night, put a Jean-Michel Jarre CD in, and Jonathan read a book while I fell asleep curled up next to him. And we goofed off the whole next day and had a good day doing nothing in a way that's hard to explain. Say what you will about what was wrong with our relationship, at the time I felt like having an angst-free day like that was worth the price of admission.

Running up that Hill

Thanksgiving came a few days later. Jonathan had insisted I double-check with Remo about whether we were supposed to bring something, and Remo told me to tell him that if he felt it was necessary not to walk into someone's home empty-handed for etiquette reasons that we could bring a bottle of wine. Which was what I had said in the first place but whatever. Jonathan went to a wine shop the day before Thanksgiving and was gone for two hours. I was glad I stayed home, because between hating traffic, hating crowds, and hating talking about things I don't understand, I don't think I would have enjoyed the trip. He seemed extremely happy about the wine he bought, though, which was a California wine, which was somehow symbolically important to Jonathan. So I guess it was worth the trip to him.

We had no traffic getting to Remo's, though, on the day of. What was more of a challenge was figuring out where to park. The driveway wasn't really designed to have cars in it. It was narrow and curvy until it got to the top, where it widened for the double garage. Three cars were already squeezed in there, plus one behind them, and another behind that in the middle of the curve. One car was already on the street, and we parked behind that. The problem was that the street itself was curvy and hilly and wasn't really made for parking on, either. But whatever. It wasn't like a ton of people were going to be driving past today.

We walked up the driveway and rang the front doorbell. I'd never been through the front door instead of the garage door, and that made it feel ridiculously like a formal occasion. I couldn't help but grin a little nervously as I rang the doorbell. Jonathan cradled the wine bottles in a paper sack.

Remo opened the door. "Happy Thanksgiving!" He gave each of us a big hug as we came in. "Turkey won't be done for a little while yet. Have a drink. Jonathan, have you met all these guys before?"

"No, not yet," he said.

"They're the easiest-going group in rock and roll, as Daron can attest. Come on."

We didn't get far. Two feet past the threshold, Martin grabbed me in a bear hug and wouldn't let go, mock-crying and pounding me on the back. "It's been forever!"

"No, merely years," I said.

"Years, how did it get to be *years*? We can't let that happen again. You have to come visit more often."

"Well, how about you? You could visit me once in a while, too."

"When neither of us is on the road," Martin pointed out, while steering me toward a table laden with appetizers and a cluster of bottles at one end. "Shit, I've really missed you. And double-shit, look how grown up you are! It's like... like..."

"Like I went off to college and came back?"

"I was going to say army, but yeah, same thing." He poured something into two glasses, handed one to me, and then made a toast. "To seeing each other more often."

"I'll drink to that." I took a cautious sip. It was bourbon.

"Okay, so I hear you've been tearing up the studio work around here lately."

"Who'd you hear that from? Besides Remo, I mean."

"Everybody. So are you liking LA?"

"Are you kidding? I hate it." I followed him out toward the pool.

"Yeah, well, everything here sucks but the weather."

"You call this weather?" I raised my open palm toward the sunny afternoon sky. "I can't even wrap my head around the fact it's Thanksgiving. The whole thing feels weirdly like a dress rehearsal. Like, it has to be fake. At the real Thanksgiving it should be cold."

We sat down on the diving board. "Yeah, well. Can't have everything. I haven't really settled here, either. I have a place here and a place in New York, and I'm only in either of them part of the time anyway. It's like having a vacation house in each place but no real house. Since we're on the road at least four months a year, anyway." He shrugged. "I figure when it's time to settle down, then I'll actually decide where to."

"How are you going to know when that is?"

"I figure I'll feel like it? I don't particularly feel like it." Martin's hair was sun-lightened, shaggy as usual, his curls bouncing when he jerked his head toward me. "But what about you? You've been here but you're still there?"

I knew what he meant. "I don't think I'm here for long. Getting a place here with Jonathan was kind of an accident."

"He treating you right?"

I blushed and snorted into my bourbon. "Yeah. He's really the nicest guy ever."

"Good. Remo likes him, so I figure he's okay. Not a lot of writers Remo will say that about, you know?"

I sucked down a bit more bourbon. "He's special. He's been good for me."

Martin gave me a look then, like I'd come too close to using the past tense or something. But then he slapped me on the arm, with one of those *I'm not going to pry* looks on his face, and changed the subject. "Hey, did you see Matthew's photography thing?"

"I did! I was there for the opening night."

"I missed that. Well, but you know that, obviously. I got to see it but I missed seeing him, and then we left the country."

"What did you think? Of the show, I mean."

He sucked on his whiskey for a moment. "Deep," he finally said. "That is some heavy shit going down in Matthew's community."

"Yeah." That was an understatement. "It was an eye-opener, all right."

"So how is he? I know Remo tried to talk him into coming to Japan, but I guess his partner took a turn for the worse."

"I hadn't heard that." I promised myself I'd call him soon. Maybe later today, even, on Remo's dime. "We met him. After the opening, we went out to dinner, me and Jonathan, and Matthew and..." I felt like a complete shithead for not remembering Matthew's partner's name.

Apparently Martin didn't remember it either, or he was humoring me. "Yeah? Like a double date?" he joked, teasing me like we were in junior high.

"Yes, exactly like that," I said, as if I was offended, which got him worried for a second that I was offended, but then I grinned to make it obvious I was teasing him back. "And I met Steve Lillywhite at the gallery, did I tell you that?"

"No, is he interested in working with you?"

"Who knows. I don't know what's happening next." I filled him in on the weirdness with BNC. Apparently Remo hadn't told the rest of them the whole deal with me firing Digger and Moondog Three being dead in the water.

"Wow, you really dumped the old son of a gun?" Martin insisted.

"I really did. And the weirdest thing happened to me the other day. I ran into him at a party, and I had this insane urge to hit him again. Like an urge so strong it gave me a cramp in my bicep."

"That doesn't sound too weird to me. Dar', maybe you're so close you can't see it—I mean, I don't mean to disrespect your relationship with your father or whatever, but..." He took a deep breath and looked me in the eye. "Your dad's a total dick."

"Why didn't you ever tell me this before?" I whined, half-joking.

"Had to wait until you could see it yourself. I mean, I wasn't going to get blamed for ruining your relationship with him, you know? And besides, I couldn't talk bad about him because he was Remo's best friend. For a while."

"For a while."

"They're still friends, far as I know, but seems to me they get along best when Remo doesn't see him very much. You know what I mean?"

I shrugged. "I'm not about to dictate who Remo can be friends with. I know they go back a long time. I just can't. I had to cut him off completely."

"It's a good thing you did." Martin nodded seriously. "A really good thing. Hey, so I saw you on TV the other day, some thing you went to surrounded by supermodels. Get me on the list for that next time, willya? I could use the help!"

"Are you sure? My drummer hasn't had such great luck with dating one." And off we went, talking about Lacey and the insanity of supermodels. And then we got onto another subject and another and another, and the next thing you know it was time to sit down to eat and Martin had monopolized me that entire time.

We really did need to see each other more often. I needed to remember that I had friends.

Don't Dream It's Over

I barely got introduced to the Mazel brothers' wives before we were shooed into our seats for dinner. Remo sat at the head of the table, with me next to him on the corner, Martin directly across from me, and of course Jonathan next to me.

Maybe I shouldn't say "of course." I could imagine plenty of families who would have split us up. Maybe that would have been to make sure we weren't holding hands under the table. Or maybe so we could each be grilled at opposite ends of the table about each other. Either way I would have been uncomfortable. I sat there thinking that fortunately, unlike my blood family, my chosen family didn't have a stake in making me uncomfortable.

The caterers put the turkey on the table so we could see it and then whisked it back to the kitchen counter to actually carve it up while they put out all the other dishes. It was about as traditional a Thanksgiving as you can imagine. Mashed potatoes, stuffing, gravy, cranberry sauce. Since it was all cooked by professionals, the gravy wasn't lumpy, the potatoes weren't too salty, the stuffing wasn't burned... in short, it was great.

Jonathan stood up to pour the wine and got to give a spiel about what kind it was. The caterers had decanted both bottles into a glass thing I had always thought was a vase. Everyone seemed to appreciate the spiel, which made Jonathan happy, which made me happy.

I wondered what it was like to be that quickly accepted by a group of new people. It wasn't only that this was an easygoing, accepting group. Jonathan was good at meeting people. I tried to figure out how he did it. Maybe I could pick up some pointers that would help me if I met his family in a month, you know?

The wine tasted good, too. I tried to keep the topics of conversation off of what was happening with the band and record company. That was kind of tricky: since music was the family business, as it were, it was a hard subject to avoid. But I got to talk about some of the bands I'd played with in the past several months, and people we knew in common, and I got to hear lots of road stories about Germany and England.

But you know how things go. You can't always watch every word you say, and this wasn't exactly a group where I felt like I had to be watching what I said. So somehow we got onto the subject of our last tour and the accident. The explosion, I mean. And everyone wanted to hear about it. "Ziggy and I were side by side, and the can was right at our feet, next to a wedge monitor. And... whoosh." I made a motion like I was splashing my face with water.

"Flames?" Martin pointed upward.

"Hot sparks, like sparkler sparks, but bigger. And when you get 'em in your eye, it's no fun."

Alex visibly shivered. "My worst nightmare, man. I don't even like to get too close to the lights."

Remo gestured for the decanter, which was empty, and passed it to a caterer who went to refill it with some other wine. "You got away lucky. Thank goodness it wasn't a bigger firework and the damage was minimal."

Martin leaned across the table. "Yeah, you can barely see the scars."

Jonathan looked closely. "I can't see them at all anymore, actually."

"Not in dim light, anyway." There was still an obviously discolored patch on the back of one hand, but I didn't even notice it anymore and figured it would fade with time.

"Well, what goes around comes around," Martin said. "Didn't Megaton break up?"

"Last I heard," Jonathan said.

I didn't even remember hearing that, but I nodded in a knowing way. So did Remo, who then had to defend himself from the good-natured ribbing of his band over a recent incident where he'd tripped over his own feet on stage.

"How's that ankle doing?"

"You know, the whole point of running wireless is no cords to trip over."

"Now you know why Jerry Garcia sits on a stool these days."

"Better trade in those cowboy boots for orthopedic shoes."

Et cetera.

Quite suddenly I yelled out, "Archie!"

Martin clapped his hand on his forehead. "Yes! I can't believe I didn't remember that."

Remo looked back and forth between us. "What are you...?"

"Hey," I said, now that I was thinking about it. "You want to call Matthew and say Happy Thanksgiving?"

"That's a great idea. What say we do that while we make some room for dessert." Remo stood up. "There'll be pumpkin pie, hot apple pie a la mode, and a chocolate pecan pie."

"*Now* you tell me," Martin said, gripping his stomach and groaning.

"You in a hurry?" Remo chided. "Let's take a break."

The Mazel brothers moved to the pool table while I followed Remo into the office to the phone. He dialed and then handed it to me. "You first. I'm going to check on the caterers."

"Okay." I sat down in the desk chair and listened to the phone ring. A machine picked up. "Hey, Matthew, it's Daron, calling from Remo's house to say Happy Thanksgiving. The whole gang's here in LA. If you're there, pick up; if you're not there, call back. We just finished dinner, and dessert won't be for a while, and I get the feel—"

"Daron?"

"Hey! Happy Thanksgiving."

"Happy Thanksgiving to you, too!" I could picture how his eyes crinkled when he smiled. "How's LA?"

"Smoggy, crowded, and drug-infested. How's New York?"

"Same as always. Tsk. And here I've been thinking you moved to paradise with your beau."

"Well, you know, fairy tales always end before you find out the castle needs a new moat."

"But you guys are doing all right?"

"Honestly?" I got up and closed the door. "Matthew, you're the only person I can imagine saying this to. I feel like an ungrateful son of a bitch. He loves me like crazy, but I can't wait to get out of here."

"Oh, that's not good. It must be really bad for you to come right out and tell me like that."

"Hey, Remo's been trying to teach me to be a straight shooter my whole life. By which I mean someone who speaks plainly and directly, of course."

"No kidding. Okay, so there's trouble in paradise." There was a whoosh of white noise as he must have sighed or forced out a breath. "You must really feel like you're drowning."

My throat tightened up as he said it. "Is it that hard to believe I'd tell you?"

"From how closed-mouthed you used to be? It's a miracle. But good for you. Let me see if I can throw you a lifeline, eh? You and Jonathan aren't getting along?"

I tried to figure out how to explain it. "It's not that. I feel like there's something wrong with me for even complaining, when I know so many people are alone or lonely or... you know. It's not that I don't appreciate how lonely I used to be. It's not that I don't like him, either! He's great. But I'm going crazy."

"Crazy how?"

"I like being with him. And yet somehow I can't be myself when we're together. And it's making me climb the walls. Is that insane?"

"It's not insane at all." He cleared his throat, and I wondered if maybe he was trying not to laugh. "And he is a really nice guy. I know why you feel he's a catch, Daron. But there are a lot of things to consider. When you're in a relationship, it changes who you are. The two of you together become something—"

I must've made a squeak of distress or something because he broke off and asked, "Are you all right?"

"You realize that changing who you are is the most terrifying idea there is? Oh my god, no wonder he can't finish writing this novel he's been working on. I'm changing him, too."

"Maybe he feels it's worth it to change who he is?" Matthew suggested.

"If that's true, then the mismatch between how he feels about me and how I feel about him is even worse than I thought. How do I tell him that it's been fun playing house and I like being together but I really never meant for us to become a couple?" I nearly choked on this next bit: "How do I tell him I'm not in love with him?"

Matthew was silent for a moment. "Daron, how long have you been living with him?"

"We haven't really been apart since we saw you in New York."

"That's almost half a year. You know, I think he knows you pretty well by now."

"Yeah, probably."

Matthew was silent again, leaving me trying to fill in the blanks.

Oh. "You're saying... he probably knows I'm not in love with him."

"I think you love him more than you give yourself credit for. But I know that there's a difference between loving him and being in love with him. If you wake up every day trying to figure out how to get out of the relationship—"

"If he knows that, then why keep going? Why not kick me out?"

"Well, why should he? Maybe he thinks you'll come around. And even if he doesn't, why should he be the one to do it? If you're the discontent one, it's your job to either end it or ask for what it takes to make you happy and give him a chance. The ball is in your court. If anything, the fact that you aren't serving it seems almost like proof that you might come around. If you're not asking for change and you're not asking to leave, he doesn't know what to do either."

"Yeah. Wow. I guess that makes sense." I let out a deep breath. "I'm afraid to ask for what I want."

"Because you might not get it?"

"No. I think because I'm afraid I might! And then I *really* won't be able to leave. If he does even more for me? Then I'd feel like a total heel for leaving him."

"Sounds like you think you'll feel like a heel no matter when you leave him."

"True."

"But think about what you said there. What if you actually got everything you wanted out of the relationship? Why would you leave?"

"That brings us back to the whole thing about the relationship changing me. I need to get away so I can... focus. Find that center that is totally missing right now. What do I want? I shouldn't be afraid to ask, but I feel pretty sure that what I want is not to be constantly having to... I don't know. It's hard enough to think about a career and who I am without having to put another person in the mix. Does that make sense? I'm trying so hard to make him happy, and I think he tries hard to make me happy, but I'm not making myself happy in the process."

"Sometimes trying hard to fix or maintain a relationship isn't enough. Sometimes even when you both want it to work, sometimes it's just not right. Maybe it's time to move on."

"Maybe. Maybe we should try moving back East, where I like it better and I won't feel like such a fish out of water, before I give up, though."

"Or maybe you should give it a break, and see how you both feel in six months."

"Hm. That'd be a really sneaky way of saying I want to break up without actually having to say it."

"It would?"

"Yeah. If I say I think we need a break? It's like I want the benefits of breaking up without the drawbacks."

Matthew laughed. "Maybe. I think it depends on how you say it, and on how he takes it."

"I'll think it over. I sure as hell am not telling him tonight. But enough about me, for fuck's sake, how are you? How's Archie?" Thank goodness I had remembered his name.

"Oh, Arch had a fall a couple of weeks ago that confined him to bed, and then to the apartment since he couldn't do stairs, but he's starting to get more mobile now. Honestly, his pride was the thing most seriously injured. Meanwhile, he started a new medical regime and it seems to be doing him some good."

"That's great. That's... I don't even know what else to say about it other than that's great."

"It's okay, Daron. I accept it. We're not going to have a long life together. But at least we might have a few more years, and those years might be well spent. That's a miracle unto itself at this point."

"I'm sor—"

"Don't say you're sorry. Don't feel sorry for me. It's okay to be happy at the good news. Truth is, no one knows how many years together you get. When my mom passed, she left me a chunk of money. We can be comfortable for a while, and now that he's back on his feet, Arch and I are going to see a little of the world while we can."

"You've already seen the world."

"C'mon, Daron. You know you can't see anything from the back of the tour bus."

"True. True." I sat there in silence for a minute then, out of things to say but not quite ready to say goodbye.

"If you've made up your mind to leave him, it's always better to do it sooner than later."

"But not on a holiday!" I was scandalized by the idea.

"Why not? Are you sure that isn't an excuse because deep down you want to give him one more chance? If you've made up your mind, why are you still together?"

"I guess... I want to be sure. And I keep thinking I'll come up with a way to separate that won't leave us both damaged and bleeding. I don't want to do that to him. He deserves better."

"Noble sentiment. But generally speaking, Daron, the longer it goes on, the more blood there will be."

"Okay. Point taken. Thanks for the advice. I didn't mean to dump on you on a holiday."

"You have a warped view of what happens on holidays," Matthew joked.

"Yeah, well, my family was warped."

"Did you say Reem wanted to talk to me, too?"

"Yeah." I opened the door and stuck my head out. "Except now I gotta find him."

The phone was cordless. I found Remo in the kitchen, conferring with a caterer. She was in a white shirt and a sage-colored apron, remarkably clean for someone who had been serving food. When he saw me, he came to take the phone.

"Okay, here he is. Bye now." I handed it over and then went to sit by Jonathan in the living room, where they were listening to music and drinking coffee. A caterer asked me if I wanted some and I didn't see any reason to say no, so I said yes to coffee, and yes to cream and sugar.

Then I slipped my hand into Jonathan's, hiding it between my thigh and his. I know I'd just convinced myself more than ever that I had to let him go, and yet I couldn't get the idea out of my head that we never know how much time we're given—for life or for a relationship.

Oh Daddy

The doorbell rang while I was on my second cup of coffee, which was after I had tried all the pies. The caterers had set up a big pitcher-Thermos sort of thing with the last of the coffee and had just left, so when it rang everyone assumed it was them coming back for something they forgot.

Remo opened the door and let out a forced-yet-surprised-sounding, "Well, hey!"

I could hear Digger's voice before I could see him. "It's Thanksgiving, you know? So I thought I'd drop by with this." He handed Remo a bottle of what was probably scotch. It was the kind of bottle that came in a fancy box, so I assumed it was expensive. "You got some kinda party going on here?" He failed to act surprised.

The stereo was still playing, but everyone had gone quiet as Digger stepped into the room and took his jacket off. For all my complaints about there being no weather here, it was actually starting to get a bit chilly that night.

Insert joke here about how cold it got in that room at that moment. Seriously. At first I thought it was just me, but no one said anything to him, no one else went over to shake his hand. Remo's place had this wide-open floor plan where the kitchen was more like an area off to the side of the living room, and instead of walls separating the kitchen, dining room, living room, and family room there were changes of level of one or two steps, most of it covered in white shag carpet. I was standing behind the island in the kitchen at that point, and everyone else was scattered across the space, everyone looking toward the door.

They all knew I'd fired him. They all knew I thought he'd sold me out. They also all knew that Remo had turned him down—more than once—to manage Nomad. I remembered Remo telling me, not that long ago, that one of the reasons he'd moved the band to LA was to leave Digger behind.

Most important for the silent treatment, though, was that they clearly all knew that Digger hadn't been invited tonight. Remo made appreciative noises about the scotch, apologized that dinner was done with, but said *hey, come in for a cup of coffee.* One of the wives made nice then, getting him a mug, and people started talking again while he and Remo sat down.

Fine. We could all pretend that there was no white elephant in the room. I started a game of pool with Martin, but I couldn't concentrate. Digger looked as bad as he had earlier in the week, dark circles under his eyes, his skin sallow.

I wondered for a second if Remo had dropped the hint to him that I'd be there and was going to try to play peacemaker between us. If so, I wondered if I would let him. But Reem sat on the couch talking with him, never looking my direction.

Digger gave me a couple of dagger-eye glances. Maybe he really was rude enough to drop in, in spite of the fact he must have known he wasn't invited on purpose.

Whatever. Martin and I finished—he beat me pretty quickly, actually—and then we set to making hot buttered rum in the kitchen, except there wasn't any rum, so we used bourbon instead. And maple syrup instead of sugar. I guess what we made then was pancake syrup with bourbon in it. It was delicious, even if I wasn't really relaxed anymore, with Digger there.

I went to the bathroom then, which was down the hall by the bedrooms, and Martin followed me.

"Hey," he said. "Thinking it might be time to tell Remo he's gotta choose between you and Digger."

"I would never tell him who to be friends with," I said, leaning against the door frame. "What kind of drama queen bullshit would that be? 'Him or me!' Can't picture myself saying that."

"No no, I mean it might be time for *me* to tell him he's got to choose. No wait, even better, time for me to tell him to kick that guy to the curb, regardless."

"Don't go rocking the boat on my account." I shrugged. "They go way back. You know that. Digger's his oldest friend."

"How'd they meet again?"

"In the army. Drafted at the same time, I guess? Neither of them ever talks about it, so I don't even know, really."

Martin shook his head resignedly. "Shitballs. They probably had some kind of indelible bonding experience during basic training or something."

"Probably." I then shoved him in a friendly and loving manner back toward the living room so I could shut the door to the bathroom and take a leak in peace.

Thus, I was not in the room when the shouting started.

Maybe it doesn't matter what Digger shouted, because he was drunk, and the rest of us were not exactly un-soused either. Maybe he would have spouted anything he thought would hurt regardless. Maybe he didn't mean any of it.

But maybe I was done making excuses for him. Here's a taste of what he was spewing:

"Listen to me, you goddamned piece of shit!" (Unclear whether he meant me or Remo at that point.) "You wouldn't have got anywhere without me! You'd still be playing fern bars on the Jersey Shore for fifty bucks a night!" (Amusingly enough, decent restaurant gigs down the Shore paid more than that, but whatever.)

"Don't you dare fucking blame me, you faggot, it's your own goddamned fault. Everything's your fault." (Okay, that one was definitely aimed at me.)

Remo apparently had some kind of mental three-strikes-you're-out going in his head, because the third time Digger used the word "faggot," he went ballistic.

"Don't you *dare* talk like that in my house," he roared. It was weird. He didn't yell, but he was loud enough to drown out Digger. I guess when you've got the lung power to fill up Giants Stadium, you can do that. "Don't you dare talk to my guest—*your son*—that way."

"*My* son? It's my fault, then? What a fucking joke." Digger was still sitting on the couch, a glass in his hand. "I did all I could to keep his mother from turning him into a girl like his sisters, but he was always a crybaby. I always knew he was going to end up taking it up the ass."

Remo was on his feet then. He was a bit drunk, too, as I might have mentioned. "Fuck you, you fucking fuck," he said, which seemed to me an excellent point to make. "You know who raised your kid to be who he is today? I did. We did. For chrissake, *Martin* over there, who was barely over being a kid himself, probably took better care of Daron than you ever did!"

Digger pointed at me then with the hand that held the glass. "Who put a fucking roof over your head, huh? Who fed you? Who—"

"Who bought him his first guitar? Oh yeah, I did." I had never heard Remo so angry before. "Who paid for his lessons? Oh yeah, the kid paid for them himself. Gee, who put the kid through school? Riiiight, he got himself a scholarship—"

"Fuck you, Mister Sarcastic, you don't know shit about raising kids. But you wouldn't, would you."

Remo's nostrils flared, and I thought he was going to belt Digger then. He sputtered. "You dare bring that up?"

"Don't get all high and mighty on me, Remo Fucking Cutler. You stuck around all those years just because you wanted to keep an eye on the kid? Yeah, right. I think it was Claire's ass you wanted to keep your eye on."

"You're out of your mind." Remo pointed to the door. "Get out. Get. The Fuck. Out."

Digger clucked his tongue while he leaned forward to set his glass on the coffee table. "Touchy, touchy! The truth hurts, don't it?"

"Out. Of. Your. Mind. OUT!" Remo bellowed and charged him. Digger scrambled over the back of the couch, skirted a big potted plant, and ran right into the pool table.

Kids, don't try to flee from friends you've enraged while drunk. Drinking and baiting only leads to accidents. Digger hit the pool table at top speed and fell to the carpet with a thump and lay there not moving.

I swear my first thought was: *If he's dead, I hope Remo has a good publicist.*

He wasn't dead. He was unconscious, and one of the wives checked his pulse and pupils and called an ambulance.

Remo seriously considered not going to the hospital. We discussed telling the EMTs that he was a party crasher. But as he sobered up, Remo decided that he'd better go. If nothing else, it would cut down the chances of Digger suing him later. Besides, someone had to bring back the news of what happened to him.

So Remo went to the hospital, the Mazel brothers and their wives went home, Martin crashed in the bed in the office, and Jonathan and I took the guest bed.

And Jonathan put his arms around me and said, "Wow." Which about summed it up. Oh, except for this: When Remo got back, we found out why Digger looked so terrible. Liver failure.

Couldn't've happened to a nicer guy.

Pretending

I was expecting a bout of insomnia, but I guess all the alcohol and turkey outdid the stress, and I passed out not long after J and I got in bed.

Jonathan, on the other hand, apparently lay awake thinking about everything he had seen and heard, and, Jonathan being Jonathan, made up stories to explain it. Which means when Remo came back at like four in the morning and we got up to groggily receive the news that Digger was alive but his liver wasn't in such great shape, Jonathan was basically bursting with theories.

Jonathan being Jonathan, though, he didn't really want to confront Remo with his theories. He inquired kind of casually, while Remo got a glass of milk to drink before he went to sleep. I'm not even sure why I was awake at that point. Martin slept through it all. I remember sitting on a stool at the end of the kitchen island, Jonathan on the stool next to me, while Remo leaned on the counter next to the fridge, drinking milk out of a high-ball tumbler.

"You're a good friend to go with him to the hospital like that," Jonathan said. "You and he go way back, I guess?"

"Yeah. Did Daron not tell you this story? We met in the army, drafted in the same year."

That was, literally, all I knew of the story. "Yeah," I said, like that contributed anything.

"When was that?" Jonathan asked. "Wasn't the draft discontinued in—wait, hang on, that was after Viet Nam..."

"It was '59. I was eighteen. Digger was older, but young enough to get conscripted, I guess." He shrugged. "There wasn't really a war on, then, so it was mostly us fucking around and making trouble. Not a lot to tell."

"In New Jersey? My dad did some stuff at Picatinny."

"Oh yeah? We trained at Fort Dix and then were stationed in West Orange. I was fresh out of high school, had never even been to the East Coast before, hadn't been living in Jersey more than a couple of months." He took a gulp of milk. "There were some real hard cases in our unit. It was a thing judges did in those days: if they wanted to give you a chance, they would give you a choice, the army or jail."

"Wait," I said suddenly, "was Digger actually drafted? Or was he a hard case?"

Remo chuckled. "Drafted. I was the hard case."

"What?" I was way too groggy to be having this conversation.

"Not as hard as you think," Remo said. "Just the kind of trouble an eighteen-year-old could get into in those days. A drunken fight over a girl. Well, to be honest, two drunken fights, which was enough for the powers that be to think I might be developing a problem."

"And the army was the solution?" Jonathan said, incredulous. "Did you drink less in the armed forces?"

"Hell no, but I guess they figured I could get my aggression out in a more constructive way. I was young and dumb."

And full of come, I heard in my head. That was an expression I'd heard before. *Young and dumb and full of come.*

"I think they figured you had a better shot at life if they sent you to the army instead of jail. At least you didn't have the ex-con label hanging over you the rest of your life." Remo drained the rest of the glass and then turned toward the sink. "It was a different time."

"I'll say," Jonathan said.

I yawned.

Remo rinsed the glass and then opened the dishwasher, then remembered it was full of clean dishes and shut it again. He put the glass in the sink. "Well, I'm beat. Don't expect me up early."

"Us neither," I said. Jonathan and I went back to bed.

That was when I got to hear all the theories.

"So if Remo was eighteen in 1959, that means he was born in like 1941."

Math wasn't really happening in my brain right then. I burrowed under the covers. "Uh huh."

"Is he the same age as your mother, then?"

"What?"

"You said Digger said he was helping her with her career when she was a budding starlet. How old was she then, sixteen? Eighteen?"

"I have no idea. Remember, Digger told me that when he was drunk off his ass, and he's a liar."

"Okay, but think about it. Did Digger already know Claire when he was drafted?"

"Jonathan." I may have actually whined.

"What?"

"Why are you asking me all these questions?"

He focused on me and rubbed my head and gave me a kiss. "Sorry. They're more speculations than questions. I'm not expecting you to have the answers."

"Oh. My head hurts."

"You should drink some water."

Before I could say anything, he had turned the light back on and retrieved me a glass of water. I had to sit up to drink it. While I was doing that, he finally laid out what he was thinking.

"So Remo was a naive kid from the Midwest who came to New Jersey. Why? Seeking his fortune? Girl trouble at home? Both? He gets there, gets into trouble, gets into the army, falls under Digger's wing. Digger, I imagine, is not all that interested in the army either, and he has other irons in the fire. He's already wooing your mom..."

"Bam, she gets pregnant, they get married and settle down."

"You ever wonder why Remo settled so close to your family, though?"

"No."

"Digger seemed to think it was because Remo was interested in your mother."

"That's just the kind of shit Digger says. Remo was not interested in my mother."

"Maybe not by the time you were old enough to notice. But maybe by then he had another reason to hang around?"

"What?"

"Daron, did you ever wonder if Remo's your real father?"

"Don't be ridiculous. Remo and my mother said maybe two words to each other my whole life."

"Which might be proof."

"No." I set the empty glass down on the side table.

"Think about it. Your parents would've been married like four or five years at that point, and—"

"No!" I pulled my knees up, making a tent with the blankets. "It doesn't add up, J. For one thing, Remo and I look nothing alike. Digger and I, on the other hand..."

"I didn't think there's that strong a resemblance."

"Same height, same shoe size, and neither of us can grow facial hair," I said. "Stop fantasizing."

"Did you ever wish Remo was your father?"

"No!"

"Really?"

"Really! Why the hell would I want my best friend to be my father?"

That shut him up suddenly. I hadn't expected that. I could see him gap-mouthed, like whatever he had been about to say had been completely derailed. Some major pillar of Jonathan's worldview had apparently crumbled.

"What?" I demanded. "What now?"

"You just... when... I don't..." He never did formulate whatever it was he was trying to say or ask.

"Can we sleep now, please?" I lay down and buried my head under my pillow.

"Daron, I'm sorry, but literally burying your head

isn't going to make this go away."

"Make what go away?" I had to unbury to talk and to keep from suffocating. "What, exactly, is it I'm ignoring? Your wild speculations about what my parents' generation was up to before I was born? Newsflash: I don't care. I don't want to know. If it would change the world for the better, great, but it won't, so who the fuck cares?"

"You really don't care?"

"Isn't that what I just said?"

"Yeah, but did you mean it?"

I don't know why that was the point where I went ballistic. Maybe my fuse had finally burned down, whether that night or that month—I don't know. I sat up and flung the pillow across the room, two-handed, like passing a basketball. It knocked some books off a shelf. "Don't you *ever* question if I mean what I say. You know what? It takes me a huge amount of effort sometimes to get any words to come out of my mouth at all! You had better fucking believe every single one. Or you know what? I may as well never say another word."

He tried to backpedal. "I... that wasn't what I meant by it. It's not that I don't believe *you*. It's just... it's so hard to believe that *anyone*—I mean, that's why I was checking."

"Get it through your head. You're not having a relationship with 'anyone.' You're having a relationship with *me*."

"I... well—"

I do wonder what he would have said if I'd let him get his feet under him. I do. But I didn't let him get a word in there, and I barreled ahead with, "I know. I'm not like the other guys. I've tried, Jonathan. I've tried. I've tried to do what you want and be what you want."

"Daron—"

"You want to know how it's made me feel? Do you?"

He got a word in edgewise. "I hope it's made you feel secure and stable. You really needed that, Daron."

"Did I?"

"You did." He scooched around so he was facing me cross-legged on the bed. He sounded quite reasonable. "You were never going to get comfortable with your sexuality if there was always a crisis around it. If there was ever going to be any hope of you calming down and accepting yourself, this was what it would take."

I, on the other hand, sounded quite angry. "So you know better."

"Daron, honestly, you're the one who constantly moans that you don't know how relationships work and that you suck at them."

Now I was the one who was gap-mouthed for a second, but only a second. The queue of things I hadn't said from this argument alone was starting to get longer than I could remember. "I'm pretty sure one of the things that makes relationships work is listening to each other."

"No kidding. We're great at listening to each other." He patted my leg.

I stared for a second. "We are?"

"Of course we are."

"Great. Tell me how I feel, then."

He blinked. That wasn't at all what he was expecting me to say, I guess. He took a stab at it. "You're hurt and angry because of all the baggage Digger dragged in, so you're sensitive, and I apologize, by the way, for aggravating you when you're sensitive with all the talk about your parents."

He tried. He really tried. I really appreciated that. But it didn't fix things. "J. I meant how I feel about our relationship."

He thought for a second but didn't say anything.

"Were you about to say 'secure and stable'?" I asked, so angry that it felt like steam must be coming out of my mouth. My face was that hot. "Because if you were, that was what *you* said. Gee, I wonder what I said about how I felt? You know, I don't think my partner actually let me say. I think my partner is great at picking out what I *should* feel. You're right. You *do* know better. I'm sure I'd be perfectly happy if I just felt the way you wanted me to all the time!"

I was shouting by the time I got to the end of that. I wasn't even thinking about how I might wake up Martin or Remo. For once I didn't give a fuck who else heard.

He took it, though. And I have to give him credit for not just shouting back at me some defensive bullshit. Oh, I saw the urge to resist well up, but I think I kind of took his legs out from under him, too. How could he be defensive in the face of the fact that he'd literally just glossed over me trying to tell him how I felt?

He knew it, too. His voice was quiet. "Daron. I'm sorry. Please tell me how you feel."

"I feel like you're not in a relationship with me. You're in a relationship with your fantasy image of what a relationship should be like. Maybe that's my fault because all I've done since we moved in together is try to live up to that, and it's *driving me fucking insane.*" My vision went white when I said those words, like I was being struck by lightning for speaking the truth. I blinked and ignored it and told some more: "I feel like a stray cat you trained to be a good pet. I feel like you could've had any cat from the pound, though. When I'm gone, you'll get another one and train him up the same way."

He frowned. "You need to get into therapy. You wouldn't feel that way if you didn't have such damaged self-esteem."

"Fuck you, Jonathan. That was the wrong answer." I got out of bed.

"Where are you going?"

"Another room. Somewhere where I'm not having this waste of an argument. For the record, you're right, I need therapy, but I don't think I need a therapist to tell me that when your boyfriend says *hey, you're not listening to me*, the right answer to when he finally tells you how he feels is not *hey, your feelings are invalid, here's why.*"

"That's not how I meant it!" He jumped out of bed. "No, really, Daron, I'm sorry. I'm sorry. I'm usually a better listener than that. It's late, I drank too much wine, we—"

"I don't need to know the excuses." I pulled on some clothes and got a blanket out of the closet. "It's just another example. You're not having the relationship with *me*. You're having it with your idea of what I should be like. That's why instead of talking to me about what I said, you told me what I should have felt."

To my utter shock, he kind of admitted I was right. "Daron. I can see the person you could be. The person you are underneath. I try to bring out the best in you."

"You see what you want to see," I said. I wrapped the blanket around my shoulders.

I went into the living room. He didn't follow. He was right about the excuses, actually. What a stupid time to try to talk about our relationship. Tired, stressed, sleepy, drunk, overwrought, and peopled out.

Of course, it was me who brought up our relationship. Wasn't it? So that just goes back to the whole I'm-stupid-at-relationships thing. At least I knew when it was better to stop fighting than to keep going and make an even bloodier mess. And at least Jonathan either agreed or at least knew me well enough to leave me alone.

I walked barefoot past the swimming pool. The concrete felt freezing cold but the carpet in the studio wasn't. I put the space heater on for a few minutes while I made the blanket into a nest in the corner behind the amp. I got the small pillow from the stool at the DX-7. Then I turned off the space heater since I didn't want anything happening like, oh, burning the place down while I was asleep. There was already more than enough tragedy to go around.

Reasons to Be Cheerful

If I were prone to cliché, I'd say the next day dawned gray and gloomy. But come on. It was another sunny, mid-sixties day exactly like the day before, like most of the days in November in Los Angeles, except for when it was even warmer.

I want to go home, I thought from my cocoon, staring at the high ceiling in the studio. When I thought of home, I thought of my room in Allston.

"Daron, you in here?" Remo.

"Yeah," I croaked. I climbed to my feet. "Sorry."

"What are you apologizing for? You're allowed to sleep there if you want." He was wearing sweatpants instead of jeans, a worn-out tour T-shirt, and shearling sheep slippers. "I just wanted to ask if you want some coffee. Or bacon and eggs."

"I won't need food again until Christmas, but coffee, yes, please," I said, balling up the blanket and taking it with me.

While we walked across to the main part of the house he said, "Jonathan said to tell you he's really, really sorry and he wanted to give you some space. So he went down the hill for breakfast."

"What?" Apparently my listening comprehension was at an all-time low.

"Why don't I tell you again after you've had coffee."

"Okay." I left the blanket on the couch and sat at the end of the counter. Two mugs and coffee fixins were already sitting there. Moments later Remo poured coffee into the mug closest to me from the glass pot. I added milk and sugar and drank some while mulling over last night's fight. Remo fixed his own coffee and then leaned against the counter by the sink.

"Where's Martin?" I asked.

"Went windsurfing with some girl. She came and got him this morning. He might be back tonight if you're hanging around." He watched me as he sipped his coffee. "So, Jonathan said he'll come back and get you later if you want, or he'll leave you be, if you want. He sounded... like he couldn't have more egg on his face if he fell into a three-egg omelet."

I swallowed. "Did you hear the fight we had last night?'

"No."

"Truthfully?"

"I heard you shout at one point but couldn't make out what you said, if that's what you mean."

"Ah. Okay." I put more sugar into my coffee. I think the sugar made me feel more awake than the caffeine. "It probably doesn't matter anyway. The gist of it was I was trying to tell him I felt like he didn't listen to me and ironically he managed to miss what I was saying, so that only illustrated the point, made me blow my top, and made us both realize that the middle of the night while hungover or drunk was the wrong time to try to actually communicate."

He nodded sagely. "Well, I'm happy for you to spend the weekend here if you want some time apart. It's my last chance to rest up before we leave for Japan."

I put my hands on my forehead. "What does it mean that I just thought 'I can't do that because Jonathan will be so sad if he's alone all weekend'?"

Remo got a loaf of bread out of the freezer and put two slices into the toaster. "It means you care."

"It means I'm trained to worry about what he's thinking and feeling at every turn, is what it means."

"Not to get all Doctor Joyce Brothers on you, but how about you think a little about what Daron's feeling?" He pulled a pack of bacon out of the freezer, too, and started a pan heating up.

"Daron's feeling like he hates LA and like he liked his boyfriend better when it was an affair and not a relationship."

Remo gave me a *been there, done that* nod. "Anything I can do?"

I took a gulp of coffee. "Yeah. Tell me what the hell all that was with Digger and you last night."

He looked a little startled. "I thought you didn't want to know!"

I jabbed him right back. "I thought you didn't hear the fight last night!"

"I didn't." He looked puzzled. "I seriously thought you didn't want to hear about me and your old man. I'll tell you anything you want to know, Daron. I will. But there's a lot of ancient history I'm not too fond of dredging up, either."

The toast popped. If I was curious if he was intending to give me one, he answered it by getting out two plates. Then I realized he'd made four pieces of toast anyway, two for each of us.

"Reem, if there's something you'd rather keep buried, then keep it buried. I'm the last person who wants to drag people's secrets out."

"I know. I just want you to know, though, that if you ever decide you want to know, I'll let you look at the skeletons in the closet."

"Thanks."

"Did I tell you last night he listed you as next of kin at the hospital?"

"He did?"

"In case he dies. I don't think he's going to die, though, the tough son of a gun."

We sat there listening to the bacon frying for a while. I mulled over my relationship with Jonathan. Could I really blame him for having a relationship with the fantasy-ideal me, when I was the one who tried to become that for him? Was it my fault for not asserting myself? Or did I need a partner who would dig a little deeper, who could coax me to express the stuff I was biting my tongue on? Or did I just need to stop biting my tongue?

I decided to try the speaking-my-mind thing on Remo, right that second. "Can I tell you what I really want?"

"Of course."

"I know it's unfair. To ask this. But I'm going to anyway."

"Ask." He flipped the bacon with tongs, separating the pieces that thawed loose.

"I know he's in the hospital, and that's a crappy time to abandon a friend, but honestly, Reem, I think it's time you cut Digger off."

"Oh, I'm right there with you. Did you think me throwing him out last night was just a stopgap measure?"

"I wasn't sure. I mean, you were both drunk. Some people would make excuses."

"I'm not big on excuses." He flipped some more bacon. "I wasn't even going to go to the hospital, remember? If he hadn't had something seriously wrong with him, I was thinking about pressing trespassing charges. I mean, if that wouldn't send a strong 'stay the fuck away' message, I'm not sure what would. But one of the EMTs said in the ambulance he looked like a liver case so I kept my mouth shut."

"Martin said last night you had to choose between Digger or me."

Remo looked me right in the eye. "He's right. And I'm choosing you. And before you get any crazy ideas, no, you're not my kid. Not biologically, anyway."

I'd be lying if I didn't say it felt good to hear that. All of it. "Good. Biology is overrated."

"Here." He put the bacon onto the toast. Apparently there were no eggs. He spread a little mayo onto the other two pieces of toast and voila, bacon sandwiches. He handed me one and then sat down on the stool next to me.

We sat side by side eating bacon sandwiches. And I felt happy about it. Yeah, worth noting. I felt happy about something.

I'll Be There for You

Jonathan called a little while later. I took it on the kitchen phone, and Remo made himself scarce.

"Hey," I said.

"Hey. I..." J cleared his throat. "I wanted to check in."

I kept it light. "Like to a hotel?"

He let out a little huff of breath, and I knew he was smiling, though he hadn't gotten all the way to a laugh. "You want to come get some lunch down here? I'm at the place down the hill."

"Why, so I won't yell at you like I did last night?" Well, so much for light.

He paused a moment. Then, "You're right. If you're ready to talk, let's not do it anywhere you might feel like you have to censor yourself."

"Sounds like you're ready to talk, anyway..."

"I am, but don't let that rush you, Daron." He started out sounding all reasonable and calm, like he always did. But the panic was starting to set in as he dug himself a hole: "You want to stay there tonight? Or for a couple of days? I'll head back to town. I'll come get you anytime you want. If you want. That is, assuming, you might want—"

"Jonathan. It's all right. Come get me tomorrow around dinnertime, okay?"

"O-okay."

Shit. It was breaking my heart to hear how panicky he sounded. "I'm not trying to hurt you, you know."

"I know. It's okay, Daron. This is good. Clear our heads."

"Yeah. Exactly. I promise we'll talk tomorrow."

"Okay. Call me at home later, though, if you decide you can't wait."

"Unlikely but noted."

I hung up and went to see where Remo was hiding and let him know it was okay to come out. He was changing a light fixture in the master bathroom.

"Do you think Eric Clapton puts up his own fixtures, or does he get an electrician?" I wondered aloud.

"Trying to get an electrician to come on a holiday weekend because it's the only time I'm home is a lot more trouble than doing it myself," he said. He was up on a stepladder with a screwdriver, fiddling with something. "I bought this fixture, what, a year ago?"

"You're asking me like I know."

"I figured I'll get it done before we hit the road. I've got a laundry list of dinky things I've been meaning to do."

"You want help?"

"Sure."

So I spent the afternoon helping Remo do stuff like change the weatherstripping on the front door. I'm not even sure why they have weatherstripping on doors in LA. Habit, maybe. We put up another shelf on the wall in the office, then did the same in the studio. I learned some things about walls I didn't know.

We also added something crucial to the studio equipment: beverage holders.

When we got tired, we ordered a pizza. Remo had rented a couple of movies for the weekend, so we had a stack to choose from. Martin came back from his windsurfing adventure to eat a little pizza and get his stuff and then off he went again to meet a girl. The same girl, I think, but I didn't ask. While he was there, though, and we were sitting around the coffee table with the pizza, I told him how we'd spent the afternoon.

Martin's response: "Remo never did learn to start acting like a millionaire."

"Nope, started too late," Remo said. "And since I want to stay a millionaire, I'm not big on wasting it on hookers and blow."

I tried to do the math in my head. "So, wait, you're forty-nine now?"

"No, but I will be on my next birthday. And you know what happens in three years?"

"You'll be fifty-two?"

He nodded. "And you'll be the age I was when you were born."

"Shit, that hardly seems real." It really didn't. In my mind, Remo was sort of perpetually in his mid- to late-thirties. Possibly in Remo's mind that was the case, too.

"We should do something special when you turn fifty," Martin said to Remo. "Have a party. Something."

Remo shrugged.

After Martin left and a movie was watched, we did what I think we'd both been kind of expecting to do but neither of us really wanted to be the one to bring up, I guess, which is play around in the studio. That we were hesitant at all was what was weird. I mean, since when was it a big deal to sit down and jam together? But I was sort of thinking maybe he saw the time off before going on the road as an actual vacation, and so he might not want to play, so I'd gotten all second-guessy and tentative about it. And he'd sensed I was tentative but thought I had some reason for it, so he didn't want to impose.

Which just goes to show that if two old friends who have no real communication issues can almost fail to do the thing they enjoy doing most together because of imaginary concerns... well, just imagine what happens to lovers around issues that are actually fraught with emotional danger.

We played for a couple of hours. He taught me one of their recent songs. I taught him a thing I'd started to work out but hadn't firmed up completely.

And after *that* my head finally felt clear enough to vent to him some more about the legal stuff and my name and my fears that my career was actually kind of over already and that it was just taking the rest of the world a while to catch up to that fact.

We were sitting in the studio, trying out the newly installed beverage holders. I finished my rant/worry-fest.

Remo waited until I was good and done. Then he said, "Your career'll never be over so long as I'm around."

Sometimes I'm thick. I mean really, really thick.

"I've said it before, but maybe it hasn't really sunk in, or maybe it was never the right time." He was sitting on a stool, had put his guitar down, and was leaning toward me, resting his arms on his knees and interlacing his fingers. "There is always, always, *always* an open invitation for you to join Nomad."

Talk about something that gave me a complicated mix of feelings. Most of them good. "I... Thanks. I didn't want to assume."

"And I didn't want to assume you want to. Or want you to feel pressured to. Roll your own, Daron. You decide. If you just want to tour, or just record but not tour, or just for a year, or just until this thing with BNC plays out... we're flexible. Well, up to a point. You know we're barbecue."

We laughed a little. He was referring to an interview I did once, where I said Moondog Three was a buffet and Nomad was barbecue. And I liked barbecue but didn't necessarily want to have it all the time. "I'll think about it."

"Good."

Come to think of it, it was the *Spin* interview I did with Jonathan. A million years ago.

"Now that we've got that clear, give me some relationship advice," I said.

"What kind of advice?"

"How do I leave him without breaking his heart?"

"Whew. That's a tough one." He stretched. "I find that if I'm on the road enough, they move on on their own. Because inevitably they meet someone while I'm gone, someone who meets their needs better, and so there it goes. Thing is, if they're fine with me being gone most of the time, and taking care of themselves, then there's no incentive for me to try to leave, either, if you see what I mean?"

"Unless you're not in love?"

"You're telling me you're not in love with Jonathan?"

"Not as in love with him as he is with me."

"Ah. You love him enough that you don't want to trample him on the way out the door. But you really want to make a break for the door."

"Yeah. And I'm sorry. I probably shouldn't have brought him here and introduced him to everyone and got everyone invested in a relationship of mine that I'm not even invested in."

Remo looked for a second like he was going to laugh, but he stopped himself. "You should stop apologizing. Don't feel like you need to stay with him on *our* account. Jeez. It's not like you got married and made us all send you gifts and start calling you a different name." Then he paused and said, "Check that. Even when someone gets married, their family's reaction to their divorce should not play a part in the decision whether to divorce. You've got to do what's best for you."

"All right. I'm still trying not to hurt him, though."

"I've stayed friends with a lot of exes. I think it helps to be honest about what you want, and if you both agree like mature adults that you can't give each other what each other wants, then moving on is the best thing for both of you. I try to date level-headed realists. It takes the passion down a notch but is made up for by longevity and the plus of staying friends."

He'd said something similar to me once before, but you know, sometimes I have to hear things more than once for them to sink in.

The thing is, there was a level-headed realist in my love life already. Named Jonathan.

Stop the merry-go-round. I want to get off.

Ashes to Ashes

When your lawyer calls on the Saturday of a holiday weekend, it's rarely a good thing.

I took the call sitting on the overstuffed leather couch in Remo's living room with the cordless phone tucked on my shoulder.

Carynne and Feinbaum were on the line together. I wasn't sure if they were in the same office on different extensions or if it was some kind of three-way call. I didn't ask. I had other things to worry about.

"I'll give it to you in total layman's terms," Feinbaum said. "Fortunately it's real simple. It boils down to BNC is not budging, not an inch, not on anything."

"Which means?"

"We're rapidly coming to the point where the only action left to take is to start lobbing lawsuits their way, and the problem with them being so aggressive is that they may try to pre-emptively file against us first."

"Which means?"

"Do not, under any circumstances, use your stage name. Don't even walk into a record store and introduce yourself. If you play a gig for some reason — I don't care what, coffee shop, opening act, whatever — do not have them put 'of Moondog Three' on the flyers. Don't even put it on a handwritten sign if you play on the sidewalk, you got that?"

"I got it, but it's okay because —"

"What name have you been working under?"

"My real one. That's what I was about to say. I've been using nothing but my real name for months."

"Okay. That should be okay. If they decide that 'Daron Marks' infringes on 'Daron Moondog,' just to be dickish, that's a case we can win. In fact, I'm pretty sure there's precedent. Good move." He cleared his throat. "They may send some nastygrams to some of the other record companies about it."

"Why?"

"To be dicks. Honestly, I know the biz is full of slimewads on one end and corporate incompetence at the other, but I've never had to deal with a more assholish bunch of people than I have for your case."

"I feel special."

"Don't take it personally. I can't imagine it actually has anything to do with you."

"Or our former manager?"

Carynne cut in. "You think Digger fucked us over somehow?"

"I wouldn't put it past him. Car', I haven't had a chance to catch you up on this weekend's news."

"Wait, what news?"

"Digger showed up here uninvited, got in a drunken fight with Remo, then collapsed from liver failure."

"What!"

"But let's not talk about that right now. Feinbaum, what do we do next?"

"Lay low. We still need to run the audit."

Carynne jumped in again. "We're going to wait until the end of January to do it, so we can get the full fiscal year's reports. I think it's fucking insane that Mills slapped us with the unrecoupable tag before the Christmas retail numbers. That's bad faith."

Feinbaum huffed. "But not actionable bad faith. You heard from your singer?"

"No. I take it that means you haven't either."

"Not a peep," Carynne confirmed.

Feinbaum: "Make sure he's not using his stage name either. He just went by 'Ziggy Moondog?'"

"Yeah, when he bothered to have a last name." Hell, I hadn't even known his real name until he signed his band contract with me.

"Ziggy's his real first name?"

"Far as I know."

"You better check with his manager, make sure the word gets passed—"

"That would be the asshole with the liver failure," Carynne explained. "Daron, I'll call you back later to get the gory details."

"Okay. I'm here until around dinnertime, then I'm heading back to West Hollywood, but I don't know if I'll be available by phone."

"Call you in a bit." She hung up.

Remo reappeared when I went to put the phone back in the charging cradle. "What's up?"

"You know it's bad when even your lawyer uses the terms *dick* and *asshole*."

"That bad, huh?"

"That bad." It was starting to sink in, for the first time since that day Mills had dropped the bomb, that Moondog Three might actually be dead in the water. I'd really felt that firing Digger had been a huge step in the right direction, but was it too late? And I'd really felt that Feinbaum going to bat for us was going to shake something loose. Now I wasn't so sure.

The feeling I had then was just plain awful. I can't even describe it. I felt ill, almost sick to my stomach, except it wasn't only my stomach, it was like an all-over ill that only intensified when I thought about people like Watt, who had worked so hard to get the band off the ground, and Carynne, who could have had a much better career with someone else if I hadn't dragged her along with us. I didn't want to cry. I wanted to... turn back time.

And that only deepened the feeling I'd been having, ever since arriving here from Mexico—no, ever since the last show in New York—that something had happened that night that sent us into the Twilight Zone. So many times I'd felt, with Jonathan, with LA, with gigs, with Lacey's drama, like it wasn't real. Like I was merely going through the motions of a rehearsal of some kind. Because I was waiting for my real life to start again.

Maybe it wasn't going to start again. Maybe Moondog Three had been the dream, and now I was awake and this was reality.

"You want to sit down?" Remo asked.

Apparently I had been standing by the phone for quite some time, staring into space like I was shell-shocked. "Um."

"Is there anything I can do?"

I looked at him. "You've already done everything I can imagine."

"Okay."

"Reem. What if I never get my band back?"

His face was grave, but his words were sensible. "Then you'll move on to the next thing."

"Like a so-called nomad," I said, too serious for a pun.

"Really, Daron, don't think it's all downhill from here. Moondog Three's only the beginning, not the peak."

"And if it isn't?"

"Then it isn't. Thank god you can work."

"True. True." I took a few deep breaths, trying to dispel the feeling I didn't know how to process. I looked at him again. "I need to go home."

"You want a ride? Or you want to call Jon—"

"I mean *home* home. To Allston and the guys." I counted Carynne among the "guys."

"Yeah, okay. That's too far for me to drive. But I'll drop you in West Hollywood. I think we should swing by the hospital, too."

"Why?"

"So you can find out the medical details on your old man."

"Seeing him's the last thing I want to do."

"So don't see him. Talk to the nurse, maybe a resident, at least."

"No. I'll call on the phone maybe, but I'm not showing up there. You know he only listed me as next of kin so I'd be in line to pay for the funeral if there was one, right?"

"Or the medical bills," Remo deadpanned. "Yeah, I know."

I picked up the phone. "What's the number of the hospital?"

He told me and I transferred around departments a bunch, almost got transferred to speaking to Digger himself at one point I think, but I finally got across that I was trying to get an update on his condition from an actual medical professional not from the patient, at which point they put me on hold.

And then Carynne came through on call waiting. I clicked over to her, told her I was on hold with the hospital and didn't have time to give her the rundown on Digger's hate-filled tirade at the moment, then went back in time to hear someone hanging up. Dammit. I went through the hospital phone tree again, this time got to the right person a bit more quickly, told them we got "cut off," and finally they put me through to a doctor of some kind. The kind of doctor who works on holiday weekends, I guess.

The conversation went something like this: "Mister Marks, it would appear that your father is a very lucky man."

"You mean lucky to be alive?"

"And lucky that he's being treated at an early stage in his liver damage. The cirrhosis is minimal for a man who drinks as heavily as it would appear he does, and if he never touches another drop, chances are high his liver will recover. Are you who we should speak to about getting him into a treatment program?"

I started to laugh. First Christian, then Ziggy, now it was Digger's turn to detox? Jeez. I sobered up to try to explain. "I'm actually estranged. If my father wants to get into a treatment program, he's on his own."

"Ah, understood."

"Let me make sure you have the phone number of his secretary, though, in LA."

After that, I called Carynne back but got her machine. I left her a message with the same gist the doctor had given me, and then I told Remo I would take that ride into town if he was still offering. We had lunch on the way to fortify me before my big talk with Jonathan, which I knew was coming.

At the apartment, I went inside braced to launch right in. But he wasn't there. I looked everywhere to make sure he wasn't doing what I might have done, i.e., hide in the shower. Or the closet. Yeah, that would be really literal-metaphorical, wouldn't it? He must have gone out shopping or walking or drinking.

I tried the thought on for size that maybe he was already out cruising for someone else, but it didn't fit. More likely he was in the coffee shop writing a journal entry about everything.

I searched the house again, this time to mentally catalog my stuff, in preparation for moving out. I didn't have a lot. I hadn't accumulated anything while I'd been living there and I hadn't brought much with me. Two guitars and some clothes.

I sat down and tried to figure out if it made sense to pack up and get out and just leave him an "I'm sorry" note.

It took some staring at the ceiling, but I eventually came to this conclusion: It made sense if my goal was to get the hell out. It made no sense if my goal was not to rip his heart to shreds on my way out the door.

Was how little I'd brought to the apartment a sign of how little I'd brought to the relationship?

I contemplated how different this was from my sudden exit from Providence. Was it? It was difficult to even compare. Living with Roger hadn't been anything like this. Well, except that it really did seem like I was barely camping out in both places. And the whole waiting and hoping for the other person who lived there to show some interest in sex because otherwise there wasn't any.

That was the point where I nearly started to cry and Jonathan wasn't even there. Was that really what the fuck was going on here? Was I re-living some kind of fucked up pattern I got programmed into back when I was too fucked up to know better? At a basic emotional level, I wasn't even thinking about it that sophisticatedly, though. I was just thinking: I'm doomed. It was as if it didn't matter whether I was with someone like Roger, who acted like he could barely stand me, or Jonathan, who loved me and wanted the best for me—the end result was the same: I was like the hungry orphan in Charles Dickens, except instead of an empty bowl I had my dick in my hand, begging for scraps.

Roger used me. I knew that by then. I wouldn't say he abused me, because I think it would be disrespectful to people who have been abused to compare Roger's push-me-pull-you shenanigans to that. I was never threatened with violence. I always felt like I could walk out if I had the balls. And that's what I did, without looking back. I assume he didn't even miss me and maybe even felt relieved to be rid of me.

I wondered what Roger was doing, then.

I wondered if Roger was even alive. Probably. He was so paranoid about sex that he sometimes put a glove on just to jerk me off. We never had penetrative sex.

Something clicked. Duh. I had known almost nothing about HIV when Roger and I had moved in together. Granted, most people knew almost nothing then. But gay men had been in the know. Somehow I'd made the assumption early on that Roger wouldn't fuck me because he didn't care enough about me. But maybe he was just paranoid...?

No, examined in the light of what I then knew about safe sex and Roger's habits, I decided it was still the case that Roger didn't care about me. I'd felt remarkably little guilt walking out on him, effectively firing him as lead singer and leaving him in need of a roommate who didn't mind living on a fold-out couch. There was no "relationship" there. By mutual denial of there being any such thing.

My palms were sweating from thinking about it. Four years ago. Four years ago, I would have punched you in the face if you'd said I was gay. Four years ago my idea of "good" sex was my roommate quelling my protests long enough to rub his dick against my spine until he came. See, this is why it wasn't abuse. I didn't lie there in the dark at night praying he wouldn't do that to me. I would pray *for* him to.

Was Ziggy Roger all over again? I admit—now—that I jerked Roger around musically. He was a good singer and had good presence, but he couldn't write to save his life. I guess there was a weird way in which I needed someone like him and he needed someone like me, both sexually and musically. But it was too dysfunctional to last. "It." There *was* no "it." It wasn't just that Roger didn't care about me. I didn't care about him, either.

Ziggy once accused me of caring about staying in the closet more than I cared about him. He didn't use those exact words, but thinking about it now, yeah, that's what he was saying.

Well, you know what, Zig? You know what I was afraid of? It's happened. Band dead, contract in dispute, persona non grata to the record company, career over. And you know and I know that "homophobia" doesn't actually explain low album sales, but that doesn't make it not the cause of all the destruction and ruination.

It's happened. It's happened. Does that mean I should have tried harder to stay hidden or that I should have said fuck it, it's going to happen anyway?

If it meant you stayed, if it meant I got to tell you that you were *more important to me than the closet, I would have thrown caution to the wind. Because hindsight is 20/20.*

These were the thoughts I was having while Jonathan was on his way home. So by the time he got there, I was tear-streaked and on my knees in the living room, with my face in the couch.

Breaking the Back of Love

Say what you will about Jonathan, one thing he was always good about was letting me preserve my stupid shreds of masculine dignity.

When he came in, my head was so far up my ass it took me a moment to even remember where I was and why. *Oh fuck.* I stood up quickly and wiped my face and said, all pretend-ignorant, "Oh hey."

"Hey," he said calmly, letting me get myself together while he took off his jacket and acted like everything was normal.

I'm terrible at acting normal. But it was important to me for some reason to try to regain some kind of footing. So I tried too hard. "How was your day?" Cringe.

He played along. "All right. I had a walk. Picked up the newspaper. Worked up a thirst. You want some juice?"

"Um, sure." I followed him to the kitchen, where he poured us each a half glass of orange juice because that was all we had left. Yeah, insert relationship metaphor right here. "Read anything interesting in the paper?" I was still trying too hard.

"The hard-line communist regime in Czechoslovakia fell yesterday," he said earnestly, and then drank his juice in one gulp.

I sipped mine but discovered I couldn't actually stomach it. "Ah. Wow."

He looked like he was going to say something, then stopped himself and put his glass in the sink. He swirled some water in it and then put it down with a quiet click of the glass against the thin metal.

"I'm ready to talk," I blurted out, before I could chicken out. "I mean, I know I don't seem like I'm ready, but, I guess what I'm trying to say is we better get it over with since really there's no such thing as a good time for it, you know?"

"I know. Should we sit down?"

"Good idea. Living room?"

"Sure."

I abandoned the juice on the kitchen counter. We went and sat somewhat stiffly side by side on the couch. I wasn't sure where to start. It was just as well, because Jonathan, on the other hand, had been rehearsing what he was going to say.

"This is all my fault," he said. Like many prerehearsed speeches, a bunch came out in a rush. "I'm sorry I've been so emotionally unavailable. I think if I weren't trying so hard all the time to convince myself that the writing-for-television thing is working out well, then maybe I'd have enough emotional energy to actual participate in this relationship. I've been living the ultimate 'fake it 'til you make it' scenario, and that's only supposed to be for careers and not for relationships and I'm sorry."

I stared for a second. None of that was what I was expecting him to say, so it took some extra time to process. "Uh. And here I thought I was the one who wasn't putting my heart into it."

He sighed. "Daron. I've known you've just been playing house to humor me for a while."

Those were my words: "playing house." But I'd never said them to Jonathan for fear of hurting his feelings. And now that he was saying them to me, they hurt *my* feelings. "You make it sound like I didn't even try to make it work."

He winced. "Did you?"

I closed my eyes for a second. "Is trying to figure out what you want all the time 'humoring you'? Because if it is, then yeah, that's all I've been doing."

"Wait, what?" For once it was Jonathan who seemed to feel that the conversation had taken a sudden left turn. "What do you mean *trying to figure out what I want all the time*?"

"I mean... *trying to figure out what you want all the time*. You want me home for dinner or you don't eat. Then you want me to figure out what we should eat for dinner. If I don't pick the right thing, you're unhappy. You want me to figure out when it's okay to ask for sex and when it isn't. We never have sex unless I ask, so it's up to me figure out when you want me to ask, because if I even *ask* at the wrong time we have a fight." I cleared my throat. "Just to name the two biggest examples."

His mouth hung open a little. "You make me sound like the world's biggest prima donna."

"No. No, that's not it at all. Jonathan, I've been in

relationships with two prima donnas, and you're not even close. What I'm saying is... in the spirit of genuinely trying to improve myself... is that humoring you? Is that me being a therapy case? Or is that what people who love each other are supposed to do?"

His breath caught, because I caught him by surprise again. "You've never said you love me."

Fuck. Somehow I had become the adult in this conversation and Jonathan had become the trembly-lipped five-year-old with no filters. "I know. I—I know. I... never felt the time was right for it."

"Then you never felt it strongly enough to mean it," he said, not at all like an accusation, just like a fact. A sad fact.

"I'm sorry." My voice was rough. "I'm... Listen. We were talking about not putting enough emotional energy into the relationship. Most of my emotional energy was used up on the road, and what I had left? Left the country a couple of months ago."

"I know," he whispered, looking defeated.

I wasn't sure if it was okay to hug him at that point. I mean, I'd just admitted I didn't love him and he'd admitted he knew it, in which case was I even allowed to try to comfort him or was that just plain wrong?

I pressed on. "So, is that what went wrong? Was I doing the right thing but it came out as humoring or pandering because I didn't love you enough?"

He shook his head. "I..." He shook his head again, trying to get his words together. "I had no idea you were shouldering so much."

"What do you mean, you had no idea?"

"I didn't even realize you were doing it."

"I was doing everything I could to make it all work smoothly and be as good to you as I could."

He put a hand over his eyes. "Including monogamy."

"You pretty much accused me of wanting to go out and get my dick sucked when you said no," I pointed out.

"I know. And that wasn't at all how I meant it. I was... Never mind how I was. I was out of my mind. If I had even half a brain, or any energy to deal with this, I would have realized what was going on much earlier. I wouldn't have been such a nutcase about sex, either." He gently pounded his fist against his thigh. "How did I end up the one holding out on sex? That doesn't even make sense. I'm usually the one who wants more."

"Maybe you really don't know how to handle someone with a higher libido than yours."

"Okay, say it's a learning experience." He gave a small nod, like he was determined to figure something, anything, out. "How often do you think the ideal is?"

"We had sex every day in Mexico," I pointed out.

"But that was a vacation. I mean long term."

"With work and stuff...?" I considered it seriously. "I'd still say once a day, mostly quickies or just hand jobs until the weekends, maybe, but... yeah. "

Jonathan bit his lip. "We've really gotten into a Saturday afternoon rut, haven't we."

"Yeah." I felt like the gears had shifted, like we forgot we were having a breakup conversation and slipped into talking about the relationship in the present tense again. "I didn't really want to make waves by asking for more, and I wasn't sure I was entitled to. Part of me says if we're only going to fuck on Saturdays, then I could just come over once a week without living with you. If the other six days of the week we're just housemates, fine, but... my other housemates don't insist I do laundry with them. And yeah, it's nice to eat together, but none of them nearly pass out from low blood sugar because they're waiting for me."

"Well, of course not. They're living separate lives. A relationship is exactly the opposite. It's that giving up of autonomy to be part of a pair."

"And that's what I did, J. That's exactly what I did."

"Yeah, you did." He looked a little terrified, then. "Can I tell you? How won—wond—" He paused to swallow hard. "I could not have made it through these last few months without you being here for me. Part of me... hoped you liked it better than you let on. Or that you would come to like it better. And even though I knew you were just going through the motions a lot of the time, it helped me. I love you being here with me. I love that you tried." His voice got stronger. "No, you weren't 'humoring' me. You're right. You were doing your best. You were doing great. It's like I said. It's my fault for being so drained."

"Okay, back up. So... you were only putting in a fraction of the necessary emotional energy, and I was only putting in a fraction..."

"It's a miracle we lasted this long?" Jonathan hazarded.

"Basically." I took a calming breath. "But if we've each only invested a little... then shouldn't it be easy to break up?"

"You'd think." He pressed his hands together. "I know you've been fantasizing about leaving. The fact that you haven't gives me hope that we can still work it out."

"Work what out?"

"The relationship. That maybe now that all our cards are out on the table we can still deal a winning hand."

"Are all our cards on the table?"

"Let me see if I'm missing anything. You're in love with Ziggy, your career's stalled, you need sex every day, and you love me enough to work really fucking hard to please me even if that's not enough to make you say it. Right so far?"

I nodded.

"And on my side of the table we've got this. I never in a million years dreamed you'd actually take me up on moving in with me, Daron. I didn't think I'd see you more than a quickie here or there in New York during the tour, and instead you ensconced me in your bed every night. I didn't expect to go to Mexico with you. At every turn you gave me more and more. Can you blame me for thinking we *had* more than we did? You not only moved in, you turned yourself into my artistic sounding board, my muse, my confidant. Whenever I doubted myself you got me back on track. And whenever I did need something—food, sex, a boost to my self-esteem—you were there. My self-esteem is completely shot to hell. That's made me into a person I don't know. But you seem to know me pretty well."

"We both need to get out of LA," I said.

"But—"

"No buts. Turn in your resignation, move to a student apartment in Providence, finish your fucking novel, and tell them where to send the fucking royalty checks."

"But—"

"Tell them you had to check into isolation rehab if you have to. Happens all the time. Get the hell out, Jonathan."

"My agent would kill me."

"Your agent will fix it. You want to know why you can't write the end of your fucking book? It's not because the TV people keep moving the goal posts. It's because you're in love with writing the book. You're addicted to writing the book. You're in love with *the idea* of writing the book, of being a novelist. But until you do it, you haven't done it, you see what I mean?"

I must have touched a nerve. His eyes were round and he was sitting up straight like he'd been shocked with an electrical cord. Then his defenses kicked in. "Why does every fight about our relationship end up about me and my writing?"

I may have shouted. "You just said it yourself! Your self-esteem is shot because of this fucking TV series, you're not yourself, and I'm trying to have a relationship with the real Jonathan, not this zombified shell. You started this by saying you were sorry you're not all here!"

"Ah. Right. Yeah." He put his hands over his face and scrubbed it, then let them drop. "So you think I should quit."

"Yes."

"Will you run off to Mexico, or to Providence, with me if I do?"

That was where I lost it and started to cry. He hugged me and I let him, even though the reason I was crying was the sudden feeling of helplessness that I was never going to break free.

"I'm sorry," he said. "I didn't mean it in a pressurey way."

"Just like you didn't pressure me into moving in with you."

"I didn't!" He let go of me, angry now.

"I know you didn't." That was the truth. He really did *not* pressure me into moving in with him. I could have said no, right? All he'd done was clearly and honestly expressed his desires. Maybe clarity and honesty had seemed like the best thing ever at the time. Clarity and honesty were easy to crave.

Right now, being clear and honest about what I wanted was the most painful thing. But the right thing. So I said, "I want to go home. I want to go back to Boston and lick my wounds and figure out what to do with my life."

"Without me."

"I can't figure it out if I'm with you," I said. "Maybe I'm explaining it badly. But it's like when I'm in the same room with you I can't even think clearly. Like I'm out of focus and not really there. The 'us' takes over my brain. Even when you're not in the room. It's like... I'm not me anymore. I'm half of Daron-and-Jonathan." I realized that was what Matthew was saying, too, that the couplehood takes over the individuals. I'd told him that the idea terrified me. What wasn't clear until this moment, though, was that it had already happened to me. "And I think it's happened to you, too. We're both wrapped up in being a twosome here. You said it. Lack of autonomy. But neither of us can reach our artistic goals while we're wrapped up in that."

He appeared to be giving serious thought to my idea. "But there are plenty of accomplished artistic couples..."

"I'm not saying it's impossible for some people. But it's impossible for us."

"You sound really sure about this."

"I am really sure about it."

"Which means if you're wrong, well, we still have to treat it like you're right, since anything you think about the relationship is the reality of the relationship."

"Wow, I understood what you said there." I cracked a smile. I couldn't help it. "But seriously, do you see what I mean?"

"I do, but I still have to do the Ivy League argument thing."

"Which is?"

"Play devil's advocate. I mean, I have to ask: is art more important than love? Than people?"

I know he didn't mean to offend me. But on some very deep level I was completely offended by the question. I edged away from him, and my voice came out very grave. "What were you put on Earth to do, Jonathan?"

"What do you mean?"

"I'll ask it another way. Were you put on Earth to write? Or to love me?"

"Real life doesn't happen in absolutes, Daron."

"It does. This is the world of the mind. Of art. Of ideas. So I get to define what's absolute and what isn't." I don't know why I was angry. I guess I didn't like my unshakable convictions being questioned. This was an absolute for me. "I was put on Earth to make music. I believe that. I believe that above and beyond and underneath everything else I believe. If I stop believing that, I stop believing I have a reason to live."

"You really don't seem like the type to play the suicide card, Daron."

"You better believe I'm not. Because I have a reason to exist. I'm not here to father children or heal the sick. My purpose in life is to make music. And I don't mean to sound ruthless about it, because that's not my intent, but if a relationship is stopping me from doing it..."

"But is our relationship stopping you? Do you have to be single to be a creator? Most creative people aren't."

"I don't know. Maybe it's me, and I can't have someone else in my brain. Or maybe it's this relationship in particular that ties me up. I don't know. But you have to hear me when I say I need to get away to clear my head."

He heard the criticism in "hear me." He knew I was calling him out about not listening to me the other night. Jonathan was a good guy, really. He really was. So he did his best to listen. "Okay. I... You're saying you need to get away."

"I'm saying I think we both need to get away from each other. Don't get me wrong, Jonathan. You were right about being good for me in a lot of ways. I still like you. I still have a lot of affection for you." And I was still attracted to him, though I didn't bring it up. If anything, all the honesty and intimacy of this conversation was making him even more attractive than usual. This wasn't a good time to express my desire, though. "I want the best for you, and I think you want the best for me, too. But speaking as your artistic confidant, this Hollywood gig is killing you. Get yourself into a fancy writers' colony if you need to, but go do it, don't just talk about wanting to. And let me go back to Boston and figure out my shit."

"You don't even know if Ziggy's alive or dead," he said—not in a cruel way, but yeah, I know.

"Moondog Three is probably done for good," I said softly, like I didn't want to admit it too loud or it would become true for sure. "I talked to Feinbaum this morning. We're on the verge of escalating to lawsuits all around or letting it all drop and walking away."

His face fell. "Oh, Daron, I'm so sorry."

"Don't be. We... did a lot better than six out of ten bands." I felt guilty that I sounded more heartbroken about the band than I did about him, but when you think about it, which relationship was more important to me? I'd been with the band a lot longer and had been through a lot more with them. Maybe it was appropriate that I sounded more broken up about it.

"Okay. But think about this. I'm not trying to talk you into anything. Just consider. If Moondog Three is really kaput, wouldn't it make more sense to be in Los Angeles? You've worked with dozens of bands here. You have a ton of contacts. Whatever you do next, strategy-wise..."

"Hmm."

"Looking at it from an industry standpoint, seriously, Daron, even if you move out of here, go back to Remo's, whatever... What I'm saying is, don't be biased against Los Angeles just because of you and me."

"It's a little hard to separate, but I'll try."

"Chernwick, Keith, the guys at Sound City, the list goes on. You have the contacts here. If you go back to Boston, do you fall off the map? Do you fall off the radar and disappear? That's what I'd be worried about."

"Yeah." He did have a point. "But you're not trying to talk me into staying?"

He looked down at his hands. His eyelashes always looked long and blond when he did that. "I... I wish I could talk you into staying until the first of January. The lease is up then, you know? I think you're right. I do need to get out. And the thing is... my part of the development should wrap by then. Hell, it should have wrapped already. I... I'll give notice. I'll tell them they have me until then, and then I'm going back to journalism."

"You mean you'll go back to journalism or that's what you'll tell them?"

"That's what I'll tell them. Who knows if I can get back in the door at *Spin* or if I have to start over." He sighed. "That's my wish, though. Stay with me, only a few more weeks, keep me sane, keep me going. I... I'm sorry it's been so hard. Maybe, though, maybe knowing what we know now, we could at least have a good last month together?"

God, he sounded so hopeful, so fragile, so optimistic, so vulnerable. That's how you sound when you lay your heart out there for someone else to see. A wish is like a soap bubble, beautiful, perfect, full of colorful swirls that could be anything—and ripe to be popped.

I couldn't do it. I couldn't say outright *no.* So I said this: "All right. But there's no way I'm going to meet your parents for Christmas."

My acquiescence took his breath away. His mouth was open but he couldn't breathe in or out, and tears glittered in the corners of his eyes. He was paralyzed with shock. The argument was over and he was stunned that he had won.

I took one of his nerveless hands in mine. My anger and angst had drained away and left me with the lust that had been burning since we'd started slinging the truth at each other. "So."

"So," he managed to echo.

"Is it okay for me to..." Oh shit. Panic welled up suddenly. I thought I'd figured this shit out.

"Is it okay for you to *what?*" He asked, gentle and concerned.

"To ask—" That was as much as I could get out. I could not say the words "for make-up sex."

"To ask... for what you want?" He prompted.

I nodded, but I couldn't do what he did and make a wish. I couldn't put myself out there to potentially be shot down so plainly. Not again.

His voice was an urgent whisper. "Daron. Please. Ask for what you want. *Please.*"

I fell back to one of my coping mechanisms. Ask for something close, not everything you hope for, just a little piece. That way you don't jinx it. Ask for something that might lead to what you hope for. I did that with Colin, I remembered, and it worked out okay. Perfectly, in fact.

"Can I kiss you?" I finally said.

That was it. I broke his heart with those words.

The look on his face said the knife went deep. He said, "Yes, of course," and he meant it, truly meant it, but I think in that moment he saw how it all might have been different, and how now it was too late to heal the wound that had left me afraid to even speak the words to ask for love from my lover.

They call it make-up sex, but it wasn't enough to make up for everything.

The Pretenders (Stop Your Sobbing)

The next day I felt better but worse. Better because I felt like I'd gotten a lot off my chest, worse because I felt like I'd been run over by a truck. They use that phrase "through the wringer" to mean emotionally, but physically I felt about the same, tender and stiff.

I had one of those hot showers where most of what I did was stand there with my hands against the tile, letting the hot water hit me in the head. The sound of the water wasn't "soothing" so much as numbing. It blotted everything out like static on the radio.

What the hell did you do, Daron? Did you really just agree to stay with him?

No, I broke up with him, just... later.

Do you really believe you're getting out by Christmas?

I have to believe that, or I'll go insane.

You're already insane if you're arguing with yourself like this.

Jonathan, for his part, seemed in a good, if subdued, mood. "It's Sunday," he said. "Let's brunch."

"When did that become a verb?" I asked.

"Probably in 1920s New York," he said, either missing or ignoring my sarcasm. "Come on. I'll drive."

He drove us to a place that I felt we could have walked to, but, you know, no one walks anywhere in L.A. (Well, except me.) We ordered our usual things, but now that I was thinking of myself as broken up with him, it seemed unusual that he liked his eggs runny.

I could not decide whether to feel normal or not. We acted normal, by which I mean we *acted* like we hadn't had an epic breakup the night before. But I still *felt* like we'd had an epic breakup. But maybe I *should* feel weird about sitting there like we were still together. Jonathan was his usual chatty self, reading me bits of the newspaper as we paged through a Sunday *Times* someone had left behind.

Then our upstairs neighbors walked past our table. One of them gave me a starkly obvious venomous glare.

More surprising to me was that the other one gave *Jonathan* a look of disapproval, and then they went on their way without saying anything.

Almost simultaneously, we both said, "What was that all about?"

"I thought Jerry liked you," Jonathan said.

"I thought they both liked you," I answered. "I'm betting they're disappointed you didn't toss me out yesterday."

Jonathan shook his head. "It can't be they're mad that we're moving out on the first. I haven't told anyone yet."

"Maybe our ceiling is thinner than we think."

"Oh, probably." He folded the paper, then his hands. "Well, I did tell Robert we were having some troubles."

"Oh, really." That was my neutral, unemotional "oh, really," not my accusing, warning-bells "oh, really."

"Jerry thinks you're sweet, if a little dumb—"

"What?"

"Which made me wonder when he's talked to you. I was under the impression you never talked to them."

"I guess Jerry's the one who gave me the basil."

"Basil?"

"That first time I did the candlelight dinner in the courtyard? Jerry got curious what I was doing with the furniture outside and he gave me the fresh basil for the tomato salad." I remembered that both times I'd set up a romantic, candlelit dinner, Jerry had come to chat. I also remembered that both times Jonathan and I had sex afterward. And both times we'd had a talk about how the reason I'd done it hadn't been to try to get him to put out. One time we had the talk first, then the sex, and one time the reverse. I wasn't sure what to make of it. It was a good thing we were breaking up so I wouldn't have to test the theory of what would happen if I set up a candlelight dinner and then we didn't have sex just to prove that I wasn't being manipulative or that Jonathan wasn't that easily manipulated...

My head hurt.

"He got all inquisitive the second time, too, and asked me a bunch of questions about your parents and stuff. He thinks I'm dumb?"

"No, not like that." Jonathan chuckled. "And who gives a fuck what they think? You're smart, Daron."

"Just not about relationships."

"No one is smart about relationships. It has to be learned." He squeezed my fingers and sipped his coffee. "Trial and error."

We did some record and book shopping on the way home and then had a quiet day at the apartment, reading and listening to things. Jonathan bought a box of Christmas cards at the bookstore and wrote a bunch of them out to his old editors to remind them he existed. He sorted out the magazines that had been piling up and got rid of the ones he didn't want. We had mac and cheese with tuna and peas in it for dinner. All in all, a very "normal" day.

Later, we sat on the couch listening to the Stone Roses album. I'd liked what I heard on the radio, and I liked the sound of the band overall, which was unique and interesting. But the album as a whole was kind of bland.

Sometime after I'd lost interest in the Stone Roses, Jonathan began coming on to me, tentatively, like he wasn't sure it was going to be okay.

I caught his hands and kissed him. "You sure?"

"Well, we are technically still on vacation," he joked lightly, "plus you did say you thought every day was reasonable."

"True. I meant it when I said I'm game whenever you are, J."

"Let's go to bed, then, before I chicken out for some reason."

So we had considerably gentler sex than we'd had the day before, with considerably less crying. I'm not sure it was any quieter than usual, though.

Afterward we lay there and I wondered about our upstairs neighbors again. "If they can hear us, though, how come we never hear them?"

"Maybe they neither fight nor have sex," Jonathan suggested. "I'm pretty sure they see us as the sitcom that moved in downstairs. The nerdy writer and his heavy-metal boyfriend."

"You're not nerdy."

"And you're not heavy metal. But they don't know that." He sighed, and I guessed he was thinking about how we had run into them earlier today.

"Good thing looks can't kill," I said.

"Yeah. Oh well. I guess they didn't like us as well as I thought. You're probably right. They think I should kick you out. How wrong they are. About everything."

"You could still kick me out if you decide it was a mistake to talk me into staying for another month."

"Not likely," he said, and squeezed me tighter.

"I guess I should book my flight back to Boston," I said. "I already told Carynne and Courtney that I'm coming back around the holidays, but that was it, haven't made any plans other than that." I left it unspoken that I hadn't firmed up the plans yet partly because I had been thinking I needed to be in New Jersey at Christmas.

That was what did it, you know, said the voice in my head. *The last straw. New Jersey at Christmas? You dodged a bullet.*

Telephone Operator

Monday was the day Remo was due to leave the country and Jonathan was due to leave the TV-writing business. I got up that morning to remind him/cheer him on.

Of course, I'm never at my most articulate in the morning. So rather than some eloquent encouraging speech, I said, over cereal and coffee, "Don't forget to quit."

"I won't."

"What are you going to say?"

"Still working on that. Don't worry. Words are what I'm good at."

We both chuckled about that. Then I said, "Call me if you need a pep talk."

"Seriously?"

"Yes."

He took a deep breath and accidentally breathed in some coffee or a Rice Krispy or something, and coughed, but when he stopped coughing he said, "When you say I have to quit, I know it in here," he patted his chest, "that it's true. But coming up with the explanation that makes sense to my head, and to other people's heads, is a lot harder."

"You need a reason?"

"Trying to cook up a justification, anyway, that's good enough to tell other people, even if I know the underlying reality is more complicated. I mean, I need to say something to them that doesn't just translate to

'I'm a selfish, fragile *artiste*. Woe is me.'"

"See, but that's the thing. Who cares if they think you're a selfish, fragile *artiste*? You have to do what you need to do to protect your..." I needed a name for that flame burning inside me. "Creative core." I knew beyond any shadow of a doubt: if that flame went out, it was curtains. I had to wonder if Ziggy's suicidal thoughts had anything to do with creative burnout. Probably not, because he was writing so much, but... In other words, for the millionth time since the summer I wondered what was up with Ziggy. That had been happening to me multiple times a day for months, so it wasn't anything new.

"I know. I just hate the thought of coming off that way."

"Have you talked to your agent?"

"She doesn't start taking calls until ten."

"J. She's in New York. It's three hours later there."

"Right! Wow. I'm that out of it, I can't remember basic facts. I'll call her as soon as I get to the office."

"Are you all right to drive?" I stood up, as if I were going to drive him in his own car.

"Yes. I'll be fine." He stood up. I gave him a hug. "You're my best friend right now, Daron."

"I know." And Jonathan was mine. Well, maybe I had Remo. But I was thinking that Remo had left the country on a flight at the crack of dawn. "We'll get through this, J. Seriously. If you need to call me, or need a drink, whatever, I'm not planning to go anywhere today."

He left. As soon as he was gone I started rearranging the apartment. Our stuff in the bedroom closet was all intermixed. I separated my stuff to the left, his to the right. I separated our CDs. I made a small pile of the books I'd collected, then decided it was probably better to let J have them. Assuming that looking at them or reading them wasn't going to make him so miserable with missing me that he couldn't stand it? Hm. Better to ask him if he wanted them. Better to put too much thought into it than too little.

I know the word "breakup" is supposed to be about the two of you breaking from each other and going your separate ways, but I felt like everything I touched that day, everything I thought about, could split into fragments of possibility. Even Remo going to Japan. I could imagine a future where I went with him. I could imagine one where I moved into his house again to babysit the place. I could even imagine a fragment where I went with him and Jonathan came along. A very slim fragment, that one. But if that was what I really wanted? I felt like I might be able to make it happen. Nothing was completely impossible. That is, nothing regarding *Jonathan* seemed out of my reach. Ziggy, on the other hand... Ziggy was in a different universe.

I wondered, for the millionth time, where the hell he was. Of course, the person who was most likely to have heard Ziggy's whereabouts was in the ICU right now with liver problems.

Let's put it this way: there was no way in hell I was calling Digger.

That did remind me to call Carynne, though. I picked up the cordless and dialed, cradling it on my shoulder while I poked through the kitchen cabinets to see if there was anything I wanted to keep. I was not going to miss this phone. I'd been on it way too much, and it felt like it was making a permanent dent in my shoulder. This is what happens when everyone you need to talk to is three thousand miles away.

"Carynne Handley's office," she said when she answered the phone.

"Is that so you can pretend you're not there?"

"Yes. How the hell are you?"

"You didn't call back."

"I heard from Remo that you were probably, um, busy. How'd it go?"

"Under the assumption that what Reem told you was only vaguely accurate, I broke up with Jonathan yesterday."

"He thought you might. And where are you now? Remo's?"

"No, I'm still here. I convinced him that not only should we break up, he should get the hell out of LA. So he's giving notice on the apartment and we'll be back on the East Coast by Christmas."

"Wait wait wait, but you broke up?"

"Yes. I didn't mean we'll be there *together.* I agreed to stay until he moves out next month. You know how people always say they want to let the other person down easy? I'm trying to actually do that."

"You think that's going to work?"

"I don't know, but my conscience wouldn't live with me jetting like a heel."

"But it'll live with you talking him out of a big money-writing gig? Daron, I—"

"He's not writing. He's in endless development meetings. This gig is killing him."

"Is it? Or is this your way of leaving scorched Earth behind?"

"It isn't. I swear. Carynne, honestly, I really think it's best, and half the reason this relationship didn't work."

"But if you're breaking up anyway, why shouldn't he keep the job, then?"

"This isn't just about the relationship." I realized I'd been staring into the cabinet without really seeing the contents for a couple of minutes. I closed it and leaned on the counter. "You know, he said it today. We're breaking up but I'm still his friend."

"I hear rumors about people who stay friends after they split up..." She sounded skeptical.

"Quit it. Point is, I'll be home for Christmas. Will you?"

"You bet. Want to have a party or something?"

"Sure. Hey, how's Courtney doing? I got email from her a couple of weeks ago but nothing since."

"She's fine. A little nervous, since she'll be hearing in like two weeks whether she's been accepted as a transfer student at Emerson."

"Wait, when did Courtney apply to Emerson?"

"Dumbass. We told you she was applying."

"You told me you were thinking about applying. You didn't say you actually did."

"Well, you know, if you were here, you'd be in the loop."

"Ouch. Okay, tell me seriously, was this entire thing with Jonathan a huge mistake? I feel like my entire life took a left turn down a rabbit hole and I can finally see the daylight again."

She was silent a moment. "I suppose if you get out of it with your heart in one piece, then no. What would you have been doing if you'd flown back with me to Boston from Cancun? You'd have been sitting around with your thumb up your butt, that's what. At least out there you worked. Hey, speaking of which, I hear through the grapevine that certain parties at BNC are pissed that the best song on Sarah Rogue's album is the one you wrote."

"Co-wrote," I corrected. "Speaking of which, you need to tell me if publishing rights on 'Candlelight' are going to bring in enough this year to pay for Court's tuition."

Silence—then I realized she was stifling a giggle. "You are so sweet. Yes, dear, it should. She applied for financial aid, too. But right now everything is covered for the coming year. Her school, your mortgage, I think we'll be okay. That is, assuming you don't pick up a coke habit and we don't blow a hundred thou' on a lawsuit against BNC."

"I can't see gambling that kind of money on a lawsuit, especially since Feinbaum doesn't think the chances are good."

"We'll see what the audit turns up, but I am inclined to agree with you."

"So there's no band right now. Essentially."

"Essentially."

"So what are you going to do, Car'?"

"Daron, the band may be dead in the water, but your assets still need managing, your solo career such as it is also needs a manager, and I only need one or two other aspiring bands to keep me busy. I'm really doing okay, and you still need me."

"Oh god yes, I wasn't saying you *should* leave. I was working up to saying please don't."

"Not going anywhere, honeybunches of oats."

"Okay, good."

"You want me to book your return flight?"

"Please."

"Then hang up so I can call a travel agent."

"Yeah, love you, too, Carynne."

"See you in a couple of weeks."

I hung up and then seriously considered calling Jonathan to see if he needed moral support. But I didn't want to seem like a nag or a control freak. So instead I went out and pruned the dead flowers off the vines growing on the wall of the courtyard. I did not see either of our upstairs neighbors.

When the phone rang I figured it was Carynne calling me back with the date of the flight, or maybe

Jonathan, so I was surprised to hear Remo's voice. "Daron?"

"Aren't you supposed to be on the way to Tokyo right now?"

"Flight's at midnight. I've got a couple of hours."

"All right. What can I do you for?"

"I wanted to call and see how you were doing."

"What, with my epic breakup?"

"Well, yeah."

"Almost there. I told him I'll play out the string and then we'll go our separate ways."

"How long is this 'string'?"

"A month. I'll be in Boston by Christmas."

"Ah."

"You sound disappointed." I wasn't sure I could take Remo criticizing my breakup strategy.

But that wasn't what he was disappointed about. "You remember Philip Constantiou?"

"Um, no?"

"The guys call him Flip? He remembers you. You talked to him at some party for an hour about Guitar Craft."

"Oh, him! I liked him, I just forgot his name. What about him?"

"Well, he was going to be my guitar tech on this trip."

"What do you mean *was*?" Cue the anticipatory violins sneaking up on the soundtrack.

"Broke his ankle this morning while loading the shipping container. He's still game to go on the trip, but... he's going to have the crutch under one arm while he carries a guitar with the other? He's a trooper, but still."

"So have another roadie do the mobile stuff. He can still do all the tuning and maintenance and restringing."

"Or I could hire someone else."

"*No.*"

"Whaddaya mean, no?"

"You're about to ask me if I'll go with you to take his place and tech for you."

"Well—"

"*No.* You rescued me once with this story, remember, Reem?"

"I'm not saying that you can't—"

"I said no. If you were desperate, you know I wouldn't leave you high and dry. But you don't really need me. So don't be doing this to try to gallop in on a white horse."

"You know..." He paused to get his gumption up. "I still feel guilty about leaving you behind in New Jersey."

Hearing somebody admit their guilt years after you've ceased to care... still feels pretty good. But I didn't need to rub his face in it. "When I was too young to come with you. I'm over that, Reem. You should be, too."

"All right. I don't have a lot of mother hen in me, you know, Daron, but what little I do seems to come out around you."

"Back into the shell, mother hen. I've got it under control."

"Roger that. I'll send you a postcard."

"Send it to Boston. That's where I'll be by the time it gets here. When's the first show?"

"End of the week. Rest of the band doesn't leave until Thursday. I'm going early to do some promo stuff at the Takamine headquarters."

In my mind the thick, warm sound of the Takamine guitar he had given me was associated with the foggy air in San Francisco. So different from the crystalline sound of the Ovation. "Have a good trip."

"I will. Have Carynne check on your dad once in a while, will you?" I guess he knew better than to ask me to do it myself.

"I will."

And then I thought I was done with the phone for a while, but then while I was sorting the laundry that had accumulated on the floor of the closet, it rang *again.*

Sarah Rogue. "Wow, Mills really hates you," she said, after the initial helloes.

"Does he? What did I ever do to him other than be hard to categorize?"

"He is so livid about that song. But everyone else there loves it. It's going to be the first single. It's amazing. You should hear the arrangement. It's brilliant."

"Did they let you play the piano?"

"We compromised. There is a piano track. But Gregg Rolie played it. Can't really complain too much about that."

Rolie is a legendary keyboard player. If you don't recognize his name, you might recognize the names of some of his former bands: Santana or Journey ring a bell? "Yeah, no, can't complain too much about that. When's the album come out?"

"Next year. Hey, are you going to be in New York for Christmas?"

"Not likely, but I haven't figured out exactly what I'm doing. Why?"

"I want you to come see the tree with me."

"What?"

"You know the big tree in Rockefeller Center?"

"Yeah?"

"You should come and see it. It'll be great."

"The big tree right near the BNC offices? Where they hate me?"

"Aww, busted. Come on. It'll be fun."

"Annoying your record company is not a formula for success, Sar'."

"Are you sure? Hey, have you heard the latest about Digger?"

"I was going to ask you that. Last I heard maybe he was getting out of the hospital today. Did you hear I cut him off completely?"

"Yeah, before."

"Remo cut him off, too. He showed up uninvited on Thanksgiving, got drunk, and spouted abusive bullshit at me. Remo threw him out, or was trying to, when he collapsed. And then we found out about the liver problems."

"Holy hell, you're kidding."

"I'm not. Called me the f-word—I mean, the other f-word—said my career tanking was my own fault, yadda yadda."

"Ugh. Well, my mother's finally getting with the program and thinking about firing him. But we're moving carefully, you know, making sure we do it the right way and don't get sued."

"Yeah, I know a little about trying to extricate yourself without leaving maximum damage to both parties." I was talking about Jonathan, of course.

"It'll happen after the album release. That way if he tries to fuck us over, you know."

"Smart. Yeah. Okay, but seriously, what the hell are you asking me about Rockefeller Center for?"

"Daron, honestly, if there's even the slightest chance Mills is right and your big problem is that people perceive you as queer, the best way to combat that is with a pretty girl on your arm at one of the most romantic spots in the world. Which just happens to be right outside their offices and also crawling with paparazzi, or at the very least we could arrange for it to be."

"Wait. You're saying to do this on purpose to generate publicity—*fake* publicity about us dating?"

"Yes."

"Okay, but let me be clear about something, because I don't want you getting the wrong idea." The last thing I wanted to happen the minute I got out of this accidental relationship with Jonathan was to fall right into another one. "I'm actually gay."

She laughed. "So am I, stupid!"

"Wait, what?" I wonder how many people, when I tell them I'm gay, feel like a sledgehammer hits them in the face? Because that's how I felt right then. "You're not joking?"

"Wow, are you that thick? I thought you knew."

"How would I know?"

"Does your gaydar not work with women? Some guys are like that."

"Holy shit, no, it does not work with me, and remember, I was raised under a rock."

"Well, also when you met me was when I'd just had my straight 'it girl' makeover. Maybe it was convincing."

"I'll say. Now that you tell me, I'm thinking about your previous album and... okay, yes, I can see it. So you thought I knew all along?"

"I was sure you did! I thought that's why we got along so well. And you seemed so understanding about so much."

"Well, in a general sense, yeah. You're one of the first people I can think of, actually, to know about me without me having to make a big speech about it." It only occurred to me right then that she was. "You seemed to know."

"Because first, you never made a pass at me, which was clue number one, and then, yeah, other stuff filled in the picture."

"Wait, you mean every guy you meet makes a pass at you or they're gay?"

"In the music business, yeah. No exceptions."

"Jeez. I wonder who else I've given myself away to

by dint of being a polite guy. But back to the topic. If we do this, it'll be to make us both look straight, is that what you're saying?"

"Yes. I'm not saying we make any kind of declaration. Just start the rumor going. It'll make Mills shut his face and it will drive your father up a wall, too. Don't tell me that's not tempting."

"It is, but I don't know, Sar'. I've got to think about it. I'm not big on being in the tabloids."

"That's fine. Think it over and let me know. I'd way rather it was you than I look for some jerk who will actually take it as an unwelcome opportunity."

"You don't know any other gay guys to ask?"

"Well, see the thing is, three reasons you're perfect. One, you're straight-acting, straight-looking enough to be believable, when a lot of other guys would be too obviously a ploy. Two, we just wrote this song together and the tabloids love the whole 'creative juices leads to love' storyline. Three, repeat previous comment about how it'll drive Mills crazy *and* who knows, maybe solve your publicity problem. Or at least remove that crutch from their argument."

"Okay, I'll think about it. Don't be too disappointed if I say no, though."

"I promise, no pressure. Take my New York number so you'll have it."

I was writing the number down when I heard the sound of Jonathan's car in the driveway. A glance at the clock showed it was only two in the afternoon. "Sarah, I've got to run. Talk to you later."

"Okay, *ciao*." She made a kissing sound.

I stuck the phone in the cradle and noticed the light was blinking, telling me the battery was low. I'd been on the phone all day.

Jonathan seemed to be having some trouble opening the front door. I pulled it open and he was standing there, carrying a cardboard box full of papers and knick-knacks and things, which was making it hard for him to get his key into the lock.

He looked a bit dazed. I still hadn't figured out why he was carrying the box.

"Did you quit?" I asked.

He shook his head.

It sank in, though, that the box was everything from his desk at the office. "Did they fire you?"

He set the box down, then sat down heavily on the couch, like his legs wouldn't hold him up anymore. I sat down next to him, waiting for him to tell me what was going on. I know I'm usually the one who's speechless; the least I could do was be patient.

"They called off the whole project," he said, so quietly that I barely heard him.

"Because you were pulling out?"

He shook his head. "Had nothing to do with me. I didn't even get to deliver my resignation speech. Apparently they were going to can us before the holiday party, but someone decided that was heartless. Isn't that funny? Heartless! So they decided to hold off until after Thanksgiving! But not Christmas, no, that was too much to ask for, I guess. Ha, heartless."

He started to laugh and put his arms around me. Then he started to cry.

Shattered Dreams

Once I thought about it, I realized that I heard things all the time about television series being cancelled. You hear more about the ones that are on the air and then get cut off. I was vaguely aware that there were those that never made it to air in the first place, but I had not given it much thought. It was just one of those things—like tornadoes or famine—that you hear about in the news but which seem distant and unlikely to hit you directly.

It had not occurred to me that it could happen to us, to Jonathan. I honestly had tried not to get sucked into the details of what all was going on, which had been fairly easy to do since Jonathan, for the most part, had been trying to hide how shitty it was to work as part of this development team in the first place. He hadn't been successful at hiding that part, of course, but I'd had no idea something like this was coming. And J? J was caught by surprise because of the "stealth" way they did it.

He had a good cry. The phone rang at one point

and he let the machine pick up. It was his agent. She sounded livid and mournful at the same time.

When he was done crying he felt better. I wasn't sure how to feel, other than because of my own situation with BNC, I could sympathize. We were still sitting on the couch, wrapped around each other. I was starting to hate that couch, though.

"I want to wash my face," he said. "But I don't want to get up."

"Wash your face later," I said. "Here. I'll lick it for you."

I licked him on the cheek and he laughed and tried to get away, and I got in another good lick on his ear before he managed to escape.

He was laughing again, and I felt triumphant, which was good. He took the opportunity to wash his face, then came back. "Ugh. Now I have to tell everyone that I'm a failure."

I was stretching while I had a chance, trying to touch my toes, and I snapped upright. "Whoa, waitasecond. You are not a failure."

"I know, I know, it's just an expression."

"No, seriously, you don't think them pulling the plug had anything to do with you, do you?"

He sighed. "I... really hope not."

A cold, creeping thought spread insidiously inside my brain and I shivered. What if this *was* the same exact thing for J as it had been for me? What if someone higher up didn't like gays? "You don't think it was a gay thing, do you?"

His laugh was bitter. "Daron, honestly. At least half the writers are gay, maybe more of the management."

"Oh. Really?" I tried to touch my toes again. In the months since I'd been off the road, I'd gotten out of shape.

"Really. Hollywood is full of gay power brokers. We run this town."

"Huh. I don't even know what to think about that."

"What do you mean?"

"I mean, if we run this town..." *Why is it such a shit-hole?* "Why is everyone still in the closet?"

"Well, you know, things are changing."

"Not fast enough," I said, pretty much without thinking.

Jonathan was standing on the step up from the living room to the "dining" area, his work shirt untucked but still buttoned, his hair damp around his face. He crossed his arms. "You know, everyone who is still in the closet is part of the problem."

Bam. Just like that, we were having a fight. "I'm part of the problem? Is that what you're saying?"

"Think about it. Every person who is in the closet encourages everyone else to stay there. To maintain the status quo—"

"You're saying I did this to myself?"

"No! I'm saying, though, that if you insist on keeping it secret, you prop up the very structure that oppresses you."

"So you are saying it's my fault. Mills put a bullet in my career because I'm gay, and you're telling me it's my fault?"

"This isn't about *you*, Daron!"

"The fuck it's not! You're the one who just gave me the hairy judgmental eyeball and used the word YOU."

And then we stared at each other for several long seconds, like two tomcats all puffed up and ready to start clawing.

Jonathan deflated first. "I'm sorry. That was totally uncalled for."

I deflated a little bit, from outright angry to merely frustrated. "You know, I just noticed how often you say those words. They're starting to not mean anything to me."

He looked puzzled. "What do you mean?"

"I mean, you say them like rote, which now that I know you makes them sound insincere. Like when guys belch and then say 'excuse me' to be so-called polite when actually that doesn't make it polite, does it?"

Jonathan did a double-take. "I think I missed something here."

"It's just this. I'm trying to tell you. I know you're probably genuinely apologetic. But when those exact words pop out so easily, you come off sounding fake. Like, do you actually believe that was uncalled for? Or was that just a phrase you learned to say to placate people?"

He blinked at me. "I never thought of it that way."

I felt a breath of relief. I'm not sure why. I guess

because not only was the fight, brief as it was, over, but it seemed like maybe I had made a valid point.

He was looking at the ceiling above my head. Or, well, he wasn't looking at anything. "Examined subtextually, that's really fascinating," he said. "The whole subtext of apology is... that what causes the need for apology is transgression against the status quo. So as long as the status quo is repaired, that is, if the transgressor conforms to the rules that were broken by stating the correct, proscribed words, then the needs of status quo are maintained. So a guy rudely burping but then muttering an insincere apology is still within the status quo, and therefore approved of. In that way, the entire form of social interaction is morally bankrupt and devoid of genuine semantic meaning."

"Spoken like a true Ivy leaguer," I said. "Does that mean you're actually sorry?"

"It does."

I went and kissed him to prove I believed him. "Can we go out and get ice cream now? I feel like we deserve ice cream after everything that's happened."

"You sure you don't want to go out for a stiff drink?"

I snorted. "Too conformist. Besides, I like my liver."

"Ice cream it is, then."

We drove to a place for ice cream. After that we got a little hungry for real food, so we drove around, and we went past one of the clubs where we had gone to shows a lot when we'd first moved there, and we ended up going to eat nearby so we could wait around to go in, and we saw some local bands, totally forgettable but adequately loud and entertaining for an excuse to be out of the house. It made me realize how long it had been since we'd gone out. Was that all about Jonathan trying to toe the line at the job he didn't have anymore? Or was that how it would have been anyway?

Hard to know.

It was past midnight when we got home, but I could see the living room light on in the apartment upstairs. I have no idea if that is partly what led to us having sex on the couch, which we had never done in that apartment. We'd always gotten in bed. Or the shower. Though it was a long time since we'd done that, either.

We left a fairly huge come stain on the couch, in fact. Maybe I hated it less after that.

Original Sin

The next day, Jonathan walked around the house on the cordless phone, telling his parents, talking to his agent, telling a college friend who worked in film but was in London for a movie shoot for the next two months, all while he wrapped his cups and plates in newspaper and stacked them in a box.

"Can I ask you a huge favor?" he said, when he was between phone calls.

"You can always ask. What is it?"

"Would you go to the grocery store and see if you can get more cardboard boxes from them? I'd go, but I'm waiting for a call back..."

"Of course." I kissed him on the cheek and headed out the door.

It was weird, I admit it, that part of me couldn't wait for the relationship to be over already, and yet part of me was enjoying it the most I ever had. Because I wasn't holding anything back now. Because now that I knew it was over, there didn't seem to be any reason to hold back.

Which brings up the question, of course: what was the reason I was holding back in the first place? Was it really that I was holding my breath waiting for Ziggy to waltz through the door? Or was it my own fear of commitment (or whatever Lacey called it)?

Or was it that deep down I simply was not committed to the relationship and so somewhere in the back of my mind I had my foot on the brakes all the time?

I brought this up to Jonathan after I got back from the store with a couple of sturdy fruit boxes. I haven't even told you half the relationship-processing talks we had because I can't even remember them as separate conversations now, they were coming so fast and thick in those final days. But we had gotten into this thing where, since we were breaking up, we each wanted to tell the other things that would be helpful in our next relationship. He asked me what I thought he could've done differently, and I asked him the same.

So I asked him what he thought of my theory.

By that point he was in the office rearranging the books by size and shape, but not yet putting them in boxes. He sat down in the chair in front of the computer. "You know, that's a good question. It's hard to say, Daron. I mean, on the one hand you say you were holding me at arm's length, and yet you wanted to have sex more often and you were bending over backwards to make sure everything was going smoothly."

"I was just trying to do it right."

"Oh, you dear thing." He hugged me. His chin hit me in the sternum since I was standing up and he was still in the chair. He looked up into my face. "You did as right as you could. I'm going to say something now, though, that I don't want you to take the wrong way."

"Okay."

"I think if, after you walk out that door, you're still holding your breath for Ziggy—?"

"Don't," I said. I didn't even know what he was going to say. I wasn't ready to hear it.

"It's okay," he said, changing tack. "Even without him hanging over you, it... it wasn't the right time for you and me."

I leaned down and kissed him. He was really a handsome fella, that Jonathan McCabe. I was already thinking of him as fondly in my past even though he was still in the room. And I know that's weird, but there was some way in which it was working for me. It took that breakup, maybe, that "learning experience," for me to really start to see the ways that affection and friendship and affinity and sexual attraction actually can fit together.

I had never realized how huge affection is. I'd never even realized *what* it is, really, before that. And yeah, Ziggy was still haunting me, because I would have one of these revelations about how I felt about Jonathan... and then a few seconds later some memory of something Ziggy said or did to me would roll through my head and give me goosebumps or make me feel like I had to sit down for a second. When Ziggy held my hand or touched my hair, maybe he wasn't trying to manipulate me or arouse me. Maybe he just *liked* me. What a concept.

I think, in my head, I was trying to break up with Ziggy, too. But it wasn't working. Not the least of which reasons was because he *wasn't there*.

I think Jonathan had hoped, when he first asked me to stick around for another month, that maybe a month with cleared air and cards on the table would lead to a renewed relationship. I'll tell you the truth: I wanted to keep an open mind. I wanted to be open to discovering the key to happiness, to staying together if sudden clarity showed that to be the way, but I was also open to using that grace period together as my last chance to learn a bunch of shit I still hadn't figured out.

So I wasn't falling in love with Jonathan all over again. Through all the talks, the sex, the feeling like we were "on vacation" again, I was giving myself a very full sort of closure with him. Great. But the byproduct of it was dredging up all the raw unprocessed emotions I had about Ziggy, which had been lying there under the surface ever since New York.

"Hey," Jonathan said, nothing more than a whisper of breath, but it brought me back to reality. He still had his arms around my back. We were still in the office.

"Oh, hey."

"You were a million miles away."

"Just thinking."

"About Nomad?"

"They're only ten thousand miles away," I said, one of my lame jokes. "Right? How big is the Pacific Ocean? Wait, they might not have even left yet. I've lost track."

"I'll admit I don't know the distance from here to Tokyo." Jonathan loosened his grip on me. "It's your turn to tell me something."

"What?"

"You haven't told me yet what I could have done differently."

I had come close to telling him once or twice, actually, about the one time I came close, *so close*, to falling for him. Not merely loving him, but falling *in* love with him. There was one moment. Do you remember it? I wouldn't blame you if you didn't, because it had only happened a few months before that and I got it wrong when I tried to remember when it was.

"I'm not sure there was anything you could've done differently," I said. "You remember the day I went to get Ziggy?" Yeah, that day where I nearly gave myself heat stroke and cried so much that I had to replenish water and minerals in Gatorade form at every exit?

"Of course I do," he said gently, like he knew how

painful it was for me to think about.

"And you were having a meltdown about your story, and afraid to talk to your agent—"

"Those weren't on the same day," he said with small frown.

I paused to think. "Are you sure?"

"I'm sure. You came home and I had been on the phone trying to figure out where he was."

"Right." I pressed the heel of one of my hands to my eye, like that could help me see into my memory. "When was your meltdown?"

"Admittedly, it was right before that."

"Ah, okay. I guess it's blurred in my head." I'd somehow mixed Jonathan's emotional crash with my own. "Anyway. You'd had this total collapse of your artistic confidence, and we were on the couch at Remo's talking, and it turned into sex, and I just... I just—" I started to hyperventilate instead of finish the sentence because I couldn't even figure out the words for what I was trying to say. I settled for: "I almost fell for you right then." I remembered the moment with great clarity, even if I had forgotten which day it had happened on. It was the absolute closest we had ever been... until the past few days, anyway.

"Why almost?" Jonathan whispered, like it was something we should be afraid to speak of aloud.

It took me a moment to connect the memory with the correct day. But once I did, the rest of it came rushing back, too. "We had a fight right after that. Don't you remember? The time you bit my head off because I was done with my project and you weren't?"

The look in his eyes was the most crushed I'd ever seen him as what I was saying sank in.

"The 'twenty-four-hour sex dispenser' comment," I said, to make sure he was thinking of the same thing.

He was. His eyes filled with tears. "I'm an idiot. Did I ever apologize for saying that?"

"Many times. But you never really stopped *acting* like you felt that way," I pointed out calmly. "Like you had to withhold sex because someone had to, and like you were drowning in your creative world while I excelled in mine and you couldn't really come to terms with it. It's been all downhill since that moment, J. And everything I've tried to do to make it up to you has failed."

He blinked hard, and it made the tears spill. "Wait, why would *you* be trying to make it up to *me*?"

"You want to know Lacey's theory?"

"Lacey knows about it?"

"No, she doesn't, but she spouted a lot of theories at me and when I couldn't escape from her I actually listened to some of them, and maybe one of them was even right."

He took a deep breath. "I'm listening."

"What happened that night? When you got irrational and blamed me for stuff that was really yours... Part of me stopped trusting you. The part of me that hid behind an amplifier without even thinking."

A glimmer of light came in his eyes like maybe he understood. Jonathan was always getting one step ahead of me.

"The same part of me that only knows two ways to handle an adult who's acting crazy and unpredictable."

"Oh, Daron." He knew what I was going to say.

That only obligated me to say it. "The traumatized kid part. The two ways are run away and hide, or just try to be the absolute best little boy I can be so there won't be any more trouble."

"Oh, shit, Daron." Now he was sobbing openly. "I'm so sorry."

"It's all right. It's all right. *I'm not hurt.*" I wiped the tears off his cheeks with my thumbs and looked down into his cradled face with my own, wide, dry eyes. "I wish I had figured out a little sooner what was going on, but I don't know if it would have made a difference."

He nodded. "I can't believe I was such a self-centered shit not to see it sooner. The fight we had at Remo's over Thanksgiving..." He trailed off.

Yeah, I'd ended up hiding in the same spot, hadn't I? I hadn't even made that connection. When I go into survival mode, apparently I don't even register what I do or why half the time.

"Listen to me," I said, as earnest and serious as I could be. "Enough with the self-pity. This is why I said you had to get out of that job. You have to get back to your real self, J. I bet it's not just me who probably can't stand to have a relationship with you when you're like this. You've been emotionally crippled by the whole thing."

"You're right." He let out a long breath. "And you *keep* being right about that. You want to know my big underlying fear? It's that writing a novel is the most self-indulgent thing a person can do. As if doing it makes me a complete waste of space on the Earth."

"You don't seriously believe that?" I asked with some alarm.

"No. Not at all. But I think a lot of people want writers to feel that way. Like we don't even deserve to live. While you're writing the novel... it's not like music, where you can stand on the street corner and play and people actually enjoy hearing it. This is... you go in a room by yourself, don't answer the phone, don't talk to your family, don't pay attention to your boyfriend's emotional trauma—"

"I told you, I'm fine now."

"—isolate yourself from all the voices of people in the world so you can listen to the voices in your head. I've been raised to believe that literary pursuits are acceptable, at least partly."

My turn to be one step ahead. "Is this why you're so hung up on writing The Great American Novel? Because if it doesn't win a Pulitzer, the naysayers might have been right? Or... your father might be right?"

He slumped. "Maybe."

"Is that how you give yourself writer's block, then? Trying to write for the critics instead of yourself?"

He nodded. "And I know it so well. The first thing every writing teacher tells you is you have to shut off the internal censor. But it's so hard!"

"Especially here. This is the most judgmental place in the country, Jonathan! People here will get on you for wearing the wrong brand of shoelaces, for fuck's sake! Even our gay neighbors judge us! And you've just spent, what, three months trapped in committees and meetings day after day trying to get approval from one another, from advertisers, from the networks, from the parent company, being judged at every fucking turn, for an idea that is going to fucking *die* if it doesn't please the one person it actually needs to, which is *you*."

"I know. I know. And thank god you were here to pull my head out of my ass."

"Well, I'll take the credit, but then again, they did can the project, so maybe you would've escaped without my help."

"Maybe. Or maybe I would have lost my sanity a while back, and by now I'd never write again."

"Jeezus, don't say that." The idea gave me chills. "Now, seriously, when are you getting back to work on the real thing, the novel thing?"

"Soon as I get back East," he said, starting to smile. "I'm going to do it the classic way. From my mother's basement like a real novelist!"

That set us both chuckling. Then he went on. "Well, or possibly from a coffee shop, which sounds at least a little more dignified. But I've been meaning to ask you something."

"What?"

"Two things actually. The first one is what else can I do to help your sanity, Daron, given that you've done so much for mine? And the second one is, what do you think about..." He hesitated, and I knew he was about to bring up something he thought was a land mine. "About clearing out of here tomorrow."

I was so surprised I think he took my shock for dismay, because he added quickly, "Or maybe after the weekend."

I overreacted a little, because that's how much I wanted him to *not* get the wrong idea. "Shit, no! Tomorrow's *great*. I thought it was *you* who really wanted me to hang on as long as possible."

He took one of my hands in his and kissed my calloused fingertips. "Letting go of you is very, very, very hard. And I cherish every moment with you. Even the ones where we're fighting."

"J—"

"But you've been right about everything. I don't want to put *you* behind me. But it's definitely time to put LA and this whole... *episode* behind me."

I hugged him so hard right then I think I actually pulled a muscle in his neck. He was way too polite to say anything about it, though. "I can totally go to Remo's."

"My mother said she'd fly standby to Las Vegas and I could pick her up there."

"Did you rent a truck?"

"They've got one down at the depot on Western Ave., but they're still trying to get the tow hitch for my car. Good chance they'll get it tomorrow, though."

"Okay, well, shit, we better get packing!" I kissed him hard, but quickly, and then broke away to start taping back together some of the boxes he had flattened but kept when he'd moved in.

After we'd packed the whole office together except for the computer itself, we had moved to the bedroom and were filling our suitcases and I said, "There's only one regret I have to this plan."

"What's that?"

"We're going to be packing all night. I would kind of like our last night together to be memorable."

He laughed. "I'll make it as memorable as you want, Daron. If it takes a little longer to pack, that's all right."

"All right." I was grinning like a fool and I didn't even mind.

A little while later I took a break and tried to call Remo, to be sure it was okay if I went to his house. For one thing, a) I didn't want to surprise the pool cleaners or anything like that, and b) for all I knew it was possible he had someone else crashing there right now. I didn't get him, left a message, and figured it would be another day before I heard from him.

But I got a call pretty shortly after that, while I was putting all of J's CDs—plus a few of mine I'd decided he needed more than I did—into a box.

"Daron, everything okay?"

"Everything's fine. I wanted to ask, I mean I'm pretty sure it's okay but in case it wasn't, you know, if you have somebody—"

"Hang on, hang on. The line's a bit noisy. Can you get to the point? It's a little hard to hear you."

"Is it okay if I go to your house for a while? Couple of days, maybe a week?"

"Why? I thought you were—"

"He's leaving. Tomorrow. Back to Jersey. So I'm—"

"Jeezus fucking Christ, that is the best news I've heard all day!" He sounded positively ecstatic. Then he sobered to add, "Not that, I mean, condolences on the relationship and all that."

"So I can stay at your place?"

"No, doofus, you can get your butt on a plane to Japan!"

"But—"

"No buts! Are you kidding me? If he's cut you loose, if you're done, get the hell over here. I need you."

"Are you sure?"

"Hell yes. You rescue me this time. Which guitars do you have?"

"An Ovation and a Fender Strat."

"You won't need the Strat. Or, well, maybe you will, bring 'em both. You'll have to carry them. The gear left Tuesday. My people will book you a flight. Shit, I can't wait until you get here. This place makes New York look like a podunk town."

"Wait, did I say I was coming?" I said just to jerk his chain a little.

"Daron. If you have a good reason not to, don't. But give me one good reason why you can't."

"Just tell me when to be on the plane. And which airport. For fuck's sake, there are too many of them around here."

"You got it. See you soon."

So that's how I ended up having to tell Carynne to cancel my plans to come home for Christmas. She was disappointed, and so was Courtney, but right then, getting on a jet plane to cross the ocean sounded real good. Exciting and different and a fresh start and all that. I know I said I wanted to go home and lick my wounds, but you know, the three? four? however many days it had been since the epic breakup conversation had really given me a lot of perspective and made me feel good about myself.

I mean, *I did it.* I wanted to come up with a way for me and Jonathan to split up without leaving each other in bloody tatters. Given how abandoned I felt by Ziggy, there was no way I was inflicting that on someone else, and in the end I didn't have to. To use an LA analogy, I rode it out until the wave came all the way to shore. Cue Frank Sinatra's "My Way" as I coast majestically onto the beach, sunglasses on, a guitar in one hand and the Trophy of Intact Friendship in the other.

On the Turning Away

We didn't have sex that night. We went out for dinner, saw two bands at a local club but didn't stay for the headliner, and instead ended up sitting in the driveway in the car having such an intense—but good!—conversation that we didn't want to interrupt it enough to go into the house. It was... kind of like how it was when we were still just friends and figuring out if it was going to become more. I had no idea it was possible to turn that knob up and down, that it wasn't just a one-way thing.

It only got serious at one point, when we were talking about LA.

"I was surprised when you said you'd move in with me," he said.

"I surprised myself, actually." Partly because of what I'd said before about the relationship being doomed after I went into Trauma Kid mode, but partly because "shacking up" had never been on my agenda. I said the second part. "It had never occurred to me that we could shack up."

"Well, me either. But then one thing after another fell into place with the gig." He shrugged. "I thought we were going to be at Remo's for a month tops and then we'd be back East."

"Funny how these things work out."

"Did you ever think that maybe you decided to stay here because Ziggy seemed likely to come back here?"

I shook my head. "No. That never entered my mind. If I had known there was going to be a movie premiere or something, maybe? But I haven't heard a release date yet."

"Hm, me either. I'll keep an eye out. Speaking of which, when's that documentary you did the music for airing?"

"Check the Discovery Channel. I think it's coming up." I'd almost forgotten about it. I'd done so many things while in LA I didn't have any chance of remembering when they were due to actually appear.

And the conversation moved on, like conversations with Jonathan do, and eventually I was thirsty and he had to pee and we gave in and went into the house.

The message light was blinking. It was a message from Remo's "people"—a travel agent—saying that she had booked me on a 6 AM flight and that an airport limo would be coming for me at 3 AM.

So it was a good thing we didn't stay out too late.

Jonathan said, "Hey, so, how do you feel?"

"Excited to be going to Japan, you mean?"

"I mean, about what you want to do now."

I looked at him. He was the same, blond, angular genius who had thrown himself in my path enough times back when that I had finally gotten the message that he was interested in me. He was as attractive as ever. But I didn't feel like I needed sex right now.

I know, let me repeat that. I didn't feel needy right then. I had reached some kind of emotional satisfaction that day, or that night, and I didn't feel like I needed anything else. "Kind of depends on what you want to do now," I said. "But I'm for spending all night packing, if you are."

"Oh god, you read my mind!" he said, and hugged me. "Are you sure?"

"I'm sure."

So we spent the rest of the night packing, and actually by the time the limo pulled up there wasn't much left for Jonathan to do on his own. He was going to run one more load of laundry in the morning and then dismantle the bed, and that was about it. We really didn't have that much stuff.

Jonathan was looking pretty drowsy by the time the limo came for me, but he wouldn't have missed saying goodbye to me for the world. I had the two guitars and my duffel bag and suitcase in the courtyard behind me. The limo driver ferried the stuff back and forth to the trunk while Jonathan and I had a last, lingering goodbye kiss.

"Thank you, for everything, for being here for me," he said.

"I'll see you back on the East Coast, I'm sure." I added a kiss to his cheek.

He looked a little angst-ridden then, a flicker of doubt creasing his eyes.

I took out my wallet, tore a hundred dollar bill in half, and handed one half to him. "There. Dinner in New York on me. Next time I see you."

He grinned, all trace of angst gone. "Okay. You're on. Rock star."

Part Eleven

December 1989

The Passenger

One of the best things about being a small person physically is that it's not a big deal for me to spend eighteen hours on an airplane in coach. They had booked me on whatever they could get at the last minute, which meant that I changed planes in Seattle and then went nonstop to Tokyo from there. The trans-Pacific leg in those days took over fourteen hours because of the need to dodge Russian airspace.

Fourteen hours is a long time to think about something. Not that I sat there thinking about Jonathan, or Ziggy, or anything for fourteen straight hours. Sleeping and eating occupied a fair amount of time, too. But the thing you find about long-haul trips like that? Fourteen hours actually *isn't* that long. Time passes. What seems beforehand like it's going to be "forever" actually goes by a lot quicker than you think it will.

Yeah, yeah, insert relationship comment here.

The thing is, have you ever had one of those moments where you suddenly realize something that could go horribly wrong and you obsess over it until the time comes when it either will or won't happen? Like I was saying, I did a lot of thinking while on that plane. With the relationship over, it was like a whole bunch of areas of my brain that had been shut off now opened up again. Memories and thoughts that had been in dark corners got light shined on them again.

In other words, when we were a few hours from landing, I started to give some thought to the future instead of the past, and started to think about the reality that I was about to tour a foreign country with a band I hadn't actually played with in years... And all of a sudden I remembered that my denim jacket that was packed in my duffel bag had a piece of tinfoil in the pocket that had I don't know how many tabs of acid in it. Christian had given it to me the night of the Jingle Bell Rock fundraising show. The night I came out to Carynne. The moment I remembered was one of those "frying pan into the fire" moments: you know, *oh shit, what next.*

I had rediscovered that piece of foil and forgotten it two or three times since the night I got it but had never done anything about it or with it. I spent the last hour of the flight in a state of total anxiety wondering what the laws concerning illegal drugs were in Japan.

That kept me good and preoccupied from worrying about what I probably should have been thinking about, which was, one, how was I supposed to hook up with the Nomad entourage, and two, why exactly was Remo so anxious to get me there? In my whirlwind of a breakup with Jonathan I'd gotten so spun around that Remo's urgency really hadn't sunk in. I'd just thought he thought I needed to get out of there.

Well, I needn't have worried about the drugs in my jacket in my suitcase. Customs was most interested in the guitar cases, and gave me some odd looks, but when a cursory search didn't turn up anything of interest to them, they sent me on my way. I should clarify: I *think* they were odd looks, but it was a little hard to tell. Their demeanor was a bit different from the rent-a-cop attitude I was used to, and I didn't know how to read the cultural signals. For the first time in months I thought about how long my hair was. It was the longest it had ever been, all the way past my shoulder blades, and yet by LA standards for guitar players that was short, you know?

Anyway. They didn't find anything, and I quickly found the person picking me up, a car driver with my name computer-printed on a sign. He spoke only cursory English, and I fell asleep on the drive to the hotel.

It was the last rest I'd get for a while. Talk about frying pan into the fire. Waldo nabbed me in the lobby.

"Hey, kid," he said, with a hand on my shoulder. "You legal yet?"

"Yeah, how about you, Waldo? That sense of humor is criminal."

"I forgot what a kidder you are. Good to see ya." We shook hands. "I'm getting your stuff sent up to your room. Grab the Ovation and let's go."

I didn't ask where we were going and Waldo didn't give me any additional information. I was used to him being taciturn and shifty around me, so that didn't rouse any suspicions for me. We went straight to a rehearsal studio. At least, that's what I thought it was. I was disoriented from jet lag and from the fact that the signs everywhere were not in English. You don't realize how much you rely on that until it's gone, I guess. So here we were in a room that had microphones and chairs and instruments set up, and I got my first inkling of how in over my head I was.

Remo had a cast on his right hand—his right arm, really, from midway down his forearm up to his knuckles, his fingers clear at the end.

Pretty sure the first words out of my mouth were, "What the fuck happened?"

He was sitting in a folding chair with a guitar in his lap. "Nice to see you, too, Daron. How was your flight?"

"Oceanic. Seriously. What the—"

"Fell off a ladder the day before I left."

"Putting up a light fixture or something?"

He nodded. "I can grip a pick okay, for a while—"

"Remo!"

"Calm down, jeez."

"Why didn't you tell me before? You told me Flip broke his ankle."

"Well, that too. I'm thinking of changing the name of the band to Doctor and the Medics. Except it's already taken. Oh well..."

I could see he'd settled into being funny about it and there wasn't any shaking him. The quicker I caught up to whatever level of acceptance of the situation he had reached, the better. "All right. What am I doing, then? Everything?"

"Don't sound so worried. It's not like you've never played with us before."

"Three-and-a-half years ago, and that was only half the set." They'd done two albums since then.

"This is Japan. It's a greatest-hits set. There won't be much new. I was already planning for Cray Lucas to play some pedal steel and rhythm guitar, then I thought all right, I'll play rhythm when I can and he can take over the lead, but with you here it makes it all easier."

I sat down in a chair and took the Ovation out and started tightening the strings I'd loosened for transport. "Easier, huh."

"I didn't say easy, just easier. Here, tune to me and let's go over that thing we did at my house."

So the next forty-five minutes were spent with me learning the actual parts for a song that we'd played together once. And then we spent fifteen minutes playing around with an arrangement of one of the songs we'd done on that warm-up tour I'd gone on with them in 1986. The tour where I met Carynne, come to think of it. So after an hour we had two songs we could basically do with him singing and me playing, and I kept wondering, *All right, but when does the rest of the band come in?*

And then they set up microphones, and two Japanese people came in and sat down with us and I finally clued in that we were on some kind of live radio broadcast. One of them was the interviewer and one was a translator, and I didn't have to do any talking at all, I just had to play the guitar when the time came. I'd say it was terrifying except that it wasn't. I didn't feel the pressure of millions of people listening or anything. Sitting in a room with three other people, it felt more like an audition than like a performance. Okay, and auditions can be terrifying, except this one wasn't. The only person I was concerned about liking it was Remo, and I had confidence he was going to like it just fine if I didn't flub it, and the way to not flub is to not stress. So I stayed calm and did my job and it was fine.

The whole show was over in under half an hour. And then came a lot of the same rituals that take place in American radio stations: autographs and photographs and shaking hands. That, at least, was familiar.

Then they took me to eat. I honestly had no idea what time it was. They told me it was dinner, but I think it was the early afternoon. It was daylight, anyway. And on the chilly side for someone who was used to Los Angeles, but not that chilly when you consider that it was December. I think in my mind I considered Tokyo to be like New York, but it was slightly warmer. I wasn't really dressed for it, but you know the drill, whisked here and there by handlers, it's not like I saw much of the outside.

Let's see, though, I should try to tell you at least a little about Japan. If you wonder why so many bands seem to tour there, it's because after the USA it's the country that spends the most money on records. If you're on an international label with strong ties there, you're going to be going there, regardless of your genre.

Honestly, much as I want to give you a travelogue of

how cool and exciting and different Japan was, I basically spent every waking moment of the next 72 hours learning as many songs as I could. "Waking moment" is a key concept when everyone's so jet lagged you can't tell if it's day or night.

Flip. I should tell you about Flip. So this was the guy I had met at a party in LA at some point in my sojourn there, and we had talked about the Guitar Craft school and bonded over falling in love with the Ovation Celebrity guitar sound. Guitar Craft, for those not familiar, was a thing started by Robert Fripp. I'm sure I've mentioned him before. Fripp is legendary, not just for playing on those Bowie albums like *Heroes* and *Scary Monsters*, or for being the one guy in all the incarnations of King Crimson, but for being a guitar sonic innovator. And my hero, in case you couldn't tell. Despite me idolizing him, I still didn't know that much about Fripp, and had never met him.

Flip had. Flip shelled out the six hundred bucks to take a six-day seminar with Fripp at a ramshackle mansion in West Virginia that was, from his description anyway, kind of like going off and being a shaolin monk for a week, except instead of learning kung fu you were learning guitar. I had heard about the seminars and about the New Standard Tuning, but Flip was the first person I met who had taken one of the seminars and who kept a guitar in NST all the time.

I'll try not to get too technical, but NST is basically this: what if you tuned a guitar like a violin, with the strings evenly spaced in sound by fifths? The bottom string has to get lower, the top string has to get higher, and the fingerings you had to learn for chords that rely on the weird way the notes are spaced normally all go out the window. Scales suddenly become standard no matter where you start. I'd played with it from time to time the way I'd played around with the DADGAD open tuning.... never mind. Too technical. The point about Flip was he was someone I could geek out with and who knew what a crazy undertaking it was to learn the entire set in two-and-a-half days.

It was and it wasn't. There are two reasons it was doable to get me up to basic competency in that short a time. One, I really do pick things up quickly. Two, the songs aren't that hard, and I did know some of them already. Flip did some smart things to help me, too. Like he made a tape of all the songs that would be in the setlist, in order, including the covers, and gave it to me. There were times when I was the only one awake and I sat there with a guitar and headphones and my Walkman and learned.

I suppose a third factor in my favor is that I knew the band pretty well and they knew me.

Except for Cray, that is. It was a little difficult to size him up at first. Like a lot of people Remo employs, he was not a showboater. He was a head-down, get-the-work-done kind of guy, or at least I assumed so at first. He looked to be in his mid-thirties, with a Lee Majors in *The Six Million Dollar Man* haircut, in jeans and cowboy boots. He had a bluegrass background, and I didn't see that much of him except when the full group was together. When I say full group, this was with all stops pulled out, complete with two female backup singers, a two-man horn section (tenor sax and trumpet), and a percussionist in addition to Cray, me, and the four regular members of Nomad: Remo, Martin, and the Mazel brothers.

That's a lot of people to keep track of, and we're all professionals, so I didn't go out of my way to butter any of them up because I didn't have to. The road crew was fairly large, too. It seemed like a lot of people for a smallish tour, but I didn't know the economics behind it. I guessed it was expensive but worth it.

So, the thing is, normally they wouldn't have rehearsed after getting to Tokyo. They'd rehearsed back in LA. But with me needing to come up to speed, they rented a conference room in the hotel where we were staying and Remo got us all together a couple of times.

I got my first inkling that things were weird with Cray after the last one of the rehearsals before the actual soundcheck of the first gig on the tour. We rehearsed in the morning, and at one point Remo pointed at me in frustration and said, "You! You need a nickname. Since I'm forbidden to call you what I called you."

He meant "kiddo." Which was not a nickname, as far as I was concerned, it was just lazy. "Call me anything but Moondog. BNC owns that," I joked.

"How 'bout Matilda," Cray called out.

"What?" Martin scratched his head with a drumstick.

"For waltzing in at the last minute," Cray said with a little snicker. That got a couple of bemused smiles out of the others.

"Mad Dog," suggested Martin.

"What do you call a worrywart guitar player?" Alex asked.

"Fret," his brother answered, and Martin punctuated the punchline with a comedic drum hit, *badump-bump.*

"Something'll have to suggest itself," Remo said. "Okay, pack up and give everything to the crew. Meet in the lobby for the transport to the venue no later than two o'clock."

Those who could scattered at that point. I took a little time getting the Ovation put away. Flip had changed the strings the day before. I looked through the case to see if I had anything in there I shouldn't, like cash. I was closing it up when I remembered, duh, customs had already gone through it, but my brain had been so fried at that point I hadn't remembered.

Cray came up to me then. "You want to grab something to eat?"

"Sure." When a guy you're touring with says that, it usually means he wants to get to know you better. "Got something in mind?"

"Let's get out and see the city a little."

"You got local cash?" I realized I hadn't been picking up a per diem like we would in the States. Everything so far had been catered or eaten in the hotel, and it hadn't even occurred to me.

"Yeah, should be enough. We've got a couple of hours."

Two hours, to be exact. Seemed reasonable. The hotel was right in the middle of a busy area that I guess I would compare to Times Square, only less scuzzy around the edges. We walked out the door and wandered for a bit. It was a lot to take in. I felt a little chilly. I was in my leather jacket with a hoodie underneath. We ended up sitting at a counter where you could point at the food, and the girls who served us laughed a lot at the fact that we couldn't speak any Japanese except for "domo arigato"—which I only knew because of the Styx album. They graciously corrected my pronunciation and then dissolved into giggles again. We got bowls of soup and something fried on sticks (chicken skin?) and then something else fried on sticks (some kind of seafood and dough ball?). And generally I thought we had a good time.

But I'd had a lot of practice up to that point trying to suss out unspoken aggression, you know what I mean? And when we got back to the hotel I had the nagging feeling in the back of my mind that Cray Lucas didn't really like me.

Big in Japan

What book is it that has that "best of times, worst of times" line? I hope it's a good one, because I'm going to rip it off and it's best to steal from the best. It was the worst show ever and the best show ever.

I was not ready to go out there and give a polished performance of most of the material. That might have been fine in, I don't know, a theater in San Francisco. But for Japan? I was under the impression they liked their concerts technically clean and hewing close to the recorded album. So I was nervous as hell when the crowd was dead quiet during the first song.

The venue was a place listed on our day sheet as "Yoyogi Olympic Pool." Another memo from the driving company called it "Tokyo Swimming Auditorium Hall." I had no idea what to expect. I was kind of picturing the YMCA pool when I was a kid, with a stage at one end and people sitting in the bleachers on the side. I mean, what would you picture?

I was not prepared for a super-futuristic UFO-looking building. I know I said that some of the venues in the States looked like UFOs. This one took the cake and flew off with it to Mars. I'd read *Neuromancer* when Matthew lent it to me, around the time everyone in America was reading it, and now I understood why the book started in Tokyo. Didn't it? Man, that's two literary references in a row I probably blew, and this chapter's barely started. Anyway. The place was silver, with swoopy curves all over, and looked like it might get up and turn into a giant robot unicycle and wheel away when we weren't looking.

I watched a lot of Godzilla movies as a kid. They would show up randomly on Saturdays on channel 9, which was one of the second-rate channels from New York. Digger liked them, too. We sometimes sat in the kitchen and watched them together on the crappy little black-and-white TV on the counter because my mom or sisters had the color TV in the living room monopolized. For sports Digger took over the living room, but I guess for B-grade sci-fi he didn't have the clout.

I don't know why I'm telling you that. Oh, right. Tokyo. I wasn't afraid Godzilla's foot was going to come through the roof, which looked like a suspension bridge inside, but I was afraid that the total lack of reaction from the audience during the opening song was somehow my fault. When you're used to the way American audiences scream and cheer all the time, the quiet feels like disapproval. The opening song was one of Nomad's best-known songs, kind of their theme song, I guess: "Traveling True." It was one of the ones I knew, but I kept thinking, *Shit, they don't like it, they don't like the way I do it.*

Then the song ended and they went absolutely nuts, and I realized they weren't sitting on their hands because they disapproved. They were being polite. It was more like a jazz or classical concert in that way.

Realizing it and feeling it were two different things, though. It was hard to get used to. One thing that always got a huge cheer was whenever Remo tried to say anything at all in Japanese. All he really knew how to say was "hello" and "thank you," but that was all right, it seemed.

The details of what else went on during the show are fuzzy. Anxiety wiped most of them from my mind, I guess. I played a stilted solo in "Moonrise" and missed my cue in "Sonny's Song," but they got me back on track pretty well. I remember the deep stab of mortification I felt when I realized I'd missed it, though. I mean, when was the last time I made an actual mistake? Musically, I mean. That hissing sound you hear is my overbuilt sense of self deflating. When did I start thinking of myself as perfect? Several songs later it still stung, and that made it hard to concentrate on what I needed to, my mind dwelling on it terribly.

When Remo introduced the band one by one in the encore, I was a little stunned by the ferocity of the cheer that hit me. There was such a disconnect between how much the audience liked me and how much I hated the performance I'd given, I couldn't absorb it at first.

Remo and I both had the shakes afterward. He communicated to the translator who finally explained what he needed, and someone brought him a big bag of ice that he could stick his entire arm, cast and all, into. I sat down next to him.

"Sorry about that," I said.

"Wasn't your best," he agreed. "But pretty good on short notice."

"I'm trying to play like you."

"I'd rather you played like *you*," he answered.

"If I don't learn your way first, I won't know what the hell I'm doing, though."

"Fair enough. Don't beat yourself up, Sundog."

"That my new nickname?"

"I'm trying it out. It fit?"

I shrugged.

The thing about nicknames, at least tour nicknames, is that one of two things makes them stick. One is they're so fitting that everyone starts using them immediately, like you know who's being talked about before anyone tells you. The other thing is if the person being nicknamed doesn't like the name, and the rest of the group picks up on it, and they'll use it just to make fun of you and there isn't anything you can do about it. Nicknames are a consensus sort of thing. You rarely get to pick your own unless you already have one. Like Flip. Flip both seemed to fit and had an obvious connection to his real name, Philip.

Sometimes a group of people will all decide on nicknames together, like you know, three of you watched a movie on videotape in the bus and decided to start calling each other Luke, Han, and Chewie. But that's rare. Usually people will just try stuff on you until something sticks.

I didn't get a tour nickname on the last tour I think for the same reason I never got pranked by the road crew. No one wanted to give me a hard time—in a good-natured way—when they knew I was having an actual hard time because of assholes.

I wanted a nickname this time. I wanted the guys

to not give a fuck about that kind of stuff. And I didn't want them feeling like they had to treat me like a kid or like someone who needed help. Does that make sense?

"Earth to Daron."

"Hm?" I realized Remo was still sitting next to me. "Your arm getting cold?"

"I was going to say, got a timer you can set for five minutes? I'll pull it out then."

"No, but I'll keep an eye on the clock over there." I could see a digital clock on the wall, red. At least the numbers worked mostly the same here as in the States. The clock was on military time, but that wouldn't keep me from tracking five minutes. "Are you taking anything for the pain?"

"No. Not even Tylenol."

"No?"

"Doctor told me if I want to drink, don't take Tylenol, or I'll end up with a liver like your old man's."

"Really."

"Yep. So whiskey will have to be my tranquilizer. And ice. Fuck, this is cold."

"Are you going to make it through three more shows in a row before a day off?"

He didn't answer right away. "I better. It's not bad enough to justify a cancellation."

"Don't look at me. I'm the one who wore an eye patch and bandages for ten days last summer and thought I was going to break my neck from misjudging the distance to the edge of the stage every night." I put my hand over my eye. It was kind of fun to make the world go flat and two-dimensional when the effect was easily reversed. "But that's what got Ziggy hooked on painkillers."

"He doesn't do anything by half, does he."

"Nope."

"Still no word from him?"

"Nope."

We sat in silence for a full minute then, while I waited for the numbers to change.

Before we got to five minutes, though, a promoter or something—I was unclear exactly who worked for whom in the Japanese system—came up to talk to "Remo-san" and very apologetically asked him, in somewhat halting English, if he could beg a favor.

"Jiro-san, of course, I would love to do whatever you need, but I am kind of stuck here for a little while," Remo explained, sloshing his arm in the ice.

"Oh, so sorry, I should explain. With your permission. We have special person want to meet *you.*" He turned and pointed at me.

"Me? What kind of special person?"

"Daughter of high-ranking official."

"Sure. I'll go. I don't look my best right now."

"Is fine, is fine! Please!" He seemed very excited that I had agreed. "She will be very happy."

"Should I sign something?" I asked as I stood up and looked around.

"Please?" He looked confused.

"Autograph," I tried.

"Oh yes, please. She give me this to find you in case you would only autograph." He held up his clipboard, and I saw a magazine was folded open to a pinup photo of me and Ziggy. Ziggy was hanging on one of my shoulders giving a sideways, bedroom-eyes look to the camera. I was just standing there, looking straight into the lens. It was an old photo, and for a second I couldn't even think when we would have taken one, just the two of us? Not the whole band? And I didn't remember doing that style of pinup. The background was kind of funky—surely if we went to a photo studio with a setup like that, I would remember it.

Then I remembered. Los Angeles. The day after we'd had sex for the first time. Sightseeing.

For a second I couldn't breathe. It hit me as a feeling and as a thought at the same time. The feeling of missing him, of a moment in time, of everything from then to now, all hitting me at once, and the thought that... waitasecond... my photo was in Japanese magazines?

Which made me wonder, what were album sales like here? Mills had never mentioned it.

Anyway, I followed the guy through the place to a reception room of some kind where my appearance produced the same kind of high-pitched shrieks I was used to in America. I guess some things really are the same.

Live at Budokan

The next night, the stakes went up. It was the first of three nights in a row at Budokan. You might as well have told me we were playing the White House, Buckingham Palace, and god's own amphitheater all at once, so far as the mythic-and-important factor went. If you don't know what I'm talking about, you probably never heard the Cheap Trick album *Cheap Trick at Budokan*, which was one of the best-selling albums of the 1970s, or any number of other major live shows that were recorded there. The phrase "live at Budokan" entered the rock and roll vocabulary in the seventies and never left. Even Bob Dylan did a "live at Budokan" record.

No pressure.

Remo was obviously hurting, there was no way I was going to ask him to play any more than he had to, and I didn't even want to ask for a long soundcheck. But he was the band leader, and I felt like any request like that had to come from him. If it had been just me and the guys I wouldn't have hesitated, but it was the expanded band. They were a blessing and a curse. A blessing because with all those horns and voices and sounds, if I got lost and didn't play for a couple of bars—like I had at the Swimming Pool—there was so much going on it wasn't as glaringly obvious as it might have been. But a curse because it was a lot more people to coordinate.

I told Remo in the morning. He was sitting on the couch, nursing a pot of coffee. "I need to work on 'Sonny's Song.' I'm faking my way through 'Pull.' And—"

"I got you," he said, giving me a sharp wave of his casted hand, while he held a cup of coffee in the other, cutting me off before I could even bring up the subject of the two songs I hadn't even started on yet. "Can you and Alan and Alex work something out, though?"

"Well, we can't get at the keyboards until we get to the venue, and even when we do—"

"Fuck a duck, you're right. Everything here's so strict." He sighed. "We don't have the free run of the place the way we would in the States."

"I've got four hours right now. I can practice with the tape. But it's not the same as the big-band arrangement, and that fucked me up last night. And I'm stepping all over Cray."

"Don't you worry about Cray. Tonight you drop out on 'Sonny' and let him carry it."

Flip came crutching into the suite then.

I looked at Remo. He looked like he hadn't slept well. So much for whiskey. "I want *you* to drop out on everything, Reem. Just sing."

"I'll get through tonight. By tomorrow you'll have it all down cold."

"I don't know, Reem. Last night wasn't pretty. Even I've got some limits."

Flip looked up from where he was pouring himself a cup of coffee. "Hey, would reading the horn charts help you at all?"

"You bet it would! Why didn't you tell me it was written down?"

"Nobody asked me. Come on, I know where there's a set of them."

The horn section had long since memorized their parts, but Flip had kept a set of the pages because he was kind of a pack rat. I guess years on the road will make a guy like that. Flip had the most impressive guitar tech setup I'd ever seen. Lots of guys had a tool box and supplies. Flip had a whole road case, six feet wide, four feet high, that opened up to become a velvet-lined workbench, with drawers and tools and everything built into it. The only drawback to it right then was that he had to stand up to use the work surface, and that meant standing on his one good foot.

Flip was one of those guys who had started to go bald young and grew a mustache to compensate for it. He was still young, maybe thirty, but because of the receding hairline he could pass for a fit forty. Especially when he wore a polo shirt instead of a T-shirt. We went back to his room and he dug the charts out of a bag.

I scanned them. The chord progression was written right on top of the staff. *Yes.* "You wouldn't think a little thing like that would be so helpful... but it is." It was like any input I could get would help me memorize more, faster.

I buried myself in those for a couple of hours, and then Alan borrowed a spare Takamine from Remo's room and we worked together on a couple of songs, even though Alan technically didn't even play the guitar. It'd be like me faking my way through something on the piano. The thing is, he didn't have to be technically perfect at all, since he was just trying to get me through the changes while I figured out my part.

Crunch crunch crunch. Remo dragged out the soundcheck as long as he could. When it was over, we sat in a backstage room and had something to eat. Me and Mitch, the sax player, got into a thing, talking back and forth, singing back and forth. "You know what would be cool? Where you have that fill that goes *ba-dana-nuh-nuh*? What if I echo it back to you?" "That would be cool! *"Ba-nanah, ba-nahah...*" "Even better, yeah, like that."

It would be cool. But I caught the look on Cray's face before he looked away. It was one of those tongue-clucking, eye-rolling expressions.

Okay, fine. He didn't like the idea or he didn't like me. I ignored it.

I reached the point where I had to let my thumb rest or I wouldn't be able to play that night either. I made Flip tell me more about Guitar Craft.

"I bet you'd have a different experience there than I did," he said. "You're a much better player than I am. And I had all kinds of bad habits to unlearn. I'd never played sitting down with my foot on a stand before."

"That's a really standard classical guitar thing. When I was in school I had a little folding footrest and everything." I wondered where that footrest was now. I had kept it, but I hadn't used it in a long time. The last time I practiced classic style, I just propped my foot on whatever was around. "The thing is to reduce the stress of curving your wrist and your arms so you can get more directly at playing the strings."

"Fripp's whole trip is about you being more free to make the sounds you want instead of the sounds the guitar wants," Flip said. "I mean, so much of the standard way guitars sound, even in classical music but especially in rock and roll, is based on the chords that are easiest to play, that sound the best. So with the new tuning it doesn't fall into those patterns, and with the better posture you don't get stuck in the guitar-player ruts, either."

"In other words, he makes the guitar into a fretted piano." Something clicked in my head. I'd always been all about getting as good as I could, as technically perfect as I could, so that I could play as freely as possible, so I could play anything I could imagine without *me* being the thing constraining what my solo sounded like or what my songs sounded like. But to actually do it as a kind of spiritual practice, like yoga, or maybe more like a martial art... Every note equal. And equally available, like on the piano.

I wondered if I'd be struggling to memorize these songs if I played like that. For a brief moment I entertained the fantasy that, if I only followed the Fripp way, I could become a guitar superhero and conquer anything. But then reality set in. These songs, this sound... I had everything in my hands already to make them happen. But there was no shortcut. I had to put in the time, practice the songs, memorize them, learn them, so I could make myself part of the soundscape that Nomad needed. They didn't need a shaolin monk with six strings. They needed Remo. They settled for me.

"Don't even tune his guitar tonight," I told Flip. "Strap his arm to his body. I want him to get better so someday we can play these damn songs the way they're supposed to sound, when *both* of us can play."

I buried my head in the charts until a half hour before showtime, like I was cramming for an exam. When there were thirty minutes left, though, I put them away and got the Ovation, and then closed my eyes and sat with it. I didn't think of any specific song. I just took deep breaths and imagined that everything flowed. Everything flows. Breath, sound, anything that comes in waves. Sound is waves. Radio is waves.

Love is waves? Okay, not sure about that one, but that's what happens when my mind blanks out.

Flip tapped me on the shoulder when it was time to go on.

"Did you give him a guitar?" I asked.

"Nope."

"Okay, then."

I never got an explanation for why we played two different venues in the city of Tokyo. Three nights at Budokan. Had they sold out and couldn't add one more because of other things being scheduled at the venue, so then they added a show at the Olympic Pool? Or was it something else entirely? Two different promoters? I don't know. If I hadn't been so focused on trying to learn so much music in so short a time, I probably would have asked all kinds of questions. But I didn't.

At any rate, the Budokan crowd was louder. The cheers when we came onto the stage were forceful. People were really excited. Good.

This time, when they shut up to listen to the opening number it didn't stress me out. And without Remo even trying to strum rhythm everything actually went better. I worried about him less and probably so did everyone else.

In the second song I laid down a very nice solo that recalled the album but wasn't the same, and I turned to the band to signal I was ending it, and I think that was when it happened. It's hard to remember exactly, because afterward my time sense of what happened when is often wrong. But I think that was when everyone started following me. I hadn't intended to turn myself into the de facto band leader, but that's what happened, the horns and the singers' eyes tracking me across the stage, and you know, it made sense, because in Nomad the guitar was always the lead instrument.

I didn't plan it that way, that's just how it happened. And it worked. I couldn't get lost when I was in the lead, I guess, and I was keeping track of the songs more like a conductor than like a backing musician. I was used to leading Moondog Three on the stage, and I guess that instinct kicked in.

I'll give you one guess who didn't hop right into the program, though. Cray. But after one or two more songs he settled in, too, because I would hand the lick around.

This description probably makes no sense if you haven't played that style. I've said before that a lot of Nomad songs are blues-based. Remember when I was teaching Colin how to improvise on top of a blues progression? You can have as many go-rounds of the progression as you want, and in a traditional performance each instrument would get a go-round to solo for themselves. We weren't there to play a jazz show, of course, but there was a lot of room for the backing instruments to trade off the lead, even during the lyrics.

So in a way, I took over as the band leader, but that meant I actually gave more people the spotlight. It threw the idea that we were recreating the album sound out the window, but so what. I should've thrown that out to begin with. If they wanted the album sound they wouldn't have added the full backing band anyway. I don't know where my head was.

It worked. When music works, it's like everyone's telepathic. It didn't matter that there were still parts of the songs I didn't know, because the group as a whole knew them. It was kind of magic that way.

Afterward, Remo caught me in a hug at the bottom of the stairs from the stage. "You're fucking brilliant. All that from reading the horn charts?"

"No. It just... sank in," I said. I didn't say I thought it helped that he didn't have a guitar. Everyone's ears had turned to me. "Thank the band. They're the ones who locked onto me and didn't let me go."

"Top notch, baby!" Martin enthused and high-fived me. "Top notch all the way."

Everyone was in a much better mood for hanging out after that show than the previous night, and we ended up back at the hotel in the bar. Not only had the show gone better, everyone was less jet lagged. Remo was the first to say goodnight.

I wanted to check with Martin, but I couldn't come up with a diplomatic way to ask him, hey, is Cray a dickhead or is it me? And then Martin got very snuggly cute with a woman, and I wasn't about to interrupt him.

So when Cray went to the men's room, I followed him. I didn't follow him in, because that can freak a guy out, you know, so instead I hung around outside the door, where there was a small lobby and two pay phones.

When he came out, I had psyched myself up to be really direct. But at the last second I decided to try casual. I pretended I was on the phone, hung up when he came out, and then walked with him back toward the bar.

"I thought that went better tonight," I said, like I was talking about the weather.

"Course you do," he said, and shook his head.

So much for casual. I stopped him in his tracks. "Cray, if you have a problem with me, I want to know what it is."

"What's this, the third degree?" He shrugged. "What

I think doesn't matter. Leave it."

"Sorry, not happening." I tried to keep my hands relaxed, not ball them up. "Last time I let something go on too long on a tour, I nearly lost an eye and my singer lost a chunk of his arm. Not doing that again." Haha, it only just then occurred to me that you could say the Megaton bomb blew up in my face. I wasn't laughing, though.

Cray had an opinion of that, though. "Yeah, I heard you were such prima donnas, you threw a band off your tour."

I was too taken by surprise by Cray's obviously misinformed take on the events to react for a second. "What?"

"I heard you crying to Cutler the other night about how your record company doesn't know how to categorize you. What the fuck do you think they're going to do, asshole, when you replace a metal band with god-squadders and then boot them and replace 'em with goths?"

I should have just walked away right then, because he clearly had some pretty messed up ideas, and while I was having the urge to pound his face wasn't the best time to try to straighten him out. But I took a breath and tried to remind myself that violence wasn't an answer. And this guy wasn't important enough to get that upset over.

"You don't know what the fuck you're talking about."

"Sure I don't." He shrugged and shook his head, like he was pretty sure he was looking at the sorriest excuse for a human being in the world: me. Then he started to walk away.

I couldn't. I couldn't just let him go. "Hey. I'm not done talking to you."

"Too bad. I'm done with you." He was sauntering away.

The thing about that cool saunter, though, it's slow as shit. I slipped in front of him. "I'm serious, Cray. This isn't some fucking summer camp ego trip."

"Sure it is. It's all about you. Little Lord Fauntleroy. You think you're hot shit, and you want everyone to know it. That's fine. No skin off my nose. When you get to my age, maybe you'll calm down."

Okay, that definitely wasn't what I was expecting to hear. Then again, what was I expecting? I guess I was expecting the usual: homophobia. But this was starting to sound like something else. "How old are you?"

"None of your fucking business," he said, and this time when he walked away, he stalked more quickly and angrily. Yeah right, no skin off your nose, Mr. Cynic.

Last of the Famous International Playboys

I think I said before that our hotel was in a part of Tokyo that was kind of like Times Square: a really busy area with lots of tourists and commerce and neon. Since now I felt like I didn't have to spend every waking minute rehearsing or learning—only three hours this time, with Alex and Alan and a spare guitar and a portable Casio mini keyboard—I went out and wandered around a little with Martin. There was enough English on signs that we could feed ourselves if we weren't too finicky. Turns out the one thing you can get just about everywhere is fried octopus balls.

Stop snickering, that's not what I mean. They're sort of like a ball of fried dough the size of a golf ball with a chunk of octopus meat in the middle. One shop we passed by had a huge griddle for making them, pocked with half-sphere indentations. The cook would put a piece of octopus into each one, then ladle in the batter, and then flip them over with a long utensil, kind of like long metal chopsticks. He could do like two hundred of these at a time. They sell them like donut holes, in boxes of a dozen or more. We burned our tongues tearing through a box with disposable chopsticks.

The thing I was looking for was a newsstand, though, curious if I could find a copy of the magazine that I'd autographed the other night at the Olympic Pool. I'd tried to ask the girl about it, like, was it recent or had she had it a while, but the language barrier was too much, as was her giggling. It had been her and three friends, and I couldn't tell for sure but I think they were really excited that I was their height. "Cute" was a word I heard a lot.

I don't think I'm that cute. Especially not with my hair that long and sweat-soaked from performing. But maybe the definition of "cute" was a little different there.

Anyway. We ended up in what was more like a bookstore than a newsstand, but they had a large number of magazines. Many of them were in plastic bags, which made it difficult to look through them. Some had headlines in English, others didn't. It was kind of fascinating but frustrating at the same time.

And I couldn't help but think, pretty much everywhere we went, *oh, Jonathan would like that*, or *Jonathan would know what to do with that*. It was like I was imagining what Jonathan would think about everything if he was there to see it. Which was actually really annoying. I did not need to be seeing Japan through Jonathan-colored glasses.

After wandering the bookstore, which was massive, for nearly an hour, Martin suggested we give up and ask our translator for advice on where to look.

While we were walking back to the hotel I finally asked, "Hey, is Cray kind of a dickhead or is it just me?"

"My impression is he's kind of a surly loner. He did the US tour with us two summers ago and was in Europe this year. Why, he giving you trouble?"

"All kinds of attitude. I don't get it." The sidewalk was crowded, but no one was really paying attention to us. It was kind of like New York that way, too.

"Nobody needs that. You want me to talk to him?"

"You think that'll help? I feel like he's staring daggers at me whenever my back is turned."

"Huh. Wonder what wild hair he got across his ass." Martin shoved his hands under his armpits while we walked. It was a tad on the chilly side. I had a hooded sweatshirt on under my leather jacket and wasn't feeling that cold, but Martin was just wearing a pullover sweatshirt with the Nomad logo embroidered on the chest. "He's a solid player, I mean, probably one of the top lap steel players in the country, you know?"

"How'd Remo find him?"

"For a while Remo was slumming around folk festivals and stuff, remember? It didn't hurt that his girlfriend at the time was a singer in a bluegrass group. I think Cray's from that same group? I figure Reem wouldn't have picked him up if he wasn't good. Overall he's been professional, so I guess if he's a pill I can live with it."

"I still can't figure out how Remo does relationships."

"Yeah, me either. I mean, I kind of can, but he's on a different part of the spectrum."

"Spectrum?"

"Okay, you know, a spectrum." He held out his arms, which were quite long, as if measuring a big fish with his hands. He made a chopping motion with his left hand. "At this end you have the one-night stands and fucking groupies by the dozen without even getting their names, and at the other end," he waved his right hand, "you have monogamous marriage."

"Okay."

"And I'm right about here." He moved his left hand toward the middle. "Once in a while a one-night stand, but it's mostly flings."

"What's your definition of a fling?"

"You know. It lasts maybe a week or even a couple of months depending on the circumstances, but I know it's a fling, she knows it's a fling, and we just have fun. If it's not fun, it's not a fling."

"All right. And where's Remo on the scale?"

"He's about here." He moved his right hand toward the middle. "Like he has these serious relationships, these deep-love relationships that run anywhere from six months to a couple of years. But even when they're pretty serious he ends up moving on."

"Like a nomad?" I joked.

"Quit that. But yeah. I don't think he has an actual objection to settling down. He just hasn't met the right one yet. It'd have to be someone who could put up with all the travel and everything. He needs a June Carter type."

"June Carter?"

"June Carter Cash, I should say. Johnny Cash's wife? They're, like, made for each other. But they didn't get it right the first time. They each married other people first and then were sorry. But they got it right in the end."

"Okay." I had no idea how Martin knew so much about Johnny Cash's private life, but then again, maybe it was a commonly known story and I just didn't know it. That was likely. "Has he got anyone right now?"

"Don't think so. He was pretty active in Europe,

a bunch of different women a week or two at a time. Remo really likes European women. Then again, they're easy to like."

"I'll take your word for it." I wondered if Japanese women were different. Or if having a hurt paw was putting a damper on Remo's extracurricular activities. Broken? Sprained? I had never gotten the full medical description.

"Which reminds me, I've got to see if I can get a ticket for Svetlana tonight."

"Who's that?"

"The woman I met in the bar last night. She's in town for another couple of days. Coincidentally, so are we." He grinned. "Perfect fling!"

I chuckled at him. Martin was so gleeful about his partners, it was hard not to be happy for him.

It wasn't until later, in that dull gap between soundcheck and the show, that I got to thinking about myself, though. I was making the assumption that I was going to be celibate for a while. Partly because, having gotten untangled from Jonathan, I knew I didn't want to get into another relationship right away, and partly because I assumed that trying to pick up gay sex partners in a foreign country was a non-starter. Seriously, though, a couple of weeks without sex shouldn't be a big deal.

That's easy to say in theory. In practice? Our second night at Budokan went well, and the audience seemed more responsive. I wonder if a lot of them were the same people coming back again, and knowing what to expect they were a little looser on the second go-round? I'm not sure. The band was pretty much ready to take their cues from me right from the start. The whole show was smoother, and with such a talented group it was fun to improvise and one-up each other and see how high we could take it. Pretty high. Cray and Alex got into a thing trading a lick back and forth between the pedal steel and the piano. The pedal steel was up on a riser at the same level with the keyboards, so they were eye to eye. It was grand.

I've said it before, and I'll say it again: playing a hot show pumps the juices. I'm not the only one who has that reaction, I know. So what do you do when you just rocked a city of 13 million people and your dick is hard and you have nowhere to stick it?

Hello washcloth, my old friend.

Big Time

Our last night at Budokan I got around to asking our translator about the magazine thing. He was a kind of skinny, nervous guy with glasses, who I would have described as nerdy in America, but in Japan I think was normal. His nickname was Rocky. I asked for his Japanese name, but he assured me I should call him Rocky. He said he would ask around about the magazines and would get me some as a souvenir if he could find them.

While talking to Waldo after soundcheck that day, I found out about the three Australian dates at the end of the tour. He was futzing around with the daybook and I asked him, "Hey, Wald', did you book me a flight back to LA at the end or to Boston?"

He looked up with that long-suffering look of his. "LA. You want to go somewhere from there, you're on your own. Besides, flying all the way from Sydney to Boston would be a bitch and a half."

"Sydney? We're going to Sydney?"

Long-suffering look got longer. "Did you not even look at the itinerary?"

"No one's given me one to look at."

He grumbled and dug out a copy of the schedule and handed it to me. "Don't tell me Remo didn't mention Australia."

"Now that I think about it, maybe he did, way-way back? But that was before I knew I was coming on the trip."

"It's real convenient that their summer is our winter. They've got festivals and all that going on. Their concert season is when ours is dormant."

"What about here, though? It's winter in Japan."

He shrugged. "I guess winter here doesn't keep people home the way it does in the States. All the big acts tour here in the winter. Clapton's coming through on our heels, Metallica was just here..."

I guess it made sense that if all the big English language acts were tied up all summer with the North American concert season and the big festivals in Europe, Japan would have to get them in the winter. Not that half of what goes on in the music industry even makes any sense, but maybe that was how it worked. "Hey, you talk to your niece recently?"

"No. You?"

"I should call her, now that I think about it."

"Well, it's two in the morning there now, so you might want to wait until tonight to try her."

"Yeah, true." Halfway around the world, it was easy to forget things like my father being hospitalized and Ziggy being AWOL. I figured if anything had happened with either of them, Carynne would call me. But it was probably a good idea for me to check in.

The show that night was not as fantastic as the night before, but it was still quite good. Cray and I had been avoiding each other since the non-conversation in the bar, but, like Martin had said, he was a professional, and what came out onstage was terrific. I could certainly live with that. I'd gotten a little more of his life story from Alex, too. Apparently Cray and I had more in common than I thought: he'd been playing in his family bluegrass band since he was tall enough to stand on the stage. His mother was a singer of particular repute.

Now that I'd looked at the schedule, I saw we had two days off in Tokyo before we were leaving for Nagoya. Which meant we didn't have to get up early to go anywhere. That meant we were having a small party for the Tokyo crew at the hotel. Which meant that I did a little drinking and was mostly a wallflower, which suited me just fine. I talked for a little while with Svetlana, actually, the woman that Martin was hanging out with. She was smart and funny and was ethnic Russian but had been raised in Belgium and now lived in France. She spoke seven languages. Japanese wasn't one of them, but that didn't stop her from coming here on an art-collecting trip. She was some kind of a curator for a big institution, but I wasn't clear on what exactly. She was kind of fascinated by the whole rock star life, you know, something you hear about but don't think you'll ever get to experience.

She and Martin went off together after a while, and the number of guests dwindled. I thought about going back to my room to call Carynne but did the math and realized if it wasn't quite midnight here, that meant it wasn't quite ten in the morning there, and maybe I should give her another hour. And then Flip and I got into a conversation about guitar playing, and the next thing you know he and I were sitting together with guitars. I half-jokingly picked up the Ovation classical style, and we played through a couple of things, a Spanish-sounding progression of his that was probably a song I couldn't place, "Sonny's Song," a Beatles song ("Here Comes the Sun").

Cray was one of the people sitting around with us. When we wound down at one point he said to Flip, "Hey, I play guitar, too," or something like that.

Flip said, "Be my guest," and handed him his guitar.

"What should we play?" I asked.

"I bet you know this one." He lit into a version of the Beatles "While My Guitar Gently Weeps." It's actually a sort of tricky song to play entirely on the acoustic guitar, because the recorded version that everyone knows relies so heavily on the piano. If you just play the actual guitar part, it doesn't sound like much, and you have to be a pretty accomplished player to manage to get it all going: the melody line, the chords, and the flourishes people recognize from the album, which are the bass and piano.

I think it's probably one of those songs that nearly every young guitar player tries to do, though. I know I had a version I used to play on the floor of Remo's living room.

Cray's version was pretty decent. A little swingy, like he put some syncopation in that didn't make sense to me because I felt it took away from the earnestness of the song. But it wasn't bad. I picked up when he got to the change into major mode, and he was able to carry the melody, and then we went back to the verses and we started trading the solo back and forth, improvising on the melody and taking it into other worlds. Because that's what any solo improvisation is, really, it's a transportation into a parallel universe where the underlying stuff is the same but the result is different.

He didn't have the facility I had, he couldn't go as many places as easily, but the six-string guitar wasn't his main instrument like it was mine, so I didn't expect him to. When we wound down the George Harrison, we moved on to another Nomad song, "Safe Haven," one of the older hits that I knew well. It was a shame Remo couldn't join in. I could see he was itching to.

"Sing," I said.

"No, *you* sing." Remo pointed at me.

I chuckled and sang the chorus when it came around. I wasn't much of a singer, you know, but my pitch was good and I at least had a modicum of expression in my voice.

We got to the end of the song, and I had to crack my knuckles and pop my thumb. "I always think of that song as being about your living room," I said.

Remo laughed. "That's because it's about my living room."

"Really?"

"I wrote it about you, Sundog, back when you had nowhere else to go."

"Okay, that is hilarious, because I always thought the song was metaphorical."

He laughed again and tousled my hair. "You never see yourself in things." Then he stood and stretched. "I'm hitting the sack. You all stay up as long as you want."

Once he wandered away, though, the crowd dissipated until Cray was the only one still sitting there, staring at me.

"Nice rendition of Harrison," I said to him.

"What was that about?" he asked, like I hadn't said anything.

"What was what about?" I took a quick glance around to see who was within earshot: nobody.

"All that about you and Remo's living room...?"

There was no way around it, then, I was going to have to be the one to tell Cray my own superhero origin story. I decided to keep it short. "When I was a kid, my mother wouldn't let me play the guitar in the house, so I played at Remo's, couple of hours a day. He wasn't even there all the time, working a day job, so I let myself in, put albums on his stereo, and taught myself the entire classic rock oeuvre."

"No kidding."

"No kidding. When Nomad got their first big record deal, though, they went to LA to record it and never came back. I would've probably gone with them except for the little fact that I was only fifteen or sixteen at the time." It occurred to me then that if part of why Remo had moved the band to LA was to get away from Digger, then that was one more reason why they couldn't've come up with a way to keep me around. If they'd taken me, they would've been saddled with him forever. Or at least until recently.

Maybe I would've come to this moment either way, touring Japan with Remo and the guys. But I was probably a better musician now than I would've been. Music school had taught me some things. And so had Moondog Three.

Cray digested what I'd said, his face a little flushed. "How old are you?"

Of course I'd asked him that the other night and he'd refused to answer. I couldn't resist throwing it back in his face. "None of your business," I said, same as he had.

"Yeah, yeah, point taken." He got up, holding his guitar by the neck and no longer looking at me. "See you in the morning."

That was a retreat if I ever saw one. I guess that means I won that battle.

New Direction

So the next day was a day for being tourists. As Remo put it, they built two days into the schedule for "Christmas shopping." I didn't think it would actually take me two days to do my shopping, so Martin and a couple of the other people from our entourage got together with Rocky to go to a famous temple.

I'm glad we had Rocky leading us because we took the subway, which could be confusing at the best of times, and then the temple itself—despite being a major tourist attraction, judging from the number of people there—was kind of hidden in a crowded but intriguing neighborhood of shops and restaurants and such. The temple grounds were very beautiful, and there were moments when you could lose sight of the crowd and get caught up in looking at a tree or a bell or a statue in a nook that looked like something out of a painting. Rocky explained a little bit about Shinto, from which I gathered that everything could be a god of some kind. As he put it, if you want good weather, you pray to the god of sunny days. This would be different from the god of catching fish or the god of good transit connections. I told him in Boston we have a goddess of good parking spaces, and he agreed wholeheartedly with the concept.

I didn't feel comfortable faking my way through any of the devotions, but under Rocky's urging Martin did wave incense on himself from a big communal brazier and clap his hands and put some money in a box. Many locals seemed to be doing the same, and there was something a bit comical about a tall, wild-haired white man standing among them, his eyes closed in prayer.

Martin and I broke off from the group after we were done seeing the temple itself and got happily lost in the side streets around it. Once we ventured off the main tourist drag, the shops became more interesting and the prices got better, which is how those things work in every city I've ever been to. We didn't get much actual shopping done, except I bought some games for Christian that I was fairly sure he couldn't get in the States.

And then we came to another temple. Rocky had called it the temple district, but I thought he had meant because of the one big one. But I guess if you have a religion that has an infinite number of gods, you could have an infinite number of temples. This one was much quieter and smaller than the big one and was mostly just one archaic-looking building with a courtyard. We were just entering the courtyard when I heard something like an accordion playing, and then a pair of voices singing a long note in unison, like a warm-up note. Which I think it was. We found a group of five musicians sitting on a blanket in one corner. A woman was playing a kind of accordion-organ (I'd later learn it was a harmonium—even I don't know every instrument ever invented) and singing, and there were two other singers and two percussionists, one with a pair of tabla drums and the other with a long, narrow drum with heads on either end.

Well, Martin being Martin sat right down in front of them, and I somewhat more slowly sat down next to him, and not long after that we had about twenty-five people in the audience, as the song got going from the warm-up stage into the actual thing. The musicians appeared to all be Japanese, but I knew the tabla were Indian, and they were wearing clothes that looked more Indian than Japanese, but after a while I stopped thinking about that and let my mind be taken up by the spiraling upward of the music and chanting. And suddenly I recognized two of the words in what they were saying—"Hare Krishna"— and it clicked. I used to go to the Hare Krishna "feast" once in a while in Providence because, hey, free food, and there would usually be this kind of singing, sometimes with ecstatic dancing.

I hadn't thought about that in a long, long time. I used to go because I was hungry and broke and too proud to make Bart feed me, even though he would have if I'd asked. (This was the same pride that made me too proud to ask him about moving in together, and I ended up with Roger, and yeah, well, never mind about that.)

I'd completely forgotten this music. Far as I could tell it was completely improvised, and yet somehow the musicians all knew when it came to a peak. Not knowing what their signals were or their expectations made it thrilling to listen to, like watching acrobats on a trapeze and not knowing if there's a net or not. Martin clapped his hands, and one of the drummers, whose eyes were open, unlike the woman leading them, smiled at him and nodded approvingly. The leader, the woman, would somehow kick them into a higher gear and they would all speed up at once, and then she would do it again. The music got faster and more ecstatic.

I felt too much like the polite Japanese sitting around me, though, like I should be quiet and respectful. I think if I hadn't been so rooted to the spot, Martin would have gotten up and danced. The whole performance was basically one song (I'm not even sure song is the right word) that went on for half an hour and ended in a big flourish, and then a slow reprise of the chant again. Then a monk came out, made a brief speech in Japanese, and passed the hat. Okay, it wasn't a hat, it was an ornate box with a slot for money, but same concept. We had no qualms about sticking a bunch of yen into the slot.

I followed Martin around for the rest of the afternoon feeling like I had been hypnotized and hadn't really snapped out of it.

On the train on the way back to the hotel, even the wheels of the train sounded like music to me, screeching and wailing in a turn and then becoming rhythmic as the train picked up speed in a straight tunnel. I was having thoughts like this: *Is all music a way to turn the sounds of the world, the sounds of life, into art? Wait, of course it is, of course that's what it is.*

I wondered, on the whole, how much of the world's music was improvised, like the Hare Krishna chanting and blues and jazz, and how much was set in advance, the way Western classical music and most pop music were. In the West we take for granted that composition and songwriting are the highest forms. The symphony. But the writing of the symphony and the *performance* of it are two different things. I remembered a class on Mozart I took at RIMCon. One little fact I had tucked away in my head and forgotten until then was that some of the arias and solos we have written out today were actually improvised by the performers. Mozart wrote parts for his friends, wife, and family members to perform. Over the course of the performances, they would eventually settle on a best version, I guess, and then write that down for posterity. So even within what we think of as the strict Western classical composition tradition, there is still room for that element, that discovery.

Martin must've been thinking along similar lines, or he was reading my mind, because he said at one point, "Have you ever seen Ravi Shankar in concert?"

"No. Why?"

"You should. If you think a couple of Hare Krishnas in a park is mind-blowing, go see some actual Indian classical music."

"There were a couple of concerts when I was in school, but I never got around to them." Too often, I was working nights trying to make ends meet.

"It's really cool. The orchestra has the percussion on one side and the melody instruments on the other side. And the melody guys decide what raga they're going to do, while the drummers decide what rhythmic pattern they're going to do. And so it never really comes out the same twice, even though it's really rigidly defined."

"Really? Do they tell each other what they're going to do?"

"I don't think so. I think that's part of the fun. And it scales up and down. You can have a concert that's just one drummer and one instrument. The cool thing is the raga will be a certain length, and the rhythm pattern will be a certain length, but they're not the same, so it's only every so often that the end of both coincides, and it's like... amazing. We're probably in the wrong country to find a classical concert to go to tonight, though."

"How do you know so much about Indian classical music?"

"Had a fling with a sitar player in Berkeley." He shrugged. "I never got any good at the tabla, though. Those are some tricky drums. Takes a lot of finesse to make them sound right. Hey, I think this is our stop coming up."

He was right. We came out into the station, which was massive, and eventually got aboveground, and it took us a few blocks to make sure we were going the right direction. We ran into Flip in the lobby and convinced him to come out to dinner with us, and we got in a cab and let the cab driver pick where we were going, which was a bit of a trick since the cab driver didn't really speak English. As Rocky explained it, "If they could speak English, they would have a better job than cab driver." Flip just kept saying "sushi" over and over to the driver until he finally said "Okay" and drove.

He let us off at a place that looked traditional—or at least looked traditional to white folks like us—with the little curtains in the doorway and rice paper windows. I proceeded to talk Flip's ear off through the entire meal about what percentage of human musical performance was improvised and the place of art in the human condition, et cetera.

Flip was always receptive to that sort of stuff and basically added fuel to my fire. Martin cheerfully went along with whatever we decided about the grand state of musical endeavors.

And we ate a lot of fish.

And after two bottles of sake (each) my head suddenly went something like this: Hare-Krishnas-tabla-Indian-drums-India-hey-wait-Ziggy-went-to-India.

So, India. Hm. India.

As Long as You Follow

In the morning my head hurt from drinking too

much without realizing it. But the bigger discomfort in my head was the feeling that I'd discovered my entire worldview was skewed. Now that it had skewed another direction, it was like walking off balance all the time.

Let me see if I have it right. Buddhism, the martial arts, spiritual enlightenment, musical modes, most of the ancestors of the instruments we play, the highest form of improvisational music, and the classical tradition all came from India? How could it be that I'd never even given the entire country more than a passing thought?

Bart and I used to eat in an Indian restaurant in Kenmore Square sometimes, and they would have Bollywood movies playing on a tinny, piece-of-crap television above the door. Gave me the impression that current Indian music was a lot of screechy yet overproduced pop that all sounded the same. I suppose that was the equivalent of judging all American music based on the *Miami Vice* reruns played in a bar.

They say the point of traveling the world is that it changes your perspective. Mine had changed so much in a single day I felt like my clothes didn't fit right.

Was that why Ziggy went to India? Did he have the same experience? Or was he still looking for it?

I was in a kind of daze, deep in thought, when Remo found me getting something to eat in the hotel restaurant and asked if I wanted to go with him to some Japanese shopping district. I didn't catch the name. "Huh?"

"In English they call it Guitar Street," he said.

My ears perked up. "They do?"

"Come on."

We took the train and no translator. I think we were relying on the "universal language" of music to get us by. As it turned out, that works pretty well in music shops where they let you try the merchandise.

"Guitar Street," which is actually called Meidai Dori, should probably be called Musical Instrument Street. Yes, there were at least ten shops selling nothing but guitars, but there were also ones that specialized in violins, or school instruments, or pretty much anything else you could name. That made for an interesting mix of people on the street, because there were, on the one hand, all these school kids in uniforms pulling their parents around by the hand while they looked for their first trumpet or viola, and, on the other hand, there were these rock and roll types complete with fringed jackets and bandannas around their heads and the whole Sunset Strip look to them, except they were 100% Japanese. There were some punks, too, with textbook-perfect mohawks and facial piercings, and some glam rockers in the vein of Prince. All of which made me wonder what the cultural signals of dressing like that really were. Did it translate from one culture to the next? If it wasn't really language, what was it? Was a mohawk a statement of rebellion here the way it was in the States and in England? Or was it more of a costume? Or a commodity? For that matter, wasn't it a costume no matter where you were? And wasn't a "look" a commodity the second it gained popularity?

This only increased my indecision about what to do with my hair, by the way. It had been growing nonstop since Ziggy had trimmed it. Was that in May? It had grown easily six inches. It was uneven because of the part they'd cut after of the explosion, but I had gotten used to that.

One of the shopkeepers had met Remo before. He spoke reasonable English, and I gathered that Remo had been brought here by a Takamine rep earlier in the trip, or on a previous tour. Amusingly enough, in his shop we played a pair of top-of-the-line Martin guitars, though only for a few minutes because Remo didn't want to stress his wrist. We thanked him and moved on.

Others sussed out who we were easily enough, though. It's not like we were hard to identify. Two obvious white guys looking pretty much like rock stars. Everyone was polite and respectful, though, and I didn't feel stalked.

In one shop where they had traditional Japanese instruments I got into a long discussion with an English-speaking clerk about the shamisen and koto, and a bunch of instruments I didn't even know about, which led to us talking about the lap steel guitar and the sitar, two more instruments with strings that have some common DNA with the guitar but clearly went off in other directions. I was tempted to try to buy a sitar from the guy, but it would either have to get shipped all the way to Boston from here or come along with us everywhere. I told myself I should wait and see if I actually wanted one when I got home.

Maybe it was talking about the lap steel that conjured them up, but it was at that point that Cray, the Mazel brothers, and Flip came in, kind of surprised to run into us there and yet not surprised because it made total sense for us to go somewhere like that. I mean, that's as close to the temple of guitar as you get, right? And I made Cray come over and talk to the clerk about the lap steel, and the next thing you know he was trying to get us play some instruments. I fussed around with a biwa, which I was told was an antique and to be careful with it, and then while the first clerk was showing Cray an elaborately decorated koto, another one swapped me the biwa for a shamisen.

The koto is kind of like a big zither, and the shamisen is sort of like a square banjo. The clerk was showing me how to hold the gigantic piece of bone they used for a pick, which filled my whole hand.

Remo came over to stir up trouble. "You boys gonna play something for us?"

Cray and I looked at each other. I had the easier instrument, I figured. I could pick out a melody without too much difficulty now that I had figured out the relation of one string to another. It was up to him whether he could pull anything useful out of the thirteen strings he had there. It was kind of like he had a harp lying on its side in front of him. Or maybe like he had the interior guts of a piano ready to be plucked.

He didn't break eye contact with me except to glance down every few seconds to see where his hands were on the strings, and he started to slowly play "Twinkle, Twinkle Little Star." This produced exclamations of amazement from the clerks and curiosity-seekers. The mode was a little funky, but I joined in easily enough, and before long we'd had three go-rounds of it, each of us with a jazzy solo, and then a round in unison.

We ended before we pushed our luck too far and received congratulatory handshakes and bows from all and sundry. It was kind of ridiculous, given that we'd played one of those songs that in the US was almost always on page two of your lesson book, no matter what instrument you were learning. ("Mary Had a Little Lamb" was on page one.) But music is music, and we accepted the praise humbly.

Later, we were all sitting around in a noodle shop not far down the street. The place was noisy, the only people I could really hear were the two nearest to me, Flip and Cray, and Flip was going on about something to Martin. So that left me talking to Cray, who told me his secret. "I had a girlfriend once who played koto. She showed me a little."

"No shit. Well, it impressed the hell out of me, anyway."

He snorted like I was kidding.

"No, really. And it blew the minds of the people there."

He gulped his sake out of a tiny cup. "Yeah, I'm sure they thought they were going to make fools of us."

"I doubt that. They're too polite for that."

"Yeah, right."

I really didn't understand his relentlessly negative attitude. "Cray, not everyone is out to get you."

"Yeah, and not everyone is out to crown you king of the universe." He looked at me with round, brown eyes, betraying little emotion. But like I said, I was sensitive to underlying aggression.

"I couldn't care less whether people crown me or not," I said. "I just do my thing, you know?"

"And that's a really privileged, self-centered attitude," he pointed out. "Though, sorry for calling you Little Lord Fauntleroy before. I should be better than name-calling."

"Call me what you want, Cray." I took a pull on a ricey Japanese beer. If his tactic was to be overly blunt, I could do that, too. "Well, anything but fag. I'd break your nose for that."

He almost spat sake out his nose. "What?"

I delivered the following in a calm manner, only loud enough so he could hear it. "I'm saying there's some shit I'll put up with and some I won't. You've got some kind of inferiority complex? Fine. I don't care. But I've got no tolerance for homophobes. If that's what it is, we may as well have it out right here, right now, and then one of us can go home."

He blinked and stuttered. "That's—that's not... Wait. Are you gay?"

"I am. Got a problem with that?"

"No! How the hell did you even—"

"Then I've got no problem." I liked that beer. And I liked having Cray totally off balance. I decided to yank his chain one more time, since I could. "What the hell did you mean by Little Lord Fauntleroy, anyway?"

"Shit, you know. Spoiled brat."

"Let me get this straight. You, whose mother has a lifelong career in music and who cleared a career path for you, is calling me, whose mother wouldn't even let me practice in the house, a spoiled brat."

He got up suddenly and walked out, at which point Flip turned to me. "What did I miss?"

"Nothing."

"No, really, what did you say? You were so calm I thought you guys were just talking."

"He's got a wild hair across his ass. All I did was pluck it." I shrugged.

I was a little less calm when Remo cornered me about it on the train. "He's a big boy and can take care of himself, but should I be aware of something going on between you and Cray?"

The last thing I was going to do was turn tattle-tale. "No. I've got no problem with him, Reem."

"You two are actually a lot alike."

"Other than he's a moody sonofabitch."

Remo gave me a look. "Oh really. I hadn't noticed." That was his way of saying he could have called me out for being the pot that called the kettle black, but he would pretend to ignore it if I would. "He'll come around."

Or he won't and I won't care, I told myself.

Mystery Achievement

We took the train to Nagoya—not the subway train, the fancy, high-speed train. The equipment had all gone ahead of us already days before, so we didn't have that much to carry. By car it would have been four or five hours—the same distance as going Boston to New York.

By "bullet" train, it was 100 minutes. Whoosh.

That left just enough time to get bored enough to read a book, not enough time to get a significant amount of reading done. I don't remember what I read on that trip. I should tell you I was reading something really deep, so you'll be impressed. But it was probably a mystery or science fiction. I think that was around the time there was a lot of cyberpunk in the airport bookstores. I remember reading several that were all set in the middle east, in a kind of futuristic "Casbah." I wasn't good at keeping track of which books in a series I'd already read, though, and I'm pretty sure a few times in those years I bought the same book twice. More importantly, that meant I read them twice, and sometimes it wasn't until halfway through the book that I realized it. Which just goes to show that sometimes books kind of go in one eye and out the other and I don't retain a lot.

Then again, who said you have to retain a lot to enjoy a book? They were something to keep my brain busy. They succeeded at that.

The hotel in Nagoya was nowhere near as fancy as the place we'd been in Tokyo, but I didn't really mind that. The place in Tokyo had been kind of over-the-top fancy, actually, and it was kind of a relief to move to a place where I didn't feel like security guards might, at any moment, ask me to leave. It was a much fancier place than I expected from Remo. I was under the impression that much, much more of the details on the tour were handled by people in Japan than by Nomad's own team. I was still pretty focused on learning the material and figured I'd absorb more details at some point.

I was still having that problem where everything I saw or did, I imagined what Jonathan would think of it. Would he like it? Not like it? Have an opinion about it?

Why the fuck did it matter to me what Jonathan would or wouldn't think about a guy I saw on the train, or the train itself, or what? I wouldn't think about him for a while, but then something would trigger it, like I'd see someone drinking from a glass and they'd hold the glass the way he held it. That kind of thing.

It was driving me a bit nuts, actually. You'd think that crossing the Pacific would be the perfect "getting away," but it was almost worse. Everything I saw was new or different, and I hadn't realized how often when we were together if I wanted to know something more about something all I had to do was ask him.

That might have been why I spent more time than was healthy grilling Flip about various topics. Martin and I had told him at length about the troupe of singing Hare Krishnas we saw. Okay, actually, *I* had told him at length about it. Don't ask me where he got it, but the next day, in Nagoya, after soundcheck, he handed me a cassette. I figured it was more Nomad stuff, something else for me to work on, but it was actually a tape of George Harrison's "My Sweet Lord." You've heard the song. Everyone in the world has heard the song. Maybe I'm the only one who never really thought about the fact that the chorus is "Hare Krishna"? I heard that song hundreds of times when I was a kid. And I never connected what those words meant. Not even after I had sat through the Hare Krishna meal in Providence. And yes, I knew The Beatles went to India, but somehow I'd always just digested the music without really thinking about where the influences had come from. It hit me particularly hard because of how we'd picked apart "While My Guitar Gently Weeps" a few nights before, and I'd been continuing to pick it apart in my head ever since. How can it be that I know things but I *don't* know things?

The place we were playing in Nagoya was a big concrete "gymnasium" building, not that different from the sports arenas I was used to. No super-futuristic architecture this time.

The show went well. I wouldn't say we were quite working like a well-oiled machine, but the lubrication was at least beginning to seep in. Bunch of professionals, good at what they do. Now that they'd all adjusted to me being the de facto bandleader, things clicked pretty well and Remo could just go be the front man.

Flip and I got into a jam session at the hotel that night. It went on for easily two hours. People were in and out of the room, but I wasn't really paying attention to them. They weren't paying that much attention to us, either. Two guitars in the corner of a room. When I had to stop because my thumb was starting to ache, like it always did when the weather was cold and I played too much, I went back to grilling him about everything he knew about Indian music.

"Okay, so first of all there's so much to know about Indian music, that's like asking somebody to tell you all about European music," he said.

"Yeah, but if someone asked me to do that, I could give them the rundown about how church music turned into classical music, the orchestra was developed, Mozart, Beethoven, boom."

"Okay, and where does rock and roll fit in there?" Flip challenged.

"Seriously? Come on. Bach relied on the same three chords as Elvis. When your music's built on the twelve-tone scale, that return to the tonic is hardwired. Rock and roll just comes out of the same root, but instead of coming out of the concert halls, it comes out of the back rooms and the bars."

"Is that divide because of class? Race?"

"Yes, and yes, and the fact that music doesn't stay in the box you put it in. If you're going to have music that is defined by the concert hall, by definition you're going to have music that *isn't* defined by it, also. It's exactly like food, Flip. French cuisine with white tablecloths is not the only food there is, and thank goodness for that. Anywhere there are people, there is going to be food. And music."

"Yeah, okay, I guess if you look at it like that." He gestured for me to hand him the Ovation, and I did. "I guess I hadn't quite thought of it as a universal human endeavor, but yeah, sure."

"So, India."

"Right. Honestly, Daron, you've picked my brain clean of what I know about Indian music. I can't tell you what the relationship between Indian classical music and folk music and Bollywood and Hare Krishna-type chanting is." He pulled a string winder out of his pocket and started taking the strings off. "Other than to say it all is. Have you heard *qawwali*?"

"Koala-ie?" I imagined koala bears with sitars.

"Qawwali. It's not Indian, it's more middle eastern. Or maybe Pakistani? It's another ecstatic chanting/singing music, using Sufi spiritual texts. It's sort of like if you make a cross between all the stuff on the *Passion* soundtrack by Peter Gabriel and the Hare Krishna stuff you've been talking about." He suddenly stopped winding. "Wait. The guy I'm thinking of actually sings on the *Passion* album. What the hell is his name? He was a huge hit at WOMAD a couple of years back."

I hadn't realized Cray was standing a few feet behind the couch where I was sitting until he spoke up. "You mean Nusrat Fateh Ali Khan."

Flip nearly leaped out of his chair, except he remembered his ankle was in a cast, and he fell back with the Ovation in his lap. "Yes! That's who I mean."

Cray slunk over to us. "Surprised the hick knew something, huh?"

Flip was usually quick with a comeback and was good at smoothing shit like that over, but this time he was caught off guard, and I jumped in with, "Who thinks you're a hick?"

"Forget it." He turned to go.

"Cray, get your ass the fuck over here and explain yourself," Flip said. "Seriously. If you're going to accuse me of dissing you, at least have the balls to look me in the eye."

Cray came around to my side of the couch, his hands jammed in the pockets of his corduroy pants. He was dressed like he always was, flannel shirt over a T-shirt, which he wore usually buttoned up and tucked in. Come to think of it, he dressed basically like Remo did.

I should explain stage dress for a band like Nomad. The backup singers and the horn section got dressed up. It was kind of a tradition with them. But the rest of the band usually looked like we could have pulled up in a pickup truck straight from our working-class jobs and walked onstage. Getting too fancy was considered not right for the blue-collar image of a band that had so much blues in its DNA. So we didn't look all that different onstage and off. The main difference was what you sent to laundry and what you didn't.

Anyway, Cray came over and told us off. "You think I don't see what you're doing? All your hoity-toity music-theory talk. You think I can't keep up."

Flip blinked, his mouth hanging open slightly. I should mention that we had been drinking. Not that much, I thought, and beer only, but you know. It's important to know. He finally got his jaw in gear. "Wait. You think we've been talking about what we've been talking about specifically to exclude you because we think you're too stupid to participate?"

Cray just smoldered.

Flip: "Cray, I never thought you were dumb about anything musically, but that is the stupidest thing I ever heard."

Cray: "Don't deny it."

Flip: "Deny what? How about this: not everything is about you."

Cray: "Something better came along. I see the writing on the wall."

Flip (exasperated): "You want to come hang out, just sit your ass down! I'm not your babysitter!"

"Hang on, time out." I twirled my hands like a conductor cutting everyone off. Amazing how well that works with musicians sometimes. "Cray, sit the fuck down."

He sat.

Here's what I said: "Look. I know I'm kind of the new guy here—" at which Flip snorted "—so I don't know everybody's history. I didn't come here to steal your friends or your spotlight. You said you couldn't care less about my sexual orientation, but you seem to have a big chip on your shoulder about me. Now you're dragging Flip into it, and that's just not cool. You want to hang out with us, just come hang out. You're the one with the chip, not me. Clear?"

"Besides." Flip set the unstrung Ovation aside. "If we wanted to keep you out, we'd just go in a room and shut the damn door. You want to come jam? Bring it, man. We know you can."

Cray's face looked even more pinched than it had when he sat down. "Seriously?"

"Seriously," Flip and I said at the same time.

I went on. "Now what was that name you said?"

"Nusrat Fateh Ali Khan," Cray said. "Blue Licks String Band played the same WOMAD he did."

"Yeah, I was at that one." Flip remembered that he had a partially drunk beer on the table and sipped cautiously from the bottle—in case it had gone bad, I guess. "I missed Blue Licks, though. Which stage were you guys on?"

"We played two sets actually, one in the daytime that was on the instructional stage, and then a night show on the east stage." Cray unhunched a little as he talked.

"Cool." Flip took a more confident swig. "Okay, but

seriously, what's your issue with Daron?"

Cray and I were both goosed by the sudden return to the previous topic. We'd clearly both been lulled into thinking we were letting it blow over.

"Oh, come on, Flip," he said. "You don't really believe that he walks on water like the rest of them, do you?"

"Uh, walks on water, no. One of the top six-string players in the world, yes."

"You can't be serious."

"I'm quite serious. Have you looked at this guy's resume? I don't just mean playing with Nomad as a teenager. RIMCon, two Top Forty hits before he was barely old enough to drink, soundtracks, made the *Guitar Player* list two years in a row now. I'm not making this shit up." He finished the beer and set the empty bottle down. "Which doesn't mean we should kiss his ass or anything. I'm just saying it's not like Remo picked him up as a charity case."

That made me smile inside, because of course the last time I had toured with them I *had* been charity case.

Cray looked straight at me. "Enjoy it while it lasts. You think you're hot shit now, but see what the world thinks of you when you turn thirty."

"Aw shit, is that what this is about?" Flip pushed himself into a standing position using his arms, then hopped on one leg over to the fridge to get three more beers. He could carry all three in one hand by hooking the necks in his meaty fingers. He hopped back, handed us each one, and then cracked the top off his own with the string winder. I had previously been unaware that a string winder could be used in that manner. "Happy Birthday, Cray. When did you hit the big three-oh?"

"Last week," Cray said glumly, and took the winder to pop his own. I followed, and we all clinked bottles.

"Okay, now we're getting somewhere. So you're in the dumps because you're thirty. What else? You're single..."

"Yeah. My mother is continually trying to fix me up with this girl she wants singing with Blue Licks but it's like, man, she's not that good a singer, and if the only reason she's carrying her is because she wants her for a daughter-in-law... that's just a bad scene all around."

"Yeah, well, you're with us now. What else. Come on, spill it."

Cray shook his head. "It's all right, you guys. I'm over it."

"Now now, I'm not convinced you are." Flip waggled his bottle in Cray's direction.

But Cray had clammed up. "I'm sorry. You guys are all right. I'm not the type to get into a pissing contest, you know? I still don't really get how you"—meaning me—"magically became band leader, but I guess I should shut up about it since it works."

Now *I* couldn't keep my mouth shut. "Maybe Remo should've said something, but I think he didn't want to put too much pressure on me. But it's basically two things. One, I'm used to being the band leader, and two, the guitar's really the lead instrument in these arrangements. So it was kind of inevitable if Remo couldn't do it. I didn't intend to grab the reins, but when they were flopping around somebody had to."

Cray thought that over.

"And it had to be somebody who could make eye contact with everyone else on the stage. I'm the only one up there with the mobility to do it. Especially since I'm not singing."

Cray sighed. "Why didn't Remo just say so, then?"

Flip was all over that. "He didn't think he had to. Come on, Cray. Remo's a laid-back dude. You know that. He's going to let things happen and just see how they come out. That's his style."

Cray nodded. "Yep. Yep, that sure is his style." He drained half his beer. "This shit tastes like rice." He got up then and went into the bathroom to pour it out.

When he came out, though, instead of sitting back down with us, he slipped out the door. Like we weren't going to notice?

"He's a moody one, isn't he?" I said.

"To put it mildly, yes. I don't get it. That guy has had everything in the world handed to him, and he can't get along with anyone for more than five minutes. While you, who are on top of the world, are the easiest person to get along with, ever."

I shrugged. "I wouldn't say getting sued by my record company puts me on top of the world."

"Relatively speaking," Flip said. "But really. You're so easygoing. You're like Remo that way. You don't create problems where they don't exist."

"Anymore," I said. Being out of the closet, at least with this group, helped simplify life a lot. "You ever meet Matthew, Remo's previous guitar tech?"

"Coupla times, yeah."

"I went on the road for the warm-up tour in 1986. And I was a withdrawn, terrified teenager starved for advice about how to live my life."

"And did you get that advice from Remo?"

"Hell no. I got it from Matthew. Thank goodness he was around to keep an eye on me, though. He's a terrific guy, really. I didn't appreciate at the time what a little lost lamb I was. I'm better now."

"I'll say." Flip tipped his bottle back until it was empty and then smacked his lips. "I think I like this beer."

"Me too. I think I like the rice flavor."

"Yeah, it's nice. Crisp."

I still really didn't understand Cray better after that night. But at least I felt like Cray had picked up some clues. The next day he was much less of a pill about everything, anyway. Maybe sometimes what a person needs most is to feel like someone listened to them.

Silent Running

The kind of dumb thing about the next day was that we took the train almost all the way back to Tokyo, to do a show in Yokohama. I guess since it only takes a hundred minutes by train, it didn't matter that much, but in my mind that was like playing a show in Boston, then New York City, and then Great Woods in Mansfield, Mass. Then again, I know there were tours set up like that, so maybe I should just enjoy the fact that for the most part Moondog Three's last tour had so few switchbacks in it. How much of that was clout and how much was simply Carynne bullying the hell out of the venues, I don't know.

The kind of cool—yet disturbing—thing about the next day was the venue, which was brand new, not even a full year old, but which was remarkably similar to Madison Square Garden inside. A little smaller, but it was like the same architect must have done it. It felt a little like time traveling to when the Garden was new.

Who am I kidding. It felt a lot like time traveling to the last big show we did as a band. For the first time this trip, I felt less haunted by Jonathan and more haunted by Ziggy.

This meant that at various times throughout the afternoon, before, during, and after soundcheck, I would space out, my mind drifting back to various memories that felt particularly vivid. It wasn't just that this place resembled MSG. It *sounded* like it.

It was in one of those moments—not the one where I was reliving him collapsing in my arms, but the one where I was remembering meeting his mother—that I got goosebumps and the hair on the back of my neck stood up. I'd realized quite suddenly that she was in an old folks home of some sort, right? Would Ziggy have told her where he had gone? Would he have left his physically ill mother with no contact for months? He was paying for her care, so that meant...

Damn it. That meant Digger knew where she was. Was I desperate enough to try to contact her that I'd call Digger and eat crow?

For that matter, Digger might flat out know Ziggy's whereabouts. He might. But what were the chances he'd tell me? Or that he'd extort something from me in exchange for the information? No. Not happening. I felt a little queasy from the mere thought of capitulating.

The only way to clear all the crap out of my head was to focus on music. Remo razzed me a little for being a space case toward the end of soundcheck. "Okay, Sundog, come down out of orbit now."

"Sorry." My cheeks flared red. "My head is in the fog today."

"Two suggestions," he said. "One, lay off the drinking tonight. Two, I think we should add a real jam to the set tonight."

So just like that we ballooned a song in the encore to a twelve-minute epic round of jazz-style solos. It still wasn't what it was like when Remo and I could jam with each other, tossing stuff back and forth all throughout the set, but that was all right.

Two days later we were in Osaka, to play at the Osaka Castle Hall. Osaka Castle Hall was not at, nor in, Osaka Castle, but we got to see the castle on our day off, so that was okay. The main memorable thing for me about the show, though, is that Remo did it again: he threw a suggestion out to the band that we took as a direct order. This time he told us to add a jam to something in the main set, and he basically said me and Cray should volleyball it.

I think he had been wanting us to do that all along, but he wasn't blind, he saw we weren't getting along at first, plus I had so much to learn anyway. But I'm sure he was aware that we were at least in some kind of a truce by then, too. He had waited until we had a chance to succeed at working together that closely before asking us to.

It takes a certain kind of trust and a certain kind of knowing each other to go out on a limb together musically.

I sometimes wonder. Did the people who were at that charity show in New York, the one where Ziggy fell, understand how before that happened they were witnessing an extraordinary performance, a one-of-a-kind performance that we couldn't have recreated if we wanted to? Improvisation never goes the same way twice.

Improvising with Cray was actually easier in some ways because two stringed instruments can mesh together in ways that a guitar and a human voice just can't. But we weren't ready to take big chances. That was okay, though. Little leaps, little risks, they're fun, too.

Remo liked it. I couldn't help but notice that Cray and I had basically the same reaction to Remo trying to get effusive about it, which was to shrug and act like it was no big deal. Piece of cake. Which it was, partly because that was how we acted about it.

That night after the show was over, Cray and I shared a cab back to the hotel. "Hey, I have an idea," he said.

"Is it a good idea?"

"Well, let me describe it and you tell me. I want to ask if you'll come work on turning my version of 'While My Guitar Gently Weeps' into a duet."

"'Work on' sounds like you want to do more than have a song you can play at parties."

"Yeah. I think we could do a thing in the show. Remo would let us. Just the two of us. And it'd give me a chance to get downstage."

"And play the guitar." He opened his mouth, but before he could say anything I continued with, "And yes, you're plenty good enough to play with me. But let's practice it."

"Now?"

"Yeah."

We stayed up most of the night working on it, actually, only getting a few hours sleep after sunrise. That meant I slept most of the train trip from Osaka to Kanazawa the next day. It was only a three-hour trip, up the western coast of Japan, so really only good for a nap. Cray and I didn't have a chance to work on the song that day at all. We didn't discuss it specifically, but I think there was an unspoken understanding between us that we weren't going to rehearse it with other people listening. We'd let them hear it when we'd worked it all out.

Cray was still a moody bastard and seemed to be fighting himself all the time, but he had given me the perfect distraction from my other obsessions.

Hot Water

The next day was a day off. The whole entourage relocated to a hot springs resort where the main order of business was soaking in hot water. Some of the tubs were outdoors, and there was much talk about how zen-like the experience could be when sitting in geothermally heated spring water while snow fell. Like something from a haiku. Yeah:

Get me out of here
Sitting still is my nightmare
Get me the fuck out

And it wasn't even snowing.

Flip, as usual, saved me. We ended up in a round wooden tub by ourselves—one of the hottest ones, which Remo declared too hot for his taste—with a view of the lagoon. Flip, in case I haven't made it clear, was kind of a hefty guy, built more like a "roadie" than

Matthew was. I don't mean he was built like Arnold Schwarzenegger, not at all, but he had big fingers, a big forehead, and big biceps. When he took the medical boot off his ankle it was big enough around for my whole head to fit in.

I wondered aloud why he was in the water in a baseball shirt—the kind with three-quarter colored sleeves and a white middle.

"Dude, did you miss the whole thing with all the bowing and apologizing at the door?"

"I did. What's going on?"

"The manager was very apologetic but trying to explain to me that basically tattoos are considered obscene here."

"They are?" That was totally news to me.

"It's a gang thing, a Yakuza thing," he said, in a lower voice. "So it's totally frowned upon in polite society to let your ink show. I'm cool with it. This is totally different from that time I got thrown out of the pool at the Ritz in Dallas."

It wasn't hard to get Flip to tell a story, ever. "What happened to you at the Ritz in Dallas?"

"Some junior manager took it upon himself to express that he didn't like my kind of people, by which I think he meant anyone with a tattoo was obviously some kind of demon-worshipping lowlife. I'm not sure which was the worse sin to him, the devil worship or being of a lower socio-economic class." Flip sniffed and shrugged.

"So he threw you out?"

"Yep. The funny part is that I was there teching for Willie Nelson's Fourth of July festival, which is this huge deal. A bunch of the bands and guests were staying there. When someone in the chain of command found out what happened, they pulled us all out of there. Nothing like costing a place a hundred thou in business in one day, eh?"

I did the math in my head. Let's say the place was $500 a night, and if the festival ran all weekend, each room was probably booked for five nights. So that would be $2,500 a pop. Say it was 40 rooms. Holy crap, that *would* be $100,000. "Where'd they send you?"

"Some friend of Willie's had a Holiday Inn on the outskirts of town that was closed for renovations, but the renovations hadn't actually started yet, so we all moved there. And that place turned into party central, let me tell you! No one but us there. I never heard for sure if pulling everyone out was Willie's idea or just something he endorsed. He's a pretty cool dude. Sticks up for his people."

"Yeah. Okay, but this wasn't like that, you say?"

"No. First of all, they were really apologetic here. Second, it was clear that it was the tattoos themselves that were the problem, not *me*."

"Ah."

"The manager told me he wanted me to understand it wasn't that they believe anything bad about me or my intentions, but they wanted me to understand that it's like a taboo here. And they knew that I didn't get inked up specifically to come here and bust their taboos, so could I simply cover it? That would make it okay."

I meditated on that for a while. "But, wait. Isn't part of the point of getting tattooed exactly to say *fuck you* to the societal norms that Dallas hotel junior managers follow?" That was pretty much how Colin had described it to me.

"Well, yeah."

"So—"

"But those are *American* social norms. I didn't do it to offend these nice Japanese people."

"Um." The hot water was melting my brain. I couldn't quite get my thoughts to line up. "So which came first, the idea that tattoos are taboo and so that's why the Yakuza get them? Or is it because it's something the Yakuza do that it has become taboo?"

"Oh, I see—you mean, is the only reason the yakuza do the tattoo thing because it marks them as outsiders? Or did they end up monopolizing tattoos because people here automatically assume tattoo means yakuza? I have no idea. I'll have to ask Rocky later."

Then I quit talking for a while because a couple of the other guys came along then and got in the tub next to ours. They started talking to Flip about something, and my mind wandered off.

Shortly after that, I was thinking I should really get out of the water because I had this vague idea that being in too long wasn't healthy. Cray came scuffing by in his slippers and caught my eye.

Yeah, I would much rather be upstairs working on the duet. That was what we were both thinking. So I got out of the water, said so long to the guys, and went to get dried off.

You want a sign of how far I'd come from my terrified and in-the-closet days? I didn't even blink or think twice about hopping out of the tub and following a guy into the changing room, despite what that might have looked like. Maybe it was because I wasn't as freaked out about how things "might look" now that I wasn't trying to hide anything. Maybe it was because I was concentrating more on wanting to play and to have an excuse to go.

We got dried off and dressed and went upstairs to play until it was time to go to dinner. The arrangement was coming out sweet, and it got to where we weren't "working" on it so much as enjoying playing it, meshing with each other. Cray really was decent at the guitar, better than Flip, though Flip could hold his own in a jam session.

When we wound down, Cray asked, "Hey, did you see if they have a shop that sells postcards?"

"I noticed a shop, didn't notice if they had postcards or not. But what hotel shop doesn't?"

"I better send one to my mother now or I'll be home for a month before she gets it." He stood and stretched.

"Good point. I better send some, too."

So we went down to the shop and bought some postcards. Some I bought to keep for myself, since I didn't have a camera and these were nicer pictures than I could probably take anyway.

One of the horn players, a skinny guy named Mitch in a skinny tie, came into the store right as Cray had finished paying and I was digging out my own wallet to finish my own transaction.

I swear what he said sounded innocent to me. Well, not *innocent*. But what he said was meant in a joking, good-natured way, not to be nasty. I think.

He said, "You two sneak off to the honeymoon suite?"

I didn't see what happened exactly, because they were behind me. But my take is that Cray went ballistic. Mitch ended up with a black eye, and postcards ended up all over the floor.

And I ended up all over Cray to keep him from beating Mitch's face in.

"What the fuck, Daron? Let go of me!"

"Yeah, as soon as you calm down."

"I am fucking calm!"

"Uh huh. Sure you are."

Waldo appeared first, at the same time as hotel security, and Remo hurried over next, dressed for dinner. They both ended up giving me the "make yourself scarce" look, so I slipped back to my room. The phone rang a little while later.

Remo. "You want to tell me what was going on there? You don't have to, but I'd kind of like to know."

"Mitch made a joke. Cray didn't take it as one."

"Well, Mitch can be kind of snide sometimes. Did you hear what he said?"

"Yeah. He asked if Cray and I had sneaked off to the honeymoon suite together. And Cray took exception to that."

"And you didn't?"

"It was just a joke. I mean, if someone else said it? Or it was to put me down? But it didn't feel like that." I thought about how I'd told Cray I was gay and kind of challenged him to have a problem with it. I didn't think he had. "Wait, you don't think Cray thought I was offended and so was defending me, sort of?"

Remo snorted. "Don't think so. I think he acted like a meathead getting called fag."

"Mitch didn't use that word."

"I know. Mitch wouldn't, because Mitch is gay."

"What? Are you sure?"

"Listen to yourself, Daron. Yes, I'm sure."

Okay, so I still had some stereotypes and bullshit to get past for myself, and my "gaydar" was crappy. What else is new? "Then, you know what I think? I think Mitch sincerely thought there was something going on with me and Cray." I paused, wondering if my gaydar was even worse than I thought. "Wait. Please tell me Cray is straight."

"As a whistle. I am curious, though, what you two have been spending so much time doing."

"We'll show you tomorrow at soundcheck."

"If I don't send Cray home on the next plane across the Pacific."

"Oh."

"He's not some green kid," Remo said. "He's thirty years old, for Pete's sake, and should know better than to punch out another band member, and has been a pain in my ass since the day I asked him to come on this trip. Give me one good reason why I should put up with him any longer."

"Because this thing we're going to play you tomorrow is going to blow your socks off."

There was silence at the other end of the phone for a while. Then Remo said, "You've really come around about him."

"If you'd asked me three days ago, I would have probably felt differently, yeah. But the band is starting to gel."

"One punch could fracture that."

"True. It's up to you, Reem. But if you want, I'll talk to him? And Mitch?"

He chuckled. "No need. Mitch isn't taking it too hard, actually. Feels like he brought it on himself. They made up already."

"Well, jeez, Remo, then why give me the third degree?"

"Just getting a fresh take on it, that's all. Come down to dinner. Everyone's going to be there."

"I'll put on a nicer shirt."

"And comb your hair. It's a mess!" he said—I *think* jokingly.

I gave as good as I got. "Yes, papa."

"Ha!" He hung up on me, and I did a little end-zone dance because I knew I'd really got him with that one.

Quiet Life

Dinner was a formal affair, on flat cushions at a low table like the ones they had in the back room at the fancy sushi places in Boston. The waitresses were all in traditional kimonos, and they refilled the sake and plum wine in our glasses whenever they dipped under half-full. As a result, everyone was too plastered to care that the seats weren't that comfortable.

I thought the whole scene was kind of cool—the rustle of the kimonos, the rice paper walls... it felt like we were inside a samurai movie. It occurred to me that it had taken until that day for the feeling that we were in Japan to really soak in. (No hot springs pun intended.) So much of the time we could have been anywhere: hotel, soundcheck, van. In Tokyo, we'd gone to the temple and to Guitar Street, but it was like I'd needed to recover from jet lag and from cramming before I had the brain capacity to absorb anything.

The group was pretty jocular. Any animosity about Cray's blowup seemed to be gone. In fact, he and Mitch had a bottle of some special sake between them and seemed to be having a great time.

Speaking of sake, I'm not sure to this day if it's really strong or if the reason it gets you so drunk is that it seems so mild that you drink more than you realize. The way they keep refilling the tiny cups doesn't help, either. I went up to my room rather tipsy, and by tipsy I mean the kind of drunk where when you lie down you swear you can feel the Earth turning. I then had what felt like a very long, peaceful time lying on the low futon bed (*hey, just like home... how weird is that...*) not thinking too deeply about anything. Yeah, it was like the hot tub relaxation and calm finally caught up to me. How about that.

I have no idea how long I had been lying there when there was a knock on the door. I answered it without thinking.

Cray was standing there looking like his usual wound-up, surly self. "Can I come in?"

"Sure." I went to look for a glass to put some water in, but in a Japanese hotel like that there were only teacups. Good enough. I filled one from the tap, then realized there was a pot, too, and filled the whole thing with cool water. I put the pot and both cups on the low table and sat down. He came and sat and took a teacup of water and drank it without comment. Either he agreed that it was perfectly sensible to serve plain water using the teapot as a pitcher or he didn't actually notice that what I gave him wasn't cold tea.

Alcohol had made his eyelids droopy. "I want your advice."

"About what?"

"Remo."

"Okay." I leapt to the conclusion that Cray had a crush on him, then immediately decided that was crazy.

Cray's idea of dressing for dinner was he'd put on a

kind of string tie, and now it was half-undone. He tried to pull it the rest of the way off, failed, and unbuttoned his collar anyway. I was pretty sure that was all stalling from actually saying what he was there to ask, but it's not like I was in a hurry.

"What's the secret," he finally asked, "to getting along with him so easy?"

"Vaseline," I said, without missing a beat. "Makes everything smooth."

It took him a moment to realize I'd made a joke. Actually, it took *me* a moment to realize I'd made a joke, and there was this half second where I thought he was going to be furious at me. But, like a good joke should, it hit him unexpectedly enough that he started laughing before he could help himself. Which made me laugh, and then the two of us were cackling like fools for a while before we could get ourselves under control.

"Okayyyy," he said when he was done wiping tears out of the corner of his eyes. "Sorry. That was kind of a dumb way to put it. But do you get what I'm asking?"

"Cray, I get along with *everyone* better than you do, Remo's no exception. Hell, I even get along better with *you* than everyone else. I'm just a more easygoing person than you are. There's no secret."

He frowned.

"I'm not saying it's bad to be so intense, but you seem like you're mad at everybody all the time."

He sipped water out of his cup, and when he put it down I poured more into it. Rehydration was probably a good idea. "Well, you guys are making fun of me all the time."

"Cray, this group makes fun of each other all the time. Fun is supposed to be fun, not painful."

"Okay, but seriously, it didn't bother you when Mitch acted like we'd... we'd..." He sputtered and got red in the face.

"Hang on. First of all, if he was serious, then what's the big deal? He's wrong. And if he was just joking, why should it bother me?"

"Well, it wasn't supposed to bother *you*. It was only supposed to bother me. And it did."

My turn to take a sip of water, because I felt like the argument had just made a loop and I couldn't figure out how to get back inside the circle. "Look. I know how it feels to be upset when someone makes a joke or hints or even just says something the wrong way so it could be construed that they're saying that you're gay. I know because I was in the closet and I used to overreact to that shit all the time. And this looks like a pretty classic overreaction to me."

"You're saying I'm an asshole."

"I'm saying take a chill pill and don't worry that people are judging you all the fucking time, whether they are or not. Most of the time they're not, and when they are, fuck 'em. Unless they're signing your paychecks."

He nodded with his eyes closed like he was trying to make that sink in. "That's exactly how I feel, though. Like everyone's judging me constantly."

It took me a second to realize what the unspoken part of that sentence was. "You mean like everyone's judging you and they think you suck, you mean."

"Well, yeah."

"Cray, Flip told me you might be the best lap steel player in the country. In the States, I mean. That doesn't sound to me like he thinks you suck."

"Flip said that?"

"Yeah. In fact, I think you were sitting there when he did, weren't you?" I couldn't remember.

Neither could Cray. "I probably thought he was just joking around."

"See what I mean about you being mad at everyone all the time? So if someone gives you a compliment you're still looking for how it could be a backhanded joke at your expense. Is it really not possible for you to just... calm down?"

He shook his head. "Not with Remo breathing down my neck all the time."

"Okay, now you can just take a hike. Remo is the least—" I tried to get the word "judgmental" to come out but it wouldn't work with my sake-swollen tongue, so I fell back to "—*judgey* person in the world."

"You don't know him like I do."

"I think I know him pretty fucking well."

"He didn't fuck your mother and decide that gave him the right to treat you like you're his kid."

Actually, I kind of think maybe he did—or wanted to, I thought, but I managed not to say it. Instead I just raised an eyebrow.

Cray's memory caught up with his mouth then and he shut it because he didn't know what to say.

"Yeah, I'm the one who grew up playing the guitar on Remo's living room floor." I poured water into the cups. "My own father is a piece of work, too, so I guess it was a good thing I had a decent role model around."

Cray blew air out his nose like he was steaming. "My mother kicked my father out of the family band when I was four. He moved to Nashville, drank too much at a gig a few years later, and died in a car crash on the way home."

"I'm sorry."

"Don't be. He was a jerk who beat my mother." Cray shrugged.

"So Remo's a step up...?" I hazarded.

"I guess." He drank some water. "He's a pain in my ass."

"Okay, that may be true, but you came here to ask me how to get along better with him."

"Right." Cray looked at his hands. "Maybe it's a lost cause."

"Hang on a second, I just finally put two and two together. So your mother's the one Remo was going to all those folk festivals to see?"

He nodded.

"And you resent that he, what, tried to be overly parental toward you?"

"I guess. I mean, where does he get off?"

"Maybe he was just being nice?"

"So that's why I'm here? Because Remo's being nice?"

"Stop skipping ahead! One thing at a time." Damn sake. "Is he still going with your mother?"

"I don't think so. They couldn't make it work."

"Then what incentive does he have to 'be nice' to you? I'm pretty sure he hired you because he likes the way you play."

"Maybe," Cray grudgingly admitted.

"This song we're working on, Cray. What's that about."

He shook his head. "Forget it. That was a stupid idea."

"No, it wasn't. He's going to love it. And he's going to make us do it in the show if he loves it, you know. Isn't that what you're hoping?"

"I guess."

"So you want to impress him. That's okay. What's the problem?"

"I don't know."

"The problem is that on the one hand you are hanging on his approval like you think you're never good enough and you think this time you're going to get it, and on the other hand you want to tell him *fuck you, I don't care what you think, you're not my father.*"

He stared at me. "Um. Yeah."

"We're the closest thing to kids he's ever going to get. But he doesn't want us to act like his *kids.* He just wants us to be family. If you don't want to be part of Remo Cutler's traveling circus family, don't take the gig the next time he offers it. But why don't you just try relaxing a little and roll with it?"

"Yeah." He let out a long breath. "It's easier now that you're not on my case, either."

"When was I on your case?"

He rolled his eyes. "Okay, not on my case exactly, but you know. You waltzed in like the king of the universe."

I was about to argue, but I realized he was kind of right. "Yeah, I did. But we're each the king of our own universe, Cray." I doubt a lot of things about myself, but it came home to me again that when it came to my talent, my artistic ability, *that* I almost never doubted. I had some rocky moments when I was pushing myself, when Moondog Three did that shakedown tour, but that was more about developing a stage presence, and about me and Ziggy, than about my performing ability.

"I don't want to come across as a spoiled brat." He had gone from looking surly and suspicious to looking tired.

"There's a difference between acting like you want everyone to kowtow and earning everyone's respect. I earned this group's respect a long time ago."

"What do you think I should do, then? To get the respect of the group?"

"Bust your ass in rehearsal, blow the doors off during the shows, and just be nice to people the rest of the time. How's that?"

"You make it sound so simple."

"I kind of think it is. You also might want to apologize to Mitch for jumping him and to everyone else for being a pill."

"You think so?"

"Or just try the being-nicer thing and maybe everyone will take that as a kind of apology anyway. You know. Make up for it."

"Yeah. Okay. I might still lose it if there are too many jokes about anal sex, though."

"Wait, have I been missing the jokes about buttfucking?"

"Oh, come on! You're the one who mentioned Vaseline! And what Mitch said! And—"

He went on with a bunch of other things that to *me* were clearly not about anal sex unless you really were stretching the implications. But I think I'd done about all I could for Cray's state of mind that night. Adjusting his attitude about Remo I could do. Curing him of his obsession about gay sex was outside my purview. Way, way outside.

Time the Avenger

The next day's show was in Hiroshima, which I had been pronouncing wrong my whole life. In my history class in tenth grade the teacher called it Hero-SHE-muh. Rocky spent a while trying to get us all to say Heh-ROE-shima. I think, as Americans, we felt like, having bombed the crap out of the place, that the least we could do was try to respect its name. At least, that's how I felt about it, and I tried to get it right.

Rocky, who until then had seemed to go about his business with a kind of earnest cheer, got pretty stoic when talking about The Bomb. But there's really no way to not bring it up when you talk about a place like that.

Quick, name me a song from the 1980s that was about nuclear war or the fact that we all thought we might die in a Russian missile attack. "99 Luftballoons," Nena. "Two Tribes," Frankie Goes to Hollywood. "Land of Confusion," Genesis. "Two Minutes to Midnight," Iron Maiden. "Every Day Is Like Sunday," Morrissey. "Enola Gay," Ultravox. "Red Skies at Night," The Fixx. "Just Another Day," Oingo Boingo. "Russians," Sting. "When the World is Running Down," The Police. "Ronnie Talk 2 Russia," Prince. "The Final Countdown," Europe. The "Unforgettable Fire" that U2 wrote about was supposedly the Hiroshima bomb itself. And this is just what I came up with off the top of my head.

It gets to the point where you think, wait, what else did people write pop songs about in the '80s? Oh right, the top two subjects continue to be love/relationships/sex and music/dancing. But the idea that nuclear disaster was right around the corner was pervasive enough that my elementary school still had bomb drills. They said it would supposedly take twelve minutes for the radiation from New York City getting bombed to reach our town, so we had to get everyone into the basement in twelve minutes. The first time we did that drill, I was five and I was terrified. By the time I was seven or eight it had become an annoying disruption of the class routine, and when we got to junior high they didn't bother to do anything. The building had a sign that said "Fallout Shelter" on the door, but there were huge windows in every classroom and we never practiced what to do. I guess we tweens were expected to fry.

Was I creeped out in Hiroshima? Yes. Rocky apologized that we could not go see the ruins of the one building that had been left more or less still standing near ground zero. It had been made into a peace memorial, but it was undergoing some renovations to stabilize it, so the best we could do was drive past the site on the other side of the river, where we could kind of make out the scaffolding and such. It was just as well that we couldn't see it, I felt, because anywhere you went, you had the feeling that people could have been vaporized right where you were standing.

We didn't have time to see an actual museum, and that was fine with me. I spent plenty of time chewing over the thoughts and implications of the atomic bomb and the United States. When I was a kid I'd had a few macabre daydreams I used to obsess over, trying to imagine what I'd do if I knew I had only twelve minutes to live.

I'm pretty sure the twelve minutes thing was bogus, by the way. I have no idea how they calculated that time, but I don't think it actually had a basis in reality.

I had always thought as much, but reading some of the plaques and signs—which were in English, by the way—on various buildings we did see while in Hiroshima convinced me I was right.

Not that I'm trying to be a downer, but the thoughts were pretty inescapable. If I had twelve minutes to live, would I try to call home? Would I call Jonathan? Or Bart? Or Carynne? Or would I write a letter to everyone and hope that whoever found my corpse would deliver it?

Jeez. I'm starting to get myself down just remembering it. Let's just say it was a fairly stark reminder that life is short even if there's no bomb at the end of it, and it forced me to confront some of the nagging questions in the back of my head, like what was I going to do next? With my life or my career? I felt like both Moondog Three and my relationship with Ziggy had run aground. In both cases, although I may have been at the helm of the ship when it happened, a lot of other factors akin to weather (i.e., outside my control) had contributed to the shipwreck.

A wrecked ship can be made seaworthy again, sometimes, but is it worth the effort? BNC seemed to be saying they were letting it sink, but they wouldn't let me sail again, either.

I could get on Remo's ship, like I was now, but I'd never be the captain of that ship. I'd always be the second in command. Not that that was bad. But doesn't every lieutenant want his own ship? And what's the point of the ship anyway, is it the sailing or is it the destination? That's a fancy way of saying, I think, is it the music or is it the success?

Maybe that's a false division, though, because if I were to win the lottery and never have to make another dime from music, that doesn't mean I'd just sit around in my living room playing to my heart's content. Sharing it with people was part of what music was. Is. Yes, I needed to make a living. I think I had proved I could do that with guitar in hand if I wanted to establish myself as a session player. But here's what I couldn't explain to Jonathan, and which I didn't even really want to admit to myself while I was in Los Angeles: playing other people's music was going to drive me insane if it was all I did.

And I realized that was true whether it was filling in parts on a metal album or playing the part of Stunt Remo like I was. It was fun. I was enjoying it. But it wasn't going to sustain me for years on end.

I could almost hear it in Digger's voice, though: spoiled brat. You're playing guitar in front of thousands of people a night for good money. You could have real problems, like radiation sickness.

Digger would not be on the list of people I called if I had only twelve minutes to live. He had worked hard to earn my disdain. He'd earned it.

Anyway. Everyone felt a little somber and uncomfortable in Hiroshima, I think, and that made it a good time to show off our somber guitar duet. We played it for the whole band during the soundcheck, with Cray taking Remo's guitar and microphone, and in the completely empty auditorium it sounded heartbreaking.

Remo stood off to the side, watching and listening, his arms folded. When we were done, he walked up to Cray and said, "You know. I was thinking we needed something in this set that we could dedicate to the city. This could really work. You ready to do it tonight?"

"Of course we are," Cray said, sounding eerily like me. "Just say when."

"And thank you for not trying to recreate the Eric Clapton solo parts," Remo added.

A light went on in my head. "That's *Clapton* on the *White Album*?"

"No, it isn't," Cray said immediately.

Remo nodded, though. "Yep. You know he and George are pals."

"Wow. That explains so much." Of course it was Clapton. The second he said, it I had known it was true. I'd always assumed it was George Harrison, possibly trying to sound like Eric Clapton. "But, yeah, this isn't a rendition so much as a deconstruction of the song."

Cray looked annoyed. "Now you've got me worrying Clapton played it on his last tour here."

Remo shrugged. "Does it matter? I love it, the audience will love it."

"Yeah. Okay." He still seemed deflated, but by then I was used to Cray always seeing the lead lining in any cloud.

It went beautifully in the show. I didn't sing. I left that all to him. The vocal harmonies that people identify with the song I hinted at in places where I played in unison, then in harmony, with the vocal line. But more than half the song had no lyrics the way we did it.

I say again: it went beautifully. But something about the performance, and the city, and the thoughts I'd been having, left me emotionally raw.

When I get like that, my usual strategy is to hole up alone until the feeling passes. But Cray wanted to bask in the success after the show, and I knew that if I disappeared he'd think I was avoiding him. Plus I wanted to prove to Remo that if there was a moody son of a bitch around, it wasn't me. So when everyone was hanging around the hotel bar, I drank too much and ended up literally face down on the bar, making that little prayer—you know the one—the one that starts out *please don't let me puke* and eventually the bargaining gets to *please don't let me puke right here right now* while you desperately hope you can make it somewhere appropriate first.

Maybe prayer does work. Remo came to play guardian angel, and the next thing I knew he had helped me to my room. And how's this for a miracle? I didn't puke.

I did something worse.

When he got me sitting in bed with a bottle of water on the side table and my shoes off and my hair in a pony tail just in case, I asked, "Did you fuck my mother?"

And he said, "Once."

Don't ask me why—at that moment—that was the worst possible answer. I don't know why it turned my entire emotional landscape upside down, but it did. I had no unpickled brain cells with which to process the news, of course, so my heart had a complete flip-out.

Not that Remo could tell, I thought, since by then I was sitting up with my knees bent and my face buried in my arms.

There were so many things about it that I did not want to know. Whose idea was it? How did it happen? Why only once? Did Digger know about it at the time or did that come later? Why did he and Digger stay friends? Was I alive when it happened?

I didn't want to know any of that. Which is to say, I *did* want to know, but I was sure that the answers, no matter what they were, would make me feel even worse. Why the fuck did I ask him that?

The can of worms kept right on squirming. Did he mentor me as a favor for her? Did he stay close to Digger so he could stay close to her?

I raised my head. "Why did you tell me that?"

"You asked. I thought that meant you were ready to hear it."

"For fuck's sake, Remo." I put my head back down.

"You want me to apologize?"

"No. You're sure, absolutely sure, you're not my real father, though?"

"Unless you were born two months late. Scared me to death when Claire started showing signs, though."

"Remo!" I did not want to know that.

"If you don't want to know, quit asking," he said.

"For fuck's sake," I said again, because I couldn't come up with anything else.

He stood to go. "Maybe we should talk about this when we're both sober."

"You think?"

"I'm gonna get Flip to come babysit you. I don't want you choking on your own vomit or something."

I couldn't really argue with that. He left. A little while later the door opened and closed. I hadn't moved. I peeked over my forearm expecting to see Flip.

It was Cray.

He was carrying two bottles that looked more like soda than alcohol, but in this country it wasn't always easy to tell.

He handed me one. "Rocky swears this is the stuff."

I assumed that meant either a nausea or hangover cure. "Gimme."

He sat down in the chair next to the bed that Remo had vacated, popped open both bottles, we clinked them, and I took an experimental sip.

What do you know, it did settle my stomach somewhat. Now where was the drink to settle my blown mind?

I Heard a Rumor

I know it makes no sense that Remo saying one little word freaked me out. Especially in light of the fact that

I pretty much suspected the truth all along. Well, not *all* along, but certainly recently. I mean, part of me felt like I had when he'd said that Clapton played the lead guitar and not George Harrison on "While My Guitar Gently Weeps." Like it was so obvious, and yet until I heard him say it, it wasn't part of my worldview. (And by the way you know there was a whole love triangle between Clapton and Harrison and George's wife Patti, right? Oh jeez.)

In this case, something with Remo and my mother was something I strongly suspected, and even joked about, and we had even talked about once before, though we'd stopped short of a bombshell. But somehow hearing him admit that he'd had sex with my mother was different from merely being pretty sure it was true.

Why would hearing it aloud suddenly make me question things when speculating about it hadn't? I don't know. But it did. I suddenly questioned my talent. I hadn't expected the answer to shake the bedrock of my self-image, but there you go—I suddenly wondered. I'd always assumed the sole reason Remo had put up with me was because my talent was unquestionably prodigy-level. The only possible explanation for all the bending over backwards he had to do to drag a 12/13/14-year-old into his band was that I was simply that good. Right?

Why did I question that now that I knew he and my mother had played hide the salami?

"You doing okay?" Cray asked.

I still had half a bottle of whatever the stuff was he had brought me to drink. There was no English I could recognize on it, but then again my eyes were too crossed from alcohol to read the fine print. "Uh, think so," I said.

"Because you look like you're either having constipation or an angst fest between the ears." He swigged back the last of his own bottle and put the empty down on the side table. Remo must have pulled the chair he was sitting in over by the bed.

"Uh, the angst fest. It's all right. It'll pass." I leaned against the wall, thumping my head a little harder than recommended against it, but I couldn't feel well enough to tell.

"You want to talk about it?"

"You remember what you were saying about how him fucking your mother gives him the right to treat you like a son?"

Cray shook his head. "Doesn't give him the right. *Does-n't*. But you don't seem to mind it."

"Except all of a sudden, I do."

"Clearly I'm a bad influence on you." Cray smiled thinly. "How'd he meet your mother?"

"No fucking idea."

"No?"

"Well, okay, he was my father's best friend." I felt a wave of queasy pass through me, and I thought maybe this wasn't from drinking. "Shit. Remo never struck me as the kind of guy who would have sex with his best friend's wife."

Cray merely shrugged.

"Seriously. What the fuck."

"I thought you said your dad was a piece of work?"

"He is. But back then, Remo and he were friends. Close friends." I couldn't imagine Digger actually approved of the tryst. Could it have been a threesome? Ugh. I thought maybe I'd be sick again.

I slammed back the rest of the drink instead. "I don't want to think about it. I don't. God. But now I can't stop."

That'd be like, like... if I got interested in women and had sex with Michelle. I could not fathom how such a thing could possibly come about.

Somehow that tore the scar tissue off a really old wound, a wound so old I had pretty much forgotten it was there. Remember when Ziggy and Carynne were sleeping together? She'd been afraid I would be angry at her. As it turned out, I was all too ready to place the blame squarely in Ziggy's lap, but somewhere in the back of my head I'd felt a little betrayed, too. She knew she should have said no, but she hadn't.

Then again, it's not like I could get on my high horse. I'd slept with both of them. And Colin. Why did I feel guilty about Colin? Why? There was no downside to it. Was it just that I'd told myself I wouldn't? And then when I did I discovered how morally weak I was?

"Doesn't anybody have any fucking morals anymore?" I whined.

Cray, who I'd half-forgotten was still sitting there, murmured an answer. "Not in this business, my friend."

"Don't call me friend. I'll just feel even more betrayed when you sleep with someone close to me," I said, joking but bitter, very bitter.

Cray, amazingly, didn't take it personally, and joked right back. "Tch. Your mom's not my type."

I tried to retaliate by hitting him with a pillow but missed.

"Seriously, Daron, you don't strike me as a prude."

I hunched over, my arms crossed. "Not a prude."

"Then why's it such a big deal who sleeps with who?"

"There should be rules," I insisted.

"Okay. What should those rules be?"

"I don't know, but I'm pretty sure your best friend's wife is off limits. And so is anyone in your band."

"You're kidding, right?"

"You don't think so?"

"I don't think I've ever known a band that didn't have somebody sleeping with somebody else, unless the situation was they were all straight guys, in which case I guarantee you one of them slept with one of the other one's wives."

"That can't be good for band harmony. And I don't mean the musical kind."

"Maybe not. I'm sure it leads to a lot of strife. But maybe that's just how people are."

"People suck." I hid my face in my arms again, fully aware that I sounded like a surly seven-year-old.

"Maybe so," he said after a while. "But people need to fuck. It's hard-wired, just like the need for food. People need it so bad guys will even turn gay in prison."

Here we go with the anal sex obsession, I thought. "Just because I need to eat doesn't mean I'd take a sandwich away from a friend."

"Yeah but fucking, unlike food, is infinitely sharable. Just cause you get some doesn't mean your friend doesn't."

"Ah, fuck you, Cray, stop making logical sense when I'm trying to be miserable!" I pulled the pony tail holder out of my hair so I could hide behind it.

I think he was trying hard not to smirk. "I think you need to get laid."

"No I don't!"

"Okay, maybe you gays are different, but if you haven't dipped your wick since the States—"

"Shut up!" This time I hit him square in the face with a pillow. It came right back at me, and then it felt to me like the whole bed flipped over. But no, it was just me that flipped, and Cray had me pinned face down on the bed. And, damn it, I was hard as a rock. Even though I'd been drinking heavily. Even though I knew he was straight. Even though I wasn't the slightest bit attracted to him. It was like my body didn't care about anything like facts, or like the only fact that mattered was someone's body was close to mine.

I had to clench my jaw—my whole face really—to keep from bursting into tears. I remember Ziggy approaching it so matter-of-factly on tour: where and when are you going to get your rocks off, Daron? You need to plan for these things.

"You going to simmer down, or do I have to get Flip in here to sit on you, too?" Cray said.

He didn't seem aware that I was horny or on the verge of losing it. I forced myself to go limp. Relax. "Sorry. Got carried away."

He patted me on the back and then let go, stepping back from the bed. "Thanks for sticking up for me with Remo, by the way."

I rolled onto my back so I could look at his face. "What? Oh. You're welcome."

"Really didn't think you would."

I tried to shrug, but the effect was lost when I was lying on my back. "Reem said you've got anger management issues. All I said was he should hear this song we've been working on."

"Well, thanks. Didn't want you to think I was an ungrateful sonuvabitch." He cracked his knuckles. "I'm thirsty. I'm going to get more of that drink. Don't go anywhere."

I shook my head. "Not planning to."

He left, and a few minutes later a knock came at the door. I opened it, expecting it to be Cray again.

It was Mitch, the sax player. He had two more bottles of the soda, the long necks threaded through the fingers of his left hand. He held them up invitingly and said, "Hey, wanna fuck?"

"Yes." I pulled him into the room and slammed the door.

Send Me an Angel

You know, I didn't think I was particularly attracted to Mitch Moreland, but the second he said the word "fuck" it was like a magic word that turned him from a frog to a prince or something. Not that he wasn't attractive before. Mitch is cute in a sax player kind of way. But I hadn't allowed myself to see him that way until *abra cadabra*.

I know, I know, a few minutes earlier I'd been whining about how there should be rules, and one of them should be no fucking your bandmates. There were a million reasons why not. Drama could ensue. Professional standards. Ethics.

But when you're the only two English-speaking gay men in the whole prefecture, so far as you know, and you're horny, then trust me, all of a sudden it makes totally perfectly logical sense to hook up.

We wasted no time in stripping each other's clothes off at the foot of the bed. Pretty much the entire negotiation of boundaries consisted of Mitch saying, "Promise me it won't get weird after this," and me answering, "No reason it should."

And pretty much the entire negotiation of safe sex boiled down to this:

Mitch: How many condoms do we have between us?
Me: Um...
Mitch: I have one. Okay if I do you, then?
Me: Sure.

I don't know if all sax players have oral fixations or what, but he went down on me for what was definitely a long time, used his spit for lube, and did me face down on the edge of the bed. He wasn't a big guy in either sense, which suited me fine.

When we were done I said, "You don't have to rush off unless you feel it would be weird to cuddle."

"Move the fuck over," he said, and I climbed all the way onto the bed and he lay down next to me. "Thanks."

"Likewise." Now that I had empty balls, I felt a lot better. "Whew. I needed that."

"Yeah."

I think we both dozed off for a minute or two.

Then he said, "I was going to try to hold out until Australia. But this was better."

I opened my eyes, and for a moment the ceiling of the room looked like the ceiling of any hotel room anywhere in the world. "What's in Australia?"

"Everything. Sydney has an insanely huge gay pride parade."

"How huge is insanely huge?"

"Ten thousand march and a hundred thousand spectators, I've heard."

"Jeezus."

"Yeah. Plus they speak English. Bars. Cruise spots. You name it, they've got it."

"Good to know. You know any bars in particular?"

"I've got a list. There was one place in Tokyo, went there the first night here when I was jet lagged and couldn't sleep."

I turned to look at him. "How extensive is this list?"

"Forty or fifty cities. Mostly in the US, of course." He was still looking at the ceiling but he talked with his hands, which meant he held them up above his face. "A couple in Canada, UK, Germany—"

"You really plan ahead."

"You don't?"

I pointed out that if I did, I would've had a condom, which made him laugh. I resolved to make sure I kept some in my road cases from then on. He agreed to take me along if he went out in Sydney. We'd have a couple of days there, after all.

We dozed off again. I woke up feeling sticky.

"Are you the shower-afterward type?" I asked.

"I'll soap your back if you soap mine," he said.

Sensible. While we were toweling off afterward, though, I asked him the one potentially awkward question in my mind. "So what did Cray say to you?"

He tossed it off nonchalantly, doing a credible job of Cray's clipped, not-quite-Southern accent. "'Daron could use some company.'"

"'Daron could use some company?'"

"Yeah. Just like that. I figured there was at least a fifty-fifty chance that he meant what I hoped he meant. Or at least that *you* meant what I hoped he meant."

"Glad he ran into you then."

"Me too." He hung his towel on the rack. "Are you the kissy type?"

"Not really." At least, not after a recreational fuck like this one.

"Good. My lip got a little overworked in the show tonight." He patted his lower jaw. "Hey, do you know what time we're leaving tomorrow?"

As if on cue, a piece of paper came sliding under the door. In damp, bare feet I went and picked it up. "According to this, we're on the eleven AM Shinkansen to... *Fuck-you-okay*?"

He burst out laughing as he reached for his clothes on the floor. "What?"

"Says so right here." I showed him the itinerary that said our final show in Japan was in the city of *Fukuoka*. Fuck you, okay?

"Why, so it does." He pulled his jeans on, holding his briefs wadded up in his hand.

At the door he said, "Thanks, again."

"Right back atcha. See you in the morning."

He gave me one of those little "see you" points from the corner of his eye with his index finger and sailed out the door.

He was whistling merrily as he went down the hallway. I felt about the same. I checked the clock. Huh. It was probably a good time to call Carynne, so I did.

"Tell me something," I said when she picked up the phone. "Do I make sex into a much bigger issue than it has to be?"

"Yes," she said. "Hey, I was hoping you'd call. I have good news and bad news."

My heart jumped into my throat as I suddenly worried it was something about Ziggy. But then, I thought, she wouldn't be so flip or calm if something had happened to him.

"The good news is that my gamble paid off."

"What gamble?"

"I sank ten thou into a new, Christmas-themed 'Candlelight' video, and all the stations are playing the crap out of it. Watt stickered the old single with some kind of holiday sticker, and we've sold through nearly all the old inventory that was lying around."

"How much inventory was that?"

"Over fifty thousand units. I was amazed they were still around. BNC won't admit it, yet, but I'm sure that means *Prone to Relapse* has moved a ton of units, too."

I lay back down on the bed. I wondered if it was intentional on Mitch's part or merely convenient that fucking on the edge of the bed left no wet spot. "Okay, but how does that affect the sales of *1989*?"

"It probably doesn't. But it does A) clear out the back stock of that single they were claiming was a liability, B) pull in a metric ton more publishing revenue for us, and C) bring in royalties on the single."

"I thought we weren't going to see another dime in royalties until *1989* earned out."

"This is the brilliant part. Those singles in inventory belonged to Charles River. It's complicated, but it boils down to they don't count in that basket."

"That's a major, major coup, then, Car'. That's excellent!" I wondered if that pulled in enough for a year of Courtney to go to Emerson. Or for us to re-carpet the basement. "But what's the bad news?"

"The bad news is they're suing us. Notice came yesterday afternoon at five PM. Feinbaum's filing the countersuit as we speak."

"Shit."

"He still thinks they'll back down. I told him our goal is reduction of monetary outlay. He's keeping it in mind." She yawned. "But how are you? How's Japan?"

"Japan is awesome. We stayed overnight at a hot tub resort."

"Hot tub resort?"

"Hot springs, I should say. I sent you a postcard, but I'll probably be home before it."

"Cool. How's Remo?"

"He's all right. I saw him taking the cast off part of the day today, anyway, so I think that's a good sign. Not like he talks about it."

"Of course. How's my uncle?"

"Ornery as always. I told him I'd say hi, though."

"Tell him hi back."

This was the moment when we should have said goodbye. Instead I sat there in silence, working up the nerve to ask her one more thing.

She was ahead of me. "No, I haven't heard anything from Zig," she said, before I could open my mouth.

"I had a thought," I blurted out. "His mom. She's in a home or something? Do you know where? Which one?"

"I can find that out easily enough."

"I wonder if she's heard from him."

"That's an excellent question. I'll get right on that. After this conference call I have with the merchandisers. Gotta go, honeycakes."

"All right. Love you, Car'."

"Love you, too, D."

And then I was out of energy, out of drive, out of emotions, and I slept like a rock.

Tears Ring Eyes

I didn't see Remo when we were getting ready to go the train station, but Waldo didn't seem perturbed by his absence so I figured he must be off doing promo or something. We got settled in the train for another high-speed trip. This one was going to cross the "inland sea" of Japan.

I wasn't looking out the window, though. Remo showed up shortly after the train started to move and sat down next to me with a guitar. He took it out of the case, then sat down again, and I noticed that he'd swapped the big cast on his hand and wrist for a smaller brace. He held a pick in his fingers and strummed experimentally.

Then he started to play a song and sing, quietly, singing just for me, not to attract an audience. I forgot all about how I had intended to be mad at him today so I could work through the crap about him and my mother that was messing me up. He'd written a song about the bullet train, and you could hear it as a love song, but I kind of heard it like it was about us, about how life is short and the faster we go it only gets shorter. And how he wanted no regrets. It had a cool lick that led into the verses.

Honestly. A cool lick makes me forgive so much.

Then, at the Fukuoka soundcheck, Remo announced that he wanted to try playing in the show, too. He'd injured himself on November 26th and now it was December 18th. The doctor had said four to six weeks. Somehow, in Remo's mind, 22 days had become four weeks.

"I'm just trying to hold a guitar pick, not do brain surgery," he groused.

I didn't try to talk him out of it. You know how grumpy and unpleasant I had gotten before Mitch showed up to take the edge off? I think that's how Remo was going to get if he didn't get to play with us at least a little.

He was a little sensible in that he limited himself to the opening number, then the song before the big jam, the jam itself, and then the encores.

It was good. It was really good. I pretty much made up my mind while we were onstage that night that some day, not sure exactly when, I'd do a whole tour with them when we could both play at our fullest.

I pretty much also made up my mind that night, though, that being a part of Nomad wasn't some kind of ultimate destiny for me. I could see how that would make a good story. The whole "full circle" kind of thing. But just because something makes a good story doesn't make it true. Nomad was an excursion, not a destination.

Especially since I'd seen beyond the horizon and I wanted to explore Indian music, or maybe Middle Eastern, or both, because in my head the seeds that were planted were growing into something and I had to water and fertilize that to find out what.

So, how does an A-list rock band spend their last night in Japan partying? That heavy drinking would be involved is a no-brainer: I mean, what else. I wouldn't have guessed it, but did you know there are all-night karaoke bars? We took the entire band and crew to a place that was "pay one price" from 11 PM to 5 AM. It appeared to me there was an open bar, but I was unclear whether that was part of the "pay one price" deal or if Remo was just running a huge tab.

They had a huge catalog of American music, and Cray brought the house down when he did a baritone rendition of Journey's "Who's Crying Now." Flip, crutch and all, did Van Halen's "Jump." (He did not jump.) I decided I had to top both of them by going straight to Cheap Trick, "Surrender."

I picked it, of course, because it was one of the songs on the Budokan album, but it had been a hit before that, and everyone in the place knew it. Yes, I got a little drunk first—did I mention the open bar?—otherwise I would have been worried I didn't know the words well enough. Karaoke gives you a prompter though, duh.

I had kind of forgotten, though, that the song is about how parents are weird.

After coming off stage triumphant, I drank a little more and fended off some attention from some of the women there, which wasn't hard to do because Flip and Cray were pretty much monopolizing me for a while then. I told you, I don't have a great voice. But I'm an expressive singer. And when my inhibitions are down, I know how to go for it. That's true of a lot of people. Rocky got up and showed a side of himself we'd never seen when he did Michael Jackson's "Beat It," complete with dance moves, though he blushed and hurried off the stage at the end like he was embarrassed.

A little while later, the liquor in my brain decided that it was a good idea to go for a second song. Remo had even finally been enticed to get up there, and he blew everyone's minds with a Frank Sinatra impression that had us all checking our eyes to make sure it was really him. I sorted through the catalog trying to find something I knew well enough to sing even if I was potentially too drunk to read the lyrics.

Hey. They had some Moondog Three in the listings. "Candlelight," "Wonderland," "Why the Sky"... What was "Intensive Care" doing on that list? Had it been released as a single here? It hadn't been in the US, but maybe it had in Japan. We usually did it in our shows. Maybe it had gotten some college airplay and deep AOR...

What the hell. I decided to do it.

The first draft of the lyrics? I'd written them back when I still had that initial crush on Ziggy. Back when I felt so strongly about him, so intense it was painful. It was a love song, but it was about how much love hurts.

I wish I had remembered that before I picked it to sing. Not only did it remind me exactly how much it used to hurt, it reminded me of the exact size of the current Ziggy-shaped hole in my life. I swear I hallucinated him sitting in the audience and then disappearing before my eyes. When you wish hard enough for something, I think you can make yourself see it. But that doesn't mean it's there.

And the thing is, I wrote the song, but he's the one who sings it, you know? I get to stand behind a guitar usually. What the hell did I think I was doing going out there with the microphone? There's no going back, you know. No matter how embarrassing or ridiculous your performance is. Karaoke, standing there on the stage alone, demands commitment. Songs take on a life of their own.

I did not do something so dramatic as cry onstage. I can hold it together. That's one of those things, though: when you feel like you're being sliced up by knives in your chest, holding it all together only makes it hurt even more.

I might have made other people cry, though. I'm sort of ashamed to think I might have, and so I've never found out for sure. I don't remember anything else from that night other than learning the word *Suntory*. (Japanese for whiskey.)

Parents Just Don't Understand

Remember, I'm a professional. Don't try this at home. Also, don't try it in a foreign country when you have a fifteen-hour flight with a change in Hong Kong the next day. I'm talking about drinking yourself nearly blind two nights in a row.

But like I said, I could handle it. With Flip's aid (he carried No-Doz and other such essentials) I was upright, dressed, and walking like a facsimile of a human being by the time our van left for the airport. Sunglasses work wonders.

They served Cup Noodle on the plane. Yes, actual Cup Noodle brand (no s), in the styrofoam container and everything. I ate it, every noodle, every drop. Cup Noodle cures all.

I have no idea which meal that was intended to be. I slept a lot. By a lot, I mean all total I probably slept four hours in the hotel, two hours before the change in Hong Kong, then another three or four on the HK-to-Australia leg. Trans-oceanic flights are long enough that you don't count them in hours, you count them in how many ginger ales they serve you. (That trip: 5.)

When we were still a few hours out from Australia, Remo came and sat with me.

"How's the wrist?" I asked him.

"Stiff, but not too bad." He yawned. "How you doing?"

"All right. Might be a good idea for me to go easy on the drinking tonight, though. Do we have to be anywhere?"

"Nope. No official function until tomorrow, sound-check." He looked me in the eye. "You're sure you're all right."

I knew this time he wasn't asking me about the drinking. Maybe he was worried I was still upset about the thing with him and my mother. "I'm fine."

"I told you, you ever want to know, I'll tell you, but if you don't want to know, I'll keep my mouth shut."

That was definitely about my mother. "I guess... I guess I want to be an adult about it, but I can't figure out if that means forget about the whole thing because it's none of my business or find out more because... it seems kind of relevant to recent events."

He shrugged. The ball was in my court.

"Okay, here's what bothers me. Two things. One, I always thought you liked having me around because I was good at the guitar, not because you actually felt parental responsibility for me, and two, I never thought of you as the kind of guy who would cheat on his best friend—even if Digger probably did something to totally deserve it." There, that came out almost mature-sounding.

Remo chuckled. "I'm probably going to have to tell you a lot more than you really want to hear if I'm going to explain why you're wrong."

I sighed. "Of course you are."

"First of all, though, I thought we had the 'charity case' discussion before."

"We did."

"You don't seem like the type to doubt yourself. Musically, I mean."

He was right. "I'm not. But it still made me wonder."

"Quit wondering. Talents like you don't come along too often, Daron."

"Okay, fine. I'm awesome. Now tell me why I'm wrong about... the rest of it."

"I'll try to keep it to a minimum. One thing you should know is that after Claire had her second child, she not only swore off having any more kids, she swore off sex."

"Okay." That sounded like the sort of thing my mother would do.

"That was tough on Digger. In those days he doted on her. But she had lost all interest. No sex drive at all. That is, until she suddenly found herself interested in me."

I looked at him, then away, so it wouldn't seem like I was staring at him.

"Digger saw it. He's not blind. They used to have me over for dinner or for a barbecue, or to watch the game on Sunday—"

"Really?" That was surprising to me. In all the time I had known him, he'd steered completely clear of our house. I'd assumed it had always been like that.

"Really. And of course once Claire got interested, she contrived to invite me over more often. This was around when Lilibeth was in kindergarten and Janine was in pre-K, and all of a sudden Claire had her mornings to herself, alone at the house."

"Uh huh." Of course it was. I was born when my older sisters were five and six.

"It was driving Digger a little crazy, but you know, he and I would go out drinking and eventually he got it into his head that it was an act. That she didn't really want me, she just wanted to make him crazy. And it started to make sense to him to tell me to push her, see if her flirtations actually went anywhere. Like it would prove something if she would go all the way with me. I'll admit, I was very attracted to her. I asked if he was absolutely sure he wanted me to go through with it if she offered. His opinion was that unless we did, he'd never be sure it wasn't just a game of chicken. The very next day after he convinced me I should see how far I could get, your mother called out of the blue at ten in the morning to say she needed help moving the refrigerator. I went over there ready to help, but, as you might have guessed, it was an excuse to get me alone."

"Wow." I remembered what Digger had told me

about how manipulative my mother could be.

"Well, the thing is, that snowballed and snowballed, and it all blew up a few weeks later, at which point I was banned from the house."

"Okay, that explains that."

"And during that period of time is when your parents had some kind of epic make-up sex, during which you were conceived."

"Wow. Epic *unsafe* make-up sex."

"I guess. I have no idea if they weren't careful or what. But to answer your other question, yeah, I felt kind of responsible for your birth, since without me cracking the ice, as it were, maybe they never would have had you. But I'll tell you, if you hadn't been a little prodigy, I can't say I would have seen you but once in a while, or from afar. The guitar kept landing you in my lap, though. And I did not mind. I did not mind at all."

I leaned back in my seat. "That's kind of twisted. Then again, my parents are twisted."

"Yep."

"Did Claire resent you after that? For not coming around again?"

"Oh yeah. She was pissed. She wanted me at her beck and call! I eventually had to break it to her that it wasn't that I didn't find her attractive. It was that my loyalty was to your father first and foremost. Well, when she found out that Digger had practically sent me over there to see her that first time, all of a sudden she wasn't interested in me anymore! Thing is, I'm pretty sure she was only interested in me because I was Digger's best friend. The whole thing was she wanted not just to cheat on him, but for me to be cheating on him, too. When that wasn't the case, she banned me from the house and never wanted to see me again."

"Jeezus." I had definitely heard enough now. "Wait. I think I..." I blinked, thinking through the idea that had just popped into my head. "That was why she didn't want me playing the guitar in the house. Because it reminded her of *you*."

"Could be."

I ran my fingers through my hair, trying to jump-start my brain. "All this time I thought she hated me because I was too much like Digger. And she even used to say I was no good because I was turning out like my father." I looked at him. "You're absolutely sure you're not my biological father."

"Absolutely. But that doesn't mean that Claire didn't kind of consider you my kid."

"That is very true." My mother had a personal version of reality that often bore little resemblance to facts. "I kind of wonder if Digger considered me your kid, too."

Remo pressed his lips together for a second. Then he said, "*I* always considered you my kid. A godson, at least. But I was always afraid if I told you that, you'd push me away."

He was clearly afraid that might still happen. I put my fingers lightly over his braced wrist. "When I was younger, I probably would have. I wanted a friend more than another parent."

"And I never wanted kids. But you? You were always more like a little adult than a kid. It was like we got along instantly."

That pretty much matched my memory of it, too. "I don't remember the first time he brought me over to your house. I must've been around ten? It was like there was the period before we would go over there, and then there's the period of my life after, but I don't remember the day it all changed. It was like I'd known you all along."

"Digger used to say he couldn't explain it but that we just stuck like glue." Remo shrugged. "Anyway. What I don't want to happen because of all this, though, is for us to change."

"We won't change," I said. "We're finally at the stage where we can be real peers, Reem. This is what we've been waiting for. For me to grow up so we can be friends. We'll always be more than that, but you know what I mean."

"I know exactly what you mean." He seemed to relax, relieved, I guess. "Worth the wait."

"Very worth the wait. Hey, so when are you hitting the road next? I'm not making any commitments yet, but I figure I should ask."

"Summer. Two months in the US, then Glastonbury and a slew of UK dates."

The schedule that Moondog Three had been on earlier this year. I was suspicious that Mills had been behind the scuttling of the UK trip. Some other band he favored more had ended up with those gigs. "Did I tell you I talked to Carynne? We're at Defcon One. Lawsuits have been launched."

"Jeez. I'm sorry."

"Not your fault."

"You got my sympathy anyway."

"Yeah." I felt like we'd run to the end of the conversation, but I had one more thing I felt I'd better say before I chickened out. "Reem, I want to come on tour with you. But I want to come because I want to, not because I have to. Does that make sense?"

"Sure does. No need to decide now. Let's play it by ear."

"We're good at that."

"Yes, we are."

In a Big Country

So by the time we got to Brisbane, it was the next day, which meant we didn't see much of the place other than the concert hall and the hotel, since the day after that we flew to Melbourne. The main thing I remember is having breakfast in the hotel and feeling a sense of relief that everyone spoke English. I'd gotten used to everyone around me speaking Japanese and had forgotten what it was like to be able to assume everyone around you could understand you, and vice versa. The main thing to say about the Brisbane show was that we played the same set as in Fukuoka, including Remo playing on those songs we'd agreed on.

Also, after the Japanese audiences, playing in front of Australians was like drinking rocket fuel. Man, they get into it.

As promised, things between me and Mitch did not get weird.

They also did not get weird between me and Cray, perhaps partly because I didn't see that much of him once his girlfriend joined the entourage in Melbourne. I gather she liked the guitar duet we played.

I don't remember a lot of Melbourne either. Maybe getting hammered really, really hard two (or was it three?) nights in a row wasn't good for my head after all. Or maybe there wasn't a lot to remember because nothing went wrong. Everything was finally clicking smoothly. I didn't have any memorable arguments, conflicts, fights, disagreements... Too bad the tour was almost over.

Australia is really large. It's basically the same size as the lower 48 States. All three cities we visited were in one "corner" of the continent, but they were basically the equivalent of doing New Orleans, Washington, DC, and Atlanta—in that order—in terms of distance from each other. So unlike Japan, which is about the size of California, in Australia we spent a lot more time getting from place to place.

Australia is also on the other side of the world. Not in the same way as Japan, I mean the other-other side. Let me put it this way: it was summer there.

On December 23rd we arrived in Sydney to play the last show of the tour. As Remo described it, the plan was to play the show, then relax and enjoy the holidays on the 24th and 25th, and then on the 26th fly home. That was all he had told me. He hadn't yet told me what his Christmas surprise for me was going to be, since then it wouldn't have been a surprise.

We were staying at a place—I kid you not—called Manly Beach. Don't get excited. That's just the name of the town.

We were at a little beach resort where they didn't really care that we were international rock stars. One of the things that was nice about Australia was that people there didn't give a fuck who we were. Which didn't mean they didn't know, just that they didn't let it faze them. It was a lot like New York City that way, only friendlier.

The show was fantastic. Remo didn't put down his guitar when he was supposed to, but I guess he figured he would have plenty of time to recover after that, so why not go for it? There were two points in the show where he took off leading the band in a different direction from expected, once turning a song into a ten-minute-long jam, and once, spontaneously, breaking into a cover of "Money (That's What I Want)," which the whole band was able to jump in on. It's a blues tune, after all, and everyone in the world has heard the

Beatles version, plus a ton of other bands from the sixties covered it. You really have to be paying attention to improvise with a ten-person band, but you know, when everyone does pay attention it's not that hard. It's kind of magic.

And the thing is, if you really pull it off, the audience doesn't even know you didn't rehearse it. It's kind of like you're putting on a show for yourselves.

Remo pulling a song out of his hat wasn't the surprise, though. Carynne, Courtney, Bart, and Michelle showing up was. They made it there barely in time for the show, so I didn't get to do anything more than hug them hello beforehand. Afterward, though? Come on, it was the last night of a tour, of course we had a big party. And what with them being jet lagged and all, it wasn't like anyone was getting any sleep.

We took over a terraced dining area at the resort for the party. A caterer had set up a makeshift bar and was pouring champagne into glasses. Bart picked up two, handed me one, and we clinked them together because isn't that what you do?

"What'd you think?" I asked.

"Of the show?"

"Do I ever ask you about anything else?"

He snorted. "It was good. Do you ever wish we could just take off running on a song on a whim like that?"

Of course Bart would pick up on something like that. "Sure. But that's hard to do unless one of us is singing."

"True." We were both silent a moment, trying to imagine what it would be like starting a song Ziggy didn't know. I did it all the time in soundcheck, but I'd never sprung it on him in front of an audience. Well, unless you counted some of the improvisational stuff we did, just the two of us, that show in New York.

That show in New York. Was that really the last time I saw him?

Bart nudged me on the shoulder. "What are you thinking about?"

"Nothing."

"Like hell, nothing. Your face says you're thinking there may not be a band anymore."

"Well, that's true, isn't it?" I couldn't separate the pain of losing Ziggy from the pain of losing Moondog Three.

Wait. Was Ziggy lost? When did I decide that? When did I give up? I stared at the bubbles going up and up and up in my champagne flute and had the urge to smash it. Not that my angst was the glass's fault or anything.

"Anything new on the lawsuit?" I asked.

Bart shook his head. "They sent theirs. We sent ours. Our auditor gets a look at their books on January eighth."

"Who's our auditor?"

"A friend of my dad's whose specialty is forensic accounting. And because he needs an assistant, Colin."

"Oh, good."

He raised an eyebrow questioningly at me.

"I'm happy Colin's helping out." I don't think that explained what he was asking, but I didn't have an explanation. Colin: good. That's it.

Carynne came over and kissed me on the cheek. "You look tired."

"I'm fine." I set my empty champagne glass down, thinking I had better switch to beer. "Bart and I are talking about the lawsuit and the audit."

"Yeah, Merry Christmas. Sorry about that."

"The timing kind of sucks, doesn't it? Not Christmas, I mean, that they tried to sue us right before we're about to audit them?"

"Well, I'm sure it's related. They think they'll get some kind of advantage, I'm sure."

"But will they? They sue us, we countersue, they know we're going to audit, now they have even more incentive to hide stuff from us though, because of the suits."

She shrugged. Bart wandered off with Michelle. Courtney, who must have been reading my mind or something, came over with a couple of cans of beer, still dripping from being in ice. She and me and Carynne drank to the holidays and being together.

"So tell me all about Japan!" Court said. "Is it as cool as I think it is?"

"I dunno. How cool do you think it is?"

She hit me on the arm, like only a sibling can hit a sibling.

"Ow. It's kind of neat. We went to see a big temple with a giant Buddha statue in it. And there's a whole street of music shops in Tokyo they call Guitar Street."

"You said you stayed in a hot tub place?" Carynne asked.

"Hot springs resort. There's geothermally heated water, and they pump it into tubs of varying temperature, and you sit around in them and look at the lagoon. It's neat."

And I told them about fried octopus and our translator and how audiences in Japan are super polite. I did not tell them about Hiroshima. Too heavy. Talking about Rocky reminded me, though. "I have to show you this." I looked around for the Ovation's case—after all, I never went to a party without it—and dug out a copy of the magazine Rocky had found for me. "Check this out."

I paged through the glossy photos until I came to a two-page spread. Me and Ziggy.

They oohed and aahed. Then Courtney said, "But what does the text at the bottom here say?"

"I have no idea."

"You didn't ask the translator?"

"Um, no."

They were both disappointed by this. I didn't imagine that the text said anything other than what it would in an American teen magazine. Probably something about our favorite colors or how we met or whatever.

Cray appeared at my elbow. "Hey, wanna jam?" He'd seen me digging around in the guitar case.

"Sure."

I introduced him to everyone and then we went out to the terrace that overlooked the beach. Someone in the crew had a little dumbek and joined in. I don't remember what we played. I cracked out "Here Comes the Sun." I know we played around with a bunch more songs, including one that must have been a Blue Licks String Band tune, but I'd be lying if I told you I knew which one.

Remo couldn't join in. He'd overdone it onstage and was wisely resting, but he really looked like he wanted in. He sang a little.

I handed my guitar to Flip at one point and rotated out to get another drink. Water first: jamming is thirsty work. And then another beer, which tasted very bready—yeasty, maybe?—compared to what we drank in Japan.

I held the cold can against my thumb, which was throbbing a little, and sat in a chair listening to the music and looking at the empty beach.

Remo sat down next to me. "You want an ice pack?"

"Was gonna ask you the same thing."

He shrugged. "I'm fine. I'll be fine."

I took his word for it. "Thanks for bringing my people here. That can't have been cheap."

"It was Carynne's idea."

"When did you talk to Carynne?"

"A while back. Seemed only fair, since I kicked your dad out." He was half-joking, but neither of us laughed. "They're going to stay a whole week."

"I take it that means I'm staying, too?"

"Dunno. I left that up to Waldo and Carynne to work out." He waved in their general direction. "Carynne said something about snorkeling."

"Doesn't that require going out in sunlight?"

He chuckled. "Moondog," he said, affectionately.

Then we sat there drinking in companionable silence, listening to the music. Bart had taken over the dumbek, someone had added an Irish flute, and a woman I didn't recognize was belly dancing. Cray's girlfriend, possibly.

I had a moment then, one of those deja vu moments where you think you must be remembering something from a dream, since you can't think of when it happened in real life. In the deja vu moment, I was playing the guitar, some guy right next to me was playing a drum, and a woman was dancing. Was it from school? A party? Or was it something that hadn't happened to me yet?

Or maybe, despite my efforts, I'd had too much to drink again tonight and my brain was pickled?

I sat there trying to hear the music in my vision, trying to feel what I was playing, but the actual party around me was too loud for that.

"I'm going to take a walk on the beach," I told Remo.

"Don't go in the water. Sharks," he said.

"All right." I walked until I got near the water's edge, then took my sneakers off and tied the laces together to make them easier to carry. And then I walked until I couldn't hear the party anymore, but whatever my mind had been trying to tell me with that flash of guitar-dancer-drum had slipped away.

No One Is to Blame

When I got back to the party, the jam session had broken up and the Ovation was in its case. I could tell from the way everything was arranged that Flip had been the one to put it away. Once a guitar tech, always a guitar tech.

I went to find him to say thanks. He was expounding about posture to Martin, who was nodding like he'd heard this one before.

"Hey," Flip said to me. "I picked up my messages from home. I've got two questions for you."

"Only two?"

"Funny guy. Two for the moment. One, do you have six hundred dollars."

"Not on me."

"Two, if there was an opening in a Guitar Craft workshop next week, would you want to go?"

So that's what the $600 was for. "Absolutely. Why? Is there an opening?"

"Might be. There's normally a waitlist, but there were six guys all coming from overseas together as a group, something got fucked up with their visas or something. I didn't get the whole story. And it's short notice. Not everyone can jump on it. So I got a call asking if I knew anyone who might want to go."

"Tell Carynne when and where, and she'll handle everything."

He grinned. "Must be nice having a secretary."

"Manager," I said automatically. "Never mind. I'll tell her myself." I patted him on the shoulder so he wouldn't think I was pissed at him or something, because I knew that came across a little snippy. I needed some rest and to have drunk two or three fewer beers.

I resolved to find Carynne and tell her before I forgot, and then go to bed.

I found her sitting where I'd been with Remo earlier, looking at the beach. I got some water and sat down with her, starting to feel drowsy now that I had resolved to call it a night.

She spoke first, though. "You know, if you join Nomad, you don't need me anymore."

I had been half asleep, but I was suddenly wide awake. "Whoa, wait a second. First of all, I'm not joining Nomad. Second, even if I did, what makes you think I wouldn't need you anymore? Are your other bands doing that well you need to move on?"

Her eyes went wide, too, like what I said woke her up. "Holy shit, no, I was thinking you might want to fire me."

"Quit that. Quit even thinking about that kind of thing. I'm not firing you; I'm not leaving you. Even if I gallivant around the world from time to time."

"Okay, good. I'm not leaving you, either."

We both sat back and rested a moment, and then we both burst out laughing.

Which made me ask, "Are we starting to become alike or something?"

"Hope not."

"Can I tell you about my next round of gallivanting?"

"Where are you going next?" She gave me a critical look.

"Virginia. Flip has the details. For a guitar workshop with Robert Fripp. Can you figure out how to get me there and all that?"

"I'll talk to Flip. Can I tell you my latest dating failure?"

"Sure."

She told me about a guy she had gone out with a few times and the various reasons why she thought they weren't compatible. My impression was that the main problem was that she liked his "resumé" but didn't like *him*. She liked a laundry list of things about him—his build, his hair color, his job, his background, his hobbies—but that didn't mean she liked his personality.

When she ran down, I pointed this out.

"I don't think it was that," she said. "I think it was that he can't handle what I do for a living and he can't handle that I used to fuck rock stars as a hobby."

"Used to?"

"Used to. Come on, D. It was one thing when I was just a kid with no real responsibilities. Now if I'm going to have any respect in the industry, I can't."

"And you told him about your... hobby?"

"Of course. How the hell am I supposed to get intimate with someone unless we exchange sexual histories?

If he can't handle where I've been, I shouldn't let him in."

"Ah. Well put."

"So he was a bore in bed, really repressed, I suspect because he was comparing himself the whole time to who he imagined I slept with when I was like eighteen." She shook her head. "And that's the real dealbreaker. If a guy is not good in bed, then there's really zero reason to date him. Everything else a boyfriend brings to the table I can get somewhere else."

"Everything?"

"Everything but the sex. I've got all the emotional attachment and fulfillment and income handled for myself already, thanks."

So it seemed. We sat quietly for a minute or two. Then I asked her, "Did you ever think that every guy you date turns out to be a bore in bed, though, because you've slept with all these rock stars?"

She shrugged. "Some of them weren't that great."

"But rock stars are what turns you on. Not nice guys with nice resumés."

She looked into her beer. "Point."

"This hasn't occurred to you before?"

"I hadn't thought about it quite like that." She sighed and then looked at me. "Why aren't you straight? That would solve all my problems."

"It would?"

"Yes, because you and I would have the perfect friends-with-benefits arrangement. You would totally handle it. I know you would."

I felt good and bad about this. "I love you, Carynne. But not like that."

"Except that one time."

"Yeah."

"I love you, too, Daron. But I wish..." She shook her head again. "Sorry. Don't mean to make you flip out. This is not a pass, okay? But you happen to be the only friend I can really talk to about it."

"I totally understand." I did. I knew all about the person who was your affliction being the only remedy, too.

We sat there not saying much then, and although I was happy she was there, I was a little depressed. End of tour. Although it was going to be nice to have a few quiet days at the beach.

I said, "Find out anything about Ziggy?"

She shook her head.

A thought came to me then. Now that the tour was over and I didn't have to think about anything regarding that, I had space in my brain to have other thoughts. The thought was this: I didn't want to go home to Boston unless Ziggy was there.

Which was stupid.

But there it was. I wondered if I would have to go directly to Virginia. No reason not to, really. I could send my excess stuff home with Courtney. Which reminded me:

"How's Christian?"

"He's all right. He thought about coming down here, too, but his family asked him to spend the holidays with them and he decided to go along with it."

"I thought he and his father didn't get along?"

"They don't, but I guess he felt like maybe this would be the time to try to make one more stab at reconciliation."

"Don't use the word 'stab.' They had a violent relationship, from what I remember."

"Yeah."

I told her my thought. "I don't want to go home if Ziggy's not there."

"Oh, honey." She held me then. I didn't cry. I'd reached a state of fatigue or numbness, I guess, where I felt awful, but not the crying kind of awful.

She held me for a long time. I could hear water, waves. At one point I said, "Please tell me I'm not doing to you what he did to me."

She kissed me on the hair. "No, honeybunches of oats. It's not like that at all with us. I'm very happy with how much I love you and how much you love me back."

"You're sure."

"I'm sure. Even if I bitch that I'm not getting laid enough."

"Let's find you some hot Australian at least," I suggested.

"That would be great. What about you?"

"Yeah, I could use a hot Australian, too, I guess."

We fell silent again. Then, at pretty much the same moment, we both tried to make the exact same joke: "Think Michael Hutchence is available?" Which set us both to laughing so hard that when Bart came to find out what was so funny we couldn't even stop laughing long enough to tell him. Which was just as well, since it couldn't really be explained.

It's the End of the World as We Know It

I remember it as a good Christmas. I remember it fondly.

We had actual Christmas, with gift exchanging and everything. I finally understood why Remo had designated a day for Christmas shopping in Japan.

I also finally understood one of the things Cray really hadn't said—maybe couldn't bring himself to say—about why he was so touchy and insecure. He called his mother to say "Merry Christmas" and I guess with the time change woke her up in the middle of the night, and it turned into an argument. A yelling-into-the-phone kind of argument, which meant I could make out bits of what she yelled, too.

Of course, the only reason I overheard this was because after all the gift exchanging and a huge meal, Cray, his girlfriend, me, and Flip had gone back to Cray's room to drink some Australian whiskey that either Cray or Flip had gotten for Christmas.

The relevant bit of the phone conversation for my realization was when Cray said something to his mom like, "You could've been here, too, you know."

I'll say one thing for alcohol. It may mess up my logical thinking in such a way that trying to figure out whether it's faster or better to take a cab or the subway in New York City ceases to work. But it frees up my emotional thinking as if somehow, when I drink, I have to drop all my baggage. It's like I simply can't carry it anymore when I'm well-lubricated, so I let it drop. The result is that sometimes my own crap stops getting in the way and I can see other people's crap instead.

Anyway. It hit me that Cray, deep down, was worried that the only reason Remo "dragged him along" on the tour was to try to entice his mother—whom I gathered Remo was still interested in—to come along, too.

This struck me as ridiculous, because I don't think that Remo would do that. For one thing, as we established, Remo didn't do charity cases. And to me, Remo didn't seem likely to compromise anything musically for the sake of interpersonal pursuits. But that didn't mean Cray didn't have hangups—and I remembered him telling me he thought his mother *would* compromise the musical integrity of their group for the sake of interpersonal pursuits. So maybe it made sense for him to jump to that conclusion, even if it was wrong.

Our visions are always colored by our experiences. And by our parents.

Remo bringing Carynne and company down made sense to me then, too, if he had been thinking of it as a chance for everyone's families to get together. There were a few others who joined in, and I think maybe there would have been even more if we hadn't been completely on the opposite side of the globe. I was a little queasy thinking about how much it all must have cost, but I felt a little better when I overheard Alan trying to tell him that he and his brother wanted to pay Reem back for their dad's airfare, and Remo's answer was: "It's only money. I can't take it with me when I die, may as well spend it now."

If we hadn't been having the problems with the record company, if the next album had been on the horizon and we'd been looking at a string of successes, maybe I'd get to that point, too. The point when I could say it was "only" money. I mean, yeah, if Chris and I cashed out of the house, that'd probably put a hundred thousand in my pocket? If I did nothing else to earn, I could probably live off of that for six or seven years.

You want to talk math? Here's the math that still was in my head:

I could live on about seven bucks a day in food costs. Round that up to $3,000 a year.

A closet-sized studio in the Fenway would run me about $400 a month, or $4,800 a year.

Let's say $500 a year in clothes, shoes, etc.

$500 in equipment, just strings and repairs.

Say $500 for riding the T.

That all adds up to under ten grand.

No car, no health insurance, but it was actually doable to make ten grand a year busking. The busking permit in Cambridge cost $40 a year. There was really only one decent place to busk in Cambridge, which was Harvard Square, but on weekends there were plenty of people and lots of room around every corner for many different performers. I knew people who pulled in $200 a night on the busy nights. Of course, you only really had two big nights a week, and only when the weather was nice. But say six months of the year, 26 weeks, you played those two nights, and took in $200 each time. How much would that be? $10,400 cash.

The reality, of course, was that you'd get a gig to play in a club on a weekend night where your whole band would only get $200 to split between you, but you'd do it for the chance to get on the stage and play in front of hundreds of people for an hour or more, instead of standing for four to six hours in one spot, playing for indifferent passerby, many of whom considered you little better than a homeless person begging for change. But you know, fuck them.

Anyway. Where was I going with this? Right. Money. "Only" money. When I think that what Remo spent to fly me and my four friends to Australia and back was about equal to what I could live off for an entire year? It made me queasy.

But then I thought to myself, *You're not going back to busking. Carynne would never let you. You've got much better prospects than that, even if you're depressed as hell about the lawsuits.*

Yeah, I was depressed as hell about the lawsuits. It was a worst-nightmare kind of scenario, wasn't it? This wasn't just "your album is a flop." This was "your album is a flop and we hate you." It took me some down time, vacationing, to realize how depressed I was.

Two days after Christmas, many folks had left. A small bunch of us made our unhurried way to the beach. A while later we made our unhurried way to lunch. Some folks went on a boat—I was unclear if fishing was going to be involved or just... boating. I was starting to feel a bit crispy-fried from the sun, so I took it upon myself to retire to my room for a bit. I needed to sort out my clothes. Remember, I had everything I'd brought with me to Mexico and then Los Angeles in one bag, and then everything else I had brought to Los Angeles with me from Boston in another. It kind of worked out, you know? Everything I wore in Mexico, I wore in Australia. And then the stuff I had packed for the cooler weather I could wear in Virginia.

I did a load of laundry. They had coin-operated machines in the back of the hotel. I know, I know, glamorous rock star life. I needed the help of the front desk clerk to figure out which coins were which. Then I sat there waiting for the stuff to spin so it could be put in the dryer, reading a magazine and wondering if there was any kind of medicine for sunburn, because the tops of my shoulders were actually starting to sting.

This is going to sound weird. But I actually felt less depressed while folding my laundry than I had at any other point in the day. In fact, I'd say my mood kind of lifted at that point. Something about putting all my things into some kind of order helped. This is why I say metaphors are reality.

Also, maybe it was calming to think that standing on a street corner with a guitar, if I was diligent and organized, would probably get me through, regardless of what kind of fuckage might go down with BNC and the music industry as a whole.

So I packed to go to guitar camp in Virginia. One small duffel bag and the Ovation. Bart and Courtney were going to take the Strat and the other bag back to Boston for me. I almost wished I was on the way already, but we weren't due to take off until January 2nd.

The group eventually dwindled down to the five of us by New Year's Eve. Over a late breakfast, we were discussing what to do that night.

"The fireworks are supposed to be amazing," Courtney said. "Like, they blow up the harbor bridge and stuff."

"They blow it up?" I asked.

"I mean, not like destroy it, but shoot a ton of stuff from it and it's cool," she said. "It's a huge deal."

"It's like July Fourth on the Esplanade," Carynne explained, translating it into Bostonian terms.

"Ah, okay." Huge civic occasion with a million-plus people. "Sure. We'd probably kick ourselves if we skipped it and we were right here."

"I wonder what the rules are concerning alcohol

consumption," Carynne mused.

"This is Australia. There are no rules," Courtney joked. "Except when there are."

"Honestly," I spoke up, "I feel like I've been drinking way too much since we got here." Really, since I got to Japan. Nomad was a heavy-drinking crowd.

"Fine, don't drink, then," Court said. I think she'd really liked that the drinking age was 18 in Australia. Not that any of us ever stopped her from drinking back home, but the freedom to walk up to a bar and order... I understood that. "But—"

I cut her off suddenly. "I have another idea."

"Besides fireworks?"

"Besides drinking."

They all stared at me, waiting for me to reveal my idea.

"I've got like ten tabs of acid in my jacket pocket."

"Really!" Court's eyes were wide with interest. "Where did you get that?"

"From Christian, like a million years ago, and I keep not getting around to trying it."

Bart gave me the hairy eyeball. "You've never tried it?"

"Never. You?"

"In school, yeah. I guess I never did with you, though. That was mostly before I got to RIMCon."

What ensued was everyone giving me their advice about psychedelic drugs. Michelle seemed to be the most savvy, actually, but she'd studied some actual science in school, plus had a bunch of suitemates who were regular trippers on mushrooms and LSD.

So the advice basically boiled down to this:

1. Vitamin C before.
2. Lots of water during.
3. Vitamin B after.

Except we didn't really know where to get vitamins in Australia, so the plan of action basically came down to the following:

1. Drink lots of water.
2. Carry the address of the hotel on a card.
3. If you get in trouble, tell people you drank too much.
4. Treat all cars as if real.

If you've never done psychedelic drugs, the one thing I'll say is that they're exactly like what you think they'll be like. Because it's your brain, whatever you imagine it will be like, that's what your brain will make it be like.

For me that meant the trip was exactly like I'd walked right into the Beatles movie *Yellow Submarine*. I first saw it when I was about six years old. It was randomly on television one Saturday morning or early afternoon. I don't remember why no one else was around, but I was the only one watching it. And I was completely transfixed. I mean, the music of The Beatles always grabbed me by the ears anyway—I was already listening to the *White Album* on a daily basis at that point, every day after getting home from first grade, right after playing *Free to Be You and Me*. And this was the music of The Beatles with cartoon animation. Psychedelic animation. It quite literally sent my little six-year-old brain on a psychedelic trip of its own, making me a space case for the whole rest of the day.

We decided to have an early dinner, then drop once we got where we were going in Sydney. I was content to let Carynne and Courtney figure that all out. They were the planners of the bunch, you know?

I remember we were in a park. We'd each made sure we had cash in our pockets, our driver's licenses (but not our passports—those were in a safe at the hotel), and the address of the hotel. The weather was warm, tons of people were out, and we sat down under a tree. I got out the piece of foil and separated the bits of paper. They didn't look like much. It was twelve tabs, actually, in a sheet like postage stamps, except that each little square was smaller than my pinky nail. I tore them apart on the perforations. We decided one each should be plenty, unless it turned out it was no good because it had been in my pocket for so long, in which case we'd double up.

One was plenty.

We were sitting there under the tree, and two guys came along and started busking nearby, with a guitar and a didgeridoo, and maybe a half hour later? forty-five minutes? I looked up and pointed to the sky. The sun was setting.

The sky had taken on a kind of three-dimensional texture that it normally doesn't have. And it was like I could see the sound waves of the music sweeping across the sky, perturbing the ridges and swirls like leaving a wake through water.

And my first thought was, *Hey, all of a sudden, I understand what* Yellow Submarine *was about. It was this.*

What no one told me, or no one impressed upon me, was how long acid lasts. It was around seven or eight in the evening at that point. An acid trip lasts a full twelve hours, sometimes more like sixteen. So we were still going to be tripping our brains out at breakfast-time the next day.

At the time, though, I wasn't thinking about that. Time stops moving while you're tripping. Literally, sometimes, where I would get focused on a flower or a leaf or the pattern on someone's shirt, and I would kind of disappear down into looking at it on the molecular level, like zooming down a wormhole into the atoms. Time doesn't move down there on the atomic level.

And then, zoom, I'd come teleporting back out to the regular world and time would move forward again. So yeah, it lasts twelve hours but it feels like a week goes by.

The fireworks were amazing, but I think they would have been amazing without drugs. Fireworks, in fact, looked exactly the same as they do without drugs.

But the *smoke*. The smoke was amazing. Like Chinese dragons come to life. Really.

I can't even remember all the things we did and the places we went that night. Different ones of us were coherent at different times. I wasn't hungry at all, but at some point Bart got us into a restaurant and made us try to read the menu. The only words on it I could read were "black olives." I'm pretty sure they were the ingredient in a salad or something. I resolved when the waiter came around that I was going to point and then just see what I ended up with. But when he came to me, all I could say was the words "black olives" and show him where it said that on the menu.

All he said was, "okay," and moved on like that was totally normal. I was pretty sure what he wrote on his order pad was "totally nuts" or something like that. But then he brought me a large glass of water and a bowl of black olives with a tiny fork.

I decided I was in love with the tiny fork. Actually, maybe I was in love with the waiter, who really seemed to understand my needs. You know? But I probably couldn't take him with me. So I stole the tiny fork, named it George, and left four Australian twenty-dollar bills under the empty bowl when we left.

There was also a point at which Bart and Courtney played Frisbee with someone's dog. That must have been earlier, when it was still light out? I don't know. Time didn't work right, and my memory is suspect at the best of times. The Frisbee left trails and streamers in the air that made me think, aha, the guys who animated *Tron* did this.

In fact, the number of movies that suddenly made sense to me during that trip convinces me that psychedelic drugs must certainly be a part of any film school curriculum.

The biggest revelation came toward the end of the trip, though. By then the sun was rising and we were starting to feel a little tired, but everyone was still completely high and groovy, and we sat on a balcony at the hotel and I played the guitar.

And I was playing a thing, kind of picking around with my right hand and hammering on the strings with my left, when it hit me that the entirety of existence is contained in the vibrating string.

Saying it like that doesn't really express the enormity of what I had realized. It was like I could see to the ends of the universe by understanding this basic component of existence.

I still didn't say it right. Plain truth is that words are inadequate to describe or explain what I then knew in my brain. Knew, felt, saw, understood, heard—all of the above. They say the senses are actually all one sense, and it's only that as humans we chop it up into these different sensory inputs, as if the universe itself is separated into things you can see, smell, taste, touch, or hear. Or know. But that's wrong. Things aren't separated. Things are just things. Things *are*.

I sound like a nut, probably. But I had never had a spiritual epiphany like it, and I've never had one since, but I found it not only mind-blowing, but also immensely and intensely comforting to know that the universe was *knowable*. That a puny being like me, a tiny pinprick of light in a universe with billions of galaxies in it, could know this and experience this one basic thing.

The vibrating string.

I tried to explain it to the others. But apparently I couldn't use words and maintain my state of communion with the universe at the same time, so I contented myself with being non-verbal and kept playing.

If there is such thing as a state of grace, that was it.

I'll tell them later, I thought.

Later—much later—I got hungry and time started to move forward again. We had breakfast, drank large amounts of water, and all ended up asleep in Bart and Michelle's room. I'm not sure why, it just seemed like the thing to do at the time.

And I should stop there. I should leave off with us all contentedly sleeping, my brain completely empty of thoughts but full of knowledge and understanding.

But you know it doesn't end there. The future was going to be full of lawsuits and dealing with Ziggy and Digger and Mills and who knew what else. The next time I opened my eyes, that would all rush in like a tide. But I had found something, between when I left LA and that morning, whether it was the epiphany or all the thinking or my growth as a person or what, I had found something that let me bob on top of it all instead of getting swamped. From up there on the surface, I could look down into the swirling chaos that my life had been and realize that an era had ended. And that I felt good about that.

That's right. The next time I opened my eyes, the trip was over. The tour was over. The motherfucking *'80s* were over.

And my eyes were as clear as they'd ever been.

Ziggy's Diary

Ziggy's Diary: 1

Dear Diary,

How many times have I resolved to keep a diary and then I don't keep it up? Well, how's this for a test of the new leaf I turned over. Hello! The whole fucking tree is new! If I really mean it, then here's the proof. Or at least when the entries stop I'll be able to see the exact day I fell back off the wagon.

New leaf new leaf new leaf SONG IDEA?

At the center we had writing assignments. It was like taking a test in school, except the subject was your own twisted mind, and you think you wouldn't have to study up on that but you do! So much learning at the center. Psychology, medicine, neurology, biology. I was crap at the therapy assignments, but they got me back in the habit of writing stuff like this. So, diary. Here I am. On the plane to London, where we change planes for India. Bought this notebook in a shop in Burbank. Three continents in one day. After not being allowed to leave the center for 28 days, you think I'm overdoing it? I'm not. I'm doing everything I can to preserve my sanity, not break it.

Jenn's asleep on my shoulder. Aww. Fortunately she's not on the arm holding the pen. She's a sweet girl.

Why did I just write that? No she's not. She's a cynic. What I don't know is whether she was a cynic before she got to Hollywood or if that came after. Maybe once upon a time she was a sweet girl. Or maybe she just plays one on TV. If you believe her, and I do, by the time she was sixteen she had decided if blowing the casting director was what it was going to take to get famous, she'd do it. I admire that kind of drive and that kind of sex-forward thinking. She never let herself be victimized by the business. (No, it took drugs to do that.)

You'd think someone that forward—someone who let me fuck her on camera for a movie where zero percent of that footage was going to get onto the screen just because she, and me, and the director got off on it—would be a good match for me. You'd think.

But honestly, I'm utterly sick of her in bed. I'm not sick of the comfort of being close to someone, of the cuddles afterward, or the talks we have. She's a friend. She knows it, too, but lovers is easier to explain. Lovers is easier to understand. Friend? She told me once that I don't know how to be a friend, and she's right. She doesn't know either is the thing. Like me, she relates to everyone through sex. For most of the world, the second they touch your dick they can never be "friends" again. I don't get that. I don't get that at all. It's a spectrum, a continuum. You don't magically stop being friends just because sex happened. But people act like the dick is a magic wand. It touches you and poof, you are magically tossed over the wall to the other side.

I guess most people can't understand that there isn't a wall between gay and straight either. Yeah, touch a guy's dick, ever, and you're gay. Cooties.

These days, cooties are fatal.

Jenn doesn't mind that I've had men. She sees us as equals that way. We had sex every day in rehab, some how, some way. 28 days in rehab, 28 sexes. (There needs to be a word for that.) We went there to get off drugs and to get off dependency. They keep you busy there, you know. Up at 6:30 AM every day! I think they do it so the ones who were addicted to sleeping pills will be good and tired every night. Crack of dawn and then a walk before it gets too hot, and then chores and meals and group therapy sessions. The center is like summer camp without the fun.

The center. Everyone calls it that. Like it's actually at the center of everything. But god help me if the center of my world is ever rehab itself. If it comes to that, suicide starts sounding reasonable.

The center is a hospital. I get that. They're trying to get your body clean without you dying. Some of the people there really needed the serious medical intervention, too, organs failing and that kind of shit. Me, not so much. I was by far the youngest person there, and my addiction was so recent, comparatively speaking, that I was the healthiest of the bunch. Some of these guys drank a bottle of vodka every day for twenty years and you can barely believe they're alive. Or the women who can't make it through a single day without a regimen of uppers and downers and prescriptions for every situation. I know what that's like. I know. I know the strategies that go through your head, and how you structure everything in your entire day, your entire life, around what pill to take when. At the center, they break you of that.

Instead, I structured every day at the center around when to get off. No, I didn't tell my counselor that. I was warned not to turn sex into an addiction. Sure. But he seemed to find it a good sign that I could get pleasure from something other than the drugs. Some of the people there couldn't physically experience pleasure because they'd wired themselves to their drugs. Some of them couldn't emotionally or spiritually experience joy for the same reason.

Jenn's one of those. That's why we're going to India.

I have a feeling the sex between her and me will stop as soon as we get where we're going. That'll be fine with me. We needed it in rehab. It was the only pleasure we could get. But now we're out.

God, I'm tired. I'm going to close my eyes for a little bit. I'm sure the second I fall asleep the damn pilot is going to make an announcement.

Ziggy's Diary: 2

Heathrow. Waiting for the flight to Bangalore. We shot off a couple of faxes from the specialty lounge. I don't have enough miles to qualify as special, but she does. Nice lounge. Swanky. We were not dressed for it, but Brits are too polite to say anything. We only did faxes, no voice calls. I wanted to talk to Daron except what the fuck did I have to say? It's all water under the bridge. If he's still going to be mad about the canceled show, I can't risk some bullshit like that sending me spiraling down again. Not right now. Leaving Betty Ford was like getting a cast off a broken leg. Now I have to try walking again for a while before going back to backflips.

I want to backflip, of course. But at the center they really sell you on the idea that you're saving your life there. That it was even worse than you think it was. They scare you. I slip at times into thinking it wasn't that bad. Then I look back at the pages where I did "homework" like "List 12 Things Your Abuse of Prescription Drugs Negatively Impacted."

Daron's name is on there a lot of times.

"The center." The center of everything. If I write a song about rehab, that's what I'll riff on. But I don't want to think of the center as my center. Which is probably why I'm traveling so far away. One reason. Of many. I'll have plenty of time to examine why when I get there. Instead of "the center" why don't I call it "BF" from now on? Betty Ford. Half the reason the place succeeds, I swear, is because with a name like Betty Ford it sounds friendly, like the mom next door is going to take care of you. If it were called the Hedwig Wilmington Center it wouldn't be half so successful, I bet.

England. I know there's a reputation about drinking here. But in the airport they are handing out free samples of booze to passersby! FREE SAMPLES. I took one before Jenn knocked it out of my hand, apologized profusely to the clerk and pressed some tissues into the guy's hand, and then dragged me to the lounge. I tried to tell her alcohol was never my problem but she was freaking out so I just said okay, sorry, and now she's fine again.

We're waiting to board, and I am bored. hahaha

I was expecting a room full of humongous egos at BF. But truth is that most of them were so beaten up and battered down and desperate by the time they were at the point where they checked themselves into detox that they actually NEEDED some ego to care about themselves enough to rebuild their shit. Oh sure, a lot of them bounced back fast. Some.

Me? I don't think I ever was that low. Even back when I was thinking about ending it all in some dramatic, headline-grabbing fashion I wasn't that low. That's the ultimate ego trip, isn't it? Seems obvious now.

A lot of things seem obvious now. The problem with all the drugs is they make you miss the obvious stuff and focus on the bullshit.

Truth is, by the time I got to BF I had figured out what I wanted to do. The idea of disappearing, NOT in a dramatic or permanent fashion at all, NOT as a placebo for suicide.

PLACEBO SUICIDE song idea?

I needed to disconnect. Unfortunately, what 28 days

of intensive rehab therapy requires is connection, not disconnection. If they could stick wires in your heart and soul and connect you directly to their belief-fixit machine, they would. You have to talk. To people. To your counselors. To your therapists. Talk talk talk. I think if they left me alone for a month and just slid healthy food under the door, that would've had a better effect on me in the end. But you get points off for withdrawing. You get brownie points for connecting. Collect enough brownie points and you win your freedom in the end!

I'm a good brown-noser. So good there's shit stuck in my eyebrows. I had everyone at BF eating out of my hand by the end of the first week. Then it was counting the days until they'd let me go.

Jenn had the connection in India, the guru she met at a meditation center in LA. Sounded good to me. Her people booked our tickets. It all went pretty smoothly. They were savvy to sneaking her out of the country with no one the wiser, which suited me perfect. Last thing we need is a tabloid scandal about it.

Okay, now we're on the plane again. This whole plane smells like the lobby of a Las Vegas casino. Like the carpet's impregnated with years of cigarette smoke and a tinge of anxious sweat. I'm supposed to be on this flight as part of a journey to become as spiritually clean as I am now physically clean. So of course I feel surrounded by filth. Irony. I'll never escape it. Might as well live it.

Ziggy's Diary: 3

Well, Diary, we made it to the swami's place in the city. Guess what? This place is unbelievably filthy and we go everywhere barefoot but that's because, they say, it's even dirtier outside. So we left our shoes at the door. We left our clothes, our bags, pretty much everything. We're all swathed up like Hare Krishnas, basically, except everything's beige instead of orange. They let me keep my notebook. They seem to think I'm some kind of poet. That's fine with me. I don't think anyone here really knows who we are except maybe the guru himself, who met Jenn before. That's fine with me, too.

The guru has an incredibly long and multisyllabic name and he wants us all to call him "Veddy." Okay, fine.

It's ironic that we "escaped" from BF to come here and the first thing they did today was wake us up at dawn and make us do therapeutic chores. It was an unpleasant deja vu! But then BLISS OH BLISS instead of forcing us to talk with each other, an hour of blessed SILENT meditation takes place. An hour where breathing is our only job.

Breathing is a wonderful thing. I suppose if I buy what the counselors at BF are selling, I'm lucky to be alive. I don't know. I have moments when I think I could have pulled back from the brink on my own. Maybe with my regular shrink's help. Then again, she was one of the people who recommended an inpatient no-contact-with-the-outside-world program. I don't know. Maybe she was tired of me. Not that she'd seen me in over a month

Shut up stupid negative thoughts, that's probably bullshit.

So yeah, I have moments when I think I could have handled it, then I have moments when I think thank god I went there and they saved me. It's hard to know how much is just that I bought into the rehab mentality and how much is actually true. I guess the idea is this: if buying into the rehab mentality might have possibly saved your life, then it's worth it to believe it, even if maybe it didn't actually save your life in your particular case. Certainly it saved some of the people there, but then again you can ask yourself if they were worth saving. I don't mean that in a callous way. I'm sure their families and husbands and wives would rather have them breathing than in a hole in the ground. This is where the suicide thing gets me. When you convince yourself that the people around you would actually be better off with you in the ground, it invalidates all arguments about the value of therapy.

The number one value of therapy is that it convinces you that breathing is better than putting yourself in a hole in the ground. Having been convinced of that, an hour where my only purpose is to breathe, breathe, breathe is complete bliss. Nirvana, enlightenment, is probably something else entirely, but I'll worry about getting there later. Right now, breathe. Good.

I'm supposed to be emptying my mind of all thoughts while we meditate. Right.

Ego is dangerous. Here's the trap I get myself into. What if ego is just a self-sustaining parasite? If the only purpose of ego is to sustain the ego, then existence is selfishness, and the release of that existence (i.e., death) is to cease being selfish. Nice piece of philosophy, but in the real world there are consequences: people love you, care about you, need you. When you kill yourself, you take yourself away from them. If the pain is great enough, though, you trick yourself into thinking they would be better off without you, and the ego wraps around and eats its own tail, because at its root, suicide is the ultimate selfish act. It can only be undertaken with the inward-facing view that the self is all that matters, and this is why we try to annihilate it. To end our pain. But if we do it to end our own pain, THAT is selfish. In other words, only god has the right to end your life, you sorry motherfucker, so just keep on going, keep on suffering, because you don't have that power to judge.

Of course, what if you don't believe in god?

I had a lot of time to think about these things during the meditation sessions today. Because I'm crap at meditating. Then again, so is everyone. We're all hyperaware Westerners. Two guys are here from France, a few from New York, one from England, et cetera, but mostly from the same Beverly Hills ashram where Jenn met Swami Veddy. We're a group of twenty, four women and sixteen men. There seem to be about a dozen monks who assist the guru but rarely say anything to us, and when they do it's the bare minimum. Maybe that's all the English they know. *Wash here. Eat here. This way.* Or maybe it's an act. Verbal asceticism. One of them led the afternoon yoga session today, but he mostly did it by example, not with words.

The only time there was really talking was over dinner, the communal evening meal. Everyone keeps their voices down, but a few people are trying to establish camaraderie/dominance in the group.

I'm practicing being invisible. It's working. No one's taken any notice so far of the mousy poet in the back. So glad I cut my hair before I went to BF.

I'm writing this at night from the mat on the floor where I'm supposed to sleep, in a room with three other men. This isn't a monastery where we are. It's more like a big house right off a busy street. There's a courtyard inside that is cool and quiet. But right on the other side of this wall, the city is teeming. The window doesn't shutter all the way and light comes in, and that's what I'm writing by.

The first day is over. No one wants anything from me here. It's glorious.

Ziggy's Diary: 4

I'm tired. Sleepy. This is the craziest jet lag ever. It's like my eyes try to shut and my body slumps over right in the middle of a sentence. Of course, this makes meditation impossible. I end up curled up on the floor like a cat, snoozing away. This is probably not advancing my spiritual journey, but fuck, let me get some rest and when I'm awake I'll work on my self-awareness and connection to the universe, okay?

Of course the problem is that I'm awake now when I'm supposed to be sleeping, and in a few hours they'll come wake us for dawn meditation...

At least they aren't judgmental. No one beat me or scolded me for falling asleep during meditation. This ain't Catholic school. I guess they figure it's my own loss if I'm not getting out of it what I came here for.

I was more awake in the afternoon session. I'm supposed to "follow my breathing." Instead I daydreamed intensely about Daron. Perhaps I am exorcising him? Or exorcising the drug memories. Vivid conversations with him returned to me with startling clarity.

Some of those conversations are taking place through music, without words. I figure if I can't actually get to meditating, at least I reached something kind of like an altered state? No drugs necessary. That's progress, right?

It's only the second day. I'm sure Swami Veddy would say I'm being an impatient American. If he spoke to me. No one, other than Jenn briefly, has spoken directly to me in two days.

Swami Veddy told a story today about a guru who

went and lived in a cave near his master's monastery and would come out once a week to talk to his master and then go back in.

That cave is sounding really good right now. Instead, I make myself the cave. When they look at me, they see only the gap, the emptiness.

Ziggy's Diary: 5

Well Diary, I was right. No sex with Jenn, and we've been here four days. It'd be tricky but not impossible to sneak it in. After the evening meditation session they have begun to let us have an hour of free time. We have nothing to do in that hour but talk with each other or meditate more on our own. There are places in the courtyard and throughout the house suitable for solo meditation. Each of those places would be perfectly suitable for a quick fuck, blow job, or hand job, too.

I find myself noting this without much emotion, though, like a man who isn't hungry noticing a sandwich shop in a train station. Like it might matter later. But right now it doesn't. It's an odd sort of relief, this not being hungry for sex. No one here needs me. No one here wants me. I'm not interested in any of them. There's no need for any sexual connection of any kind and so there ISN'T one. Kind of amazing and, for me anyway, kind of an altered state of being all its own.

Speaking of food. It's good. Not as fancy as what you get in an Indian restaurant in the States—this is more like home cooking—but at least it has flavor. After a month of the institution food at BF, maybe anything would taste great to me. But I think this stuff is pretty tasty. How can you go wrong with rice and beans? Okay, the beans are different ones, lentils and chickpeas mostly, but seriously.

Jenn hates it. You'd think she was being forced to eat cat food from a can. I guess she'll get used to it or starve? The only rice she's ever eaten, apparently, is Uncle Ben's. This blows my mind. Rice is the staple of the cooking from so many different countries! She insists she's never even had fried rice take-out. Never had sushi. Never had rice and beans in a Cuban or Caribbean restaurant. Never had paella. Never had Greek grape leaves stuffed with rice pilaf. Never had shawarma on rice. Never had a burrito stuffed with rice. And obviously she's never had Indian food. The mind boggles. How could you live in Southern California and never have Mexican food? Well, she's had tacos. No rice in those.

I guess only poor folks eat rice and beans. Not that she grew up rich, no, then she'd probably be more worldly and have wider experience, too. No, she comes from that bland, blind, middle-of-America middle class. I.e., the People Who Eat Uncle Ben's. I didn't think of her as "sheltered" because she took charge of her sexuality so young. But I guess there are other ways you can be sheltered.

I begin to appreciate growing up in New York City and eating everything without caring what country it came from. If it's sold from a cart or a truck or a restaurant with a window onto the street, I've eaten it. And that's pretty much everything you can think of.

Yeah, no, the food isn't what makes me feel like we're a million miles from home. It's the sanitary conditions, or lack thereof. Everyone says it's worse in other places. At least we have a modicum of running water in the building here. They say don't drink from it, but it's only a matter of time before the local gut bugs get into you and make you sick. I guess it's like Montezuma's Revenge, only the Indian version. Kali's revenge.

So far so good on me. But it seems to be making its way through the whole group. Only a few have actually puked—it mostly comes out the other end. When can I go to my cave?

Ziggy's Diary: 6

Kali's Revenge got Jenn today. Maybe she was already feeling ill, which was why she didn't like the food. She won't be eating anything for a few days anyway, other than rice gruel and tea. The important thing about the tea is they boil the water, so you know it's clean.

The only bad part about not getting sick myself is it's taken away my invisibility. I'm pretty much the only one who hasn't had it now, and they're all looking at me with baleful eyes, like, why are you special? Why aren't you miserable with us? They are all in lots of tummy distress. That's putting it mildly.

I spent the afternoon meditation session writing a song entirely in my head and memorizing the words.

Here they are. Let's see if I actually wrote a song in my head or if I only hallucinated that I did:

She puts me in a cage
Says I'll show my stripes
Right now it's all the rage
Don't worry, I won't bite

She makes me show my face
Tells me to be nice
But nice isn't what they pay
for, another show tonight

They wanna see teeth
They wanna see gore
Heart of a lion
Hear me roar

She puts her top hat on
and then cracks her whip
I'm helpless to say no
As in the cage I go

And then we're moving on
A new town every night
Come see me in my cage
I promise I won't bite

You wanna see teeth
You wanna see gore
My claws are unsheathed
Hear me roar

I guess I did.

Ziggy's Diary: 7

Everyone who's here met the guru in either LA or London. I find myself fascinated with his accent and his manner of speaking. In the States, the more sophisticated the topic of your speech is, the more refined your accent is. That's just how it is. But when Veddy speaks, there's a twist—because of course he's got a heavy Indian accent but there's also part of a British accent in his English. And sometimes when he is getting deep into a speech about some deeply sophisticated philosophical point, his accent and his grammar both get more and more British-sounding and less Indian. But then he catches himself, and he reverts to almost pidgin English, as if his message is better absorbed as exotic and mystical and deep if he sounds more like a guy who lives in a cave than one who got a degree at Oxford.

It takes a faker to know a faker. Trust me.

I'm not saying he's not a good guru. I don't have much point of comparison, though. He makes some thought-provoking points about the self and enlightenment. But so do a lot of books, right? There's a room with shelves of the Indian classics here, the Upanishads, the Bhagavad Gita. None of them are in English. A few are in Spanish, but my Spanish is too rusty and weak to read philosophy in it. Isn't that sad?

My mother didn't want me speaking Spanish when I was growing up. It was one of the only reasons she ever beat me, because of Spanish coming out of my mouth.

She thought it would hold me back in life if I had an accent.

She also didn't want me going out in the sun because it would make my skin brown. My father must have been a light-skinned man, because she's right. If I don't get sun, I'm white.

If I speak English, I'm white.

It's a little disturbing to think that my mother wished for a white child the way other women wish for a boy or a girl. I think my mother didn't care what sex I came out, but she cared about my color. My older half-brothers are both very dark with kinky hair.

She wanted a white child who would get somewhere in society and take care of her.

That's what I've done.

Children know, though. They know if you're different. They're trying so hard to put names on things—isn't that what half those children's books are about?—they look at you and they know right away you're not like them. I got those questions all the time as a kid. "Where are you from?" As if I came from some other country. As if only white people ever lived in America? "What are you?" They want a label, black, white, Indian, Japanese—I didn't have a word to give them. "What are your parents?" I don't have a father. If I wanted to give an answer and didn't want to give a huge explanation I would say my mother was Turkish Brazilian. Because at least those were countries people had heard of and then I wasn't saying she was Spanish-speaking, since I knew she wouldn't like that. I sometimes said Turkish Portuguese, which was fancier-sounding. Europe was more prestigious than South America, anyway. You learn that shit quick on the playground when respect is in short supply and the bullies are trying to figure out who to target.

My mother doted on me. Spoiled me as rotten as possible. But I will never forget that beating. How vicious her fear was. She was having hysterics, her voice distorted into a high screech. I don't know who cried more, me or her. After that, I never dared ask her about where we were from or what kind of blood we had.

Which wasn't to say I didn't speak Spanish when it suited me, as long as she wasn't around. When I was in high school and wanted to blend in with a Puerto Rican gang in New York, I had no problems. Can't even call it a gang, really, since it was just some kids, not like organized crime. More like gang wannabes, I guess. I hung around them because they had the best drugs and the girls all did anal because they were saving their chochas for marriage. I didn't spend too much time with them, though. Too macho. After I got the ringleader to suck me, it was going to end badly—and I mean West Side Story badly—if anyone found out. Not worth someone getting hurt or dead over. So I disappeared after that. Easy to do. New York is big, but people mostly swim in their own little ponds. Jumping to the next pond over is easy.

Veddy knows how to jump ponds. I think he genuinely wants to help people but doesn't think he can do it by being genuine. Or maybe the genuine Veddy is too hard to believe in. People want to believe he simply crawled out of a cave one day a Jedi Master. They want to believe in Yoda. But no one talks about how Yoda got to be that way. Wasn't he a hotheaded young apprentice once who had to be schooled and make mistakes and all that? These people aren't here for that. They're here to stare at the complexities in their own souls, the selfish fucks, and they don't want to have to contemplate the complexities of their guru.

So Veddy puts on the pidgin-English cave-dwelling yogi act, they buy it, and everyone's happy. Even me, since I get to have a feeling of smug superiority over seeing through the whole thing.

I know. Smugness and superiority are two things I'm here to let go of. But how can I when I'm literally the only person here whose shit doesn't stink?

Ziggy's Diary: 8

Guess what? Two of my roommates are fucking. There are four of us. One's asleep. I'm writing in the strip of light from the window like I always do. The other two snuck out together a few minutes ago.

So much for this being a sexless paradise. My dick is hard as a rock imagining what they're up to. One of them is the mouthy Frenchman who keeps trying to control the whole group, always dominates the conversation at dinner, and is always trying to get Jenn and the other few women to like him. The women are supremely uninterested in him. I wonder if, having struck out with the ladies, he's decided he has to plant his flag somewhere else. The guy he went with is one of those quiet-mild-mannered guys who is so effeminate it can come across as an advertisement. I don't mean he's clownish about it, either, but most American guys wouldn't dare act like that because that's how much they fear being mistaken for faggots. Which is fucked up and is probably my least favorite thing about the United States. But anyway, having been raised in America, it raises a flag to see anyone not conforming to the minimum acceptable standards for demonstrating a standard heterosexual demeanor. It makes it hard to believe that any somewhat feminine mannerism is innocent and not a come-on.

Because of this, my mind figures it must be Frenchman on top. I know it's probably not that simple. Sex rarely is. But I'm curious. And my dick is curious.

Okay, just tried meditating to see if I could make my erection go down. No. Because when I meditate my consciousness expands, and I hear every little sound in the whole house, and I can hear them. They're all the way across the courtyard, on the first floor, by the kitchens. They're in the common room. I heard one little scrape of a table against the floor. Femmy is bent over it, I'm sure. I could hear his breath. Frenchy has his hand over his mouth to keep him quiet, but that means his panting goes through his nose.

This is not my imagination. I could hear all that. Now I'm trying not to listen. I'm writing. Let's write about... something else. How about this. Is music a privilege or a right? In the States we treat it like a privilege, a luxury, but how can something that is a basic component of all cultures be that? It's a right the same as food is a right. Everyone has a right to sing or clap or make sounds together with others. People have a right to music the same as the right to food or the right to their own language. I'd think that would be obvious. But in the States we've skewed it so much—or the dominant white culture has skewed it so much—as if the only music that can be made at all these days is made by a privileged class: musicians. And only the privileged of the privileged can make a living doing it. But if people were honest and open about their need for music, would more musicians be supported in doing it, or would fewer? I think more. More would make better livings while fewer would be multimillionaires. Jenn thinks the same about sex, I think. She has this idea that if people were as open and honest about their need for sex, we wouldn't have the entertainment industry as a whole. She's not just talking about porn films, but regular films too. If people didn't lust after movie stars because their own lives didn't have enough sex in them, then not enough people would go to the movies to sustain a multibillion-dollar industry.

I think maybe she goes a little far with that assessment and has her own internal self-esteem reasons for wanting to believe that being a professional actress is the modern equivalent to being a sacred whore.

I know what I forgot to write in yesterday's diary entry, and today's: I haven't said a word in several days now. Not to Jenn. Not to anyone.

It's freeing to do it by choice like this. When I couldn't speak because of the way I ripped my throat to shreds on the tour, it was like being in chains. At first, anyway. But there were moments when I realized that so much of what I say in a given day is obligatory stuff. Hello, goodbye, thank you, et cetera. I fantasized a little about what it would be like to live free from the obligation of speech.

I haven't taken a vow of silence, but I can understand why someone might.

Ziggy's Diary: 9

Femmy couldn't sit for meditation today. Wonder why.

Ziggy's Diary: 10

I've lost count of the days. I think we've been here three weeks? A month? I should have written every day, and then it would be easy to count. But I've been living the experience. That's more important than recording it.

Had to write about this, though. We had a field trip today to a temple. I think this was promised at some point in the sales pitch by Swami Veddy. Given that I never heard the sales pitch, I had no expectations other than Jenn told me we were coming here to meditate and commune with spiritual whatever. Anyway.

The temple was in a cave. So I finally got to a cave. Funny, right?

It's a pretty big place, carved deep into the rocks, with pillars and separate areas for worshipping Shiva in one part, Parvati in another part, and they tell me that there's one holy day a year where, the way it's built, the sun shines through the pointers on a trident sculpture outside and right down into the cave. Like an underground Stonehenge.

A family was undergoing some kind of ritual with water. The entrance is right on top, in the "roof." It's been built over, so it really looks like the roof of a building, only irregularly shaped. This isn't what you'd think a sacred cave would look like if you wrote about it in a fantasy book or something. That's the thing, though. Enlightenment probably doesn't look the way people expect, either, and that's why it's so hard to find.

I'm still not talking, so I didn't ask any questions at the cave. I was content to wander and see and experience and soak things in.

God, the people. There are so many people here. There are roving bands of chanting monks and throngs of families and just plain THRONGS. I can understand Jenn being a little freaked. I was a little freaked. But I don't think Veddy's about to let any of us get kidnapped or something, because I would bet that would be bad for his little ashram-getaway business plan. Besides, nothing bad was going to happen to her when everyone there was looking at her. I get that it freaked her that everyone was staring at her, but she was making it so obvious that she was the only white woman movie star there. Why did she change out of her kameez and put on sunglasses? Did she think some paparazzi were going to be there and she wanted to look glamorous? Put a damn scarf over your hair and wear long sleeves if you don't want people staring at you. Everyone else went in the kameez and salwar we were given when we got here. Kameez has to be the same word as camisa, doesn't it? It's a tunic blouse thing, and salwar are the baggy pants that go along with it. I don't understand her.

I think the thing that freaked her out the most is that she lost me while I was standing practically right next to her. Because I blend in with the crowd. I can make myself invisible. It's especially easy because I've browned up since we got here. I've been sitting on the roof for some meditation sessions, and I'm looking varnished. And this has always been true: my face could be almost any face from almost any sunny part of the world.

I am this close to being able to disappear completely. It isn't death I'm seeking. It isn't oblivion in the traditional sense. It's death of the ego, only the ego, I'm seeking, and that's something I don't even have a word for.

Ziggy's Diary: 11

Dear Diary,

Well, so much for being invisible. Up until yesterday I think the only people in the ashram who actually noticed I haven't been talking were Jenn and Swami Veddy himself. But now everyone knows because Jenn made a big deal out of it.

She made a scene, accusing me, yelling at me. She got exasperated that I haven't been answering her for weeks. You'd think she would have caught on by now and given up asking me things. But no, the only reason she asks me things is to try to force me to talk to her. And so now she's decided that the REASON I'm not talking is so that I won't have to answer HER. As if this is all about her. She actually went to Veddy and told him to make me talk! Like you'd go to an elementary school teacher to make that boy in your class stop hitting you with spitballs.

Veddy told her to respect my walking my own path on the journey and to respect that my path and hers may not lead to the same place. That really wasn't what she wanted to hear, and she spouted some bullshit about how she paid my way here so she was entitled to me "being there" for her. Gee, if she'd said she wanted a minion to come with her and support her, I might have said "no, thanks." So much for all her claims that this trip to India was the absolute best thing for ME and that she "would do anything to help [me] find the key to happiness." She's a better actress than I realized, I guess, because that hadn't sounded like bullshit at the time. Then again, maybe my bullshit detector was out of commission because of everything at BF.

Anyway. Veddy clucked his tongue and shook his head a lot when she said I owed it to her to speak because she'd paid for me. He then dressed Jenn down, but in his gentle folksy pidgin-English way. He is always smiling and seems to be laughing at his own private joke all the time. So even when he criticizes, it isn't like a scolding. But he really told her off, I thought. He told her to focus on her own path and not mine and basically to leave me alone, that being fixated on me was holding her back, etc. Then he sent her off to meditate. More likely she went off to fume, but at least she did it in private.

Then he took me aside and told me a story. God has many faces, he said. (My immediate thought: Can this guy read my mind?) The story was that Brahma, the creator, is pictured with four faces or four heads. Brahma, by the way, he said, is considered the god of creativity and music. "Lord of Speech and Sound," he called him. I have no idea if Veddy knows who I am or that I'm a singer. Obviously he knows I've chosen to keep my mouth shut, so maybe that's the big relevance there.

Anyway, the story goes that Brahma actually used to have five heads, not four. Brahma had ten sons and one daughter. One day, his daughter was flying away from him and a fifth head rose up above the others. Make all the Freudian inferences you want—you'd be right, because that fifth head represented LUST and also EGO. Apparently Big Daddy had a lot invested in his lone daughter. Shiva didn't approve of this and cut off Brahma's fifth head with a sword.

End of story.

Veddy may be a faker, but that doesn't mean he doesn't have insight or that he doesn't have something to say.

The question the story poses is this: is it possible for me to let go of lust and ego on my own or do I need someone to come castrate me? Even the otherwise-benevolent god of creation couldn't keep his lust from getting out of control. Obviously it's better to come up with a way on my own than to need the sword method, though. How?

Oh right. Meditate. This is all supposed to work if I meditate.

Ziggy's Diary: 12

What I did during the evening meditation session today was write another song in my head by memorizing it line by line.

It's a terrible song. But I'll write it down anyway, having made the effort. Maybe get it out of my system.

The year I lived
At the top of a tree
On top of a mountain
So far away

A giant eagle
Flew up to me
Majestic and fierce
And so very free

I tried to calm it
So scared of me
Eagles fight wars
We're all enemies

What nobody knows
Is the top of the tree
Is a prison cell
Trapped in the sky

My one chance
To fly and be free
Was the golden eagle
That flew up to me

Majestic and fierce
And so very free
With feathers like knives
Wings wide as the sea

I loved the eagle
I was gentle and sweet
I won it over
And made it love me

And one by one
I took its feathers away
So I'm no longer alone
Trapped in the sky

I'm cringing because I think the song is terrible. But right after I write something is the worst time to try to judge it. Sometimes I look at things later and they seem good. Other times after finishing a song I think that it's awesome, but when I look later it's crap. So who knows.

I want to stop feeling the angst that drives me to write this kind of thing. Even if the song is good. Is that reasonable?

Ziggy's Diary: 13

Ugh. Was afraid this would happen. Jenn's little flipout about me not talking made everyone else realize that A) they had missed the whole fact that I wasn't talking, and B) now I'm teacher's pet. So they all hate me, basically. I thought it would blow over, but a week has gone by and ugh.

This is what's wrong with people. They all want me to give a fuck what they think. Are they insane? Isn't the point of a spiritual retreat to get away from bullshit like worrying about what other people think?

I don't give a fuck what they think about me
or my silence
or my lack of giving a fuck.

But they've cohered as a group now, and all this negative attention is pointed in my direction. Which means when I sit down to meditate in the back of the class, it's like every person meditating in front of me is mentally turning around and glaring at me.

And now my silence becomes a prison because I feel like I have to keep it up or they'll ridicule me. If I actually don't give a fuck what they think, then why does their ridicule matter? It's not supposed to, but suddenly it does, and THAT SUCKS.

Veddy is unhappy about this turn of events. I can see it in his eyes, but he's a good faker, he keeps on smiling and laughing, and waiting for the children to settle down and come around. I just realized what a demoralizing business this must be. He takes a group of two dozen spoiled Westerners like us every couple of months and spends time with us and does all this, and do any of them ever actually change? Probably not. But they pay their money, right? They probably don't learn squat, but at least maybe they go back home feeling better about themselves.

This is what happens when I don't charm all the people around me and make them love me. They hate me. I tried to stay invisible. I tried to stay on the fringe, in the back, forgotten, unnoticed. It almost worked.

I've got two choices now. Start talking, take over, seduce as many as I have to, and make myself the ringleader... or suffer.

I'm not here to be a ringleader. It'd mean elevating Jenn along with me, too. That's not what she's here for, either! And there would be casualties. There always are. Frenchy's ego would take a beating, for one.

Suffer. Let's try it. Plenty of spiritual leaders have claimed to attain enlightenment through it. Somehow I feel it would be easier if they were actually beating me with sticks instead of just thinking daggers of hate at me through their minds, though. If they were beating me, I could disassociate.

Wait. Disassociate. Can it be done purely mentally? Yes! Of course! Because the me that they're aiming the daggers at is MY EGO. It's the part that cares what the fuck they think. Separate that and they can hate that all they want because the rest of me... isn't there! Cut that head off right now!

Where am I? I'll be over here in my cave of enlightenment not giving a fuck because this is the part of me that doesn't!

Well, we'll see if it works. When we're actually sitting there in meditation tomorrow. Can I do it? I don't know.

Ziggy's Diary: 14

Was it Veddy or Jenn who took up the sword of Shiva to castrate me today? Guess what! It doesn't matter! Because I don't care! Veddy and Jenn are fucking, and I don't care. Jimmy crack corn and I don't care.

No, seriously, I feel nothing. My dick doesn't even stir the slightest bit when I hear them. I take that as a sign that my lustful ego is dormant if not dead. Finally.

It's fascinating because I can see through a prism into the parallel universes where I WOULD have cared. Where it would have wounded me deeply. In one: "She betrayed me." Another: "HE betrayed me." Another: "Why was I not invited?" None of those are me as I am now, though.

I heard them during the evening meditation session. All the hate in the room felt like it was trapping me there, but my mind fled as best it could, searching the house for the sounds of the monks washing the dinner dishes, the trickles of water down the drain in the back courtyard...

At one point Veddy got off his perch at the front of the room and wafted out, as he sometimes does. Jenn slipped out a short time later.

God bless Daron for forcing earplugs on me years ago.

The attention of the group is split now, because some of them noticed that she left at the same time as him, and you don't have to have ESP to guess why.

Ziggy's Diary: 15

Dear Diary, apologies for shaky handwriting. I'm safe and calm now but my hand is still nervy.

I almost undertook a new experiment in disassociation tonight. Almost. I almost lay there silent and let Frenchy fuck me to see if I could do that. But no.

No. He pissed me off too much. Couldn't maintain my Zen-like calm, and it feels so good to say the motherfucker deserved what he got.

Hard to say if I injured him seriously or if it was merely that painful to him? Funny what you remember from when you're young. In junior high we had a guy come to our gym class to teach a self-defense workshop. This was ostensibly for the girls in the class—I think there had just been some high-profile serial rapist in the papers—but they didn't have anything else for the boys to do, so we all took the class, too. The instructor was a short guy built to the max, and he taught us a couple of ways to twist out of holds and included in the instructions how to kick the attacker in the balls if the opportunity presented itself. We practiced in slow motion, but, you know... it was good for an hour of hilarity with a bunch of fourteen-year-old boys whose idea of perfect comedy is kicking each other in the nuts.

The muscle memory remains, though. At full speed, in the dark, with my blood racing from adrenaline and rage because what he said was, "you're going to have to talk to say no to me," and his pants already down, I kicked him really hard.

And then once he was down, I confess: I kicked him a couple more times.

And then I left. Might not have been the smartest thing, but I guess I'll find out. I can't see him going to the police. I don't think they treat either foreigners like him or gays very well, and I can't imagine he'd get much of a welcome reception from the local authorities.

Want to know the funniest thing of all? Femmy got up off his sleeping mat and kicked him a couple of times, too. I gave him a thumbs up for that. I doubt Frenchy could tell. After that first whack, I don't even think he felt the other kicks. Anyway.

I've got my travel pouch with my passport and wallet in it, but I left everything else behind. I didn't have much stuff anyway. You're hardly allowed to bring anything to BF in the first place, and so most of what I left at Veddy's was drab clothes.

I'm writing this from the top bunk in the far corner of a dormitory hostel. Three dollars a night. No one here has the slightest idea who I am. It's wonderful.

Ziggy's Diary: 16

Tried to send a fax to Carynne today to say I'm okay, but it didn't go through. I was trying from one of these communications offices in a train station where they'll fax a page for a fee. But it would not go. It was very nice of them to give me my money back, I suppose.

I got the idea to fax her just in case Jenn had a freak-out and called the embassy or *Hollywood Reporter* or who knows what. In case news reached the States that I had gone missing from my already-being-missing, haha.

The thing is, I was also hoping Carynne would call to check on my mother. I'd send the message to Digger, but that motherfucker won't actually do it. As I was tearing up the page I'd written out to throw it away, it occurred to me that I don't know what I was expecting Carynne to do either. Call up the home and say is she okay? And if they say no, then what? It's not like I was giving her a way to get back to me. I guess I just wanted someone to be checking on her, even if it isn't me. I don't know. Actions that are spurred by emotions don't have to make sense because emotions don't have to make sense.

Train stations are easy places to meet people. There are so many beggars here. But also so many monks and mystics. And backpackers and tourists. I've been at a different hostel every night for the past three nights. I've had to talk a little. But mostly I've been listening. There's a lot to know.

At the second hostel the authorities came and took a boy away. I say boy, but he was over eighteen, though not by much. He was from Ireland, and his parents had been looking for him. He had disappeared into India and they had feared him dead, kidnapped, something. Kidnappers usually ask for a ransom though, or so the clerk at the hostel told me later. He also told me that the doctors at the hospital, where his second job was, said that Westerners who came to India often went insane. Western doctors called it "India Syndrome," he said. I didn't ask him what Indian doctors called it, but maybe I should have. "Westerner Syndrome," maybe.

He was not, by the way, making hints at me about myself. The universe might have been, though.

See, apparently it's a thing where folks not from here come in search of spiritual enlightenment and instead go crazy. They're just not ready. You also hear stories about people who try LSD for the first time and lose their minds. That didn't happen to me when I was a teenager, and India isn't about to flip me out now, either. It's about being open to new experiences and letting your mind open. Some people will never be able to handle that. Whether that's something about them or something about Western culture that damaged them beyond repair, who knows.

What I do know is that meditation is still not working for me. I've tried a couple of different temples, a couple of different ashrams, that I've been finding through the hostels. They all give the same basic speech as Veddy did. Follow your breath. Suck in the air, let it out, and think about nothing but that. You'd think after months of steady trying I'd be getting further than I am.

All following my breath does is clear my mind enough to think about everything I haven't been thinking about. It's something different every time. I go back to the list I made at the center, the twelve things I regret doing most while I was on drugs. The thing is, what about the list of twelve things I DON'T regret doing despite the fact I was on drugs? Yes, it would have been even better to do them NOT on drugs. But why has no therapist ever asked for that list?

I know why: because Western therapists disapprove of spiritual pursuits. They want to heal your spirit with science. With medicine. They disapprove of drugs because, well, we're in the middle of a War on Drugs, remember? So if you take peyote or mushrooms or drop acid or even if you just dose yourself with painkillers to skew your view of the world into something less fraught with misery, well, that's frowned upon. Tsk tsk tsk. You're supposed to talk your way through it. Talk talk talk.

While I agree that I am off drugs and should never do them again, I don't agree that seeking altered states for the sake of enlightenment is bad. And I also realize that there were things I did while on drugs that I would not have had the courage or clarity to do otherwise at the time. And I do not regret those things at all. Not at all.

Maybe I'll make that list now. Here goes:

1. Kissed Daron
2. Sang my heart out
3. Overcame pain
4. Overcame fear
5. Brought ecstasy to tens of thousands of people
6. Fulfilled my professional obligations (all but one)

Why are these lists twelve, anyway? Let's start with six. Could I have done them all with no drugs and just meditation? Meditation and yoga, maybe? I think maybe I could have if I could only get this meditation thing working. It sounds like it should work. I feel like I have an inkling of it. Like I have peeked through the open door into the room, but I haven't actually set foot in the room yet. And in the room there's a chest that, once you get to the center of the room, you can open. And in the chest there's more to see. And so on. But I'm still standing just outside the door.

But at least I know the door, and the room, exist.

Ziggy's Diary: 17

New ashram. New revelation. This one uses mandalas. Having something to look at changes the experience completely for me. My mind still wanders, but it wanders more into the realm of fantasy than my earthly problems, blames, etc., and a little bit into philosophy, but only a little. And this guru told me that the wandering is part of the experience.

It's a kind of gift, he said, that each time your mind wanders you have the opportunity to return to meditation. And the more times you return to meditation the easier it will be to return again in the future. Interesting way to think about it, but even better a good way to quit beating myself up about failure.

Part of me wants to immediately apply this trick to the rest of my life. Like if only each fight with Daron were a gift from the universe to allow us to get back together, making coming together easier and easier over tim

Ziggy's Diary: 18

Last wrote a week ago. Threw book across room as I came to realize something. Painful realization: holy fuck, that's exactly what was happening with me and him. I'm so stupid. I was too impatient. Too needy. Too drug-eroded. Too destroyed in my own inner life to see that each fight with him was an opportunity to close the gap between us, not widen the breach.

We were getting closer. We WERE.

I can't even write his name today. I can't. I'm too destroyed now again, laid waste by my regrets. This is my fault. Entirely my fault. The drugs are my fault. I have to own that responsibility. Say what you want about Megaton or bad luck or whatever. I'm the one who let myself be seduced by the drugs and blinded myself to what was actually happening right in front of my face. Fuck fuck fuck.

I've been living with this regret for a week, and it's heavy. So heavy. Today was the sixth day in a row that they asked me to leave the ashram because my weeping was disturbing the others. This time they asked me not to come back. Can't see the fucking mandala through tears anyway.

I've accepted now, though, that I have to start over. I have to let go of the crap I did. I can't move forward if all I do is pine over opportunity lost.

The pining is painful. I must let go of it.

Tomorrow I'll look for another place.

Ziggy's Diary: 19

You know how I keep saying I have to let go of the fact that I'm so stupid? But here's how stupid I am. How obvious is this? There's a form of meditation that involves singing. That involves voice. In fact, there are probably many of them! Duh! And the thing is, if I stopped and asked myself before I came to India what was the one thing I thought of when I thought of meditation, what I would have answered was "Om."

Right?

Maybe it was necessary for me to try and fail at everything else first. Not fail. Not fail. LEARN. I learned a lot. I learned I don't sit still and my breath isn't compelling and having something to look at helps but my best sense is my hearing and the key that unlocks my inner self is my FUCKING VOICE DUH IT'S SO OBVIOUS NOW.

I chanted for two hours today, and I thought it was two minutes. The vastness of the universe presented itself, which made time seem small by comparison.

I'm a bit calmer now. If still a bit hung up on the fact that I could have, should have, started with this. But that's all right. If I keep it up, regrets should fall away and the wounds should heal.

I wonder how many hours of meditation it will take to heal the wound I made from hating myself for being stupid about meditation? What's the prescription?

I suppose I'll know that I've healed the wound I made from hating myself over being blind to what was happening with me toward the end of the tour when I can write his name again.

I once wrote a song that had a riff about loving him more and loving myself less. I see now that it was only my ego I needed to love less. I still needed to love my true self more. That void was what I tried to fill with drugs. Or that I wanted him to fill, but no one can ever fill that hole for you. It just becomes a wormhole that eats them alive and is still hungry for your soul.

hole/soul

heal/seal RHYME SONG IDEA?

Ziggy's Diary: 20

It's been a while since I wrote. But I wanted to make sure I wrote about this. I had a vision today. Is vision the right word? I didn't see anything. I felt it. Hallucination, then, in the tactile realm.

He was standing behind me. And I felt his hand on my shoulder. And I wept. But because we were chanting, I didn't break down and sob. I kept chanting, but tears ran down my face.

I wasn't overcome with a feeling of acceptance or any bullshit like that. I was crying because I knew all this meant was that I am so desperate that my mind hallucinates he's here when he's not.

I have to get past that, too. But I don't want to. I'd like to feel his hand on my shoulder for another few days. Wouldn't that be nice? Pretend everything's all right between us?

But it would be pretending and I know it, and so move on. Cry tears for the fool you are, as well as your knowledge that you have to leave even the most comforting hallucination behind.

Meanwhile, on the earthly plane, I got a fax through to Digger, telling him to check that the payments were being made for my mother and to see how she's doing. I tried from a different train station. Couldn't get through to Carynne, but at least I did get one to Digger.

I should tell you, Diary, that I'm living in this ashram, now. It's a nice one, with a public temple in front and a couple of small dorm buildings in back. Pretty much no one here speaks English, but then no one speaks much at all, and yet we communicate perfectly well with gestures and pantomime and facial expressions. They seem to have basically taken me in without any formal agreement or paperwork. Everyone helps cook and clean and polish the bells and sweep the courtyard and collect alms out front, me included, and everyone meditates. It's all men here, by the way. Some of them have shaved heads, but most don't. One of the other men gave me another set of baggy pants so that when I launder mine I don't have to stand there naked. Not that I think anyone here would care. The ashram down the road is some sect that doesn't believe in possessions, apparently, and that includes clothing, and so they're seen begging in the street in literally nothing. This group I'm with is a bit more modest than that.

When people try to talk to me, they never try English, so I'm learning some words. I don't even know which language it is. Hindi? They speak something called Kannada here, too. But, you know, words are basically when we make a sound, and it communicates something, or maybe it fails to. The more people understand the sound you made, the better it is for that use. The tones here are the same as in English—I can tell when someone is asking a question, when they're angry, when they're curious, when they're amused. That's the music in speaking, the music in the human voice. You can hear the song even if you can't understand the lyrics.

But I'm learning some words. Here and there. Some of the others staying here don't speak the native language either. Far as I can tell I'm the only one who speaks English and Spanish. I speak back to them in Spanish sometimes just for fun. No one's here to beat me for it.

Ziggy's Diary: 21

Haven't written in a couple of weeks. It isn't that I haven't meant to, but it's felt like what's going on in my mind is so unprocessed, it's not ready to be nailed onto paper.

But one thing happened today that I felt I needed to write down, even if I can't figure it out. Maybe writing it down will help me untangle it.

The guru here is a chubby man with salt-and-pepper hair, grown very long and unkempt as if caring for it is beneath his worry. Most of the holy men you see here are skinny as alley cats, but this one isn't, though I've never seen him eat. He smiles and joins us for meals, but I never see the food enter his mouth.

Anyway. When he sits to chant with us he sits with us, not facing us. I am under the impression that he hardly speaks to those like me. After someone has been at the temple for a year or two, then he will make an occasional comment. After ten years, perhaps an actual lesson. I have gleaned this information slowly with observation and what I can gather with the limited languages I have available.

Today, though, as we chanted, he roamed among us, and when he came to me, he put a flower behind my ear and smiled at me.

And I lost it. I burst into tears as feelings of helplessness poured out of me. Helplessness. I have no idea where that feeling came from. As I sit here writing I can try to rationalize it, but it feels like trying to explain why the bicycle wore glasses in a dream. Was it my own emotions that made me helpless, my intense but ignored need for affection and love, suddenly kindled and leaving me gasping? Or was it merely the touch of an enlightened being returning me to the state of being an infant, a creature helpless but full of needs?

Or was it something darker? Did I feel feminized in that moment? Forced into a role? Was it fear that the flower meant my victimization before a powerful figure? Or my fear that an idol had fallen?

His smile never wavered. He cupped my cheek and then moved on. I do not understand what happened.

I do feel calmer now. I feel serene. But not enlightened. These are not the questions I want to be asking.

Tomorrow after the morning chores are done, I will move on.

Ziggy's Diary: 22

I am back at the hostel that I started in when I first left Swami Veddy's ashram. The one by the train station. Been here a few days, talking to people, hanging around, waiting to figure out what my next direction to go in will be. This one gets some foreign backpackers, so I've been able to practice my Spanish, my French, and even fake my way through some Portuguese. They think I'm a native because they can't tell my fake Indian-English from real Indian-English. I give them advice about where to go in town. I tell them to go see the cave temple. I pepper them with questions about the outside world. Today I saw an English language newspaper for the first time in months. I am surprised to say it's November. Since the weather here never changes, I feel like time hasn't been passing. But it has.

Jenn must be back in the States by now. Or did she stay with the swami? I wonder. I'm not curious enough to go back there now, though. Actually, I'm not even sure I could find that ashram again. It was not well marked and was just a house on a side street.

I am glad I did not stay there. Thinking back on them now, it's clear to me that the entire group was looking for the spiritual equivalent of plastic surgery. They want to pay a bunch of money to come out beautiful. Veddy wasn't going to turn them away, but he also wasn't about to say, you dumbasses don't work anywhere near hard enough to get past your shit. It isn't the swami who changes you. Hell, even god isn't the one who changes you. You have to change yourself.

They're going to go home and brag to everyone that they went on a spiritual retreat in India, and the only real "change" they will have had is that now they feel better about themselves. Like their egos needed the polishing? Please.

Maybe if I had stuck around I would have eventually seen Veddy break them down. But I think more likely he was going to shake them down for more money. More power to you, Swami. I think you provide exactly what they want. Can't fault you for that. But I'm glad I didn't stay.

I bet Jenn is still fucking him. I don't know what to think. I see so much of my own behavior in her, but women have it different. How much is she's a sexual creature who ignores society's rules about why one should or should not have sex, and how much is that she's got an obsessive need to control anyone with power over her with sex and to bolster her self-esteem through the desire of others? It's so obvious to me now that's what I do. What I did.

I had a therapist once who tried to tell me that. He never said it in those words exactly. Part of his whole thing was trying to get you to come to the conclusions yourself because then you'd actually believe them. I tried so hard to seduce that therapist. So hard. I couldn't help myself. He tried so hard to get me to stop trying. "I can't help you if you're spending the entire session flirting with me." "Try to think a little more about yourself and less about me." Etc. But I knew I had him hooked, and at that point I wasn't going to give up. I think I was sixteen? I somehow talked him into letting me give him a blow job under his desk. After he came, before he even pulled up his pants, he wrote out a referral for me to see someone else. So then I guilt-tripped him into blowing me in return, since after all, if I wasn't going to be his client anymore, what was the point in holding back? He tried to give me some bullshit about being twice my age. I told him I'd let him off the hook if he was married, diseased, or had a religious objection to the act. He admitted he had none of the above. I had sex with him twice after that, both times at my insistence, and both times in the pillow talk afterward learned a lot more than I ever had in his office. So maybe it was worth it. Of course, maybe I would have learned something if I had been—like he said—concentrating on why I was there instead of on trying to get into his pants. But until I got into his pants I couldn't concentrate on anything else.

At the time I thought of it all as proof that I was at the top of my game, well-adjusted, and not in need of regular therapy. All therapy was going to do was tell me to conform to be happy. While that's true, I also see now what he was trying to tell me about the way I used sex. This is all so much clearer when I don't feel the need for sex. I haven't had it since I was last on US soil, right? This is by far the longest stretch I've ever gone without sex since I was fourteen. And the longest I've gone without an orgasm since I learned to masturbate.

A couple of guys came into the dormitory late tonight. They are carrying hand drums of some kind and they're dressed traditionally, though they're both obviously not from India. One of them settled in the bunk right under me, and they carried on a conversation in Spanish that I'm sure they had no idea I could understand. Sounds like they're looking for an ashram. If they go out looking tomorrow, maybe I'll go with them.

Ziggy's Diary: 23

They sing the names of god.

Gods.

All of them.

The names of the gods unlock the shuttered spiritual rooms inside us. Each one a key to a different lock. And when you sing them you invoke them inside yourself. How did I not know this before?

Shiva, Ram, Krishna, Govinda, Gopala, Radhe, there are so many. Om is like a sledgehammer beating on the door. These names are lockpicks and keys and screwdrivers for taking your soul apart. They're the vitamins of the soul, the balanced diet. How did I not know this? Or a better question: why doesn't everyone know this? Because I did know it, sort of, I just didn't have an explanation for it.

More later.

Ziggy's Diary: 24

I didn't realize how many days have passed since I last wrote. In fact, I don't know how many, but a lot. I'm at an ashram now that's maybe more of a collective than the previous ones? Because it's all full of musicians. I mean, there's a head guy, but he's not always the one who leads. Whatever. The details don't matter. It's the singing that matters.

We sing the names of the gods over and over. Sometimes with drums and flutes and musical accompaniment.

I can lose myself entirely in singing the names of the gods, as if my entire body fills with a light so bright that it is the only thing that can be seen and all else disappears. Is that why they call it enlightenment? I realize I have felt this before. Onstage. That's an odd place to forget who I am, but it's that the music itself takes on a life of its own. This time the scope is bigger though, the entire universe is the concert hall.

The trick is that, of course, singing engages my ego tremendously—but the same singing has the ability to overcome ego entirely and leave it behind. To lose one's self is so rare and precious. People are afraid of it and yet they crave it. Why else would people drink until they black out? Presented with the cliff, do they shrink from the edge because they fear falling or because they fear being unable to resist flinging themselves into the void?

I have to be careful of my talk of oblivion, I know, because that's how one lands in forced hospitalization. But you know what, Diary? Suicide isn't what I'm talking about here. It's so difficult to put into words in a way that anyone who hasn't been inside my head will understand. This is also why one doesn't get enlightened from a book or just from hearing some guru talk. Words only get you so far. To actually understand, you have to do it, you have to live it, you have to get all the parts of your mind wrapped around it, not just the wordy parts.

We're singing. We sing every day. Everyone sings. There's a leader, but we all answer in one voice. I know no one here, yet I love them all. And I feel loved. Because the love of the gods is the love that can fill the void where humans can't.

Ziggy's Diary: 25

Ecstasy is seductive. Like drugs, except without the bad side effects. It's blinding in its way, too. I've been through every kind of emotion while singing here. Sometimes the entire group will float upward in joy. Sometimes we'll mysteriously all cry. This spiritual cleansing and energizing is very seductive—of course it is. It feels good beyond all meaning of the word "good."

But as my awareness grows, and it has taken time for that awareness to develop, I realize that the white light that fills me has a shadow deep within. The scar, the blockage, the dark space into which no light seeps, is the damage I did to myself by turning my love into a weapon and his love into a bunker.

I did that. I am responsible.

Can a god absolve me of that?

Ziggy's Diary: 26

While collecting alms in the street today I overheard one tourist tell another, "Merry Christmas." At first I thought, *What an absurd idiosyncrasy for two grown men to have in their manner of addressing one another.*

Then I realized, no, wait, it must be Christmas. This doesn't seem possible, and yet it is.

I knew immediately upon realizing it that I must call my mother. I must. If I don't call her on Christmas she will assume I'm dead. That's the only possible excuse. New York is ten-and-a-half hours earlier than here. I have no idea how that half hour gets in there. It's one more thing that says that India is not on the same plane as the rest of the world. So I had to wait until evening, and then I begged to be allowed to use the ashram phone.

They're actually quite nice here, and no one cares that it is some other religion's holiday today. Can you imagine if I was away at some Jesus spiritual camp and I said I needed to use the phone to call my mother for some non-Christian religious holiday? I'd probably be beaten with sticks or something. Or made to beat myself mea culpa style. Here, they think it's quaint.

Anyway, I eventually got through to a carrier that would let me charge the call to the credit card number I have memorized, and I eventually got through to the home, but they told me she was sleeping. I made the poor person who answered the phone promise me under pain of violence that when she woke up he would deliver the message personally that I had called. Some enlightened avatar of peace, love, and understanding I am, eh?

Okay, I did not actually make threats. But I was very vehement.

After all the peace, love, and understanding, vehemence feels like violence.

Ziggy's Diary: 27

The Christmas spirit caught up with a couple more of the musicians from Western countries today. So I guess yesterday was Christmas Eve. The result was... a bunch of us had a party? Is that what I should call it? We went out, anyway, and had food and rotgut alcohol at a place I hesitate to call a restaurant—more like an alley that had been commandeered to serve food in. But we drank and sang Christmas carols until they literally threw us out. I drank only a tiny bit—it was terrible—but after nothing for so many months it went straight to my head.

Christmas carols are a kind of *kirtan*, you know. Songs about baby Jesus. I've had this revelation (no pun intended) before, that singing hymns can bring you closer to God. The only times I can really say I believed were times like that.

I know how it's supposed to work. Those good feelings, we're supposed to say they came from God, and the evil feelings that make grown men who have taken chastity vows make passes at teenage boys, we're supposed to say they came from the devil.

I reject that idea. Because if that is true, then I am a devil, and I should end myself. No true good can ever come of that worldview. Only temporary reprieves that drive people to desperate measures. The ability to experience sensual pleasure has to be a gift from God. It has to be. It is the only pleasure we experience, aside from eating, that makes us feel whole. It is not like the high of drugs or the oblivion of alcohol. It is something we're born with.

Turning that gift into something ugly, that is my definition of sin. Of evil. Which means the church is evil.

Not that I can ever have that conversation with my mother. But that's not what I'm calling to tell her. I'm calling to tell her I'm alive, that I haven't forgotten her, and to hear that she's alive, and hasn't forgotten me.

Of course she hasn't forgotten me. She wouldn't be in such good care without me.

I tried to call again a little while ago and got a busy

signal. My guess is that so many people are trying to make their Christmas calls that the lines are overwhelmed. That guy yesterday had better have given her my message.

I tried to meditate after the call did not go through. I sat still and quiet. I followed my breath. My heart slowed.

It slowed so much I nearly passed out.

Ziggy's Diary: 28

And today I have a hangover. Headache. I feel awful. From two ounces of alcohol. Well, I'm no longer used to it. I suppose I was asking for it.

Maybe it was trying to make that Christmas phone call that brought me to my latest realization. I chant and my mind opens and I see the universe and I feel the ecstatic joy that is to be alive. But then I realize that to remain in that state of grace I have to leave behind all that I know. All that I am. Not merely ego, not merely sin. All. ALL.

But didn't I come here to purge myself of the urge to self-annihilate? How is being swallowed whole by the entire universe different from death? How is it different from leaving those in my life bereft of me?

It isn't different. And I suddenly remember that I came here to supposedly heal myself SO I CAN become a functioning member of society again. Right? How is singing the name of god being functional? How long have I been here, anyway—six months? Does everyone think I'm dead?

I've been chipping away at that block of darkness, that scar, that damage I did to myself by being untrue about love. But I have come to think that even the unconditional love of god is not enough to heal that wound. There are only two choices.

I can forsake my entire past life, cut the memory of him out like a cancer, and move forward spiritually free into utter ego-less abandon. Or I can go back and try to heal the wound, return to my former self for the sake of doing so. The dilemma is the same as before, in a way. Oblivion beckons on one side, the love of others on the other. My mother, too. Can I leave her so easily? No. I really can't.

The weight of it all feels crushing as I allow myself to remember what awaits me on the North American continent. The movie release. Has it happened yet? Are they searching for me? And what about Moondog Three? Am I ready to face Daron yet?

Daron. There. I wrote it. I found my mind chanting his name, spelling it out and making silly songs for call and response, even while the afternoon *kirtan* was going on. I thought of things like this:

Does
Anyone
Remember
Old
News?

Doubts
About
Romance
Orbit
Nightly

Don't
Ask
Right
Or
Not

I need to go home.

Ziggy's Diary: 29

Tried to call my mother again today. Different time of day, different person, same answer: she's asleep. I tried to impress upon them that I'm calling from very far away. They tried to impress upon me that she's very hard to wake.

I worry. This worries me. Is she asleep or unconscious?

Ziggy's Diary: 30

It's no good. I can't meditate, can't sing, can't even sit still. I've tried to call twice more. Two more times, "She's asleep."

They're not even very good liars. If they were, they'd vary the story. I fear the worst and I can do nothing but obsess over it. This is the worst possible thing for all the learning I've done. But this is my mother we're talking about. This isn't about learning to let go of suffering. My own suffering is one thing. The fact that my mother may be in a diabetic coma or something is different.

I called Carynne and got her answering service and was told she's out of the country. Out of the country! What! Outrageous. Yes, I know. I'm the one who started that trend. I am not allowed to complain about it. I didn't leave a message.

I tried to call Digger and was told he's in the hospital. What the fuck is going on over there in the United States? Did I leave and everything immediately fell apart? Or did it take a few months?

Ziggy's Diary: 31

A month since I last wrote. A month.

I can explain. The problem with lies is that they can become the truth. This happens to me often, and always has. I would lie to stay out of school, for example, tricking my mother into thinking I had a fever by sipping her coffee when she wasn't looking and then putting a thermometer into my mouth. At least once, the next morning, I woke up with a real fever and then was out for a week with the flu. Did I bring it on myself? Or had I somehow known I was getting sick and that was why I wanted to stay home in the first place?

I'm writing this from the hospital. I still don't know if I wished myself here, or if this is all part of me wishing myself home. Or maybe some other twisted way in which my inner self is still, restlessly, trying to end itself, like a cat in a cage that throws itself against the bars until it tires, but only ceases temporarily.

Or maybe Kali's Revenge finally got me.

I had decided I needed to leave. I don't really want to face any of the things that await me, but being chickenshit is NOT enlightenment. But getting home from here is a little more complicated than just hopping on a train. If Carynne or Digger had been available, I would have tried to have them arrange it all. As it was, I had to ask around quite a bit at the hostels to try to find a travel agent.

The first one I went to literally chased me out the door, screaming in Kannada that beggars were not welcome.

Okay, yes, the only clothes I've got I've been wearing for months, my hair's a mess, and I'm as brown as a mahogany chest. I look the part. And I had been feeling awful. The headache that came after that Christmas "party" had never really gone away, and I had started to wonder if I ate something bad, as well. So I probably looked even worse than I thought.

At the second one, I went in brandishing my American passport and speaking American English. The guy at least listened to me, though he kept looking at me like I was getting mud on the chair I was sitting in. There's a caste system here, I know, is that what's going on? Anyway. He was able to look up flights and information and give me prices. But he wouldn't just take my word for it that I have a credit card number memorized. I know, that's fraud if it's not my card. I got a little testy with him and then I ended up disengaging and leaving without further argument because I got a feeling he was going to call the police next.

Which set me to thinking whether there was some other way I could get home. And I thought, what if I got really sick? You read news stories about Americans who get airlifted back to the States to take care of grave injuries, right? What if I caught cholera or one of the things they suggested we get vaccinated for but which we didn't because of the secretive way we arrived? I wondered if taking a dip in the river would work.

I didn't actually take a dip in the river, though. I eventually went to the hostel and asked the clerk who was kind of my friend there what people did if they lost their credit cards. He said there's a number on the back of the card that you can call, collect from outside the US, to the card company to report that it was lost, and they would send you another one. Brilliant. But the problem was that since I didn't have the card, I couldn't call the number, since I didn't know what it was.

I left the ashram at that point and moved back into the hostel. But there were no Americans there with American credit cards.

Two days later an American came in and I asked him if he had VISA or Master Card and what flavor he had. He was quite skeptical at first but I assured him that I didn't want to see his account number, just the customer service phone number on the back because I had lost my card and actually I was kind of stuck in India until I could replace it. He gave me the number. It wasn't the same card company as mine, but I called it, collect, and managed to wrangle the actual phone number of the correct company! Amazing what the helpfulness and kindness of random strangers can do. Some nut calls you from India with a weird request. Then again, if you work in a call center, maybe my call would have been the highlight of the day.

Anyway. I got the correct number. I called it. They grilled me about who I was. My social security number. My mother's maiden name. City I was born. Et cetera. I didn't blame them. I mean, what's to stop some random con man calling them up and getting new credit cards mailed to a sketchy hostel in Bangalore? Eventually they decided I had to be real, and at first they told me they would mail a new card to my billing address in Boston, which I said was okay, but my manager wasn't there to get the card, see? I was really trying to get myself out of India and didn't want to wait for her to get home and then FedEx the card to me, did I? They eventually got it and said a new card would be sent directly to the hostel, but it was going to take four days to get there. Okay, four days.

That night I began to have cramps. My stomach was in intense pain. And my fever must have spiked so high that I passed out.

I'm lucky that instead of just stealing my passport and leaving me to die in a ditch, the hostel clerk had me hospitalized.

I remember nothing of the next two weeks, my fever was so high. Nothing. I can remember details from a week when my brain was obliterated by painkillers better than I can remember the previous fourteen days. Well, okay, I remember a lot of pain. That's not a memory so much as a sense. Like remembering that you had a dream but not the details.

I know it's fourteen days because I just read the notes on the clipboard attached to my bed. Some of them are in a language I don't know, some are in English, but the chart of dates and vital signs is easy enough to interpret.

My fever was 40 degrees C. I think that's quite high. When we were in Toronto I remember the poem they taught us to figure out Celsius:

Thirty is hot,
twenty is nice,
ten put a coat on,
zero is ice.

If thirty is hot, say eighty-five? Forty would have to be what? A hundred? 105? Probably 105 if I was delirious?

Was it cholera after all?

Ziggy's Diary: 32

Not cholera. Typhoid. I'm here for another two weeks, they say. The fever is down, but there are various reasons why they have to keep me here. I have only grasped the bare minimum. They don't talk to me much. Maybe I'm contagious, still?

The clerk brought the credit card to the hospital while I was unconscious. So I have that now. As soon as I am stable enough to walk I will try that travel agent again. As soon as I am cleared to return. I feared this might be something they won't let me into the country with, but as far as I have been able to determine from peppering the staff with questions, I'm not the first American tourist to come down with it and the others were allowed to go home.

There's no phone here that they will let me use. But I would not call and worry people now. The last thing they all need to do is freak out that I'm stuck in an Indian hospital for two more weeks.

No, I'll fly home, get my game face on, and meet everyone on my own terms.

Part Twelve

January 1990

Spanish Fly

I didn't go to Spain looking for love. I didn't go there looking for fame, either. I'd spent the better part of the previous three years of my life chasing after both of those things, with mixed results. Maybe it was time to look for something else.

So here's what happened with me, and Orlando, and flamenco, and my quest for something I can't really put into words... but I'm not going to let that stop me from telling this story.

When I decided to go to Spain, I'd just been on tour in Japan and Australia, with all the highs and lows that come with playing rock and roll in front of thousands of people. I'd dropped acid for the first time in Australia, on New Year's Eve, and it Roto-Rootered my 22-year-old brain. During the trip I decided that the vibrating string was the central principle of the universe. After the trip I decided I still agreed with that thought. Another thing to consider: at that point, my guitar had taken me to three separate continents in very short order. A fourth seemed almost logical. Or at least not that far to go. Maybe when you're an internationally traveling musician the whole world seems smaller than it really is. Or maybe it really is that small.

Final important note about my state of mind: I confess, I didn't want to go back home because of my broken heart. Plain and simple. It hurt more there. I don't know why, it just did.

So all that is why it made *perfect sense* for me to go to Spain.

Okay. I can tell by the look you're giving me that I still haven't explained why. So let's back up a little. When I left Australia, a lot of things in my career were up in the air, and through various connections I had managed to get a slot in a Guitar Craft seminar with Robert Fripp. Fripp taught these six-day courses every so often at a sort of run-down mansion in Virginia, and I was keen to try it.

Guitar Craft is hard to explain. It's kind of like yoga with guitar. It's an art form unto itself, but if you're a dancer—say—you don't go on the stage and perform Downward-Facing Dog. You practice yoga so that whatever your own art form is, you can perform better. The way yoga changes and improves how some people relate to their bodies, Guitar Craft changes how you relate to your guitar.

The first night, I arrived at the mansion completely jet lagged from having just flown most of the way around the world. This was a few days after the acid trip, and I think I was still sort of susceptible to falling into a hallucinatory state. Or maybe it was lack of sleep. I was shown to a room where I put down my guitar and my bag, but I was apparently the last one to arrive so I was ushered directly from there to the main room, where the introductory session was to be.

Many of the others had been there all afternoon and had already been talking to each other. I was the only one who took a seat in that circle of chairs who hadn't yet met anyone but the guy who had picked me up at the train station and shown me to my room.

An interesting moment occurred when Robert Fripp walked into the room for the first time. Everyone's heads turned like a follow spot had come on the second he appeared in the doorway. And everyone's eyes stayed fixed on him as he crossed the room and took a seat and began talking without fanfare.

He reminded us that we were to keep our hands off our guitars until tomorrow's first session. He probably said a few things about philosophy. I'm not really sure. I was either too zoned out to absorb what he was saying, or else it was absorbing directly into my bloodstream before I could process it.

Then began a round of introductions where we went around and told our names, which I floated through. In other words, I didn't absorb anyone's name, and when it was my turn all I said was, "My name's Daron. I'm from Boston. I've been playing guitar professionally since I was a teenager."

One of the other guys was clearly confused that I didn't sound the way he expected. "Wait. Aren't you the one who came from Australia, though?"

"Had a gig." I shrugged, and the next guy introduced himself.

I'm sure Orlando introduced himself. He must have. Everyone did. But I don't remember it.

What I do remember is that night, after I finally went to the room I had been assigned and collapsed on the bed, I was so overtired I couldn't sleep, and I lay there thinking about what I had said. My introduction wasn't calculated, but I realized it might have been the first time I introduced myself as from Boston instead of New Jersey, and it might have been the first time I thought of being a teenager as long enough in the past to be notable.

There's nothing I can really tell you about the actual sessions without it being about as boring as describing a yoga class. We had re-tuned all our guitars to even fifths... if you don't know what that means, don't worry about it. Blah blah music theory blah blah.

Most of the sessions involved us sitting in a circle with our guitars, but on the first full day we did something I didn't expect. They had us work with a movement coach, who analyzed our postures and tried to correct them. I was a bit surprised to find my posture was generally considered good. For one thing, I didn't slouch. "I'm too short to slouch," I joked, but it was true. For another, all that classical guitar practice in my formative years had properly trained me for the right ergonomics when it came to playing while sitting down. The guys who had only played rock and roll or who were self-taught all had problems with their posture: bent wrists, bowed heads, pigeon toes, you name it. The idea was that if we were positioned properly, then music, energy, creativity, et cetera would flow better. Kinda hard to argue with.

I'd fallen into practicing classical style a few months before, working on getting those chops back even though at the time I didn't have a reason to. Now I had a reason. Funny how things work out.

I sleepwalked through the first three or four days. I didn't think jet lag or acid flashbacks could be the only reason for it. I think I kind of hypnotized myself into a state where I was just a sponge, soaking it all in, but in a really passive way. Then I started to wake up a little, as facility with the tuning began to sink in and as ideas for ways to use Guitar Craft in songs or performances started to pop up in my head. I resisted writing anything down. I tried to hold myself in that space of creativity where all possibilities are equally open.

Basically, I went. I did the practice. I had my understanding expanded of what one could do with a vibrating string.

Or did I? I had arrived there pretty much convinced that the vibrating string was the binding principle of the universe, remember. At the seminar, I was caught in a bubble with two dozen other people who happened to believe it, too. Good.

The result was that six days later I was back in the real world, my posture refined, my fingers lithe, my ears open... and the real world was still the real world, and full of aggravations like, well, the usual bullshit at airports when flights are delayed. My roommate, my best friend, my sometime lover, my sister, and my manager were all waiting for me in Boston. (That's five different people, by the way—don't want you getting the wrong idea.) It was January. There was snow. There was no telling when, or if, my flight would take off.

When was the last time I was home, anyway? I wondered. I mean, for more than a week? Between the warm-up tour in the spring and the US tour in the summer, that was when. Then had come the tour, and then the trip to Mexico, and then the side track to living in Los Angeles, and then the tour of Japan and Australia, and then six days in Virginia.

I was sitting in a coffee shop in the airport with my guitar against the wall thinking this over when another guy carrying a guitar case came in. I recognized him from Guitar Craft but couldn't remember his name. He was a little taller than I was, with straight black hair chopped off right at his shoulders and a hint of a black goatee and mustache.

I saw him scanning the seats, no doubt trying to figure out where he could sit where his guitar would be safe. I waved him over. There was room for another guitar on top of mine where I had wedged it between my seat and the wall.

He leaned on the back of the chair opposite me with both hands and gave me a very intense look.

"Put it here," I said, gesturing to the guitar. "It'll be safe. It's fine."

He nodded, handed me the case, and I settled it atop mine in a kind of nose-to-tail arrangement. Mine was a road-worthy clamshell that could survive a nuclear attack. His was a more modest fake-alligator-pattern case that was probably mostly cardboard and probably had fake fur inside, if it was anything like the one I used to have for my old Yamaha classical guitar, my "school" guitar.

"Orlando," he said, and held out his hand to shake mine.

I figured he didn't mean the city in Florida. "Daron," I said.

He made an attempt at saying my name, and it came out sort of like "Deern?" I didn't try correcting him. At the time it didn't occur to me that I'd be spending more than an hour at most in his company.

Then he said, "You, here?"

"I'll watch the guitars if you want to get some coffee," I said.

"Café, sí," he said.

That was my first tipoff he was Spanish. He took his leather jacket off and slid it over the back of the chair. Underneath he was skinnier than I was, rangy and whipcord. Not that I was a hunk of beefcake myself, you understand. I was still never going to be taller than five-foot-four, but I'd put on some weight while I'd been living in LA with a boyfriend (now ex-) who liked food better than sex. Some of what I'd put on was muscle.

I pretended to read the newspaper while Orlando got a coffee and two muffins. He sat down with them, and we made eye contact and kind of stared at each other across the table while he picked one of the muffins apart with his fingers, eating it piece by piece. He didn't look away, so neither did I.

He pushed the other muffin toward me and I clued in that it was for me. So that was the first time Orlando fed me.

While I ate it—in the same manner as him, pulling it apart and eating the pieces—he watched me with an interest I would have said was sexual only because what else could it be? When else does someone stare at you like that? But as we made a few halting attempts at conversation, halted entirely by the lack of words we had in common, I decided it wasn't sexual at all. It was that I was the closest thing to a person he could talk to there.

We did have some basic words. "Where?" he asked me.

I pointed ahead of me, "Boston."

"Ah, Boston. The Cars."

"Yes, that's right, The Cars are from there."

"Eliot Easton."

"Yes!" I smiled. Only a total guitar geek would name Eliot Easton as the first member of The Cars they thought of. "How about you? Where are you headed?"

He gave me a blank look.

"Where?" I asked then, the way he had done.

That time it sank in. He pointed like he was lobbing something over the table. "Sevilla."

Something clicked at that moment. Something that had been trying to gel in my head for months—maybe years?—about the guitar, and the weird hybrid instrument it has become, with the classical tradition on one side (especially the Spanish tradition) and the folk/rock tradition on the other.

One of the things that was driven home during my acid trip epiphany was that every culture has music, and every culture has rhythm and melody. We're born sensing the inherent difference between higher frequencies and lower frequencies. We call those "notes" in music, but ultimately it's a physical property of reality that we sense. It's physics. And rhythm? Every human has a sense of time moving forward. Cultures cut that time up different ways, but it's the same principle. Just like different cultures cut the frequencies up in different places, so they have different notes, different scales. It's still music.

Having grasped this basic tenet of human existence, I wanted to explore that territory immediately. It's hard to describe what I mean by that, but I didn't mean sit alone in a studio recording things for myself. I wanted to throw myself into a situation where I could play within a structure but improvise at the same time. Like the blues, yeah, but because I'd just spent six days at a Guitar Craft seminar, it had kind of reset all my expectations and made me feel like I didn't want to settle right back into an old rut. I'd blown my mind on Indian classical music and Hare Krishna chanting and Sufi Qawwali singing, too. I'd been doing all this thinking about Indian music, about how their "classical" tradition still had a deeply ingrained improvisational aspect, how there was a way in which it was a highly different artistry from the rigid,

rigid, rigid world of Western classical music, and yet no less rigorous or demanding.

And I was wrapped up in this wish that I could do something like that… but with the guitar, which is my instrument.

When Orlando said "Sevilla," though—which is Spanish for Seville, as in *The Barber of*—everything coalesced. "Flamenco," I said. I felt like my head was on fire, but in a good way.

"Sí, sí, flamenco," he said and snapped his fingers. That was pretty much the limit of that whole conversation. His eyes were bright and he had a little smile in the corner of his mouth.

Here's the thing. I didn't really know much about flamenco at all. Or Seville. In fact, most of what I knew about Seville I had learned from the Spanish language textbook we used in ninth grade. There was a whole section on the "Tunas," which were described as roving bands of college students who would play guitar for tips and food in Seville, a tradition that started in medieval times. On the page there was a line drawing of a guy who looked kind of like me playing a guitar in a short cape and floppy hat. In my wildest fantasies of that era—that is, the ones that didn't involve being jerked off in the gym shower by someone whose face I couldn't see—I imagined I could run off to Sevilla at any time.

Anyway. What I knew about flamenco was only enough to realize, in that moment when it all seemed to come together, that flamenco is the place where the guitar takes on the role of the melodic instrument in Indian classical music, improvising while at the same time being forced into a rigorous structure.

"Flamenco," I said again, like I was taking a taste of the word in my mouth, rolling it around like a fine wine.

Orlando's smile widened.

Now do you see why it made perfect sense for me to go to Spain?

Pump Up the Jam

Two more relevant things happened before we left. Maybe they're one thing, actually, though they happened a few hours apart.

The first is that, to kill time while we were waiting around, we went to a gate that wasn't in use and we played together. My flight to Boston was still showing "delayed" by several hours, so we had nothing better to do. A little while later, my flight was cancelled entirely. I'll spare you the gory details, but add this up: massive blizzard in Boston plus a zillion frequent flyer miles plus Carynne being a kickass manager and making some phone calls equals a transatlantic coach ticket and a hotel voucher.

When I tried to explain to Carynne over the pay phone that I needed to take a detour to try my hand at flamenco, she didn't try to talk me out of it. All she did was make me promise to find out the phone number at whatever hostel I ended up in so that if there were any emergencies she could call me.

Anyway, Orlando and I clicked right away when we started to play together. No audience, no goal, just jamming and playing around and teaching each other things with notes and licks. I forgot we couldn't actually talk to each other for a while there.

The other thing that happened, though. The other thing. Turns out Orlando was booked on the same flight to Seville that I would take if they could get me on. It also turned out that his plan had been to squat in the airport overnight. I took him with me to the hotel the airline had provided instead. There was a bed for each of us. We played again for a while when we got to the room… I wish I'd had a tape recorder, because playing it for you would beat describing it.

He was good. And he was used to improvising. He was as fearless as I was when it came to trying stuff out musically. Maybe Guitar Craft had helped that, but I think that's just how he was. He was a lot more versed in flamenco than I was, but that only meant he could show me a lot, which gave me a lot to mess around with.

At one point we had put down our guitars to get some sleep. The wake-up call was coming at 4 AM. We still couldn't really talk to each other. But he took my hand to look at my nails. He held up his own hand, comparing them. All the way back in LA, I had started growing the nails on my right hand so that I could play without finger picks. I had a bottle of clear nail polish in my guitar case and had been putting on a coat every few days.

Next thing I knew, Orlando was rubbing my hand up and down the stiffie in his jeans.

"Are you gay?" I asked.

"No," he said, which left me wondering if he had understood the question. He unzipped.

I was perfectly willing to stroke him. I unzipped, too, and he seemed perfectly willing to reciprocate. Getting off with a stranger was an unexpected but not unwelcome end to a very odd day.

It didn't take long to both get off. We're both good with our hands.

Money's Too Tight to Mention

So I ended up spending the entire next day in the airport because I didn't make that standby flight after all. They did book me on another flight late that night, though, for certain. I didn't complain. Orlando flew ahead and said he'd meet me on the other side. At least I hoped that was what he had said.

Orlando and his girlfriend Carmina were there to meet me at the airport. She was Italian, supposedly, so she spoke about the same amount of English as Orlando did—i.e., almost none—and from what I could tell her Spanish was a little questionable, too. From Orlando's perspective, I think, she could have been speaking Martian and it wouldn't matter so long as she had that long dark hair, glowing with auburn highlights, and those long, long legs that made every dress she wore look too short. Maybe he *had* understood me when I'd asked if he was gay and he said no.

They brought me to the apartment they were sharing with a guy and another couple and ceremoniously showed me the couch, which had visibly been cleared of clutter to make room for me, given how the rest of the place looked. Understand, the place wasn't dirty, but it was a jumble of books and cassette tapes and half-burned candles and you name it.

My arrival was apparently a good excuse to open a bottle of red wine, and the other woman, whose name was Gabriela, washed out a glass for me. Her boyfriend's name was Rafi, which I think was short for Raphael, and the other guy was Vicente. They mostly drank out of mismatched coffee mugs, some of which were missing their handles, and their voices grew faster and more raucous as we drank, meaning I went from catching every fifth or sixth word to catching none. That was all right. I can't explain why, but I felt at home, even though Orlando had introduced me as "Dión." He simply couldn't say "Daron," not the way I say it anyway, with my "r" crushed up against the "n" as if the "o" had jumped out of the way of an oncoming Camaro on the New Jersey Turnpike.

When the wine was done, Vicente went back to studying, and the two couples took me out to eat. The apartment was on the second and third floors of the building, while the entry door was at street level. The street was narrow, only fit for smaller vehicles. The building itself was three stories, stucco on the outside with bright yellow plaster molding around the windows and shiny black wrought iron bars across them. It was one of the lower buildings in the area. The small street we were on ran to a larger street where the buildings were eight and ten stories high, and that one ran to a main drag that had apartment complexes that were twenty or thirty floors. We walked along that main street to a wide bridge over a small river. Off to the left there was what looked like one fat turret of a castle standing by itself.

"Is that a castle?" I asked.

Orlando said something, then Carmina said something, and I put two and two together to make out something that sounded partway familiar. "Oro! That's gold, right? Tower of Gold?" They were enthusiastically supportive of my interpretation of what they said. I never did find out why it was called the Tower of Gold, though.

They led me into the old part of the city. When I say old, I mean some of the buildings were actually medieval. And yet still had taverns and restaurants in them, and I don't mean in some cheesy historical recreation way. They took me to a tapas bar and introduced me to a bartender. I tried to tell the bartender my name was "Daron" and he said "Dión," too.

Food and wine flowed freely. Orlando and the rest must have been regulars at this place because many people dropped by the table to say hello. I was introduced as "an American" to some of them and as a guitar player to others. Those two words I heard over and over, *Americano, guitarra.*

One older woman, her face set with heavy jowls, her hair dyed black and pulled straight back, spoke at some length to Orlando after cursorily meeting me. The woman glanced at me a few times, but I couldn't tell if this was because Orlando was saying something about me or because she really wasn't listening to what he was blathering on about and was more interested in looking at the new guy.

That night I think we ate everything. Tapas can be sort of endless. The servings are small, and there are so many things you can have. Imagine a restaurant with an appetizer menu a hundred items long. It's about like that. I would end up eating a lot of meals in that place and in other tapas bars, and I swear every dish I later tried we had that night. It was an epic night. I lost count of the number of bottles of rioja we drank.

The bartender didn't, though. He said something to Orlando when we were stumbling out. I found out what in the morning. At the time I was more concerned with getting home and taking care of my last order of business for the night: figuring out the phone number of the apartment. Gabriela wrote it down for me, and I called Carynne and left it on her machine and then curled up on my couch. Even the sound of Orlando and Carmina fucking enthusiastically wasn't enough to keep me from conking out. I slept quite contentedly until morning.

Okay, by morning I mean the early afternoon, when we actually woke up. The couch was pretty comfortable, as they had given me a pillow and a blanket and I'm not a tall person to begin with.

Anyway, Orlando explained, as he washed his face in the kitchen sink a few yards from where I was struggling to sit up, that it would be a good idea today for him and me to go out and make enough to pay back what we'd eaten. I think he said something like this—"Good food, sí? We need it. Pay."—followed by him miming playing a guitar. This was the point when I realized they really, really had no idea who I was. They also didn't know that tucked away in my guitar case was a credit card with a twenty grand limit. For emergencies.

This didn't sound like an emergency. This sounded rather like business as usual. I got myself up. They had running water. I had my own towel in my bag because I hadn't been sure what there would be in Virginia. The place wasn't in any worse shape than the places Roger and I had lived as students.

We got our guitars, tuned in the living room before we left, and hit the streets. We got strong coffee from a place that served right onto the street out of a window. It would have burned a hole through my stomach, but there was a kind of roll that went with it, like a sandwich roll, only softer, sweeter... and no sandwich inside. It was good.

We went back into the old section of the city and scoped out the areas around the cathedral, where there were a lot of tourists. Orlando hurried me out of one courtyard and into an alley though, and I assumed he had seen a policeman.

"Is busking legal here?" I asked. I mimed playing. "It's okay?"

"It's okay," he assured me. Then he jerked his head back in the direction we had come. "Gypsies."

"Wait, what?"

He waved his hand in a gesture I was starting to realize meant "I can't explain."

We skirted around an old wall and then around another building that must have been as old as the cathedral. A young woman was walking there with a small bouquet of flowers in her hands, as if she had just picked the flowers herself. When she saw Orlando she frowned suddenly and barked something at him.

We hurried along again then, but a man came out of a side alley and blocked our path. I immediately looked behind us. No one was there. Okay, good, if we had to run for it, we could, I thought.

We didn't have to run. Orlando and the guy, who didn't look much older than we were, exchanged angry words, complete with some dramatic hand gestures, ending with Orlando muttering a few sullen things and then pressing past the guy. I followed, trying to mind my own business, though I was trying to guess what that could have been about. Was the woman we saw Orlando's ex-girlfriend and the guy her protective brother? Did he owe them money? I could only guess.

I followed him through enough winding narrow streets that I would have had trouble backtracking alone. We ended up in a fairly large park, and he set me up in a spot by a fountain, with the clamshell case of the Ovation open to catch money.

He threw a couple of coins into the empty case. You have to do that when you busk, you know. It's called "salting the basket." If you don't put some money in to start with, you won't get more. I don't even know who taught me that. Remo, probably. Except I never played on the street with him.

Orlando went to find a different spot.

I was hungover, jet lagged, and had no idea where I was, but that really didn't matter. This I understood. This I could do. Busking was something that came pretty much second nature, and two hours went by before I knew it.

Orlando dragged himself back to me at that point, looking somewhat dejected. He brightened when he saw what I had in the case, though.

"How much did you make?" I asked, racking my brain for the textbook-Spanish question words. Who, what, where, why... "*Cuántos*?"

He showed me his meager take and then tossed it in with mine.

"Really, that's all? Orlando, that's pathetic."

He shrugged.

"Look, go get a bottle of water. *Agua.* Get agua, then come back and I'll show you how to do it."

He understood the agua part anyway, and took some of the money and went to the snack stand that I could see not too far away. While he was doing that, I picked up everything and moved us closer to the snack stand.

He looked at me, puzzled.

"It's a much better spot over here. Look. People will sit and listen to the music while they eat their ice cream, and here they have to get out their money anyway, so more change will fall to us. Also, you can hear the guitar better without the fountain right there."

"Better here?" he asked.

"Yes. Better here." If he hadn't understood what I said, he'd see for himself soon enough. I wondered how these things weren't obvious to him. "Plus, with both of us together we'll attract more of a crowd. Louder." He was giving me a blank look. I tried fewer words: "Louder is better."

"Aha."

Of course there was the problem that we didn't know that many things in common. From the bit we'd played in the airport and in the hotel, I knew we only had a little overlap. But that was all right. This is how you learn new things.

We did a lot better in that spot. I was kind of surprised there wasn't someone there already, but I would later learn that there were so many places to play in this city that they weren't all full all the time. Also, the weather was in the mid-sixties, which some Sevillanos would consider too cold, so we were among the few out that day.

Another factor was that a lot of them had gigs at night and didn't come out until sunset at the earliest. But I didn't know any of that yet.

And we played so freely with each other. We passed things back and forth. It was the opposite of the way Remo and I played with each other. Remo and I knew each other well. Orlando and I didn't know each other at all, and everything was new and different, and yet it wasn't because it was still the guitar. More stuff I can't put into words. Me, Orlando, guitars, music. Sound, music.

We played until it started to get dark, when the park emptied out and the snack stand closed. We had a much more respectable take by that point, and we sat and counted it on one of the stone benches.

"Is it enough?"

"Is enough," he said, folding the bills and putting them the interior pocket of his jacket and sweeping the coins into a bandana.

He handed me the bandana and I tucked it into a pocket inside my guitar case.

"You good," he said then.

I looked up from the case, and he was giving me that open stare again, like he had when we'd first met in the coffee shop.

"Orlando," I said. "Are you gay?"

"No," he answered again, but gestured to me to follow him around the back of the snack stand. I carried both guitars.

Against the concrete wall in the dark he reached into my jeans and I wondered if maybe he had a sort of fetish for hand jobs or what. The air was getting chilly, but I didn't much care about that. What I did care about was getting deported or thrown in jail if the police here didn't like gays, but when Orlando used his mouth, did I stop him? Hell no.

So it was that I had a streak of his come dried on my boot when we walked into the restaurant where we had been the night before. Orlando undertook some kind of a negotiation with the guy tending bar, who I was beginning to gather was more of a manager or an owner than merely a bartender. That's how we ended up having a somewhat more modest supper there, with a lot less wine than the night before, and then I played a gig by myself in the courtyard in the back of the place. Which was really amusing, because although I played a tiny bit of Spanish-style stuff, it was only a tiny bit, and the rest of the time I went through my usual repertoire of pop and rock. An American couple sat near me and complained to one another, assuming that I couldn't understand them, that they didn't come all the way to Spain to hear Van Halen. Of course, they weren't clueful enough to realize that "Spanish Fly" was also Van Halen, but whatever. No skin off my nose.

Anyway, that's how I ended up playing two gigs in one day and got my dick sucked on my first full day in Spain.

No Myth

A week went by where Orlando and I got up around noon pretty much every day, fortified ourselves with bread and coffee, and then busked until sundown. The others were in and out for classes and their various jobs.

Everyone gave their rent money to Vicente. I was unclear on whether this was because Vicente was the one whose name was on the lease or if he was actually connected to the landlord somehow. He had a little chalkboard on the wall by the refrigerator where he would mark what people had given him that month. That made perfect sense, given that everyone was working cash gigs that paid unevenly. In that way, busking was a lot like waiting tables, which Carmina did a few nights a week.

Every other day or so I would ask Orlando, "Flamenco?" Sometimes when I'd ask, I'd be pointing to what looked like the ad for a flamenco concert or show in the newspaper or posted on a wall. "Orlando, flamenco?"

And he would say something like "soon" or "later" or "not tonight." He was teaching me things bit by bit, riff by riff, while we stood playing for hours in the park, but he hadn't taken me to see any flamenco or to meet any other musicians. Yet.

The other thing that happened about every other day was at sundown we'd go back to the apartment before going out that night and have some kind of sex, usually oral. Orlando always initiated it, and I always asked him "are you gay?" and every time he said "no" before proceeding to peel my jeans off. He seemed unconcerned about the fact that we were in the middle of the living room every time. I never tried to take it into the bedroom he shared with Carmina. I assumed that would be crossing a line... and that was assuming we weren't already crossing a line. I figured he would have been more secretive if he didn't want her to know.

Orlando, flamenco? Not tonight. Orlando, are you gay? No. So it went.

He finally brought me to a flamenco show after I'd been there almost two weeks. Some acquaintances of his were musicians in the show, and apparently it was an off night. That meant we could get in for free since there were empty seats. It was a dinner show, but we were seated at the table farthest from the stage and given only the baskets of bread and a pitcher of water. Which was fine with us. I could not have cared less about the food. I was there for the music.

Orlando kept trying to tell me something. As usual, this was like a game of two-way charades where we each latched on to what words of each other's we knew, even though that sometimes sent us barking up the wrong tree. I eventually gathered that he was warning me this was sort of a "tourist trap" show, i.e., not the "real" thing. I wanted to ask how it could get any more real than being performed in Seville by actual Sevillanos, and that raises the whole question of a "performance" not being a "real" thing no matter what, right?

My mind hung those thoughts out to dry while we sat there, and I watched the ideas twist around from all angles, unsure how I felt about any claims to real/not real in regards to music. It's kind of a dangerous concept, isn't it? There were those who said John Lee Hooker didn't play "real" blues because he played the electric guitar instead of the acoustic guitar. Nowadays that sounds ridiculous, but at the time I guess the change felt so drastic it was enough to spur claims of inauthenticity. Makes you think, if no change is ever allowed then the only "authentic" music has to be, what, people banging rocks together?

Real or not, that show included several numbers of flashy group choreography, kind of like the Rockettes—with matching dresses and frills—but showing a lot less leg. One had about a dozen dancers, all women, moving together. Another had all pairs of men and women, moving in unison through a choreography tableau. But a couple of songs had all the pairs in a semicircle, and they would each take turns dancing in the center, like break dancers. And just like with break dancers, I couldn't tell how much of that was choreographed and how much was improvised. While one pair was dancing, all the others would clap their hands rhythmically and stamp their feet at prescribed times in the song and in specific rhythms. I loved the rhythms. Some had twelve counts, some had eight... I didn't know the patterns off the top of my head, but they were easy enough to figure out.

With all those dancers on the stage, though, it was hard to see the musicians. They sat in chairs behind the dancers, in a line along the back of the stage. They had three guitars, two regular ones and a basso—not a bass guitar, like you think of in rock and roll, which is basically the same size; this was more like the size of a cello. Plus two male singers, one of whom also played an anvil (an actual anvil, like you'd make horseshoes on), and one man who sat on a box and played it with his hands.

I would eventually learn that the percussion boxes were called "cajones," which sounds very similar to but isn't the same as the Spanish word for testicles. However, when you have one between your legs and you're beating on it, it's hard to keep from thinking about that. Especially when the guy on the box next to you sucked your testicles a few hours before. But I'm getting ahead of myself.

After the show, we spent some of our day's earnings taking one of the guitar players out to dinner. Ramon was older than I realized until we were sitting down with him, but he had learned enough English that, at last, I could pick somebody's brain. It was still slow going; he had no classical training at all, so he wasn't familiar with some of the language I was using.

I asked about a million questions, mostly the wrong ones, but that's how it is when you know so little and the thing you want to know about is so different from your experience. I think I offended him with some of them, in fact, until finally he demanded, "Why *you* want to learn flamenco?" With that extra accusatory "you."

I babbled about how I had put together this idea in my head about the world of music and human beings and the balance between structure and improvisation and the nature of music, and Indian classical music, and Qawwali singing, and American blues, and the guitar, and the vibrating string being the binding concept of reality and life in the universe...

He got the gist and nodded his head. "Gloria," he said, and I thought maybe he was praising god.

Orlando made a distressed noise, though, and rattled off some sentence of protest.

The guy sighed, and rubbed his face, and then cracked his knuckles. "Gloria, she know everything," he said. "You go to her. If she like you, she tell you everything." Then he smiled and chuckled to himself and said something I took to mean I might be sorry once she got started.

Orlando shook his head but seemed resigned. Ramon said goodnight shortly after that and left us to finish the bottle of wine we had started. We split the last glass between us, the wine almost chewy it was so strong, so concentrated with the essence of dark grapes. Orlando grimaced at me and showed me his teeth stained temporarily with it.

I wanted to lick his mouth, then, my intellect satisfied for the moment, my stomach content, but my neglected sexual hunger for him coming to the fore. He had long lashes and very round eyes, giving him an earnest look, even when he was trying to be subtle or surreptitious.

He went into the men's room. I put cash on the table as the waitress came to clean up and then followed him.

He beckoned me into a stall, and I pressed him against the tiled wall with my body and took the kiss I had been dreaming of. He made a surprised sound, then kissed back enthusiastically. I don't even remember which one of us did the stroking that made us both come.

After that, though, I tried to separate from him carefully so I didn't get come everywhere, but before I could pull away, he pecked my mouth like a bird, demanding and tentative at the same time. I kissed him slowly, then, with careful explorations of his lips and tongue and teeth, tasting wine and salt. When I pulled back, he licked his lips and nodded at me, like he had decided kissing like that was not only okay, he was adding it to his mental checklist of things we should do again.

Everywhere I Go

Two days later Orlando took me to meet Gloria—the woman with the jowly face whom I had met briefly on my first night in Seville.

He brought me to a house across from a university building. Unlike most of the houses in this area, which had the door at street level but the living quarters up above, this one had a large ground floor parlor that was her classroom. We went there directly from busking, so we were carrying our guitars (as well as a lot of loose cash). Gloria was sitting on a stool in one corner of the room, a ragged oval of cajones around the perimeter.

She had more English than anyone I'd spoken to in weeks, other than American and British tourists (who were always amused to hear me singing in English when I was busking). "Pull up a cajón," she said. "Show me what you can do."

I put a cajon down in front of her, sat my butt on it, and took out my guitar. And foot stand. Two of the three guitarists in the show we'd seen had played with the neck up in classical position. I figured that was a majority: go with that.

I spent a few moments tuning. The Ovation always held its tone better than my other guitars. I don't know if the difference was the strings or the pegs or what.

I played. While busking I had been working on a Spanish-style reworking of "Grenadier." The song is built on an E minor and A minor progression anyway, so it was a fit. The flamenco show had featured the guitars being played very hard, very loud, to be heard over the stamping and clapping. So I attacked this song—it was an aggressive song anyway. My eyes unfocused, and away I went.

When I was done I focused back on her face. "This is what you want to do?" she asked.

"No," I said. "But you said I should show you what I *can* do. Right now, that's what I can do. But I want to learn to do... more."

She looked at Orlando. He was hunched down on a cajon looking like he was trying to hide in plain sight.

She looked back at me, her lips pursed. "How hard do you want to work?"

"I'm not afraid of hard work."

"Can you be here every morning at nine? Then you can take the guitar class at ten. One hour. And percussion follows that."

"Is that one hour, also?"

"Yes."

"I think if I have my afternoons free to busk, that should be fine."

"Busk?" She didn't know the word.

"Play for money in the park."

"Ah, yes. You would have plenty of time for that. Be here tomorrow morning at nine sharp. Do not be late."

I was not late.

Midnight Oil

I went home that night and wrote my name on the chalkboard for rent. It seemed only fair, since I got the feeling I was going to be there a while. Carmina pinched me on the cheek and then kissed where she had pinched, babbling approvingly in Italian or Italian-accented Spanish (I could never tell the difference). Then she took Orlando into their bedroom and fucked his brains out, which was a regular occurrence.

I curled up on the couch and slept like usual.

People ask me sometimes, if I have such sensitive ears, how do I sleep through a lot of noises? Well, it's like right in the very center of my head there is a chamber, a dark chamber like an eight-sided cabinet, and once you climb in and shut the door behind you, no light or sound gets in. Oh, you can still kind of hear, and the door never seals completely, but it's good enough for getting to sleep.

Maybe that's why I sleep so well on the tour bus. Because climbing into the bunk to sleep is kind of like getting into that space in my mind. I don't know.

Anyway. Orlando woke me up in the morning with his mouth in a very stimulating fashion. I still didn't understand why Orlando had this sexual appetite or if it was supposed to mean something. I was pretty sure it wasn't, and it felt good, and there didn't seem to be any harm in it. And that day I was glad of something to get me going that early in the morning.

I hadn't expected him to come with me at that early hour to Gloria's, but he did on that day, at least. She made me clean the classroom. Orlando sat on the stairwell that went up to the apartment upstairs, watching me while I swept the floor and the front hallway and then ran the vacuum cleaner around. I was a little surprised he didn't get out his guitar during the guitar class, though. Then again, it was a beginner class. Maybe he was too far beyond it.

After that day, though, Orlando chose to sleep in most of the time. Turned out that aside from cleaning and getting the classroom ready for the day, what Gloria needed me for most was to clear out and renovate a whole courtyard behind her house, and Orlando was not one for physical work. I eventually figured out that half the conflict between him and Gloria was that she wanted him to help out and he resisted.

Renovating the courtyard involved a lot of pulling weeds and small trees out, moving big stones around, scrubbing and plastering, and a lot of other things I didn't know anything about but could do once someone showed me. Ramon and one or two other people from her circle came to help out on some days, too—it was clear to me there was no money to pay a contractor or anything like that. It only dawned on me after we'd been working on it for a while that what she was doing was building a performance space that would be a lot bigger than her living room.

I soon picked up the class routine. Two days a week the guitar class was for beginners, two days a week intermediate, and one advanced. I took them all and went headlong into a daily schedule that basically guaranteed I never got more than five hours of sleep. Every morning I was working on the courtyard, then taking classes; in the afternoon I was busking, and in the evening I downed a quick dinner of tapas so by ten o'clock I could be at one of the flamenco bars with either Gloria or one of her cohort, listening and learning. That meant I wasn't getting back to the apartment until three in the morning or later. Oddly, Gloria and her coterie of flamenco performers never seemed the slightest bit tired, even though I knew they were keeping late nights and early mornings, too. Was it just the strong Spanish espresso that kept them going?

Gloria eventually clued me in to the idea of the siesta, a nap in the middle of the day after lunch. I wasn't really eating lunch, though, and most of the busking money to be made was when the tourists were out and about in the mid- to late afternoon, so a nap wasn't really an option for me.

Well, it could have been. I could have pulled cash out of the bank and not worried about it. But somehow that didn't feel right. I was sort of enjoying living hand to mouth. I can't say I ever enjoyed it in Providence, nor when I was scrounging retail hours at Tower Records when I had first moved to Boston. But here it seemed so... *doable*. I guess after all the touring and record contracts and complicated finances that were waiting for me at home, there was something satisfying about being so self-contained.

I can do this, I thought.

And I was learning so much. Gloria basically crammed as much into my brain as it could hold. Remember when Ramon had said she knew everything? He might have been right. I learned that the cajon came from Peru and that the gypsies came from India. (India again!)

I also eventually learned that nearly everyone in the flamenco community I'd met was gypsy or part-gypsy, including Orlando himself. Gloria was somehow related to him. So was Ramon, but more distantly. The word she used was "cousins," but I think she used it as a catch-all word to mean "relatives."

One day, the guy who had yelled at Orlando on that first day we'd gone out busking came by the park where we were playing. I'd caught sight of him once or twice before, and at those times Orlando had magically made himself scarce. But this time, before Orlando could run off and hide, the guy came right up to us and said something aggressive. Orlando shrugged calmly, which seemed to enrage the guy. I don't know where I got the balls to do it, but I stepped in front of Orlando and said, in English, "What the hell's the matter with you? Can't you see we're working here?" I pointed to the guitar case, which had a respectable number of pesetas piling up in it.

The guy scowled at me, gave a last glare to Orlando, and then left.

We stayed another fifteen minutes to save face, and then I made us pack up and move. Orlando was kind of shaken up and was playing for shit at that point, anyway.

I took him into a cafe, and he ordered coffee with sweetened condensed milk in it. I got one also, and we sat there being soothed by the hot, sweet drink.

"So what is it with him?" I finally asked. "What the hell?"

We had taken by this time to basically speaking to each other pretty much in our native languages and figuring some small percent must sink in. We still did a lot of shrugging and giving each other blank looks, but that was all right. It's not like we were discussing philosophy or something.

Which meant he rattled off a fairly long paragraph, of which I understood pretty much nothing until he mentioned Gloria.

"Gloria?" I asked, to be sure I had heard right.

Apparently the guy was another cousin, whose name was Adan—which I guess is Spanish for Adam—and was Gloria's son.

"Wait, but if Adan is Gloria's son, and he's your cousin, then she's your aunt?" Or maybe just another flavor of cousin?

He shrugged. "But Gloria and Adan, quit." He made a throat-cutting gesture. "She quit him."

"You mean she disowned him? Threw him out of the family?"

"Sí, sí. Adan very bad."

I would later learn from inquiring carefully from some of the others that Adan was in charge of a group of women who would make money from tourists by handing them flowers or twigs and then trying to tell their fortunes. Ramon warned me about them and then spat on the ground. Later he added that it would be fine if all they did was tell fortunes for the tourists, but unfortunately the same group were also pickpocketing and running other scams on the unsuspecting. Ramon apparently disapproved of this. So did Gloria, which I gathered was why she had run Adan out of the house. My guess was anyone who was part of an organized ring of petty thieves was probably also involved in drugs and prostitution, even if no one said anything about it. Maybe that was my New York City bias showing. But that was my assumption.

But when I wasn't trying to figure out Orlando's strange family situation or his aversion to physical labor or his attraction to my dick, I was cramming my brain with flamenco. The biggest thing I learned was that flamenco could be an improvisation not only among the musicians, but also among the singer, the musicians, and the dancer. The dancer was a percussion instrument unto himself or herself, and the singer was very much like a Qawwali singer, riffing on a specific theme or story. Sometimes the theme was flamenco itself, sometimes it was gypsy life or the hardship of life. Gloria was a singer.

She had been trying to open this flamenco school

for years and hadn't even been in operation for a year at that point. It took me a while to figure all that out. And it was a while before she started treating me like I was serious about learning and not just a source of free labor.

I think it took about five weeks. I think in weeks because the only day that was different was Sunday. There was no class. Instead, there was church.

I have never been much of a churchgoing type. But Carmina insisted that Orlando go, and Vicente and the others went, and I ended up going with them. We did not go to the huge old cathedral, but to a church nearer to the apartment that was still probably older than any church I'd ever been in. It was a lot like Catholic Mass in the States, except in Spanish, and the singing was mostly in Latin.

I've always liked the singing.

Anyway. I think four Sundays had passed, but maybe it was five, before Gloria started telling me to bring a guitar to the flamenco bars when we went at night. In other words, she started throwing me to the wolves. I shouldn't say it that way, because I make it sound like it was a bad thing. It wasn't, but it was a little bit terrifying at first to be suddenly on the spot in a new art form. So I didn't play as much as the other guitarists, who pretty much played all night, but I held my own for a song or two, here or there.

I have no idea what Gloria thought of how I played, because she never said, but the other guitarists took me under their wings immediately as a result. I was never sure how much was they were impressed with me and how much was that it was like having a mascot, a funny American they could teach tricks to. Didn't matter to me, really, because everything they showed me was another something I could use. They started trying to get me to come to more *juergas*, which are like jam sessions except there are dancers, too, and I started convincing them to show up at the park or wherever I thought Orlando and I might be busking. That way they could teach me on the spot *while* maybe we made a little money. They made fun of me for that, saying that only an American would do that. Multitasking. But I didn't know how long I was going to be there. I wanted to get as much into me as possible.

It was difficult and yet it wasn't. I was force-feeding myself, but my head was completely cracked open so it was easy to pour stuff right in; and given the training I'd done with Guitar Craft, it was the right time for my fingers, for my body, for everything. My chronically sore thumb didn't even hurt after two or three hours of playing. Gabriela, who was training as a flamenco dancer when she wasn't in a university class or working tables, started coming out to the park with us, too, and dancing, which meant we could draw a much bigger crowd. We developed a ten-minute "show" that we would do a few times in an afternoon, while the rest of the time it would be more of a juerga. We started drawing in large amounts of cash during a hat pass at the end of the "show."

Orlando started bringing a cajon and some days left his guitar at home since now we had me and sometimes one of the other guitarists, plus a dancer. The only thing we didn't have was a singer. That was okay, though, because I was still learning how to read a dancer. There were things she could do, twisting her hands in certain ways, for example, that would cue us to repeat a section. In flamenco the dancer is an instrument, too, but it's a bit like she's leading a solo all the time.

Gabriela and I got good together. We practiced one night in the living room, which was probably bad for the apartment floor. We got so good together that her boyfriend Rafi started to get a little jealous, and came and hung out when he could. I'll admit, playing for her so she could dance was a lot like making love, so Rafi can be forgiven for being jealous about it. By the time he convinced himself that I wasn't the slightest bit interested in her sexually, though, he had become the group's hawker and designated hat-passer.

So, after another month, we had basically almost a full troupe of our own just with our roommates. The only ones who weren't involved were Vicente, who had too much studying to do, and Carmina, who wasn't Spanish and wasn't interested in singing, dancing, or playing an instrument.

The only drawback to having such a group at the park with us was that Orlando and I had to stop making each other come behind the snack kiosk. Honestly, that was probably for the best, because we were bound to get caught. Orlando was creative, though, keeping his eye out for restrooms, alleyways, and other opportunities for privacy.

One day Gloria came to see our troupe when we were set up in a cul-de-sac not far from the art museum. She must have been watching from behind us so we wouldn't see her. When we were packing up for the evening she came stalking over like she was angry. She and Orlando exchanged what I would have thought were angry words. Then she walked away.

I asked him what she had said.

He rattled off some words, the only one of which I made out was "gig."

"What? We have a gig? Where?"

"Her place."

I didn't press for more details because I knew I'd get them from Gloria in the morning. Which I did. She was opening the performance space for two concerts a week and wanted us to play one of them. She anointed herself our singer for those shows. She would sell the tickets and we would get paid: half the proceeds to us, half to the school. This was also the point at which she put up a sign outside saying that the house was a flamenco school. Me and Ramon hung it one morning. I never did find out why she and Orlando had sounded so angry at each other, though. I think maybe some of the reason there's a stereotype of the "fiery Latin" personality is they simply yell more than uptight Anglo folks do, and they sound a lot more vehement when they do. Maybe that's just how Spanish sounds. I decided I couldn't judge.

Once our little troupe had the school gig going for us, one of the restaurants we frequented with an outdoor patio suitable for shows also hired us, sans singer, for one night a week. I sent Carynne a postcard from the place. I wrote: "You probably won't be surprised, but I have a gig here. Will send you 15% of all the rioja I drink."

We quit busking on the days we had night gigs, and I started the afternoon classes, too. Palmas (clapping), cajon, flamenco singing, and, of course, dancing.

I didn't actually do the dancing. I played guitar for the dance class. It was very useful for me to learn with some of the beginners, who were doing things more slowly than the "pros" and were learning the beats.

On gig days, even with me doing all the classes, I had time for a siesta. The only thing I love more than staying up late at night is sleep. I know that sounds weird. Spain is a stay-up-late country. In Seville a lot of the bars and restaurants closed at five or six o'clock for a very late siesta and then re-opened at nine or ten: nightclub hours. Some didn't re-open until midnight. At three in the morning there would be plenty of people on the street. Not tourists, either—they were already in bed by then.

When I went for a late-afternoon siesta, Orlando was usually there, and that became a good time for us to get off if the others weren't home.

Now we had shows to promote when we went out busking, and we had flyers for the flamenco school, and the classes started getting fuller, and the shows were all pretty much sold out. The courtyard only seated about fifty people, maybe sixty in a pinch. But Gloria was charging them a lot for this "private concert" that was being billed as the "authentic" flamenco. It wasn't all that different from what you could see at one of the good flamenco bars after midnight, but like I said, tourists didn't seem to want to stay up that late. We added two more shows: one for us, and one for Gloria's older crowd on the one night of the week that the big "tablao" was dark. That meant Ramon could come play, too.

If you couldn't tell, I was pretty wrapped up in it all. And why wouldn't I be? I was performing every day, I was learning like crazy, I was getting my dick sucked on an extremely regular basis, and my only sense of time passing was marked by the weekly church day. I've never been good at keeping track of time.

But one thing I couldn't miss was when summer arrived, and the academic year ended, and Carmina and Vicente both packed up to leave. Vicente went back to Madrid, where his family was, and Carmina was getting ready to return to Italy.

I came in one afternoon ready to take a siesta, but Carmina and Orlando were in their room. They were having an argument, that much was clear. It sounded more like the bickering kind of fight than a tearful one. The weather was heating up. I was barefoot, in a T-shirt and shorts, getting ready to nap and hoping they'd quiet down when the bedroom door opened and Carmina stalked out.

"Dión. C'mere." She gestured for me to follow her.

I followed her to the bedroom. Orlando was sitting on the bed, blindfolded, his hands behind his back where I couldn't see them. Naked.

"You guys look like you're in the middle of something," I said, hanging back at the doorway.

She smiled sweetly and began to unbutton her shirt. "You help me, yes?"

"Um..."

She gestured at Orlando and, with a hollow hand, mimed giving head. I pointed at myself. *Me? You want me to...?* I mimed back. She grinned and pointed.

Well, that was clear enough. If it got weird I could always say no and walk out.

I knelt at Orlando's feet and took him in my mouth.

"Dión!" he swore.

At which point Carmina started yelling at him and smacking him in the face. He clearly wasn't having any of that, trying to dodge her, and I tried to get out of the way but then realized he had his hands tied. She was hitting him pretty hard. I grabbed her by the wrists and said, "You can't go hitting him like that. Carmina, what the fuck."

At which point she burst into tears, broke free, slapped me in the face, and then marched out. I was trying to get Orlando untied when I heard the door to the apartment slam, too. Orlando still had the scarf around one wrist as he hurried to the window. I looked with him and saw her get into a taxi. We needn't have hurried to catch a glimpse of her: the taxi driver struggled for a while to get her suitcases into the trunk of the car, and she stood on the sidewalk haranguing him. Eventually he gave up and put one of them on the back seat. She got in the other door and they drove away.

Orlando turned to me. "Sorry."

"Orlando, what the fuck is going on?" My cheek itched a little where she'd smacked me.

He shrugged. "She leave. Every summer she leave."

"Do you mean she left you for good? Like, broke up with you?"

He shrugged. "Every summer." He mimed an explosion, complete with sound effect. "When she come back, she love me again."

"You mean she breaks up with you before she leaves every summer?"

"Every summer," he repeated and shrugged. He looked a little stunned, probably from her smacking him in the face so many times, though not so stunned he forgot his erection, which he stroked as if soothing himself. "Dios mio."

It was a common enough swear; I heard it all the time. The literal translation was "my god," but it was used more like "for chrissakes."

"Dios mio yourself, Orlando," I said.

He sat on the edge of the bed and shrugged. If he'd given me hurt puppy eyes, I think I would have smacked him and walked out, too. But he didn't seem interested in manipulating me emotionally. Orlando was just Orlando.

He lay back then, the whole skinny enchilada of him, curly black bush around his balls and his face and neck browner than his chest from playing all those sunny afternoons in the park. He didn't make "bedroom eyes" at me or anything. He merely jerked his head like he was inviting me to lie down next to him.

Why the fuck not. I slipped my shorts off and stretched out beside him. I folded one arm behind my head and jerked off while Orlando did the same next to me. I had no idea what was going through his head, but we both looked at the ceiling, and after we'd both come we took a nap side by side on his bed.

Do You Want to Dance?

It gets hot in southern Spain in the summer. Although, was it any hotter than most of the other places I'd lived? Maybe a little. It was regularly above ninety degrees. The apartment had air conditioners set in the walls next to the windows, but only in the bedrooms.

Not sure that's really why I moved into Orlando's room with him, though. We were only busking maybe two days a week by then, even though he and Gabriela didn't have classes to go to. We were too busy with nighttime gigs, and I was still spending a lot of time at the flamenco school. One day, though, he and I had gone out without anyone else. And the park was kind of dead because it was hot. But somehow that didn't faze us, we just kept on because we were enjoying playing with each other.

Flamenco, as you might have gathered from what I've said, is a really structured thing—but that's what lets it be freeform at the same time. Even the structure of a show, though, could be either on a kind of strict form or more freewheeling. It really depends on the situation. When we went to the little cafes and bars at night, it was more of a jam session—and I wondered if the word for that, *juerga*, was related to the word *juego*? Juego was one of my textbook words, which I knew meant "play"—not in the sense of play an instrument, but as in play a game. Then there were forms we used for the concerts, like how a symphony has an overture and other specific parts. Like with Indian music, in a flamenco performance the melody instrument (the guitar) plays an introductory solo, introducing the theme to everyone. It's improvised, but it's within the form.

Gloria had eventually let me know she approved highly of the things I did when I played the introduction.

That day in the park, I started the introduction to a *farruca*, thinking it would be fun to improvise on it with Orlando. The farruca is both a dance (like a waltz) and a type of piece (like a chorale). We hadn't been doing one in our shows because we only had a female dancer and the farruca was a traditionally male dance. (I would eventually learn there were women in history who danced the farruca... but always in men's clothing. So maybe I should say it's a masculine dance?)

Anyway, I played an intro to this farruca, and Orlando did something I had never seen him do before, which was put down his guitar and dance. We had no drummer, no singer, but it didn't matter. I played, and he danced.

I might have mentioned that doing a dancer/guitar duet with Gabriela was kind of like having sex with her. So you probably won't be surprised, then, that what happened after the song finished was we went back to the apartment.

We left our guitars sitting in the living room on our way to the bedroom door. I was a little surprised that after flipping the power on the air conditioner, Orlando produced a strip of three condoms from somewhere and tossed it onto the bed.

I was pulling my shirt over my head, but I heard the sound of it hitting the sheets and looked. "Are those for you or for me?"

"You," he said, then frowned, realizing that it kind of depended on what I meant by that.

Whatever. We'd figure out who was doing who soon enough.

Actually, I really hoped I was doing him. There was no lube in evidence. That wasn't why, though.

Sex has a lot of back and forth in it, I know. Just like a duet, things shift, ideas come to you, your goals emerge and then merge.... You have to be open and listening. I listened to Orlando. I listened with my fingertips and with my eyes as well as my ears.

Yeah, it became clear I was going to be doing him.

It had been a long time—six months?—since I'd last fucked. I hope I did him well. I'd managed to forget how much I needed it. I'd managed to forget what it was like to let the lust I had running through my system boil out through my hips instead of through my hands.

It felt very, very right. I can't say that about a lot of the sex I'd had in my life up to that point.

"You okay?" I asked afterward, since he was facing away from me and I couldn't see his face.

"Fantástico," he said, sounding like he did after the first bottle of rioja.

I put an arm over him, and he clutched it to his chest and then kissed the backs of my fingers. Okay, that was a clear indication he was feeling good. I answered each kiss on my hand with one on the back of his neck and let the incense of his sweat intoxicate me almost to the point of unconsciousness.

Then I asked, "Orlando, are you gay?"

"No," he said, like usual.

The next day was church day. I wondered what Orlando thought about when he closed his eyes and put his hands together.

My mind drifted like it usually did during the service. In the summer, you could feel the heat from all the racks of lit candles in the saints' alcoves along the side of the pews. So many people wore their "Sunday best" that I had to wonder that more of them didn't faint from the heat. (Me, I didn't have any Sunday best, really.) I watched a sunbeam crawl across one of the stained-glass windows.

And the next thing I knew, I was praying. Okay, maybe it's a little strong to call it praying, since I wasn't on my knees or anything. I was just having a little one-way conversation with God in my mind. It went something like this: *Dear God, please let this thing I have going with Orlando actually turn out to be as good as it feels like it is. As good for us both.*

Maybe sometimes prayers get answered. For the most part, after that—same as it had been before—I let Orlando dictate when we had sex and what kind. Instead of leaving me feeling powerless and antsy, though, I was perfectly fine with it. Maybe because I never felt like there was a shortage? Not quite every day, but not exactly every other day, either. Unpredictable and yet consistent enough that I had no anxiety about it.

In other words, sex with Orlando *wasn't* the thing that changed on the day Orlando danced in the park. No. The day after church, he showed up to the afternoon dance class.

Gloria glared at him but said nothing to him during the class, treating him like any of the other students. That day the class was working on tangos. In flamenco, what they call "tangos" is not the same as the Argentine tango, which is the ballroom dance you're probably thinking of. The guitar part is really strict in the flamenco tango, with the strums falling in very specific places—the guitar is as much a percussion instrument as a melodic one. (Well, there's a reason they call it "rhythm guitar.")

I've talked before, haven't I, about how there's a purity in the E chords? Maybe it's been a while. The E string is the lowest string on the guitar. When you play an E major or E minor chord and you let that bottom string ring, you are basically giving the guitar its full throat.

Well, the A is a close second to the E. The A is the next string over. So the A chord, and especially A minor, is another really resonant one. Most of what you think of if you hear someone playing "Spanish guitar"—think of what the soundtrack would be if a matador suddenly appeared in your movie—is the E minor and A minor chords.

I can't remember where I was going with this other than to say those are the chords you first fall in love with when you pick up one of those Yamaha classical guitars when you're ten years old. And you never stop loving them. You can go and play all kinds of things. You can even re-string and re-tune your guitar. But it always feels like going home when you return to them.

Right. So the farruca is played in A minor. The flamenco tango is also in A minor. Not to get technical, but it's in the Phrygian mode.

It took me a while to figure that out, of course. No one who was teaching me used anything like music theory to describe the notes or even most of the chords. The other guitar players would just show me and I'd do it. Some stuff you simply internalize and parrot and trust that you're getting it right because you read the reactions of those around you. Come to think of it, that's about how I learned what little Spanish I learned, too. But I learned way more guitar than Spanish.

After class that day, Gloria and Orlando had a screaming match. I really couldn't understand a word of it, but there wasn't anywhere to go to escape the argument either. When they were done, Orlando marched out. I wanted to ask Gloria what it was about, but I wanted to stick with Orlando, so I picked up my guitar and followed him.

We ended up sucking on salty, bitter olives in a dark tapas bar and drinking red wine at three in the afternoon. Orlando lined up the pits from the olives and pushed them around with his finger morosely.

"She didn't like you dancing?" I asked.

He shook his head and made the "I can't explain" gesture.

"Will you dance tonight? In the show?"

He shrugged.

We went home and had a siesta (but not sex, and that was fine), then went back to the school for our evening performance as usual. I was expecting there to be some tension between him and Gloria, but they seemed to be over whatever spat they'd had.

And at one point in the show, while Gabriela changed her costume and Gloria went to help her with it, I played and Orlando danced a farruca. It was a great hit, so far as I could tell. I guess the audience loved watching his narrow, bony hips and his long, expressive fingers as much as I did.

I fucked him very hard that night.

Out of Touch

We went to three tapas bars regularly. There was the place where we had the gig, there was the place we had gone on the first night when I had arrived in Seville, and there was a place that the older flamenco crowd liked, one of the ones where regular jam/dance sessions broke out. Oddly enough, that was the place that had a radio behind the bar that they turned to a station that played pop music in English from time to time.

By mid-July it was really too hot to busk outside in the afternoons. Not that we would have minded the heat ourselves, but no one would linger to listen or watch. So we left off going to the park entirely and concentrated on our evening gigs, two shows a week at Gloria's school and, by then, two nights a week at the bar. It was one of those hot July afternoons when we were in the bar early for some reason. I was sitting with Orlando while he was talking to the bartender, a twenty-something woman with skinny arms but prodigious breasts. I wasn't really listening to what they were saying since I could barely make out any of it anyway.

A song came on the radio. My ears perked up: something new, something that sounded kind of good...? Then Sarah Rogue's voice came in and I realized it was the song I'd written with her. Which made me snort with laughter. Orlando wanted to know what was so funny. I did my best impression of his "I can't explain."

August is as hot as July. They say tempers flare when the weather is hot. I don't know if that's true. I do know that Adan showed up at the bar one night and went ballistic when Orlando got up to dance. Fortunately the bar had a fairly large, fairly undeniable bouncer named Hector who threw Adan out on his ear.

I spent the entire walk home that night looking over my shoulder, though, convinced that a gypsy gang was going to jump us.

They didn't. When we got home I tried to ask Orlando about it, but it was useless. And then he distracted me, anyway, using his mouth for something other than talking.

So I asked Gloria the next day, telling her about the incident. We were sitting in the classroom after the guitar class, and Ramon was lurking around somewhere. "What's the story between Orlando and Adan?"

She made a disgusted noise and waved her hand in that Spanish "I'm not going to talk about it" way.

"Adan showed up at our gig last night, and he and Orlando almost came to blows."

She looked at me sharply. "Orlando fought?"

"Well, Hector grabbed Adan before it got to that, but it looked like he would've given as good as he got."

She didn't quite follow that expression, I could see from her face.

"I mean, if Adan was going to go at him, Orlando was going to hit right back."

She leaned tiredly with her elbows on her knees. "Those boys. Adan is trouble. Orlando..." She shook her head and changed the subject. "I want to hire you to teach the beginner guitar class and to play for the dance classes."

"Gloria, I've only been playing flamenco a couple of months." Okay, maybe it was six months, but still. "I can't teach the beginner class."

"Yes you can," she insisted. "Most of them can't play at all."

"And I don't speak enough Spanish!"

"No common language hasn't stopped your teachers from teaching you," she pointed out.

"I really shouldn't," I said, as the other shoe dropped: "I don't know how long I'm going to be here."

At that she gave a little self-satisfied nod, like "aha, I thought so." She stood. "It's true. You'd need to get a work visa. I need to run a clean business here."

By clean she meant legal, I think.

"What about Orlando? He could teach and play."

"He's too lazy."

"Not if you're going to pay him."

She gave me a skeptical look.

"He's not the most motivated person in the world, but the one thing that gets him out of bed in the morning is money. Why not, Gloria?"

She gave me a stone-faced look.

"Come on, Gloria. Why wasn't he already working for you when I started here? What's going on with you and him and the family?"

But she closed the subject. "Family is family." To make sure I knew the subject was closed, she added, "I don't need you this afternoon. Go."

So, for snooping around Orlando's situation, and maybe for admitting that I wasn't there for the long term, I got thrown out. At least for that day. I was pretty sure if I showed up in the morning, she'd pretend the conversation had never happened.

I went home and tried to talk to Orlando about it, but that was the usual complete exercise in frustration. Even if he was willing to talk, there were too many gaps in what we could say to each other.

I finally said, "You know I'm going to go back. To the States."

"When?" is all he asked.

"I don't know. Sometime. Not yet." I wasn't really prepared to think hard about it. "Sometime but not yet" was about as much as I knew.

I showed up at the school in the morning, and, as predicted, Gloria tolerated me and pretended the day before had never happened.

Two nights later we were at our usual bar, and Josué, the bartender/manager, came over to tell Orlando he had a message. Spanish is full of words that are similar to English words, which makes them easy for me to remember. "Mensaje" isn't pronounced anything like the word "message," but two years of textbook Spanish back in the day was enough for me to grasp stuff like that.

Orlando asked who the message was from.

"Carmina," the bartender said.

Without batting an eye, Orlando then asked, *Oh, when is she coming back?*

Josué shrugged and handed Orlando a piece of paper with a phone number on it. Orlando frowned and asked another question. The only word I made out was "why."

Josué had no answer, apparently, other than a shrug. So I asked Orlando, "Why did Carmina call here? Why is the message here, instead of at home?"

To which Orlando just shrugged like he hadn't made out a word I said.

I had a sudden ice-water-down-the-back feeling. What if our phone didn't work? How would I even know? It's not like it ever rang. There was an answering machine hooked up to it. Now that I thought about it, it was never blinking anymore. I had assumed that was because, with Carmina and Vicente gone for the summer, maybe there were fewer phone calls. Carmina was the one who had used it the most.

"Orlando," I said, miming the phone. "Is it broken? It works?"

He shook his head. I tamped down a sudden surge of panic. It was August. I'd been here since January.

Calm down, I told myself. I was sure the phone had worked when Carmina was here. So it had only been two months I'd been incommunicado.

"Why?" I insisted.

He tried to give me an explanation. I made out the word for summer and Vicente's name. I took that to mean Vicente had the phone turned off when he left for the summer.

I was seized with the sudden urge to call home. I had been depending on that phone. If Carynne needed me for anything, she would have called. What would she do if it didn't work?

I went to the bar and asked Josué if there were any messages for me. Josué had a little English, enough to joke around with me sometimes. "Why, you got hot girlfriend, too?"

"Yeah," I said, far too seriously. "She'd be calling from America."

He shrugged. "Francesca answer the phone, not me."

I had a sudden suspicion. I went back to Orlando. "Let me see the message. The mensaje. Let me see."

Orlando dug the piece of paper out of his pocket and handed it to me. I put my forehead in my hand. The number was Carynne's. "Oh, shit."

He asked me what was wrong.

"This isn't from Carmina. It's from *Ca-ri-neh*," I told him. "It's not for you. It's for *me*."

His eyes widened. "Oh, shit," he said, in a passable imitation of me. "You girlfriend?"

I almost said no, she's not my girlfriend. But given that I couldn't explain who she was, or who I was, for that matter, it was easier to simply nod.

We hurried home and I picked up the phone and, sure enough, the line was dead. I stared at it for a few moments, trying to remember where I'd seen a pay phone.

"I call Carmina," Orlando announced.

"From where?"

"Come." He led me out again. There was a pay phone a few blocks from the apartment, on the side of a building by the post office.

Orlando used it first. I probably should have walked down the block to give him some privacy. Somehow that didn't occur to me. I leaned on the wall next to the phone and waited my turn.

He sounded casual as he spoke to Carmina, then happy as he confirmed when she'd been returning. Next week. That much I got.

Then it was my turn. I called Carynne's number, collect. It was three in the morning in Seville, so it was something like 10 PM in Boston. A reasonable hour to call.

I got her machine.

The message I left went something like this.

"Hi, it's me. Guess you're not there. I just got your message at the bar and found out our phone hasn't been working. I'm still in Seville, just, I guess when one of my roommates left for the summer no one paid the phone bill? I hope everything's okay and that you were just leaving the message because of not being able to get through on the phone. Anyway, yeah, I know, it's been a while since I've called—actually I know I've never called, but I hope everything's okay there? I guess if you need to reach me the two places I can usually be found are the Triana Flamenco School, which I guess is probably Escuela de Flamenco Triana if you have to call Directory Assistance, or call the tapas bar again, and make sure to ask for Josué—and by the way they can't say my name here, so call me Dión." Dee-own.

Her machine cut me off at that point. I hoped she had just been calling to check up on me, but somehow I felt a little ill with dread.

We went back to the apartment. In the bedroom, I stripped Orlando out of his clothes, and because he was taller I waited until we were lying down to climb on top of him and pull his head back by the hair so I could kiss him as hard as I wanted. So hard I almost wanted to bite him on the mouth.

"What happens when Carmina comes back?" I asked him, but then I kissed him again before he could answer. When I took my mouth away from his I spoke again: "I think I should leave."

"Maybe," he said.

"Do you even know what that word means?"

"Maybe," he answered.

I kissed him even harder, hard enough to inspire him to leave gouges in my back from his right hand.

Understand that I wasn't angry at him. Not at all. But a certain amount of frustration had been building up because I knew there were things going on that I didn't understand. And I was a little angry with myself for not checking in at home more often. (And by "more often" I mean "at all.")

I fucked him in a rhythm of eight, and then in a rhythm of twelve, and he gave a frustrated growl and pushed back against me, four on the floor. There's a reason they call it rock and roll. We sank into a steady beat then, the drone of the air conditioner thrumming, and my mind wandered.

I realized I had made up my mind to leave before Carmina got back.

When we were done, and I was lying there sandwiched between the cold air blowing on my back from the A/C and Orlando's hot, damp body in my arms, I asked, "Orlando? Are you gay?"

And he said, "Maybe."

Disappear

If I hadn't made the decision to leave, then that last show at the flamenco school might have gone differently. Or maybe if Gloria hadn't told me right before the show started that Carynne had called, I wouldn't have been so on edge. It's possible my memory has gilded my performance a little, but I really think it was good. I remember it as being the best, but maybe it's just that one always remembers the last time of something with such fondness. I don't know. Ramon was there that night, too. He'd been hanging around the school more and more, and I was happy to have him play with our group.

I remember Gabriela's dress was black and white with polka dots, ruffles all around her ankles, and Orlando was in a black button-down shirt with the cuffs rolled neatly. Gabriela's hair was up in a twist. Orlando's was hanging down at his shoulders with that Prince Valiant cut of his.

When he danced the farruca, every time the fingers of my left hand gripped the neck of the guitar I thought about the way I gripped his hip bone to pull him onto my cock.

The memorable thing about the performance for everyone else, though, was that when we were nearing the end of the set, Adan showed up and called out Orlando.

I heard the front door open and close and saw one of the girls who helped hand out programs get up from her seat to go see who it was.

A few moments later, Adan burst onto the floor in the middle of the chairs, standing at the edge of the flat wooden platform the dancers danced and stamped their feet on. The girl followed behind him, wringing her hands. A song had just ended, and it took me a second to focus on him, and then I had a feeling like everything was rising: my heart rate, the temperature in the room, my hackles. It was like I was floating upward out of my seat even though I was still sitting down.

Some in the audience tittered nervously when Adan made his opening statement, pointing at Orlando, who was sitting on a cajon next to me at the time. I think they thought it must be part of the show. Adan was certainly dramatic enough, like something out of a Shakespeare play. He was wearing black slacks with scuffed shoes, a plain white T-shirt under an untucked button-down. To an American eye, he didn't look dressed like a thug, but I'd seen him before, and though I couldn't understand what he was saying, his tone was undeniably aggressive.

Orlando stood, eyes burning, and Gloria got to her feet, too, her face reddening with rage. But before Mount Gloria could blow her top, Adan charged Orlando.

He never reached him. He got the carbon-fiber back of my guitar to the face, and then, after he fell to his knees, my boot to the head, which laid him out flat on his back. It was over that quickly. Wham bam, thank you ma'am.

I hadn't even gotten out of my chair.

At that point, Ramon, who had been spending more and more time at the school, and a couple of the older guys dragged Adan by his arms through the classroom and out the front door to the street. Gloria hugged Orlando and then I stood up and patted him on the shoulder. The other men came back in pretty quickly, so I wondered what they had done with Adan. Left him unconscious in the alley next door? Called the police? I had no idea.

Ramon spoke to the audience, apologizing for the interruption, then asking them to leave.

After they had filed out, he came back and said something to Gloria that I think was, *What are you going to do about your son?*

And I'm pretty sure she said both *I have no son* and *This is my son*. She was still hugging Orlando.

We didn't go to the bar that night. We all went upstairs, where I had never been, and another woman I had never met but who was clearly another cousin or aunt cooked, and we drank wine and ate sitting around in the upstairs parlor. The musicians alternately acted out the story gleefully of how I had dispatched Adan with the Ovation and shook their heads gravely about what was going to happen next. The phone rang. It was someone with news. After telling the others in Spanish, Gloria eventually sat down next to me and said in English, "He's hurt. Cracked his skull on the stone when he fell. They say he'll be all right but he is in the hospital now."

One of the others said something about the police.

"No police. They are not our friends." By "our" I think she meant the gypsy community. "We will take care of this ourselves."

Orlando said something from across the room, pointing at me.

Gloria put a hand on my arm. "Thank you for all you've done, Dión. Did you know, Dión means 'chosen of God'? Maybe you're an angel sent down to guard Orlando when he needed you most."

"I didn't mean to hurt him," I said, meaning Adan.

"We know. You're not one of us, though. Adan's men

will blame you."

"You don't worry for Orlando?"

"We will take care of Orlando from here." She patted my arm again, but Ramon stood, looming over us.

"You should go," he said. "I'm sorry, my friend."

"It's okay," I told him. "You're right. I should."

Gloria squeezed my arm. "Back to America?"

"Yeah." I caught Orlando looking at me from across the room then, his eyes as flat and unreadable as my own. "I probably shouldn't have stayed this long. But Spain has been so good. Everything, the music, everything. Has been so good."

"Angel," Gloria said again, and then she hugged me.

My takeaway from all that was that she was grateful to me for flattening her disowned son but that for my own good, I had better leave. Something about the way it had all unfolded had resulted in everyone accepting that she was taking Orlando in as her own—including Orlando himself. No one ever told me where Orlando's parents were in all this, and I wasn't about to ask.

Ramon and a couple of others escorted us home. When Orlando and Gabriela and I went upstairs to the apartment, I started to pack. To my surprise, Orlando did, too. He erased both of our names from the chalkboard in the kitchen.

Gabriela asked something in Spanish, and I think I asked the same thing in English: "What about Carmina? Isn't she coming back next week? I thought you were getting back together."

He shrugged, then said, "Carmina crazy. Adan crazy. Enough."

"Where are you going, then?"

He told us he was moving in with Gloria. Gabriela shrugged and kissed him on the cheek and went upstairs to her own room.

Once she was gone, Orlando tugged me close to him until we were fly to fly. "You leave, now I have to work."

"You'll have to take over playing for the dance class, and the guitar parts for the palo, yeah," I agreed.

He kissed me then. "Dión. Angel."

"Not an angel," I told him. "And my name is Daron." I pronounced it with a Spanish accent this time, making the "a" long, rolling the "r" and rounding the "o."

He chuckled and gave me a hickey under my ear.

Knowing it was the last time made me even hungrier for him, but it was odd. We were more affectionate, more tender with each other during foreplay, and then fiercely energetic when it came to the deed itself. Like playing the guitar so hard your fingers hurt. Like yelling at someone as if you're angry because you actually love them. I guess.

Orlando let me do whatever I wanted that night until exhaustion set in. Then I slept with my arm around him, my nose buried in the back of his neck, drinking in every last moment with him. And in the morning when we parted, I had the oddest feeling. I felt sated, finished, like that deep thrum in the gut when you get all the way to the bottom note of the guitar and there's nowhere to go. You've reached the root note and you're done, gloriously done.

Part Thirteen

August 1990

Prodigal Blues

When the only thing I could get on such short notice at the Seville airport was a British Airways flight to London, I decided I might as well take it. One more country to check off the list, right? I took the flight, since it wasn't insanely expensive, and booked the seven-day-advanced flight from London to Boston while I was at it, since the amount I saved was more than enough to get me a hostel and feed me for a week.

It was so much easier to get around an English-speaking country. I found a hostel pretty easily. I called Carynne from the pay phone there and got her machine again. I gave her the number where she could leave me a message. The next day I got up and went to see the spot where the Abbey Road album cover was photographed. Then I went to Picadilly Circus and gawked at crowds and stuff. In the afternoon I went to the Tower of London and was surprised to find it wasn't actually a tower. When they say tower they mean fortress, I guess.

I was standing in a tourist-trap shop not far from parliament and Big Ben (which *is* in a tower) when I thought about sending Jonathan a postcard. I hadn't thought about Jonathan in months. I felt a little bit guilty about that, but then I thought, why should that make me feel guilty? We had a relationship. It ended. I had no regrets about it. So I stopped thinking about it. Isn't that how it should be? I felt so calm about it.

I was less calm, though, when I was looking through a bin at a hip record store and realized the flyer tacked to the wall was for the opening of *Star Baby*. So that was happening. My breath got a little short looking at the grainy photocopy of the photo of Ziggy and the actress whose name I could never remember in each other's arms.

And what about Ziggy, anyway? I hadn't exactly stopped thinking about him, but I'd run out of new thoughts to have. It had been over a year since I had last laid eyes on him.

A year. Jesus.

A voice in my head that sounded a lot like Carynne's asked, *How do you feel about him now?*

And a voice that sounded a lot like mine said something I was pretty sure I'd said many times before: *That really depends on him.*

I was still in love with him. I'd given up fighting that. But whether I let myself experience the feeling was going to depend on him. Whether there was even a way to experience it remained to be seen. Was there still a band? Had Ziggy ever come home?

Back at the hostel, there was a message from Carynne. It said, "Call Me. Urgent." The hostel had a pay phone in the lounge. A Madonna sing-along was going on in the lounge, though. I went back out to the train station two blocks away and used the phone from there.

This time, at last, I reached her.

"Daron, holy fuck, where the hell are you now?"

"London. I got your message at the hostel."

"Okay. When are you coming home? It's... I've been trying to call you for weeks."

"Shit." I felt like a ball of ice had formed in the pit of my stomach. "I was afraid of that. I had no idea the phone in Seville was cut off."

"It's all right, other than the ulcer I gave myself worrying about you. But there's a lot going on here."

"What do you mean 'a lot'?"

"I mean, for example, lawsuit shit ramping up and a ton of other things to tell you."

Before I could ask her to elaborate, she blurted out, "Like Ziggy's mother dying."

"Dying!" I clutched the phone. That sucked no matter how you looked at it.

"Well, she was. It happened a couple of months ago."

"Oh, shit." How long I had been away hit me like a guitar to the face. Not that it might have made any difference if I had been there. It's not like I could have saved her. And it's not like I could have helped him or been there for him if he didn't want me to.

Would he have wanted me to?

"Have you... have you been in touch with him?"

"Not really. He's been in LA and New York mostly. But anyway."

"I'm sorry."

"It's all right, sweetcakes. But I really need you here now."

"All right. All right. Can you re-book me on an earlier flight? Otherwise I'm here for six more days."

"If I know you're coming home in six days, that's—"

"No. It sounds like I've put it off long enough. I should get my ass home now."

"Call me back in an hour. It's still business hours here. I'll call the travel agent."

"Okay. I'll call you. If I need to get on a flight at the crack of dawn, I can do that."

I left the next day. When I landed at Boston Logan it was shortly after 12 noon local time, the sky was dark with oncoming thunderclouds, and it was humid and hot. The A/C in the customs area seemed to be broken, and I carried my leather jacket draped over my guitar case in one hand, my duffel bag in the other.

Outside customs, Carynne was waiting for me. She ran and hugged me and I stood there a little awkwardly until she let me put the stuff on the floor so I could hug her back. Then she took a look at me and squeezed my biceps.

"Shit, did you join a gym in Spain?"

"No, I helped demolish and rebuild a stone courtyard," I said. "You don't like it?"

"I love it. Jeezus, I've never seen you so buff. I guess they fed you good over there, too."

"Chocolate and churros and red wine every day."

She hugged me again. "God, I'm glad you're back."

To everyone else in the terminal, we probably looked like a couple. I didn't care. "I didn't mean to be away so long."

She picked up my jacket, I picked up the guitar and bag, and we started walking to her car. "Did you have a good time at least? I mean, did you learn what you wanted to?"

I nodded. "I got adopted by some gypsies, and they taught me everything they knew."

She said nothing.

"No, really," I added.

Well, it was true.

Night and Day

Let me tell you what it's like to pick up a Fender Stratocaster for the first time in seven (or was it eight?) months. Onstage I had pretty much always split my time between the Ovation and the Strat. Switching between them had become second nature to me. But then I had spent most of the year in Spain, where I played the Ovation every day.

I couldn't believe how heavy the Strat felt. I had criss-crossed North America with it strapped to my body; how had I never noticed how heavy it was? A Stratocaster is solid wood. They say Les Paul made the very first electric guitar from a railroad tie. I believe it. Ovations have carbon fiber shells, as light and tough as scarab beetle wings.

(It always comes back to The Beatles.)

I had found the Strat's case sticking out from under the futon frame in my bedroom. I still wasn't used to the frame, which Courtney had bought for me and which lifted the futon off the floor by about ten inches. But I hadn't slept on it yet. Had I? No, wait, I did when I was here for Thanksgiving. Nine months ago. The frame wasn't new anymore, but it was new to *me*.

Court had also cleaned the room within an inch of its life, the CDs all on the actual shelf, the books likewise, the knick-knacks lined up like a small army. Cat Elvis was hanging from a shade pull. I wasn't sure, but I think she had repainted the walls, too. I honestly didn't own that much stuff, and previously there had been hardly any real furniture either.

Ziggy's notebook was in a niche in the shelving unit at the head of the bed, the one that had replaced the pile of milk crates. I didn't open it. I wondered if he wanted it back... then quickly slammed the door on that train of thought, which would lead to me obsessing over everything about what Ziggy might or might not want. That took real will power.

I almost weakened again when I opened the closet and sitting there was Ziggy's shoulder bag of clothes, the one that had ended up in my hands after the tour had been cut short. But then I slammed the door literally. I picked up the Strat's case and headed directly to the basement.

The basement rehearsal room hadn't changed much. The evil, lumpy shag carpet was finally gone, replaced with a utilitarian gray. This was where a lot of the milk crates had ended up, holding rolled up cords, microphones, random audio equipment, and a pair of Chris's ratty sneakers.

I sat down in a metal folding chair and put the Strat in my lap, thinking *Jeez, this fucker weighs a ton.* The strings felt sharp, like something from the guts of an infernal machine. I ran my fingertips over the paint job. It felt slick and smooth, then satiny in the spot where my sleeve had rubbed it a million times.

I plugged in, tuned, and warmed up. It took me a couple of minutes to rediscover my internal settings for the spacing of the strings, but then I was off and running. Letting my mind and fingers wander across songs I knew, or half-knew, or half-remembered.

After a while, that half-awake state that can only be jet lag took over. I decided I should unpack. I left the Strat in a stand, intending to come back to it relatively soon.

Upstairs, Courtney was lying in wait. She pounced with a simultaneous hug and expression of annoyance as soon as I emerged into the living room. "God! Finally!"

I hugged her back and did my best impression of our father. "Hey, kiddo, how's it hangin'?"

"Ugh! Don't tell me everyone in Spain talks like that." She hit me on the arm, which I deserved for yanking her chain like that. "Seriously. How was it?"

"Fantastic. I kind of ended up in a flamenco troupe."

"I saw the postcard. Carynne showed me." Court led me into the kitchen, where she popped the top off a Rolling Rock from the fridge. She handed it to me before I could ask her for it and opened a second one for herself. "So, what'd you bring me?"

"Help me unpack and you can see," I said, taking a pull. The clock said it was 4:30 in the afternoon. It felt later. Well, of course it did. My body was still five or six hours ahead. I focused on her clearly for the first time. She had cut her hair and colored it subtly, with deep auburn highlights. I realized then that she was wearing makeup, too. All in all, the effect was that she'd aged a couple of years since I last saw her. Ridiculous. "Um, nice hair."

Her eyebrow quirked. "You disapprove."

"Did I say that?"

"No, but you're thinking it."

"It looks good on you."

"But? I hear a 'but.'"

She could read my mind. Or my face, anyway. "But you gotta admit it's a little on the conservative side, don't you think? I mean, so far as my taste is concerned."

She swigged her beer, then belched loudly. "Yeah, I've become such a conformist to traditional womanhood."

"Um..."

"Don't worry, big brother. I'm not going to turn out like mom and our sisters. I had a meeting with my academic advisor today, though, and it's better not to freak them out." She smirked and ran a hand through her hair, fashion-model style, and I could see that underneath she had shaved the sides.

"Stealth punk?"

"That's the name of my next band," she joked. "Come on. Unpack."

We went up to my room, where I praised the redecorating job and sorted my clothes, most of which were technically clean, but Court declared they smelled too much like cigarette smoke and consigned them all to the laundry. I gave her some souvenirs I'd picked up in the airport: a folding fan and a tall hair comb she put on right away, exposing her stealth mohawk. I also had castanets for Christian, olive oil and saffron for Bart, and a leather-tooled purse for Carynne.

"What did you get for Ziggy?" she asked, looking through the assortment.

"Nothing. I was trying really hard not to think about him."

"Is *that* why you went there?" My sister: the direct one. I had forgotten she was like that.

"No. Well, maybe." I sat on the edge of the bed. "Have you seen him?"

"Only on television," she said, giving me a sad, appraising look.

Room at the Top

Christian came home a little while later, in jeans and work boots that were obviously covered in plaster dust. I was sitting in the living room at the time, reading through a stack of *TIME* magazines that were sitting there and feeling like I'd been not just in another country but on another planet.

"Hey," he said, looking a little startled to see me.

"Hey." I looked him up and down. "Helping someone renovate?"

"Um, yeah." The pseudo-guilty way he said it smacked me like an unexpected wave. He didn't want me to know he was doing construction work? He didn't think I'd approve? He was shy about it? Ashamed? He cleared his throat and spoke with forced casualness. "How was your trip?"

"Long." Now I was the one who felt guilt-ridden. Was it my fault Chris was acting so skittish again? Was I gone too long? What had I missed? "You, um. You okay?" I cringed inwardly. Wrong question, and wrong way to ask it.

"I'm fine," he huffed. "Be down in a bit." And he ran off to take a shower.

The phone rang. I picked it up and was glad it was Carynne. "So when do I find out everything that's been going on?" I asked.

"I just talked to Bart. He'll come over tonight. We'll get take-out and catch you up. Tell Chris when you see him."

"He just came in." I coughed nervously. "Um. Is he doing all right?"

"What do you mean?"

"Is he working construction again?"

"I don't know."

"I thought you said we were okay for money for a while."

She was quiet a moment, and my heart sank. "Let's talk about it tonight," she said.

"How soon is tonight?" I'd forgotten how anxiety made it feel like a rubber band was winding up tighter and tighter between my shoulders.

"I'll be over in like an hour. Just chill until then, okay?"

Sigh. "Okay."

I went back to the pile of magazines, wondering if Chris was going to dare poke his head out again.

Understand that when I was in Spain, bits of news did reach me. But since I couldn't read the newspaper and pretty much never even looked at a television except once in a while when it was on in one of the bars, and even then I couldn't understand what was being said, I had missed a lot of fairly drastic changes in the world. Communist Russia had fallen? The Cold War was over? Holy crap. I'd known about some of the little communist countries, but Russia? Nelson Mandela had been freed. East and West Germany were reuniting.

Oh. And we were going to war. Iraq had invaded Kuwait just a few days ago, and the US military was mobilizing to their defense. I turned on CNN and wallowed in war porn until Bart came in, turned it off, and asked, "Are you okay?"

"Um."

"Jet lag?"

"More like culture shock." I shook my head to clear it. "I was only gone for months, not years, but it feels like... I don't know."

Bart shrugged and sat down in the armchair across from me. "It's like the world woke up and said, holy shit, it's not the 1980s anymore, we better get with the program."

"And what is the program?"

"That remains to be seen." He shrugged. "So how was Spain? Are you, like, a flamenco master now?"

"Pretty much, I guess. The week before I left, the flamenco school where I was working asked if I'd start teaching classes."

He chuckled. "How did I know you'd end up doing something like that?"

"I'll show you some stuff later, if you want. So how's Michelle?"

"She's good. She's in New York this week. Which is just as well, since the contractors tore our kitchen out yesterday."

"Wait, does that mean you bought something?"

"Yeah. Beacon Street. A townhouse."

"The whole thing?"

"Yep." He looked a little sheepish in that way I knew meant Bart didn't like to show off that his family was made of money. "Terrace view of the river and everything. We took possession of the place right before the Fourth of July and had a big party up there even though we hadn't moved any furniture in yet."

"Wow." That meant I had been out of the country two July Fourths in a row. I started wondering if we were ever going to do one of those big summer tours again or if we were dead in the water. Part of me was saying that was some trivial shit to be obsessing over when we were dropping bombs on other countries, but part of me was freaking out over the possibility that everything we'd worked so hard to build with the band could be gone.

"Do you think there'll be a draft?" I asked, but he was already walking away from me.

Bart opened the front door and there was Carynne, coming up the front steps. I had been so deep in thought I hadn't heard her car.

I hadn't had Thai food in like a year, so we got it delivered, and I scalded my tongue on coconut milk and dried red chili pepper soup and packed my guts with tangy, starchy pad Thai noodles. Courtney came and ate with us. I was dreading the band meeting by then but also hypereager to finally find out everything I didn't know yet. Chris barely said a word while we were eating, and neither did I, but then again both our mouths were too full to talk.

When we were done, and the containers all in the fridge or the trash, Carynne started the meeting. "Okay. I'm going to try to bring you, Daron, up to speed, while also giving everyone some news I've been sitting on for a couple of days. So try not to interrupt me so we can get to it."

"Okay," I said.

"Let's see. The timeline on this. BNC declared the album unrecoupable near the end of the year."

"Actually, it was like August," I put in. Wasn't it? That day when Mills showed his true colors and I fired Digger in Los Angeles.

"Okay, August. We put the wheels in motion to audit their books. They stalled us until the end of the year."

"Meanwhile, though, you did the thing with the Christmas video and the sales of the Charles River inventory," I added.

"Yes. Yes, that's true, but *Daron you said you wouldn't interrupt me.*"

She gave me one of those if-looks-could-kill looks. I shut my mouth.

"Anyway. Audit happened. We found a few little things, but nothing on the level of outright fraud. Some numbers got moved from one column to the other, but nothing that changed the fact that the record just didn't sell anywhere near what it should have. In fact, when all was said and done, they moved fewer units than Charles River moved of *Prone to Relapse*."

"What?"

She glared at me.

"That was an interjection, not an interruption," I said, in my defense.

"I repeat," she said, "BNC sold fewer copies of *1989* than Charles River sold of *Prone to Relapse*. But they manufactured far more copies, and that's one piece of what's killing us. We've been through all that. Anyway, we're now at the point where we've each threatened the other with a lawsuit, neither of which have a ton of merit, but—"

"Wait, what's the basis of the suit?"

"Theirs or ours?"

"How about both?"

She made an exasperated noise and put her hands on the table. She tapped each finger, moving from her left pinky to her right pinky, as if she were playing a keyboard, as she enumerated each point. "Ours: they made internal decisions that we are paying for. Like they paid bonuses to executives based on high laydown but now are penalizing us for excessive inventory. And they incorrectly are charging us for tour-support costs that they promised to pay. Among other things. Theirs: well, for one, they'll sue to recoup the tour support they claim we owe. Which is bullshit, by the way, except maybe we can't prove it, because Digger's an ass."

"Can we make this a drinking game?" Bart asked. "I think meetings will be more fun if we have to drink every time someone says Digger's an ass."

"Be my guest. In fact, give me a beer." Carynne waved impatiently toward the six-pack of Sam Adams at Bart's feet. He opened one for her and put the rest on the coffee table.

"Okay," I said, since there seemed to be a pause in her story, "but neither of these lawsuits has actually happened yet?"

"No." She took a long swig of her beer. "The whole point of our threatening to sue them was to try to get them to negotiate. Well, I think I finally know what they want."

I bit my lips and waited for her to spell it out, whatever it was. Our fate.

"If we want to do another Moondog Three album, which we're technically bound by contract to do, they won't front a dime for it. But if we want to bankrupt ourselves to get them a product, well, then, they'll deign to put it on the shelves for us."

I couldn't stay quiet. "And they'll do such a great job, like they did with the last one? Fuck that."

Carynne was nodding. "Exactly. They'll let us take all the financial risk. Even making the record on the cheap? Tape alone is going to run ten thousand dollars, you know. We'll probably have to market it ourselves, too. We'll have to make our own videos. At fifty thousand minimum, each. Like I said, they'll let us bankrupt ourselves, and for what?"

Bart cut in. "Would they let us out of our contract after that?"

She sighed. "Technically they would have the *option* on one more record. Only an option, though, and if they decline to pick it up, that would be it. But," she held up her finger. "But there's a new twist. They've floated an idea I think you're going to hate, but I really wanted you to hear and discuss before throwing it out."

Bart and I looked at each other, then at Chris, then back at Carynne. "Okay, what's the idea?" I asked.

"Mills is talking about the possibility of... an image makeover for the band." She cringed a little as she said it, and I knew she was trying to make it sound better than it was. Carynne could never keep up bullshit for more than a few seconds, though. She gave it to us straight the second time. "He wants Ziggy as a solo artist. He wants to break him out as a pop singer and rename the band 'Ziggy and the Moondog Three.'"

There were so many reasons why I hated that idea that I couldn't even pick one of them to start with, so my mouth hung open for a few seconds.

Bart said, "And that helps us how?"

"Well, if you wanted to get out of working with BNC, this would be one way to do it without a lawsuit and without owing them any money," Carynne said.

Bart again said what I was thinking. "How would that get us out of working with BNC?"

"Ah. Because you wouldn't necessarily have to be 'the Moondog Three.' Mills wants to replace you with session musicians."

Chant No. 1 (I Don't Like This Pressure On)

There's a moment in one of Shakespeare's plays—maybe more than one, they blend together in my head—where a guy gets stabbed and then he has to comment on the fact that he's just taken a knife to the gut and what it feels like. I don't actually remember what he says, but it was one of those things that always struck me as ridiculous. The absolute last thing you can do when you've been stabbed in the gut is talk.

Or at least, when *I* feel like I've been stabbed in the gut, I can never say a word.

I had a large plastic cup in my hand (empty), and to express myself I flung it as hard as I could across the room. It hit the front door with a surprisingly, satisfyingly loud sound.

"I take it you're not thrilled with that idea."

I tried to ungrind my teeth enough to speak. I failed. Bart spoke up. "I think what Daron's trying to say is 'over my dead body.'"

I managed a nod and a croaked "Yeah."

Carynne took a deep breath. "Okay. Trial balloon went down like a lead zeppelin. But seriously, Daron, could you live with becoming, essentially, Ziggy's backing band?"

"Hang on, hang on." Bart held up his hands. "Are we talking about just for, like, marketing purposes? Is it all image? Or would this change the actual financial relationship?"

"We haven't talked about it in detail yet. But I think they're trying to keep all the contracts intact. You know, their suggestion of re-launching the band with a new image is the way BNC can get on board with supporting you again, which suggests to me that the whole point is they don't want to renegotiate on the back end."

I finally found my voice. "And you know what happens after that. Ziggy goes on to a solo career and the rest of us go home."

"You don't know that."

"Somebody want to tell me where the guys in Foreigner who weren't named Lou Gramm are now? When was the last time you heard from Stewart Copeland or Andy Summers since Sting went solo? Where are The Smiths now? The GoGos? Journey? 10,000 Maniacs—?"

I could have gone on, but Carynne cut me off with a gesture she learned from me: the conductor move that ends in a closed fist. "Worry about what happens down the road later. We need to concentrate on right now. Once the contract is up, if you four want to stay together, there won't be anything stopping you from signing with another company."

"Except there's no going back to just the band's name." Or original image. What category did they want to put us in, I wondered? "And do you really think Ziggy would let us take his name *off* the bill?"

She opened her mouth to argue but closed it again as she thought about it.

"There's no going back if we go this route."

"We don't have to make a decision now," she said.

"You just said we need to concentrate on right now!"

"Don't you fucking bite my head off, Daron Marks, just because you're upset things went to shit while you were gone!"

I blinked, as stunned as if she'd reached across the coffee table and slapped some sense into me. "Holy shit, I'm sorry. That wasn't what I meant. I mean, yeah, I'm upset, but I don't mean to take it out on you."

She looked equally stunned. "When did you get so good at apologies?"

"Trying to keep up bullshit is a lot harder, I've decided." Also, I had Jonathan to thank. He was a good role model when it came to honest apologies, quickly served. "Let's set the image question aside for a second. Can you bring me up to speed again on our financial situation?"

"If you're worried about Courtney, don't, that's all figured out."

"I'm more worried about Chris."

Chris jerked in his chair like I'd goosed him. "Who, me?"

"Yeah, you. Were you on a contracting job today just because you felt like getting out of the house?"

His face reddened. "I've got some debts."

"Drug debts?"

"Not directly, no, but you know. Car' says the mortgage is taken care of, but I don't have anything saved...." He rubbed his face. "Do we have to talk about this now?"

"No, of course not, but you know, if you need money—"

"I don't want charity."

"It's not charity if it's band earnings. The whole point of a fucking band is that the money we made is for us to live on."

"Yeah, but I've run through everything we earned on the road."

I glanced at Carynne.

"Most of what's in your bank account, Dar', is from songwriting. It's your publishing stuff and the session stuff, too," she said calmly. "And what Remo paid you."

"Wait. What did Remo pay me?"

"Duh, remember the tour of Japan and Australia? You were on the road for almost a month."

"Yeah, but..."

"Did you think he wasn't going to pay you for that?"

"Honestly, we never discussed it."

She made an exasperated noise. "Union scale is $180 a day on performance days, $90 on non-performance days, plus $30 per diem, which you almost never took. And he threw in some for promotional appearances."

"Oh." I had forgotten about the union, frankly. Remo had signed me up for one the first time I'd gone on the road with him, but I hadn't given it much thought since then. Carynne had been paying my dues, I guess. "So how much was it?"

"Five thousand, give or take."

"And you took fifteen percent, right?"

"Actually, I was waiting for you—"

"Carynne, you don't have to ask. Fifteen percent of everything I make is yours. Everything."

"Yeah, well, but I'm not as cavalier as you about it. Anyway. You're in good shape right now, is what I'm trying to say. Chris..." She looked at him. "Is it mostly just the IRS?"

He shrugged. "Yeah. But you know, I would've had the cash to pay them off if I hadn't put so much of it up my damn nose."

"Oh, so is this a kind of guilt-redemption thing?" I asked.

"Yeah, kinda." He cleared his throat. "By which I mean yeah, definitely."

"All right. All right. But don't lose a finger on a saw or something, for fuck's sake." I held up my fist and he bumped it. "I'm the last person to say you shouldn't take honest work."

Carynne was holding back a sly smile. "Weren't you working construction in Spain?"

"I helped build a flamenco school and a performance space, which I then gigged in two nights a week, if that's what you mean," I said. I realized from the way they were all looking at me that they were hoping I'd say more. "It's not that big a deal. I met this guy at Guitar Craft from Seville, he started teaching me flamenco, then he introduced me to his aunt, who was teaching classes in her living room, and we built her courtyard into a sixty-seat venue."

I shrugged, and they all sat back like they knew that meant I wasn't going to say anything more.

Carynne stretched. "Well, we should meet with Feinbaum. How about everybody sleep on the idea and we can talk about it again tomorrow."

"Anyone know where Ziggy is right now?" I asked.

Carynne stood. "Movie premiere is next week."

"In New York?"

"LA."

"Fuck."

"Why, were you thinking of crashing the party?"

"Quit reading my mind." I went and picked up the cup I had thrown earlier and tipped it into the trash. "All of you. Now, who wants to rehearse?"

Social Distortion

It was a little unfair for me to spring a rehearsal on Bart and Chris like that. I think I expected them to laugh off my suggestion and tell me to go jump in a lake. But either they really wanted to, or they felt that now that I was back... I was back in charge.

I'll say this: I felt like I was in charge.

Rehearsal consisted of us playing our way through a song and me saying something like "wow, it's been a year," repeat with next song. Despite that, we sounded pretty tight for not having played together in that long. I reminded myself that Chris was a much better drummer than he gave himself credit for. He really had a great touch, whether he was playing hard or soft. It's hard to explain.

I think we all felt better afterward. I sat down on a milk crate. "Tell me honestly. Do either of you imagine the three of us, five years from now, with some other lead singer?"

They both shook their heads. There were bands who tried. But it was like TV shows that changed lead actors. It just didn't work.

"Unless we cut down to just a trio," Bart said.

"No," I said automatically.

I didn't expect him to push back. "Why not, Daron? You sing perfectly well."

"But I'm not a singer."

"Neither are half the people in this industry."

"And that means I should do it?"

"It means you should seriously think about it. I've never understood your whole not-a-singer shtick. You've got a good voice, good pitch, and good expressiveness."

"Which, as far as I'm concerned, are the bare minimum requirements." I laid the Fender into its case.

"I'm just saying let's not be too rigid in our thinking. Whatever's going to come along next, we need to be open to it."

Chris had been silent through all this, so I asked, "What do you think?"

"I agree with Bart," he said.

Bart went one step further, though. "Maybe we should look at this like an opportunity. No one needs or wants anything from us musically right now. This is the best time to step outside our comfort zone and see what we can do, don't you think?"

"Do you have something in mind?" I asked.

"I inherited a cello while you were gone, and I've been teaching myself to play it. Chris and Colin have been doing stuff with keyboards and MIDI. What happens if we put all that together with whatever you want to bring to the table?"

I looked at Chris to get his opinion again.

"I've been hearing about this fucking cello for months. About time you brought it over."

Well, that settled it. "All right. And you're right. It's not like I have something else to do right now." Laundry? Redecorating? Yeah, right. I had nine months of the electronic music mailing list to catch up on reading, and not much else on the to-do list. "Tomorrow?"

Chris stood up. "I'll be home by late afternoon."

"I'll bring dinner," Bart said.

We went upstairs. Chris went to bed because he had to get up early. I should have been dead from jet lag around then, too, but I wasn't, so Bart and I sat around on the back porch talking for another hour or two. We didn't talk about the music industry and we didn't talk about Ziggy, but we talked about everything else. Spanish food, granite, the fall of the Soviet Union, recumbent bicycles (he had bought one), shoe repair, broccoli. Like I'd never been away.

"You and Michelle getting along all right?" I asked at one point.

"Man, it's weird being the one at home when she's the one on a business trip," he said. "I thought we had the whole non-monogamy thing down pat, but I discovered I was too creeped out to bring a girl home. Like, that just felt wrong."

I felt like that was maybe too much information, but what the hell, he's my best friend. "Why?"

"I guess because I feel like the house is this place that we've built for the two of us? Maybe?"

"But then how will you feel if she brings guys back there the next time we hit the road?"

"Shit, I don't know. I never used to mind one way or the other, but that was before we bought this place...." His hair had grown out again, and his shaggy curls partly covered his eyes. "I guess, yeah, it would bother me."

"Is that a sign that deep down it bothers you overall?" Listen to me, all talking about relationships and stuff.

"No, I don't think so. Part of me says I'm being stupid. I mean, if it doesn't bother me if she wants to get some when I'm not around, why should I care where they do it?"

"Maybe you just have to live there for a while. You're still in the honeymoon phase with the house itself."

"That's possible. I guess part of it, really, is that it's not about sex. It's about how much of your life you're going to share with somebody else." He sighed.

"Have you told her you feel this way?"

"Yeah. She thinks it's cute. Let me tell you, it feels like such a blessing to be this in love with her after all these years."

"How many is it, now?"

"Four. Going on five." Bart shrugged. Once upon a time, a girl lasting five months with him was considered long. "Over and over I feel like she's the absolute right one."

Which was cool. But got me thinking about Ziggy.

Was the only reason I fell so hard for him—both the first time, and each time since—because we had been spending so much time together, playing music and traveling together? Would it even work, would there even be an "it" to speak of, if we weren't in a band together?

Well, I'd just spent a year separated from him. Was I any less interested in him? No. Was I less obsessed? No. Was I less in love?

No.

But that only made contemplating breaking up the band even harder.

And it made contemplating seeing him again even worse.

Don't Want to Know If You Are Lonely

I slept three hours and then was wide awake in the morning, more because of jet lag than because I was worrying or something. I went back to the basement where the Mac was still set up and checked my email, working backwards from the most recent.

After a while I came across one with Jonathan's new phone number in it, wrote it into my notebook, and then went back to bed for a bit. When I woke up again, hungry this time, I called him while I was making toast.

"Hello?"

"Guess who's back?"

"Daron! I heard through the grapevine that you were in Spain."

"I was. Which grapevine?"

"Carynne, who else. Are you caught up on everything?"

"Not even remotely. When did you talk to her last?"

"A month or two ago? Why, what's happening on your end?"

"Hang on. Let me eat this piece of toast so I don't have to go into it all on an empty stomach. Tell me about you. I'm guessing from your phone number that you moved to Manhattan?"

"Yes, at least for a while. I'm subletting a place in Chelsea, friend of a friend's, rent controlled so it's ridiculously cheap compared to what it's worth."

"How long are you there?"

"At least a year before he comes back. I lucked out. Let's see. Oh, I finally finished a first draft of the novel!"

I nearly dropped the stick of butter. "What? Congratulations!"

"Yes, I know, it seemed like I was never going to finish it. After I moved back east I couldn't focus, was living in my parents' basement, and I thought, okay, you know what? It's now or never. If I take a job somewhere or I go back to the freelance grind, when am I ever going to have time to focus on this? This is why people go to writers' colonies. When was I ever going to be able to take a month or two off? To do nothing but write? I looked into a couple of programs and destinations, as well as the possibility of just going to a Motel 6 somewhere for five or six weeks. I got accepted to a place in Vermont and was there all of May and June. And, you know, you go to one of these places and there is literally nothing else to do but write."

"Wow. So you did it."

"I did it."

"So what did your agent think of it?"

"She looked it over and fast-tracked it straight to the editor at the publishing house who's been waiting for it."

"And what did he think of it?"

"I haven't heard from him yet. He's only had it a few weeks, though."

"So that's normal?"

"It often takes them a couple of months to get back to you. I can hardly blame them, though. I was so late getting it to them. Now they can take their sweet time."

I refrained from asking what he thought of it. If he hated it, he wouldn't want me picking at that soft spot, and if he liked it, well, he liked it. "Well, it's great that you got it done. In the end, I guess it was really a matter of time."

"Yeah. Also, I finally realized there was a character in it I had to change. Things just weren't clicking, weren't working, it wasn't making sense." He chuckled a little nervously. "The character based on you, actually."

I bit into the toast instead of answering. I had sort of known there were things in there based on me, us, but he'd never talked about them. I mean, to me it was as natural as breathing that my art would reflect the loves in my life—aren't most rock songs about either the people you wish you were with, were actually with, or were no longer with?—but Jonathan had been especially close-mouthed about it when you consider how much else he told me. So I had never pried.

"I guess finally having the relationship with you I had been wanting and then getting over you finally freed me to stop trying to turn that character into a version of you. Or something." He sighed. "Anyway, let's just say I really sympathize now with that urge to get away from it all."

"Yeah. So when did Ziggy reappear, anyway?"

"I'm not sure exactly when he came back. His first public appearance was maybe a month ago?"

When Carynne started trying to call me. I felt stupid all over again about the dead phone. "Carynne told me his mother passed away."

"Oh, I'm sorry to hear that. I take it you haven't been in touch?"

"I haven't. I've only been back for a couple of days, and I hear he's in LA anyway." I put the butter back in the fridge. "Okay, I'm fortified. Are you ready to hear the latest twists and turns in our BNC legal bullshit?"

"Absolutely."

"Off the record, of course," I said, just to be sure.

"Of course. I am freelancing again, though, by the way. I'm finally getting to do some more political work, actually."

"That's awesome. You've wanted that for a long time."

"And it's like all hell is breaking loose in the status quo politically! Mandela, end of the Cold War, fall of communism, war in the Gulf, it's like what the hell is going on? All of a sudden a lot more pages are being devoted to geopolitical stuff and less to the antics of poodlehair bands or what have you." He cleared his throat. "But I'm listening."

I went back to my room to give him a fairly detailed account of everything I knew about what the audit had turned up, the contract, and the Mills image makeover idea. Jonathan was one of the only people I knew who had a good grasp of the ins and outs of the industry and who knew enough of our band dynamics to be able to give some advice on the matter.

Of course, leave it to Jonathan to zero in immediately on my biggest deficiency. "You can't make any decisions without talking to Ziggy first."

By then I was lying on the bed, looking at the ceiling. "You know how sometimes I get terrified of fucking things up?"

"Yeah."

"Well, this is undoubtedly the most terrified I've ever been of fucking things up with someone. I mean, essentially, I'm afraid I'll find out it's already way too late. A year apart from him... J, it's been a year! You know how he is, a chameleon, what if he's not even the same person he was?"

"If he's not the guy you fell for, Daron, maybe that'd be a blessing in disguise. If he's changed that much, then maybe you can move on, too."

"Shit, I hadn't thought of it that way." I shivered as if the thought were making me cold. I rolled over, and the futon frame creaked under me. "I don't know which would be worse, he's changed, or he hasn't changed."

"Can you get his phone number? Maybe you should at least try to chat a little before you meet face to face."

I made a sound of dismay.

"Daron. Is this the real reason you went to Spain? To avoid him?"

"No! But I'd half-convinced myself he wasn't coming back by that point."

"But he did. And you did. Don't make it into a bigger deal than it is."

"Fuck."

"Or you'll make it into a self-fulfilling prophecy. You'll worry about messing it up so much that it'll be messed up from the start."

"That, right there, is the description of my entire history with him."

"Oh, D."

"It's true, isn't it?"

"What can I do to help?"

"You're already doing it. Listening and being a voice of reason." It suddenly hit me how fortunate I was that I could have such a good friend for an ex. "Which, by the way, thank you. I can't tell you how much I appreciate it that you're there for me, J."

"Of course," Jonathan said. I think he felt that people who hated or avoided each other after they broke up were vulgar and un-evolved.

"In other news, Bart learned to play the cello."

"Did he?"

"He says it's not that different from the stand-up bass, which he learned a long time ago, but the cello you can play sitting down. I don't see why that's an advantage, but then again I've been playing sitting down for months now and my shoulder's sore today from the strap of the Fender."

"You know Gary Hunter, from Geozilla? He was having shoulder pain from his bass being so heavy. Says he cured it with acupuncture, though."

"Really? Interesting."

"Yeah. You've got to take care of yourself, D. You're not a kid anymore."

"I'm only twenty-three. I'm sure I just have to get used to it again."

We were on the phone for another hour after that. I told him more about Spain and he told me more about the articles he'd been writing and some of the travel he'd done for research. It was kind of nice to know that even after going through a fairly dysfunctional relationship, a kinda wrenching breakup, and then many months without even speaking to each other.... we were still friends. In other words, we were actually friends, and not just guys who had been friendly because we were flirting.

In my mind I was dividing people into two types: those who didn't change if I didn't see them for a long time, and those who did. Bart and Jonathan and Carynne were definitely in the former group, while Chris was in the latter.

I feared Ziggy was, too.

Home Sweet Home

Of course, the other person I had yet to connect with, besides Ziggy, was Colin. When it comes to people who don't change if you don't see them for a while, I figured Colin would be one. And I was right about that, other than that he'd gone bleach blond. When he came in the front door that afternoon he startled me. Which was only fair, since I startled him just as much.

"Daron!" He jokingly put his hand on his heart as if he needed to recover from the scare. "When did you get home?"

"Couple of days ago. When did you get blond?"

"Eh, when tax season ended." He tugged at where a lock of it hung in his eye. "Huge mistake. It's breaking off all over the place now. Man, if I'd known you were here, I would've come back sooner."

"Come back from where?"

"Some girl you don't know and don't want to." He ducked into the kitchen and came out with a can of Coke. "What're you up to now?"

"Waiting for Chris to get home and telling you all about Spain—or so I'm betting, since you don't look like you're going anywhere."

He threw himself down into the armchair. "Sounds like a plan."

So I filled him in on the adventure, including the trip to Japan and a little about Australia, which he'd heard about from Bart. I wanted to go back to Japan at some point to see the actual country. Colin said I definitely should, and that I should bring him with me, even though I told him the story about Flip's tattoos freaking the locals at the bath house.

Colin filled me in on what he'd been doing, which lately was mostly nothing. After the forensic accounting stuff he'd done for us, helping out Bart's dad, tax time had rolled around, and he'd hooked on with a tax prep office for two months of absolute crunch work running up to the April 15th deadline—for which he'd been paid well. He'd been coasting ever since.

I had a sudden pang of panic remembering the subject of taxes, then remembered Carynne had already told me she'd filed an extension for me. I still wasn't clear on whether that meant she forged my signature, or if she even had the power to do that.

"You're staring at my head," he pointed out.

"Put on a hat or something, man, you're too pale as it is, and with bleach-white it's like you're a ghost, or a dandelion... or something."

He sniggered. "Dandelion?"

"You just look wrong."

"Well, I guess adding black on top of the already-bleached can't actually make it worse." He twisted the strand in front of his face and wrinkled his nose at it. "Give me a hand with it?"

"Sure." I followed him up to the second-floor bathroom, the same one where Ziggy had dyed his hair the previous spring.

I got out the box of latex gloves that lived under the sink, and Colin gave me one of those inquisitive eyebrows.

"You said give you a hand," I said. "I'll give you two, even." I pulled on a pair of gloves and pulled off my shirt.

He gave me a grin. "You been working out?"

"Working. I was moving a lot of heavy stones and things." I shrugged and looked him up and down. "You going to take yours off, too?"

"It's actually best to get stripped down to nothing." A hint of blush hit his cheeks when he said it.

"So Ziggy used to tell me. He also said it was better to get in the bathtub."

"The man spoke the truth," Colin said solemnly, as he began undoing his belt buckle. "I swear."

Pretty soon I had a naked Colin in the tub, a plastic garbage bag over his back and shoulders, and a squeeze bottle of dye in my hand. I held his hair in one hand and soaked it with the dye from the bottle in the other. When it was pretty well sopping I set the bottle aside, wrapped Colin's hair in paper towels, and clipped the bundles on top of his head.

"Ah, this shit burns," he remarked. "Thanks. Doing it solo always makes a mess."

"No problem." I realized I was casually appraising him. He was sitting in the bathtub with his legs bent, his arms resting on top of his knees, and his erection pointed at his chest. I think Colin liked having his hair touched.

Or maybe he just liked having me around. He cleared his throat. "So this lover you had in Spain, what was his name again?"

"Orlando."

"You were safe with him?" Colin gave me one of those looking-out-for-me looks.

"I should probably get tested, just on the theory that it's a good idea," I said. "But, you know. In the short term, it wouldn't matter as long as you and I were safe with each other."

There was a twinkle in his eye. I swear. An actual twinkle. "By the short term, do you mean today?"

"I mean before Chris gets home." Hey, look who learned to quit beating around the bush.

Colin turned on the water. "I'll get this shit out of my hair and be right in."

"All right. My room or yours?"

"Your bed still needs breaking in."

"True." I went to my bedroom and pulled back the covers. I stripped the rest of the way down and then crawled onto the bed, looking through the wall unit of shelves at the head of the bed where the milk crates had been. Everything that had been in those crates, Courtney had rearranged neatly into the cabinets and shelf modules. A few years' worth of *Guitar Player*, including the recent issues I hadn't seen. Demo cassettes. My old lyric notebooks. The clock radio.

I wondered if there were condoms somewhere in there. I looked into one small cabinet with a sliding door. Yep. A couple of "gold circle" were sitting there. I blushed a little, wondering if we'd get to using them or not.

I lounged under the top sheet then, paging through a magazine that had arrived while I was away.

Colin came in, still damp, and lay down next to me, mirroring my pose. "I didn't know if you'd still be interested in being physical with me," he said.

"Honestly, I didn't know if I would either," I said. "But I really can't think of a good reason not to be right at the moment."

"OK, good."

That was when I discovered just how loudly a brand-new futon frame can squeak.

Relax (Don't Do It)

I really hadn't expected to fall into bed so easily with Colin. Well, to be clear, I hadn't expected it at all. But I felt really good about it. Like mutual pleasure with someone I trusted and felt close to was something reasonable to expect, without the expectation itself creating anxiety.

I had a couple of little revelations though, thinking about it. The last time I'd had sex with Colin, that night in Cleveland, I'd been a complete emotional wreck. The contrast to how I felt now was so stark, even I grasped how much of a basket case I had been. By extension, I think I was starting to understand how much of a basket case Ziggy was when he wanted me but couldn't have me. Maybe I even had a hint of how much of a basket case Digger was while married to my mother. Not that

that excused anyone's bad behavior, but at least I felt like I understood something I didn't before.

I was still lying there feeling pleasantly sticky when I heard the doorbell ring.

"Oh shit, that's Bart," I said, jolted by suddenly remembering that we were due to rehearse. Was Chris home yet, I wondered?

"Come on, then." Colin shepherded me into the shower, brought me dry clothes while I was hurriedly rinsing off, and then got in himself while I combed my hair and pulled on the shirt and jeans he'd brought me.

I opened the bathroom door, ready to dash downstairs, only to run nearly headlong into Chris, who looked from damp me to the bathroom door. The sound of the shower still running was quite loud.

"Who's in there?"

"Colin."

Chris coughed lightly. "Oh. Um."

I tried to change the subject. "Was that Bart at the door?"

"Yeah. I'll, uh, meet you downstairs." He disappeared down the hall. *Whoosh.*

I felt a little dizzy and weak in that moment, like the shower water had been too hot, like the sex had taken it all out of me. But I knew it wasn't that. I knew it was something darker.

I leaned against the wall and took deep breaths. I wasn't going to let Chris being freaked out about me being gay freak *me* out about being gay. Or about having sex in my own damn house. I wasn't. *I wasn't.* I'd come too far for that. But I knew exactly how weird and icky Chris felt because of how I used to feel myself, and I felt a chill, like the ghost of that feeling passing right through me. And then I felt hot and cold, having quick flashbacks to Colin on top of me, and a throb in my gut because I wanted him to do that again.

That want, that *need*, that sudden craving, I knew why Chris equated it to drug addiction. Maybe he couldn't see it any other way, and that was why he was always going to be uncomfortable with it, even if he could get over the usual homophobic crap he'd grown up with?

I forced myself to move rather than analyze someone who wasn't even in front of me at that moment. I went downstairs barefoot to find Bart in the basement, sitting in a chair, tuning the cello. I put the shoulder strap on the Ovation. Given what Colin had just done to me, I figured I shouldn't sit down.

Chris appeared a moment later, carrying a beautifully tooled metal dumbek I didn't remember seeing before.

We both said "Sorry about that—" at the same time, and then laughed at ourselves.

For once, I recovered first. "I didn't mean that to come as such a surprise."

"Er, it wasn't, I mean, I kinda thought maybe last summer—" His blush went all the way down his neck. "This isn't coming out right."

"It's all right, Chris."

"No, it isn't," he said. He sat down and rested his arms on the dumbek as if it was a tiny table. "I mean, talk me through this one, will you? I'm fine with you being gay. I really am. I really *really* am. But this kind of threw me for a loop, and that's probably just... I don't know. Is it normal for gay guys to... to..." He flailed, waiting for me to pick up the explanation.

"Like I give a fuck what's normal?" I said. I know, I know: I used to give a fuck about that a lot, even though I knew "normal" was a lie.

"But Colin," Chris managed, with a grimace.

"Colin's had a crush on me forever. Where's the harm in it?"

Chris fished around for what was really bugging him. "But he's your housemate. Tenant, technically. Isn't that weird?"

"It'd bother you less if there was some total stranger in the shower?"

"That's not what I mean."

"Then what do you mean?" I don't think I was doing my best to convince him of how to get over it.

"I mean, who's off limits then? Or now that you accept your sexuality are you just a—" He cut himself off before he could call me something he would regret. He tried again. "I thought that's what bothered you about Ziggy. That he'd fuck anything that moves."

Oh. My cheeks got hot in spite of myself. "You're okay with me being gay but not me being a slut?"

"Well, yeah...?" He didn't sound too sure of himself, possibly because I was giving him a death-ray sort of look.

I closed my eyes for a second to turn off the death ray. "Me sleeping with Colin doesn't make me a slut. Honestly, Chris, think about that for a second."

"I know, I mean, I heard what you said, about Colin having a crush, and I wasn't exactly blind to it, even if I was wrapped up in my own shit when we were on the road, you know."

"But you've extrapolated that to, if I'll sleep with Colin, I'll sleep with anyone."

"No. Yes. I don't know."

Bart decided to cut in at that moment. "You've never had a problem with *me* sleeping with anyone I wanted to."

"Well, that's just it, though," Chris said. "You've slept with half the Eastern seaboard but not with, like, people we know. That's what makes it weird."

Bart thought about that for a second. "So you'd be okay with it if Daron was doing random groupies who happened to be male."

Chris's fingers tapped nervously along the edge of the drum head. "I guess. I mean, now that I think about it, I can see why you wouldn't. AIDS and all."

Bart shrugged. "Is that why, Dar'? I kinda think it's the whole thing about how you don't like strangers in the first place."

My cheeks got hotter. "What do you mean I don't like strangers?"

"Are you kidding me? You hate having to talk to anyone you don't know."

I tried to argue. I really did. "Don't be ridiculous. I do perfectly well at cocktail parties."

"But you hate it."

"Doesn't everyone?"

"No, D, in fact, some of us really like parties."

Oh. I thought about how Jonathan often seemed in his element in a crowd he didn't know, while I was happier sitting in a corner watching everyone, preferably with someone I knew on either side of me. "Okay, so talking to strangers is not my favorite thing."

"That's why Carynne never inflicts her boyfriends on you. The last one was the guy she brought to your birthday party who you never said a word to."

"What guy?" I literally couldn't remember a guy.

"That time we surprised you at the No Name?"

"Oh, wait, maybe I do remember she brought someone." I didn't remember his name, though, or what he looked like. "Was I supposed to say something to him? What was I supposed to say?"

"Never mind. That's not the point. The point is you don't like new people for anything, really, why would you like them for sex? Heck, you taught Colin about guitars instead of hiring a professional."

"Colin needed the money, and I didn't need one of those guys who thinks they're a race car pit mechanic just to keep track of three guitars."

Bart sighed. "Yes, I know, but that just proves my point. I don't think it's a gay thing. I think it's a Daron thing to stick with the people you know. For everything."

"Hey, I met a total stranger and went all the way to Spain and lived with him," I pointed out.

"Which only proves my point. Chris or I would have probably slept our way across half of Europe in the same amount of time." Bart shrugged; he wasn't boasting. "Anyway. I have no problem with you being fuck buddies with Colin. Or whatever you are. As usual, my only concern is how any of our interpersonal relationships affect band unity."

At that point, Chris got a little upset with Bart. "Oh, like you'd have the right to tell me not to get involved with someone?"

"No, no, I never said that—"

"Because if you thought Lacey was a mistake, you should say so."

"I didn't think Lacey was a mistake. I had no idea she was going to turn out to be bugfuck crazy!" Bart made an exasperated noise. "What I'm saying is I *don't* have the right to vet who anyone in the band sleeps with or otherwise gets involved with. None of us have that right. But when those relationships threaten the group, we have to speak up. Because we all have a vested interest in the group."

Chris seemed mollified. "Okay."

"So my only question for Daron is... is this thing with Colin going to turn into something else?"

"What do you mean, something else? We're not boyfriends, if that's what you mean."

"I mean, is it going to turn into something that will

freak Ziggy out."

"Ah. Ziggy's slept with Colin, too, you know," I pointed out.

Chris made a surprised noise. "When?"

"In New York."

Chris winced. "Colin always struck me as straight."

"I always struck you as straight, too," I said, then paused for a second. "Wait. That's what's really bothering you, isn't it? That you think I turned Colin gay or something."

"There used to be a steady stream of pussy in and out of his room, you know."

Bart snorted. "And there still is. Colin gets laid more than anyone else we know."

"True." Chris fidgeted uncomfortably on the stool. "Okay, but then is there, like, a competition between you and Ziggy for Colin's affections or something? Is that why you and he aren't getting along?"

"Me and Ziggy aren't getting along because Ziggy disappeared and hasn't spoken to me in a year," I pointed out. "Maybe when I finally talk to him everything will be just fine."

Bart grimaced. "When are you going to talk to him?"

"I don't know. I guess I have to talk to Feinbaum first."

"When are you doing that?"

"Tomorrow, supposedly. And then I'll try to call him, I guess. He's in LA this week for the movie premiere, so who knows if I'll be able to catch him."

We all pondered that for a few seconds. Bart said what I think we were all thinking: "It'd be better to talk to him in person."

"He can't just blow you off as easily that way," Chris added.

"I know, that's what I've been thinking, too," I said. "But I've got to figure out when. Where."

Another couple of beats of silence passed. Then I said, "Okay, so have we settled the issue of it being okay for me and Colin to have recreational sex when the mood strikes us?"

"Yeah," Chris said. "Yeah, I'll get used to it. Come on, now, let's play some music." He moved his chair closer to Bart's, angling toward him halfway.

Standing up was going to be awkward if they were both at a similar eye level. I somewhat reluctantly put a chair facing them both and then gingerly sat. Colin had been energetic, and I hadn't been on the receiving end since Japan, many moons ago.

I was a bit too obvious about my discomfort, I guess. Chris put his hand over his eyes, exclaiming, "Oh, for crying out loud!" Which made Bart and me crack up laughing.

When Bart could stop laughing long enough to get words out, he said, "Okay, so that was what was really bothering you all along, wasn't it?"

Chris was red in the face. "What?"

"It's the whole taking-it-up-the-ass thing that makes you uncomfortable."

"Well, shouldn't it? I mean, c'mon!"

Bart sighed and shook his head. "How can you even say that if you've never tried it? Michelle's got a strap-on—"

"*That* is officially too much information," I said. "I'm about as uncomfortable talking about you having anal sex as Chris is talking about me."

"Okay, see, but if we get it all out in the open we'll never have to discuss this topic again," Bart said. At which Chris and I both sniggered, knowing full well it never worked that way.

"For the record, that was the first time Colin and I went all the way," I said.

"*Can we stop talking about buttfucking!*" Chris roared and then put his face down on the drum head, his long, feathered hair hiding everything. "Oh my god," he moaned from under there.

Bart and I exchanged holding-in-laugh smiles. Later I would ask him if he thought we pushed Chris a little too far and he'd say no. Chris had talked to him a lot about the value of getting stuff out in the open and how hard he'd worked with his counselor to do it, and especially not to bottle stuff up inside with us, his bandmates. Bart had always been ridiculously frank about sex stuff, so that was easy for him. And I guess I was still trying to undo all the damage of years of silence and hiding on my own part.

I let the silence stretch out for a couple more seconds and then I started to play something. Bart watched my fingers and began to play along—well, actually, he began to play counter to me, but you know what I mean. Chris picked up his head, started tapping the drum with his fingertips at first, until I had established a rhythm, and then he started using his palms, too.

I had a lot of bits of songs and riffs and things that had been building up over the last year. So I had a lot of things to choose from when I decided what to play. But once we had jammed for a bit we started building it into a song, just like we always had before, discovering bits we liked and then gluing them together bit by bit. With no lyrics in mind and no specific goals, and only the riffs and melodies to guide us, we discovered some cool stuff, letting some really exciting sounds grow.

It was well after eleven when we finally quit, because we were getting hungry and needed a break. It was the quietest rehearsal we'd ever had, and we realized that with no amplification and only the hand drums our neighbors probably couldn't even hear it.

Bart convinced Chris to come with us to Chinatown for a bite to eat then, and we went to our regular place, which hadn't changed at all while I'd been gone, thank goodness, and I stuffed myself on greasy beef fat and chow fun noodles. It was almost like old times. Chris apologized for being, as he put it, "an ignoramus" about my "lifestyle," and he was so sincere about it I accepted it.

He really did calm down a lot after that night, though.

Public Image Limited

The meeting with Feinbaum was useless. Carynne and I went to his office for it. I had jokingly asked her if that meant I should wear something *without* any holes or something with. (Without.) The weather was stupidly hot, and inside his office it was refrigerator cold, suitable only for people wearing three-piece suits, I guess, which neither Carynne nor I were. Feinbaum had seemed rushed, like he didn't have time for us, and I was just as glad to get out of there quickly anyway.

We got in Carynne's car in the depths of a parking garage where it was slightly cooler than outside and I asked, "Do you get the feeling he didn't really want to talk to us?"

She shrugged and started the engine. "Maybe now that it seems like we're not about to try to sue the pants off BNC, he's not having as much fun."

"Or making as much money."

"Yeah." She took me into Cambridge so we could stop at the little guitar shop that carried all the strings I liked so I could restock. They were surly in there in that way that passed for friendly in New England, which is why I think I liked them.

She dropped me off at the house. As she was pulling into the driveway she said, "The premiere is on Thursday."

"What day is today?"

"Tuesday, D."

"Okay." I took a deep breath. "Can you get me a phone number for him? But I think I should wait until the weekend to call him."

"Oh?"

"Have a heart, Car'. This is his big moment. Let him have it without me nipping at his heels. And then I'll give him a day to recover."

"He's supposedly off drugs...."

"Drinking and drugs aren't the only things people need to rest up from," I said. "I'll try him Saturday or Sunday. That's assuming we get a number for him."

"Oh, speaking of numbers, Sarah Rogue called and left a new one for you. Here." She put the car in park and dug in her big purse for her address book. She copied a number onto a piece of paper and handed it to me.

I went into the house and didn't call Sarah right away. I set to restringing everything and adjusting the truss rod on the Ovation. Hitting Orlando's cousin in the face with it had knocked it out of true, so there was a slight buzzing in the strings. Colin came down and helped me restring, which was nice, since otherwise it's kind of tedious.

When I say I restrung everything, I mean six guitars. The Ovation, the backup that was just like it, the 12-string version, both Fenders, and the Yamaha we'd found in the junk room back when. The other guitars

I had sitting around I hadn't played in years now and didn't have plans to. So they could wait.

I played a couple of the classical guitar pieces I'd memorized forever ago, back in school, on the Yamaha. Something about going back in time like that seems helpful to me. It gets me grounded and gives me a kind of benchmark. I needed to file my nails. If they get too long, they break too easily, and then you're kind of up a creek until the broken one grows in.

Colin had painted his black.

We walked to the pho place and stuffed ourselves happily on beef brisket soup and rice noodles, and when we got back to the house I called Sarah.

I lay down on my bed to call her. Her machine picked up. "Hey Sarah, it's Daron."

She picked up the handset. "Heyyyyyy! The world traveler returns."

"Yep. How are things with you? Did you fire my dad yet?"

I'd said it as a joke, but her voice dropped immediately. "Oh, jeez, Daron, I need some advice about that."

"What kind of advice? Give him the boot. That's my advice."

"Seriously. This is the thing. My mother was all for getting rid of him. We were getting the paperwork together for me to move to a full-service talent agency. An agent there was all gung-ho, I really liked him, and then all of a sudden, poof, they turned me down."

"Was it Weiland Thomas?" I asked.

"Not him, but someone else at WTA, yeah," she said. "How did you know?"

"Digger used to work there. And I'm sure he has his grubby fingers in somebody's pie there. Blackmail? Someone owed him a favor? Who knows."

"Or maybe the rumor that I'm a lesbian scared them off."

"Is there such a rumor?" The back of my neck prickled.

"Not so far as I could tell, I mean, nothing in the press. And yet there was this sense... something the guy said to my mother made me think that was what was going on. He wouldn't come out and say it directly, because then we'd deny it. But you know how you can sometimes tell?"

"Yes." The prickling spread across my shoulders and I rolled over onto my side. "How much you want to bet it was Digger himself who spread the rumor to them?"

"But he's the one always going on about how I shouldn't ever let my image slip or people will whisper!"

"You told him?"

"No! But he's concerned that my image will slip within the industry..."

"Not to mention that your contact at your record company is a homophobic shit who would think nothing of eighty-sixing your career if he thinks you're a dyke," I added.

"Mills, you mean."

"Yeah."

She was quiet a second. I could hear a siren in the background. Ah, New York. "Daron, there's something I think you should know about Mills."

"What?" I was imagining she was going to tell me something about BNC, or that she'd heard him say he didn't believe in guitar-oriented rock anymore, or something.

"I think he's a closet case."

It took me a second to understand what she said. "What? I mean, I heard you, but... what makes you think that?"

"You told me yourself that your gaydar's broken."

"Even still!"

"He's the only man in this entire industry who doesn't flirt with me or outright try to get me to sleep with him."

"Maybe because he's your rep? Or because he's been there done that with some other acts and it's old hat to him now?"

"Are you seriously defending the guy?" She was almost yelling at me. Almost.

"No! But back up a second. That's a really big leap to make."

"You don't understand. Every man. Every. Man."

"Oh shit, are you telling me Digger came on to you?"

"Of course he did." I think I could hear her rolling her eyes at me. "Daron, wake up, this is what it's like for a woman in this business. They think if I'm a sex symbol that means it's okay for them to proposition me right and left. Every single one thinks maybe he'll be the one to get lucky."

"Is that why it's called getting lucky? Like luck is the deciding factor? Because a guy finally asked the right girl at the right time if she wants to fuck?" I was thinking out loud. "Um, now that I think about it, that's kind of how cruising works."

"Because when you're cruising you're looking to find someone else who's cruising too, right? This is what I'm telling you, though, straight men, at least in the business, are cruising for pussy *all the time.* At least all the time I'm around. It's like I walk into the building and all their dicks point at me like divining rods."

"That's... Sarah..."

"That's reality. It's okay, I'm used to it. Anyway. The thing that makes me think Mills is a closet case is that he's the only one who never gives me that vibe. And I used to think what you said, that it was because we had an actual business relationship and maybe he was too principled a dude for that. But then after what he did to you, after what he said..."

I was putting two and two together. "You mean, he's a homophobe because he hates himself."

"Bingo." She let a couple of beats go by before she asked me, "So when are we going to piss off him *and* Digger by going out together?"

"You haven't found someone for that yet? It was a year ago we talked about that, Sar'."

"Oh, I did. I was seen in the tabloids getting felt up by Ryan Rasner. But that's old news. And he was kind of a head case anyway."

"Like I'm not."

"No. You're not. Not in comparison. Plus you have talent. What are you doing this weekend?"

"Nothing."

"Come to New York. We'll catch a show or something. I'll see what guest lists I can get on. Come on. Now that you're back in the States you need to show your face." She let me think about it for a couple of seconds before she added, "Call Carynne. You'll find out she agrees with me."

"Okay, but did Carynne tell you what's happening with us and BNC?"

"No."

I opened my mouth to tell her and then realized I didn't want to be on the phone for another hour, which was what I knew would happen. "I'll tell you when I see you."

"When will that be?"

"Friday. I'll take the train. Should I pack rock star standard?"

"You mean like what you wore for house parties in LA? Yeah. Call me when you know what time your train gets in and I'll have my driver pick you up."

"Your driver?"

"I know, I know. But come on. Like I'm going to drive myself around New York Fucking City." She snorted. "See you in a couple of days. I'll alert the media."

"Wow. That's the first time I ever heard someone use that phrase in a non-sarcastic way."

"Oh, hey, and bring a guitar."

"I wouldn't leave home without one."

After that I called Carynne to check that it was really okay for me to go to the city and be seen gallivanting around with Sarah Rogue on my arm—or more likely me on her arm. That woman was like an Amazon once she put heels on.

Carynne agreed that I should go.

And she gave me a phone number. Ziggy's. In Los Angeles.

Put the Message in the Box

I lay there with the phone in my hand, imagining all the ways it could go if I threw caution to the wind and just called him.

Hey, Zig, it's me. I just wanted to know when you were going to come pick up your stuff. You know, the clothes and stuff you left with me when they carted you off to the loony bin that time...?

Yeah, no.

Hey, Zig, it's me. How was India? They got good chicken tikka masala there...?

Yeah, right.

Hey, Zig, it's me. I'm horny as fuck. What are you wearing?

Hah, no. No no no.

Hey, Zig. I hear The Man wants to put us between a rock and a hard place. Which one you gonna pick?

A sudden idea for a song grabbed me, and I spent the next two hours writing and playing around with it. The last thing I expected to write just then was a rock anthem, but that's what it was shaping up to be, about choosing between "rock" and a hard place. So yeah, it was another song that, underneath, was about me escaping New Jersey through music, though I didn't refer to myself specifically. You know how that goes.

Hey, Zig, I just wrote a song. You wanna hear it?

I went down and made myself a midnight snack. Peanut butter on toast. With honey.

Chris came down to the kitchen looking bleary-eyed and poured himself a glass of milk. He had on a big, brown terrycloth bathrobe, and his feet were bare.

We sat down together at the kitchen table. "Can't sleep?" I asked.

"Yeah. Dunno what it is."

"Stressed out?"

"Not really. I mean, I kinda want to know what's going to happen with the band, but that's nothing new."

I wasn't really digging for the answer, you know. I was just trying to be supportive. "You seen your old man lately?"

He jerked his head a little like that had stung or something. "Jeez. You go right for the jugular, don't you."

"I didn't mean—"

"No no, it's okay, I didn't mean in a bad way." He waved a hand at me. "I meant more like you hit the nail right on the head."

"It was sticking out," I said. "Wasn't it?"

"Does anybody get along with their father?" Chris asked. "Well, I guess Bart does, now that he's successful. Or was. Or, you know."

"I know." I did.

"I swear, there are days I think the only way I'm going to quit feeling like lightning bolts of rage are hitting me every time he opens his mouth is to just beat the shit out of him. But, you know," Chris said. "Violence isn't the answer."

I knew exactly how he felt. "But really," I added, "who's to say that would actually make that feeling go away? Or that it wouldn't be replaced with a worse one?"

"Or that I'd end up going to jail, which he sure as shit isn't worth going to jail over." Chris drained the glass and set it down empty. "I guess I thought maybe we'd get somewhere, what with me being cleaned up and all."

"You mean, you thought because you went to counseling and got your head together, that would make him less of a shit?"

"When you put it that way, it sounds stupid." Chris yawned. "But yeah. I thought, let's see if I am enlightened enough to repair this relationship."

"Both sides of a bridge have to be on solid ground for it to work."

"Yeah. Yeah, basically. I have my shit together, but that doesn't change the fact that he's the same shitbag he always was." He sighed. "I mean, maybe the real problem, I thought, is that now that I've been through rehab, it's just impossible to talk to him without seeing him as a chronic alcoholic. Like I can't see him as a real person until he admits that. But no. Even without my rehab goggles on, he's a shitbag. There are addicts who don't beat their wife. The bottle doesn't make you do that."

"He beats your mother?"

"They're separated, remember? He's living with this other woman now. She drops him off at the job site if he can't get a ride and it's ugly sometimes, I tell you."

"Ugly how?"

"He can't drive himself. Lost his license because of drunk driving. But you know. In his eyes the state took his manhood away, and so he resents her driving him even though she's doing him a huge favor. So he takes it out on her. Meanwhile the person he should be blaming for his problem is himself, because it's his own damn fault."

"Jeez, yeah. That's fucked up." I licked honey off my fingers. "Hey, so have you given any thought to what I said about me paying off the IRS for you?"

"I don't want you to do that."

"I think it'd be better if you didn't have to see your father on job sites every day," I said. "Have you thought about doing session gigs?"

He nodded, his hair flat and limp. "The problem is the number of gigs that could turn into a coke fest or a party."

"Here, too? I thought that was just LA."

"Here, too, Dar'." He shrugged. "Not every gig obviously, but I didn't want to risk it."

"What if we did them together? Sell ourselves as a package deal. Or you, me, and Bart."

"You mean, become the backing band that we're about to become for Ziggy anyway. But for anyone."

My blood ran a little cold at that. "Um. I hadn't thought of it that way, but..."

He stood up. "Thanks for looking out for me, Daron. But..." He trailed off, frowning.

"Yeah, I know, I don't like that thought either," I said. But we'd be a really good studio band. There wasn't as much call for it around here as in New York, but...

"We can think about it later," Chris said. "Let's keep our options open."

"I still think you should get away from your dad."

"I agree. I'll try to get transferred to another crew. Or pick up with another company. Goodnight."

"Goodnight." I watched him cross the living room and shuffle back up the stairs.

Hey, Zig, you're the only one without Daddy issues. Because you didn't have one. Um, forget I brought it up, okay?

Hey, Zig, I miss you. Do you miss me, too?

Metropolis

Have you ever had a connection to someone where it was like you had the same sense of humor so you didn't have to explain a lot to them, like you can get halfway through an explanation, or even give no explanation at all, and they just click with you? I'm doing a terrible job of explaining it because, well, I don't click with that many people. I mean, it's like music, sometimes you just go the same place without discussing it: it just happens.

Maybe I should give an example. The escalator at Penn Station was broken, and I was in a crush of people climbing up the steps to the main waiting area. I can be tough to pick out of a crowd because of my height... unless I have a gig bag on my back, which I did. Sarah picked me out of the throng at the same moment I picked her out of the people waiting. She threw open her arms like a movie starlet in some kind of 1950s Hollywood epic welcoming her soldier boy home from the front, and we stage-ran across the floor into each other's arms, quickly collapsing into ugly-snort kind of laughter.

She took a deep breath and deadpanned, "How was your trip?"

"The short one or the long one?"

"Both. Come on. The car's outside." She took off for the escalator to street level.

"Well, you've learned to walk like a New Yorker," I said, when I caught up. "The city treating you well?"

"Pretty well. I mean, it's weird though. Like everyone here knows who I am, but they want to act real cool, like it's no big deal I was in the top ten." She made a hair-fluffing motion on her otherwise spaghetti-straight hair. "If someone stops me for an autograph, it's always a tourist."

Her driver saw us coming, hopped out of the car, and opened the trunk. He tried to take the guitar, but I put my backpack into the trunk and then brought the guitar into the back seat with us. Too many bad things can happen to a guitar in the trunk of a car, especially in the soft gig bag I had it in.

"Daron, this is Ray," Sarah said. I shook Ray's hand. He was wearing a polo shirt and sunglasses and looked to be in his mid-thirties, his brown, cop-short hair starting to grow out on top.

In the back seat we picked up where we left off. "What's weird about that?" I asked.

"Weird about what?"

"About New Yorkers not asking for your autograph."

"Isn't that weird? I mean, it's like the more famous I get, the more disdainful they get."

"Is it disdain? Or is it just a total lack of fawning? New Yorkers couldn't give a fuck who you are, no matter who you are. I kind of like that."

"I guess it's just different from everywhere else," she said. "I mean, LA is a little like that, too, except not."

"LA is at the opposite end of the fawning scale. There, once people figure out you're 'somebody' they fall

all over themselves." I shook my head. "God, I really hated it there."

"I liked the weather."

"I'm not an outdoorsy person. I could give a fuck about the weather." A thought occurred to me then. "It's like New York is all one giant backstage party. Broadway's here; everywhere that isn't the stage is backstage."

"Except that's true in LA, too. Everyone either works in the business or could."

"Maybe it's just that New York and LA take totally different approaches to the strategy 'fake it till you make it.' New York is all about showing up and paying your dues. That's how you become a New Yorker. Everyone here came from somewhere else—or your parents did."

"You're from here, aren't you?"

"Yeah. I guess. New Jersey anyway, but as they say, the 'New York metro area.'" I hadn't thought about it before, but probably where I was born wasn't any farther from Manhattan than Simi Valley or Long Beach was from Hollywood, but people there still said they were from "Los Angeles."

"But you grew up here."

"Yeah."

"So you can show me all the cool places."

I chuckled. "I don't know about that. But if you want to go out clubbing I should call Tony and see if he can hook us up at Danceteria."

"Who's Tony?"

"One of our security detail on the last tour. He used to be a bouncer there and still has a lot of friends working there. Or at least he did last year."

"Cool, check this out, use the phone." She opened a compartment between the two front seats and pulled out a phone handset. We were in a town car that was limo-like without being an actual "stretch" limousine.

She handed me the handset, which had number buttons in the handle, and I dug my notebook out of the Velcro pocket on the gig bag and paged through looking for Tony's number. There it was. On the same page as an angsty scrap of junk lyrics about Ziggy. Sigh.

I called him and reached his mother, who gave me another number to try. I wrote that down and tried that number, and, with amazingly good luck, reached him.

"Antonio?"

"Who's this?" he said suspiciously.

I busted his chops a little. "Don't you talk to me like that. Your mother gave me this number. It's Daron Moondog."

"Daron! How you doing, man?"

"Not bad. I'm in town."

"Well, that is righteous. What can I do for you?"

"How do you know I'm not just calling to say hello?"

"Moondog, you are *not* the type to jaw on the phone. Am I right?"

"You're right. Okay, but it *is* nice to talk to you."

"Nice to talk to you, too."

"So, do you still have connections at Danceteria?"

"I do. You looking to party?"

"Yeah. You know Sarah Rogue?"

"I know the name. You want I can reserve you a little party nook. How many?"

"Her and me and...?" I looked at Sarah questioningly.

"Um, do we need an entourage?" she asked. "What am I saying, of course we do. Tell him three or four others and we'll see what we can do."

"I heard her," Tony said. "Tonight?"

"Tonight."

"Early or late?"

"Late. Um, she's going for maximum exposure." I wasn't sure how to explain that this was more than just a night on the town.

"Oh, I get you. Publicity impact."

"Exactly."

"Not a problem. I'll put the guys on alert for paparazzi. You know we can't let 'em in."

"That's fine."

"Crowd to get in should be good and thick by about ten, ten-thirty. Come then."

"You got it. Okay, last question. Can I hire you for the night, too?"

"You don't have to do that. This is a favor for you," Tony explained.

"I know. But anyway."

"As it so happens, I am free tonight. I'm booked tomorrow and through the weekend, though, so you know."

"Got it. See you tonight."

I figured out which button to press to cut the call off

and stuck the phone back in the arm rest.

Ray spoke up. "What was that about? Did you just hire a bodyguard?"

"Yeah. I figured you'd be more comfortable if we had someone official on the inside."

"Smart man. Sarah, where'd you find this guy?"

"The cover of *Billboard*. Don't start with me, Ray."

"Oh, sorry." He cleared his throat and went on in a Jeeves-like voice. "Will the lady and her gentleman caller be dining out tonight?"

"Yes, but drop us by the apartment so I can get changed."

I had only been vaguely paying attention to where we had been going, but I had the feeling we were on the Upper West Side. Ray dropped us off at a building where a uniformed doorman welcomed us in, and up we went in a small but fairly fast elevator.

Inside the apartment the entry hall was narrow and lined with bookshelves, floor to ceiling, all completely full.

"Do you read a lot?" I asked.

She laughed. "I'm subletting. The place came completely furnished, including books, knick-knacks, and shower curtain."

Said curtain was clear plastic except for a giant opaque silhouette of Albert Einstein's head. The place managed to be bohemian and upscale at the same time. I followed her into the somewhat more spacious living room, and a fluffy gray cat wandered out from behind the couch and rubbed against my leg. "Your cat or the apartment's?"

"Next door neighbor's, but I take care of him when he's away. He's a show promoter at Radio City Music Hall, but he goes to Puerto Rico three or four times a year for business."

"What was I saying about everywhere in New York is backstage?"

"Yeah yeah." She poured beer into mismatched glasses and handed me one. "So where should we have dinner?"

"Well, we could go down to the Indian restaurants on Sixth Street—"

"Did you say restaurants, plural?"

"Yeah, it's a whole block. I don't know why there are so many of them there, but there are. Then there's—"

"I have a lot to learn about this city," she said. "Will we be seen there?"

"No. Let's have an actual dinner without publicity. Tomorrow let's do something fancy-ish in midtown. Wherever the A-list are seen. That'll give them a night to come up with a table for us."

"Good plan."

While Sarah set the rest of the wheels in motion and did her makeup, I looked through the magazines on her coffee table. And finished drinking my beer while petting the cat.

We were in the elevator on the way down to the car when I said to Sarah, "Antonio knows I'm gay."

"I figured."

"How demonstrative should we be in public?"

"You mean like should you kiss me or something?" She seemed to be considering it seriously. "Don't take this the wrong way, Daron, but if you try to kiss me I will blacken your eye."

"Good. I'm not sure I could make it the slightest bit convincing."

"Your arm around my shoulder is a good look, though."

"As long as we're sitting down. When we're standing up you're too tall for that."

"Ugh, you're right. Maybe I should go change into flats—"

"It's fine, it's fine," I said. "Besides, you'll still be taller. What about hand-holding?"

"Holding hands is good, too. In fact..." She laced her fingers in mine. "Sometimes there are photographers hiding in the garbage cans of the building across the street."

So we exited her building, the doorman holding the door for us, with my fingers getting a little sweaty in hers but hopefully looking sufficiently smitten with each other. The doorman certainly gave me an approving nod behind her back. I wondered if Chris had gotten affirmations like that when he had dated Lacey. Undoubtedly.

Glamorous Life

So I learned a very important lesson about tequila.

The lesson was this: I remembered way more about what happened when I was on LSD than I did after two drinks of tequila. At least, I think it was two. Like I said: I don't remember.

Let me back up to what I do remember. We had Indian food downtown at a little place where a sitar player and a tabla player sat in the window and serenaded us all night while we were eating, and I kept getting sucked into listening to what they were doing instead of what Sarah was saying until they finally took a break, and then I told Sarah what I'd been learning about Indian music and about flamenco and the connections from there to jazz, and she told me about a jazz piano player who had taught her how to improvise ragtime. I was ready to say forget going out, let's go back to your apartment and play with the piano. But there'd be time for that later, I supposed.

Antonio met us at Danceteria, and yes, there were flashbulbs as we got out of the limo. I'm pretty sure we spent some time in the same exclusive area where Ziggy had glued himself to me while on Ecstasy. I think that was where the tequila was administered, because it all gets really hazy after that.

Dancing ensued. That much I know. I have a sense-memory of the sound system being much louder on my left, but maybe I only think that because my left ear rang louder later. Did I really forget to put my earplugs in?

Anyway, I don't remember much of Danceteria, but what was there to remember? Dancing, and then not dancing. It's too loud to talk, so the not-dancing part isn't going to be particularly memorable, anyway.

I know we left there and got back in our limo because later I saw photos of it. Sarah's handler had gotten a tip about a party going on at Limelight, and off we went.

Limelight is the place that used to be a church. We'd done a press conference here once, a long time ago, to announce the signing of Moondog Three to BNC. I told Sarah this and we went looking for the room that it had been in, but nothing looked the same to me. I think maybe the room where we'd had the presser was now done up like some kind of high-tech opium den.

We were holding hands while she led me through a bunch of tuffets with spaced-out people sitting on them, and somehow we ended up in a different area. Another exclusive sort of area.

I clued in that we had found the party when I saw a familiar face. "That's Jordan Travers, the producer," I said to Sarah.

"I know." She dragged me in his direction.

"Trav!" I shook his hand.

"Daron!" He gave me a half hug, patting me on the back. "What's this about you going to Spain to learn flamenco?"

"Who'd you hear that from?"

"Everybody." He shrugged. "I thought I was going to see you guys in the studio sooner rather than later."

"Yeah, well." I was sobered up enough at that point to wonder whether it was a good idea to tell him what was really going on. "Did you hear about the lawsuits and stuff?"

"Not very much," he admitted. He shrugged his skinny shoulders and rubbed his hand over his short-shorn hair. The hair on his head and in his goatee was the same length. "Just rumors."

Mine stood on end when he said what he said next, though.

"Speaking of rumors, what about the one that you guys are breaking up?"

"Who'd you hear that from?"

His expression was quizzical, and he spoke slowly, like he was trying to puzzle something out. "You guys have been silent for a while."

"Some bands take breaks after a big tour—"

"And everyone knows about Zig running off to India, and you running off to Europe."

"Yeah."

"That seems like odd behavior for a band that just hit it big if said band was going to be staying together and doing a follow-up. People gotta assume."

I had to agree that's what it looked like. "We're not splitting up intentionally," I insisted.

Trav's face was far too serious, I thought. "You'll be at the thing tomorrow?"

"Thing?"

"That isn't why you're in town?

"Trav, which thing are you talking about?"

"The screening of *Star Baby.*"

"In LA? Wasn't it yesterday?" God, I hate that feeling like poisoned ice water is creeping through my veins.

He cleared his throat. "Okay. I knew you were out of the loop, but I didn't know you were this far out of the loop."

"Zig and I haven't spoken since he left for rehab." *In an ambulance*, I didn't add.

Jordan's eyes scanned the room, I guess making sure of who was potentially listening. Like anyone could hear us over the pulsing music in the background? He leaned closer, talking into my ear, the way you do when you're both wearing earplugs. "They cut a B-side," he said.

"Who? A B-side to what?"

He gestured at me to follow him. He took a pack of cigarettes out of his leather jacket and tapped it like he was getting ready to take one out, but he led me into the men's room in the back.

It was dark in there, despite the jewel-like track lights, which were mostly aimed at the black walls. This was a small restroom, three stalls, and looked barely used that night, I guess because it was in the A-list party area. Celebrities don't actually piss or shit, you know, we just slowly decompose into fairy dust.

Anyway. In there the music was quieter and I could hear it when he said, "They're releasing that song you cut in New Orleans as a single. And they needed a B-side, so they grabbed Ziggy to cut vocals—"

"And stuck him with some backing musicians."

Jordan nodded, and put a hand on my arm, because I guess I must have looked or sounded really wounded by the thought.

That's because I was really wounded by the thought.

Call me weird. But I barely cared if Ziggy fucked everything that moved compared to how I felt at that moment, not merely entertaining the idea that he might perform with another band, but knowing that he'd already done it? I'll put it this way: It's one thing to realize your wife is flirting with other guys. It's something else entirely to come home and find a slimy condom in the middle of the bed.

It had been years since I felt the surge of rage I felt at that moment. Years. That time when I'd knocked Adan out cold? That had been cold-blooded. Even when I'd fired Digger I hadn't felt like this. Right now I had that burst of static in my ears that meant my blood was pumping so hard it was like my head was going to explode.

"Who else knows?" I managed to say.

"It's not in the press, if that's what you mean," he said. "It's just a B-side. Seriously, Daron."

"Mills wants to replace us."

"Don't jump to conclu—"

"Carynne told us that Mills asked her to ask us to bow out."

"You're fucking kidding me." The incredulity and anger in his voice was a balm to me. So fucking good to hear. Understand, Jordan Travers was a cool cucumber who rarely showed much emotion. If he smiled, that was the equivalent of cracking someone else up. If he gave a little nod of his head, you knew he really loved a track you had laid down. So to hear him express some outrage... I felt like at least I wasn't alone. At least I wasn't crazy.

He squeezed my arm where he had been holding it, and I realized that my hand was balled in a fist. And that my nails had cut crescent moons into my palm.

Awful thoughts come into a person's head when you feel like that. I knew that, so I tried very hard to ignore the voices telling me to hate everybody, to lash out at anybody. So it took me a while to try to come up with a way to ask Jordan the question I wanted to without it coming out like some kind of accusation. It did anyway. "I take it you were at the board?"

"Yeah. I produced it," he said, wincing a little because I think he knew that made him complicit in my betrayal. But I wasn't blaming him. I just wanted to know everything.

"If it's just a B-side, why you?" I know I sounded suspicious as hell. In the back of my mind, a fantasy of me, a shotgun, and Mills was playing like a movie. I've never touched a gun in my life, you know.

"I know it seems odd," he admitted, "but they called me in because I've worked with Ziggy before."

"For musical reasons?" My skepticism dripped so

hard it splashed on the floor.

He shook his head. "For personal reasons."

My eyebrows did the asking, then.

"He's been through a rough time, Daron," Trav said. "He's a little fragile right now. And they needed someone he trusted."

Way to put a knife through my heart, Trav.

"And nobody called me?"

"You were in Spain."

"Nobody called Carynne to find out if me and the band were available?"

"I don't know, D. I got the call from Patti, never even talked to Mills myself, I have no clue what's going on there."

"Patti... Marsh?"

"Marshfield."

Why was I even asking? Like the details mattered? I don't know. I couldn't help myself. "Mills told me that album sales failed because I'm gay."

Trav's eyes sort of flared then, and one of them started to twitch. "That is... fucking insane. Are you sure that's what he meant?"

"I'm sure. This wasn't some kind of insinuation thing. He told me flat out that it's my fault."

"Yours and not Ziggy's?"

I put my hands on my head. Apparently I was not in any shape for a counter-interrogation. I could answer, though, because that fucking conversation with Mills was burned into my brain. "He pulled out paparazzi photos of me and Jonathan and told me because people call AIDS the gay plague, the album didn't sell."

"These photos were in a magazine?"

"No. He paid to keep them out of the magazines."

"But then the public doesn't know..." Trav's eyebrows scrunched together while he tried to figure this one out.

"Exactly. Which means that the reason me being gay resulted in the album not selling has nothing to do with what the American public thinks and everything the fuck to do with what Mills the homophobic asshole thinks."

"Fuck," he agreed.

I leaned against the sink and put the heels of my hands in my eyes. *This isn't your fault*, I tried to tell myself, but in my mind I was going around again, thinking, if I had been here, if I hadn't been gone, could they have gotten away with just plopping Ziggy in a studio without even calling Carynne or me? If I had been around, I would have already talked to Ziggy. Maybe we would have split up of our own accord. Maybe. But maybe not. Maybe we would have worked everything out.

If I had been here. Dammit. Fuck.

"Who wrote it?" I heard myself asking.

"The track? Ziggy. If they had wanted a surefire hit they would have bought something else."

Was that a consolation? Just a B-side, just a B-side, I tried to tell myself. No big deal. That's why they didn't call. They just needed something quick and dirty. It's the movie, so it's him, not us.

But it was a Moondog Three single. Wasn't it? "Do you know the billing? Is it listed as an M3 track?"

"No idea. It was a one-day job. I figured it was just that you were out of the country."

"Am I making too big a deal of this?"

"Normally I'd say yes. But given everything else, no. You're getting screwed good and hard, man, and that's for an industry where asking you to bend over is standard operating procedure." He had lit a cigarette at some point when I wasn't paying attention, and now he blew smoke at the mirror with a frustrated twist to his lips. "I don't know what else to tell you. I normally try not to let big company politics get to me. But fuck, man, fuck."

My rage had ebbed down a bit. I no longer felt quite so much like if a baseball bat had been handy I might have smashed all the mirrors. "When is this opening?"

"Not an opening, just a screening. Tomorrow. Times Square. Some press and stuff and they're giving tickets away on the radio stations. You know anyone at Power 95? They've got hundreds to give away."

I didn't know anyone who worked at WPLJ, but I was willing to bet Jonathan did.

"Are you sure you want to be there?" Trav asked.

"Will Mills be there?"

"Probably. He's bucking to move up in BNC Media, into the Hollywood division."

"Hollywood division?"

"BNC merged with American Pictures, and probably within two or three months you'll see Columbia folded in, too."

"Columbia Records or Columbia Pictures?"

"They were already the same company," Jordan pointed out.

"Ah." So Mills wanted to move out of radio and records and up the corporate ladder that had grown a few more rungs. Interesting. Ugh.

Jordan tapped the pack of cigarettes again. This time he tapped until a joint came out. "You wanna?"

"Yes, please."

So I smoked a joint in the bathroom of Limelight with a Grammy-winning producer who, at that moment, felt like my best friend in the world.

She's So Unusual

I don't know if you noticed, because I certainly didn't at the time, but I came out to Trav in the course of that little conversation. It was only later that I realized it was no big deal to him. Maybe it's more important that for once it was no big deal to me. Or at least in comparison with the other stuff I was dealing with, you know?

Sarah wanted to know where we'd disappeared to when I found her again. She was a little drunk.

"Can I lean on you?"

"If you kick your heels off, maybe," I said.

She promptly came closer to my level and I put an arm around her. After smoking a joint I often get very quiet. Not that I am talkative in the first place, so maybe no one else notices the difference? But it meant I didn't feel at all hurried or like I had to say anything. I just held her close to me and she didn't seem to mind.

A little later she said, "Do you want to dance?"

"Didn't we do that already?"

"At the other place. I mean here."

"If you want to dance, I'll dance with you."

"I thought maybe you'd want to."

"Do you want to?"

"Now that I took my shoes off, no."

"Maybe we should go home."

"Hmm. You might be onto something there. I'll page the car."

She disengaged from me and went up on tiptoe to get the bartender's attention, and I guess borrowed the phone or something... I had stopped paying attention and went back into my own little world for a bit.

I waited until we were in the car to tell her what Jordan Travers had told me. It came out somewhat bare bones because I was still feeling the effects and wasn't talky, but she got the gist quickly.

Back at the apartment, I should not have been surprised to find out she knew Jonathan's number. Outside the tiny kitchen was a short piece of countertop and two stools. She sat me in one and used the phone hanging on the wall there.

"It's two in the morning," I said. "Maybe we shouldn't be—"

"Hey! Jonathan? It's Sarah. I have a favor to ask you."

I heard the tinny notes of his reply but couldn't make out the words.

"Can you get me and Daron on the guest list for the movie screening tomorrow? Yeah, he's here. Here."

She handed me the phone. "Hi," I said.

"I'm sure I can add plus two," he said, "but couldn't you guys just call Mills? And hi, by the way. I was just thinking about you."

"Um, I think we don't want Mills to know we're coming."

Jonathan made a skeptical noise. "He should at least know Sarah's going, though. In fact, I'm kind of surprised she's not already invited."

I said to Sarah, "Jonathan wants to know why you weren't already invited."

She sighed. "I probably was and I turned it down. I'm sure Digger said I should go and I said no. Which is why I don't want to call him and say I changed my mind."

"Okay, but if you show up with me, won't it be kind of obvious that you're giving him the finger by bringing me? I mean, he and I aren't even on speaking terms."

"You want me to fire him anyway. Maybe pissing him off is a good idea," Sarah answered.

"Point. But—"

Jonathan spoke. "Tomorrow I'll go pick up my press pass from the station and either get tickets for you or make sure you're on the list when I go down there. I'll come up to Sarah's place to meet you and we can go down to Times Square together? I have something for you, assuming you didn't see tonight's *Entertainment Tonight*?"

"Why would I watch *Entertainment Ton*— Oh. Is it about the movie premiere?"

"Yeah. I taped it. I thought you might want to see it."

I did and yet I didn't. "Thanks."

"I'll meet you guys around three? That okay?"

"That sounds great."

"But I really do think Sarah should alert BNC's publicity people that she'll be there. Maybe don't tell Mills directly, but publicity will want to know, I think."

"Okay, I'll tell her. See you tomorrow."

"Love you. Ciao," he said as he was about to hang up. Then said, rather awkwardly, "I mean, sorry, old habits die hard."

"It's okay, J. Love you, too. Just, not like *that*."

He laughed, still sounding sheepish. "Exactly. See you tomorrow." Then he hung up before he could say anything else embarrassing.

Sarah seemed to have heard everything, or at least guessed it. "He still have a thing for you?"

"Maybe? I was pretty sure we had a clean break. We're still friends, though."

She nodded knowingly, though I wasn't sure what it was she thought she knew. "I guess I'll let Belle know I want to go. Now that I think about it, I don't want Jonathan getting blacklisted because of this."

"Am I that toxic?"

"No, hell no. It's not like that. You wrote a number three *Billboard* hit, Daron. You deserve some respect from these people. But I know Mills is going to flip out when he sees you anyway."

"Number three, huh? Why didn't it go to number one?"

"Couldn't knock Phil Collins and Janet Jackson off," she said with a shrug. I finally noticed she was wearing a bathrobe. "You hungry?"

"Maybe a little."

She pulled a take-out menu from a folder taped to the wall next to the phone and waved it in front of me. "Chinese okay?"

"Yes, please."

"You like anything in particular?"

"I eat everything."

"Great. Everything coming up." She picked up the phone and ordered fried rice with everything, lo mein with everything, the everything appetizer platter, and a couple of other things.

She then handed me a wad of cash. "For when the delivery boy shows up."

"Okay."

"I'm getting in the bathtub. You should come talk to me, though."

"Um—"

"Seriously, Daron, you don't have to look. I'll pull the curtain."

"The one that's clear as a window except for the part with Einstein's face on it?"

"It'll steam up. Do girl parts freak you out?"

"What? No. I just... Making sure we know each other that well."

She snickered a little. "You can be as shy as you want. But I'm getting in the bathtub and I don't think you should be alone right now."

"Okay, sure. Wow, and I thought Carynne was bossy."

"I am not bossy. Just practical. Now get your ass in gear."

She led me to the bathroom, where an old claw-foot tub stood. She started the water, dribbled in some nice-smelling oil, and then got in the water and drew the curtain so that Albert Einstein was more or less between us. I sat on the toilet lid and caught her bathrobe when it came sailing over the rod.

"Okay, so tell me what you're thinking," she said, once she had shut the water off and it was quiet again.

"I spend at least ninety percent of my time thinking about Ziggy," I said.

"That sounds par for the course."

"I'm going to call him on Saturday. Or Sunday maybe."

"What are you going to say?"

"I don't know." Sounds of water splashing are supposed to be soothing, right? Maybe that's why I felt sort of calm right then. Or maybe I was just tired of being stressed out. "It kind of depends on what he says first."

"Except you're the one calling him."

"True. I guess I'm just going to say… hey, I'm back, thought you should know."

"That sounds like a perfectly good way to start."

"I suppose we're going to actually sit through the movie tomorrow."

Splish splash. "If we get up and leave in the middle it'll probably be noticed. Were you not planning to see his movie?"

"Honestly? I wasn't. Unless he wanted me to."

"Why wouldn't he want you to?"

Because he's Ziggy and he's not like a normal person, I thought, but didn't say. "He might have his reasons. I always figured I'd leave it up to him."

"You don't sound like you want to see it."

"I'm not particularly keen on seeing him fuck Jennifer Connolly."

"Wrong Jennifer."

"Her either."

"I think maybe you better tell me the story of you and Ziggy."

"Haven't I told you?"

"You've told me some of it, at least. Tell me again?"

"You're sure you want to hear this?"

"I'm sure."

"I'm sorry about this," I said. "I know you wanted to have a good time this weekend. Listening to my problems—"

"Daron, partying like a rock star is not the only way to have a good time. Now come on, before the food gets here or the water gets cold."

So I told Sarah the story of me and Ziggy, of meeting in the park, and trying to get Artie to sign us, and Watt getting us into college radio, and the opening gig for MNB. And I had gotten up to the part where Ziggy had his flipout in Los Angeles and ended up in my room when food arrived.

Show Me Your Soul

I told her the rest over lo mein. It was weird laying out the whole thing, the whole trajectory of me and Ziggy, and I told her so. "I've never spilled it all at once like that, from beginning to end."

"End? Is it over?"

"I sure as hell hope not," I heard myself say.

"You mean for the band or for a relationship with him?"

"Both." I flexed my fingers like I was trying to grab something out of the air, something I couldn't see or even touch. "Okay? I admit it."

We were at the coffee table with the containers spread out all over, sitting crosslegged on a braided rug. "Admit what?" she asked. "That you want him back?"

"Yeah, I guess."

"Daron. You don't spend ninety percent of your time thinking about somebody and not want them."

"Are you sure? Because I think that might just be obsession, not love."

"Okay, granted, but didn't you just tell me that you'd fallen in love with him all over again right before he went into rehab?"

"Yeah." I put down my chopsticks. I'd gone from the munchies to unable to swallow.

"And you didn't even get a chance to tell him?"

"No."

"And you haven't spoken to him since?"

"Well, when you put it that way…"

"Duh. Of course you're still in love with him."

"Or at least I'm in love with the person he was then. But he's probably not still the person he was then. I mean, fuck, I'm not even the person I was then."

"Except you pretty much are," she pointed out. She took a bite of a chicken finger. "Far as I can tell, anyway. Except possibly with even less bullshit."

"You think?"

"Yeah. You had enough food? Let's play the piano." She hopped up, wiping her greasy hands on her bathrobe. "Come on."

"I told you you were bossy."

So that's how Sarah and I stayed up all night playing music. She wrote a song called "Falling Star." I don't know if it was about me or Ziggy. I didn't ask.

When dawn was starting to break, she put a pillow and a couple of blankets on the couch for me, and then she went to bed. I got out of my jeans and thought about getting in the shower, but although I felt pretty grungy at that point I didn't want to get wet. I don't know. You know how it is with negative thoughts. They can sneak in at weird times. I wondered what would happen if I slipped and fell in her bathtub and hit my head.

Then I wondered what would happen if Sarah died in her sleep. Weird, right? Why would I even think about that? I told myself: she didn't drink that much. She didn't do any drugs as far as I know. This is crazy. Go to sleep.

But then I lay there having random dire thoughts. I had plenty of actual dire things to think about, like the imminent demise of my career and/or band and/or relationship with my singer, but instead I was thinking about slip-and-fall fatalities.

I put my head under the pillow, but then I was hot, and I ended up standing in the window of the apartment watching the sun rise.

"Hey."

I turned and saw Sarah standing there, her hair a tangle, a quilt wrapped around her shoulders.

"Can't sleep?"

I shook my head.

"Nightmares?"

"I'm not even getting that far," I said.

"Bring your pillow and stuff. Come sleep in my room."

I did what she said. She rearranged my blankets on the floor next to her bed. It was very dark in the room, the tiny window completely covered by a heavy curtain.

"I like to go to sleep with the radio on," she said.

"You know, I used to do that as a kid. I got out of the habit the last couple of years."

She hit a button on the clock radio by her bed. WNEW, the AOR station I'd listened to a lot as a kid, came on. A Pink Floyd song was playing.

I think I said "thank you" before I fell asleep. But I'm not sure. Because the next thing I remember is waking up in the morning.

I mean afternoon. It was almost two. Sarah was nowhere in sight. I emerged to find a note that said she was getting her hair done and there was cereal on the counter. I helped myself to a bowl of Lucky Charms with half and half because there didn't seem to be any milk.

I was emerging from the bathroom after a shower, with my jeans on but bare feet, when Jonathan arrived. Sarah had come back while I was in the shower, and I pulled a shirt over my head as she opened the door. I took a breath, determined not to turn this hello into something weird and awkward.

She gave Jonathan a hug.

So did I.

It worked. We grinned at each other, and we really meant it when we said it was good to see each other.

He'd lightened his hair a little, which I know sounds funny because he's already blond, but there you go.

He handed me the videotape, which Sarah snatched and pranced with to the television somewhat gleefully. All right. I supposed we were about to see a piece of either ridiculously fluffed hype or ridiculously hyped fluff. I was prepared for the usual red carpet bullshit about what dresses the women were wearing.

Jonathan's mouth was in a tight line, though, as Sarah put the tape in and searched for the remote to turn on the TV, and he caught my eye just before the picture came on. I wondered if he felt sorry for me somehow.

The anchors were blathering like always, and then came the footage from the red carpet. Jennifer Carstens stepped out of the limo. She was wearing black high heels that really looked like they could be used as murder weapons, and the anchors were blathering on about her outfit. When she stood up it looked rather like a dress, but with a top that looked like it had the black satin collar and lapels of a tuxedo jacket, while her back was completely bare. When she walked, though, you could see that the "skirt" part was actually pants. One of the anchors used the term "prom culottes." Her hair was short, what they called a "pixie cut," very different from how I'd usually seen her.

"You might almost say she's going for a kind of gender-bending look," one of the commentators said. "Very stylish and smart. I give her an A for execution."

"Well, if you think that was gender-bending, take a look at what her co-star wore."

The footage came from a shakier camera, as someone hastily noticed that someone was else was emerging from the still-open limo door. One foot came first, another stiletto heel, but this one at the end of a tapered leg in fishnet stockings.

A Hollywood starlet from the 1940s emerged, black pencil skirt, mink stole, pillbox hat and veil.

"Barbara Stanwyck?" Sarah asked.

"Ziggy," I said. Whispered, really, because my throat had tightened up.

"Seems to be some kind of homage to Faye Dunaway in *Chinatown*," said one of the commentators. "Perhaps we'll understand the outfit and its statement better after we see the film."

As the footage of Ziggy walking slowly up the red carpet, clutching the mink around his shoulders, continued, the prattle also continued. "Carstens' co-star declined to speak to sideline reporters."

Then it showed the commentators in the studio again. The male one said, "Well, I'm often baffled by fashion, but that was an especially baffling choice."

"You idiot," I said, my voice somewhat louder. In fact, I shouted. "Isn't it obvious? Leave him the fuck alone! He's in fucking mourning!"

Hello I Love You

"Where is the phone?" I asked, like I didn't know it was on the wall by the door to the kitchen. "Where is the phone?"

Sarah knew what I was actually trying to come up with. "Why don't you use the extension in my room," she said. "It's by the bed."

Jonathan gave me a little encouraging nod. He knew what I was thinking.

I'm grateful to them for both being right there with my need for privacy. I pulled my notebook out of the guitar case and went into Sarah's dark, quiet bedroom.

I sat on the edge of the bed and picked up the phone on the night table. It took me a moment to find the page where I'd written the number. I noted the area code and the exchange. Had to be someplace close to where Jonathan and I had lived.

I listened to the out-of-tune buzz of the dial tone for a few seconds, working up my nerve while simultaneously beating myself up for everything. Everything.

I know. Not the best frame of mind for me. And exactly how I got myself gutted and shredded in the past, right? By making myself totally, irresponsibly vulnerable.

I dialed. It rang.

And rang.

And rang.

If I had been having dire thoughts about slip-and-fall accidents the night before, well, just imagine how dire my imagination was getting now.

An answering machine finally picked up, with a generic robot-like voice saying, "Please leave a message."

I froze. I should have just hung up. But what if he was there? What if he was screening? But likewise, what if someone else was listening? I didn't even know if it was Ziggy's own place or if he was crashing on Digger's couch or what. I had no idea.

A few seconds had gone by after the beep, and I settled for an almost voiceless, "Hey. It's me."

A few more seconds of silence passed and then the machine hung up on me.

I hate the dial tone. Hate it. I would have thrown the phone across the room except I had no strength left in me. I could barely muster the strength to hang up the phone.

I guess I sat there without moving for so long that Jonathan came to check on me. He peeked through the door, which I had left open, and then came and sat next to me, tentatively putting a hand on my shoulder.

"What happened?" he asked, which I think was his way of asking why my cheeks were all wet.

"Nothing," I said. "Not home. Or not answering."

"Oh, D."

I let him hug me then even though that squeezed a lot more tears loose. I can't tell you how much I hate being a basket case like that.

"If you're this upset and you haven't even talked to him yet," J said, "you must really be twisted up inside."

It took me two tries at clearing my throat before I could speak. "Have you ever known me not to be?"

He didn't answer other than to rub my back with

the palm of his hand. Remind me I still owe him that medal that says "Supportive Ex" on it, will you?

Jonathan checked his watch. "We could wait a half hour and try again," he suggested.

"Or we could go see the damn movie and I'll try him after that and then I can say I saw it," I said, kind of in a rush.

"That sounds like a plan."

"Yeah."

"You going to be okay?"

"I could use a drink." My head lifted. I heard how that sounded. It didn't sound good. "Of water," I added.

"Good plan," Jonathan said, standing up and then helping me up, too. "Good plan."

Ultra Vivid Scene

So the free screening of the film was at a movie theater in Times Square. For those of you who have never seen a movie in New York City, it's a little bit like going to a gospel church, where people yell at the preacher when the spirit moves them. If you're used to the kind of mass where everyone sits quietly, it can be kind of startling at first. In New England, not only do people not yell at the screen, they sometimes don't even laugh out loud at the funny parts. In NYC, there's no such problem. If anything, there's too much laughing at inappropriate moments.

This is why going to see a movie in the city is fun. If you're not in love with the person being laughed at, anyway.

I'm getting ahead of myself again, though.

Sarah's driver dropped us off a block or two away from the theater, and we walked. There was a pretty big crowd outside under the marquee, and they had gigantic blowups of the movie poster flapping on the exterior walls like tapestries. There were three versions. One had the two of them in a romantic mutual hand-clutch, framed as if they were standing on top of a giant spotlight pointed upward. The other two had the same spotlight effect, but one was Jennifer Carstens standing alone, a wireless mic raised in one fist, and the other was Ziggy alone, no mic, just both arms outstretched, palms upward, face upward, so you couldn't really even see his face.

The way it had worked out was that Jonathan had gotten tickets for Sarah and me, so our names weren't on a guest list—yet. He used his press pass to get inside to see if he could pull us out of the crowd.

Sarah and I were game to stand in line, actually. I mean, why not? Well, other than the fact I was kind of a wreck, but you know, I can put on a normal face when I need to. In fact, being there among happy people who had no big emotional stakes would probably be good for me, you know? We got in line, and at first no one around us realized who we were. We can both be pretty unassuming. We were wearing sunglasses, and Sarah was not overly dressed up or anything.

And New Yorkers being New Yorkers, when they started to recognize us, it was mostly with little nods of recognition. A couple of people craned their necks as Mark Goodman and one of the other MTV veejays got out of a car and headed to the door, shaking hands and giving high fives as they went.

But there was a palpable shift as people realized we were staying put in line and not going inside. A guy in a polo shirt who looked like he was playing hooky from his office finally turned around and said, "Everyone's kinda looking at you because you look like Daron Moondog."

"That's because I am," I said.

"No shit! Well, let me shake your hand."

I shook his hand.

"What are you doing here?" he asked.

"Just here to see a movie," I answered, which got a laugh from the people around us.

See, I told myself, *everything's fine, you shouldn't worry so much, it's just a movie, and later you'll call Ziggy and have a big laugh about the whole thing.*

That was when the girl ran up to us, put her hands over her mouth so she wouldn't scream when she saw me, and burst into tears. She had done herself up sort of like Ziggy's Statue of Liberty look from last year. She swayed like she was about to faint.

I caught one of her arms, and Mr. Polo Shirt caught

the other. "Oh my god oh my god I was outside the hotel that time you almost got arrested and I love you so much it's been so hard when you were gone I didn't know what to do," she said to me. And then she passed out.

We couldn't really hold her up, and people started waving for security while we lowered her gently to the sidewalk. I crouched down next to her while Sarah fanned the girl's face.

Next thing I knew, a big man was elbowing people aside and kneeling down next to me.

I did a double-take. It was Antonio. "Was this the job you had to do?" I blurted out.

"Yeah," he said, holding the girl's hand. She was blinking now. "Um, yeah. What the hell are you doing out here?"

"Waiting for the mov—"

"Come the hell inside," he said, and helped the girl to her feet. The crowd parted for us, and he guided her slowly inside, while Sarah and I followed.

In the lobby there were various industry types milling around, but I was kind of focused on making sure the girl was okay. Tony gave her a sip of ice water from a soft drink cup, and she took a couple of deep breaths and said, "Oh my god, sorry about that. I've never had that happen before." I couldn't make out her natural hair color or skin color, but she had a Puerto Rican lilt mixed in with her Long Island accent.

"It's okay," I said, "if you're okay."

"I'm fine now, thank you." She took another deep breath. "You are so nice. I mean, I knew you were, I was there outside the hotel. That time? When you were letting girls come in a few at a time when you were eating?"

"At the Penta."

"Yeah. I was there when you almost got arrested, too."

Antonio gave me a *look*, remembering that. I guess I didn't exactly make his job easy.

The girl went on. "It's just that I didn't think you were going to be here. I mean, I kind of hoped you would? But I thought it would take a miracle." Her voice dropped to a stage whisper. "I prayed for it to happen. I've never had a prayer answered before! So it was a total shock!"

I prayed for as ecstatic a reaction from Ziggy the next time he laid eyes on me. "Well, we should take some pictures or something," I said. "You've got a camera?"

"Of course, of course!" She pulled her camera out of her bag, and Antonio took some pictures of her and me, and also of her and me and Sarah.

Then he escorted her out, and she happily went, blowing me a goodbye kiss as she did.

"Wow, you're so calm with them," Sarah said. "Fans, I mean."

"Shouldn't I be?" I watched Antonio cross the lobby again, then, and disappear through the double doors into the auditorium.

"I guess I get more affected when a girl screams and faints in front of me," Sarah said. "I get all jittery, too, like it's catching, like I want to jump up and down and scream, too."

"You look cool as a cucumber."

"But inside I'm spazzing out." She hooked an arm into mine.

"You'll probably get used to it," I said, "when you tour. Speaking of which, why aren't you on the road? Number three Top 40 hit, and it's summer..."

"I'm doing a bunch of festivals here and there. Come over here, they've got swag." She steered me toward the scattered industry schmoozers at the other end of the lobby. "They're not sure I've got the stamina to do night after night."

"Seriously?"

"Yeah."

"Well, given what went on with Ziggy's vocal cords, I can't say that I blame them for being careful."

A young PR assistant of some kind, wearing an extra-large promo T-shirt over her regular clothes and tied in a knot at one hip, handed us T-shirts from behind the table where she was sorting them into piles. Sarah and I disengaged elbows to look at them. On the back was the logo of the radio station, while the front seemed to be the movie posters. She had the one with the Ziggy image on the front, mine had Carstens.

Sarah swapped them, twitching the one out of my hands and giving me hers. I rolled the shirt up small and put it in my back pocket just as Mills came through the doors from the actual theater into the lobby.

I will confess it was kind of satisfying to see him stop in his tracks for a second when he saw me. He was goosed, and the thought that went through my head was *you can't get rid of me that easily.* Then Sarah waved to him and sauntered over in a really jaunty-but-sexy way. He smiled and kissed her on the cheek, plastering a fake smile on his face. Or at least it looked fake to me.

Then he spoke to another guy, maybe mid-thirties, also wearing the promo T-shirt in too large a size over his button-down shirt, which, let me tell you, was not a good look. I guessed he was the PR director for the station. He cleared his throat and made an announcement to the scattered group. "We're letting the crowd in starting in two minutes, so get your swag if you want it and sit anywhere inside that you like."

We went in and found Jonathan and what had to be a bunch of other writers and press people sitting in the first couple of rows. They were each holding a press packet, and I guessed they had been having a sort of press conference in here while the rest of us milled around outside.

Sarah plopped down next to Jonathan and began to regale him with the tale of the fainting fan. I gave him a little wave as if I were going to hit the men's room or something and he gave me a little nod back while listening intently to Sarah.

I didn't want to sit in the front. I wanted to sit somewhere I could slip out without anyone noticing.

I went up to the second level, where there was a large upper-level balcony, but I was searching for a way to get to the ornamental opera boxes. That is, I was hoping that they weren't merely ornamental.

There was a rough door that had a latch on it like a closet door would, with a hasp and a padlock, but the padlock was open and hanging from it. I figured that either it had to be a supply closet or else it went where I wanted to go.

I pulled it open and heard a gasp.

I took in a lot of things with my eyes at that moment. The bruise purple of Ziggy's lipstick. His wide-eyed what-the-fuck-are-you-doing-here look. The stylish, well-cut suit of the man with him. Ziggy's hand down that man's pants.

I panicked. *I can't do this.* I don't know if I said it or if I only thought it, but there was too much, too much to think about, too much to remember, too much to handle, and I panicked, shut down, and fled.

This Is How It Feels

You know how in cartoons they often depict someone having an internal debate by putting an angel on one shoulder and a devil on the other? And the little angel and devil each put forth their arguments?

I didn't have an angel and a devil on my shoulders. I had two pathetic, ineffectual weak versions of myself. One of them was saying the following: *what the hell is wrong with you? you've got people who love you downstairs, you're strong, you're over that shit, you're talented, you're good-looking, people like you, you wrote a hit song, girls faint when they see you, hot men would line up for you if you let them...*

The other one was saying *oh shit oh shit fuck fuck fuck fuck fuck fuck fuck fuck.*

What the fuck is wrong with me, indeed.

You shouldn't have been surprised by that, voice one said.

But I was! voice two insisted.

I went into the men's room because I didn't have enough brain power to think of anything else. I could hear the sound of the crowd starting to take their seats. I locked myself in a stall.

I wasn't crying. I was kind of hyperventilating.

Voice one: *There's got to be a rational explanation, don't jump to conclusions.*

Voice two: *fuck fuck fuck fuck shit shit shit.*

You remember how thrown for a loop I was that time I lashed out and hurt my thumb? There's a reason they call it "losing it." It's not just losing control, it's losing your mind. And what I felt like right then was like I was losing my mind. Like every other time I'd lost it was happening to me again simultaneously.

No wonder I was afraid to talk to him. No wonder I'd been so chickenshit about calling him. I felt like I was having a heart attack or a seizure or something. It was like after having kicked the Ziggy habit, my resistance was at an all-time low and a single look was an overdose.

Voice number one wouldn't give up, though. *Are you sure that was him and not some fan impersonating him? They do that, you know. Are you sure you didn't just imagine it? Why the fuck would he be here, for this? He was in Los Angeles yesterday.*

But that was yesterday. *He could have taken a red-eye.*

The thought struck me then that if Ziggy was here, Digger was probably lurking around, too.

Shit. That straightened me right up. Like hell was I going to let Digger see me like this.

Like hell.

I could hear applause, and I could make out the baritone squawk of the PA system. Someone was making some kind of introduction in the auditorium.

I splashed a little water on my face but, like I said before, I wasn't crying. I dried my face and then slipped into the back of the main balcony.

Down on the stage they were introducing the director of the film. He was in a stylishly cut suit as he waved to the crowd. Was that him? The one? In my mind I could definitely picture him in my memory, but I felt like maybe I'd gotten too quick a glimpse to be sure. I might have been retroactively adding him in. But it would make sense, given Ziggy's m.o. of using sex to control whoever held the creative strings.

The director was one of those guys who didn't really know how to hold a microphone and who kept turning his head away from it so that some of his words were lost. He said a couple of things about why he wanted to make the film. Then he said he had a special surprise for everyone.

He introduced Ziggy with a wave of his hand toward the balcony I'd been trying to get to.

Ziggy stepped out of the shadows and waved. There was a swell of cheers from down below, and he threw some T-shirts, but up here in the balcony the crowd seemed to be mostly guys in their late teens and twenties whose "yeah"s were kind of derisive. Maybe I was being oversensitive. I supposed these were the guys who were there to see Jennifer Carstens's tits and they were only grudgingly acknowledging the guy who actually saw them in person.

I doubt they were put off by Ziggy's outfit, like the *ET* guy had been. This one was quite a bit more butch; though he did have on black lace gloves, the rest was a long-cut tuxedo jacket with black satin lapels. When he ran out of T-shirts, he sat down with as much dignity as he could muster.

The lights went down, plunging him into shadow as the film started.

He was hurting, that much was clear to me. *Maybe you're seeing what you want to see*, I told myself. No. I knew him too well. This was the last place he wanted to be.

I didn't last ten minutes into the film. The audience was not swayed by the angst evident in the first couple of scenes. Some of them were there because they were Ziggy fans, some were there because they wanted to see Carstens's tits, and some were there because what the hell, they had won free tickets. The upper balcony wasn't even full.

I wondered if that boded ill for the success of the movie. I had no way to know.

I went back to the men's room to make a plan. Okay, what were my choices? Leave? Stay but hide in here? Leaving would probably result in Sarah and Jonathan panicking unnecessarily. I didn't exactly relish the thought of hiding out in the bathroom for two hours, though. I also didn't want to see Digger if I could help it.

Antonio. If I could find him, he could tell Sarah and Jonathan I'd slipped out. They could meet me in the lobby of the New York Hilton. Wasn't that the place Jonathan had said the concierge was the best?

I prowled around a bit. If I knew Antonio, I didn't think he'd sit through the movie. He'd be checking on things.

I was right. I met him coming up the stairs as I was about to go down. "Tony."

"He still up here?" He meant Ziggy.

We were stage-whispering. "Far as I know. Why didn't you tell me Zig was going to be here today!"

"I thought you knew!"

I shook my head, trying to think of what to say.

"I mean," Antonio went on, "it was supposed to be a surprise for the people, but I figured you would know."

"I haven't talked to him since the night he fell from

the stage," I blurted out.

"In Chicago?"

"No! The show here in the city!"

"Oh, oh, oh, that one." Tony looked pained. "I still don't know what the fuck happened there, boss. I'm sorry."

"It's not your fault."

But Tony took it like it was. "Look, it's time for me to get him out of here."

"Where are you taking him?"

"Back to the hotel."

"Which one?"

He looked around to make sure we weren't being eavesdropped. "Carlyle. Room 408."

"Where's Digger?"

"Downstairs. I'm leaving him here to gladhand afterward."

I made a decision. "Get Ziggy out of here. I'll catch a cab to the Carlyle."

"You got it, boss."

Voice number one had won. *You're not a kid anymore. He's not trying to hurt you. Sit down and talk, for god's sake. There's nothing to be afraid of.*

Just keep saying that. There's nothing to be afraid of.

Here I Am

I had a lot of time to think in the cab. We were in traffic for over an hour trying to get to the Upper East Side. I hadn't known where the hotel was, and neither had the cab driver, and I'd stupidly caught a cab headed downtown, which meant that with the driver talking with his dispatcher about where the hotel was, we went south for quite a while. Sounded to me like the dispatcher looked it up in the phone book. I hoped we were going to the right place.

Nothing like an hour-plus of worrying to undermine a guy's confidence. By the time we pulled up at the hotel I was about ready to crawl out of my own skin. The fare was outrageously expensive but I didn't care. I handed the driver a few twenties as the doorman opened the door on the curb side.

He gave me a much more gracious "Welcome to the Carlyle" than I expected to get, given that I was wearing torn jeans and a denim jacket.

"Thank you," I said, and waltzed into the lobby like I owned the place. That's the only way to play it, you know, when you're trying to get upstairs in a New York City hotel where you don't have a reservation. You have to act like you belong there. I learned this from Courtney, who explained this was how groupies sometimes got upstairs, despite hotel security.

I went directly to the elevators and pushed the up button. The place was small but swanky, much, *much* nicer than the Penta. A chandeliers-and-black-marble kind of place.

On the way to the fourth floor I wondered if I should have called from the house phone before going directly up. When I came off the elevator, though, there was a telephone on a stand, flanked by two little stools that had a 1920s look about them. I sat on one and picked up the handset.

The hotel operator answered. I asked for room 408.

"I'm sorry, sir, but that room has asked that no calls be put through."

"Oh, um, can you take a message?"

"I can do that, sir."

"Thanks. Uh, the message is..." I could not think of what it should say. I didn't know who would pick the message up or anything. "Um, never mind. No message. Thank you."

She wished me a nice day.

I walked over to the door marked 408 and knocked very quietly.

A few moments later, the door opened a crack. I could see a sliver of Tony. He unchained the door, came out into the hall, and quietly closed the door behind him.

We went back to the stools by the elevator, even though Tony looked kind of ridiculous perched on one; he was large and it wasn't.

"He's asleep," he said, meaning Ziggy.

"I figured. He must have come in on a red-eye."

"Yeah. Sorry about that, boss."

"No, don't wake him, don't apologize. I..." I took a

deep breath. "Tony, you know how it is."

"Actually, I don't, but I can guess," he said. "But you can tell me if you want."

"Short version: BNC is trying to break up the band, and I'm a wreck because of the whole not-talking-to-Zig-for-a-year thing."

"Okay," Tony said, sounding skeptical.

"I mean, I don't know if he loves me or hates me."

"That's rough, boss. You two need to work your shit out."

"I know. I guess that's why I'm here."

"You guess?"

"Well, to try. I don't know if it's going to work."

Antonio nodded. "Still. You gotta try."

"But how are you, man? We didn't really get to catch up last night."

He seemed a little surprised I was asking. "I'm good. My momma had a fall but she's fine now. My brother's working as a physical therapist, so he got her in at the place he works."

"Ray-Ray?" The only brother of Tony's I had met so far was a skinny kid in Chicago who was still in high school.

"Naw. My big brother."

"Is your big brother as big as you?"

"Bigger. He's the one who tried out for the NFL. Tore up his ankle, though, and that's what got him interested in being an athletic trainer. Took him a while to get the credits to go to school, though."

I nodded like I knew what he was talking about, though I only had a vague idea what was involved in a job like that. "How about you? You been keeping busy?"

"Pretty busy. I had to turn down a road gig to help out my mother after her fall, so I've been trying to keep busy here in the city, but now that she's back on her feet? I might hit the road."

"With who?"

"Not sure." He jerked his head toward room 408 and the short braids at the back of his head brushed the top of his shoulders. "Your man there's been making noises about wanting a full-time bodyguard."

"He likes you," I said. I didn't ask about why Ziggy wanted a bodyguard or where they'd even be going. Instead I asked, "How is he?"

Tony shook his head very slowly. "You want my honest opinion?"

"Always. If I want bullshit, I'll ask Digger."

"He's a wreck. Ever since his mother, I guess? I'd be a wreck, too."

"When did it happen?"

"Not sure. Couple of weeks ago, maybe?"

I tried to imagine Ziggy being in that much pain for weeks, months, and I did not feel good. "He looks exhausted."

"He's a tough little motherfucker," Tony said. "But yeah, he's wrung out."

"What time is it?"

Tony showed me the watch on his wrist.

"Shit." I wanted to make myself scarce before Digger got there. "Tell him I miss him. Tell him I really need to talk to him." *Tell him to keep his hands out of other men's pants...* Hah, right. Not that I had any right to even think that, but I thought it anyway.

"Wait, are you leaving?"

"Avoiding my old man," I said. And even if I wasn't, once he got there I couldn't have the conversation with Ziggy I wanted to. "I'm staying with Sarah. Take her number. Give it to him? I'm not leaving the city until either I talk to him or he leaves."

I wrote the number on the little message pad on the phone stand. Tony stood up and tucked it into his pocket, but he said, "Let me just check on him before you go."

"Okay."

I wasn't in the mood to laugh then, but I feel I should point out that it's hilarious when someone as big as Antonio tiptoes. He opened and closed the door to the room with ninja-like silence while I stood there by the elevator with my heart getting louder and louder.

The door opened again, and Antonio gestured for me to come in.

Never Enough

The room was a corner suite. I stepped into the parlor

room. The furniture looked like it was someone's grandmother's house. Someone's rich grandmother, I should say. Tony waved me toward the door to the bedroom, which was open.

"I'll be right outside in the hall," he said in a low voice. "I'll knock three times if Digger's coming." And then he—very thoughtfully—left the room completely.

I stepped into the doorway, my hands jammed into the pockets of my denim jacket, and leaned on the doorframe.

Ziggy was lying in the middle of the king-size bed, tangled in the bedclothes but otherwise naked. His skin was strikingly tan against the white sheets. He had a pillow over his head.

I assumed he'd been awake enough to tell Tony it was okay to let me in. Right? Tony wouldn't have just sent me in there without warning Ziggy first, would he? If Ziggy had fallen back to sleep I didn't want to wake him. I held my breath, caught between wanting to crawl into bed with him and run away.

Far, far away.

You tried that already, I reminded myself. *So did he. Yet here you are.*

What if he doesn't want me here, though? What then?

He looked like he'd lost weight. I wondered if that was from grief or if he'd gone vegetarian or what.

His arm moved sluggishly as he pulled the pillow off his head.

"I can try to come back later if you're too sleepy," I said.

His head turned suddenly and his eyes flew open. "Oh shit, you're really... I thought I was dreaming that Tony told me you were here."

"He did."

"Oh."

Neither of us moved for a while. I was sort of frozen, every sense of mine tingling. I had heard his voice, heard it for the first time in so very long. That voice. God. Coming out of his mouth, not out of the radio.

"Come here," he said then, very quietly, but I heard him perfectly well.

I took a breath but not a step.

"Come here, please?" he tried, and I found myself gripping the doorframe. Not sure if I was holding myself back or keeping myself from running away or what. Tears pricked at my eyes, and I was feeling entirely too many things at once.

I tried to say his name then, but it came out a whisper.

Ziggy struggled to sit up, then, when I guess it was obvious I wasn't coming any closer. His makeup was a complete mess and his hair was epic. He blinked as if trying to focus on me. "Hey."

"Hey." I could barely swallow, and my mouth was suddenly crowded with shit I knew I should not say. *Who was that on the balcony? Do you have any idea what I've been through?* Etc. I groped for something safe to say. "Are you all right?"

Wrong thing. "No, I am fucking well *not* all right, no thanks to you!"

Maybe there was nothing I could have said. Maybe the powder keg was going to spark no matter what I said. And maybe he had as much a right to be angry at me as I did at him. That didn't stop me from answering in kind: "Me? No thanks to me? How the fuck is it my fault!" I probably wouldn't have been so explosively defensive, of course, if I hadn't feared exactly that. *Of course* it's all my fault. "I didn't tell you to give executive hand jobs at the theater today."

"Don't you judge me. Don't you dare judge me!"

"And what am I judging, exactly? Your choice in men? Or your choice to act like a fucking whore!" Why did I say that? Why?

"You don't know what it's like!"

Angry, scared, desperate, hurt. This is what it sounds like: "What *what's* like, to have sex with someone other than because I want to? I've never had sex for any reason other than that. Oh wait, except with one person. You."

He started to cry, as tears spilled over quite suddenly and his chest shook with dry but nearly silent rasps. I wanted to hold him and shake some sense into him at the same time. Everything in my chest was shredded—heart, lungs, voice—and that must have been how he was feeling right then, too.

He found his voice first. "Well, aren't you lucky, then. Aren't you lucky." He pulled the sheet over his shoulder like he suddenly felt the need to hide his nakedness, and in one of those upended-ice-bucket-down-the-back moments I realized what he was implying—that I'd never been the subject of unwanted sexual advances, but he had. As usual, everything turned upside down or inside out in Ziggy's vicinity. I'd meant it the other way around, that I'd never made advances at someone to try to get something from them, but I knew he had, I knew he did. This flip to thinking of Ziggy as sexual victim instead of aggressor...

...combined with his opening accusation that this was my fault...

I couldn't take it. I couldn't. "You're as full of shit as ever."

That sparked full on hysterics. He began throwing pillows at me as he screamed, "So are you! So are you!"

What a time for three little knocks to come at the door, eh? I pulled the bedroom door closed just as the door from the hallway opened.

Something loud hit the door and I jumped back. Ziggy must have moved on to throwing things other than pillows. I couldn't really worry about that right then, though, because in came my two least-favorite people in the world. They looked at me like the feeling was mutual.

Ball and Chain

Digger and Mills weren't wearing matching suits, but they might as well have been. No ties today, but button-up shirts undone at the top.

"Doesn't sound like His Highness is too happy to see you," Digger said, as something else hit the door. "Tony, would you escort our friend here to the street?"

"Wait," Mills said mildly. "Now might be a good time for us to talk over some recent issues. Why don't we go somewhere a bit quieter?"

I probably should have said "fuck you" and taken off at that point, except I would have had to have my wits about me enough to realize that, and truth be told, I didn't want to leave without trying to talk to Ziggy again. "Do you think we should leave him like this?"

Mills looked sidelong at Digger, who just waved in Antonio's direction. "Tony'll get him calmed down. Won't you, Ton'?"

"Yes, sir," Tony said, folding his arms across his chest.

So I went with them to the bar. They didn't frog-march me there, but it felt like they did, what with hostile vibes coming from all three of us. I pretended to be reading the notice posted inside the elevator. It was the lineup of artists playing in the hotel's cabaret that week. Eartha Kitt. Huh.

In the bar they stuck me into the leather banquette, and Digger slid in next to me, trapping me there. Mills took the seat across from me. Okay, I knew that was standard rock star protocol: the most one most likely to cause fan hysteria was always seated least accessible to the public. But it didn't feel like that was why they did it.

The bar was very lightly populated at that hour. There were maybe two tables besides ours, and they were on the other side of the room. One guy sat alone at the bar itself. That was it.

A waiter in an impeccably white shirt and black pants came in our direction. He skirted around an empty table on his way to us and I thought, *oh no, not a gay waiter. I have enough to deal with right now.* He stopped in front of us and folded his hands instead of taking out an order pad. Something about the way his weight was slightly more on one foot than the other, and the extreme shortness of his hair, and the way he moved... *I could be wrong,* I told myself. *Your gaydar sucks, remember? Maybe you're wrong.*

Then he spoke. "What can I get you gentlemen?" Something of a lilt in his vowels and the way he hung onto his consonants. Gay.

"A Manhattan," Digger and I said simultaneously. I quickly added, "No, wait, make mine a Sazerac."

I got an eyebrow twitch for that from the waiter, but he was smooth, turning his eyes on Mills, who asked for scotch and soda. "Very good, gentlemen." I watched as he went directly to the bartender and some kind of debate ensued. The bartender was older, maybe forty, heavyset, losing his hair, and he shooed the waiter away as he reached for the bottle of Pernod on the back shelf.

Mills didn't wait for the drinks to arrive. "You're looking well," he said, playing nice.

"Thanks. What did you guys want to talk about?" I was surprised my words flowed pretty easily. I guess

I was getting better at faking it. "You know I'm not supposed to say anything to you in case we end up in court. Feinbaum will have my testicles on tongs if I say anything I shouldn't."

Mills spread his hands. "Nobody wants to go to court."

"That isn't what your legal department says."

"Legal doesn't make that call," he said, and looked me in the eye.

Mr. Magic Pen. Mr. Vice-President-to-Be, too, I remembered. "And you do."

He pursed his lips a little as he nodded, like he was liking the music he was hearing in his head. But he went on in a friendly tone. "This is all about trying to find common ground, and protecting our common—our *mutual*—interests."

I am interested in drop kicking you onto Madison Avenue, I thought, but of course I didn't say. I thought of something better. "Like it was in our mutual interests for *you* to be the one who blackmailed me instead of the paparazzi doing it."

I was not playing nice. Mills had a good poker face, though. He grinned like I'd told him we'd all gotten puppies or something. "I don't recall blackmailing you, Daron. I do recall it being in our mutual interest to have those pictures out of circulation, though."

"Don't do me any favors, Mills." I paused as the waiter delivered the three drinks, setting them down and then zooming off, as it must have been obvious we were deep in the thick of something. I took a sip of the cocktail. It was the thing Crystal had made for Chris that time he was trying to get over Lacey. It was strong. I pretended it gave me the courage to say what I said next. "Funny thing. Turns out Jonathan knew that photographer."

The smile on Mills's face dimmed. I was half-lying, you know, which is why it took such balls to say. Jonathan had told me he knew who took the photos, not necessarily that he knew the guy personally. But it was close enough. I saw how that thought made Mills falter. Whether it was because he was the one who put the photographer on our trail in the first place or maybe just the thought that Jonathan or I might have been able to handle keeping the photos out of circulation ourselves, I'm not sure. Either way, I had set him off-balance.

I pressed my advantage as best I could. "Tell me what you really want, Mills. You really want me out of your hair, out of your life?"

"It's nothing personal," he tried to stutter.

"Tear up the contract. Release Moondog Three. We'll drop our lawsuits. Everyone can go home."

Mills snorted from deep in his throat. "You think it's really that simple? If only it was."

"So what do you want, then?"

I had to wonder if he'd ever been honest with me or if honest wasn't in his makeup. Or his job description. There's a chance that what he said next was true, though. He cleared his throat, had a sip of his own drink. "What do I want? Look. I know you think you're an artiste and you've had a pretty good run. You got a lot more out of it than a lot of musicians in your place. But I'm here for the dollar signs, and that little junkie prima donna running up the property damage bill upstairs? Is on the verge of a commercial breakout. I know I can make it happen. I know it. I can feel it, I can smell it. I can make him the next Terence Trent D'Arby. If he doesn't self-destruct, I can make him the next George Michael."

I knew what he was implying. That if Ziggy was George Michael, I was Andrew Ridgeway. Ziggy was Tom Hanks, I was... whatever the other guy's name was who co-starred in Bos*om Buddies*. I was trying to think of a snappy comeback—or at least a logical one—when Mills went on.

"Are you really going to get in the way of success like that?" he asked. "Are you really going to shoot down his chance at stardom by tying yourself like a noose around his neck?"

Yeah, Mills really knew how to mix a metaphor. "This isn't about me."

"Isn't it? If it's about Ziggy, and you really care about him, you'll do what you can to contribute to his success, not tear it down."

"Okay, but then where do our mutual interests come in? I thought it was in our mutual interest to sell a shitload of records, and we did everything, absolutely everything, from our end to hold up that bargain." A creeping suspicion was forming in the back of my mind.

Had Mills sabotaged the band's success because he wanted to get Ziggy away from us, to turn him into a commercial pop solo artist? Was that why the weird homophobic excuses didn't make any sense, because they were not what was really at the root of all this?

Mills nodded like he agreed with me. "I know you did, and that just proves the drawing power of your front man. So listen. I know legal's been champing at the bit on a lot of things lately. That's what lawyers love to do: sue. I think we've got a pretty good case we could slap you around with regarding exclusivity—"

"I never used the Moondog name in other work and you fucking know it," I burst out, livid.

"—but this is what I'm getting to about our mutual interests. I'll tell legal to back off. You want to tear up the old contract? Maybe you have a point. Maybe starting fresh is the way to go. That'd release you to do whatever other work you want. Anything that doesn't use the name or infringe the trademark. Cut you loose, free and clear. You and the other two. No muss, no fuss. And then we sign Ziggy to a fresh, new deal."

He held up his glass of scotch, and Digger clinked his glass against it. "A multimedia development deal," Digger said. "This isn't just some band deal we're talking about."

He was making it sound like the gold record meant nothing, like a mere hit record was piddling compared to whatever they had in the works for Ziggy: more movies? TV shows? jingles and sponsorships? I had no idea.

I tried not to let my imagination run wild. Digger had a way of making me feel like I was out of my league; it was one of his favorite tactics. I couldn't let it succeed.

It was dawning on me, though, how stupid it was to go into a conversation like this without Carynne or a lawyer or somebody sane there. I'd told Mills that what I wanted was to get rid of the contracts. Cut us free. Now he was telling me he would, in fact, do that. But he was making it clear it meant I wouldn't get what I really wanted, which was to keep the band together.

My head was spinning and I'd had only a few sips of the drink. "Ziggy and the Moondogs," I said derisively.

"I told you he wouldn't go for that," Digger said to Mills.

"That's because Daron is an artiste," Mills said. "Not a hack. He's not about to put on a fake spacesuit for the sake of getting on the stage. Am I right?"

"You really are trying to get rid of me," I said to Mills.

"Nothing personal, I told you," Mills said. "But it'd be a lot easier if you were out of the picture."

Digger cleared his throat, and I think he was trying to kick Mills in the shins. I wondered what he was trying to tell Mr. Magic Pen. The fact that they weren't on the same page would have helped me, maybe, if I could figure out what they were up to.

The only thing I knew for sure was what I had said: they wanted to get rid of me. So I dug in my heels and resisted that however I could. "You can get rid of me if Ziggy wants to get rid of me," I said.

"The same Ziggy who was throwing furniture at you upstairs?" Digger chided.

He had a point. But I knew better than to think a tantrum was the same thing as the truth. "When I hear it from Ziggy's sober mouth that he doesn't want me around anymore, I'll walk away," I said. That made sense, right? Because what was the point of trying to keep the band together if that were true? "If Ziggy tells me it's time to move on, I'll move on."

The two of them looked at each other, and I saw Digger looked a little panicked. Or maybe just surprised. I hoped it was panic I read in those slightly widened eyes, though.

Mills downed the rest of his drink. "Why don't you two make an appointment to talk in a couple of days, then."

Right. So you and Digger can pull these same strong-arm tactics on him that you're trying to pull on me right now? *Like hell*, I thought, but didn't say. "Sure. How long are you in town for?"

"Coupla days," Digger spat.

"Me, too," I said. "I'm staying at Sarah Rogue's. I'm sure you've got her number."

They exchanged another look, like they were none too happy about that idea. I was making myself very hard to get rid of, wasn't I?

"Let me go take a leak," I said, half-standing up, which was as much as I could do with the banquette and the table the way they were.

Digger slid out and let me go, seemingly without suspicion. Good. I asked the waiter which way the restroom was. He pointed me back toward the kitchen. I thanked him, thinking: *this is going to work.*

They couldn't see the kitchen doors from where they were sitting. I slipped into the kitchen and made my way quickly through to a service elevator. Perfect. No one appeared to have noticed.

Moments later I was on my way to the fourth floor. I had decided I wasn't going to let anyone's idiocy or pettiness get between Ziggy and me, not Digger's, not Mills's, and especially not my own.

Justify My Love

I had two options when I got to the fourth floor. I could knock on the door to 408, or I could knock on the door to 409, which was the actual bedroom that Ziggy had been in.

I worried that I'd put Tony in a compromising position if I knocked on 408. Digger had pretty much told him I wasn't approved for entry. If I knocked on 409, though, and Ziggy opened the door himself? Well, it wasn't like he wasn't allowed to, was he?

Honestly, now that I had a moment of quiet I was replaying some of the crap Digger and Mills had said. Digger had called him, what? "His Highness?" And Mills had called him a junkie prima donna.

The problem with remembering every sound you hear is that you can replay the sound like a tape. It's how I know things I said when I was too upset to even know what I was saying while saying them.

I didn't like what Digger and Mills had said, but I liked even less what I heard now in my memory of the fight Ziggy and I had just had. I'd said he acted like a "fucking whore."

You know who used the word "whore" a lot? Digger. You know who didn't? Me. Or so I thought.

I decided slipping a note under the door was a better idea than knocking. I hurried back to the telephone table by the elevator, conscious of time slipping away. Any second Mills and Digger might figure out I had flown the coop and come right back up here.

I tapped the pen against the paper trying to think of the words. I wrote the "I" in "I love you" before it occurred to me that was going to come across as desperate or possibly sarcastic, which would be another disaster. So instead I wrote:

I'M
SORRY

Hadn't he left me a cryptic note once in a New York hotel, with the word SORRY so prominent, so out of place with the rest of the note that I wondered why he'd bothered to write the rest? I wished I had a song lyric ready to add to it now, but there was no time for that.

I went back to his door and slid it under as far as I could, then held my breath.

I heard the hiss of the paper against the carpet as it was pulled the rest of the way into the room.

A moment later the door opened and I was looking directly into Ziggy's raccoon eyes. I had forgotten we were exactly the same height.

"They're coming," I said. "Or they will be."

"Okay. One sec." He closed the door to a crack but didn't shut it all the way, and long seconds ticked by while I wondered what he was doing.

Then he slipped out into the hallway with me, closing the door silently behind him. He'd put on a jacket and pulled on a pair of short boots. "Where are we going?" he asked.

"Somewhere Mills or Digger can't have me thrown out of?"

That earned me the "oh really?" look, and he gestured for me to lead the way.

I took us to the end of the hall, where I hoped there were fire stairs. There were. Thankfully we were only on the fourth floor. At the ground floor there was a door to the outside that said it was alarmed. I didn't want to risk it. Fortunately there was another one, unmarked, that led into a service corridor. We came out the loading dock at the back of the building and then onto Madison Avenue. The doormen never saw us.

We walked a block on Madison while I tried to hail

a cab with no luck. We were both being really calm and cooperative with each other, you might have noticed. I didn't know if that was because we'd both gotten the explosion out of our systems or if we were trying to avoid it again or what.

I think we both knew we had things to say and we wanted to say them, whether we agreed on what those things were or not.

"Let's just go to the park," Ziggy said.

Central Park, he meant, which was a block away. It was night. Not the best time to be walking through there.

"There are benches on the edge, come on," he said. "We'll stick to where it's populated."

Like he read my mind. Okay, maybe it was obvious to anyone who had spent time in New York City that Central Park at night was something to carefully consider. "All right."

When we reached the edge of the park, though, he pointed and said, "We're right by the Alice statue."

"Alice statue?"

"Alice in Wonderland. You haven't seen this? It's one of my favorite things."

That settled it, I suppose. I followed him into the park, where a giant bronze sculpture of Alice and various characters from the book were sitting on a magic mushroom. It being like nine at night in the summer and it being New York City, there was a gaggle of kids climbing all over the statue while their parents stood or sat around on the edge. A guy with a boombox was off to one side, rollerblading/dancing in front of it without a care in the world for whether anyone watched him or not. His T-shirt was hanging out of the back pocket of his cutoff shorts.

A woman stood up from a bench, pushing a stroller and yelling for her kids to join her. Ziggy made a beeline for the bench before anyone else could get it and threw himself down tiredly.

I sat somewhat more gingerly next to him.

"So are you actually sorry or was the note just a ploy to get me to open the door?" Ziggy asked.

I was glad I hadn't written I LOVE YOU, then, because if he'd said that to *that*, I think I would have walked away and never looked back. Or worse. I turned to face him, heat spiking through me, but I kept my voice down. "I'm not one for ploys."

"Ah, I forget that." He looked genuinely troubled by it.

"I can believe it if you've been spending most of your time with my father and Mills."

He sighed heavily.

"But let's not talk about them," I went on. "Let's talk about us first."

"Okay, what are you sorry for, then?"

"For blowing up at you. I don't know what got into me."

"I take it you were upset by what you saw."

"Or what I thought I saw, anyway." I wanted to patch things up between us enough that I tried to give him an out.

He didn't take it. "I'm sorry. I'm surrounded by closet cases who can be led around by their dicks. Literally. Sometimes I can't resist grabbing them by the handle."

My skin flashed hot and cold again. "Like you did with me."

His mouth dropped open a little and his eyes widened with sudden panic. "That's not what I meant. Daron—"

"Yes it is. We both know I was a terrible closet case and that you used it as a way to control me when you thought you needed to get creative control of the band. You've already apologized for that, Zig. I'm still working on forgiving you for it."

He swallowed. "Okay. I guess that's something. Is that why you react so badly when I do it to someone else, though?"

"Maybe. I think this time, running into you by surprise, I... it brought it all back full force."

"Full force?"

"Panic-attack level," I admitted.

"Ow. Those suck."

"They do."

We fell silent on that point of agreement, while my defensive inner voices began to chatter: *Why the hell are you trying to patch it up with someone who sends you into panic mode? This is why your relationships are doomed.*

Okay, but you know what? I'd tried the other extreme, I tried stability with Jonathan, and it didn't work. I'd also tried a sort of no-strings-attached thing with Orlando and that had worked, but the whole thing about there being no strings meant there wasn't anything keeping us together, either.

With Ziggy, there were strings. Even the strings had strings. I wasn't ready to cut them unless I absolutely had to.

"We both need to get out of our old patterns," I said then.

"We do?"

"We do. You have to stop doing that."

"Or you'll have panic attacks."

"That's assuming I'm around you enough to see it, of course." I held up my palms and looked at them, as if I could measure my worth, as a partner, as a musician, as a friend, based on what I saw there.

"Hey," he said, and I knew he meant *look at me*, so I did. "Do you want to be around?"

"Mills is the one who wants to break up the band, not me."

Ziggy's spine straightened. "What did he tell you?"

"A load of crap, so far as I'm concerned. What did he tell you?"

"That while I was in rehab you whored yourself out to a lot of other bands, looking for a new job, and in the end you re-joined Nomad."

I should not have been defensive, but I was. "That's called making a living."

"Oh, so you did what you had to do? How's that different from me?"

"For fuck's sake, Ziggy, I'm a professional musician. So are you. You are not, however, a professional *professional*." I couldn't bring myself to use the word "whore" again, not even though—or maybe because—he'd just used it.

"I'm an entertainer," he said.

"Fine. Entertainer, actor, celebrity, fine. That doesn't mean you have to have sex with whoever's in charge."

"But I like the sex."

"Is that why you do it? Honestly? You just like it?" I had a sudden feeling of deja vu. Didn't we have this conversation once before? Or had I imagined it? In the time we were apart there were so many things I wished we'd said, I wondered if I were mixing fantasy with memory. "Let me be clear about this, Ziggy Ferias." Yes, I was using last-name-level vehemence. "I get jealous. I do. But I could live with you sleeping with whoever you wanted if that's all it was about, freedom and being yourself and enjoying sex for the sake of sex. But when it's this control-game bullshit? It makes me want to run far, far away. If you're lovers with Richard Whatshisface, the director? Okay, fine. But you just told me he's a closet case you control with his joystick."

To which Ziggy had only three little words to say, in a very small voice. "You get jealous?"

Fuck. Had I come here to say it? Had I come here to confess, to admit it, to leave myself open to what torture he could inflict?

I was suffering anyway. That much I had already admitted. He knew, or at least he guessed. And I'd just set myself up as the one who didn't use ploys, who was the honest one, right?

Right. Time to say it. "Of course I do." My voice was almost as small as his. He leaned toward me to hear my words over the sounds of the boombox and the cavorting of children. "I wouldn't be here if I wasn't in love with you."

His intake of breath was sharp, sudden, like my words had cut him.

I kept talking, unsure if continuing was a balm or like salt in the wound. "You know how long I've been waiting to say that? A year. Maybe longer. I wanted to tell you... when I couldn't deny it anymore. We were right here in New York." Noisy, roiling, grimy New York. "The charity show. I..." Why was I telling him this part? I could barely stand to think about it myself. "I had half-convinced myself to tell you after our set, that amazing, amazing set. But I couldn't find you during the break, and then came the accident."

He already had raccoon eyes, so the fact that his eyes brimmed wet now didn't matter, makeup-wise. But he still held it in. "You could have told me in the hospital."

Oh, for the love of... He thought I hadn't come to see him on purpose? "They kept everyone but Digger from you. Because we're not family."

He pushed back. "You never called me when I was at Betty Ford, either."

"They told me you were in isolation and no one was

allowed to talk to you except for Digger."

"And you believed that? Who told you that?"

"Digger."

Ziggy clenched his teeth. "I was allowed to name two contacts. I named him and you."

"No one ever told me that." I shook my head slowly, trying to imagine how this entire year might have gone differently if I'd spoken with him. I wasn't angry, I wasn't outraged, I was just... sad that our understanding of each other was so weak that he could believe I hadn't wanted to talk to him. Maybe that was my fault, for holding back so much from him. For not telling him sooner. For not realizing it sooner.

The case against me wasn't looking very good. "I heard you went off on vacation with Jonathan, while I was in there."

So much for not angry, though maybe now I was as angry with myself as anyone. "Because I thought we weren't allowed to talk to you for twenty-eight days! And Carynne and Jonathan decided that I was going to gnaw my leg off like a zoo animal if they didn't do something with me. And I picked Mexico so we'd be closer to you!" Unfortunately my voice got louder and my anger more heated the longer that statement went on. And I wasn't done yet. "Then I refused to go back to Boston so I could be there when you came out and I even fucking drove all the way to Palm Springs so I could beat Digger to get you, and gave myself fucking heat stroke only to find out you had skipped the country with Jennifer Carstens! So don't you fucking play this 'I hear you went to Mexico with Jonathan' game!"

His face shuttered like a window. He looked down, his shoulders hunched, and he closed off. When he looked up again his eyes were like pinpricks of light down a long tunnel. "I'm not allowed to be mad at you for going to Mexico with Jonathan?"

I slumped against the bench. "You're allowed to feel whatever you feel, Zig, if I'm allowed to feel whatever I feel, how's that?"

"What do you mean?"

"I mean, let's get all the feelings out in the open and see if there's anything left but scorched Earth when we're done."

"I thought you said you came here to tell me you loved me."

"I actually didn't know you'd be in the city at all, if you recall. But once I knew you were, yeah. There was no way I was leaving until we'd at least talked. And I didn't know if I was going to have the guts to tell you. But I did. So there you go. I love you, motherfucker. There were times I tried to stop thinking about you, tried to forget because it hurt to think about you, but I thought about you every damn day."

He looked down, tears dripping, and put his hand to his forehead, as if shading his eyes, but actually trying to block me from seeing. The splatters of water on his black jeans were obvious, though.

"Here." I dug in the pocket of my leather jacket for a piece of paper towel I'd folded up in there after I'd splashed my face with water in the movie theater restroom.

He looked up but didn't take the paper out of my hand.

I reached out slowly and dabbed at his cheeks. I steadied his head with one hand and wiped at the sooty smudges under his eyes with the towel. He leaned heavily into my hand then, like a cat. I scritched him like one.

He took my hand in his then, but didn't seem ready to say anything yet.

"I don't want to make you miserable," I said. "And I can't live with you making me miserable all the time either. If there's no way to make it work, then there's no way to make it work. But I couldn't let another year—or another day—go by without telling you. All right? I fucking love you, I am in fucking love with you, and if that fucks things up royally there's nothing I can do about it."

He kissed me so suddenly that his head knocked into mine hard enough that I saw stars, or maybe that was the lack of oxygen from his squeezing his arms around my neck so tightly. Then just as quickly he let me go. Would you be surprised that he was the one who looked around us to see if anyone had noticed us? I know I was.

"Now can we talk about Digger and Mills?" he said, with a slight snarl in his voice.

"Sure," I said.

"But wait." Ziggy turned to sit sideways on the bench, his legs crossed. "We didn't finish talking about us. You said we both have to break our old habits. We talked about mine. Now let's talk about yours."

Remember how I said I knew confessing I loved him was going to open me up? I could practically hear Ziggy sharpening his knives. But maybe it was about time I had some bullshit surgically removed.

Welcome to the Real World

"Sex has always been easy for me and hard for you," Ziggy said. The statement would have come out more clinical sounding if he hadn't also leaned over and wiped his eyes on the sleeve of my black T-shirt. His face was less raccoon-like now than it had been when we started talking. I felt that was a victory of sorts.

"It's not quite as hard for me now," I said, a little afraid to admit too much and set him off. "At least, not when there's not a lot at stake."

"Ahhh." He nodded like he knew what I meant: I didn't mean just that "casual" sex wasn't a big deal to me anymore, but that sex between him and me always had a lot at stake. He got it: "And there's more at stake right now than ever."

"Feels like it, anyway." I took a deep breath and tried to let it go bit by bit.

"So what old habit are you going to kick?" He leaned against the back of the bench, but it was too careful, too posed to be actual nonchalance. Maybe that didn't matter. He was signaling to me that he was relaxed and ready for whatever answer I gave.

"What did Digger tell you about me firing him?"

Ziggy made a dismissive noise. "Nothing, really. Acted like it was no big deal, like it was all status quo. Made it out as if you and he and Carynne had been talking for months about a 'transition' once she was ready. I mean, I knew you wanted to fire him, but the only way I knew you actually did was Alex Mazel told me."

That surprised me. "When did you see Alex?" From Nomad.

"At some function in LA. He commented to me he was surprised to see Digger walking around upright because the last time he'd seen him he was being taken away in an ambulance." Ziggy was looking past me, his eyes glittering. I didn't think he was focusing on the statue. "Digger of course hadn't bothered to mention his hospitalization to me."

"So you know about how he showed up at Thanksgiving at Remo's house, uninvited? Remo read him the fucking riot act and would have kicked him out except he collapsed and, yeah, ambulance."

"That's pretty much all I know. That wasn't when you fired him though, was it? You aren't the type to kick a guy when he's down, Daron. I really can't picture you standing at his hospital bed and telling him to take a hike."

I took another one of those deep breaths. "Am I that soft?"

"You make it sound like it's a bad thing."

"It is if keeping him for as long as I did is what sank us." That was one of those thoughts that kept me up at night. What if I'd had the courage to fire him earlier? Or not hire him at all? Would a better manager have worked things differently with BNC from the start? Then again, maybe it would have been worse. There was no telling. Ziggy was giving me a bit of a blank look. "Wow. You really don't know what's been going on?"

He shook his head.

"I fired him the day he wouldn't stand up for me or the band when Mills called us in to the office to tell me to my face—" I had to stop and take another deep breath, and to remind myself not to shout. There were kids close by. "—that they were dustbinning the album as unrecoupable because I'm gay."

Ziggy gave me—or that thought—the hairy eyeball. "I thought the album didn't sell."

"The only reason the album didn't sell goes all the way back to what Digger himself said the month it was released: they didn't put enough copies out there. It's a fucking travesty that we could fill a twenty-thousand seat arena in Houston and not have a blip in sales there." I paused to try to remember what I was actually trying to say, though. It was hard to remember because it made no logical sense. "The whole business about them not knowing what bin to put us in, yada yada. Mills mentioned that but then handed me a pack of paparazzi photos of me and Jonathan holding hands in a parking lot and tried to lay on some bullshit about how that kind of thing turned off the American public."

"Like people would give a fuck?"

"Well, even if they would, the American public never saw those photos. Because Mills paid off the photographer. And as far as I know there's been zero word in the tabloids or wherever about me. So how could it be a PR problem? It's a scapegoat problem is what it is."

Ziggy nodded gravely.

"There was one of you and me in there, too. A photo, I mean."

"There was?"

"Yeah." I remembered so clearly what his weight had felt like on top of mine that night he'd collapsed after the show at Madison Square Garden. God, I missed him. I had missed him. "Backstage at MSG."

He bit his lip, which trembled a little.

"But anyway, at that meeting—which was while you were still at Betty Ford—I fired Digger."

"Your hands are shaking." He took hold of mine, one in each of his.

"Smartest thing I ever did," I said.

"But traumatic." He squeezed gently. "Was there violence?"

I had to think. "I smacked him in the face. Digger, I mean. Mills had already waltzed out. Digger said something vile and I just couldn't take it anymore."

Ziggy nodded. "He didn't hit you back?"

"Nope. Maybe he thinks we're even now. I dunno."

"Even?"

"He smacked me that one time, that one awful time, and now I got him back? I don't know." I squeezed Ziggy's fingers in return. "Anyway. About old habits. I vowed no more violence after that."

"You're not exactly a violent person, D."

"No. But..." It was odd to hear Ziggy say that, when he was the only person, other than Digger, I had hit. "Are you sure?"

He raised one of my hands to his lips and kissed the knuckles. "I'm sure."

I shook my head. "I should never have raised a hand to you."

"You learned it from him."

"That's my point. That's what I'm trying to stop. That's what I'm trying to get rid of."

"You're trying not to be like him. But I'm telling you, Daron. You're not like him."

"I keep thinking I'm not, or that I've moved on, but his bullshit seems to keep cropping up again and again."

"When are you going to stop giving a shit about what he thinks?"

"I stopped giving a shit about that a long time ago." *Especially after firing him*, I thought. "That's not what I'm talking about. I mean shit like... I'll say something and it'll sound like it came out of his mouth. And then I'll hate myself."

"Don't hate yourself. What kind of things?"

"Like calling you a whore earlier."

"Ah." His eyes fluttered closed for a second and I wondered what was going on inside his mind. "That was... not the best moment for either of us."

"Yeah, no." Apparently we were both ashamed of our outbursts. Him staying calm helped me stay calm.

"I'll make you a deal," he said, looking down at our hands instead of at my face. "Call me on it if I try to play the victim card, and I'll call you on it if you're acting like Digger."

"Okay, deal." For the sake of being specific, I added, "And I won't hit you or call you a whore."

Ziggy pursed his lips. "I'd say that was a pretty reasonable word to use, given that what I'd done was fully deserving of the label. But, you know, if I'm going to stop sleeping my way to the top it won't be because I'm ashamed of it."

Sex has always been easy for me and hard for you.

"Why will you stop, then?"

"I already told you, but I'll tell you again. For you, Daron."

"Thanks, I think?" From one angle that seemed really straightforward. From another angle it was twisted. I decided the only logical thing to do was stay at the angle where it looked straightforward. "Do you like it, though?"

He shrugged. "I like exerting control. But there are ways I can do that without being a whore."

"You're the only person I know who can use that word with a straight face."

"To mean what it actually means? Someone who trades sex for something else?"

"Yeah. I mean, seriously, would I have even called you that if I hadn't grown up hearing it? Digger liked to throw it around whenever he was upset with my mother. I mean, even when he shouldn't have been. For fuck's sake, she would get dolled up to go out with him, to look pretty for his sake, and he'd make comments..." I trailed off, remembering what Remo had told me in Japan, about Claire and him.

"What?" Ziggy asked, while my brain tried to integrate what I knew with my childhood memories. Digger calling Claire a whore took on a different dimension in light of what I now knew. Was he rubbing her face in it all the time?

"Digger's an asshole," I said, which was the only reasonable conclusion. "My mother... cheated on him. He knew about it. They tried to manipulate each other constantly. I can't..." I felt a little ill, thinking about it. "I can't do it that way."

"You need honesty," Ziggy said seriously.

"Doesn't everyone?"

"Some people can't live without the lies that prop them up," he said, without any apparent irony.

Fine. "What about you?" I asked gently, more a plea than a demand.

He licked his lips. "For me, truth and lie aren't two mutually exclusive states with a wall between them. You know that."

"That doesn't make sense, though. If you ate the last piece of blueberry pie, either you did or you didn't."

"Okay, let me rephrase. When it comes to matters like identity and relationships, I don't think there's always a binary between honesty and dishonesty. And trying to break everything down to this or that is just wrongheaded and reductive."

"Give me an example?"

"Okay. For example, it's reductive to say you had to be either happy or sad after you fired your father. It's perfectly possible you could have been both."

"Huh." In the case of firing Digger, I was more like neither. But after I had broken up with Jonathan? Hell, while I was still living with him? I could see it. There were things almost every day that made me feel both happy and sad, relieved and anxious, and so on. "I guess... I guess I can see that."

We were silent for a while. The children were quieter now: there were fewer of them. The park was emptying out a bit. Mr. Boombox had gone. That probably meant we needed to go, too.

"What next?" I asked.

Ziggy sighed. "I go back and play nice."

"You do?" My hackles rose, literally, the hairs on my scalp standing up and my heart picking up pace.

"Daron. There are a lot of pieces in play when it comes to career here."

"Career."

"Calm. Calm." He was still holding my hands. He squeezed them gently until I relaxed my fingers. "Let's not make any decisions yet, okay? I won't make any commitments. But I need to feel them out, find out what they're actually thinking, and find out what's on the table."

"They want me and the guys to quit and to reposition you as 'Ziggy and the Moondogs' with a backing band," I said, sounding nowhere near as calm as I wanted to.

"And what do you want, Daron?"

I want you, I thought. *I want you, and you and that's it, I don't care about the details, I just want you beyond all sense or reason.*

I didn't say that, of course. Because I knew the details mattered, and I knew I'd be miserable if I went along with what Digger and Mills wanted.

"I want you at a band meeting on Tuesday," I said. "Allston house. Basement. Seven o'clock."

A smile spread slowly across his face. "I think I can manage that. Now let me go before Tony has a coronary."

I had tightened my grip again, I guess. "All right," I said, but I didn't let go.

He leaned over and kissed me then, gentle and almost tentative, until his tongue coaxed my lips to part, and then he sucked the breath right out of me. I wanted to pull him closer, but once I let go of his fingers and reached for him, he skipped away. He turned in a circle and then blew me a kiss goodbye before running away, laughing gleefully.

His laughter was infectious. Despite my doubts, despite my fears, as I sat there I found myself smiling.

Roam

I found a pay phone and left a message at Sarah's saying I hoped they weren't worried, I was fine, and I'd fill her in when I got there and hopefully she'd be there when I arrived. She had the kind of voice mail you could call to retrieve messages, so if she and Jonathan were out searching for me they could at least check to see if I'd called.

Then I called Jonathan's, in case he'd gone home, but got his machine, too. I left him a similar message.

I wasn't quite ready to talk with anyone yet. I wanted to let the things I'd said and the things Ziggy had said sink in for a while. New York is an outstanding city to be alone in. You can wander around lots of places full of people and no one bothers you. Sarah's place was on the Upper West Side. I was on the opposite side of Central Park from there and wasn't stupid enough to try to walk through the park, but skirting along the edge was just fine.

Don't think I didn't notice, by the way, that in all we'd said, Ziggy hadn't said "I love you" back to me. I noticed it but I felt like it didn't bother me. Whether it was that he wasn't ready, or he wanted to make me wait for it, or he wanted to wait for some moment of maximum dramatic impact, whatever, it was fine. For all I knew, any reluctance on his part might have boiled down to him avoiding the cliché of saying "I love you, too."

I know it doesn't seem like me, but I wasn't worried.

I spent more of my time thinking about the band stuff, and about how Digger had completely let Ziggy believe that various things were my fault or that I wanted them that way. The fact that Ziggy might have thought I didn't want to talk to him all the time he was in rehab...? It was like he was in a different reality from me. A painful universe that wasn't reality.

Thank goodness I'd decided to come to the city. Thank goodness I'd had the balls to confront him. Or who knows how much longer I would have believed he was nothing but a fame-hungry sex maniac and how much longer he would have believed I didn't care.

I'd have to ask him later whether he really believed I was done with him. Enough of him must have hoped I wasn't so that when I finally presented myself in a sensible way, he'd jumped at the chance to run off with me.

Part of me wondered if I shouldn't have flagged down a cab, taken us to some other hotel, checked us in, and after all the talking was done we could have spent the night together. I hoped he wasn't disappointed that I hadn't. I took it as a sign of maturity in both of us that getting the business stuff ironed out was a bigger priority. I think maybe we both realized, too, that if we could get that shit worked out, we'd be seeing plenty of each other.

Besides, he'd said he'd be at rehearsal, didn't he? I had a sudden flashback to him kissing me, once hard, once soft, and for a moment I regretted letting him go back to the Carlyle.

But only for a moment.

It was around ten-thirty when I reached Columbus Circle. I'd been walking/wandering for a while, probably an hour, and I decided to try calling Sarah again.

This time she picked up. "Hello?"

"It's Daron. Sorry about ditching you guys."

"Well, to be honest, once we saw Ziggy was there, and then that he *wasn't* there, we figured you two had run off to either bang or kill one another. Apparently you survived?"

"Yeah, and you're wrong on both counts: all we did was talk. Well, okay, there was one moment of tantrum."

"From you or him?"

"Uh, both simultaneously. But we got it out of our systems. And I also got read the riot act by Mills and Digger and jeez do I have an earful for you about them."

"Uh huh. Which do you want to do more, tell me or go out dancing?"

"I'd much rather tell you about it."

"Good, because having made one public appearance today already, I'm ready to order a pizza. Jonathan's here, by the way."

"Awesome. I've probably got twenty minutes walking to get to your place."

"Pffft. Where are you? I'll send the driver."

So that's how I spent my second night in the city eating greasy but heavenly pizza (my god, you don't understand, actual New York pizza is the Food of My

People and I hadn't realized I missed it so much until I was eating it) and watching MTV and filling Sarah and Jonathan in on all the shenanigans that Mills and Digger were trying to pull.

The couch was more than big enough for the three of us. I sat in the middle, Sarah on my left, Jonathan on my right, and the empty pizza boxes on the coffee table in front of me.

"Do we know how much money is on the table?" Jonathan asked at one point. "I mean, they're talking about some kind of multimedia development deal, that means a certain number of albums, a certain number of films, and who knows what else. Would it be a big advance like they do with multi-year, multi-album deals, or would this be a monthly stipend kind of thing, like the way the old Hollywood studios had contract stars?"

"I have no idea," I admitted. I'd done my best to parrot what Mills had said. "I'm not sure they know yet. What I do know is it sure looks to me like Digger is in Mills's pocket, he's not necessarily looking out for Ziggy at all, and he's completely willing to throw me, the band, and everyone else under the bus."

"Including me?" Sarah said.

"I wouldn't put it past him."

"Ugh. Well, we're getting ready to ditch him, I told you that, right?"

"Yeah, but when?"

"Soon. That is assuming he doesn't dump me first for being seen all over the city with you. Which reminds me!" She picked up the phone and left a message for someone—possibly her driver—saying to pick up the *New York Post* and the *Daily News* in the morning.

I put the question to Jonathan, "How unusual is a deal like they're talking about?"

"Pretty unusual. But with all the mergers going on, maybe it's going to start to be commonplace. I'll do some snooping around, see what I can find out."

Sarah plopped back down. "You are good at that, aren't you!"

"It's my job, ma'am," J said with a fake cowboy twang. Then to me: "So when are you seeing him again?"

"Tuesday."

"So how long are you in the city for?"

I shrugged. "Sarah, how long am I in the city for?"

"How many changes of clothes did you bring?"

"Depends on how good you want me to smell, really."

She hit me with a pillow.

I stayed two more days in the city, including two more paparazzi-baiting outings with Sarah. The longer I was apart from Ziggy the more anxious I got, though, so I was pretty glad to head home.

I had lunch with Jonathan in midtown before I caught the train to Boston. It was nice seeing him, really it was, and it might have gone completely without a hitch if only I hadn't been stupid and asked him if he was seeing anyone. And he said no, and we had one of those telepathic moments like you can only have with someone you used to be that close with. In that moment I knew he meant not only no, he wasn't seeing anyone right now, he meant he hadn't seen anyone seriously since me. And a bunch of unspoken stuff flew back and forth between our eyes, where he saw how appalled I was, and I saw how hurt-embarrassed he was, and then he saw how hurt I was by that...

"I'm sorry," I said, for bringing it up, and for not being the one he had wanted me to be.

"Don't be," he said. "I needed some time on my own. I needed to be alone to finish writing the book."

"Ahhh." Art trumps relationships. That I understood.

"And I've been so busy since then. I know. Here I am in the city, living alone, perfect setup to see whoever I want." He shrugged. "I'm going to Fire Island with some friends next week. I wouldn't be surprised if they fix me up with someone."

In other words, he was saying: don't worry about me, don't feel sorry for me.

I squeezed his arm, which was my way of saying I cared anyway.

Jonathan and I went together down the escalator from the street. Penn Station is underneath Madison Square Garden. Somewhere above my head was the place I'd met Ziggy's mother. God, I had forgotten to give my condolences. Well, one thing at a time.

At the bottom of the escalator, Jonathan and I parted. He went off to catch the subway, and I made my way to the Amtrak ticket counter. As I crossed the polished floor I had the strangest feeling. I felt like I was the older one now, somehow, as if Jonathan had frozen in time and I had jumped ahead. Strange.

Strange.

Happy Mondays

When I got home it was early evening, and so I wasn't surprised that Christian was home. What was surprising was he was sitting in the living room with a six-pack next to him and a beer in his hand. Okay, that wasn't surprising either. The shell-shocked look on his face, though—that was.

I plopped my stuff down and said, "Hey, everything okay?"

"I've never needed a drink more than I need a drink today."

"Okaaay." I tried to remember what he'd told me about rehab and alcohol.

He saw me thinking. "I'm all right. I'm not falling off the wagon."

"If you say so. Did something happen?"

He took another swig of the beer. "Yeah."

When he didn't say anything else right away I took that as a cue to take a bottle out of the carton, pop it on the bottle opener in the kitchen doorway, and sit down across from him.

It was some kind of summer Sam Adams, different from the regular. I took that as a good sign somehow. Having decent taste in beer seemed to indicate less of an addiction to me. Not sure that was actually true. But that's how I felt about it.

When he was ready to, he said, "A guy at work sawed two fingers off today."

"Holy fucking shit, Christian," I said, when I was done spitting my beer.

"Sawed 'em off clean. Went right to the hospital. They jammed his hand and the… the fingers… into the cooler and sped him there. Crew chief said they can totally reattach those kinds of things now." He put the beer down, suddenly, looking a bit ill. Not that I blamed him. "Right? Shit. I'm never going to be able to get a drink out of that cooler again."

"Holy fucking shit," I repeated. "You're never going back to that job anyway, okay?"

"Shit, Daron, don't be such a hard ass. Def Leppard's drummer lost a whole arm and he's doing all right."

"Fuck. That's not funny."

He shrugged. "It's either laugh or cry."

"Tell me again why the fuck you're doing this job? I thought you were painting houses."

"General contracting. So that's painting and also hanging dry wall and laying tile and other crap like that." He put the empty bottle in the carton and opened another one, using the bottom of a lighter to pop the top.

"And was the guy using the saw, like, trained in safety?"

"He was trained to use the saw, anyway. I think."

"You think?"

Chris shrugged again.

"And now that he's in the hospital, who takes over the saw? You? Fuck that shit, Chris. There's got to be something better. Or with less likelihood of maiming."

"I'm not afraid of getting maimed."

I had only had two sips of my beer. "This is not about whether you've got cojones or not, motherfucker! I'm your fucking boss. Don't tell me you're doing construction because if you quit the other guys will call you a pussy."

His face reddened.

"For fuck's sake, Christian."

"It's not that. It's not."

"The hell it isn't."

We were silent for a couple of minutes, drinking and stewing. I spoke first. "I'm serious. Is it your father?"

"Of course it's my father."

"Okay, look, do you want to stay here and swap my-father-sucks stories or you want to go and get properly hammered?"

He looked at the bottle in his hand. "Hmmm."

"I'll buy."

"Deal. I take it you ran into Digger in New York?"

"Shit you're smart. Come on."

We walked down the sidewalk while drinking our beers, flouting whatever regulations there might have been, then threw the empties into a dumpster before we got to the bar we liked drinking in. It seemed like a good idea to sit at a booth instead of at the bar, given the subject matter our conversation might cover. We waited for a host to seat us. He was a college kid, or looked like one, with dark brown hair and glasses.

"Let me just check, one moment," he said, and went to check on something host-like. Whether the table was clean, maybe? I could only guess.

He came back but appeared to be rummaging around in the host stand for something. A flashlight? A sponge?

I could see there was a dimly lit booth in a corner. "Chris," I said, intending to point it out to him.

"Yes?" the host said.

"He means me," Christian said. "Didn't you?"

I looked back and forth between them. "Yeah, you. Why, do I know you?" I then said to the host.

"Doubtful," he replied. "Just moved here from Nowhereville, South Carolina."

"This must seem like freakin' paradise to you, then," Christian said.

"Came here as soon as school finished," the host said with a nod of agreement.

"Could we have that booth in the corner?" I asked. I didn't want to interrupt the conversation, but I remembered that when he's been drinking sometimes Chris can go on and on. Gift of blarney, he called it once. The kid seemed a little lonely so I hoped I wasn't quashing his one chance to talk to someone interesting that night.

Then again, who am I kidding, we were in Allston: all kinds of interesting characters probably came in and out all the time.

He didn't seem to mind. He showed us to the booth. An actual waiter came by a moment later. We ordered things with whiskey in them.

Christian didn't seem like he wanted to go first, so I did. Thus began the recounting of Digger's latest fuckery. I filled Chris in on almost everything in New York. Okay, not so much the whole story, like I left out the business about Ziggy sexing up the director of the film, but I included the bit about Mills and Digger shaking me down, and the sneaky ways they'd kept him and me apart, and how it almost fucking worked except that Ziggy and I actually talked.

Chris was as outraged at that bullshit as I was about his coworker getting maimed.

"Okay, then, your turn," I said. By this time we were on our second round and I could barely see straight. "Digger sucks. Your turn to tell me why your old man sucks."

"Because he fucking sticks his hands in children's panties, that's why."

At first I thought he was kidding. It took a minute for it to sink in that he meant it seriously. "Shit."

"Well, I don't think he does it anymore. But still. And now he's trying to quit drinking. Trying to make amends. All that shit. He wanted to make amends with me and the program he's on, you know, you try to actually make up for the shit you've caused because of your drinking. So he gets me this job like he's doing me a big favor but the more I look at it, I'm the one who's fucking doing him a favor." He let out a long, boozy sigh. "But then I think, hey, he tried. He reached out and tried. And you know, I keep thinking, if rehab is going to work for him, I have to give him a chance the way you've given me a chance—"

"Hang on, wait, one second. You never did anything as fucking wrong as... as all that." Besides the comment about being a child molester, he'd told me at various times about his father abusing his girlfriends, beating Chris, some pretty serious shit.

He rubbed his eyes. "That's not for you to judge."

"Hang on, hang on. You told me once that the reason you couldn't do the extreme style of rehab was because they broke you down and made you believe you were shit, and you couldn't hack that because low self-esteem was what drove you to drugs in the first place. So I think I do get to judge. What did you ever do, besides drugs, that made you a piece of shit? Had a little tantrum once in the studio? Big fucking deal, Christian. That's water under the bridge and you're better than that now anyway."

"Uh...." He swirled the liquor in his glass. "Jeez. You took the wind right out of my sails."

"Damn straight I did. If it was going to be a pity party, I say party's ovah." I said over as "ovah," as if using Christian's own accent would make the point sink in better. Like I was speaking his language. "Okay, I get it. You gave him the benefit of the doubt. You tried to be a good support person by being there when he was kicking booze."

"Yeah. So I went and worked with him on a job, and another, and next thing you know I'm part of the regular crew, and with my money problems it made sense, you know? But you know what? Now he's sober and he's still an asshole."

"Is he actually sober?"

"Well, funny you should mention that. I think he's cheating. He doesn't get it. He thinks he can cheat on sobriety the way he cheated on every woman he's been with. Like just a nip of vodka when no one's looking is okay. As if the reason he was staying sober wasn't actually because he needed to, but because he was going along what other people said." He shook his head. "Stupid ass."

"I thought you were supposed to try not to interact with people who undermine your soberness."

"Sobriety."

"Whatever. I have not got it at the moment, obviously."

"Yeah. Point taken."

"Okay, you're sure us drinking this much is okay?"

"We're not driving and we're not making it a habit. Once or twice a year is not a habit."

"Okay good, because I don't want to be one of the underminey people, you know, I want to be one of the supporty people. And fuck your dad."

He sniggered. "You do not want to fuck my dad."

"Fuck! You know what I mean! Oh fuck, I can't believe you said that. I've never even *met* your father."

He was laughing hysterically now though, tears leaking out of his eyes and trouble breathing and everything. And you know, that kind of laughing fit is contagious, and so when *I* was finally done laughing and could breathe again, I said, "Besides, if you keep up with that job, sooner or later they'll make you cut your hair and then I'll know you're done."

He got a horrified look. "Never."

I shrugged.

"I mean it. You know how much shit I take for this hair sometimes?"

"I think I can imagine." When was the last time I had a haircut, anyway? Ziggy had trimmed it out of my eyes in April 1989. I remembered that because it was before we went on tour. Hadn't cut it since. It hung in my eyes a lot. I think most people thought that was a "look." Intentional.

We lapsed into silence, but it was an agreeable silence. After a while he clinked his glass against mine.

Sometimes that's all you can say.

House

The next day, despite my hangover, me and Bart staged an early-morning intervention. When Christian tried to get up and go back to that job, the stubborn bastard, I hid the keys to his van while he was in the shower, and when he came out Bart told him he had a three o'clock gig. Chris didn't even ask what the gig was, just stared at us with dripping-wet hair and still-bloodshot eyes. He grunted like some kind of shampoo commercial Bigfoot and went back to bed.

I went back to bed, too.

When I woke up, it was after two and there appeared to be no one else in the house. I went downstairs to see if all the drums were there or what, saw that they weren't, and then saw the computer and turned it on to check my email.

Three hours later I stood up with a crick in my neck and the feeling I was ridiculously dehydrated. Note to self, carry food and water if you're going to go dive into the deep recesses of the electronic world. I tried to remember if William Gibson had mentioned what cyberjockeys did to stay alive while in cyberspace. It had been a couple of years since I read *Neuromancer*, though, and the main thing I remembered about it was the Rastafarian space station. In fact, that's still the main thing I remember.

Anyway. I discovered that when there's no milk in the house, do not use yogurt as a substitute if the cereal you're eating is Captain Crunch. I mean, I ate it anyway, but it was not a good combination. Froot Loops and a fruit yogurt's probably fine—in fact, I'm sure it is—but yeah. While we're on the subject, Cocoa Krispies are okay in banana yogurt but not anything else. The vanilla's too sour, and it makes the chocolate taste weird.

The thing is, I had decided to go to the grocery store when I saw we were out of milk, but you know it's always a disaster to go food shopping when you haven't eaten. Even I had learned that, at 23 years old. So I forced down a bowl of Captain Crunch smeared with Yoplait and then I put on clothes, another good thing to do before leaving the house. I was lacing up my high tops when Colin came home.

"Oh, hey," I said when he came in. "You want to come grocery shopping with me? We need milk, and two of us can carry a lot more than I can by myself."

"Sure." He hadn't taken his sunglasses off yet, and he checked his pockets for his wallet. "I've got a backpack we can put the milk and other heavy stuff in."

"Good plan."

"I'll get it." He went bounding up the stairs two at a time. As he did that it reminded me that upstairs, in my own room, under my pillow, were the keys to the van.

"Hey! Never mind!" I yelled.

Colin's head appeared at the top of the stairs, angling out so he could see me. "What?"

"I just remembered I've got the keys to the van anyway. They're under my pillow."

"Right." Colin didn't ask how that happened. He went and got the keys without complaint. I drove us to the store while explaining the business with the keys as a precaution.

We went, we shopped, we conquered. By which I mean we bought things in all four food groups, as well as sugar, caffeine, fat, and chocolate.

If people thought it was weird that a rock star did his own grocery shopping, they didn't say it to my face.

Bart and Chris came home later, and we hung around. Courtney, too. She was excited to see what we'd bought and made enough nachos for an army, which was dinner. I mean, come on, she put cheese and tomatoes and peppers and olives on, and we had bean dip and sour cream, so in my mind it was the same as eating pizza, nutrition-wise, maybe even a step up in the vegetable department. We talked about maybe having a barbecue in the driveway on the weekend and inviting some guys we knew.

It was like for a while we were everyday regular Joes. I'm sure we would have gotten bored if every day was like that, but it was kind of novel to have a day like that once in a while.

Especially when I had a feeling that, with Ziggy coming back, there wouldn't be many "normal" days to be had.

Come to think of it, the boring-regular part ended when Carynne called to say she was done wherever she was, so she could drop by so I could fill her and the guys in on what was going on. I had told Chris the night before but wasn't sure how much he remembered, and I had a feeling he'd told Bart a bunch, but again, probably with some gaps in it, so it was just as well she was coming over and they could hear it again.

The thing I hadn't told Chris, because I was waiting for them all to be in the room, was that Ziggy was coming to rehearsal. So we were all in the living room gathered around the platter of nacho crumbs when I dropped that little bombshell.

"Rehearsal for what?" Bart had asked. "For which thing?"

"Who knows?" I said. "We have to have a band meeting, all of us together, and figure out what we're going to do."

Carynne sighed. "Does it have to be on Thursday? No, wait, forget I asked that."

I wanted to ask why she'd asked, but she'd just said to forget it, so I tried to. But I suspected one of her other clients had a gig. "What time are you free? Since none of us are working day jobs right now," I said, giving Christian the eye, "we could rehearse in the afternoon, too."

"Let me get back to you, but whatever time you do it, I'll be here."

That was nice to hear.

After that we went downstairs and played around with the cello and keyboard and guitar. I never did find out what gig Bart had taken Chris to, but I didn't think it mattered.

Maybe it didn't. The thing is, the motherfucker got up the next day after that and went to the job anyway. Go on, shake your head now. Just goes to show I didn't have the monopoly on stupidity in those days.

The Emperor's New Clothes

We had the band meeting in our living room, because where else would we have it? Carynne, the four of us, Courtney taking notes, and Colin there to talk about the accounting stuff.

Honestly, it was hard to concentrate at first because Ziggy was sitting in the chair across from me and it was like he had a spotlight on him: I couldn't take my eyes off him. He was brighter and shinier than everything around him, and I don't mean his clothes, which were dark. His jeans were dyed an almost-black wine purple and he wore a loose shirt with a turquoise-and-navy blue pattern on it. There was a purple sheen to his hair, too, underneath the black.

Half of me had worried that he wasn't going to show up, but it was the half I kept gagged and tied up in the trunk of the car of my mind.

Now that he was there, in the room, in reality, it was surreal. As if he hadn't sat in that living room a million times before.

Carynne presided over the meeting. "Well, it's nice to see everyone in one place. Zig, are you around for a while?"

He gave a half-shrug. "My lease runs out September first. I'm supposed to tell the landlord this week if I'm keeping the place or moving."

"Where would you move?" she asked him.

"That might depend on what we decide here." Again the shrug.

"Okay. Here's the situation as I see it: we have an under-the-table offer from BNC to rebrand the band, which would stop all potential legal action on all our parts and they would, I believe, fix the so-called accounting problem."

"Accounting problem?" Ziggy echoed.

"Yes. They basketed the sales of the *Prone to Relapse* re-release with *1989*'s. Our interpretation is: that was wrong. The fact that *1989* didn't recoup its advance shouldn't have kept them from paying us what they owed on the sales of *Prone*, at least based on our interpretation of the contract."

"They really did that?" Ziggy's voice had an edge of sneer to it—no disbelief, more like disgust.

"The basketing bullshit is a lame attempt to hide the fact that it's their fault they didn't sell enough records," I said.

"Could be. And we dug up some other little things." She gestured to Colin, who cracked open a folder with spreadsheets in it.

He cleared his throat. His hair was down today, and his black bangs hung in his eyes. "Yeah, little things is right. Bart's dad called it 'misconduct rather than criminal.' Which means it shouldn't take much pressure to get them to make an 'adjustment' and pay us a little to make up for these things. It's stuff like they applied their standard packaging fee instead of the one we negotiated. It's only off by a quarter of a point, but when you add up all the little things their accounting department did that didn't comply with the actual contract that was signed, you're looking at a fair amount of money."

"Like ten thousand dollars," Carynne added.

"Ten-thousand, seven-hundred and seventy-six dollaroos, to be exact," Colin said. "And that's not counting the *Prone* royalties."

"So you're saying they'll probably give us the *Prone* royalties and this other ten thousand if we shut up and let them rebrand the band," I said.

"Yes."

They were all looking at me. I said, "No."

"No?" Carynne raised an eyebrow inquisitively.

"They owe us that money anyway!" I said. "We can't possibly treat it like an enticement to get us to do anything!"

"Well, if we have to go through the courts to get the money, we could spend more than we make."

Ziggy cleared his throat. "It might not come to that, though. Let's forget the money for a second and concentrate on what we want to do."

"Good idea," I said, but then I thought about what I wanted to do and that wasn't a simple question to answer, was it?

Carynne picked up the ball and ran with it, though. "In an ideal world, what would you guys be doing next? Bart? Chris?"

They looked at each other. Bart spoke. "In an ideal

world, we'd split from BNC and sign on somewhere else that would support us better. And the band would go on, building on what we did. We wouldn't be the first band to have three records with three different companies, you know."

"I wonder if Artie would be interested in a call from us," I said, thinking that sounded good, didn't it? What if there was a way to simply move on? You know, like moving on from a relationship that didn't work out? Or even one that did but that had run its course?

Carynne twirled her pencil. She was wearing what I thought of as a businessy skirt, but with a flowery top. "And that's what you all want? Or is that the only thing you can think of?"

"What do you mean?" Bart asked.

"I mean, think outside the box. What if each of you signed a solo record deal somewhere else? For example."

When she said that, everyone pretty much looked at Ziggy.

"I don't have a burning itch to go solo," Bart said.

"Don't look at me," Chris added.

"Or me," I said. "Besides the fact I think the only one of us who would probably have a viable commercial solo career is Ziggy."

Ziggy put his knees together and rested his elbows on them as he leaned forward. "I should tell you all what they're offering me."

Insert cliché here about pins dropping, held breaths, etc.

His voice was quiet, and one of his feet tapped nervously. "It's the same deal Sarah Rogue got. Five years, five million, and would include five albums and a minimum of three movies."

Colin: "Five million dollars?"

Carynne: "Up front?"

Nods from Ziggy, but he was looking at the floor, his hands, the tip of his boot—anywhere but at me, it felt like.

Mills had asked me: if I cared about Ziggy, would I impede his success? This was what he was talking about.

"They also floated the idea of ten years and ten million dollars, but I said no way." He still wouldn't look up. "Because who knows, in five years I might be worth a lot more than that."

"What did Digger say to that?" I asked.

"He said I was right, of course, and that he was thinking the exact same thing. The liar."

I looked back at Carynne, not sure where to take the discussion from there.

She had the usual look on her face she had whenever Digger's name was mentioned, like she was trying to figure out where a bad smell was coming from. "And they're presumably offering you this as a solo artist? Which would mean they would *have to* let the others do their own thing if they wanted."

"They didn't say that," Ziggy said. "They did ask me if I—ha, as if it's my decision—if I wanted to keep you guys." He sounded embarrassed to even bring it up.

Carynne sucked in a breath. "Wait. Is that why they want to do the rebranding? To get you as a de facto solo artist without actually tearing up the old contract? And keeping these guys chained up?"

"They can't," I said. "They've proved they don't give a fuck what I do as long as I don't use the Moondog name. Even Feinbaum agrees I'm in the clear on that. They can't keep me from working."

Ziggy sighed. "I think they still like the general image and concept of Moondog Three, and they want to build on the fanbase. But they think they can do that with me alone."

"What do you want to do?" Carynne asked.

Ziggy took a deep breath. "That really depends on what you guys want to do. I think if I put my foot down and say they can't have me unless they take the whole band, fix the accounting shit and the contracts and everything, they might do it. But that means Moondog Three is stuck with BNC for an even longer commitment."

Carynne went on. "And who would get the five million advance? You, I imagine. Presumably they wouldn't turn that into a full band advance."

"I don't know." His shoulders were slumped. "They don't know I'm here, by the way."

"Five million dollars," Chris said, like he was stuck on that. To tell the truth, so was I.

Ziggy shrugged again. "One, five, ten, ultimately, what's the difference? The thing I needed so much money for was my mother. And she's not..." He broke off, like he couldn't bring himself to say aloud that she was gone. His voice was rough when he went on. "That's not a concern any longer."

Carynne blinked and didn't let that get to her. "The difference is how much Digger puts in his pocket up front, that's what."

Ziggy looked a little surprised. "I meant it rhetorically."

"Of course he wants you to sign a big money deal. He gets to pocket, what, fifteen percent?"

Ziggy nodded.

"That'd be a nice payday. Seven-hundred-fifty thousand dollars." She put her pencil down. "And he gets to keep it even if you fire him later."

Which was one of the reasons Sarah's mother hadn't fired him yet. I hadn't realized her deal was quite so big. I should have guessed, given how she was spending money, but hadn't really thought about it.

"I don't know what to do," Ziggy said. "I don't know if time is running out or what."

"Why would time be running out?" I asked.

"Because." He took another breath. "I might not be the hot thing in another couple of months. The movie's not doing as well as they hoped. They're blaming Richard, they're blaming Jen, but for how long? And these deals, these multimedia development deals, they're a new thing because everyone's hot for the mergers and acquisitions, but is that going to hold up? This might be a moment. A bubble. It could pop."

Carynne took all that in, but she didn't let him off the hook. "You still haven't said what *you* want."

"That depends—"

"Don't say it depends! Come on, Zig. What do you *want.*"

Now he looked up, and he looked right at me. "Truthfully? I want it all. I want the money, and I want them kowtowing to me on both coasts. I want fame, and I want Mills's balls in a sling. And I want to keep making music with you. I want all of the above. Everything."

When he said "you" he probably meant the whole band, but it felt like he meant me. At least, that's what the look in his eye said.

Only Tongue Can Tell

When the meeting was over, and we had run out of things to say—because you know of course we rehashed everything at least twice and maybe three times—I was in no mood to actually play. More importantly, neither was anyone else. Bart made some noises about having to get up early for real, and that was all the excuse any of us needed to call it a night.

Eventually it was just me and Ziggy in the living room. I felt awkward all of a sudden. I knew how this song went, didn't I? If he had melted away and disappeared I'd know I wasn't going to see him and if he lingered it meant I would, right? Maybe not. There was that time he threw rocks at my window. Maybe any attempts I made to predict him were doomed to failure.

He seemed to feel just as awkward. He looked around at the empty room and then back at me with a hesitant look on his face, like he hadn't intended for his mere presence to be a come-on, and now that it obviously was... he wasn't sure what to say.

Don't think that I didn't want him. Don't think that where his lower lip was a little swollen from where he had chewed on it during the meeting didn't look delicious to me, like I wanted to be the one sucking on it next. But I was trying to figure out if the warning voice in my head telling me not to jump into bed with him was actually a rational, sensible one or just the same old fear pretending to be something new.

"So, how are you?" we both said at the same time, and that made us both laugh. Like we were thinking the same thing. Last time we'd talked we hadn't really *talked*, you know?

I decided right then that someone I was that in tune with I should not worry about so much. "You want to hang out?"

"Yeah," he said.

I opened a can of Coke from the fridge and offered him one. He declined and we went up to my room.

He stopped in the doorway and scanned the place from left to right. "Nice. When did you get this?" Meaning the furniture.

"I made Courtney do the shopping. She has good taste, eh?"

"It's a step up from Early Dorm Room, anyway," he said, stepping into the room. He trailed his fingers along the bookshelf. "I didn't realize you had so many books."

"I didn't either. When they were in piles on the floor and in boxes in the closet it was hard to tell." I sat down on the bed and put a cassette into the player. "Speaking of closets, I have some of your stuff."

He sat down next to me and tested the bounciness of the futon — which was to say none — by pushing on it a couple of times with his hands on either side of his hips. "What stuff?"

"I ended up with what you left on the bus." I didn't say *when you were held in isolation on suicide watch.* I didn't have to. Ziggy was always good at hearing what wasn't said. Maybe that was why we got along, since I was always holding back something? The thought gave me slight goosebumps.

"Oh," was all he said for a few seconds. "How much stuff was it? I don't even remember."

"One bag of clothes... here. You might as well take a look." I went to the closet and dragged out the bag.

Ziggy unzipped the top flap and rummaged through it a bit. He pulled out a white stuffed unicorn that he'd decorated with markers. "I kind of wondered if these had survived the trip."

"I kept mine," I said. The bear he'd decorated for me with tribal-style "tattoos" in Sharpie was in the shelf with the stereo that served as my headboard. "Oh, and this." Instead of reaching for the bear, I pulled out the notebook. Or should that be The Notebook?

He stared at it. "I thought I'd lost that."

I sat crosslegged on the bed and handed it to him. "Someone, I assumed it was you, put it into my bag."

His mouth hung open a little and his eyes unfocused as he thought back. "When?"

I kept my voice quiet and even. "The night of the charity show. You must have done it before the show or during intermission." I thought I did a pretty good job of not showing any hint of how scared and angry and freaked out I had been. After that show. After he fell. For weeks.

Ziggy rubbed his hand over the embossed cover of the notebook but didn't open it. "I guess I... Do you remember the intermission of that show?"

"Before I answer that: do you remember the opening act of the show?"

"You mean us?"

I nodded.

He nodded also, his eyelashes fluttering a little as he looked down.

I had the sudden feeling he was going to cry. I had the sudden feeling *I* was going to cry.

When we both held it together, though, I answered his question. "I remember wondering where you went between sets. But there were so many people there, from the charity, industry types, and stuff, I...." I fell silent, the feeling in my chest too heavy to continue.

He nodded again, blinking rapidly.

"And when you came back, for a second I thought you just wanted a costume change, a makeup refresh. But you... you seemed different." Colder, I thought. Much colder.

"I was on drugs," he said, his voice a resigned whisper.

"I figured that much."

He held up the notebook. "I... I want to say I had a premonition something might happen to me, so I must have put this in your bag. In case. But... but the premonition was about myself, you know?"

I wanted to ask, *Ziggy, did you plan to kill yourself?* But I couldn't ask, so instead I said, "No, I don't know."

"I... I knew I shouldn't be taking those drugs. I knew I was at the end of some kind of rope. I know it doesn't make sense. It only had to make sense when I was in the drug state." He handed me back the notebook. "I'm not ready to see this yet. I'm... I don't know."

"Are you afraid it'll... bring back that mindset?"

"Pretty much. You keep it for a while longer, okay?"

"Okay." I slid it back into the shelf so only the spine showed. Anything to minimize the enormity of the fact that Ziggy might have, at any point, considered suicide.

And then I had one of those weird moments of clarity, as if the rules of a game had suddenly presented a loophole to me. I didn't care so much whether it was "true" that he had, or had not, tried to kill himself. What I actually cared about was that he *knew* that I worried about it, and I wanted him to do something about it. Not to "tell me the truth" necessarily, but to acknowledge that I felt the way I did. And you know what would have to happen for that?

I would have to tell him how I felt. Fuck.

I let my own eyes close for a second while I drew a breath. When I opened them, he was looking right at me. *Here goes.* "I really worried you tried to kill yourself. And I really worried it was..." My throat got so tight I could barely choke out the last two words. "...my fault."

Shit. Ziggy cracked like a second-rate aquarium, and like *that* he was projectile crying. I don't know which one of us had the bright idea to hug the other. Maybe it was spontaneous. We ended up pressed together, me cradling his head while he wept into my shirt and I dripped tears into his hair.

One of us was repeating the word "Okay" softly over and over, and it took me a while to realize it was me.

Eventually he said, "No."

"No?"

"No, it's not okay. And it's not your fault. Nothing's your fault. You didn't get me hooked on painkillers. And I wasn't taking them because of you." He lifted his head and drew a deep breath. "I'm sorry."

I remembered something suddenly, then. "Digger even rubbed my nose in it. Told me that I ought to quit being such a baby and just sleep with you already because if I didn't put out, you were going to crack. And then he said *I told you so*."

"You're fucking kidding me."

"I'm not."

Ziggy's face went slack with disbelief, shaking his head slightly. "I... I don't understand his relationship with you."

"That makes two of us." I rested my forehead on the top of his shoulder. For all the upset and angst I felt, the scent of him, the solidity of him in my arms, the *reality* of him filled me with intense relief.

He freed one of his arms and took a sip of the Coke I had left next to the CD player. "This is you."

"That's the one I opened before we came up here," I said, not understanding what he meant.

"The music, I mean," he said. "I'm right, aren't I?"

"Yeah. This was a soundtrack I did while waiting for you to get out of rehab."

"It's nice." He lay back on the bed with a sigh. "Tranquil."

"Working on it wasn't, though. It was an emergency job after something else fell through. I think they half expected I wasn't going to pull it off, either." I lay down next to him and we looked up at the ceiling. "Nature documentary of some kind, whales and oceans in part of it and the American West in part of it... they didn't give me a lot to go on at first so I just did whatever the fuck I wanted. You know, hm, if I were watching a nature documentary, what would I want the music to sound like? And I did whatever I thought of. I didn't have time for anything else. I did it in Remo's home studio in Laurel Canyon."

"You and Jonathan lived with Remo?"

"For a while. And then he got this disastrous writing gig—although we didn't know it was going to be disastrous when it started—and so we rented a place in West Hollywood for several months before I took off for Japan with Nomad and he moved back east."

"So," he said carefully, "would you say you're—"

"Done? We're done."

"Okay." He smiled. I wasn't looking at him but I could hear the smile. "I wasn't sure if it was, you know, a trial separation or what."

"We're still friends," I said. "If we'd stayed together any longer I'm not sure we'd even be that."

He nodded knowingly. "So tell me about Japan."

"If you'll tell me about India."

"I have a lot of stories about India."

"Good. I want to hear them all."

That gives you some idea of why it is that Ziggy and I talked all night. I'm not even sure who had the last word. Some time after light had started to seep into the sky we fell asleep in our clothes. I woke up at one point spooned against him, my nose against the back of his neck, and I thought, you know what? There's this cliché expression, "better than sex." This isn't what they mean by it, but that's what it was.

Lust for Life

I insisted we get together and play some of the old material the next day. Ziggy never made it back to his apartment that day. He discovered everything in the bag had been laundered. I didn't remember doing it but I must have, when I was freaked out. That whole week was a blur. Week? However long it was before we went to Mexico. He changed into clean clothes and we hung around all day. I showed him the Mac in the basement. We walked to get a late lunch in the middle of the afternoon at the Vietnamese place I liked.

While we were walking back he said, "I'd forgotten how nobody in this town gives a fuck who we are."

"You mean that in a good way, right?"

"Yeah."

"I'm pretty sure in the pho place they don't even know who we are. They've been seeing us for years. It never occurs to them we're anything but metalheads from the neighborhood."

"Speaking of which, you going to keep your hair long? It's never been this long."

It was well past my shoulders now, and when I put it back, I had a real ponytail. "I guess. I haven't had any urge to change it."

"I like it long."

"Then I won't change it." I dared a glance at him, and he seemed very pleased by what I said.

Bart came over a little while after we got back, and we went downstairs while we waited for Christian to take a shower. Ziggy did some vocal warm-ups while the water ran and Bart and I tuned.

When Chris came downstairs, in a tank top and basketball shorts, his wet hair back in a ponytail, Bart harangued him about going to work. Which was good, because it meant I didn't have to.

"For Pete's sake, Christian, I thought you were going to quit that job."

"Well, they're down a guy." He hitched the drum stool under his ass and pulled out a pair of sticks. "I told them this is it, though. As soon as this job's done, I'm done."

"You mean it?"

"Yes. Swear it on my sobriety."

"Because I have a line on some other gigs. They don't pay great, but they pay what a day on a contracting crew is getting you, at least."

"I hear you. I hear you. I just couldn't leave these guys totally in the lurch, you know?"

I know, Chris, I know, you're too good a guy to do that. But maybe if they wanted to keep their workers they should've had better job safety.

Not that Moondog Three had such a great job safety record. If we ever hit the road again, I was going to make the crew put up one of those "____ Days Without an Accident" signs. Also, "No Pyrotechnics."

This was not the time to bring that up, though. "What do you guys want to play first?"

"I was going to ask you that," Bart said.

"Zig, you pick. I have no idea what you're prepared to sing."

"Mmm, let's start with something not too high. How about 'Walking'?"

So we played "Walking," and that led to "Welcome," which led to "Why the Sky." And then "Candlelight." Roughly chronological in the order they were recorded. We stuck with songs I didn't have to change guitars for.

I don't know if I can describe the way it felt to play songs again for the first time that I had played hundreds of times before, but not in a long time, with those three. It felt good. But strange, too, like I dislocated in time, like the ghost of who I had been then misted over my brain.

After "Wonderland," Bart said, "Still got it."

Ziggy nodded.

We played for about an hour, which was plenty, and then we called Carynne to see if she wanted to come with us to grab some dinner and got her answering service. Answering service? She had apparently upgraded from the answering machine. The service apparently paged her, because she called back before we could decide where we were going. I picked up the kitchen phone and Carynne started talking like we were in the middle of a conversation:

"Why don't you guys come down to Axis?"

I could hear from the background noise that was

where she was. "Who's playing?"

"One of my baby bands is third on the bill tonight." She said a name I couldn't make out. "They would love it if you guys showed, you know."

"Sure. I'll tell the guys. We can grab a slice at Pizza Pad on the way."

Whatever she said next was obliterated by the next band going on. I hung up the phone.

"Where are we going?" Chris asked, jingling the car keys in his hand.

"Axis. One of Carynne's other acts is there. They're called Stumblebum or something?"

"Oh, Sugargum," Bart said. "I heard their demo. It's a girl band. They're good."

"Okay, hang on, if we're going out I'm changing my clothes," Ziggy said. "Five minutes."

He ran up to my room. I resisted the urge to follow him and watch him undress because—come on, people—I'd just been listening to him sing for an hour. If you didn't expect it to be like an hour of foreplay, you haven't been paying attention.

He took longer than five minutes—more like fifteen—and when he came back down he had done his eyeliner and gelled his hair.

We took the van and parked on the other side of Kenmore Square where Chris knew a side street that didn't require the resident sticker and where, luckily, there was a space.

The cover was ten bucks. I put down two twenties for the four of us, not bothering to check if we were on the guest list. I mean, come on, it's forty bucks. That's as much as the band that was first on the bill got paid, probably, if they got paid at all. The second band was still in the middle of their set as we walked in. Axis looked like it hadn't changed much since the last time I was there. Most of the surfaces were painted black and were marred with scuff marks—walls, floors, even the ceiling. Chris wandered toward the stage. The rest of us took the stairs to the second floor, where it was likely Carynne and the band were hanging out.

They were. Carynne hugged me, then Ziggy, then Bart, and introduced us to the three women in Sugargum. They used stage names, which didn't help me remember who they were. The singer was some kind of Asian with bleached blond hair. We made small talk for a while. About how we'd played here a couple of times back when, as if it had been a really long time ago. Three years at most? I'd been too young to drink, so three years was about right.

"Carynne was telling us no one took you guys seriously until you got a drummer, though," one of the women was telling me. Keyboard player, I think.

"Yeah, it's true," I said.

"We had one, but female drummers who are good, they're kind of hard to find."

"What happened to the old one?"

"Tch. Got married and moved to Illinois."

"Dang."

"I know, right?"

Ziggy and the singer had broken off from the group and were conversing animatedly, complete with hand gestures. I couldn't tell about what.

The music from downstairs changed from live to pre-recorded. Carynne clapped her hands. "Showtime, ladies!"

I helped the keyboard player get her stuff onto the stage while the previous band dragged their gear off to the side.

Some people might have thought doing that kind of thing was beneath me. But I'll tell you one thing about this business: nothing is beneath you. I'm a fucking musician, not the King of Siam, okay? Just shoot me if I ever start thinking I'm too good to move an amp.

Sugargum weren't bad, talent-wise. They were fun, which was fitting for a name like that, but I found myself trying to figure out where they fit. Were they post-punk? Rock? Would they be arena rock if they had live drums and a bigger stage? Were they "alternative?"

I decided I was being a douchebag for even trying to categorize them once I realized that's what I was doing. As if I couldn't listen to the music for what it was, like I couldn't understand what I was hearing until I put it in a box or knew which filter to apply to it. Why? Had I been brainwashed by the industry? Probably. It was fucking annoying.

But there it was. I suddenly appreciated Mills's problem—and Artie's from way back. That very first meeting with me he'd said he liked what he heard but didn't know what category to put it in.

This is what I told Carynne when she asked me my opinion later. Her answer? It didn't matter what musical category they were in because no matter what they did, they'd be marketed as a "girl band." As if that was a category itself. Which was pretty fucked up in its own way, I thought, but different.

After the show, upstairs, Ziggy had that look in his eye. That hungry look.

"When was the last time you sang onstage?" I asked.

He gave me a pained grimace, and I realized with a pinprick of shock that he meant it had been that night in New York. He'd been in the studio, but not live. Somehow I'd thought for sure there would have been a press conference or a party or something....

He gestured for me to follow him into the men's room. In there, he folded a piece of paper towel, wetted it, and wiped his cheeks carefully so he didn't smudge his eye makeup. Then he turned to me. "I have a slight problem," he said, licking his lips. "By which you know I mean a serious problem."

He was being frank, so I was frank back at him. "Is this a sex problem or a music problem?"

"How'd you guess?"

"Zig, come on. You look like you're about to climb the wall." Or fuck it.

"Okay, yeah. Horny as water buffalo," he admitted. "So I'm asking. You don't seem ready to go there."

"Are you?"

"With you?"

"Isn't that what we're talking about?"

"Yes. Yes, you and me is what we're talking about." He dabbed a little more water on his face and took a deep breath. "You're right. I don't want to mess things up between us, and I know it's better to be cautious with you. I want to let you..." He had to take a breath in the middle of the sentence. "You be the one to decide when. You make the first move."

"And you're worried that by telling me this, you're goading me into making the move."

"Yeah."

"Can I tell you something? You being this honest with me is one of the hottest things you've ever done." At least, judging by the state of my dick, which was stiffer than a flagpole in my jeans.

"Can I tell you something? You being this ready to hear it: same."

"Will you be angry if I say I'm not ready yet?"

"Will you be angry if I fuck Pollyann's brains out instead?" The lead singer.

I gave myself a second to think about it. "No. But Carynne might be."

"She hasn't been giving me the hairy eyeball."

"That is a good sign."

"Well?"

"When am I seeing you next?"

"Come by my apartment tomorrow? I need help sorting stuff out."

"Okay, what time?"

"Two or three in the afternoon?"

"Should I call first?"

"I'm not sure the phone's on."

"Okay. Sure. I'll be there."

I thought that was the end of the conversation, but as he went past me to leave the room, I couldn't help myself. I snagged his arm and pulled him into a kiss. Every inch of my skin throbbed in time with my heartbeat.

When I let him go, I asked, "Why did you ask my permission?"

"Why did you give it?"

"Because you asked for it."

"There's your answer, Daron." He grinned.

I had a feeling I'd be untangling that one for a while, but that was okay. I felt good about my decision. And I felt good about the fact I was pretty sure that no matter how good the sex with Pollyann was, it was me he was going to be thinking of.

I'm Free

You might have noticed that when Ziggy went off to have a one-night stand with the lead singer of Sugargum, he didn't ask me what I was going to do. That would make you quicker on the uptake than me, since

I didn't think of it until later. It was a lot of new stuff to deal with, you know?

Me and Bart and Chris didn't stay to see the headliner, and we ended up at the Deli Haus, where we got recognized but it wasn't a big deal, and then we went to Bart's place so he could show it off, even though it was only half-renovated. It was a warm night, and we walked up Beacon Street to get there.

The place was a brownstone, narrow but they had the whole place from basement to rooftop. The full finished basement he was going to turn into a small recording studio. The first floor had a front parlor with the kitchen in the back. The second floor had what had been a formal dining room above the kitchen and would be again once the floors and ceilings were refinished, plus another parlor-type living room that Bart had already turned into a media center with the biggest TV money could buy, and the third floor had three bedrooms, one for him, one for her, and one with skylights that was Michelle's office and design studio.

"How do you decide which bed to sleep in?" Chris asked. "Flip a coin?"

"Whichever sheets are cleaner," Bart said, without any apparent sarcasm. "Check this out." He pulled on a rope hanging from his ceiling and a sort of cross between a ladder and a stairwell came creaking down. He climbed up into a space the size of a phone booth and pushed open a door to the roof. We climbed up after him. Up there was a deck with wrought iron railings and a view of the Charles. Across the river we could see the dome at MIT and the big beige building with the round thing on top of it.

"Next year, Fourth of July, this is where we'll be," Bart said.

"Unless we're on the road," I added.

"Unless we're on the road," he amended.

"Amen to that," Chris said.

We hung around until maybe two in the morning, at which point Chris declared he definitely had to get some sleep. Bart harangued him again about the job. Chris swore that all he was doing was painting, nothing with sharp objects, and that it would be done probably within a week.

When I got home I lay in bed thinking. If the things that were the most commercially successful were things that fell into categories and styles that were already known, then why didn't record companies simply recruit studio musicians and make them into bands and make them into hits?

Then again, isn't that what they actually did in the fifties and early sixties? I guess the whole thing about rock and roll, though, was this constant need for change, for new things. That's part of what made it popular. The whole "rebellion against the previous generation" thing made it kind of necessary. But now that we were on the generation *after* that generation, no one had quite figured out how to make that work. The corporations were looking at the upheaval of the sixties with psychedelia, and then the wave that was punk and New Wave, as trends that were over and done with. Like everything should just settle down now and let them market all the flavors we had, like a Baskin Robbins ice cream store or something.

But that's the problem, I thought. They've made "alternative" into a genre—like "girl band"—which isn't a genre. It's not a genre, it's a lifestyle. Okay, so not a genre, but maybe you could say it was an audience, right? But "alternative" is the audience that the mainstream *doesn't know how to fucking reach.* By definition.

I realized at that moment how fucked every "alternative" band in the country probably was at that moment. Moondog Three included. Unless all you ever wanted to do was play clubs like Axis and sell your tapes and CDs at shows. If you wanted commercial success, you had to be part of a very tiny, elite group.

The thing is, we had been a part of that group. I felt like Mills had kicked us out of the club.

Now he said he wanted to invite Ziggy into the club, on a higher level, even. Hm.

That brought me back to thinking about Ziggy, of course. So he was out there getting his "needs met," as the expression went. It had taken me a long time to admit I even had needs.

This raised the question I mentioned before: what did Ziggy expect me to do about my own needs tonight? Did he expect me to do anything? Did he know I wouldn't, which was why I didn't need his permission the way he needed mine? Or was it that he didn't care what I did, but he knew I cared what he did?

I'd have to ask, wouldn't I? I'd have to ask and we'd have to talk about it. Hm. I didn't dread that idea as much as I thought I would. It would really depend on whether he was in a mood or not.

And whether I was in a mood or not, I admit.

Which still left the question of what I was going to do that night. About my needs.

I decided I liked my needs. Knowing that the next move was mine, and that it was likely to be met with positive enthusiasm, made lusting after him so much better. Instead of painful, it was kind of nice to be on that edge of desire, to think about him without worrying whether I was ever going to see him again. It was kind of indulgent to think about him—to fantasize, even—and to know it was for the sake of enjoying how much I wanted him, rather than out of desperation because I couldn't have what I wanted.

There were nagging voices, of course. *You're going to fuck it up*, they said. *He's going to bite you. It won't last. He'll pull a Jonathan on you. You'll pull a Jonathan on him.* Et cetera.

I didn't listen. I got in the shower and took care of my "needs" and fell asleep on my bed with my hair still soaking wet.

Epic

I'll confess I got a little anxious when I tried to call Ziggy before going over to his place and got a recording saying the number was out of service. I know he had said his phone service was probably off, but I had this moment where I suddenly worried that he had left the country again. It felt like poison slowly coating my insides. I told myself I was being stupid. I was halfway there on the train when I realized I probably should have brought his bag with me. Whatever. He could get it later.

It was about half past three when I buzzed his apartment number from downstairs.

Up there I found him with a black-and-brown smudge on his cheek, wearing a T-shirt inside out and running shorts, barefoot. He had a paintbrush in one hand. The artist kind, not the house-painter kind. "Hey," he said. "Sorry. I found a piece that was half-finished, and the next thing you know I started working on it, and is it after three already?"

"Yeah. Have you eaten?"

"Good question. No. Give me a sec. I'll put on something clean and we can grab something."

He went into his bedroom while I loitered in the living room. It looked the same as the last time I was here, the night after we'd filmed the "Wonderland" video: very goth. In a draped-velvet-with-candelabras kind of way.

I hadn't thought about that day, or night, in a long time. Was that when Chris had started using drugs again? Jeez. There had been cocaine at the afterparty. I had assumed the film crew had brought it, but maybe it had been Lacey. Or some combination thereof.

I remembered Ziggy being really sensible that day. And I had really appreciated that. We had drunk too much and had barely made it here because neither of us could see straight.

Okay, put "sensible" in air quotes. Somewhere in the back of our minds we had to both have been wondering if "going home together" was going to lead to something. It hadn't, but blame alcohol for that, too.

I went into the hall. His bedroom door was open, and I could hear rustling like he was digging through a drawer of clothes. I leaned against the doorframe.

He had put on a pair of black jeans but apparently hadn't found a shirt yet. His chest was bare, and as he lifted his head to look at me it was like his nipples were staring at me, too.

So much for going out. I took a step into the room and pulled one of his belt loops with one finger until his hip touched mine. I ran my other hand up his bare stomach until my fingertips skated over one nipple.

A last shred of my rational brain made my lips move. "Are you hungry?"

He shuddered as one of my callused fingers circled the tip of his nipple. "Only for this," he breathed, and left his lips slack, waiting to be kissed. I did not miss my cue. I kissed him, wet and soft at first, then harder as I tugged on that nipple. Despite my pulling, the kiss moved him backward toward the bed. I let my mouth express all the urgency I'd been holding back, and I flattened him back atop the bedspread.

His hands pushed at my denim jacket and I shed it without breaking the kiss. To get my shirt off, though, I stood up straight and pulled it over my head.

Ziggy's eyes glittered eagerly as he shifted further onto the bed. "You look amazing."

I wanted to insist that I wasn't any different. Except I knew that I was, physically, mentally, spiritually, from the last time we did this. I'd fought hard to change, yet I still didn't want to admit it, like that would give too much credence to how much of a failure of a human being I had been in the past.

Okay, at the time, I admit, I wasn't thinking that deeply. It was later when I was trying to explain to myself why I didn't simply revel in his admiration of how I'd changed that I thought up a reason why. In that moment I shook my head to brush him off.

"Believe what you want, but you do." He ran a hand up and down my arm as I crawled over him again. I was in no hurry to get our jeans off. Well, I was, but I wasn't.

I ran my fingernails down his chest and watched him shiver. It had been a really, really long time, hadn't it? I had forced myself to forget how much I loved doing this, how much I loved making love to him. Remembering again was like going from black and white to color, from mono to stereo.

"Oh yes," he said. On that point we most definitely agreed.

Think

When we woke up I almost didn't want to get in the shower. I wanted to lie there and breathe in the scent of him forever. We were pressed together so closely that I couldn't figure out which one of our stomachs it was that growled really loudly.

"I guess that means we should get up," I murmured. (Ziggy wasn't the only one who had been kind of stupid about not eating that day.)

"We could get something delivered," he said.

"We'd still have to get out of bed to answer the door," I pointed out. "And eating would require sitting up, anyway."

"True. Probably worth getting up for real, then. Come on. Let's get in the shower together."

Okay, so that delayed us getting dinner by another hour because neither of us was feeling much in the way of inhibitions at that point. And I've always liked coming in the shower. And he had all kinds of fancy conditioners, heady-scented like incense. For all I knew they were mostly there for wanking purposes? They were certainly good for that.

It was night by the time we finally got dressed and went out. We walked to Newbury Street, and I was fairly sure that anyone who looked at us was going to be seeing a super-bright just-fucked glow. I also didn't care.

We ate in a Thai restaurant in the basement of a brownstone where my food was way too spicy and I didn't care that it was. I was feeling too good to let it bother me, and it wasn't like it didn't taste good, just that I normally don't need the pain threshold on a meal to be quite so high.

The restaurant was called The King and I. That made me laugh on our way out. Ziggy asked what I was laughing about. I said, "Nothing, Your Highness."

We went into Tower. We got a couple of sidelong looks and double-takes from people while we browsed, but nothing problematic.

"I met a buyer for Tower while I was in LA," I said while we were looking through a couple of CD bins, side by side. "I kind of thought I knew something about record retail after working here, but I think it gave me a rosier outlook than the reality."

"What do you mean?" Zig asked.

"The guy was saying that, basically, Tower figured out how to capture the alternative market, but pretty much none of the other national chains have. Which might explain why our sales are great through Tower and Newbury and shit through everywhere else."

"Hey," Ziggy said, looking at me instead of at the CDs. "Don't blame yourself."

"What? I'm not blaming myself."

"You're sure? You sound kind of like you're saying you miscalculated the album's sound, thinking it would have a spot?"

I chewed that over for a second. "Maybe. I don't think when we started writing songs that we had the record store bin in mind, though."

"Yeah. True." He went back to flipping through the inventory.

In my own bin I kept coming to stray copies of a B-52s album. It's funny. They're one of those bands I really like, but I own none of their albums. To be nice to whichever clerk had reshelving duty next, I gathered them together and put them in the front of the B divider. I couldn't stop myself, really.

We eventually wound down our browsing and it was time to move on.

"They're going to put a plaque to you in this place," Ziggy murmured to me as we made our way toward the classical department with the CDs we had each picked out. He looked at the glass door into the classical section. "What do you need in here?"

"There's always a shorter checkout line in here. Haven't I told you that?"

"Oh, you know, I had forgotten about that."

In fact, there was no one in there but the one bored-looking clerk, who happily took our money and immediately went back to being bored the moment we left. Dude, I know, I feel your pain.

We walked along Mass. Ave. out of reflex. Hey, there was the pizza place where he and I had eaten a million years ago, back before that first time we slept together. A million years before.

"Now what?" Ziggy asked.

"You mean we're not going back to your place to fuck some more?" I asked, only half-jokingly.

"That is certainly an option."

"There was some pretense of why I was coming over, wasn't there? Was it just a pretense or was there something practical we were going to get done?"

"Oh, yeah, I need to sift my crap and decide what I'm keeping, including whether I'm keeping the apartment or not."

"If you don't keep the apartment...?" I realized I hadn't thought through what that would mean.

"Well, if I sign this development deal, I think I better move to LA."

Every part of me stopped at that moment, my brain, my feet, my heart. "Wait."

He grasped immediately what had knocked me for a loop. "Isn't that one of the options on the table?"

"Is it?" I think I grabbed his hand, like an astronaut in space trying not to drift away.

"Breathe, Daron. Breathe. Nobody's made any decisions yet, right?"

"Right..."

"Including we haven't ruled out taking the offer on the table, with various caveats and conditions. Isn't that one of the things we talked about?"

I took a deep breath. "Right. You're right. I guess...." I felt my cheeks flush. I felt embarrassed that I'd somehow made some pretty huge assumptions, emotionally anyway, that once I thought about them for even a second seemed obviously that: assumptions. Wow. Like the one that now that we were attached at the hip, he wouldn't even contemplate moving three thousand miles away. Like the one that in order to keep us together, we were going to do everything in both of our powers to keep the band together.

Facts, Daron, facts. This wasn't a decision to be made with my dick or my heart. Ziggy seemed to grasp that, at least. Huh. I thought I was the calm, rational one and he was the flighty, drama-prone one, but maybe it was time to throw that idea out the window, too. I wasn't the only one who had grown up a little in the past year, I guess.

"Should we talk about it now?" Ziggy said. "Well, I mean, should we go home to talk about it, or—"

"Let's talk as we walk," I said. "Let's break it down into small pieces. I think I still haven't got my head around everything that's in play."

"Okay." He squeezed my hand in his. "Okay. One step at a time."

One step at a time.

If You Leave

We walked down Boylston Street. The night air was breezy, humid in that end-of-summer way.

"I can tell you're upset," Ziggy said.

"In the sense of, like, the apple cart in my mind flipped over, yeah." I took a deep breath of the night air. We were passing the hotel where Jonathan and I had spent a weekend, but that thought barely made it to the surface. "I'm not angry. I'm not freaked."

"It's okay to be upset, Daron. This is something that's going to change everything. Whatever we decide. All the apple carts are going to flip."

"I guess I'm still clinging to the fact I wish it didn't have to." The breeze was blowing his un-gelled hair across his forehead. It was confusing that I wanted to pull him into my arms and kiss that forehead at the same time we were discussing breaking up the band.

"Okay, first of all, on that point, are you blaming yourself? Because if you are, stop."

"I don't think I am. I think I'm pretty well blaming Mills and maybe Digger for it."

"Digger for—?"

"Being a waste of a human being, but even more for being a manager who didn't look out for us. Especially now that I know what he had on the table for Sarah Rogue was a deal like yours."

"You think he was so blinded by Sarah's deal that he didn't see what was coming on the other side?" That frown line between Ziggy's eyebrows. I wanted to kiss it.

I tried to stay on topic instead. "No. I mean he sold us out to close Sarah's deal. Instead of fighting for us, he was cozying up to Mills and trying not to make waves so he could close this other deal."

"Oh." Ziggy's eyes were as wide as I'd ever seen them without aid of eyeliner. "Oh, shit. I didn't realize that."

"Yeah. When I fired him I knew he'd rolled over for Mills but I hadn't known why. Now? Now I know why."

"Well, no wonder you're so against me signing this deal."

I stopped in my tracks again. "Ziggy, you signing this deal signs the death warrant for Moondog Three. Even without all the crap about Digger. Can't you see that?"

"Okay, but... What if it didn't have to?"

"What do you mean?"

"Hear what I'm saying. We're talking about two different things. One, you being against the deal because it plays into what these guys you see as enemies want. Two, because of how it would actually affect the band. They're related but separate."

We weren't holding hands anymore, but I didn't remember when we'd let go. "Okay."

He looked up and down the street. We were in front of the convention center. "Come on. Let's keep moving."

"All right." We started walking again, slowly. My feet were moving, but what we were saying was a lot more important to me than moving through space right then.

"Now, try to set aside the whole Digger-selling-us-out thing for a second. I know that's huge, so it's not easy. But compartmentalize a little for the sake of figuring this out."

"That's hard to do when I wonder if he wasn't thinking all along that what he was going to do was get Sarah's deal closed and then work one like it for you, which would essentially let him keep control of everything I built while cutting me out of the picture."

Ziggy made an "unh" sound deep in his throat. "God. When you put it that way... Okay, yes, I allow as to how that might have been his plan. But honestly, Digger's not great at such long-term planning. He's great at recognizing opportunity and grabbing it, though. And he's also a selfish prick who is definitely not above screwing you for spite. So I get that. But still. Let's try to set that aside and look at this deal for what it is."

"Okay."

"Which is a fuckload of money." He was looking up the street as he said it, not at me. "So let me see if I have this straight. Christian needs money because he got himself in a hole with drugs, and he knows if he doesn't keep up his mortgage payments you'll have to cover him, and that'll torpedo what self-esteem he has left and make him so unable to face you he'll probably have to move to another state."

"Wait, what?"

"You don't think that's what's going on?"

"Well, I knew he was funny about money, but—"

"Daron. Trust me on this. Chris will never live it down if he defaults to you. His pride can't take it. He's already on a self-esteem rollercoaster as it is."

I got the feeling Ziggy was more familiar with the self-esteem rollercoaster than I had previously suspected. "You might be right. Especially after I called him a motherfucker for convincing me to buy the house with him when he was pretending he was totally okay with me being gay, when he wasn't." That came out sounding wrong. "I mean, now I know it was more complicated than that. But when we were fighting that was how it seemed. You know, how could you have done that if you were actually afraid to get my cooties? We're cool now, but it was an issue."

"I'm sure he hasn't forgotten that either. So, problem one is your mortgage." He bent back his left index finger with his right, as if ticking it off the list. He added his middle finger. "Problem two, art."

"Art?"

"Music. Artistic self-determination. Whatever you want to call it. I don't want to say artistic 'freedom,' because the only way you have that is to not have a record company at all. Freedom would be us doing four solo albums and selling them on street corners, right?"

"Okay. We accept that a certain amount of compromise is necessary as part of the package. I've always known that. You don't record a single where all the lyrics are the word 'fuck' just because you feel like it unless you've got the mentality of a six-year-old."

"Which some bands do."

"True. But we never did. I like to think we've always been more mature than that, musically speaking."

He nodded. "Hey, this is the rock and roll sushi place." He pointed to a restaurant on the other side of the street.

"The what, now?"

"Rock and roll sushi. You know. Most sushi places are like some kind of modernist Zen garden. This one, they call it rock and roll sushi on weekends. Because the music's loud."

"Do you want to go in?"

"We just ate dinner," Ziggy pointed out.

"I know, but if you wanted to go in, I'd go with you." I realized we hadn't made it very far down the street.

"No no no, I'm just noticing it's here. Not saying I want to go there right now." He waved his hands and sped up walking, as if to get us away from the place. "Anyway. So problem one, mortgage, problem two, to put it more frankly: what happens to the band. Mills wants to get rid of you, that much seems obvious."

"Him and Digger both." We were walking more briskly now, as if the questions we were asking had more urgency.

"Assuming I have some bargaining power here, I might be able to do something."

"Like what?"

"Like make it a condition that the band stays with me. Or that you are totally free to start something else without them owning your ass. Or they have to liberate the back catalog. I don't know exactly, but I'm sure I have at least a little leverage."

"Ah."

"And if I sign it, a couple million dollars goes a long way to solving problem number one—and most of the other problems I can come up with. Like how to put your sister through school. How to keep Carynne employed—"

"Wait, what about Carynne? Wouldn't signing this deal mean you're keeping Digger as manager?"

"First of all, why? So I can get my money's worth or something? Second of all, you don't think Carynne would still be my road manager if I asked her to? This is assuming you don't get the rights to the band name, hire another singer, and have her locked up so busy I'd have to hire someone else because she'd be on tour with you."

My knees got weak and I had to stop walking. He gripped my wrist.

"Sorry, too upsetting?"

"You never..." I felt dizzy. "Stop for a second and listen to what you just said. You go off and have a solo career while I replace you and Moondog Three goes on without you?"

"In theory, Daron, in theory."

"In theory the entire world could end tomorrow, too!" So this was the thing about being upset but not angry or freaked out: it was a very, very short distance from upset to either or both of those things. "What happens to us, then? What happens to you and me if we're both on separate tours for half the year, and you're on location shooting a film the rest of the year?"

He took the small paper bag of CDs out of my hand, put it into the plastic bag hanging from his wrist, and then took both my hands in both of his. "That is problem number four, or five, I've lost track. And let's not call them problems anymore. Let's call them priorities. How high a priority is it?"

"How high a priority is what?"

"This." He squeezed my fingers in his. "Don't answer yet. Listen to me. I know we just had the world's most mind-blowing sex. I am so in love with you right now I am almost ready to throw five million dollars out the window, okay? But I'm also not some lovestruck teenager who believes 'if we just stick together we'll find a way.' Don't try to sell me on some kind of idea like we can live on what we'd make busking in the park on sunny days. This isn't Spain. Plus Courtney's tuition isn't cheap. Plus your mortgage. Okay?"

I tried to mull that over sensibly. But what I said was, "You thought the sex was mind-blowing?"

"Didn't you?"

"Yes, best I've ever had, but you've had a lot more—"

"*Daron*," he said, eyes flaring and emphatically knocking that train of thought right off the rails.

"Okay. Okay, you're right, if you'd asked me two weeks ago, or two years ago, which I'd pick, a guaranteed five million dollars or a very not-guaranteed relationship with you, it might have been a tough choice."

"And I'm saying let's not throw five million dollars out the window merely because love has made us stupid."

"Okay." I pulled him to me and kissed him then, a quick but deep kiss that left us both breathless. Quick because we were standing on a public street. So much for love not making us stupid? We were practically standing in front of the gay bookstore, for Pete's sake. I looked up and could see the sign in the window on the second floor where it was located. Glad Day, it was called.

Ziggy saw me looking. "You ever been in there?"

"No. And we're not going in there now."

"No?"

"No. We're going back to your place to fuck, because at this point that's the only chance we'll have to talk rationally again. I want you so much right now I can barely finish this sentence, much less a rational thought."

So we did that. Went back to his place and peeled back the bedspread to the un-love-stained sheets underneath and stained them good and thoroughly.

Be Still My Beating Heart

I meant it when I said that "compromise" is part of the package if you're going to be a professional musician, if what you mean by compromise is you accept that you might not just be able to scream the word "fuck" two hundred times and call it a song. Or any other thing that you might want to do. Understand, you have every right to scream "fuck" two hundred times if you want; it's that no one gives you a right to make a living doing it. If no one wants to hear you, that doesn't mean your art isn't valid or important or good, just that it isn't commercial.

Where the music business sucks the worst, of course, is that what if there are people who want to hear you but the only way they can find out about you is through the industry machine, and the machine itself crushes you beneath its wheels before it even notices you? or in its gears after it swallows you whole? Sorry for the Pink Floyd imagery, but it's the case that the machine wants to spit out the same sausages it sold before. It's not good at finding new customers, and it's not good at selling new sounds to old customers.

But those are the two extremes. Most professional musicians I know are somewhere in the middle: they're neither at the stage where they have no living and no audience nor at the other end where all they do is pump out imitations of what's come before. This isn't about scale or fame, either. You have wedding bands and Muzak session players and Top 40 manufactured acts all on the imitation end, and you have both the undiscovered and the so-famous-they-don't-give-a-fuck so they make inaccessible shit at the other. Most of us aren't at either extreme. We're somewhere in a very wide middle.

No judgment on the wedding bands or Muzak players, either, don't think I'm saying that's wrong or "bad" somehow. It's not. Anyone who works hard to entertain people has my respect, and if you think it isn't hard work you haven't been listening to me.

But anyway. The only real question about the future of Moondog Three was an existential one. I didn't actually know what the word "existential" meant before. I'd always heard it with "existential angst" and associated it with pretentious philosophy students in berets. But as Ziggy explained it, lying there in his bed—which had black satin sheets, by the way—the question was whether the band would still exist in the future. And if we rebranded, even if we kept the four of us together, would that count as "existing" since it might not be the "same"?

"Would you be able to stomach it if the thing with your name on it went on without you while you did something else?" he asked, while we were lying there, side by side. He had the window cracked open now, and cool night air seeped across us, cooling the sweat on my skin. He was curled next to me, holding the back of my hand to his cheek like a baby with a security blanket.

"I don't know. You know what I bet, though? I bet if you did one album as Ziggy and the Moondogs, by the next one it would be just you, they'd drop the band name completely. Did you hear what John Cougar Mellencamp is doing? On his next record, they're finally getting rid of 'Cougar.'"

"Huh." Ziggy said.

"You know he paints, too."

"John Cougar?"

"Yeah."

"Interesting. You might be right about the name thing, though. Transitional. If it's just a studio band anyway they won't think twice about firing them."

I almost felt sorry for this mythical band that didn't yet exist. Then again, they were probably going to hire veteran session players who were used to going from gig to gig...

I shook myself. I was thinking like it had happened already. No wonder I had started to feel a little ill. The afterglow of sex was most of what was keeping me calm and un-anxious.

Yeah, me. Remember when I used to have panic attacks after sex? Okay, mostly just that one time. But I thought it was worth noting.

"But what do *you* want, Daron?"

I rubbed the back of my hand against his cheek. "Maybe it's just timing, but right now I think if I knew it could always be like this with us, I wouldn't give a fuck what happened with contracts or whatever. But is that just sex talking? I kinda think it is."

He gave me his Cheshire Cat smile. "Well, maybe." He kissed the back of my hand again before he sobered, saying more seriously: "I mean, there's the question of whether it could be like this if, for example, our careers pulled us in different directions. Or if you were having angst over money."

"Yeah. But you know. When you're Romeo and Juliet, you think that drinking poison is a totally reasonable course of action."

"I know." We shifted position so that we were still lying down, but now different parts of us were glued together. "Which one of us is Romeo and which one is Juliet?"

"You're both," I said. "You're the one with the swagger and you're the pretty one."

He snorted.

Then it was my turn to be serious. "I will say this: I think if we don't come up with some way for you to get this contract, you're going to resent it for the rest of your life."

He was silent, letting that sink in, or letting the fact that I'd come out and said it sink in. When he spoke, he wrapped one of his ankles over mine. "You might be right about that."

"You said you want everything. All of it. What if there's no way to have it all?"

"That's why we're talking so much. Trying to figure it out. What our priorities are. Another way to put it: what are we willing to sacrifice? Or what can we sacrifice without losing our minds, our souls, our hearts?"

"That sounds like a song." I was half-joking, the way I often do when something gets melodramatic.

"Let me write it down." He slipped away from me on the bed, to grab a composition notebook jammed between the headboard and the wall. It had a pencil tucked into the pages, and he scrawled down a couple of lines. I was content to watch him, one leg folded under him, as he moved the pencil against the paper.

When he was done, he stuck the notebook back where it had been.

"That's a handy place to keep it," I said.

"Yeah, always in reach if I get an idea in the middle of the night. And it keeps the headboard from knocking against the wall when we fuck."

That made me laugh. Always multiple motives with Ziggy. Everything has more than one reason.

"Let's fuck again," I said. "My brain is too full to talk anymore."

"Are you ready to go again?"

"Check for yourself."

He lay alongside me and reached down. "What if I could get your mortgage paid off, Courtney's tuition paid off, Digger paid off to get out of our fucking hair, and still keep five million for me?"

"Is the five million really important?" It was going to be difficult to keep up this conversation if his hand kept doing what it was doing.

"Only in a symbolic way, given it's how much they offered, so topping it is important. Overall? It represents how hard they'll work to make back their investment, by ensuring my success. But imagine. What if I could get all that? The only question left would be the existential one about the band."

"That's too many ifs."

"There are never too many ifs. What if I could rule the universe, get revenge on everyone who'd wronged us, and justice would reign supreme?"

"Um..."

"Or, you know, hit number one, make them all eat crow, and write my own ticket from there. Well, maybe that's the same thing."

"If you could do all that, why couldn't you just get them to okay the band staying together?"

"Well, maybe I could. I'm just asking, what if. Trying to see how we feel about various scenarios, some best case, some worst case. Something to think about."

I had plenty of time to think about it then, since conversation had to cease while his mouth took over for his hand. Except I wasn't about to get much thinking done with his wicked tongue taking up all my attention.

That night I had a dream. In the dream, I worked as a busboy at the Ground Round, while Ziggy was the host who seated people. It was one of those startlingly realistic dreams, and the problems and complications at the restaurant kept getting worse, and the entire thing was grind-my-teeth stressful. Which meant that when I woke up in the middle of the night with nothing resolved yet regarding the band and Ziggy, I felt oddly relieved.

Too Much Joy

I woke up in the morning to the smell of coffee. I pulled on a pair of jeans. They were on the floor with a couple of other pairs, and Ziggy and I are about the same size, but I'm pretty sure they were mine.

Out in the living room he was perched on the odd, claw-footed antique chair, with a mug next to him and his notebook in his lap.

"What do you think?" He turned the open page to face me. I came close enough that even my bleary eyes could make out the words. The song was apparently called "Making Up for Lost Time." I smiled. "I think I'm too sleepy to really judge it. But, hah, yeah." We were each up to, what, six? orgasms in the past twenty hours? I may have lost track. I was actually starting to feel sore. Not that I cared about that.

I handed him the notebook back and picked up his mug. The coffee had gone cold. I took a gulp anyway. Ziggy liked it with a lot of sugar. "So are we actually going to sift your possessions?"

"Yeah, I guess we should." He closed the notebook and scrubbed his face with his palm. "I don't have a lot of stuff, really. Not that I care about. I've got to figure out if I'm keeping the art, though, or pitching it."

"You mean like the painting you were working on yesterday?"

"Yeah. You want to see it? It's in the kitchen."

He got up and took me to the kitchen, which was a tiny room, but with just enough floor space for an easel and a person to stand in front of it. The counter was littered with painting paraphernalia, tubes of color and such. I know nothing about painting, so I wasn't sure what all I was looking at. The easel was more or less in the doorway, so that he could get the light from the tiny window shining on it, I supposed. He squeezed past it so he was in the kitchen while I was still in the hall. He plucked the canvas off the easel and turned it around to face me.

It appeared to be an impressionistic image of deep foliage, with overhanging vines and bushes, except for two eyes peering out of the area of deepest shadow.

"You can't throw this away," I said. "People will want to buy it just because you're famous."

"But isn't that the question? What if I don't want people to buy crappy art just because of my name? What if I suck as a painter?"

"It looks fine to me."

He growled. "That's not what I mean and you know it."

"Isn't it?"

"Bad art is... I don't know if I could live with it if critics were panning it."

Oh. This was definitely too deep a conversation to have before breakfast. "What's the chance you get a fair shake from critics anyway, though? Zig, seriously, when did you decide you wanted to be a fine-art painter?"

"Well, I don't, really, but I have these paintings and have to decide what the fuck to do with them."

"Keep them. Whether you think they're good or not. They're art. You can't just throw that away."

"But is it worth moving them across the country, if I move to Los Angeles? Or New York?"

"About that," I said, but found myself pausing, trying to tread carefully on the subject I wanted to bring up.

He seemed to know it was something sensitive. He put the painting down on the counter, folded the easel, and came out in the hall, kissing me good morning as he did it. That tamped down my rising anxiety.

All right. "You could always leave the paintings at the Allston house," I said. "Or... you could just move in."

"No," he said, then quickly added, "Don't think I don't realize how serious it is for you to ask me to move in with you, Daron. But no. It would not work."

"You've thought about this before?"

"Yes. And I would go insane living with Chris and your sister and Colin. For one thing, putting me and Colin into a house together would be a terrible idea."

"I thought you and Colin got along really well."

"Too well. Do you really think it would work for me to be fucking Colin with you in the next room?"

"Um..." I was trying to think of a tactful way to say *been there, done that.*

"I mean on a regular basis," Ziggy said, as if I'd said it out loud. "And... I don't know. I'd feel really weird."

"What would feel weird?"

"Sleeping with you, in that house."

"What?" Okay, now I knew I needed coffee or a hearing aid or something. "Zig. You snuck into my room after climbing up the fire escape and—"

"Because I was desperate. If I lived there, if we were together? It'd be so creepy, don't you think? To have your sister, and a guy we've both slept with, and Chris who has all kinds of issues, all in earshot?"

I pulled him back to the living room, where the mug of cold coffee sat. I drained it and handed it to him. "Are you seriously saying that you'd be weirded out having normal, unsurreptitious sex with me in my own house?"

"Yes."

"I didn't think you had any inhibitions."

"Well, you found one." He put the mug onto the mantel of the fireplace. "That's part of the problem, I guess. It's your house. If I moved in there, would I be your tenant? Weird. All kinds of weird."

"Waitasecond. We were just talking about you paying off the mortgage on the place. Wouldn't that make you an owner, too?"

He waved a hand like that didn't matter. "I just know it wouldn't work. You and I have enough trouble making things work. Putting a monkey wrench like that in, just... no. Trust me."

"Okay." I sat down in the chair, but it hadn't hit me yet why I felt so deflated.

He sat at my feet and rested his head on my knees. "Daron. It's all right. I'm not rejecting you. Just the idea of moving into your rock and roll family commune."

I snorted, trying to smile. "Is that what it is?"

"I don't know how you stand being around so many

people all the time, actually. You're even more of an introvert than I am."

"You're an introvert?"

"I mean it, Daron. If I lived with that many people I'd spend all my time hiding in my room."

"You do all right on tou—" I didn't stop myself in time. Ziggy *hadn't* done all right at all on that last tour, and his face showed it. "Was that because of all the people?"

He sighed. "No. No, it wasn't that. And it wasn't you or the guys. I had plenty of time to myself."

The full notebook of lyrics proved it, I guess. "I used to live alone. I had a studio in the Fenway." I combed his hair with my fingers. "At first it was rough, moving into Allston. The house was more crowded then, too, with Lars and his girlfriend, and a couple of others, but I was pretty broke and needed somewhere to go. But now it's really all people I'm close to. That makes it easy, somehow."

He sighed sympathetically. "Don't ask me why. We could put all those same people in a tour bus with us and I'd have no problem giving you a blow job in your bunk. But if I lived there, in the house, no."

"What about if you don't live there?" I still couldn't get the logic of this. "Like right now. What happens if we go over there to rehearse and I ask you to stay the night?"

"That's all right. I like it here better, but I wouldn't leave you with blue balls."

"I still don't see what the difference is, you living there versus visiting me there."

He looked up at me. "It would feel different. That's all. Sometimes you just know."

"Okay. I'll accept that." My turn to sigh. "Which reminds me. Speaking of things I just know. Whatever we negotiate in the future. You have to promise me one thing."

"Which is?"

"You ever sleep with Mills, it's over." I had meant for it to come out joking, but it came out dead serious. I tried to make a joke about double-homicide but it wouldn't come out. Instead I repeated, "Over."

"Promise," Ziggy said. "I can see why that would fuck you up. For the record, I'm going to continue to treat Courtney like she's off-limits, even if she does flirt outrageously with me every chance she gets."

"La la la can't hear you!"

"That girl tortures me something fierce. You know what? I can't even tell if it's because she really wants something to happen but knows because I'm off-limits I'm safe to mess with, or if it's some kind of revenge for things she thinks I did to you."

"Seriously?"

"Seriously." He sucked air through his teeth. "Your sister's hot."

"Revenge-flirting. What a concept." There were ways in which my sister was more like him than she was like me, I think. "Thank you, though."

"Don't thank me for respecting your boundaries. I should. You do get that it's your job to set them, though, right?" He stood up and stretched. He was wearing boxer shorts so old they were wearing through at the edges, and his stomach was brown and flat where it disappeared under the sagging elastic. "Any other rules you want to make while we're on the subject?"

"Stay safe?"

"Good. You, too." He nodded.

A swirl of old arguments with Jonathan washed through my head. And non-arguments, too. Like the whole "be with me when you're with me" thing. Somehow I couldn't quite apply that to me and Ziggy, though. "I don't want to end up on opposite coasts if we can avoid that."

He looked out the window, down into the alley between buildings. "We survived being on different continents pretty w—"

"No, we didn't!" I hadn't expected my anger to flare up hot like that. I was on my feet and he turned to face me. "Are you fucking kidding me, Ziggy? This relationship barely made it through. And what if you didn't come back? What if you'd caught something fatal?"

"But I didn't—"

"What if I'd decided not to come back?"

"But you did. That's my point, Daron."

"That I'm at your beck and call?" I was burning too hot, moving too fast.

And Ziggy knew it. "Whoa, waitasecond, where did that come from? No, what I'm saying is that this relationship is the reason both of us came back." He came close, and I managed not to bristle. "Neither of us is here because some corporation owns our contracts. Don't tell me that's why."

I took my cue to slip my arms around his waist. "Don't try to tell me that you—" Wait, what was I saying? Why was I so convinced that I was the one at a disadvantage? I leaned my head against his. "Never mind. I don't know what I'm saying."

"Give it time," he said. "We're not making any decisions yet."

"I don't want to let you out of my sight." I buried my nose in his hair.

"Yet you did, the other night."

"I'd rather give you permission to have sex with someone else than drive you to it by making you feel trapped," I said.

"Wow."

"Wow what?"

"That's a really... evolved train of thought from you, Daron."

"It's true. And I don't feel threatened by Pollyann."

"But you feel threatened by the idea of me moving to Los Angeles."

"Yes. I don't know why."

"Hm. My next question was going to be why."

"Maybe because I hate Los Angeles. Or maybe because I wasn't worried you'd fall in love with Polly but I am afraid if I'm not around you'll fall in love with *somebody* and the next thing you know I'll be pawing on the glass outside again."

"Again?"

"Are you telling me this thing with this actress was just a fling? You practically eloped to India with her."

"Well, except it wasn't like we got married."

"No, just the honeymoon." Why couldn't I shut up? Why couldn't I slow down?

He made a pained noise, though, more like I was right than like he took my antagonism the wrong way. "I was never in love with Jennifer Carstens, okay? Never. We clicked. But I was never in love with her."

I didn't know what to say to that. It was good to hear, good to know, if it was true, but still. "But sometimes fucking somebody leads to love."

"Sometimes," he agreed. Then he pulled back to look me in the eye. "No, actually. That's only happened to me once. Once exactly."

My throat closed. *Don't you dare fucking lie to me about this, Ziggy Ferias...*

"You know who the one person was, Daron. You."

I don't know why I argued, but I did. Actually, maybe I do know. Because I wanted so very much to hear him say it. I wanted him to love me. I wanted it to be true. I wanted it enough that I needed to be sure it wasn't just me hearing what I wanted to hear. "I thought you had a thing for messing with closet cases."

"I do. But I had wanted to get to know you for a while at that point."

Get to know me? "Biblically?" I had the familiar feeling of needing a translator when Ziggy spoke. "Wait, at which point?"

"That day in the park."

"Wait, *what?* How could you have already wanted to know me on the day we first met?"

He moved his weight from one foot to the other, like we were slowdancing. "I know you think that was the day we met, but it wasn't. I'd seen you a couple of times before, at parties."

"Seen me? But did we actually talk to each other?"

"Maybe not, since you were always behind a guitar."

"Then I stand by my story that in the park that day was the first day we met."

"Well, fine, but if you could have love at first sight, so could I, only I saw you first." He seemed extremely pleased to have won this argument.

I was giddy-pleased to have lost it, but still wanted proof. "So when was it? The first time you saw me."

"Bart's girlfriend Michelle had a friend from art school named Susanna. Her parents have a house down the Cape. She had a lot of infamous parties at which a lot of art-school types got very drunk and had a lot of sex. As you might recall, I was, once upon a time, in art school."

"Oh." It seemed obvious when spelled out that way.

"And I would have put the moves on you all the way back then, maybe, if you hadn't been hiding behind the guitar every time I saw you."

"Maybe?"

"Maybe. Girls were plentiful and distracting. And none of my sexual relationships with men had worked out all that healthy at that point."

"Healthy?"

"I mean mentally."

"Like that kid you jerked off behind the school."

"Yeah. They'd all been like that to one degree or another: dirty and hidden and wrong. It was only women I tried to have romantic attachments to. Tried to 'date' or be a partner to. Because that was easier."

"I know what you mean." I did. I wasn't oblivious to the way people treated me and Carynne when they thought we were together.

"But you know what? I don't think I'm actually any good at intimacy with women. In fact, I think maybe I'm not any good at intimacy with anyone... except you." He sucked on his lower lip for a few seconds. "And I know I haven't exactly been stellar with you, either."

"You went to India without even talking to me."

"I know. I—" He took a deep breath, and I watched his chest rise and fall. I was expecting a long explanation to come forth. Instead all he got out was: "I was afraid."

Then he started to cry, and I squeezed him so tight neither of us could breathe.

Of course, I had to let us breathe if I was going to say anything. "Let's try not to be afraid of each other, at least, deal?"

"Deal." He exhaled, leaning against me. "I love you, Daron. I love you but it makes me stupid."

"It makes me stupid, too," I said.

"I think we're better off together, then."

"Yeah. Two heads are better than one."

"Mm. Maybe if we each have half a brain we'll be all right, then."

"Mmhm." I also had the thought that two cocks were better than one, too, but this didn't seem to be the moment to say it. "Don't move to Los Angeles."

"What about New York, could I move to New York?"

"Maybe."

"You told me once you always thought you were going to live there."

"That's true."

He stopped short of asking me to move to New York with him. I stopped short of suggesting it. Instead I said, "Let's go to Allston and work on the song you were writing."

"Why don't we stay here?"

"All my guitars are there."

"I've got one in the closet."

"Really?" That had never occurred to me. "Why?"

"You know how it is. I ended up with one. Come take a look." He got up and pulled me back into the bedroom. From within the closet he produced what looked like a brand-new hardshell case. He laid it on the floor (well, on top of some of our discarded clothes) and opened it.

Inside was what looked to be a brand-new Taylor acoustic. Without getting technical: it was a really nice guitar. If it was a hand-me-down, it was from someone with more money than sense. Then again, that described a certain segment of Ziggy's art school crowd.

I dug a guitar pick out of the pocket of my denim jacket, which was lying conveniently nearby.

I tuned the guitar. Ziggy sat crosslegged next to me, watching my every move.

I had a strong feeling this was not a hand-me-down guitar, but I also had a strong feeling it wasn't to my advantage to force Ziggy into telling me the truth about it. He had been honest about so much already, I decided it was best to leave it alone.

We started working on a song. It quickly progressed to what I can only describe as a songwriting binge. The binge lasted for two days, with breaks for sex and food delivery.

It probably would have gone on even longer, except eventually Carynne showed up to make sure we were okay. She buzzed from downstairs.

Ziggy talked into the intercom. "Hello? Are you a food delivery?"

"I sure as hell am not," she replied. "Please tell me you have Daron up there."

"I do. You want to come up? We'll put clothes on."

"No, that answers my question. Next time you guys decide to spend a week in bed, how about let someone know first, though?"

I shouted over, "It hasn't been a week."

"You sure about that?"

Ziggy and I looked at each other. Neither of us was

confident enough to contradict her. He cleared his throat. "Seriously. If you want to come up, you can."

"No, just here's a message. The guys want to know when you're getting together to play next. Give Bart a call when you come up for air, okay? Later, honeybunches."

Los Angeles

I still think it's weird how my entire outlook on life changes for the better when I'm having enough sex. More to the point: how it changes—for the worse—when I'm *not* having enough sex. Ziggy left on a business trip to Los Angeles a week later. Before he left we played around with Bart and Chris a bunch, wrote some songs, worked on some things I'd almost forgotten about, but we didn't have much drive to finish anything since no one knew quite what was going to happen next. So that was fun, if a little frustrating sometimes—like it's fun to play with wet clay, but at some point you want to finish it and bake it, you know?

For the week after he left, Bart, Chris, and I goofed around some more and played music and wrote songs because why wouldn't we? I could think of nothing I wanted to be doing more with my "free time" than making music. We cooked up some weird stuff, and some good stuff, and some wild stuff, and that was good. And it kept my mind and my body at least partly busy. That and playing with the computer, reading my email, etc. My mother used to say that sitting too close to the TV would ruin my eyes. I don't think that was true. But staring at the computer screen so much definitely wasn't good for me: I'd come up from the basement sometimes and have trouble making out the captions on CNN if I was standing at the kitchen door. Weird, eh?

And I would say it was about a week after that when I started to climb the walls. And by climb the walls, I mean if I were a cat I'd be the kind that licked all my own fur off.

I called Remo one night. "Hey, wasn't it you who said figuring out what to do with yourself when you're at home was difficult?"

He paused for a second, and I heard something that sounded like a power drill in the background. Then he spoke. "Maybe. Why, you going stir crazy?"

"A little. It doesn't help that I have no idea where my career is going right now."

"What's the latest?"

I filled him in on how the current idea in play was one we all hated yet seemed inevitable now somehow: Ziggy going solo and the rest of us... "Sitting around with our thumbs up our butts, I guess. I mean, he's basically saying he'll take care of our financial worries, but then what?"

"I saw Chernwick the other night. He wanted to know if you were back in the saddle for soundtrack work. Hang on a sec."

I heard another whizzing sound like a drill again. "Are you doing house renovation? Didn't you decide you were better off hiring somebody for that?"

"Nah. I'm making a fruit shake."

"A milk shake?"

"There's no milk in it. Frozen berries and ice cubes and some peaches that were going soft. And some powdered health stuff."

"Are you on a diet or something?"

"Or something. Doctor says I need more fiber and fruit. I figure I better work on that when I'm at home because, short of the maraschino cherry in a Manhattan, I don't see much of either when I'm on the road."

"Maraschino cherries are high in fiber?"

"They're a fruit, aren't they?"

"Hadn't really thought about it. You going to do Japan and the Pacific again this winter?"

"Nope, taking this one off. What do you think, should we do Christmas out here?"

"At your place, you mean?"

"Yeah. If neither of us is on the road, I think we should get together, anyway."

The idea that we should plan "family" Christmas had not entered my mind. The idea that Remo would assume that we should also hadn't entered my mind. Once he said it, though, it made sense. "Okay, sure. But we should go somewhere cold. It doesn't feel like Christmas with palm trees waving around."

"Damn, that shoots down my other idea, which was

Mexico."

"How about New York? Then we could see Matthew, too."

"You do have a point there. Have you heard from him lately?"

"I haven't heard from anyone. I would've thought you would hear before me."

"Huh. I guess. I thought you and him and his partner were getting close though."

I was puzzled for half a second. "Why, because we're all gay?"

Remo paused. Maybe he was drinking some fruit shake or maybe he was stopping to think about that. Or both. "Huh. Yeah."

"Reem. Just because—"

"Yeah, yeah, I get it. Sorry, I just kind of assumed. Birds of a feather and all that."

"Okay. But no, I never got close to Archie because I didn't think he was going to be around for very long, you know? Oh jeez, that sounds heartless." I felt like a shit as soon as I said it.

Remo didn't judge me, though. "Nobody needs to be Mother Teresa except Mother Teresa. It's more important you be there for Matthew when he needs you, if you want to be a good friend."

"You're saying I should call Matthew."

"You've got the phone in your hand, you know."

"Okay, but does that mean you agree we should get together in New York? For Christmas?"

"Let's say that's definitely on the table." Then he made a pained noise, like "arghhhhhh."

"Jeez, if you really don't want to—"

"No, no, it's not that. I'm just having brain freeze from this damn drink."

"Rub your tongue on the roof of your mouth," I said.

"Why?"

"It'll help. Speaking as someone who used to live on ICEEs and Slurpees, I know brain freeze."

"All right, all right. Go call Matthew and call me back later."

"Will do."

I had to dig out my notebook to get Matthew's number, since I didn't have it memorized. His machine answered. "Hey, Matthew, it's Daron. I'm at home for a while, give me a call if you get a chance. Remo has this idea of getting everyone together for Christmas and I suggested New York as more central than LA, and so I was wondering what you thought of the idea because I could totally use some help convincing him. And by the way how are you and all that. Okay, hanging up now before your machine cuts me off."

To keep myself occupied I took the cordless phone with me to the basement and messed around on the computer a bit. When it rang again a few minutes later I thought it was probably Matthew.

Nope. Ziggy.

The Stroke

So, what do you do when your lover-singer-creative-partner-relationship-person-you-can't-live-without is three thousand miles away?

If you're me, all you do is suffer a lot in silence.

If you're Ziggy, you get a pager.

I picked up the phone when it rang. "Moondog Central."

"Hey." He sounded out of breath. "Glad you're home."

So am I, I thought. I hadn't talked to him since he'd left. "Hey. How's the left coast?"

"Smoggy and ridiculous, as usual. I wanted to give you a number."

"A number?"

"A phone number. I got a pager. Since I'm kind of bouncing around and not always at the same place."

"Ah. Sure." I didn't even ask where he'd been staying. I figured if I needed to know he'd tell me. I took down the number. Then, trying not to sound totally pathetic but probably failing, I asked, "When are you coming back?"

"Next week, probably? But maybe only to New York. I don't know." He didn't sound happy.

"Everything going all right? With the movie and stuff?"

He made a non-committal noise. "Opening-weekend

box office was strong enough that no one is complaining too loud, but it got panned pretty bad by critics, and it's out of most theaters already."

"Is that good or bad?"

"A little of each, I guess. It's kind of weird. One thing that didn't get panned was my performance. And they're taking the strong opening weekend as a sign that people went because of me, whereas those who want to go to see an actual good movie aren't bothering now. So... it's all good for my career personally but it's a little tough when it might have done better."

"How's Jennifer?"

"Your rival for my affections?" he joked.

I swear I didn't say anything, didn't even breathe, but somehow he heard me freeze up.

"I'm joking, Daron. She and I are just good friends now."

"Okay, but forgive me for being like a lawyer about this but...." I spoke very delicately. "I wasn't aware some-one had to even be friends with you to get in your pants."

"Hah. True. But it's also true I haven't seen her since the premiere, and she's not even in LA right now."

"Oh. So when are you coming home?"

"Not sure."

Hearing his voice, I wanted to lick the phone receiver. No, I had not been drinking. "Shit. I finally got used to having you around," I said, meaning it as a joke, but it came out a sort of pathetic whine.

"Having me every day, you mean."

"That, too."

"Meet me in New York? You got anything better to do?"

"No, but..."

"I'll let you know when I'm coming. It'll probably be at least a week, though."

"Ugh."

"Daron."

"Ziggy."

He licked his lips. I could hear it. "You really need to do something for yourself when I'm not around."

"Like what?"

"Like... let Colin suck you like a Hoover."

His voice had already turned me on, but hearing him talk like that, it was impossible to stay cool. I pretended to, anyway. "Colin is not into cocksucking."

"All that matters is he's into you. Or, fine, just hire someone. No fuss. No attachments."

"You're kidding, right?"

"I am not kidding. Most of them are perfectly nice guys."

"Who peddle their asses because they're such upstanding, responsible human beings? No. That's too dangerous for too many reasons. Don't be ridiculous." A sudden thought occurred to me. "What about you? Tell me you're not hiring hustlers to take care of your needs."

"Uh uh." His voice dropped. "I'm holding out until I see you again."

"You're what?" My jeans were getting uncomfortably tight. "Really?"

"Really. I'm lying in bed right now. I'm pretending that's your hand on my dick."

"You're not..." I stood up to shift myself. "Are you?"

"Mmhm, I am. This abstinence thing is kind of hot, don't you think? This whole not-letting-anyone-touch-my-skin-but-you thing."

"Ziggy!" I cupped my hand over my zipper.

"You could fly out here, you know..."

"I. Am. Not. At. Your. Beck. And. Call."

"Mmm, true. Just pointing it out, though, if you can't wait. I, though? I can wait." He sucked in a breath suddenly. "Mm, that was close."

"What was close?"

"Almost came. But I'm holding out."

"Holding out? Are you waiting for me to hang up?"

"No, definitely not. I'm waiting for you to get over yourself and start jerking off with me."

"Fuck." My brain wasn't working right, and it was pretty much impossible to decide whether I should go upstairs, or lock the basement door, or just whip out my cock and have at it. I was already well past any kind of judgment about whether or not I was going to do it. There wasn't any question about that, it was just a question about whether I could be at all sensible about where.

"Are you in your room?" Ziggy asked.

"No, I'm in the basement."

"If I were there, I'd take you in my mouth and swallow every drop so there'd be nothing to clean up."

"You're going to kill me. This is torture."

"Is it painful? I bet it wouldn't be if you put your hand down your pants."

The second my hand wrapped around me I wondered why I'd been waiting. He sucked in a breath again and I heard a shuddery moan that I knew was him holding back. Fuck.

I sat down on a milk crate, moved the phone to my other shoulder, unzipped, licked my palm, and went at it in earnest.

"Go on, Ziggy," I said. "Let me hear you come."

"You first," he said.

"No, you first. When I hear it, there's no way I'm going to be able to hold back."

"Mm. All right." There was a rustling sound as I guess he changed his position.

I probably don't have to convince you that hearing him moan and groan and say my name while he came was the hottest thing I had ever heard.

When I came to my senses a little, I was sitting in the basement with my pants down and a large handful of spunk.

"So, now you have a number you can call whenever you need to jerk off," Ziggy said. "I'll try to call back whenever you need me."

"No," I said. "What happens is now whenever you call me I'll want to jerk off."

He chuckled. "You're still inside out, upside down, and backwards sometimes."

"'You spin me 'round,'" I quoted.

"Okay, now I have to actually go." He made a kissing sound into the phone.

I couldn't bring myself to be that cheesy, even if I was love-drunk right then. I said "Bye" instead.

He was right: my head was inside out. The fact that I wasn't the slightest bit freaked out by what we'd just done was proof. I succeeded at not thinking too deeply about it at all.

I'll spare you the gory details of how I got back upstairs without making a total mess. Two words: laundry day.

Somebody's Watching

The word came via voice mail a few days later that Ziggy was flying to New York on Monday, so I called Sarah to see if she was around for the weekend and if she wanted company. She said yes and yes, so I got on a train on Friday morning (where by morning I mean 12 noon) with a guitar and a book (and then slept the whole way anyway).

I thought I heard a camera shutter snapping when I walked up to the lobby of her building. The doorman greeted me like he remembered me. He was a slim Hispanic man with very short cropped hair and creases around his eyes.

"You might want to check for paparazzi," I told him. "In the bushes or something."

He shook his head. "There's one. He's trouble. Photographing everyone going in or out. We've run him off a couple of times but he comes back and comes back."

Upstairs, once we'd sat down in the living room I mentioned it to Sarah, too. She made a face. "Ugh, I was pretty low profile here until Remy Harris moved into the building. Doesn't it just make you want to stay in and order a pizza and write some songs?"

"That's my idea of a good time anyway," I reminded her.

"True. Let's do that, then, but tomorrow we're going out." She clapped her hands together with a little burst of manic glee. "I know! We'll go out for brunch. Make it look like we spent all night doing whatever decadent and deviant thing people want to believe we do together."

"Sure." I'm sure for some people staying up all night songwriting probably counted as that. "Okay if we visit a friend of mine in the afternoon?"

"You bet. We can go out dancing tomorrow night. Is your friend the type to want to join my entourage?"

"Um, don't think so," I said. "He's like forty, and I don't think he's the clubbing type. So who's Remy Harris?"

"He's a big daytime star."

"Like the sun?"

"The Son? Son of what?" Then she laughed. "Oh, the sun. I forget how funny you are."

"Hate to disappoint you, but it was actually that I couldn't figure out what you mean by big daytime star—but now that I think about it, you mean soap opera star, right?"

"Right." She still had a big grin on her face, though. "You're still funny. Okay, pizza first or music first?"

"Music. Otherwise the piano keys get all greasy."

She laughed again. "Okay, I'll put my hair up. Come on."

I followed her to the bedroom.

"I hate my hair," she said casually as she piled her hair on top of her head and twisted it in a cloth scrunchie. She was in a tank top and basketball shorts and bare feet, and her hair didn't look that different to me from usual—straight reddish brown, shoulder length, with layered sides.

"What do you hate about it?"

"I have to do so much to it to make it look like anything. But I can't do it super short: Annie Lennox already owns that look. Sinead O'Connor. It just won't go over. And I'm just not butch enough to pull it off." She sighed. "I envy yours."

"Mine? Mine definitely doesn't look like anything."

"Which is kind of the point, right? You look like you roll right out of bed and it looks exactly like that. And that's like part of your casual image, your whole look is like..." She searched for the words. "Working-class vagabond."

I chuckled. "Like a Nomad?"

"Oh yeah of course, you're right. I mean, guys don't have to get as dressed up anyway, but rock musicians especially, maybe. Like you give the impression that you dress like that because you don't have any other clothes."

"Sarah, I *don't* have any other clothes."

"Okay, but you could."

"I don't see myself having a closet full of, like, Benetton or something." I followed her back to the piano.

"Or Armani."

While I got out the guitar and tuned it, she went on. "Seriously, though, even punk bands are dressed up, in their way. If you're going to spend hours putting two hundred safety pins through a pair of jeans and spray paint on things and all that."

"If you want a low-maintenance hairstyle or lifestyle, I wouldn't recommend punk or goth industrial," I said. "It takes a good hour for Colin to put his mohawk up."

"Okay, but that's the thing, I guess. You go onstage, or to an industry function, in a T-shirt and jeans and it totally works."

"There's a reason we call that Rock Star Standard."

"I just can't get away with that, is what I'm saying." She opened the piano and started warming up her hands without touching it, stretching her fingers and cracking her knuckles.

"Are you sure? I'm pretty sure that's all Chrissie Hynde usually wears."

"Yeah, but Chrissie Hynde is badass. My image is not badass."

"Okay, well, but what *is* your image?"

She didn't miss a beat. "Quirky ingénue songbird."

"Huh. I guess you've thought this over a lot."

"You better believe it. And I had to fight for the quirky part."

"What would the options have been?"

"Well, you know, I could have been an ice princess, untouchable and inaccessible but highly romantically desired. Except I didn't think I could keep up the poise, and it would be boring as shit. I could have been a hot young temptress, except I really didn't want to go in such an explicitly sexual direction. Madonna kind of cornered that market, too—"

"Okay, okay, I get the idea. Hm. Quirky ingénue songbird. Presumably you won't keep the ingénue part in a couple of years?"

"Well, yeah, images can always change. Quirky songbird lets me kind of acknowledge my folksy past and also gives a kind of edge to the songwriting and musicality. It lets me be the smart-but-not-too-smart girl, the smart-but-still-sexy girl."

I was done tuning but found myself turning these thoughts over in my mind. "And what's my image again?"

"Six-string vagabond. You've managed to construct an image that says 'image doesn't matter, only the music does.'"

"Sar', that's not an image. That's what I really think."

"I know, but don't think that isn't an image. It's what you project." She swiveled on the piano stool so she was facing me. "It's probably one reason why Mills doesn't take you that seriously. And maybe why he thinks you're replaceable."

"Because I'm a guitar for hire? I could see that."

"And maybe why he's so worried about you being labeled gay. Since you don't have any other image. I mean, think about Elton John. His image is flamboyant arena showman. It kind of doesn't matter then if he's gay."

"Hm." I wasn't sure that all added up in my head. "Is this advice or are you just thinking out loud?"

"Just thinking out loud. It's kind of weird, but you've avoided the 'guitar god' image. Maybe because you're not really a metal guy."

"Probably."

"Although since you grew your hair out, maybe, you could go in that direction if you wanted."

"Do I look like I want to?"

"Not particularly. I do think you could put on a little more swagger when you're in public, though."

"It's hard to swagger when you're five-foot-four and your record company is trying to bury you."

"All the more reason to do it," she said.

"Okay, one more question then. What's Ziggy's image?"

That one stumped her for several long seconds while she thought it over. "Ziggy's image is alternative auteur, or maybe artiste."

"I thought 'alternative' was the kiss of death, though?"

"Mm, maybe, but I think it's more like an exception-that-proves-the-rule situation. Ziggy wants to be that one exception—and BNC is doing a good job of making it happen."

I sat back. "I've never really thought of it in these terms before."

"That's because Digger never worked on this kind of stuff with you, and Carynne is really a band and music industry person, not an overall entertainment person." She turned back to the piano. "Now it's time to forget all that, though, and just play."

I scooched over to the near end of the couch so we could make eye contact while playing. "Can you just forget it all, though?"

"I have to," she said. "My image isn't real, after all. And to write music I have to get back to the real me."

I realized then that I was the opposite. "Whereas the only reason I have the image I do is because that's who I have to be to make music. All the confidence comes from this." I held up the guitar.

"Huh," she said. "Huh."

I've Been Thinking About You

"The problem with writing songs with you," Sarah said in the morning, when I had put the guitar away and she had put some waffles in the toaster but we hadn't yet slept, "is that you write these things that sound so great with the guitar riffs and then when you're gone it sounds kind of lifeless."

I leaned against the kitchen counter. "I didn't think 'Blue Skies' sounded lifeless when it went to number three."

"Okay, but we had to get a guitarist in there who could do it some justice, you know."

"Did you ever tell me who it was? Did you get Steve Lukather or someone like that?"

The toaster dinged before she could answer, and she put the waffles on plates using her bare fingers. We put butter and syrup on them and stood at the counter eating instead of sitting down. No, I don't know why. Now that I think about it, though, maybe it was because if we sat down we might be too tired to stand up again.

That was the kind of tired I liked. I liked staying up all night playing music and then being so exhausted that I'd conk out the second my head hit the pillow. It felt right.

She started to sing with her mouth full. "Blue skies, above the clouds there are always blue skies..."

I sang harmony and almost choked on a piece of waffle, but didn't. I don't recommend singing while chewing. Professional driver; do not attempt.

I slept on Sarah's floor, on a folded-up comforter, and I slept like a stone.

In the morning, by which I mean around noon, we woke up and took showers—so much for the "disheveled look"—and went to a fancy-ish brunch place where most people needed to wait but apparently not us. I wondered how many phone calls it had taken to set that up. Fancy brunch involved much better waffles but also grilled fish and other things I didn't necessarily expect, along with some of the best coffee I'd ever had. I appreciated that Sarah could keep up with me foodwise, though she said she'd have to make an appointment with her fitness trainer to make up for it. I pointed out that we were going to go out dancing tonight, and that would probably burn off anything we'd taken in.

"So true, so true. That's the kind of truth-telling I like best," she said.

We did some Manhattan walking after brunch, a bit of Fifth Avenue that we both liked near-ish to the restaurant: Tiffany's, St. Patrick's, the big Japanese bookstore that was always fun to walk around in. While we were walking, we talked a little more about Ziggy. But, you know, it's not always about me.

"What about you, Sar'? Got anyone special?"

She snorted. "I'm too busy for a relationship right now. Besides the usual... issues."

She didn't have to say any more than that for me to know what she was talking about. "Yeah."

We went back to the apartment, where she actually *did* call up her workout coach, and while her driver took her off to the gym I took a nap.

While we were getting dressed to go out that night, we reprised the "image" conversation. I wore a pair of jeans I'd had so long I'd basically worn through them in a couple of places.

"Wow. I approve," she said, looking at them. "Jeez, I'm not even into dick and I approve."

"Thanks, I think?"

"You do know that where the guitar has rubbed against you makes the contour of your private parts really... um... visible."

I looked at myself in her full-length mirror. "So it does."

"Trust me, it's a good look on you. Let's gel your hair."

"It's just going to get all sweaty anyway."

"Which is why you gel it. When you toss your head back to keep it out of your eyes, it'll stay."

"Huh. All right. What about you? What are you going to wear?"

She stared into the closet. "I'm not sure. I have a really cute dress, but the shoes that would go with it will kill my feet. Assuming we actually want to dance, and not merely be seen in a dance club."

"We definitely want to dance." I looked into the morass that was her closet. "Why don't you do jeans and boots too, then?"

"I'm supposed to stay away from butching it up too much, you know. Oh wait, I know."

She put on a pair of jeans that had an embroidered flower on the pocket and a vine down the seam, so form-ftting they looked painted on. Stretch denim, she explained. A flower-print top and then a heap of necklaces and bangles. Not as many as Steven Tyler, but a lot. She pulled on a denim jacket then and looked herself over in the mirror.

"No," she said. "The denim jacket is too cowgirl, too C&W."

"You need leather."

"Hm. That could be a problem." She dug through the closet but didn't find anything.

"Wear mine," I suggested.

"Ooooh. Let me try it on. If it's not too big..."

"Sarah, you are an Amazon compared to me. It won't be too big."

In fact, it fit her perfectly. "Anyone who's paying attention is going to know I'm wearing your jacket," she said, examining the spot on the sleeve shoulder where Ziggy had drawn the Moondog Three rocket. "If we hadn't already cranked the rumor mill, this will do it."

"Oh, you mean in like a cheerleader-wearing-a-guy's-football-jacket kind of way?"

"Exactly." She seemed quite pleased with this idea.

Then I watched her put on her makeup. It was very different from watching Ziggy put on his makeup. Probably because I didn't get the same feelings about it.

In fact, the feeling I got was to start, very intensely, missing Ziggy. *He'll be here Monday*, I told myself.

"We should go out," she said.

"We are going out."

"When Ziggy gets here, I mean."

"Did I say that out loud?"

"You did."

So now you know the frame of mind I was in when we went dancing. We went to Limelight and danced until our clothes were soaked through with sweat, and then we danced some more. And sometime deep in the night while I was totally lost in the movement and music, a song came on that I hadn't heard before. It had a good groove and a strong synth hook, but I wasn't really paying attention to it.

Until Ziggy's voice came in. "Do, do, do it. Do, do, do it," he sang. It was that kind of vocal mix where he'd sung it really quietly but they'd cranked up the volume, so it was almost like he was murmuring in my ears, "Do, do, do it."

It clicked. The B-side he'd worked on with Jordan. Of course there was a dance remix of it: it was Jordan, and he was into that.

It wasn't until near the end of the mix that I heard a full lyric line, though, or full chorus, I wasn't sure, and I realized that "Do, do, do it" wasn't the whole line. It was "Don't wanna do, do, do it without you."

I stumbled when I heard it. Remember that notebook of songs that were almost all about me? Maybe that's why I was so sure he was singing it to me.

I Didn't Want to Need You

I drunk-paged him from Sarah's in the wee hours of the morning. She was asleep on the couch, looking like something from a Renaissance painting, hair flung everywhere and arm over her eyes. When the phone rang a little while later she barely stirred.

I answered it in her bedroom. "Hey."

"Hey. I see from the phone number you're in the city already."

"Yeah. I'm at Sarah's. Figured I'd make sure I was here before you arrived."

"You sound... tired."

And you sound very far away, I thought. "Well, it is four AM here."

"Is Sarah's mother all right with you staying with her?"

"I get the feeling Sarah doesn't give a fuck what her mother thinks."

Ziggy snorted. "From what I've heard, the reason Sarah moved to New York was to get out from under her wing, so, yeah."

I nearly said something to him then about Sarah being a lesbian anyway but then realized I wasn't sure if he already knew, and if he didn't, well, even if Sarah was sometimes cavalier about outing, I sure as hell wasn't. I also realized that maybe her mother didn't know about either her or me. I could not remember who supposedly knew what. This is the problem with secrets. I decided that not saying anything about it was, as usual, the safest policy. "How's Digger?"

"Do you really want to know?"

"Only if the answer's bad."

He chuckled. "He's the same as always. He's coming with me to New York."

"Ugh. Does he have to?"

"Promise me you won't resort to violence the next time he tests your patience." I couldn't figure out what to say to that, until he went on. "Kidding. I'm kidding."

"You know I made a promise to myself to be non-violent, right?"

"I know, which is why I joked about it. Badly. Sorry.""

"I kind of felt like that was the one act of violence in my life I had waited the longest to deliver, and once it was over I should give it up for good, you know?"

"You've really thought about this." He sounded surprised.

"Of course I have. I measure myself against the crooked yardstick that is Digger every waking minute. Or at least I used to."

"Have you been seeing a therapist?"

"No. Haven't gotten around to it."

"Because that's a pretty advanced way of thinking about your relationship with your father."

"I've had a lot of years to work on that one." I cleared my throat. "I've had a lot less time to figure out more recent relationships."

"Like ours, you mean."

"Exactly. Thank god you understand what I'm talking about. At least some of the time."

I could hear him breathing. I wished he could come through the phone and touch my hand.

"Daron," he said.

"Yeah?"

"You sound like..."

"Like what?"

"Like you're in pain."

I sucked in a breath, as if him saying that made the pain real instead of imaginary. Then again, what's the difference between "real" and "imagined" pain? They both hurt the same.

Write that down. That's a song lyric right there.

"I shouldn't be," I said. "I'm drunk, I've been dancing, and I'm going to see you in two, no, one-and-a-half days. I should be happy."

"You can be happy and still hurt," he said. "What's wrong?"

"I don't know. But now that you pointed it out, I do feel kind of like there's a sword through my chest."

"Why?"

"I guess because I miss you? Why else would I have paged you in the middle of the night?"

"I can change my flight. I can be there tomorrow."

"Thanks. But I'll live. I'm seeing Matthew tomorrow. Are you going to be at the Carlyle again?"

"No idea. You know how it is when you leave these things up to Digger. You need to get a pager so I can let *you* know where I am."

"You could always call Carynne at the office number. We pay an answering service for a reason."

"That's what I mean. So you get a pager and then when there's a message for you at the service, they beep you."

"Ahh, that makes sense."

"Or you can skip them entirely with one like mine where you can just enter the number to be called directly."

"But not leave a message."

"No. But you're the only person I gave the number to."

"Oh." I scratched my palms lightly with the tips of my fingers, one hand callused, the other long-nailed. I wanted to touch his skin so much in that moment that my hands itched. "I'm feeling very disconnected."

"You're drunk. I'm glad you thought to page me, though."

"Me too. Hearing your voice is... good." I was lying on the floor of Sarah's bedroom in the dark. "How can you tell I'm... hurting? What does it sound like?"

"Not sure I can describe it. You just sound... I don't know. How do I sound?"

"You sound kind of tired, too. You been sleeping okay?"

"Eh. It's been better, it's been worse. I'll sleep better after everything gets settled, I'm sure."

"That's probably true for both of us."

"Yeah."

I think he started telling me a story then, or maybe I dreamed it, because I fell asleep with the phone in my hand. Sarah woke me up a little while later trying to tuck a pillow under my head.

"What's wrong with me?" I asked her as she climbed into the actual bed.

"What do you mean?"

"I thought I was happy, but Ziggy pointed out to me I'm not. I mean, I guess I thought if I could reconnect with him that would be the end of my misery, the promised land, la la."

"Well, you do still have a mess with BNC to figure out," she said. "So I could see being stressed out about that."

"True."

"You're happiest when you're making music."

She was undoubtedly right about that. Well. "Let's write another song tomorrow."

"Okay," she said. "Goodnight, Daron."

All the Things She Said

I'll tell you about seeing Matthew later. I have to tell you about Ziggy first.

I expected to see him Monday. I didn't. I paged him around nine o'clock that night and he didn't reply. As you can imagine, that started to freak me out. Sarah was saint-like in keeping me calm.

When he hadn't called back by midnight, she convinced me that he was probably on a delayed flight, and probably still in the air and couldn't even get a page. She half-convinced me that he had probably told me his flight time and I had forgotten it... but I thought I would remember something like that. I'm pretty sure he hadn't told me what time he was due in or anything. She did what any good friend would do, which is distract me. And the next thing you know, several more hours went by between a bottle of Maker's Mark and a guitar and the piano. We jammed and wrote and played and drank, and I told myself not to worry.

But you know how being a worrywart works, right? If you don't worry, but then something goes wrong, you feel like it's your fault. As if your worrying could somehow magically prevent disaster, while not worrying would invite it.

I know it doesn't work like that. I know. But knowing doesn't stop me from feeling like it did.

I woke up to find myself lying on my back on the couch, my arms around the Ovation, the neck making a crease on my cheek. For a second I wondered why I was awake and whose ceiling I was looking at. Then the phone rang for what I realized was a second time. I raced to grab the handset off the kitchen wall.

"Hello?"

"Hey." Yes, it was Ziggy. He sounded worn out, that one syllable little more than a croak.

The clock read 10:00 AM. "You all right? Tough flight?"

There was a long pause. Then: "...Yeah."

"Are you all right?" I repeated.

He dodged the question. "When... Where are you?"

"Upper West Side."

"I'm at the Penta." His laugh sounded bitter. "I have such great memories of this place."

"Ziggy—"

"I need to get some sleep. Can you meet me on Canal Street in the afternoon?"

"Sure, but—"

"I need to do some shopping. I'll bring Antonio."

"Tony's there?"

"Yeah. Bring Sarah, too, eh? We'll make a thing of it."

I was annoyed he hadn't let me get a word in edgewise and that he was being evasive and maddeningly Ziggy-like. "What if I don't want to make a thing of it?"

"Then don't. Jeez, Daron, not everything has to be an international incident. Will you come or not?"

If I had not been hungover, underslept, and freaked out I might have come up with a better answer than the one I did. In hindsight I realize I could have made a counterproposal, or at least tried. Instead I said, "I'll be there."

"Let's say two o'clock at that big Japanese housewares store. You know the one I mean?"

"I have no idea what you're talking about."

"Azuma. The place you can get a Hello Kitty kitchen lamp."

"Uh—"

"Never mind. How about the East Village? Which street is Trash & Vaudeville on, Eighth? Fourth?"

"I know that block. There's a comic book store and a guitar shop across the street from there."

"Perfect. If you get there first, hang out in the guitar shop and I'll come get you there."

"All right." I was blinking, looking around Sarah's kitchen, trying to figure out why I felt so unsettled. "You're all right, though?"

"Everything's going to be fine. Go back to sleep."

"Zig—You're acting weird."

Now it was his turn to sound annoyed. "I'm trying to keep you and Digger separated, all right? Or did you forget he's not supposed to know you and I are in cahoots?"

"Um." Right. I had kind of forgotten it. Well, not forgotten exactly, but it wasn't as much in the forefront of my mind as it was in his. Okay, so maybe that explained why he was being so cagey. "All right."

"I gotta crash. See you at two?"

"Yes. At two."

He made a kissy noise into the phone and hung up.

If you think I got back to sleep after that, you're a wishful thinker. I ended up making a pot of coffee, closing Sarah's bedroom door, and playing quietly in the living room for a while with my brain off. Flamenco, bits of school recital pieces I'd memorized, you know. Noodling. I only drank about half of a cup of coffee before it got cold: my stomach was roiling too much to put plain black coffee in it. I gave up after a while and went out to buy either bagels or donuts and ended up with both, plus some other pastries, which I carried back upstairs in a paper bag.

When Sarah got up she was delighted to find the pastries on the kitchen counter. She mixed the coffee with ice cream, which was a brilliant idea I can't believe I'd never thought of, and we dipped pastries in it and it was decadent and sweet. Which was the point. Then I told her I was having a cloak-and-dagger meeting with Ziggy.

"I thought I heard the phone ring, but I thought maybe I'd dreamed it," she said. "You look worried. I thought everything was going good with you two?"

"It is. I just... I don't know. I'm worried."

"You're always worried," she pointed out. "So do you want me to come with you or not?"

"I think if we're trying not to attract attention, probably you shouldn't come." Wait, though, I thought, why would Ziggy have suggested I bring her if we were trying to keep everything low profile? It was that kind of stuff—stuff that didn't make sense—that drove me crazy about him.

"You want my driver to take you down there?"

"Nah, I'll take the subway."

We were sitting in the living room at that point, with the pastries strewn across the coffee table, crumbs everywhere, and she was in an oversized T-shirt, her hair disheveled, her legs crossed, licking ice cream off her upper lip. Looking like a lot of guys' wet dream, basically. But not mine.

"Do you actually like taking the subway?" She looked at me curiously.

"I like not being treated like a circus animal," I said, a little more vehemently than I meant to.

She sat up very straight then, her expression stern. "That's not a very nice comparison."

"Sarah. I'm not trying to put you down, believe me. I get it. Celebrity is... I get it. It means people are going to gawk at you and take photos and crowd around you like you're a giraffe or a tiger or something. That's all I mean by it. You don't take a tiger on the subway. I get that."

She pursed her lips. "I like being driven around and not having to take the subway."

"Giraffes probably like being fed every day and not worrying about hungry lions nipping their heels, too," I said. "I'm not saying it's not a valid choice. All I'm saying is I'm not a tiger. I'm just a garden-variety, commonplace..." I tried to think of a word.

"Dog," she said.

"Yeah."

"A moondog, you might say."

That made me laugh. "I guess. I like walking around on my own. No one bothers me."

She yawned and stretched. "I'd say I envy you... but I don't. I'd still rather be driven where I'm going."

I went to the window and looked down toward the street, but it wasn't like I was going to be able to see a photographer hiding in the bushes. "What are you going to do when you have a girlfriend?"

She shrugged. "No idea."

"I feel funny asking you about this because Ziggy used to ask me this kind of thing all the time and I felt really weird about it. But he was right. I should've paid better attention to my needs."

She made a dismissive noise. "We girls are different. Trust me."

"If you're sure." Why was I trying to give her advice? I'm not sure. I did anyway. "I guess I'm saying it's better to have a plan than to get blindsided."

"Why, you think if you had a plan you would have ended up with someone other than your lead singer?"

Oof. Remember how I had told Ziggy it felt like there was a sword through my chest, only I'd gotten so used to it I didn't feel it until he pointed it out? When Sarah said that it was like the blade twisted. My heart stopped for a second.

"Sorry," she said, standing up and coming closer to me. "Didn't mean to hit a nerve."

"It's okay," I said, but a little breathless. "That's what friends are for...?"

"Daron—"

I held up a hand to stop her coming closer. "Hang on, hang on, I don't want to lose my train of thought." Too much coffee and not enough sleep and too much sugar and not enough Ziggy were making that close to impossible anyway. "You might be right. You might be. But you might not."

She raised an inquisitive eyebrow.

"I mean, maybe if I had been more comfortable with my orientation I would have already been in a relationship when Ziggy and I met? Or maybe I would have at least known what I wanted?"

"But—"

"Or maybe it wouldn't have mattered because Ziggy was the right one for me all along and I should just be grateful that the universe delivered him to me on a platter right when I needed him?"

She shut her mouth, but she still looked concerned.

I leaned my arm against the window frame and looked down the street. I could just make out a little bit of green that was either a sidewalk tree toward the avenue or maybe a sliver of Central Park. "I need to get over the fact that I can't live without him," I said. "Because that fact's terrifying, but it's a fact nonetheless."

I made myself a mental note to write a song for Sarah called "Devil's Advocate." Because what she said next was, "But you proved you could live without him. You did fine in Spain without him, didn't you?"

I shook my head and looked out the window, a lump in my throat too hard to talk through.

"Okay, but which is it, then? Is Ziggy your soulmate or is he the only one of the available people in your life that you'll let in?"

More like he's the one who wheedled his way in, I thought. But what I said was, "Maybe both."

"That seems awfully convenient."

"Ain't it, though." We were silent for a while, listening to the sounds of New York City. Cars and traffic and distant sirens. Then I asked, "More convenient than having a relationship with a member of the press?"

"I thought you said Jonathan was good for you?"

"We were good as friends and pretty good as lovers, but we were terrible as boyfriends," I said. "Jonathan was a Learning Experience."

She cringed. "That sounds awful."

"He admits it. That's why we're still friends. We agree it was all one big Learning Experience." I sighed. "Ziggy is not a Learning Experience. Ziggy is..." I thumped my fist against the wood, frustrated that I didn't have the words to describe what I thought or felt.

Sarah squeezed my shoulder and made me let go some of the tension I was holding. I guess she had come closer than I realized. "Hey. Isn't that what all those songs we write are about?" Love, she meant. "Go with your heart and have no regrets, Daron."

"Sarah, when you meet that person, even if they're the most—or least!—convenient person in your life..."

"I'll grab on and I won't let go. I hope I have the sense to know them when I meet them, though."

"You'll know." If you know yourself, that is. Unlike me. Sarah was a lot more aware than I had been. I was sure she'd be fine, whenever that time came. "You'll know."

Fooling Yourself (Angry Young Man)

I went walking to clear my head and to make sure I made it there on time. If I missed my rendezvous with him, who knew what chaos would ensue? I know I predict disaster more easily than most people, but this time I could really imagine that another week would go by without seeing him, during which I would drive myself insane.

It could be months before the contract and record company stuff is ironed out, I told myself. No use getting anxious.

Then again, I was anxious that I hadn't said more about where we were meeting. The block Ziggy had been describing was equivalent to Eighth Street on the West Side, but after crossing Broadway it turned into St. Mark's Place. And the music shop we had both been thinking of wasn't actually on the block he had been describing. I kicked myself mentally and soldiered on, figuring I'd just keep circulating until I ran into him.

The comic book store was nice. Bart and I used to read a lot of comics when we were in school. He'd go every Friday to get new comics and then we'd sit around his dorm room or apartment reading them. He would buy anything that looked remotely interesting. Superhero, indie, you name it. Since we'd moved to Boston I'd gotten out of the habit, but I recognized a lot of things.

The last thing I needed right now, though, with my

financial future somewhat in question, was to pick up another expensive habit.

I lingered on the street outside the bookstore as the time drew a bit closer to two o'clock. I cruised in this bookstore once, didn't I? At least once. God, that seemed like a long time ago. The day after the show at the Pool Bar, the day I had met Artie and he told me he liked us but wasn't signing us.

Artie. I really needed to be in touch with him.

I went into the punk clothing store, not wanting to seem as if by standing around outside the bookstore I was cruising. That was the last kind of trouble I needed.

I didn't buy anything in there either. The cashier was a girl who tried to give me a jaded-as-fuck attitude, but I caught her staring at me kinda wide-eyed a couple of times. I didn't linger.

When I hit the street again, a large black limo was pulling up outside. The front window rolled down, and I saw Antonio. He hopped out immediately and held the back door open for me. I climbed in, the door shut behind me, and we were moving before I had a chance to wonder where we were going.

Ziggy was leaning back against the seat like he was too exhausted to sit up. "Hey."

"Are you all right?"

He opened his arms like he wanted to hug me. I wasn't such a stubborn idiot as to say no to that kind of invitation. I scootched up next to him and pulled him close. I would have thought the way he had been lolling back that there wasn't any tension in him, but I felt it draining out of him as I held him. Or maybe that was me.

He let out a long sigh.

"How was Los Angeles?" I asked.

"Exhausting."

"I can see that."

He lapsed into silence again. I decided I'd wait until he spoke first next time.

I'm bad at games of chicken, though. A few minutes later I broke. "Where are we going? I thought you wanted to do some shopping."

"We can go wherever you want. I just wanted some alone time." He rubbed his cheek against my chest, but not in a seductive way. "It's been kind of rough."

"Has it?"

"Yeah."

Again the silence. I began to get the feeling he had more to say, but for some reason he wasn't saying it.

I wondered if that made it my job to figure it out. I decided to try a more pointed question. "What's the latest with Mills?"

"Fuck." He squeezed me around my ribcage.

"That bad?"

He didn't answer, but he was breathing faster and the tension in him was rising.

Oh fuck, I thought. Mills finally made a pass at him. Or worse. What else could it be? My palms went prickly, and I forced myself to breathe slowly through my nose, waiting to hear the worst.

I was wrong. Mills hadn't made a pass. And that wasn't the worst thing Ziggy could have told me. When he finally looked up, and I saw he'd been silent-crying, the words that came out of his mouth were:

"I signed."

I waited a couple of beats, thinking there should be more words to that sentence. Something was missing. That didn't make sense. Then it began to sink in, and it did make sense. Terrible sense. "You what?" I asked, trying to be sure, hoping I misheard or he meant something else.

He disengaged one arm so he could wipe his nose on the sleeve of his sweatshirt. "I signed it. The development deal."

I know I sounded angry when I demanded, "When?"

"Yesterday."

"Yesterday!" And I know that sounded even worse. He moved away from me and huddled in the corner, hugging his knees. "Ziggy, we barely talked about—"

"I got everything you wanted," he burst out.

"What are you talking about? I didn't want you to sign it in the first place!"

"Yes, you did. You said you wanted everyone taken care of and you wanted Digger to get screwed."

What I wanted, but couldn't of course express at that moment because I was too angry to be coherent, was for him to have consulted me before actually putting his name on anything. "That isn't what I said at all! We talked in hypotheticals, Zig. You asked me what about this, what about this, you never said you were going to go out and sign the fucking thing!"

"What did you expect? For fuck's sake, Daron, you think this was easy?"

"Easiest five million you'll ever make!" I could barely hear myself over the buzzing in my ears. "If this is exactly what I wanted, why are you crying? Why were you afraid to tell me? Huh?"

He rocked back and forth, his eyes sullen.

"And stop acting like you're five! I'm not your father! Or your mother! For fuck's sake, Ziggy!"

He growled like he'd been raised by wolves, which was not an improvement. Then he shouted, "I didn't know what else to do!"

"Stall! Wait! Talk to me!"

"There wasn't time."

"Like hell there wasn't! What, did they ambush you with it when you got off the plane yesterday? Did they hold a gun to your head until you signed it?"

"Something like that," he murmured, not meeting my eyes.

"So now you're going to tell me they forced you into it? I thought you said they gave you everything you wanted."

His voice was still small, barely audible, but you know, my hearing's pretty sharp. "They did. Which was why I couldn't stall anymore."

A heavy silence fell between us then. I couldn't quite accept that the earth under my feet had moved quite so drastically. And I still didn't know enough about what this new reality was to get a grip on it.

"It's all going to work out—" he started to say.

"How? What's your definition of working out, Zig? Tell me."

"Seven and a quarter. You'll be free to work. Digger will be history."

He meant $7.25 million. "How."

"It's a buyout. Mills is heading up a new multimedia division. They're essentially buying me from BNC—"

"And from me." I meant to say from the band, but yeah.

He nodded. "So that leaves you free to pursue whatever."

"How? Wouldn't that leave the rest of us under contract at BNC?"

"Part of the deal is we get together on a lawsuit to make Digger the fall guy in all the previous disputes between BNC and Moondog Three. That'll put a stopper on him making anything off this deal and probably get you some cash out of his hide, too."

"When you say buyout—"

"The breakdown is like this. Five million to me, two-point-two-five to Moondog Three via BNC, who are going to take a little over a million to recoup costs, and then the rest is for you. And the guys. To do whatever you want with. Put Courtney through school, start another band, whatever."

Start another band. Just kick me in the nuts, why don't you? Did he really not know how that would sound to me?

What happens to our relationship now? I wanted to ask, but I couldn't imagine saying the word "relationship" now that it would come out sounding like sarcasm in the wake of what he had done. No wonder he was so upset. He knew this was a breakup conversation before I even got in the car.

His hand slid up my thigh. I think I can be forgiven for slapping it away and snarling, "You've got to be fucking kidding me."

He looked like I'd slapped him across the face, not on the hand. Wide-eyed and shocked.

"What?" I demanded. *Welcome to the world you made, Zig.* "You wanted to fuck me one more time for old time's sake? To prove you still could? To prove you can have your fucking way with me whenever—?" That was the point where my voice broke, and so who knows what else I might have said.

"No," he said weakly.

I looked out the window. We were on Sixth Avenue heading north, already uptown of the Penta. Heading toward the BNC offices, maybe.

I knocked on the divider between the limo compartment and the driver. The shaded window lowered, and Antonio looked back at us with that predictable big-brother concerned-face.

"Pull over. Let me out," I said.

Antonio looked back and forth between us, but Ziggy had gone into his shell like a snail, curled up and impenetrable. And silent.

"Whatever you say, boss." Antonio pulled over at an unoccupied stretch of curb.

Ziggy woke up suddenly. "You're really going to get out?"

I looked at him, wondering which of us was feeling the greater disbelief: me that he'd pulled this shit without even asking me or him that I was actually going to remove myself from his vicinity. "I trusted you," I said as I swung the door open and stepped out. I started walking away so fast I didn't even slam the door like I should have.

"I did the best I could!" he screamed after me. "Ingrate!"

I heard the door slam after that. I didn't turn around. I kept walking.

Things happen sometimes. Things that affect your whole future but that seem random. Or like coincidences. The perfect singer happens to be standing in the crowd that day in the park. Okay, maybe that wasn't a random coincidence. Ziggy had known us. Had seen us. And probably knew we were looking for a singer. I was still getting used to knowing that information.

This, though, this really was a coincidence: where I had bolted from the limo was two blocks from the Wenco offices.

I wondered if Artie was in. I didn't have an appointment.

I didn't care.

Merry Go Round

I talked my way into Wenco the way Digger would have talked his way into the best restaurant in the city. With equal parts bullshit and bravado and being nice when it counted. Lucky for me, Artie was there that day.

His office was just as cramped and cluttered as the last time I was there, three years ago. He shook my hand and cleared a chair for me to sit in. When he saw my look was kind of grim, he shut the door so no one could eavesdrop what we were saying, though he kept up his gladhandy demeanor while he worked his way around to his side of the desk to sit down. "Your name's been popping up in a lot of songwriting credits on our labels lately."

"Oh, has it?" I tried to be casual. "I did a lot of work when I was in LA last year. Didn't really pay attention to the labels." That last bit wasn't me being cavalier: that was true. I didn't know what label most bands were recording for, and the checks were mostly going to Carynne.

"Remo keeps me up to date on you when he can," Artie added. "But I'm guessing you're not just here because you were in the neighborhood?"

What's funny is that actually *was* why I was there that moment, as opposed to calling on the phone or something. But I came right down to it. "I'm being cut free from BNC. Just found out."

He looked serious. "I heard there were lawsuits being filed."

"Threats and counter-threats. It's all going to be wrapped out of court, though—well, mostly. We may sue our ex-manager jointly with them. I'm not holding my breath on that, though." I looked around at the stacks of demo tapes and press kits and the layer of dust on everything and realized how hard it was to get to where I was now, but that couldn't make me lose my nerve. "I don't know what you've heard."

He looked me in the eye. "A couple of law-dogs from BNC did come barking. When they stopped yapping, I assumed you had worked out a deal regarding recording under another name."

"Not really," I admitted. "They didn't have a leg to stand on there and they knew it."

"So what changed?"

"Buyout."

"Ahhhh." He folded his hands and sat back, like that one word explained everything.

I explained anyway. "Ziggy signed a development deal with Megastar or whatever they're calling the new conglomerate, which is paying BNC and Moondog Three to take him." My voice didn't much like those last two words, so I clammed up.

"Which makes you a free agent. I see." He leaned back in his chair, and his hair looked grayer than I remembered. Or maybe it was just the way the afternoon sun coming through the window lit him.

"Um, yeah." I suddenly felt weird for having barged in there. It wasn't like I wanted to sign a contract myself that instant. It wasn't like those days when I carried a cassette tape around in my pocket of whatever song we'd polished most recently. Yeah, I used to do that. "I thought you should know."

He nodded almost imperceptibly. Then he glanced at his watch and I thought he was going to throw me out of the office for having wasted his time.

Nope. "It's getting close to three. You want to go for a drink?"

That was music to my ears. "Yes."

So Artie took me a couple blocks away to a watering hole that was kind of a dive, but that was a good thing. I was comfortable there. It was not a "be seen in" kind of place, not frequented by the captains of industry or anything.

We didn't talk business explicitly, you know how that is? He asked about Spain since Remo had told him I was there, and I talked about how I'd met Orlando at Guitar Craft camp, which made it sound less sketchy than me taking off on a whim like I did. And we talked about Nomad a bunch.

At one point Artie said, "I'm under the impression you could join up with those guys any time."

"Yeah, so am I," I said, realizing I was at the bottom of my beer mug. We were at the bar, and I pushed it about an inch away from me. The bartender refilled it and put it back down in front of me before I could say anything. Well. "I've thought about it."

"Does the fact that you haven't done it yet mean something?"

"I was holding out to see if things might work out with M3, I guess." I turned the cold, sweating glass in my fingers but didn't drink any more. "It's... it's a little hard to let go."

"When'd you find out about the buyout?"

"Right before I walked into your office."

Artie started to laugh, then checked himself when he realized I was serious. "That's rough. I'm sorry."

"I feel like I built something and they took it away." I shouldn't have said that. This was the bad part about going out drinking. You say things you probably shouldn't let people hear. "At first I thought it was our ex-manager trying to screw me out of what was rightfully mine, creatively mine, but in the end it was Ziggy."

Artie took a thoughtful swig of his beer. "You're saying your singer engineered the buyout?"

I gave that a little thought. "No, he just set out his demands and John Mills engineered the buyout. Ziggy gets rich and I get my freedom. I'm supposed to be happy about that." I waved my hand. "I mean, literally, I should be happy about that. But as you can tell I'm kind of miserable."

Artie clinked his mug against mine. "It's a tough thing to say goodbye to something you put so much blood, sweat, and tears into. That's all right, Daron. I feel confident you have a lot more music ahead of you."

Because he had said that, so was I. We didn't talk about what I might do next, didn't talk demos or gigs. But remember that night I got drunk and ranted about musical modes at a party in LA? That had led directly to that soundtrack gig. This had the same feel, only this time I was aware of it happening.

A kind of numbness set in during that second beer, which I did end up drinking. I wondered if it meant my heart wasn't that badly broken or if I merely couldn't feel it. Maybe it was that while I was with Artie I could pretend that it was all about business, all about the band. I could pretend that I didn't feel like my creative partner, my muse, my other half, had just turned his back on me and left me in the dust.

I know. It's messed up that I could only think of Ziggy so clearly in those terms after he was gone. I thought him leaving me for India had brought about clarity. Apparently I didn't know shit by comparison.

Blues from a Gun

Artie said goodnight a little while after that. It was the dinner hour, and I was too angry and upset to feel tipsy.

I ended up in the tiny phone booth squeezed between

the restroom doors in a diner not far from Sarah's (she'd left word with her doorman for me to meet her there) using my calling card to try to reach Carynne.

I got the answering service and left a message saying I'd try again from Sarah's later. Then I called her home number but couldn't think of how to sum it all up for her answering machine so I hung up before her outgoing message finished. Then I called Remo and got his machine and left the following message:

"Yeah, hey, so I wanted to be the one to tell you it looks like I'm a free agent now. Or will be. Contract shenanigans are still going on but I think it's the end of an era, basically, and I saw Artie today and I'll call you later. I'm in the city at a pay phone. I'll call you later. Oh and by the way Matthew says hello and he's fine and I'll fill you in about that later too. Okay? Bye."

I sounded really calm and collected, didn't I?

I thought about calling Jonathan. Thought about it. Thought better of it. And didn't.

I called Bart, who listened to the whole story and didn't say much, which to me meant he felt the same as me. Use whatever cliché you want. All the air went out of the balloon. He asked if I wanted him to drive to New York to get me. I hadn't made up my mind yet when I saw a waitress gesturing quizzically at me. I had forgotten I had ordered food. I told Bart I'd call him later.

I sat down and ate a grilled cheese sandwich and a bowl of soup. I wish I could say the food was really calming and grounding, but I don't think I really even tasted it. I had reached a state of numbness.

I was sitting there with a cup of coffee trying to see if caffeine would make me perk up when Sarah came in. She slid into the booth across from me. "Hey. I guess you got the message from the doorman."

"About you being with your trainer? Yeah." I had forgotten that was supposedly why I was in that diner: to wait for her. It was hard to remember why I did anything right then.

"Are you all right?' she finally asked.

I managed to tell her a really dry, barebones version of the facts as I knew them while waiting for the check.

I didn't fall to pieces until we got upstairs. I tried to do that thing of explaining it all again to see if it made more sense—except the problem was that the whole thing made perfect sense, it just sucked. Right? I expected Sarah to tell me to back up and look at it from another angle. I thought she'd surely have some perspective I was missing, some insight from a person who had signed a multimillion-dollar deal, and that she'd tell me to calm down and pick it apart some more.

Nope. When I started to cry, she started to cry, and I have no idea how long that went on for. We were not the best match when it came to hugging—she was too tall and bony—but it wasn't like that mattered. I kept wishing for the crying to stop, but it was like falling down a hole, you can't make the bottom come any faster. My ribs hurt.

I was glad I hadn't called Jonathan. Who knows what I would have done?

When the sobbing subsided, I apologized. Her eyes were so puffy it looked like I'd punched her in the face, and I pretty much felt like I had. "Sorry. Didn't mean to ruin your afternoon."

"You're stupid," she said, hiccupping a little as she got herself together.

"I know."

"No, I mean, don't apologize, stupid. What are friends for."

"Um. Okay." I didn't really believe it but, okay, I felt slightly less guilty about the fact that she suffered through that with me. "You know what makes it all seem like it's never going to get better?"

"What?"

"The fact that it just makes it so obvious there's this huge gulf between him and me. Whenever I feel like we're two halves of the same apple, I'm happy. But the truth is we're from two different planets."

She patted my hand. "I don't know. Sounds to me like they're both stories and both likely to be equally untrue or true. All I know is that swinging back and forth between the two extremes is ripping you apart."

"Okay. That might be true." I got up and went to the kitchen and made an ice pack with a dish towel and package of frozen strawberries and brought it to her. "Your eyes look painful."

She gave a phlegmy snort. "Oh god. I'm the queen of the ugly cry." She took it and leaned back on the couch with the frozen fruit pack lying over her face. "I'm afraid to ask you anything because I don't want to start you off again."

"I think I'm out of tears for the moment," I said, rubbing my chest, which hurt. I don't think I'd ever cried so hard or so long. "This is normal, though, right? For an epic breakup?"

"I wouldn't know, but I assume so," she said. "It's kind of not fair, I guess. You're having the breakup with your first big crush *and* the breakup with your bandmate—"

"And my muse and my obsession and my other half all at once. Yeah." I stopped short of saying soulmate, which is a term that's always been sketchy to me. I went back to the kitchen and got us two glasses of water, even if that meant replenishing the tear supply. "And the breakup of the band. But it's like, under all that, I just feel this... gulf. This uncrossable space, and it's like if there's such a gap between me and him, how far am I from the rest of the human race?"

"Hm. Dunno Dar', but I feel pretty close to you right now."

"I know. And that's good, because otherwise I'd probably still be in the phone booth, contemplating sui—" I stopped myself, then forced myself to say the word because I didn't want to feel like a wimp for not saying it. "Suicide." It's one of those words that gets thrown around casually by those who haven't really thought about it that much. But I wasn't one of those. Not then, anyway.

I had a glimmer of understanding, though, how someone who seemed to have everything might still come to the conclusion that suicide was a reasonable option. When you feel like you're stuck on a rock in the dark surrounded by a lake, it seems irrelevant that people are celebrating your birthday on the beach you can barely see.

For a moment I wondered if Ziggy felt like he was back on that rock. And then I thought, *If he feels stuck on that rock it's because he put himself there. He acted, he decided, he signed.*

The simplest thoughts seemed to hurt the most. "I thought we were in it together." I didn't realize I'd said it out loud until Sarah answered.

"You really feel like he did it for himself?"

I looked at my own feelings. "Yeah. Could he have signed without getting all those concessions? Yes. But it just means me and the guys don't get screwed quite as hard, you know? Did he think that was going to buy forgiveness? He knows damn well he took things into his own hands when he shouldn't have. He knew damn well I was going to be ripshit about it. That's why he was so contrite and woe-is-me when he saw me. That's... that's the part that kills me. He knew. *He knew.* And he did it anyway."

"I'm so sorry."

That was confusing. "What are you sorry for?"

"Stupid. That was the 'I sympathize' sorry, not the 'I apologize' sorry." She handed me the frozen strawberries.

I pressed them against my own eyes. Huh. It was dark and cool and soothing. "I apologize, then. My emotions are so broken right now I can't tell the difference."

We sat there in silence for a while. Until she said, "You do know some people go to therapy to feel better, right?"

I looked up. "Um." I confess the thought had not occurred to me. Every association I had with therapy was that it was awful and painful. "Therapy," I said, like I had never thought about what the word meant. "*Therapy.*"

Aromatherapy. Psychotherapy.

Therapy is one of those words that if you say it a few times in quick succession it quits sounding like a real word at all.

"Therapy. Should make me feel good when I feel so bad, but feeling bad is all I've had," I said.

"Is that a song?"

"It is now."

It's a cliché for a reason. We spent the next couple of hours at the piano—well, her at the piano, me on the stool next to her with a guitar—working out the song. A blues song. In case that wasn't obvious. It'd sound a lot better if Remo sang it—he's got a much better honky-tonk voice than I do—but right then I didn't worry about that so much. Singing the blues is singing the blues.

I'll Be Your Chauffeur

So here's when I confess that I was stupid. Not that I did something stupid, because it was what I *didn't* do that was the proof of just how dumb I was. And I don't mean stubborn or reckless. I mean I made a dumb mistake, really. Okay, actually, this explanation will make a lot more sense later, but right now, just hear my mea culpa, because that's how much I need to say it.

One thing, of course, that you might have thought I did right—or got incredibly lucky with—was the fact that I had surrounded myself with supportive people. I had really not thought of anyone in terms of a "support system," but when therapists say those words I think they probably mean something like these folks.

I was a little surprised that Bart and Carynne and Christian wanted to drive down to pick me up. I assured them I would come straight home on the train the next day, but they insisted. My feeling at the time was that they wanted to have a band meeting even more urgently than I did. It sunk in after they arrived that maybe it was just that they were worried about me. I half expected when they pulled up they were going to tell me they had Colin and Courtney hidden there somewhere, too. (They'd left them at home: the car wasn't that big.)

We all ate together, all of them and me and Sarah—and Jonathan, I now remember—and then we got on the road. And had basically a four-hour-long band meeting with occasional breaks for pit stops. Bart did most of the driving. Around the time we ran out of things to say, when we were maybe twenty miles from home, we ran into traffic on the Mass Pike. I ended up falling asleep while we were still inching along in the traffic jam.

When I woke up I was curled into a ball on my side with my face wedged against Christian's leg. He had a hand on my shoulder. He was rubbing it the way you rub something to make it stop hurting. I kept my eyes closed for a little while, wondering if he even realized he was doing it and if he'd be embarrassed if he did. But I was getting a crick in my neck.

I shifted and sat up and saw we were pulling into the driveway of our house. Bart and Carynne didn't linger, saying subdued goodbyes.

Once we were inside, Chris said to me, "I don't know if you can appreciate this, but I sure do. You're the spark. The soul. The heart. Of the band, I mean."

"Or I was," I couldn't help saying.

He nodded. The feathered part of his hair was extra fluffy that day. "I know it's not that easy. It's hard. It's the hardest thing and the most necessary thing, but at the same time it's the thing that has no money value, because you can't put a price on it."

"What are you saying?"

"I'm saying thank you. You didn't just put the wind in the sails, you *are* the sails. I'm just a deck hand. I'm not going anywhere without you."

"And Ziggy and—"

"Ziggy's getting the money because he's the figurehead. He's the marketable piece. He's the ship. Or maybe he's the racehorse, okay? But you're the jockey. Fuck, I am such a lame-ass when it comes to analogies."

That made us both laugh.

"Anyway. I'm saying it sucks but I appreciate it. I mean, I suppose I will grudgingly thank that dumbass if I ever see him again for paying off the bills, but I have a lot more to say to you, and you mean a lot more to me. Basically."

"Thanks, brother," I said, and I meant it. At that point we spontaneously clasped fists and patted each other on the back with our free hands. "So what do you think? Should we keep playing around with the cello and keyboard stuff?"

He shrugged. "Might as well. You got something better to do?"

"Not at the moment."

"Fine. I'll tell Bart tomorrow?"

"Sure."

I guess the other thing to point out about the conversation with Christian, other than that I felt we'd very definitely repaired whatever had been broken between us, is that he clearly saw the whole thing as a breakup. A band breakup and a split between me and Ziggy. Everyone saw it that way. Like the final nail in a coffin or something.

The thing is, they hadn't been there when I'd spent

however many days attached to Ziggy's hip. They couldn't know how attached to him I still felt, or what kind of war went on in my mind when things were quiet. And I couldn't really tell them. Obviously they knew I was in pain: they assumed I would be. But part of me felt like if I talked about how much I missed him or how I wished things were different, I'd be sort of betraying their support of me. Does that make sense? They had my back. I didn't want to make it sound like I wanted to give Ziggy another chance to stab me in it.

But damn. The first thing I did when I went upstairs to lie down after the drive was wish that he was there.

You're just having trouble letting go, I told myself. Artie had even said it was hard to let go. *This is normal, right?*

Maybe only if you've entwined your entire creative life and your entire emotional life with a person who was fine to drive a $5 million wedge between you. Yeah. Those were the kind of toxic thoughts chattering in my brain.

Rehearsal is pretty much what saved me. I mean, I'm never at my best when I don't have something to do, but this would have been a special rock-bottom example.

There was still a lot of lying awake at night trying to figure things out. Feeling like I had somehow traded a repaired bond with Christian with a broken one with Ziggy. Feeling like that was a stupid thought. Feeling like feeling stupid was stupid. Et cetera.

This time, when Remo called and asked if I wanted to house-sit for a couple of months, I said yes without hesitation. Knowing that I'm not a big fan of Los Angeles, you might wonder why. Do I have to tell you where Ziggy went?

So yeah, I told Remo I'd come to Los Angeles.

And then I asked if he could recommend a shrink in the area.

Things Can Only Get Better

I'll say right off the bat: therapy is weird. The reason I say that is that I really thought a therapist would tell me that my constant need to distinguish weird from normal was wrong and that I should change it. But what my therapist actually said was that it was perfectly normal.

Weird.

I mean, you go to a doctor because something is wrong with you and they should tell you how to fix it, right? But I felt like most of what my therapist tried to convince me of was that nothing was wrong with me. This is not to say it wasn't helpful. I don't mean for it to sound like what the therapist did was take my money just to tell me essentially nothing. But the therapist in fact really *doesn't* tell you anything.

You tell yourself.

It boils down to you know damn well you shouldn't be so judgmental (for example), but if a therapist (or anyone) told you to stop doing it, you wouldn't. But when you tell *yourself* to stop doing it, at least there's a chance you'll listen.

I saw my therapist once a week, every Tuesday morning at 11 AM, for twelve weeks. This meant that for about forty-five minutes a week I cried, ranted, argued (with myself), confessed, etc... and then, as I would realize the time was almost up, I'd spend about five minutes trying to explain what I really meant, or what I wished I'd said instead, and that was when I'd often actually realize stuff. Yeah, when I was in a hurry. And then it would be the therapist's turn to talk.

At the end of the first week he said, "Sounds like you should worry more about what's going on in your own internal processes and less about what's going on inside other people."

That was as much as I ever got out of him. Once in a while, a single sentence that always began with "Sounds like..." e.g., "Sounds like you're a little isolated from your support system when you're in LA" or "Sounds like your parents had complicated emotional lives." Other than that, all he ever said at the end of my weekly rant/crying jag/confession was, "See you again next week?"

I think I'm probably giving a bad impression to therapy and I don't mean to, but maybe it's like a joke you can only understand if you were there. I should come out and say: it was fucking helpful. Remember how I felt while—and immediately after—dropping acid on the last day of 1989 in Australia? I felt a rightness, a kind of being in tune with... myself, the universe, everything. It was like acid gave me the feeling of what it was like to be on the top of the mountain. You see how incredible the view is from there. But when you come down (is that why it's called getting high and coming down?) you're at the bottom of the mountain, but just knowing what's up there makes it seem not so bad.

Well, therapy is like going on an incredibly painful hike once a week, where you climb the fucking mountain by your fingernails. But at least it somehow reminds you that the mountaintop is there, and it eventually reinforces the feeling that you can stand at the top in perfect peace again.

I told this to my therapist, George Joseph. He wanted to be called George instead of Doctor Joseph. In the end I didn't find him through Remo exactly, but through a friend of Matthew's—it being important that I find someone who was gay-friendly, obviously. George Joseph was a dark-haired guy, mid-thirties, dressed like a younger, slightly preppier Mr. Rogers. I think that was supposed to be comforting. He always looked a bit like he was on the verge of tearing up and starting to cry himself. I swear, half of me figuring out my shit was to try to make him feel better after I told him something horrible.

Hey, whatever works.

Anyway, I told him my mountain-climbing theory and that acid was like a teleport to the top, but that the feeling didn't last. This was in the one conversation we had about anti-depressants. Anti-depressants were not like acid, he said, but were probably more like a good pair of hiking boots. They'd be a big help to climb the mountain, especially if without them you couldn't get anywhere at all, but you still have to do the climbing yourself.

That was the conversation where I decided I was not going on Prozac. Or any other drug.

It wasn't until later, when I was by myself thinking about the mountain-climbing analogy, that I remembered we'd called Colin my sherpa. Huh.

Yeah, so that was therapy. Next I'll tell you about the other 167 hours per week I spent in LA. That's going to take a lot longer.

Heart Like a Wheel

So the first thing I did when I got to LA was eat. Remo took me through an In-N-Out Burger drive-thru (or was it Fatburger? not sure, he was driving, I just did the eating...) and then we went home and drank bourbon while sitting outside by the pool while I told him bits and pieces of everything that had been going on with me. So he eventually pieced together what all was going on with me and Ziggy and BNC and the various messed up situations intersecting there. He didn't say much about it, though. Yet.

I slept until one in the afternoon the next day. I crawled out of the guest room to the kitchen and stared at the contraption that I thought might be a coffee grinder and pondered whether I had enough brain cells to operate it without breaking it or maiming myself.

"That's my new juicer," Remo pointed out, when it was clear I did not have the required degree in rocket science to make it go.

So I sat at the counter while he juiced things and gave them to me in the form of a suspicious-looking brownish-greenish liquid.

"You let me sleep late," I said, steeling myself to take a sip.

"Sleeping late is good," he said. "Come on. People like us need to be at our peak at eight, nine, ten at night."

"You have a point. Although to my body it's like four PM right now."

"Just proves you needed it."

"I've been sleeping for shit lately, now that you mention it." I tried the drink. It was pleasantly carroty. Huh. "So, when do you leave again?"

"Couple of days. We're packing the equipment tonight. You want to come help?"

"Sure. Wait. What are the chances I run into Digger there?"

"He moved offices to somewhere swankier a while ago, if that's what you're thinking."

"Ah." I had not kept up. "Well, sure."

So that night I got to see the guys, all of whom assumed when they saw me that I'd decided to come along on the tour with them, and I had to explain that no, I was actually house-sitting.

House-sitting is a great euphemism for licking your wounds. Quick, someone write a song about it.

Martin had a girlfriend there. She very reluctantly left before we were done messing around with equipment: as I might have mentioned before, drummers have more stuff than anyone. Martin seemed really sad to see her go, too.

Confession: I don't remember her name. And I know I'm crap with names, but I think Carynne's right when she says I forget women's names more easily than men's. Then again, it turns out I'm terrible at remembering the names of people's significant others. Like somehow I got it in my head that Matthew's boyfriend's name was Dennis, when it was Archie. I apologize if at some point I call him Dennis. In my mind he'll always be "Matthew's boyfriend ________", and the last bit is the part that gets lost easily in my brain.

When we were done, Martin and I broke off from the others and went to get something to eat. Late night at the deli was an LA thing, you know. This was not the same deli I used to go to with Jonathan, it was a different one. That's how much of a thing it was.

"You seem like you're really into her," I said, when we were settled and had ordered.

"Yeahhhhh," he said, making the word extra long so that it was more a confession than simple agreement. "Going away's going to be hard this time."

"This time?"

"Well, you know, usually it's time to move on when a tour comes up anyway, whether we're admitting it or not. This one... I'm going to be wrecked if things can't be the same after I get back."

A busboy plopped a tumbler of seltzer down in front of me. It was hard to imagine Martin wrecked over a relationship. I'd never seen it before. "Matthew said something similar about relationships to me the other day."

"No shit? You've seen him?"

"I was in New York. He's doing great, and, kind of amazingly, Archie is doing great." (I might have said Dennis. If I did, Martin didn't call me on it.)

"Oh, yeah?"

"Yeah." When Matthew had first introduced us, it had been over a year ago, in New York that time we... you know which time I mean. At the time Matthew had said he was getting off the road because he wanted to enjoy what time Archie, who was HIV+, had left. I said what Martin was avoiding: "I didn't think he'd still be around this long."

"No kidding."

"He's been doing well, apparently. Some of it's better drugs, some of it's nutrition and supplements, and it all sounds pretty complicated, but it's working, I guess."

"Did he have it full-blown?"

AIDS was the word Martin didn't say, but I heard it loud and clear. "I don't know. They didn't dwell on the details and I sure as hell didn't pry. But yeah. Matthew felt like, even though he's doing way better, he feels like he doesn't want to hit the road because a lot can happen in a couple of months. At the same time, I think he's starting to feel a little trapped."

"Yeah?"

"He didn't say that, but that was the feeling I was starting to get."

"You sure it isn't that you feel like you want to hit the road and so you ascribe those feelings to others?"

"I suppose that's a possibility. But anyway, what about you? What are you going to do to keep the flame burning when you're not home?"

"What do you mean?"

"I mean are you going to, like, send her postcards from every city to let you know you're thinking about her, or what?"

Martin looked at me with a stunned expression. "That is a fantastic idea. Wow. How did you think of that?"

"Uh..."

"I mean, that's brilliant. I wonder if I can get one of the roadies to do it for me."

"Doesn't that kind of negate the point?"

"Isn't the point to make her feel like I'm thinking about her?"

"If you actually write the postcards, though, won't you be?"

Martin had a little while to think as food started landing on our table. While I was busy dipping my fries in my chocolate shake, he tried to explain. "See, the thing is, on the road, there's so much to think about, I really don't think about home. It'll go completely out of my mind. She will go completely out of my mind. But if I deputize a roadie to do it, at least it'll remind me? I wonder if that would work. I mean, I know it'll work to make her feel like I'm thinking about her, but wow, that's a revelation, maybe me thinking about her on a regular basis while I'm traveling would actually have a really good effect on me, you know?"

"Gee, you think?"

He sighed. "Everyone's got to deal with this somehow. Every one of us. Unless your relationship is with someone you tour with. But hardly anyone has that."

I had a pang of thinking about Ziggy. What I thought about wasn't the sex. I thought about that night in Pittsburgh (was it Pittsburgh?) when we stayed up all night talking in the bus parked outside the motel where we had perfectly good beds to sleep in.

I missed him. Plain and simple. I missed him.

Something was simple, at least.

Drive

Remo waited until we were on the way to the airport to finally tell me what he thought of the whole BNC/Ziggy situation. He was driving, and the plan was that I was going to take the Jeep from there.

"So, let me get this straight," he said. "What you had looming over you was a couple of potentially expensive lawsuits, potential blockage of your ability to perform, pretty much guaranteed death of the band, and debt."

"Well, not *guaranteed....*"

"Daron. Enough with denial."

"Okay, yeah," I gave in, not knowing that another shoe was about to drop.

"And what Ziggy did was wipe all of that out."

"Well, when you put it that way—" Why was I trying to argue?

"Listen here." Remo cut me off. "I know you're rip-shit over it all, but is it possible, just maybe, that Ziggy really did think he was doing what you wanted? It kind of sounds to me like you gave him carte blanche. And if it sounded like that to me, how do you think it sounded to him?"

I had that carsick feeling I hated so much. It almost always meant I had fucked something up. I clung to the things I had been repeating to myself, though. "He knew I was going to be pissed off, though. He knew. And he did it anyway."

"Mother*fuck*!" Remo swerved to avoid a car that changed lanes suddenly. When he had put a couple of car lengths of distance between us and them, though, he hadn't forgotten what he was going to say. "And maybe he thought your partnership was strong enough that pissing you off shouldn't be a dealbreaker. Are you sure *he's* the one who threw your partnership under the bus?"

I opened my mouth to be cranky that Remo was taking Ziggy's side but managed to stop and think for half a second: wait, there was no way Remo was in anyone's corner but mine. In which case... one of the people I trusted and respected most in the world was trying to come up with a gentle way to get me to see that maybe I was the one at fault. I felt ill. "He should have talked to me," I mumbled weakly.

"Yes, he should have. And maybe he'd apologize if you gave him the chance."

And maybe I'd pour gasoline all over my self-esteem and set it on fire and watch it burn, too. Which for some reason is what it would feel like to admit to Ziggy that I had been wrong about this. Which was why I thought I needed therapy.

"Okay," I said. "Maybe it is my insecurity. Maybe that just proves it can't work."

He sighed heavily, like I was missing the point. Or maybe like I was just depressing the hell out of him.

"I'm going to see somebody next week," I said. "I mean for counseling."

His next sigh sounded more relieved. "It's going to be good for you," he said firmly. "You're going to dredge up a lot of stuff, though."

"So I hear."

"Sometimes that can paralyze you creatively until it all settles down again," he warned. "So don't worry if it does."

"Okay. Thanks, Reem."

After I dropped him off, I headed back onto the highways of LA and promptly got into traffic. I would much rather be doing anything in the world, even shopping for clothes, than sitting in traffic. I realized I was going to pass pretty close to Chernwick's office. I decided to stop by there since I didn't remember his phone number but I did remember how to get there. I figured if nothing else I'd pick up his card from his secretary and it would be an excuse to get off the highway. Maybe the traffic would lighten up by the time I got back on.

What ensued was a several-hour excursion because Chernwick was there, convinced me to go with him to a showcase gig for a band who were pretty terrible (but Chernwick wasn't there for the band but to schmooze with all the music industry execs), and the next thing you know we're at an afterparty, and to make a long story short I'll say I woke up in Remo's SUV in the parking lot of Chernwick's office at nine in the morning. I'd smoked a little weed backstage and then pretty much didn't say anything for the rest of the night. Drank a bit at the party, but I think it was mostly jet lag that had done me in. After all, when I got back to the car at four in the morning it had felt like seven in the morning to me, right? Whatever. I got forty winks, and that was good.

I had a vague memory that we'd discussed a gig. I drove a couple blocks down to a donut shop, where I cleaned myself up in the bathroom a bit and drank some coffee, then went back and asked Chernwick's secretary about it. Chernwick himself wasn't in evidence, but she had me wait for a bit. The office had a tiny waiting room with out-of-date issues of *Billboard* and *Variety* sitting on a glass table. I paged through *Variety* and heard the screech of a fax machine from another room.

Oh, hey, look at that, a shot of me and Sarah outside the theater in New York at the *Star Baby* event. It looked to me like Jonathan had been cropped out of the picture.

"Daron," the secretary said, like she knew me—then again, she probably did. "I have a spec sheet for you and some paperwork for you to sign."

She was middle-aged and reminded me a lot of the well-meaning secretaries in the principal's office at my high school, right down to the cardigan sweater and glasses on a chain. Except with a veneer of LA glamor. It's hard to explain.

So I went back to Remo's with a gig in hand. This time I had longer to work on it than the previous time: it wasn't a rescue job. On the other hand, I didn't plan to stay in LA longer than necessary, and Remo would be back for Christmas so I wanted it done by then. And, check it out, I had a small budget to pay session musicians if I wanted.

I ate some tuna right from the can with a fork and then went into the studio thinking I'd get started noodling around on some ideas. The project was another nature documentary, another one in the series about indigenous species in the American West, wolves, buffalo, eagles, etc. It was kind of too bad Remo wasn't around, because he would have been perfect playing on it. I wondered if I had Cray Lucas's number. I'd left my notebook in the house.

I went back into the house to get it and then went back to the studio, paging through, looking for the page where I might have written Cray's number. My notebook is generally chronological, so it was probably where the notes about Japan were, right? But sometimes things got written into the margins on other pages.

I came to a song about Ziggy. I mean, who else could I have been writing about? Actually, I think I was kind of writing this one as if it was from his point of view. Maybe wishful thinking about his point of view. Draw what conclusions you will about that. When I wrote it I had a really clear idea in my mind how the melody and vocal should go, too, though I'd never sat down and worked it out exactly. A really simple song, bluesy in an almost Ricki Lee Jones kind of way. Or maybe Paul Simon from the *One Trick Pony* era.

Next thing you know, I sat down and recorded a demo of it.

I'm bad at promises
I'm bad at holding on
I'm bad at being true
I'm bad at being strong

The only promise I can make

is that every promise I will break

The only promise I can keep
is that I'll always break my promise

I'm bad at promises
I'm bad at singing songs (about)
true love and promises
I'm bad at being strong

The only promise I can keep
is that promises will make you weep

The only promise I won't break
is that I'll always promise

I Go to Extremes

What ensued was a songwriting binge that went on for… I'm not sure how long. A couple of weeks? Remo was wrong about therapy putting a block on my creative energy. Instead, each session was like a Pandora's box of (painful) song ideas. They would come flying out, and I'd scramble to catch them all when I got back to the house. I figured I was not a great person to be around while wrestling with that shit, so other than George Joseph, the cleaning lady, and the pizza delivery guy, I didn't much interact with humans.

The thing was, of course, I was working on this soundtrack that was all instrumental and that was going to be time-consuming and that I wanted to be all perfectionist about. But I'd get a little ways into it and then I could hear how this other song in my head should go, and I'd procrastinate on working on the soundtrack by obsessively writing (and recording) an entire song. I've never been a singer-songwriter type. I'd rather not be playing and singing at the same time, except for some choruses. But, you know, this was some deeply personal shit.

You'd think it would be enough to just write the lyrics for therapeutic purposes, right? Wrong. Maybe it's just that who I was and how I felt was so wrapped up in being a professional rock musician, but I couldn't leave one of these songs until I'd polished it and recorded a demo that I was happy with. Playing and singing and maybe even putting one or two overdubs on it.

Obsessive. Sometimes not eating, sometimes not sleeping, sometimes not doing the work I was being paid to do, but it felt like such an imperative to record these songs when they were bursting out of me. It felt good. I figured, well, it's therapy. If it feels good, it's a good sign. And some of them were really good songs. I'd get one done, and then I'd be able to work on the soundtrack for a couple of hours or a couple of days, and then the next session would roll around and I'd crack my skull open and more stuff would pour out.

That description makes it sound exhausting, but it wasn't. I was so energized that sometimes I had to sort of tire myself out before I could spend a couple of hours in front of the keyboard and computer fussing with them for the soundtrack. I took to swimming a lot and using the pull-up bar across the doorway to Remo's bedroom. The pool was small, and I could swim underwater all the way from one end to the other on one breath, surface, and then go back under and swim back. I would lose count after about fifty of those. I had to be careful not to go into the studio while dripping wet. I could hear all kinds of music in my ears when I was underwater.

The only part that was exhausting were the nights when I couldn't sleep because I was lonely or horny or self-flagellating. But since my time was my own, I mostly worked during them and then whenever I finally felt sleepy I could just lie the fuck down wherever I wanted and conk out. Like a cat or something. That probably wouldn't work so well on a long-term basis, but for that stretch of weeks it worked perfectly well.

Counting it by therapy appointments, I must have been about six or seven weeks into my stay when Cray and Bart showed up to play on the score together. Then all three of us had a semblance of a schedule dictated by the work, but it wasn't like we had to clock in nine to five, you know? We ate when we were hungry, and otherwise—ha, literally—played it by ear.

We got Pike to come up and engineer some tracks with all three of us playing together, which was easier than me doing it, and I learned some tricks from him about making Remo's studio work for me. I'm a pretty good engineer, but the way you learn that is by watching other engineers. Pike had worked with some of the best in the business.

One morning, after Cray had gone to bed, Bart and I had the following conversation:

Me: I'm glad you and Cray are getting along so good.
Bart: Were you worried we wouldn't?
Me: Yeah. I pictured you two stalking around each other like territorial tomcats.
Bart (looking puzzled): Why?
Me: I don't know.
Bart: Dar', that's you who gets weird around people, not me.
Me: Oh.

For what it's worth, Cray and I got along fine. He was a lot calmer than the last time I saw him, and I guess so was I. He left after a week. Bart stayed for a couple more days, during which we went to a lot of shows and ate a lot. I think he was alarmed that I was too skinny actually and felt it was his duty to fatten me up again while he was there, a vestige of our music-school days when tuna from a can with a fork was all I could afford sometimes.

Then when Bart was due to leave the next day, in a moment of weakness—or strength, maybe—I played him a couple of the "therapy" tracks I'd been recording. Next thing you know, I'd dubbed him a cassette of them all to "listen to on the plane," he said. He also took dubs of the instrumental stuff we'd polished with Pike to use if anyone needed to hear samples of his session work.

Don't think I wasn't aware that for two-plus months I wasn't dealing with Ziggy. The thing is, in my mind, I was dealing with him every day. But I was dealing with the Ziggy in my own head; even more important, though, I was dealing with the Daron in my own head.

Then came the day Carynne faxed me some papers to sign, making the buyout official from our end.

Remo's fax machine was one of those ones that used a roll of thermal paper. So I took the faxes down to the nearest copy machine, which was a self-serve machine at a drug store down the hill. I copied the pages so I could read them without getting them all smudgy from my hot fingertips.

Later, I had a phone call with Carynne that went like this:

Me: Hey, so, you're one hundred percent behind me signing these, right?
Her: Yes, why?
Me: I want to sign them without reading them.
Her: Why?
Me: Because reading them is making my head hurt...?
Her: Are you at a pay phone?
Me: ...Maybe.
Her: Daron, are you all right?
Me: I'm fine.
Her: Have you been drinking?
Me: A little. It's okay, that's why I pulled over in this parking lot until I sober up. Which is why I'm calling you from a pay phone. I'm being responsible.
Her: That's not reassuring.
Me: I promise I won't go anywhere until I sober up.
Her: No wonder your head hurts.
Me: Well actually, I didn't even try to read past the first sentence.
Her: Daron. This is really for the best, you know.
Me: Is it?
Her: I'm not saying don't be upset. You have every right to be upset. But... but you're getting paid for not lifting a finger.
Me: For my life's work.
Her: Listen to yourself. You're twenty-four years old—
Me: Twenty-three.
Her: —Even worse. You're only twenty-three and you're calling two albums and an EP your life's work?
Me: Okay, I misspoke. Life's work is... I can't explain it.
Her: I can. You wrapped a huge amount of your ego and your self-esteem and your identity in the band. Come on. Isn't it obvious? *You named the band after your persona.* But maybe it's time to stop mixing up the band and *you.*
Me: ...

Her: Daron? Are you there?
Me: ...You... In eight seconds, you just explained more about what's going on with me than eight weeks of therapy.
Her: Have you talked to him yet?
Me: I do every Tuesday.
Her: Not the therapist. *Ziggy.*
Me: Is he here?
Her: There's a thing called the phone, you know.
Me: But I don't know his—

Ice water. Panic. Nausea. I was such a stupid fuck. I *could* call him. *I had a pager number for him.* One he said he only gave to me. What the fucking fuck was wrong with me? Remember when I said I was stupid—like really, *really* stupid? This was what I was talking about. For two-something months I had forgotten I had a way to call him. I had no excuse. I was Just. Plain. Stupid. I have no way to make it sound better than it was. I can justify it in hindsight as maybe kinda good because of how much I wrote, how much I did, during those very intensely productive two months but... but that's a retrofit.

Carynne: Daron, are you there?
Me: ...
Her: Daron? You're freaking me out.
Me: Um.
Her: ...
Me: I'm going to call him right now.
Her: Right now?
Me: I gotta go.

Later she would tell me maybe I didn't "forget." Maybe I was subconsciously protecting myself until I was ready to talk to him. Yeah, and maybe Carynne was trying to put a good spin on my stupidity.

I searched around to make sure the phone I was at took incoming calls. It did. I called the number I'd memorized and then input the pay phone number.

And then I sat there for an hour, getting sober and feeling like if I drove away, the second I did he was going to call, and then if it rang and rang he'd think I was yanking his chain and *oh fuck me why didn't I wait until I went back to Remo's to call him from there?* Stupid.

It wasn't quite the level of suffering as that drive back from Betty Ford the time I gave myself heatstroke. But I was desperate enough to piss behind a dumpster so the phone was in earshot. I think I was there for about four hours? I suck at estimating time, but I was there long enough that I got offered drugs three separate times as well as two different blow jobs—one from a woman, one from a man—and was panhandled four or five times, too. Which felt pretty much like a microcosm of everything I hated about the entertainment industry, you know? I said no to all of them, of course.

Maybe the reason it felt like a microcosm of the business, though, is that the business is just a microcosm of everything I hate about human nature.

Here's the kicker: I could have been perfectly content to stand outdoors next to that damn phone for four hours if I had a guitar with me. Why did I even leave the house without one? Oh right, I had just gone to make photocopies and somehow that led to me stopping off somewhere for a drink... and it was the bar's parking lot I was in.

A police cruiser trawled by slower than the speed of traffic. I took it as a sign. I got in the car and left before I could get arrested for vagrancy or some equally bullshit thing.

Good thing I did.

It's All I Can Do

When I turned on the engine the radio came on, and the first thing I heard was Ziggy's voice.

Universe, I thought, *now you're just fucking with me.*

He was in the middle of some kind of on-air appearance. They were blathering about some charity—I eventually gathered it was some kind of fundraising event they were broadcasting live from. I wondered if I could drive to wherever they were.

"So are you going to play a song for us?" the deejay asked.

"He's going to play it. I'm going to sing it," Ziggy joked.

Who, who's going to play it? I thought. I heard someone else's voice count off in the background and then an acoustic guitar came in.

And then Ziggy started singing. The song started off kind of folky, almost like a sixties-style protest song, but when it came to the chorus I thought, jeez, that deserves to be done with some serious heavy noise, like Nine Inch Nails level or Metallica, but, you know Ziggy, he could be singing a grocery list and he could fill it with drama.

Looking at the words, you could think of it as an environmentalist song, in which case it was actually a little flat or dull, but that almost-abstract chorus...

I knew him. It was about fucked-up parent-child relationships. And/or maybe ex-lovers.

Fuck.

Here's pretty much the version he sang:

they say it's acid rain
eating away the finish
eating away the cold hard edges
ruining the varnish

they say it's toxic waste
poisoning the water
poisoning the food we're eating
killing our sons and daughters

words burn
hate churns
leave me
free me

they say it's a legacy
given to the children
living today through all our messes
inherit the world we've built them

words burn
hate churns
leave me
free me

Then the deejay came back on and they nattered a little more, laughing and joking, and then they went to commercial. When they came back from the break they had moved on to their next segment and Ziggy was gone.

I wondered if they'd given the name of the guitar player earlier, before I was listening, or if Ziggy felt he didn't rate a mention. I was aggravated on the guy's behalf if the latter.

I turned the engine off and stared at the pay phone. What would happen if I paged him now?

I dug a quarter out of the ash tray where Remo kept them and went to the phone, slotted it in. I dialed again. I punched in the number when prompted. Hung up.

Stood right there. Waited. Tried not to look around for that police car, which would only make me look suspicious.

When the phone rang I nearly jumped out of my skin. I steeled myself for disappointment. It was probably someone looking for a drug dealer or a pimp. I answered it. "Hello?"

"Oh my god, it's you." Ziggy. "You're in Los Angeles."

I decided not to tell him I'd been here for two months. "Um, yes. Hi."

Silence from the other end.

Shit. "Zig—" I couldn't make words come out. I couldn't think of what I was trying to say. "Can we talk?"

"I don't know, can we?"

Words burn. His voice dripped with bitterness.

"I... I just..." Argh. What could I say? "I'm sorry."

"So am I," he said, which sounded completely wrong. As if what I had meant I was sorry for was that the relationship was over, not for being stupid. Maybe those two things were ultimately the same, though.

"Can I see you?" I sounded pathetic. I thought about the way I'd snuck away from Digger and Mills that time, to find him at the Carlyle Hotel. How both of us had made off for Central Park. Where was that rapport now? Could I get it back?

"I don't know, Daron."

"I'm signing the fucking papers today. To close our end of the deal."

Silence. Jeezus, Ziggy, throw me a bone.

"I just want to talk."

Again, silence. Then, "Wellll, there is one thing I

could use your help with."

"What?"

"I can't discuss it now."

"I'm on a pay phone outside a bar. But I'll be at Remo's in a little while. You can call me there."

"Page me the number when you get there."

"All right."

He hung up without saying anything more.

I probably deserved that, I told myself.

I drove home in a lather, as you can imagine. Fortunately I did not get into a car wreck. And I paged him the second I got in the house.

An hour went by. Then two. I wondered how I could be sure that Remo had call waiting, still. Eventually I gave in and called Carynne.

"I'm home safe," I told her.

"Good. So about those papers."

"I'm signing them and faxing them back. I never want to see them again."

"That's a very mature attitude, Daron."

"Okay, then, seriously. Am I obligated to do anything as a result of these?"

"Well, this part isn't in writing of course, but we're going to team up with BNC to sue Digger."

"Wait, is that really going to happen? Ziggy said Digger would get screwed, but I wasn't sure he meant like that."

"Daron, seriously, Digger doesn't deserve your sympathy. I think we've actually got a pretty strong case."

"Based on what? Evidence BNC provides?"

"Well, yeah."

"Carynne, those are the fuckers who doctored their books to screw us in the first place! Yeah I want Digger to get what he deserves, but not if it means lying, cheating—"

"Whoa, whoa, I think that's too strong a way to put it."

"Now you sound like Ziggy. Are there multiple versions of the truth?"

"There are always multiple versions of the truth when it comes to contracts, dear. That's why there are courts to decide which interpretation is valid."

"Ugh. I deeply, *deeply* hate everything about this."

"Including the million dollars you and the guys are getting."

That might have made me hate it all the more. But I knew getting the house paid off would be a load off Christian's mind, and I wasn't about to let him go back to framing houses or something. Just because I had some heroic ideal about truth. "It feels like... extortion, somehow."

"Bribery, but point taken. We might not end up in court-court. It might go to arbitration."

"Is that better?"

"In an ideal world, Digger settles with us before it has to go that far."

"That makes it feel even more like extortion!"

She sighed. "Daron, for fuck's sake, there is no universe in which Digger doesn't actually owe you money, whether morally or because of specific fiscal shenanigans. I'm sure of that."

"I don't like greed."

"You're not being greedy. You're not even being vindictive, particularly. Maybe *I* am a weensy bit, but only a bit."

"Fine. I just better not have to testify or anything."

She didn't say anything about that. I signed the papers and fed them into the fax machine one by one.

And still no call from Ziggy. The motherfucker made me wait.

Instinct

I didn't get much done while waiting for Ziggy to call me back. I couldn't concentrate enough to work, didn't really feel like I could eat. Television failed to hold my interest. Remo had a bunch of books on a shelf, but I couldn't bring myself to start one. Starting a book is like striking up a conversation with a stranger, and sometimes you just don't want to get sucked into the wrong one.

I made the mistake of turning on the TV and caught a clip of a news piece on the charity shindig. There was Ziggy, being shepherded by an entourage, Antonio right behind him looking very Secret Service, two women, two other guys.... Entourage was the right word for them. Ziggy looked very small in the midst of them. The little prince. Maybe I imagined he looked sort of lonely, too. I wondered which one of the two guys had played the guitar.

I turned off the TV before I could beat myself up any more. You know what I did to distract myself then? I taught myself to use Remo's space-age juicer. I found the manual in a drawer in the kitchen and decided it was the only way I was going to get around to eating the apples and oranges and carrots I had sitting around. I suppose I should mention that I hadn't really improved my haphazard ways of shopping for food. You know how it is. You go to the grocery store, you think, hey, I should buy fruits and vegetables because they're good for me. And most of what I would buy were apples, oranges, and carrots because they last a long time without you eating them. So at least you have a chance to eat them before they go bad. Celery, too. But I never had a plan for how or when to eat them. I didn't even like apples particularly, but they could be eaten without utensils or any forethought.

Turned out when I put apples and carrots and oranges into the juicer, what came out was actually drinkable. I did a small batch first, and after I tasted it I decided I might as well run them all through. So in a really weird way the juicer solved two problems at once: what to do with the food I'd bought and how to keep my brain busy while waiting for Ziggy to call.

The juicer running is the only explanation I have for how a car could pull into the driveway without me hearing it. When the doorbell rang I nearly jumped out of my skin. Remo's house is on a canyon road out of earshot of the next house. I wondered if I should pull a kitchen knife out of the block before I answered the door.

I went and looked through the diamond-shaped window on the front door and saw Ziggy standing there. If level ten was him dressed and made up for the stage and level one was him fresh from the shower, he was at about a four here, very light eyeliner, unremarkable jeans, T-shirt, and unadorned leather jacket. (Yeah, what was a four for Ziggy was a nine for me.)

"Can I come in?"

"Of course."

"You sound like I should be sure of that."

I found myself saying, "You can come in if you're not here to rip me to pieces."

"That's not my intention," he said.

Fine. They say vampires have to be invited in, don't they? "Come in."

Then I saw him wave to a car. I didn't see who was driving, but they backed the car down the steep driveway. Tony, maybe?

I shut the door behind him and went on autopilot, completely unprepared for his presence. "Uh, can I pour you some juice? I just made it."

Ziggy sounded completely unprepared for this question. "Um. What kind is it?"

"Apple, orange, carrot."

Confused: "At the same time?"

"Yeah. It's surprisingly good."

He gave one of those glances around like he was expecting a prank film crew to pop out. "Uh, okay."

He sat in one of the stools at the island while I debated whether to put ice cubes in the drinks. Ice never tasted right to me in LA. Well, neither did the tap water. Then I remembered the beer glasses Remo had in the door of the freezer. Where all the juice collected was this section of the juicer that could be used as a pitcher. I poured it into two glasses and set one down in front of Ziggy, and then I leaned back against the part of the counter next to the sink, the island between us, feeling utterly and completely ridiculous.

Maybe Ziggy felt the same. He looked around again, like this wasn't what he expected somehow. He slid his leather jacket off, leaving it inside out over the back of the stool, looking suddenly as small and naked as something newly hatched. He took a sip, or at least pretended to, while we sort of stared at each other in this odd bubble in spacetime created by the gulf between our minds. I mean: I was wondering what he was thinking and then I realized he was probably wondering what I was thinking, which meant we were thinking the *same thing* and so how could it be that we felt worlds apart?

I felt that hot feeling behind my eyes like I was about to sneeze or cry.

"I've got some things I should say," he said, as he

put the glass down on the white countertop. He was wearing no lipstick, and his lower lip was plumper and shinier than the upper one, and that was the kind of thing I was noticing while he spoke. "But I'm not sure if I'm ready to say them."

I just nodded at him, since I didn't trust myself not to burst into tears or say something I'd regret—I wasn't sure which. All I knew is I felt like the pressure was building: inside this bubble was a vacuum, and I was swelling up with unexpressed words/feelings/angst. I was so angry and hurt and messed up, but at the same time there was a sense of relief at being in the same room with him that was so intense it was frightening.

He slipped from the stool and came closer to me. I reminded myself to keep breathing. He took the glass out of my hand and set it down, and then he reached a hand toward my face.

His thumb brushed my chin. "Don't," he said.

Don't what? I thought, but I couldn't actually make words come out.

"Don't bite your lip like that," he said, his thumb brushing my lip that time as I realized I was clenching my jaw and had done a number on the inside of my mouth. "Not for me. Not over me."

Is there any reasonable response at that point other than to kiss him? I've never thought of one. Maybe kiss isn't the right word, because that sounds kind of premeditated. This was more like I put my mouth on his mouth like I had lost my grip on the magnet and couldn't resist the force that stuck us together any longer.

Yeah, there was a chatter in the back of my head while we kissed, a flock of flittering negative thoughts like *hey, Chris was right, this is exactly like an addiction; it feels good now but what is the hangover going to be like?* And: *is it a good idea to kiss someone you're so angry at? Generally not.* And: *what the fucking fuck, Daron, is this what you called him for?* But at least the chatter was in the back of my head, not the front. The front was busy devouring him.

When we came up for air, what Ziggy said was, "Thank god."

"What?"

He shook himself, the look on his face telling me that hadn't been what he intended to say at all. "Just... happy to see you." His hands had ended up gripping the unbuttoned edges of my flannel shirt, and he didn't let go.

The PR director in my head was waving at me, trying to get my attention, trying to tell me to steer this back to business talk, or to small talk. He was shouting suggestions: *bring up the radio thing you heard! tell him about Bart's visit!* Anything but relationship talk.

I ignored it. "Happy. You don't look happy."

"It's hard to be when..." He closed his eyes, then opened them and started over. "I don't know. It just feels better over here than it did over there." He jerked his head toward the abandoned stool. "And being over there felt better than being apart."

"I feel exactly the same way," I said, a little wonderingly.

"Which would explain why you didn't shove me away."

"Were you afraid I would?"

"Yes."

That sliced me. And it brought home the fact that, for fuck's sake, we really *did* feel the same. "You're as afraid I'm going to say something to rip you up as I am that you will." It came out like word salad, but he understood me, which only proved we felt the same.

"Yeah."

I felt like the ghost of Jonathan was hovering in that house, though. I knew from him that feeling the same didn't mean things were always going to work out. Still.

Ziggy went on. "When you took off from the limo I think maybe I... appreciated how freaked out you must have been when I left the country without telling you."

"I wondered if I'd ever see you again."

"Exactly."

Wow. Remember what Remo had said? He'd asked me if it was Ziggy who'd torpedoed the relationship by signing the contract or if it was me who'd done it by walking away when Ziggy probably needed me the most.

Maybe both. "Zig."

"Yeah?"

"I... I have some things to say, too. And I don't know if I'm ready to say all of them either."

"Well, we can't say them all at once anyway."

"True." I fell silent then for a couple of long moments, caught up in experiencing his presence, the scent of him, the knowledge that he was there in the room. This is what being apart for so long did to me, I think. And then to have been glued together for that stretch of days in Boston, only to be torn apart again until now. I couldn't make sense of it: why did I want him so much, need him so much? Was it because I loved him? If so, was that a good reason? or was reason really nothing to do with it at all?

His mouth touched mine this time, tentative and searching, then more firmly as he found what he was looking for. I know that how angry I was affected the way I kissed. But that didn't mean I wanted to stop.

When he pulled back, I said, "What would you have done if I pushed you away? Just now?"

"Said some of the things I wanted to and left," he said. "For good."

I wondered where his driver had gone, but didn't bring it up.

"And I figure if I said some of those things, that was probably the last straw for you, too."

"What makes you sure the last straw didn't hit me two months ago?" I asked.

"That you didn't push me away," he said, as if that made perfect sense. Maybe it did? Maybe that's why he'd said "thank god." Because he knew I was willing to listen?

"Maybe we should take a step back," I suggested.

"We tried that once, remember? Maybe we should take a step forward."

"What do you mean by that?"

"That's for you and me to figure out," Ziggy pointed out.

"Sounds to me like figuring it out *is* a step forward."

"Which is exactly what I mean." Ziggy gave me a sharp look. "We seem to agree an awful lot for two people who supposedly aren't getting along."

"Yeah, well, neither of us has said the things we mean to, yet."

"You mean we won't know until we do whether this is going to be a breakup or a makeup conversation."

It didn't feel much like a breakup conversation, honestly, given how close he was standing, given that one of my hands had strayed around to the small of his back, but, you know, I've been wrong about Ziggy before. So I tried to keep an open mind. "You're right. I don't know which it is."

He licked his lower lip.

I was getting frank in my old age. "Sex first or after?"

He was unsurprised by my question. "I think you'd better decide that."

"Why?"

"Because if I say first, you'll suspect the only reason I came here was to get you in bed. And if I say after, you'll suspect I was trying to negotiate while you were in an impaired state."

Ouch. The truth always hurts the most. In the same kind of "logic" that had ruled the conversation so far, then, I came up with a solution. "Okay, then we should have sex before *and* after."

"And if we melt down during the talking, go nuclear and there's no going back?"

"Then we'll hate-fuck after and both write songs about it for decades to come."

I wasn't joking, but it made him laugh. I don't think he thought I was joking, either.

This is the thing. Part of my brain was telling me that sex was the worst possible idea. But the thing I was finally coming to understand (thank you, therapy?) was that my instincts about sex were badly skewed by homophobia and Digger and Ziggy himself. I was gradually learning to distinguish my actual instincts from bullshit that I'd soaked up in suburbia and from defense mechanisms I'd developed. And so, sure, "common sense" said I shouldn't "give in," but why was it considered "giving in" in the first place, as if withholding itself were some kind of virtue? *That* was bullshit, and even I could see that.

He started to sink to his knees, but I gripped him by the elbows. "Don't. Let's go to the bedroom."

I was not sorry with this decision. Not sorry at all.

King of Wishful Thinking

It's not like I didn't know we had issues. Me and Ziggy had massive issues. It's not like we were using sex to cover them over or ignore them. But I think if we were in unspoken agreement on one thing, it was that whatever it was that attracted us to each other—chemical, magical, or inexplicable—sex itself wasn't the problem.

Could it be part of the solution? Maybe it needed to be.

We didn't waste much time, both eager for it even if we were still angry at each other and hurt and all that. It was hammer-and-tongs sex: we went at it until we were both limp. When we were done, we might have even dozed off for a second or two.

When time started to move forward again I said, "Well, I sure as hell am calmer now."

"You're always calmest when you're not worrying about where your next sex is going to come from," he said. His voice was only slightly muffled because of how close his mouth was to my damp skin.

"Is that why I don't ever want to let you out of my sight? That doesn't sound... healthy."

"You don't ever want to let me out of your sight because I keep doing stupid shit like running off to other continents, or at least the wrong side of this one."

"If that's what you think, then why do you do it? Why don't you just stay with me, Zig?"

For the record, these words were coming out of me without any filter, without any forethought, and without any thought for actual facts or circumstances. I think Zig knew that.

Ziggy, though, was never unfiltered, though he could be brutally frank when it suited him. "Because I get tired of being pushed away."

"Ah." I licked the part of his skin nearest to my mouth: the top of his shoulder. "It's all my fault, then."

"No. There's a lot more going on than that." He shifted position—we both did, like ballroom dancers with long practice together—and I settled against him again. "But remember that piece of it, will you?"

"Okay." I can't say that I really did remember, exactly. The lesson that I was happier when I was with him than when I wasn't did seem very obvious at that moment, though. At least it seemed like it when I couldn't even think about all the other junk yet, the industry stuff and the contracts and the bullshit that had torn us apart in the first place.

That crap began to filter back into my brain slowly. "Remo says I overreacted to you signing the contract."

One of my ears was against his chest, so his voice sounded deeper than usual when he asked, "And what do you say?"

"I say it's taken me two months to come to terms with the fact that even if you did the right thing for me, for everyone, knowing that hasn't made me any less angry at you. I guess I have to own that."

"Ah."

"I feel like it should: like facts should trump anger, you know? I should be able to make myself reasonable about this. Or therapy should help, right? But I'm still incredibly pissed off. Therapy hasn't made me less angry; it's made me accept that I am."

Ziggy stroked my hair. "You know what's dangerous for me? Sex with you is so incredible when you're angry. It tempts me to piss you off. But I promise I did not sign that contract trying to piss you off. I swear on my mother's grave, Daron."

"Maybe I'd be less angry if I knew what was going through your head," I said, trying to sit up a little so I could see his face, but failing. Lying down with as much of my skin touching his skin as possible felt better.

"When I signed it?"

"When you decided to, yeah."

"Okay," he said, but then was silent for a while. I felt him swallow and take a deep breath. "I can admit this now that I have a feeling you're not going to shut me out again. At least... at least not right away."

"I promised we'd have sex after we talked, didn't I?"

He laughed in spite of himself. "You did. And I trust your promises."

"So what are you admitting?"

"That I was afraid of two things if I signed it. One was that you'd shut me out."

"So you *knew* I'd be pissed off."

"Um, I strongly suspected it—"

"And then I actually was. Can you blame me for that?"

"I guess not." He let out a long breath, and it was like he was deflating. "But it still hurt like hell when you ditched me."

"You do understand that it felt to me like *you* ditched *me*."

"Did it?"

"After all those talks we had in Boston? It felt like... the same old thing, only a hundred times worse. You got me completely disarmed and believing we were soulmates. And then you turned around and ripped my testicles off."

"Hm." He was silent. I couldn't tell if he was processing that or preparing a rebuttal. He ventured carefully along the same path. "I was worried because you always react badly to me taking charge of anything to do with the band."

"This wasn't just anything, though. This was everything."

"I... I see that now. I... really hadn't looked at it like that. I was thinking of it in terms of your control over my career and my control over my own career."

I clenched my jaw. "Listen to what you just said. You basically just said you chose yourself over the band."

"Except I didn't. I could have signed a deal that screwed you all good and hard. I really did try to get everything you expressed concern about. Money. Your ability to work. The lawsuits. I really tried."

"Okay." Maybe I got what I deserved there, for insisting on control when our band relationship should have been more collaborative all along? Money skews everything, fucks everything up, though. I know it was my own weird morals that made it seem like if I took the million from the deal I was somehow dirty and corrupted. Would playing martyr have been better? Probably not. I just had to get over myself, maybe. "You said there were two things you were afraid of, though. What's the second thing?"

"That I fucked it all up completely and made the wrong deal."

"What?"

"Maybe I was in over my head. I thought I played them, but maybe Mills played me."

"Wait, you were afraid it was the wrong thing before you went through with it? Or afterward?"

"Afterward. I thought I was playing hardball. I made the deal with Mills without Digger, you know, because the plan was to cut him out of the deal, right? I thought I could handle it." He was trembling. I could feel it everywhere my body touched his—which was everywhere. "But Mills agreed so quickly to what I asked for I not only had no leeway, I immediately suspected I didn't ask for enough."

I held him then, pulling him onto his side so I could cradle his head and he could cry a little, tears of fear and regret. Like he was still afraid.

When he looked up his cheeks were wet. "Are you still angry?"

"Yeah," I said, "but maybe a little less. Thank you for telling me."

"I know I did it to myself," Ziggy went on with sudden urgency. "The one person I needed to turn to for support about the decision was the person who was going to be the most upset about it. You."

I remembered him clinging to me in the limo like a child. "Was that like, I dunno, having to confess to your mom that you needed her help even though she was going to punish you for getting in trouble?"

He leaned back from me and blinked in surprise. "Whoa."

"What? Was that yes or no?"

"Yes." He looked at me then like he was seeing me with new eyes. "I hadn't even thought of it that way. But, yes. It was exactly like that. Except I always knew my mother loved me no matter what. You, I thought maybe I finally broke everything so irrevocably that there was no going back."

So, he felt as relieved as I did that we were talking like this. "You thought you poisoned the well."

He sat all the way up. He almost sounded accusatory: "You heard that song."

"From the on-air gig? That's how I knew when to page you."

"Fuck." He put a hand over his eyes and drew a few deep, even breaths. I wondered if he was meditating. "Okay, look. Are we at the stage where we can apologize?"

"I don't think I can apologize for being pissed off at you, Ziggy. I know maybe there was no real choice, I know maybe Moondog Three would be dead no matter which way we went, but it still really feels to me, deep down, like you killed something that was mine." *Or took it for yourself.* I didn't say that, though.

"I'm not saying apologize for being angry. But how about for not being there when I needed you?" He looked sad and pathetic.

I almost didn't have the heart to say what I was thinking, but I knew I'd regret it if I didn't get the words off my chest. "Okay, you know when you actually needed me? *Before* you signed that contract. That's when you should have called me up for a heart-to-heart."

"Shit." He winced and screwed his eyes shut again before looking at me. His voice was a whisper. "You might be right."

We stared at each other for a long time then, like we were frozen. Me, I was mostly savoring the extremely rare feeling that I had won a fight. I mean, these kinds of fights didn't usually have a winner or a loser, you know? My eyes began to itch, but it was like I didn't even want to blink.

He finally spoke and broke the moment. "I'm a little parched."

I wasn't sure if we were done talking, but we had definitely come to the end of a round. I felt a little parched myself. "Well," I said, "there's juice."

Can't Be Sure

We put some clothes on and sat side by side on Remo's white leather sectional, drinking the juice. I'd added ice cubes now to freshen it up. Ziggy looked around.

"So this is your home away from home," he said.

"I guess...? There's a recording studio on the other side of the swimming pool."

"Swimming pool?" He looked at the large plate-glass window, but I hadn't turned the lights on out there. I went to the doorway to the patio and flipped the switches. The lights under the water and the little ones along the landscaping came on.

"That's where I recorded that documentary score," I said, pointing to the outbuilding that was the studio. "The one you heard at the Allston house."

"Are you working on another one?" He had a very casual tone, but I knew him well enough now that I could hear it was *too* casual.

"I am, but that's not why I came to LA," I said, looking at the glow of the pool instead of at him. "I came here because you were here."

I heard his juice mug click against the glass-topped side table. "And... it took you two months to figure out what to say to me?"

"I guess." I felt my cheeks burn a little as I thought again about how I could have paged him sooner. But would I have? "Maybe it's a Freudian slip or something, but I didn't remember your pager number until today."

"What's special about today?"

"I told you. I signed the papers that make the deal official from our end. Dissolving my interest in the property known as Moondog Three so that BNC is free and clear to do whatever they want with you." I turned and looked at him. "Are you really having second thoughts?"

He shrugged. "Second thoughts are only going to bring me misery at this point. So, no." His face was set.

Now that I was feeling sympathetic to him, though, I was having second thoughts myself. Not about what he did for me and the guys, but... "It still feels like a deal with the devil."

"Maybe they always do," he said. "I'll write some clichéd songs about it. More likely it's damned if you do and damned if you don't."

Frankly, he looked miserable, which was difficult to look at given that at that moment I was feeling pretty good. It felt uncomfortably unfair.

I sat down next to him. "I know maybe I'm being a hypocrite here, but I really don't want to see you unhappy."

"I don't want to see you unhappy, either." He took my left hand and turned it back and forth looking at it. There were scars where I'd been burned by Megaton's illegal pyrotechnics. "Can you live without me?"

I tried to pull my hand away, thinking he was—what—asking for permission to leave me?

He held fast. "I mean—shit, Daron, I mean I..."

I recognized that panic. It was usually me who was saying the wrong thing and trying to dig myself out of a hole. "Say what you really mean, Zig."

He was holding my hand with both of his. He sighed. "I said... on the phone... that there was something you could help me with."

"Yeah..." I tried not to sound suspicious, but I probably failed.

"I mean, I know you're a free agent now."

He meant like in sports. Free to sign with any team for the highest amount.

"I know you've got a lot going on, too. Soundtracks. Session work."

I hadn't actually done any session work in a while, but I was sure I could if I wanted, so I didn't argue.

"Songwriting."

I shrugged like it didn't matter.

"You wrote that song for Sarah," he said, his tone suddenly accusatory, I guess because I was trying to shrug it off.

Or maybe because he was jealous? "She's a friend," I said, and it sounded exactly like it would have if he'd insinuated I was sleeping with her.

"And for all I know Remo Cutler's going to put you in his back pocket one of these days and we'll never see you again."

When he put it that way, yeah, I was a lot busier and had a lot more prospects than a lot of "failed" rock stars. "What's your point, Ziggy? I'm not going to sit at home crying in my beer? Of course I'm not."

He got up and paced restlessly to the window, staring at the lit-up pool and patio.

"What do you want, Ziggy?"

He folded his arms like it was cold by the window, though I knew it wasn't. "I know how this is going to look. I know how it's going to sound. Please don't go ballistic."

"What? What are you going to ask me, Zig? What possible favor could I do for you at this point?" What the hell could he be thinking of asking me to do that he thought I would flip out over?

"You heard the on-air thing today."

"Yeah." And it had sounded fine, from what I remembered.

He turned to face me. "I need a guitar player."

Oh. I had a moment of being stunned, merely because that wasn't what I was expecting. Then I had a moment of anger and I knew why he'd asked me not to go nuts. But seriously: didn't we just break up? What was the point of that if we were going to turn right around and, and... And then a second wave of ire swept through me: from Ziggy's point of view, this would give him all the advantages of being in a band with me with none of the disadvantages.

Put a simpler way: now he'd be the boss.

I forced myself to be calm, though. I tamped everything down. And then I tried to say something, but what came out was, "You've got to be kidding me."

"I told you I know how it sounds, how it looks, but I swear, this wasn't about you and me." He made a gesture with his hands like passing dishes back and forth between us. "This wasn't about creative control or anything. I swear. I wasn't trying to take the band away from you and I wasn't trying to grab the reins."

"But that's how it turns out."

"The guy I've got now, he's okay. But he's not you."

I was not acquitting myself well, I know. "I'm sure he's nowhere near as good in bed."

Ziggy's eyes flared. "Maybe I should find out."

"If I don't take the job, and even if I do, I'm sure you will."

"I wouldn't, if you—"

"So now you'll blackmail me into working for you by threatening to fuck this asshole if I'm not there?"

"You're the one who brought it up!" Ziggy lost it right there. Lost it.

I hadn't really meant to push him that far. I hadn't really meant to do anything in particular, though. I was just arguing because I was hurt and angry. It was kind of startling to realize that Ziggy could be pushed to the point where that was all he was doing, too, where he could lose sight of his motives and just react.

I understood that blow-up we had at the Carlyle Hotel better, then. I took a deep breath. "You said you'd stop. For my sake. Was I an idiot to think when you said that we had more going for us then than... than... coworkers?"

He made a face like he tasted something really bitter—yeah, my vitriol. "Relationship trumps business, huh? Then maybe I wasn't an idiot for thinking we had enough going for us that when I fucked up I could expect a little forgiveness and a little support from you."

"We've been over that," I said. "You would've had all the support in the world if you'd called me a few days earlier."

He stared at the carpet, literally downcast. "Then you don't forgive me."

It was dawning on me for the first time, really, how big a problem it was that our work-love relationship was so inextricably tangled. "Is the only way for me to show I forgive you to come work for you?"

He let out a long sigh. "I don't know. I... I don't know."

We looked at each other for a long time, then. I don't know what was going through Ziggy's mind, but I know I was trying to come up with a way to get us back to some kind of an understanding. Right then, though, I felt like we'd said everything that could be said, and where we'd ended up was, to say the least, not on the same page. I was reminded of some times with Jonathan, where we'd both meant well, but we'd ended up miles apart.

"I don't want to fight," I said. "I don't know what else to say."

Ziggy came and sat next to me again. "I don't want to fight either."

"Maybe you should go home."

He slid a hand onto my shoulder. "Maybe you should rage-fuck me first."

I opened my mouth to protest but he hurriedly added, "You promised."

His hand on my neck, behind my ear, felt fever-hot. Other parts of me were heating up in response. How did he know me so well? And was that a good thing? "I was kidding," I said weakly.

"No, you weren't," he whispered, leaning back, pulling me forward...

I fucked him right there on the couch. He wasn't the first man I'd fucked on that couch, you know? Maybe I lack imagination, but I think this time was a lot like one time between me and Jonathan. Maybe it was just that there was one logical way to avoid having to go into the other room to get the lube. I described what we'd done in the bedroom as hammer-and-tongs sex. I didn't think it through: this was much more hammers-and-tongsy than that. No condom.

He screamed my name, not when he came, but when I did.

When we were done, I could barely move. I felt completely wrung out. Physically, emotionally, you name it.

"What happens now?" I asked him.

Ziggy snorted, a euphoric smile on his face. "Now, we clean the couch."

See, we agreed on something.

The Only One I Know

I found it somewhat mortifying to learn that the entire time we'd been fucking, and arguing, and fucking again, Antonio was waiting around a couple of miles away.

Ziggy paged him, but I answered when the kitchen phone rang.

"Yellow. Tony, that you?"

"It is. You rang? Or was that Zig?"

"Zig." Ziggy was gesturing impatiently for the phone. I held the cradle with both hands to my head so he couldn't pry it away.

"Are you kicking him out, then?" Tony asked. "Or are you keeping him for a while?"

"I don't know. Hang on." Ziggy hadn't actually told me his preference when he'd paged. "Tony wants to know if he should come pick you up or not," I told him, so I could find out myself.

Ziggy had gotten fully dressed—white jeans, black motorcycle jacket—but had washed his face, and his hair fell in silky wisps, ungelled. "Well, are you busy?"

"Um...." How could I answer that? I knew how it would go if he stayed for a couple of days. If he wasn't there I'd work non-stop, like I had been. If he was there... I'd spend all my time paying attention to him. I doubted I would have the willpower to ignore him. Whether we were fighting or not. "A little?"

"Do you want me to stick around?" he asked.

Argh. Why were we having this conversation while Antonio was listening? Of course, what I should have done was hang up and tell Tony we'd call him back. Instead I said, "I'm afraid to let you out of my sight again. But what I'd like even more is for you to leave and come back in a couple of days."

"A couple of days? Like Friday?"

"What day is today?" I had to ask.

"Tuesday." He did a bad job of hiding his smirk. "You know Thursday's Thanksgiving, right?"

"It is?"

"Next Thursday, I mean. Next week."

"Okay, jeez, don't scare me like that." Although, truthfully, I hadn't tracked on the fact that it was next week, either. That reminded me that I had plans to go to New York for Christmas to meet Remo and the guys. "Seriously, Zig—"

"You've got wheels? Meet me Friday at this thing." He wrote down an address for me. "Come get me and I'll come up here for the weekend."

"Okay." That seemed reasonable no matter how I sliced it. I handed him the phone then.

"All clear, Ton'. Come get me." They exchanged a few more words and then Ziggy hung up and said to me, "He'll be here in five or ten minutes."

"What? Where the hell has he been?"

"Drinking coffee on a patio somewhere nearby, he said."

"Whose patio?" I was thinking he had a friend in the neighborhood or something. "He's just been waiting for you to be done with me?"

"Or you with me. It's all right. He likes coffee."

"Jeez, Ziggy."

"Well, I wasn't sure how long we'd be. And he didn't want to drive all the way back to the city if things between us blew up."

"Things between us did blow up."

"Well, but not to the point where I had to storm out. Or you kicked me out." He shrugged and opened the fridge. "Are you starving? I'm starving."

"Now that you mention it..."

"Come with us. We'll go get something to eat and then drop you back here."

That was sensible. "If we just do one of the local places, maybe."

"You'd know better than me where we should go."

"I'll put on a cleaner shirt."

So I put on a cleaner shirt and Ziggy gelled his hair and gave himself a touch of eyeliner. This wasn't a pretentious area, really. The canyon had its share of hippies (both rich and poor) and throwbacks and generally was not a glamor spot. Which was why Remo liked it, I think. Not a glamor spot, but not a slum, either.

We got in the car and I think it was the least comfortable I'd ever been in front of Tony. Thinking about him waiting around... all I could imagine was that he must have been wondering what we were doing. Fighting, having sex, or both? The entire conversation itself was about coffee, not sex, but I couldn't get it out of my mind.

"There are two basic places to eat in Laurel Canyon," I said. "One has good coffee, the other has good pie."

"I was at the one with the good pie," he said drily, looking over the front seat at us.

"You were sitting at Four and Twenty this whole time?" My cheeks were flushed.

"Yeah. Come on. The pie's worth going back for more." Tony, for his part, didn't seem fazed by anything we did or might have done.

Not even the argument we had when we got to the pie place. "Wait for us in the car, willya, Ton'?" Ziggy asked him.

"What? Don't be silly. He can come in with us."

"Daron, it's not a big deal. We can handle being in there by ourselves. We don't need a bodyguard—"

"No no, I mean, you're going to make him wait out here while we eat? He should come eat with us."

Tony cleared his throat. "I'm fine to wait in the car."

"I gotta say, though, that feels so wrong to me." So here I was arguing for Tony to come in with us despite the fact I was so uncomfortable with him at the moment. I guess I was less comfortable with us treating him like a footman or carriage driver than I was with him overhearing more of our possible crap.

Tony said, "Boss, relax. I'm an employee—"

"You're a friend," I insisted.

"I'm a confidant, certainly. I mean, I get it. You feel weird telling me to wait in the car when we've been close. So close I've seen Z-man here crawl all up in your lap when he was high as a kite on Ecstasy."

Ziggy laughed. "God! I forgot about that night. You!" He pointed at me. "You pawned me off on Colin. Fucking hell, that guy can fuck. I could barely sit the next day."

I had kind of forgotten about it, too. "Yeah. Okay. Confidant. That doesn't mean you should get left in the car like a dog."

"I did already have pie," Tony pointed out.

"Yeah, but." I folded my arms, unable to make a rational argument. It simply felt wrong to me.

"This is why I knew Tony was the right guy to hire," Ziggy said.

"Why?"

"Because he already knows all about you and me. And I know you trust him."

"I thought the important thing was that *you* trust him?"

"You know me. Always multiple motivations."

Tony laughed.

In the end I won, though, or maybe you could say pie won, as Tony admitted there was a pie of the day he hadn't tried yet. So we went in and had pie, all three of us. We were the last three customers to come in, and we were the last three to leave, too.

While we were eating, Ziggy said, "If you had to choose between us being boyfriends and being bandmates, which would you pick?"

"That's like those stupid questions people ask, like, if you had to die which would you pick, being drowned or in a plane crash?"

"You're comparing us to a plane crash?"

"That's not what I meant and you know it. It's a fake hypothetical choice. I'll tell you one thing. We're never going to be '*boyfriends*.'"

"No?"

"I tried the boyfriend thing, remember?"

"So you did. Hey, one thing you can say you've done that I haven't," Ziggy said, looking a little scandalized to realize that I was "ahead" of him on something.

"And let me tell you. After three months I was bored. And I am betting you'd get bored even faster."

"Okay, so not boyfriends." Ziggy was being kind of relentless about this, I noticed. "What, then."

"That's what we're going to figure out," I told him. "But we sure as hell aren't figuring it out tonight."

He pouted but didn't argue the point. I guess the mere fact that we could discuss the existence of a relationship even if we didn't know what to call it made both of us feel better. We both walked away reassured that there was something worth chewing on there, even if eventually we ripped it to shreds. Insert visual of two dogs playing tug of war with a moon-like Frisbee here.

By the time they let me off at Remo's again I was feeling pretty mellow about the prospects in front of me, even if I didn't decide to join his band. Of course Ziggy had hired a guy I trusted, I thought, if he wanted me to come work for him.

When we parted I told Tony to look after him, and I meant it. "Don't let anything happen between now and when I tear him a new one next time I see him," I said through Tony's open window.

"Hey!" Ziggy said, but really couldn't protest. He rolled down his own window. "Does that mean you're thinking about my offer?"

"You haven't made me an offer yet," I pointed out.

"Tell me what you want," he countered.

"Maybe I will. Friday."

"Heh." He blew me a kiss and rolled up the window and I stood there watching while the town car backed down the driveway and then sped away.

It felt inevitable that I was going to take the job, and I did not like that feeling of inevitability one bit. This was going to take some thinking.

The Way You Do the Things You Do

So I did what I did best for the next couple of days, which was avoid thinking about it. And compose and play a lot on the soundtrack thing. I'd pretty much been on the cusp of a bunch of stuff falling into place anyway, and I'd bought a secondhand DX7 from a "Gear for Sale" poster I'd seen on a pole outside the pie shop, and it turned out to be the thing I needed. I think I might have been at it for 20 hours straight. I'm not sure. Five of that was hooking the synthesizer up to the Macintosh I'd bought for Remo that I don't think he'd touched but which I had been using every day I'd been there.

Somewhere in there, when I felt a little unsure about something, I talked with Chernwick more about the specs. His take was I didn't need any more specs since I wasn't trying to score it like a movie—meaning I wasn't trying to time cymbal crashes to climax moments or something—I was just supposed to hand over a bunch of stuff that the people in post-production could paste in at will. So I just made the songs sound how I wanted them to sound. Some contemplative, some majestic, some borderline comedic... mostly contemplative, though. I know part of what was in my ears was—well—the way the universe sounded when I had been on acid on the other side of the world. I hear music all the time; in the shower, on airplanes, even in the white noise of the background it often sounds to me like there's a song there if only I could "tune" the radio in better and fade the static out. One of the effects of LSD was the static stopped mattering. It wasn't gone, but I could hear the music in the background better. The DX7 helped with recreating some of those acoustic spaces that I know were really the echoes inside my skull.

I convinced myself I was also subconsciously ripping off the background music of every nature documentary I had ever watched as a kid because some of the songs sounded so... quintessential. Was it actually like something I'd heard before, or had I only heard it in my own ears?

I asked Chernwick if he would come over and listen to what I had or if I should bring a demo tape to the office. He said he'd come over in the afternoon—by which he meant the next day, Friday—and asked if it would be all right if he brought a friend who was in from out of town. Chernwick, you might remember, was fifty-something and typically hid his receding hairline with a hat. I said "sure" to the friend comment without giving it much thought.

At lunchtime on Friday, when they showed up, I found out the friend was a slightly aging skinny blond bombshell coke queen from Belgium with huge tits and no English-language skills. We spent about 45 minutes listening to the demo, with the two of them cuddled up like love birds on the couch. Then they snorted coke and did to each other on that couch what I had done more than once, so I didn't really feel like it was my place to complain. I mean, really, if you were going to design a couch that was good for sex, this would be it, you know? Probably not a coincidence. I took a can of Coke—the soft-drink kind—out by the pool and had my daily swim.

One of the things about coke—the drug kind—is that the effects don't last terribly long. Long enough for a good, heart-busting fuck, and then it fades. The two of them were in the shower when I went back inside. I made myself a sandwich and when they came out I asked if they wanted any fresh-squeezed juice. The bombshell said something I took to be her expressing that I was kind of cute and charming. She kissed me on the cheek. They had some juice, then Chernwick said I should finish up whatever last bits I needed to on the tape and then turn the fucker in.

"It's not too cliché?" I pressed.

"And even if it was? Don't you think that would make those fuckers approve even more?"

"Huh. I hadn't thought of it that way...."

"Stop stressing yourself," he said. "It's not a cliché. It's better than that." He blinked and looked at me seriously. "Oh, yeah. Don't drop it off at the customer. Bring it to my office. Okay?"

"Monday?"

"Anytime next week. Just quit fussing with it. It's good." He patted me on the shoulder and then the two of them got into his two-seater sports car and away they went.

Huh.

If I sound nonplussed about a business associate of mine doing drugs and having sex right in front of me, it's because I was. Later I thought to myself, huh, that kind of thing probably would have freaked me out a year or two ago. Now, well, okay I had a healthy respect for how fucked up drugs could make a person, but as long as I wasn't being asked to take them it was clear to me they were "business as usual" for a lot of folks. So was boning a former Miss Belgium or whatever she was.

It did occur to me to wonder why Chernwick had brought her here to do that, but maybe it was just that they didn't want to do drugs at the office. Or, for all I knew, maybe he had a wife...? This didn't occur to me at the time, though.

At the time my main thought was this: I did sort of wonder what the best way to clean the couch was, other than to leave a note on it for the actual cleaning lady. I wasn't sure when she was coming by next, anyway, and I was likely to forget and sit on the couch myself without paying attention. So cleaning it again myself was the next order of business.

This is how my phone call to Carynne went:

Me: Hey, quick question.
Her: Is this important?
Me: No, just quick.
Her: Um, okay sure.
Me: Can you clean leather with Windex?
Her: I'm pretty sure... no. You can't.
Me: Okay. Hm.
Her: Do I want to know why you're asking?
Me: I gotta go.

Ziggy hadn't been much help with the cleaning last time. I guess I was on my own.

L.A. Woman

I looked the place I was supposed to meet Zig up on the map. Then I paged Antonio.

He called back quickly, and I grilled him. "Okay, so where are you and what should I be wearing when I show up?"

"It's a kind of publicity stunt party for Gallani Gilliman," Tony said. "Supposedly her birthday, but it's more like an excuse to get a lot of supermodels together in one place with their sullen, punk-ass boyfriends."

I wondered what brought on that comment. "You don't sound too thrilled."

"I'm fine."

"One of those guys giving you trouble?"

"Nah. Nothing like that. But I'm thinking, shee-it, if I had a girl like that, would I follow her around like a raincloud, looking like an axe murderer? Ain't the whole point of wanting a gorgeous, ultra-perfect woman that it should make you happy? These punks wouldn't know happy if it bit them on the fucking cojones. Pardon my French."

"Spanish, you mean."

"It's just an expression, boss."

"I know, I know, just busting your cojones. Maybe that's what happens when you pick your girlfriend for how pretty and famous she is and not because she makes a good girlfriend."

"Ya think?"

"Anyway, what should I wear to this place?"

"Leather jacket and jeans'll do you fine. Boots instead of Chucks though, man."

"Okay." I'd put a little gel in my hair, too. Not too much. But it was still damp from the pool. "And do you think Ziggy's going to expect me to stay? Or am I just kidnapping him?"

"Why you asking me the hard questions? I'm just a bodyguard."

"You are not just a bodyguard and you know it."

"Yeah, more like babysitter."

We both snorted. I wondered where he was calling from that he could speak so frankly. Must have been in a back room. Or on a car phone. "Okay. How about this. I'll come and stay for one drink for the sake of being polite and then we're out of there, how's that?"

"Good plan."

"Be there in forty-five minutes. Unless there's traffic."

"There's always traffic," he reminded me.

So I got dressed, got in the truck, and drove to the place, which was some kind of restaurant nightclub type deal—they all blend together after a while.

There were two paparazzi sitting on the hood of a car in the parking lot, sharing a joint. The one who didn't have the roach picked up his camera, long lens and all, as he saw me approach, but the other one said something and he put it back down. Probably because I didn't look like anybody.

Then as I got closer, though, he changed his mind, picked it up, and fired off a couple of shots. I gave him the finger.

Tony was standing by the door, wearing a double-breasted suit that made him look more like a hit man than a bouncer. He had his hair slicked back instead of in cornrows. He held the door open for me and took me inside. We sailed past the hostess stand and then past the door guard for the back room.

The place was sort of U-shaped with a bar in the middle. Ziggy was on top of the bar apparently leading a chorus line of supermodels in a rendition of "The Time Warp."

I exchanged a glance with Tony. Ziggy was clearly having a terrible time and was desperately in need of rescue. (Not.) I held up one finger, signifying the one drink I was going to have, and I went to the back of the bar where the bartender was leaning against the rail watching the proceedings with a cocked eyebrow. He was Hispanic looking and so slim I wondered if he was anorexic.

I remembered I was driving, so I asked him for club soda with a twist of lime.

"And a splash of cran?" he asked.

"No, a twist of lime."

"I mean a twist of lime *and* a splash of cran," he clarified, twirling one finger as if that would make the idea sink in better for me.

"Uh, sure."

"Gives it pizzazz," he said.

What gave it pizzazz was the little sword he put in with a twist of lime, a lemon, and a cherry stuck on it, as well as the smoldering look he gave me when he put the napkin down and then set the drink on top of it. Was he that flirty to everyone or was it me? I wondered.

I reached into my jacket pocket.

"Open bar," he said.

"Doesn't include tip." I put a dollar down and he whisked it into his apron.

I found a little out of the way spot to sit while the song was winding down. I realized the DJ was crammed into the corner on the opposite side of the bar from me and that the tables there had been hastily pushed aside to create a small dance floor, which was empty since the only people dancing were Ziggy and the six or seven models on the bar with him.

Then a new song kicked in, and the tall woman with a black mane of hair next to Ziggy squealed with delight and threw her arms around his neck and planted kisses all over his face, then began to sing. It was the song Ziggy had cut for the B-side of the theme song to *Star Baby*, "Do It," the one he'd recorded with Jordan Travers, the one that had become an inadvertent dance hit.

I wondered how inadvertent it actually was.

Now all the women were singing that. Ziggy, for his part, tried to climb down at that point, but another one held him by the wrist and he danced with her for a little while longer.

I think I could see why the punk-ass boyfriends might be a little sullen, though. Maybe.

I finished the drink, ate the cherry, chewed through the ice cubes, and then went to the men's room, thinking, *okay, when I come out, we're out of here.*

I had to go back to the main section of the restaurant to get to the restroom. It was in a back hallway decorated with a little side table and a vase of flowers. Fake flowers. Okay, that wasn't important except that it felt typical to me of LA.

What was important was who was sitting there on a chair, staring into space, looking lost and forlorn.

Digger.

Don't Go Away Mad (Just Go Away)

It took Digger a second to recognize me, and then he said what I was thinking: "What the hell are you doing here?"

"I heard the ribs here are good," I deadpan improvised. I'm pretty sure he not only hadn't expected to see me at this party, he hadn't expected to see me on this coast. I don't know why I didn't expect to see him, since I knew he was Galani Gilliman's agent. I wasn't thinking, I guess.

Or maybe I expected that either Ziggy or Tony would have warned me. Whatever. I was staring at the motherfucker now.

Is it weird to use the term motherfucker for one's actual father? Whatever.

He seemed to be on autopilot. "So, how you doing?"

"Fine." I wasn't in the mood to make small talk. Not that I ever am. But given that we were supposed to be suing him, I wanted to talk to him even less than usual. "How about you?"

"The usual. Little of this, little of that."

"Uh huh." Okay, that was it. We were out of small talk. I should have said goodbye then and gotten Ziggy and left. Instead I decided to see what would happen if I said, "I did it, you know. Gave up my controlling interest in the band so your boy there could sign that development deal."

"He's not *my* fucking boy," Digger snarled, suddenly vehement, and I began to get an inkling why he looked so forlorn. "Though maybe he's yours."

I held my hands up in don't-blame-me mode.

"Is this your doing?" He stood up. "I've done nothing for that kid but work my ass off for him. I don't deserve to get the boot like this."

"I had nothing to do with it. If Ziggy has a problem with you—"

"He never had a problem with me. Never." He put his hand over his eyes then. Was he starting to cry? Jeezus. When he put his hand down his eyes were red but he wasn't crying. He cleared his throat. "Maybe it's karma. I know. You don't give a fuck. I didn't always do right by you, Daron. I know that. I didn't always make the right choices when you were growing up. And I've paid for those mistakes, don't you think? You were right. John Mills put me in his fucking back pocket and I caved when I should've been speaking up for you. You were right about that. But I've paid for that. You already fired me. I don't deserve to lose Ziggy, too."

I tried to remember, then. Why was Ziggy firing him? Was it my fault? Was he doing it so I'd come work for him?

No. It was part of the deal with the devil. I mean, the record company. They were going to pin some shit on Digger and make him the scapegoat.

I was pretty uncomfortable with that. Looking at Digger right now—it was obvious to me he had been drinking heavily since getting the news—I was even more uncomfortable with it. I seemed to recall that heavy drinking was what wrecked his liver to begin with.

He sat back down because his legs wouldn't hold him anymore. And he hid his hands in his face again.

"I really, really, really worked hard for that kid," he said. "I busted my ass. He doesn't even know the half of it. That kid never sees past the end of his own nose, though. Never sees what people around him do for him. Everything revolves around him."

Ziggy's the sun, I thought suddenly, *and I'm the moon*.

Digger looked up at me. "You know exactly what I'm talking about."

"Uh." Yeah, I did. So Ziggy could be a self-centered shit. That was not news.

"He wraps you around his finger. I know it."

"Actually—"

"That's why you're here, isn't it? What'cha doing for him now, Daron? It's not enough he's got all the pussy in Hollywood chasing him, he's gotta have dick, too?" He snorted. "Not just any dick, though, eh? *Your* dick."

"You don't know anything about it," I found myself saying.

"Yeah yeah, believe what you want. I know how it goes. When he's got no use for you anymore he'll kick you to the curb, too. He'll give you the boot without a thought." Digger chuckled. "Oh, wait, I forgot, he paid you off. He already gave you the boot. But now he's figured out you're still good for something after all, is that it? Cocksucker, cocksuckers both of you."

Remember that promise I made to myself not to be violent? Remember how I broke it when I fired him? Remember how I ran into him at that holiday party with Jonathan and I had that sudden urge to tackle him and beat his face in, at least until I saw how jaundiced and ill he looked?

I remembered. Even though he was talking shit, even though he was saying words that should have sent me through the roof, this time the little voice that was saying "don't listen to him, he's a drunken idiot" actually made sense to me. Huh. He *was* drunk. He *was* an idiot...

Then it suddenly became clear to me that he didn't say this shit out of some kind of clueless oblivion. He wasn't on a booze rant. He knew perfectly well he was trying to get a rise out of me. The realization that this was predictable, that it would always go like this and that I could have known it would, took all the anxiety out of it for me. Digger suddenly seemed about as scary and stress-inducing as a sitcom, which is to say not very.

"Jeez," I felt like my whole body was a fist that suddenly let go. "And to think I was almost starting to feel some sympathy for you there, Dad."

His eyes narrowed accusingly. I hadn't been allowed to call him "Dad" since I was about six. I didn't remember the exact conversation. Maybe we were in the car going somewhere? I think he said some bullshit about how because I was "a little man, now" I shouldn't call him Daddy anymore. My sisters never got that talk, so Courtney still called him Dad even now.

I went on before he could say anything. "Don't worry, though. I'll make sure Courtney gets through college."

Oh, that really burned him. I knew it would. I was implying that I was doing for her what he should have done. He knew it, too. His face was getting redder by the second.

I wondered if he hit me if Tony would come to my rescue. I felt sure he would. I wondered what he'd do to Digger. If Digger actually went for me, though, I didn't think I could let him. I didn't think I could simply turn the other cheek. I took a long slow breath, though, getting ready for it just in case.

In fact, I was pretty sure I could be the one to say something really baity and hurtful and be the one to get a rise out of *him*. If I wanted him to hit me.

Instead I said, "Look. Whatever's between you and Ziggy, that's got nothing to do with me. What's between you and me goes back into ancient history. It's water under the bridge, Dad. I cut you off for a reason, you know? You don't owe me anything. I don't owe you anything. We're done."

Digger's eyes always had a kind of sad-sack quality to them, but never more than then. "He's gonna try to screw me to the wall, you know."

"Get a good lawyer," I said. "See you around, Dad."

And then I turned on my heel and marched back into the party room. I hope I looked a lot cooler than I felt. I felt like a big dork. If Tony is to be believed, though, it looked like I strutted up to the bar like I owned the place, snapped my fingers, and Ziggy hopped right down into my arms. Okay, not my actual arms, because we were playing it cool. He blew a goodbye kiss to the black-maned beauty I assumed was Galani Gilliman, grabbed his jacket, and out we went.

"Does valet parking have your keys?" he asked, as I led him across the restaurant.

"No. I self-parked."

"Why?"

"Because I was a dork and didn't pay attention when I pulled in. But it's handy because now it means we can go out the side and avoid the photographers staking out the entrance." As I said this, I was leading him to the side exit.

"Does that really matter?" he asked as we went out into the Los Angeles night, crisp with arid exhaust.

"It does, only because..." I didn't finish until we were in the front seat with the doors shut. "I want to do this."

I grabbed him by the back of the head and kissed him as hard as I've ever kissed him. I can't say I knew what was going through my head. I don't even know now. I know we had all kinds of issues to resolve. And I know trying to set up boundaries and discuss what was appropriate were among them. But my emotions were buzzing—all of them—and it felt like the thing I wanted to do most in the world. It was one of those kisses where I really didn't let him breathe.

"She's just a friend—" he blurted when he could.

"Jealousy is not what has me riled up right now," I said, much more snarly than I thought I should sound. I sat back from him. "But thanks for acknowledging my feelings."

Then I put the SUV into reverse, he put his seat belt on silently, and we got out of there before I could tempt fate any more.

I Found That Essence Rare

Ziggy was silent for almost the entire drive. I could feel he was holding back saying something, but I couldn't guess what. Maybe what he was going to say was going to depend on what I said first.

But I didn't want to be first. So instead, inside my head, I made guesses about what Ziggy might be feeling. That was an effective way to forget about what I was feeling. Was he afraid to say something because I seemed angry? I had flashes of my own child/teenage self pretending to be invisible in the passenger seat while Digger drove. Or was he sharpening his knives, waiting for the right moment to cut me up? The possibility that maybe he was simply tired also flickered by. Or maybe he was horny and waiting to find out whether he could maneuver me into bed.

You just kissed him breathless, I reminded myself. He's probably not thinking it's going to be difficult to get you to do more if he wants it.

As I drove up the canyon road toward Remo's house, Ziggy finally spoke. Extra-casual. "So. What happens when we get inside?"

"I haven't thought that far ahead."

"If you want to just hang out, you know, that's fine with me."

I tried to look at him, but I couldn't get more than a glance without driving off the road. I gripped the wheel with both hands. "As opposed to doing what?"

"As opposed to me pressuring you into either sex or a job."

"Jeez, you've gotten direct."

"You seem to respond well to it."

"True. Okay, then... what do you want to do, though?"

"*Besides* have sex and talk you into working for me?" He sounded like he was smirking.

"Yeah, okay, I rescind the question."

"Why don't I ask you instead, then. What do you want to do?"

I nearly missed the driveway while answering. "Regardless of whether I want to or not, I know we need to work out our shit."

"You think we can?"

I jerked the SUV to a stop in the driveway. Trying to get it into the garage while talking about relationships was a recipe for damage. I pulled the handbrake. "I don't know if we can or can't, but I know that the only thing to do is hammer at it until we've figured out if it's 'can' or 'can't.'"

"Yeah?"

"Yeah. Are we going to be a thing? Or are we going to be exes? Or will you be the one that got away? The best thing or the worst thing that ever happened to me? Right now I don't even know how I want it to turn out. I don't know what's best for me. I don't know what's best for my career." I realized I was staring at the ignition key, which I had pulled out and was still holding in my hand.

Ziggy reached across my lap and took the keys. "Let's go in."

I reached up and hit the garage door opener that was clipped to the visor, and we got out and went through the garage into the house. Doing it that way, you come directly into the hallway between the kitchen and the bedrooms.

Maybe that's what made the decision for me. (Or maybe if we'd come in the front door we would've ended up on the couch. Or the pool table.)

We didn't even make it all the way to the bedroom at first. I pressed him against the wall of the hallway, overcome with the desire to have as much of me touching as much of him as possible. Still trying to make up for all those miles and all those days/weeks/months apart. Clothing thwarted that desire somewhat, but I could feel the heat of his skin through my jeans, through my shirt, and it was what I wanted. I think maybe he felt the same because he surrendered to it so easily. Which wasn't to say he was passive. He was trying to push my jacket off my shoulders. I was busy kissing him and barely noticed. He managed to get my shirt off over my head, too. Which, because I had put some gel into it, made my hair into something wild.

So did his fingers. I hitched his legs around my hips. He was wearing some kind of tights or leggings, which felt like he wasn't wearing much at all.

He stayed glued to me as I carried him into the

bedroom. I guess I had kept a lot of the muscle I'd built up while moving flagstones around in Spain.

I don't remember most of the rest of it. Once we made it to the bed, I stopped thinking, I stopped over-thinking, I stopped worrying, I stopped guessing. The only thing in my mind was Ziggy and all the ways I could fit out bodies together. Or at least some of the ways.

Eventually all my physical itches were scratched. At that point I was spooning him, my hand goopy with his spunk, his ass goopy with mine. I licked the back of his neck where he'd shaved his hair short, under the longer locks from further up. Ziggy made a contented sigh.

"You're the only one who ever does that."

"Does what?"

"Licks me like that."

"None of them appreciate the way your sweat tastes the way I do," I said seriously. After all, I'd had his sweaty hair in my mouth onstage long before we ever got in bed together. "I could do without whatever mousse you're using, though."

"It's hairspray."

"Fortunately there's not much of it down here." I nibbled on the back of his neck weakly, not at all hungry anymore, simply enjoying him.

We lapsed into silence that, after a while, grew from being regular comfortable post-coital silence to being us not talking about what we needed to talk about.

"What do you want to do now?" I asked him, feeling like I should ask, like I should get something going, but not ready to dive in myself.

I wasn't ready for his answer, which maybe only made it all the more delightful. "I want to write a song."

"Mmhm. A specific song?"

"A specific song."

"How does it go?"

"That's what I want you to help me figure out."

"Hm. Makes sense. We better get cleaned up for that."

"True. Come on," he said, but he didn't move.

"Mmhm. Any second now."

"Yeah."

So we lay there for a while longer, because we wanted to. And then we got cleaned up and went into the studio.

What I Am

We went into the studio. The feeling of calm that having him in my arms gave me—quieting the annoying part of my brain that cried like a lonely puppy whenever he wasn't there—gave way to the unsettled feeling of walking across unknown terrain.

Except writing together was familiar enough ground, wasn't it?

Not when I didn't know what was going to become of the song, maybe. I wondered if I could put that out of my mind and just "get in the zone" despite that.

"Is this where you did it?" Ziggy said, poking around the studio curiously.

"Did what?"

"Wrote that song for Sarah that went to number three." He wasn't looking at me when he said it. It wasn't like there was a thunderclap and a devilish red glow in his eyes or something. He was telling it like it was. "I'm still kind of upset about that."

"I know. You said that the last time you were here."

"I know I shouldn't be, but I am." He sat down on the engineer stool at the mixing board. "But that's not why I want to write a song right now. I mean, it's not like I feel you owe me one because you wrote one for her."

"With her," I said automatically.

"Okay, with her, but it sounds like you, Daron."

I shrugged. "If you say so. I think it sounds like her. But whatever."

He spun himself in a full circle on the stool.

"So you don't like your new guitar player."

He stopped the rotation when he was facing me. "I like him fine except for the fact that he's not you."

Maybe you should have thought of that before... I thought.

"Before what," he asked, and I realized I had said it out loud.

"Before you..." Since I hadn't been aware of speaking at first I had no idea how that sentence was supposed to end. Before you signed that contract? "...wrote yourself a new ending."

"What?"

"You rewrote your future, Zig. And you wrote me right out of it."

His eyes were wide, panicked. "But—"

"Was I crazy, thinking we'd finally figured some shit out in Boston? I thought we were on the same wavelength."

"We can be again."

I gave him probably the same accusatory look Digger had given me when I'd called him "Dad." The *did-you-really-say-that* look.

Ziggy drew his knees up on the stool. He folded himself into an egg-shape almost, perched there. "You're... you're being very hard about this."

"Yeah, I am. Because if you can't understand why? Then I need to figure out how the hell to cut you off."

"Maybe I could understand it better if every time we talked about it you didn't jump down my throat."

I forced myself to take a couple of deep breaths. "Okay, but..."

"But what?"

I tried to get my thoughts in order. I was having that feeling I sometimes did in therapy, like I had dug myself a hole by talking without thinking and I had to do a lot of thinking to get myself out of it. Which maybe was the point.

"But I feel like if you didn't understand it before, I'm not optimistic you'll understand it now."

"So you don't even want to give me a chance."

"No! I mean yes, of course I'll give you a chance."

He unfolded himself slowly. "You know sometimes I have to hear things more than once for them to sink in, too. Even if they're hard to say."

I went and picked the Ovation 12-string out of its stand and sat down on a chair across from him. "Okay. I guess if we reach the point where I'm not willing to keep repeating myself I'll know it's time to walk away."

His eyes got suddenly shiny when I said that. And when I saw that, mine began to sting a little, too. The thought of me walking away, after all we'd been through...

That we both reacted like that might have been what proved there was something there. A relationship, if you want to call it that. I don't know what else to call it.

I needed to put my thoughts in order, but what I did was played a couple of my usual warm-ups that were ingrained in my fingers and then picked my way through a placid and sweet section of the soundtrack I was working on. I'd chosen the 12-string because it sounds sweet and placid most of the time, really, and I thought it would be calming.

It was. I finally looked up and said, "I know the band was always one of a dozen avenues to fame you could have tried. I know that. So maybe that's why it's hard for you to understand what it's like for me."

He rolled the stool closer to me so he could hear my voice. He had no makeup on right now, and his hair was hanging down partway over one eye, all the styled curl gone. He had pulled his leggings back on but was wearing one of my flannel shirts, I realized.

"I don't have some other avenue. All I've got is this." I lifted the neck of the guitar a little. "This thing I did every hour of my life that wasn't miserable. This is it. This is my salvation. This is my livelihood. This isn't just what I do, it's what I am."

For a second it looked like he was going to argue, but maybe he was just opening his mouth to take a breath.

"Finding a band that works, building one that works... it's incredibly hard. It takes something besides talent, besides drive. There has to be chemistry. Something has to click."

He gave a little nod like he got that.

"Maybe it's crazy and maybe it's selfish, but if I'm not expressing myself creatively I don't know why I'm on the planet. I'm a waste of space if I'm not making music. I don't mean that in a self-hate kind of way, either. It's just... a fact. And yeah, I've learned I could stand on a street corner and do it and that would be... okay. I guess. But I'm sure you understand why I want more than that. And..."

And...

"I knew I could never do it alone. I knew I wanted to do rock and I've always known that would mean finding a singer." I found myself sucking in a breath, pulling myself back from the edge of tears, feeling like this was turning into a breakup conversation before I gave it a chance. "When you find the one, you know."

He got to his feet suddenly, and I watched him beat back his anger, stuff it back down inside himself so that he could tell me something instead of screaming it at me. "You know how you said I should have asked you about it before I signed the contract?"

"Yeah?"

"Maybe *you* should have said *that* sooner, too."

Shit.

I stopped playing and put a hand over my eyes, and it felt like the world was spinning. Had I really not said that? Had I really never told him? Not at the Carlyle, or in Central Park that night, or in his apartment later?

No, I probably hadn't, because it had taken me so damn long to know it myself. "Yeah." The word came out a croak. "I should have. I've... I've felt that way for a long time, you know? In fact, I've always felt that way. From that first day we officially met and I thought, god, I'll do anything to make this guy our singer. I think I didn't even let Bart get a word in edgewise."

He was biting his lip so hard I wondered if he was damaging himself.

"But it's taken me a long time to see it for what it is. And to admit it. If that's my fault, okay, that's my fault. If it's something so wrong with me that I can't have a functional relationship—or at least a functional relationship with you—then... then... that sucks and I'm sorry."

Ziggy's eyes were wide and serious. "I haven't... I haven't ruled out the possibility that we can... work it out. Somehow. You know."

"I know. But to get back to what you were originally asking. Think of a band like a... a mansion. Every time we make an album it's like we decorate another room. We get together and figure out what it's going to be like, aesthetically. Then we build it. The band is the architects and the builders. The singer can be part of that, too, but his most important role is to be the... face of it. The museum guide who takes you through."

He raised an eyebrow as my analogy was starting to get far-fetched. I knew it, too, but I had to try to make it work.

"So this new deal is kind of like if the butler suddenly turned to the builder-architect of the house and said, by the way, I own this now, and you can run along."

"Butler?"

"The analogy kind of sucks, but do you see what I'm getting at? And now you're saying you'll hire me back as a sub-contractor to work on the house that I used to own? That I built with my own hands?"

He sat back down on the stool. "Maybe the analogy isn't too far-fetched. Maybe that's exactly why it seems so extreme. Because that's how you feel."

"Like you kicked me out of my own house? Yes."

He pushed his hand into his hair. "I... definitely never intended you to feel that way. And I see why you think I should've known you would. And I'm sorry I didn't. Even if it was partly your fault for never really telling me anything before."

My cheeks were properly red at that. We stared at each other for a while.

"Will you help me with this song?" he finally asked.

"Yeah."

It didn't feel like either of us was promising the other much with that. But it was something.

Hearts and Bones

My fingers filled up the silence between us with a wistful drizzle of notes.

"What's that you're playing?" he asked,

"Nothing yet," I said. I put down the 12-string and picked up one of the Remo-signature guitars I'd been playing on the soundtrack a lot. It had a deep bowl and a resonant voice to match. In fact, I'd tuned it down to D. I slung it over my shoulder and picked up where I left off (no pun intended). Then I paused to tune a little—

"No, leave it," Ziggy said, waving his hand.

"You sure?"

"Yeah." He was still on the stool, but sitting up so straight it was like if he'd had cat ears they would have been pointing at the ceiling.

"Now go on, play that riff."

I picked out the pattern again, went through a chord change, brought it back.

Ziggy started to hum. I took a step closer to where he was sitting because I could barely hear it, but I could see his chin moving side to side a little.

Now I could hear it. We were face to face, a foot apart, me standing, and I could hear that high thread of a hummed melody coming from his closed mouth—ever so slightly echoed in the body of the guitar.

I played quietly, listening, making the chord change again. His eyes were closed.

We jammed like that for a while. I don't know how long. Until it had been around and around a couple of times and I'd found out where the progression went and he'd followed me and found out where the melody went.

I opened my eyes, having not realized I'd shut them, to see him opening his at the same time.

We both talked at the same time. "Let's record that." "Can we get that on tape?"

It took a little fussing to get a setup that really captured that sound. Remo's studio was all one room; it wasn't like there was a separate vocal booth. We tried it first with both of us sharing one condenser mic. But we couldn't quite get the right balance, even when he was really close to it and I was far away. Eventually I set up a vocal mic for him that he could get right up against, put a screen between us, and then set up another mic for myself a couple of feet away, and then I sat back from it a ways, in the corner. This time he was standing and I was sitting and we both had headphone monitors on.

That was almost it. On the next take I opened the door and put myself on the concrete patio between the studio and the pool, and that was it. The hard reflections gave the guitar a faraway echo sort of sound, while Ziggy sounded like he was humming right in your ear. We did a take that was a couple of go rounds and couple of changes, and as we were ending it, a jet passed overhead, putting a kind of sound tail on it that was kind of neat.

"I need some water," Ziggy said, clearing his throat. "All that humming is rough."

We took a quick break, rummaging around the kitchen a little, but we didn't pause for long. When we went back he jotted down some words.

We dubbed a vocal track then, and I discovered that the melody he'd been humming was a counter-melody to something he'd either been hearing all along, or he improvised, I don't know which.

It was a song about being alone in the world.

We had a lot of stops and starts while he worked out the words. They came out sort of improvised, sort of rapped, and then he pared them down to the right number of syllables, the better word choices. I could see him get an idea and be writing one thing down while trying to remember the thing he'd thought of in the middle of it.

Alone in a crowd. A feeling I knew so well I accepted it as normal.

And it turned into a song about a song, too. The chorus was something like:

Alone in a crowd
Alone in the world
A lone wolf howls
He knows the words

I helped fill in and shape the words, but I can't remember who came up with which exactly. I think it was me that turned it into a song about a song, but I'm not sure, really. We were in a state of flow.

We took another break when my fingers hurt enough for me to realize it had been a number of hours. My thumb was starting to ache. I shook it out, and he took my left hand between both of his and massaged it.

I practically melted off the chair. "Is this song about losing your mom?" I asked.

"What makes you think that?"

"The bit that goes, 'Eyes behind a black veil of pain / Familiar song, familiar refrain.' Made me think of a funeral. And what you wore to the film premiere."

"Huh." He let my hand go and sat down on the stool across from me.

"That's what I thought, when I saw what you wore. You were dressed for a funeral. For mourning."

He frowned. "You're the only one who got that."

Not even Jen? I thought, but didn't ask. "That's what made me think it might be the message here, too."

"I... I guess. Maybe."

"Why, what did you think you were writing about?"

"*You.*" He turned away quickly, as if I wouldn't see the tears spring into his eyes. "Asshole."

"I think it's a little early to write the eulogies for this relationship if we're still sitting in this room together,"

I pointed out.

He blinked away the moment. "I still can't help but feel like you're going to abandon me."

"You going solo is not *me* abandoning *you*."

"I know! But it feels like it anyway." He covered his eyes with his hand.

"Maybe it feels like it because with your mother dying, you're extra sensitive to feelings of abandonment right now." I sounded uncomfortably like Lacey there, but I thought the theory might hold water.

He made a grumbling sound. "Possibly."

I petted his hair and ended up standing beside him, hugging his head to my sternum and letting him cry on my shirt.

At one point he tried to talk. "It's so hard to explain what it's like to lose her."

"You don't have to explain."

"I think to myself, why didn't I do more? Why didn't I see her more often? Why wasn't I there? Would any of it have helped her, or helped the way I feel? I don't know. And not knowing hurts, too."

"I know."

"And you think, god, if this hurts this much, it must be punishment for something. Like I must be a terrible person to deserve this."

"You know that's bullshit, though, right? Her dying had nothing to do with you."

"I know. I know. And yet somehow, I don't know. Maybe it's just that the hurt is so bad and the negative feelings are so overwhelming that self blame comes as part of the package."

"Or maybe everything about parents comes with guilt."

"Yeah." He looked up at me then, his eyes puffy. "Please don't think I'm trying to make you stay because I'm so pathetic."

"I won't if you don't think the only reason I'm staying is because you're pathetic."

"Oh." He gurgled a little, and I pulled away and got him a tissue. He blew his nose. "Yeah, okay, logic is starting to come back now." He looked around as if it were suddenly dawning on him that we'd been at it for enough hours that it was now long past time we should have had a meal. It was twilight outside. I don't think either of us could have told you if that was sunrise or sunset at that point.

My stomach growled. "Come on." I took him into Remo's kitchen, where no matter what time of day or night it was or how broken your heart was, there was always canned soup.

New Order

My home away from home, eh? I was feeling fancy, so I heated up the soup in a pot on the stove instead of in the microwave. We sat at the counter on the island, eating it silently, each absorbed in our own thoughts for a while. You know, it wasn't just that Remo's house was a home away from home for me: Remo was a safety net of all kinds. I felt pretty confident that if I ever needed a gig, I could get on Remo's bandwagon. If I ever needed a place to live, I could move in here. I mean, I'd probably always be too proud to, but knowing that safety net was there... that gave me a kind of footing that a lot of creative people don't have. For all I'd said to Ziggy that guitar was the one thing I had, I actually did have more options than some people we knew.

I was thinking of Christian. Then I took it back: Christian did have other options, if only he'd explore them. But instead of exploring them, he'd gone back to construction. Why? Lack of self-esteem, he'd said. And trying to avoid drugs. But I remembered how nervous he'd been during the tour. The cool cucumber we thought was Mr. Experienced was the one with fear of failure.

I didn't seem to have fear of failure. Partly because I was so confident as a musician, and that confidence was only growing the more I learned and did. Partly because I had the Remo safety net. And now—at least partly—because, technically, I had failed. And I'd found that fearing failure was worse than the actual state of so-called failure itself. Yeah, things were fucked up, but not as fucked up as things could have been if I'd rolled over and done what Mills wanted just because I was afraid. I was pretty sure if I'd done that then I'd have neither success nor artistic integrity, which was lose-lose, and at least this way I still had a whole soul. Which I needed to play and to make music. And if the point was playing and making music, well, then I was doing okay.

Ziggy had given us all a safety net, too. With the money. That was finally starting to sink in.

And I was starting to get an inkling that maybe Ziggy had more fear of failure than I thought. It was just outweighed, maybe, by his drive. And maybe he just had brass balls.

Ziggy, meanwhile, was thinking about something completely different.

"Do you ever miss your mother?" he asked, pushing the alphabet noodles around in the bottom of his bowl.

"No."

"Really? Not even from when you were little?"

"Nope. She never bonded with me, I guess. I was a difficult pregnancy and she didn't want a boy and there was drama."

"Drama?"

"Didn't I tell you this? About how she wanted to cheat on my father with Remo and all that?"

"Ah, right. You did. But you're not Remo's kid."

"Maybe only in a spiritual sense," I admitted. I got up and stuck my bowl and spoon in the dishwasher. He tipped his back with his hands, drinking the last of the soup from the rim, and then came and put his next to mine. The silverware went clink in the basket.

"It's hard to explain," he said, going back to the subject of mothers. "Those last couple of years, I hardly saw her, hardly spoke to her, you know? But knowing she was there, and now she's gone... it's like my whole world changed."

"Your whole world did change." I put my arms around him tentatively.

Ziggy wasn't tentative. He clung. I didn't mind, even if it made it hard to breathe. "It isn't even like a day-to-day change, you know?" he said. "But somehow... something's missing. Something's missing."

I didn't have anything to say to that, so I didn't.

"I mean, maybe everyone's got a hole they're trying to fill. And people pour a lot of drugs and alcohol down those holes."

"I'm pretty sure there are a bunch of songs about that exact thing."

"Yeah." He exhaled, and I felt the warmth of his breath trapped in my shirt. "Everyone's got traumas, I guess."

"Do you feel like you were traumatized by not having a father growing up?"

"Hm. Not really. I think it's different when there's someone and then they're gone, as opposed to not there in the first place."

"Makes sense."

He looked into my eyes. "You get used to having certain people in your life."

"You know I could be saying the same thing to you, Mister Indian Subcontinent."

"I know. Does that mean I don't have the right to ask?"

"Ask me what?"

"For... Hm." His eyes narrowed while he thought about how to word it. "I guess I should be clear about what I'm asking for."

"Yeah."

"I don't want to lose you."

"That's not very clear, Zig. I'm not leaving the planet and neither are you, right?" Eh, Mister Contemplated Suicide? That was the closest I came to bringing it up.

"Right." His mouth still sagged unhappily.

"So what don't you like about the guitar player you've got now? Serious question."

"The guy Mills picked? It's like I said. He's not you."

"What's his name?"

"Joe Alvarez."

I didn't know the name. "Have you recorded with him yet?"

"No. Just some rehearsals."

"You sounded pretty good together on the radio," I said casually, but I had him in my arms and it was hard to play off the fact that I gripped him tighter when I said it.

"This is stupid," Ziggy said, pressing his forehead against mine and looking into my eyes. "I want you to play with me and you want to play with me. And the reason you won't is because...?"

"Pride?"

"Are you asking me or telling me?"

"I'm brainstorming," I said. "I'm still hurt about how it all went down? Because I don't want to be anywhere near John Mills and BNC ever again? Because you'll make my life a living hell and then we'll both be miserable?"

"Maybe what I need, though, is someone who will listen to me instead of Mills," Ziggy said.

"So fire him and let Jordan Travers recommend you someone. Meanwhile, see previous point about you driving me, and therefore both of us, insane."

"Why would I do that?"

"It's not why, it's how. We've been over this."

He closed his eyes and sighed, and I hadn't won the argument but he at least retreated from it for a while.

"Let's lie down for a while," I suggested.

We got half-undressed and got in bed, and he snuggled bonelessly against me. "That was a very... humane idea," he said. "Lying down, I mean."

"Beds were an excellent invention. It seemed wise to take advantage of having one."

"You are so weird."

"I know."

In the morning he told me he had to leave for a photo shoot in St. Maarten. He also told me that the song we'd written wasn't the song he needed help with. And he told me he'd be back in a week.

I kissed him goodbye when Tony came to pick him up. After he left I called Cadmon Molina.

"You know Joc Alvarez?"

"Guitarist from Van Nuys? Yeah, decent chops, keeps clean. Why, you looking to hire him?"

"No, I was wondering if you could use him for anything."

"Are you his agent now or something?"

"Nothing like that. I just... think he'll be looking for work soon."

There you have it. If you're reading this, Joey Alv, now you know the truth. Zig was going to fire you anyway. I'm glad Molina hooked you up with those guys from Detroit.

Success

I cried through most of my next therapy appointment. That isn't as bad as it sounds. They were basically tears of relief. Even though Ziggy and I hadn't *really* resolved anything, somehow, my heart still felt better about everything. Some kind of weight had been lifted. Or something.

It's my inability to make a good explanation of what I felt—or why—that leads to those obscure songs with lots of oblique references to poetic visuals. The ones that, when you hear them on the radio in your car and you finally figure out the words, they make you say, what the hell is this song about?

Yeah.

Anyway.

I feel a little bad about doing this, because I felt pretty good for a while, and you guys only get to enjoy it for the space of one paragraph before I hit you with the existential crisis that came next.

Thanksgiving had happened but I had missed it, head down in the work, you know? I was about a week from turning in the soundtrack when Artie called. I was surprised to hear from him. Actually, I was surprised to hear the phone ring in the middle of the afternoon. At least I was awake to answer it.

After we'd shot the breeze briefly, Artie said, "You know Wenco has a New Age division," like I should know what he was getting at.

I said something highly intelligent like, "Um?"

"I want to know how much material you've got. Or, if necessary, how much it would cost to pay you to dump and run."

"Dump and run?" I was being particularly thick, I guess.

Artie was pretty sharp, though, and filled in the gap for me. "Did Carynne not tell you she was sending me the demo of your soundtrack work?"

"What? No. In fact, I didn't even send it to her."

"Huh. Well, she sent it to me, and all I'll say is you're probably being criminally underpaid for the quality of work you're doing."

"It's not actually that difficult. I mean, I get to sit around Remo's home studio and jack off all I want, basically—"

"How difficult the work is and how good it is are two different things, Daron."

"True. Okay, so, what are you saying? You got wind of this soundtrack I'm doing and you want to buy me out or something?"

"Pretty much. Or at least, I think we can put together a very good solo instrumental album, and I'm wondering how much more material you've written than what I've heard."

I felt distinctly squidgy about this. "I don't think I'm comfortable leaving a client in the lurch," I said. "I mean, maybe a lot of people don't have professional ethics to speak of, but I do."

"Of course, goodness, I don't want you to think I want you to screw anyone. There's more than enough of that in this business already. And look, it's not huge money: the advance would only be low five figures, but you know I've been wanting to get your name in ink for years."

"You have?"

He laughed. "You know it. This would be low impact, low risk. That is, if we can put together an album and you can still get your deliverable in. Or if we can swing a deal for licensing, but I think it's too late for that. I mean, to make it work, you'd have to pay *us* what they paid *you*, we'd take it as a licensing fee on the music we'd own because we'd pay *you* to put the music under contract. And they might not really want that if they want to own the music and milk it for years to come."

"I have no idea. A guy I know out here kind of brokered the job."

"Okay. If you're sanguine about just letting that stuff go below value, it's probably a lot simpler and a lot more straightforward if we don't double-dip."

"I've been writing a ton, Artie. If you're saying you'll consider an actual demo from me for a solo instrumental album, I have no shortage of stuff to send you. Hell, I can probably give you a complete album if you give me another couple of weeks and I fly Bart here one more time. I mean, now that I think about it, he's been learning the cello—"

"Okay, okay. Great. Exactly what I wanted to hear."

"No problem. For a demo, is just a cassette okay? I can dub you some stuff today and FedEx it." I looked at the clock. "Okay, actually, it's too late to get FedEx today and I need to pick through everything to make sure I'm not accidentally duplicating anything. But that won't take me that long."

"Great. That's wonderful. I'm so pleased. I have a strong feeling I'm going to love what you send."

So I sent Artie a tape, and Artie sent me back a contract, and the day after I delivered everything on the soundtrack, I locked up Remo's house and flew to New York to meet with Artie. I signed the deal, we hashed out album concept and direction, he sent a memo to the art department, and I agreed to book some studio time at a bigger, better studio in Boston when I got there.

Then I went out on the town with Sarah.

I'm getting to the existential crisis part, I promise. Okay, maybe next time. Bask in the glow of musical accomplishment for a little longer.

Golden Blunders

Since I'd last visited Sarah, her career had taken a couple of leaps and turns. (I forgot to say: we did go out to dinner once or twice when she came to LA, but nothing of consequence to report there.) She'd moved into a new apartment: this one on Central Park East, and not a sublet, so it had a lot less stuff in it and felt a lot less homey, but she hadn't been there very long. She assured me she'd fill it up with things soon enough. She was going out on tour that coming summer, North America and Western Europe, and she had this plan that she was going to come back with souvenirs from everywhere she'd been.

"You seem skeptical of the idea," she had said.

"No, just trying to think if I have any souvenirs from the tour at all." Besides T-shirts, which I seemed to pick up everywhere. I held up my left wrist with my habitual adornments on it. "Some of these things I accumulated on the way."

We were in the VIP room at Limelight, where she had become sort of a regular, and it was quiet enough to hear what each other were saying. She ran her fingers over the things I had on: a friendship bracelet made of purple and black string that a fan had made for me, the beads that Native American woman had given me, a black leather one with a silver snap I'd picked up in Spain, a couple other things like that. I'd thought the beads were lost after the explosion, but no, someone had set them aside for me and I'd eventually found them and put them back on. I'd been accumulating stuff on that wrist ever since.

"Because they hide the scars?" she asked.

"There's not much in the way of scars now." I looked to be sure what I was saying was true. It was: there wasn't much to see unless you knew to look for it. The same was true on my face: there were a couple of streaks where the skin was discolored on my cheek and near my eye, only visible in certain light. "The only one I take off sometimes is the leather one because it's not a good idea to get it wet. The rest you can't really take on and off." The friendship bracelet was knotted on, for example.

Right, but I was going to tell you about the existential crisis part. Let me see if I can remember how it started.

I can't. I don't remember exactly what I said. But I was crowing about the deal with Artie and how pumped up I was about that. Now, remember that underneath it all I was still upset about Ziggy going solo. The combination led me to say something idiotic like, "Thank god I stuck to my guns. You know what pulled me through this? My integrity as a musician. Part of me almost says Wenco could keep the money—the validation is the thing."

"Validation?"

"Of instrumental solo work? Yeah, there's something really validating about that. Possibly worth more than the twenty grand they're paying me."

"Easy to say when you're not in debt or scrounging for lunch money," Sarah pointed out.

"True. But it's weird, you know? It all happened so fast."

"But it didn't. Look at how many years it took you to develop those chops, learn to compose, build your studio skills, and make the connections! Think about it, Daron. It's years of work, it just happened to come together now."

"Huh. True. And it's weird, because part of me almost doesn't care what art they put on it, what they think it should be called, and part of me cares even more than usual, because this one is mine, really mine. It's my ultimate proof of... of... something." I had been drinking, which was not doing wonders for my vocabulary or my common sense. "And I don't need any dancing or singing or costume changes to prove it."

That was the line that did it. I said something like that. And I didn't even realize it at first that I'd really offended her.

"What, are you going to break out the tux and do a concert hall recital tour?" she asked, her voice sharp with sarcasm. "Or do you never have to leave the home studio again?"

"Well, I don't know about *that*, but—"

"Who's going to listen to this album?"

"I don't know. I used to work in the jazz section of Tower. Random people did come in and buy out of the New Age section, but not that many."

"So it's Muzak."

She said it like an insult, which is what I took it as, since who the hell wants to be thought of as Muzak? The words "Muzak" and "integrity as a musical artist" didn't go together in my brain. "It's a lot better than Muzak."

"Is it? Sounds like it'll be used as background music in those stores where they sell crystal jewelry. How do you know it's better?"

"What do you mean, how do I know?" I didn't understand why she was attacking me. "Because I'm good. Because I wrote something and played something that was really, really good, Sarah."

"And your definition of good is 'doesn't need costumes or dancing'?"

"What?"

"Obviously, the only reason music that utterly lacks integrity exists is because we bother to dress it up with vacuous idiocy to fool the masses into parting with their money. Isn't that what you're saying?"

I guess that *was* what I was saying, because my reaction to that was, "They're going to throw Ziggy into the studio with a bunch of anonymous backing musicians. Jordan Travers or Jellybean Benitez or whoever is going to rewrite all his songs—or outright write them for him—and then they're going to put him on parade with backing dancers like a trained elephant!" I may have shouted this. "For a quarter million a night. To make back the millions they spent." I flashed on this thought: if he wanted to kill himself at the end of two months on the road with Moondog Three, what was he going to be like at the end of six months in a one-ring circus? Ugh. But I didn't get to pursue that thought because Sarah was in my face.

She crossed her arms, but I don't think it was because she was cold. She was terribly underdressed for early December in New York, wearing what she described as a "sheath" dress. It was sleeveless and didn't come halfway down her thighs. I didn't know what part of the dress the "sheath" was, but right then she was sharp as a dagger. "You think I'm a trained elephant."

"No, of course not," I said automatically.

"Listen to yourself, Daron. You just put down everything I've worked so hard for."

Yes, I had. Shit. "Wait. I didn't mean it that way."

"Well, how the fuck did you mean it, then? You find it demeaning to go onstage and perform for people?"

"No, of course not. I love playing live."

"But you think going out as a rock band and going out with a stage production are different?"

"Um..." I should have shut up and said I'm sorry, but I tried to dig myself out of the hole. "They are different underneath. The priorities are different."

"Music over money? I don't think so."

"No no, I mean... how important the music is in the scheme of things. In a rock band, it's everything. It's the raison d'etre. It's..." I felt it was important to try to nail down why it was important to me, in light of what I'd been telling Ziggy. "It's the songs you would have written even if all you did was play them in your garage to your dog. The expression so important you couldn't live without getting it out."

"Oh. So it's okay if the music is an expression of what you are, and not just something you're getting paid to do?"

"Yes." The second I said that, I realized two things: 1) Yes, that was exactly the difference between what I wanted to do with Moondog Three versus what I would do if I took a job playing with Ziggy's faux band. 2) No, that's ridiculous: I just put down every working musician on the planet. "Wait."

She tapped her fingernail against her forearm, waiting for me to pull my foot out of my mouth, or my head out of my ass.

"You know that isn't what I mean," I said, trying to figure out how to reconcile the two things I felt.

"Yeah, those poor saps in Broadway orchestras, and singing on the stage, too bad they're not real musicians," she said. "And those guys in symphonies, for that matter, such frauds for playing all that music by famous composers. The only pure music is clearly the music you keep to yourself because the second you make a buck from it—"

"That's not what I'm saying. I know it sounded like it, but... give me a second. I mean, come on, how many times have you heard me say that I respect anyone who can make a living from music. Even in genres I don't particularly respect."

"Hypocrite," she said.

I was really in over my head on this one, but I kept trying to make my point. "Oh come on. The Broadway musical is a completely bankrupt artistic form."

"Is it? Is that why sixteen million people paid up to two hundred bucks a pop to see it last year? Because it's, ahem, bankrupt?"

"There's nothing new to be done artistically in Broadway musicals! Have you seen some of the things they've tried to turn into musicals? It's a fucking formula. It's a—"

"Twelve-bar blues isn't a formula?"

"Um..." How could it be that I felt something so strongly but couldn't explain it so I could make her see it? "There's a difference between a format and a formula. A sonnet isn't a cliché. A love poem about roses probably is, though. Surely you can see that."

"And what makes rock different?"

"Okay, first of all, there is clichéd, bankrupt rock. Huge swaths of poodle-hair metal, for example. Spinal Tap proved that. Some things run their course, they should go extinct if they don't evolve."

"Is classical music dead, then?"

I sidestepped that question. "The whole reason M3 was forced into the 'alternative' corner is because we didn't conform to the formulas. Because we tried to achieve something artistically, and BNC found that too much of an effort to sell. So you know what? Actually I'm fine with the 'alternative' label. It proves they can't fucking label me." This came out a lot more vehement than I expected. This was probably the wrong time to be venting my anger about BNC.

"It's called a record *label*, Daron."

"Label shmabel. It's just another fucking hand of conformity trying to crush me, Sarah. Every time I think I've escaped it, wham, another one comes down!"

"Is that all it is? Rebelling against your suburban upbringing? Wow, that's really fucking original. Not a cliché at all. You know what says angsty-white-boy pain better than anything else? Anthemic guitar solos. That's so, so much less of a cliché than a big Broadway number, oh yeah, right."

Oh shit I'm in trouble, I thought. I'm having a fight with a friend, like a serious, we're-both-mad-and-upset kind of fight, and on top of that, fuck, if she's right, and I think she is... something in the bedrock of my self-identity is crumbling away.

And that always sucks.

Even if it's necessary.

Even though I was putting the brakes on in my brain, my mouth was still going, which goes to show how upset I was. "I don't do those piece-of-shit anthem solos and you know it."

"Tell yourself that if you need to, but I thought you were over lying to yourself. I think you're saying all of that to justify what's happened and the choices you made that led to it."

"Oh yeah? I'm pretty sure you're saying what you're saying because you're about to hit the road with a fifty-person entourage, wearing a rhinestone-studded bra."

She slapped me. I deserved it.

In fact: "I deserved that, didn't I," I said. My eyes stung as much as my cheek.

She fumed at me. Projectile fuming.

"Let me... let me think about this for a minute."

"You do that."

It was going to take me a little while to figure this one out. She went to the ladies room and I wondered if I could straighten it all out in my head before she got back.

Not likely, I know.

Crystal Clear

When Sarah went to the ladies room, I wasn't entirely surprised when the next person who sat down next to me was Jordan Travers, who I gathered was also something of a regular at this hangout.

"Trav, awesome to see you." We exchanged a complicated handshake I had almost forgotten about.

"How you doing?"

"Pretty good. Did you hear I signed a deal with Wenco?"

"You what?" Trav had grown a little goatee and had shaped his eyebrows to match but had shaved his head again. The effect made his face seem extra long.

"For a solo instrumental album with their New Age division."

"Awesome. So you're keeping busy?"

"You could say that. Hey, can I ask you something?"

"Anything, my friend."

"Is authenticity a lie?"

He rubbed his goatee thoughtfully. "I have a feeling you're asking the wrong question. I'll say this. The drive toward something we call authenticity as a measure of quality, i.e., the more authentic something is the better it is, is a false or inapplicable concept when it comes to commercialization."

Jonathan probably would have got that on the first try, but I wasn't sure I did. "Can you say that again in non-Ivy League terms?"

"Sure. For example. We'll say universally that Leadbelly and the black bluesmen of the Mississippi Delta were better, more authentic, than The Rolling Stones. But we consider the Stones way more 'authentic' than, say..." He snapped his fingers, trying to come up with a comparison, and I knew what he was looking for: a white guitar-driven pop artist but even more sanitized and removed from the source.

"Bryan Adams?" I suggested.

"John Cougar?" he countered. "Well, except he's starting to build an authenticity of his own, but you get the idea. Anyway. The point is the whole concept is kind of ridiculous. What makes the Stones great is Keith Richards's originality, not their so-called authenticity, not their trueness to some legendary source. But there will be those critics—and consumers—who hold them in higher esteem because they meet some inner metric of authentic-ness."

"Okay, but what about originality, then?"

"It's kind of the same, isn't it? We have a critical metric of comparison. The Police, U2, R.E.M., The Cure, all of them display very high levels of originality, but more importantly they are viewed by the industry as being wholly original."

"So original they define a genre itself?"

"You mean 'modern rock' or 'alternative'? Yeah, that's the thing, though, if the thing that defines your genre is originality, what you're saying is the thing that defines the genre is 'not being any of the other genres.' And that's really not a definition."

"But is it wrong to want to be judged on your own terms? If this whole thing is about self-expression?"

He asked what I think was a devil's advocate question: "One can't have full self-expression unless one is outside a genre?"

"Well, I mean, that's the point of alternative, isn't it?"

Jordan cleared his throat. "Just because the genres that were created by commerce are too narrow to encompass all expressions doesn't mean that music that falls outside the narrow bands on the spectrum that are approved is *better* than the stuff falls within them."

"But originality...?" My brain hurt.

"I understand the drive to originality, D. That drive to escape the well-trod path and distinguish yourself. But that doesn't make it *better* music. Just more original."

Oh fuck, I thought. "But isn't it better to not be derivative?"

"If you're not derivative, then how are you supposed to be authentic to your source?"

"By being your own source. By being yourself instead of sounding like someone else. Isn't being yourself instead of sounding like someone else a form of authenticity?"

"So that would mean true authenticity and originality are the same thing."

That sounded good to me. "Yeah."

"Except think about it. The reason Leadbelly is revered as authentic by us is because he's seen as the 'original' bluesman. But come on. Do you really think he wasn't representing a genre? That there weren't a ton of guys who sounded at least something like that sitting on the back porches of shotgun shacks playing for their neighbors? Leadbelly's just the one we *know* about. How do we know if he was original? How do we know if what he did was authentic or if it was watered down to make it palatable to us? It's all subjective to those making the rules, those making the judgments."

"I..." I think I was curled up in a ball on the loungey banquette at that point, with my knees in my face.

"No one ever escapes their influences," Jordan went on to say. "It all goes into your ears and it comes out again in what you do. What's original to the process is that you're the filter it passes through. But it doesn't come from you. It just comes through you."

I looked at him suddenly. "You've given this pep talk before."

"I'm a producer. Of course I have."

I stared at him for a bit.

"At least this time we're not over budget and past deadline in the studio and you're not hiding in the men's room refusing to record until you get your ego glued back together."

That made me snort. "I like to think my ego isn't so fragile."

"I'll tell you one more thing. I've given this talk to artists in just about every genre. Rap, rock, dance, you name it."

"No shit."

"No shit," he assured me.

"I feel like a fraud."

"Do you?"

"Like my whole life has been a lie? Okay, that's too strong. Like my whole career has been operated under faulty assumptions, maybe."

"You'd be far from the first. Let me buy you a drink." He got up, and I realized Sarah had been sitting on the other side of him for a while.

"I'm an idiot and I'm sorry," I said to her.

"Apology accepted," she said, and slid closer. "Hey, did I tell you my other big news?"

"Other than the apartment, the tour, and the Benetton endorsement deal?"

"Yeah." She looked around and then put her mouth against my ear. "I'm seeing someone."

"Oh yeah?"

"Yeah. She's a grad student in women's studies at Columbia."

I didn't realize it at the time, but that explained a lot.

Soho

I think one step in figuring my shit out wasn't making better decisions so much as recognizing when I was making shitty ones. That didn't always stop me from making a bad decision, but it was better than the times when I hadn't even realized there was a decision to be made.

I decided not to stop drinking when I started processing what Sarah and Trav were saying. I was feeling really unmoored by the whole conversation, and being intoxicated isn't exactly a grounding thing. But at least I was aware that I had a choice of whether or not to have another drink, as opposed to it being some kind of inevitability. Does that make sense? Trav bought me a drink, and then I bought myself another one, not out of habit but in a conscious decision not to sober up yet.

I apologized to Sarah some more, but every time I ran up against something in me that felt really basic, really solid in my core: my beliefs about the superiority of my chosen mode of artistic expression.

That night, six of us ended up at Trav's loft in Soho. The other three were also music industry people. Good people, though, Trav's people. A backup singer, a producer I think I'd met before, and a third guy whose connection to the group I didn't know at first but I figured I'd either find out or I wouldn't.

I know I sail through life without people's names sticking to me. I used to think that was a failing on my part. Now I think it's normal. Everyone I know says they're bad with names. I think this means the people who are good with names won't admit it because they're such a minority. I still feel like crap when I forget the name of someone I actually like and respect, because if they realize I don't remember their name they automatically feel like I must not like or respect them. Like if I really cared, I'd remember. But that isn't how my brain works.

Anyway. I don't remember the names of the other people there, but that didn't mean I didn't like them or that I was unfriendly to them. Although I was not at my best, what with being in the midst of an existential crisis and all.

I made the decision to sober up when Trav showed me the coffee setup in his kitchen. Since he lived in a loft, the kitchen was built into one corner, and the coffee machine took up most of an entire countertop against the wall. He was showing me how it worked while we talked.

I was still kind of hung up on what we had been talking about. As you can imagine. "Authenticity isn't just about place or culture, though. It's about era and time, too," I said. "If I go to The Haight and drop acid and make an album with fuzzed-out guitars and a lot of flange effects, that doesn't make my psychedelia more authentic."

"Well, because it would lack the element of originality," Trav said, while he measured out the beans. "Thing is, now you've got a whole new generation of hippie kids, wearing the hairstyles and the bell bottoms."

"Okay, but are they into the philosophy of the whole freedom-and-love generation? Or do they just think the style is cool?"

"Is there really a difference?" he asked.

"I think the people who went and protested in the streets against the Vietnam War and stuff probably think there's a difference."

"But how many was that? And how many of that generation just liked the style at the time? And did they define their identity by the music they listened to? I thought you were against that whole concept."

Apparently Trav and I had talked about this before. Probably while we had been recording *1989*. "You mean the concept that the punks and the metalheads and the rappers can't get along?"

"Yeah."

"Well, of course. It's patently ridiculous that people who like one type of music can't get along with people who like a different type. As if there's something inherent about their identity? Something that is 'true' punk? or 'true' metal? It's bogus that you have to choose between one or the other, and it's like you're not allowed to like both. That's as ridiculous as saying if you're Italian you're only allowed to eat Italian food. You're not allowed to like Greek or Chinese."

"It's worse than that," Trav said. "If you're Italian, at least you grew up with it and so maybe there's a tradition from your family that you feel a part of. Whereas what music you listen to? No one listens to the music of their parents. That's the whole point." He had to pause because the grinder was loud. When he was done grinding the beans he went on. "I mean, I get that people use music as a way to break away from their parents, as a way to grow up and be independent. But we were talking about genre. And people choosing which genre they listen to and the fallacy that what genre they choose is therefore superior to the genres chosen by others."

"Oh shit, now it makes sense." I pressed my palms to my forehead. "That's exactly what I think, and yet when it came to myself, not as a listener, but as a creator.... Ouch. My head hurts."

"There will be coffee soon," he said, as if the reason my head hurt was what I'd been drinking.

"There's a word for that, isn't there?"

"Lack of coffee?"

"No no, that thing where you're convinced you're better than everyone based on an arbitrary thing that has nothing to do with it."

"You mean chauvinism?"

"Jeez, yes."

"So you're saying you've been a... guitar chauvinist pig?"

"Alternative chauvinist pig, I think." I called over to Sarah. "Hey, Sar'. C'mere."

She was barefoot and had an afghan wrapped around her shoulders. "You guys making coffee?"

"He's making the coffee. I'm helping by staying out of the way," I said.

Trav started doing something with mugs and got out a carton of milk. "Daron wants to know if you agree on something."

"Okay." Sarah gave me a skeptical but expectant look.

"Am I an alternative chauvinist pig?"

She dissolved into instant laughter. "Yes! Yes, that's exactly what you are. Or were...?" she asked hopefully.

"I'm working on it," I said. "God. I knew genre was meaningless. I told people I believed genre was meaningless. And yet deep down I still have this feeling..." The more I thought about it, the more it felt like a lead weight was pressing down on my head. "If I don't believe in what I'm doing, I'm not sure I can keep doing it."

"Wait. Music's only worth doing if you believe your music is superior to everyone else's?" Sarah asked.

"No. No, that's not what I mean..." But this was why it was an existential crisis. Something had changed. Something had moved out from under my feet.

Maybe it had moved a while ago, though, and I was like the cartoon character who kept running long after passing the edge of the ledge but only fell upon noticing there was no ground under him.

"I don't feel so good," I said.

"Bathroom's through that sliding door," Trav said, pointing.

"Not that kind of not good," I said, and decided I better sit. I sat cross-legged at the edge of where the kitchen tile changed to hardwood and leaned my back against the brick wall.

Trav mixed me up a cup of coffee then, heavy on the milk and sugar. I don't know how he knew I liked it like that unless he remembered from when we were working on the album. Come to think of it, that was the sort of thing he would remember. Jordan Travers was nothing if not observant.

Me, on the other hand... we know I'm not as observant as I could be. Case in point: after Trav handed a mug of coffee to Sarah, he brought some to the other three, who were sitting a couple of yards away around the coffee table. He put a mug down in front of the backup singer and one in front of the producer, but the third one he handed right to the guy I didn't know. The guy kissed him on the cheek in thanks.

Yeah, I can be pretty thick sometimes. I forced myself to look into my coffee mug so I wouldn't stare. I mean, my whole worldview was already in a shambles, what was one more thing?

Trav came to collect my empty mug a little later. What came out of my mouth was, "Have you been gay this whole time?"

"Only for the last thirty years," he said.

We're All in the Same Gang

So, hit me over the head with a brick about it.

Somehow, despite ample evidence to the contrary, I was used to thinking of myself as the only gay person I knew. I in fact knew a ton of people—Ziggy, Colin, my own sister, Jonathan, Matthew, Sarah, maybe even Mills if she was right about him—but in my head queer people were still really few and far between.

I tried to work out the math. If you believe the one-in-ten estimate, well, that would mean ten percent, right? Pretty rare. And yet clearly way more then ten percent of the people I knew were not straight.

Well, I thought, maybe one-in-ten doesn't take into account that the entertainment industry probably has a higher concentration of gay folks. And it also probably doesn't count bisexual people properly in the first place.

Right? Did that mean my impression was less stupid? Probably not.

Especially since not only had I been oblivious to the fact that Jordan Travers was gay, I had also missed the fact that *all six of us* who were hanging out at his loft that night were. In fact, the reason Trav picked us to come back to his place and hang out was that we were queer.

I didn't know how to feel about that. I mean, on the one hand, I understood it, and we had a great time and I liked it. I mean, if you're worried that I sat on the floor brooding and angsting about it the whole time, let me assure you I didn't: Trav had a guitar, which, as you know, always fixes everything for me in social situations. On the other hand, I still wasn't comfortable being counted as part of a "group" defined by queerness.

By the way, in 1990 I wasn't all that comfortable using the word "queer" yet. After all, I'd only worked up the nerve to start using "gay" not that long before, and that was what I mostly used. But sometimes people (like Jonathan and Sarah) would get on my case about using the word gay because it could be interpreted as exclusionary to lesbians and bisexuals even if it wasn't meant that way. People seemed to be moving toward "queer" as a catch-all term that would include gays, lesbians, bisexuals, and trans people—in other words, all the people who straight homophobes would label "queer." Except this was claiming the label for ourselves. At least according to Jonathan.

I could see why that made sense, but it took me a while before I could get comfortable with a word that had been tossed at me like a knife on more than one occasion. Still, I could see how it was hard to apply the word "gay" equally to me and Sarah and Colin and Matthew, but "queer" was a bigger tent. So I use it now.

I probably don't have to tell you we were up all night that night, given that it was about four in the morning when we were having coffee. The little social gathering just kept on rolling, with talking, and singing, and listening to some tracks Jordan put on from some group he was working with, and the next day we brunched. Let me tell you, nothing makes me feel more like a rock star than getting seated at the best table in a chic place despite the fact I'm still wearing the clothes I was out dancing in the night before.

Fuck existential crises. I enjoyed the company. I enjoyed the overpriced eggs and cocktails. I enjoyed not having to be anywhere or think about anything important for a while. After we ate, we all walked over to Rockefeller Center to see the tree—remember when Sarah had thought she and I should do that as a publicity thing? They always put it up the weekend of Thanksgiving, so it was there to be seen. We saw it. From there we scattered, and Sarah and I ended up in a cab back to her apartment, which was when she actually clued me in about everyone.

"I wonder who else I've missed?" I mused, going through my mental Rolodex and trying to figure out who else was gay and I had missed it. "Trav was the last person I would've thought."

"Really? The last?"

"Well, not in that he was the least likely, more like he was the last person I would have thought of in a sexual context."

"You know, you don't have to be attracted to a guy for him to be gay," Sarah said.

"I don't mean for me personally." I couldn't think of how to explain it. "I mean more like Trav doesn't seem particularly... is there a word for this? Kind of like forward but not forward. I guess I'm saying this is an industry where a lot of people strut around like sexy beasts, and he never struck me as projecting anything like that."

"Maybe because he's on the other side of the mixing board."

"No, more like because he's discreet. Is he in the closet? I didn't know how to ask."

"He's as in the closet as you and me, if that's what you mean. It's not public knowledge, and he'd rather it wasn't."

"Does Mills know?" I asked suddenly.

"About Jordan? He might. He might not. I sure as hell was not going to ask."

"So how are you planning to keep your secret from Mills? Now that you're seeing someone?"

She shrugged. I couldn't see her expression under her sunglasses. "We'll be as careful as we can for as long as we can. I'm hiding her from my mother, too."

"Jeez. And have you thought about what happens when they find out?"

"Every fucking day." She shrugged again. "If I'm lucky, I'll end up being one of those people where it really doesn't matter."

I blinked. "Which people are those?"

"You can't name any of them because the fact that they're gay or lesbian doesn't matter. So you don't even remember."

"You believe these people really exist?"

"Of course they do."

I mulled that over, though I was not at my sharpest after having been up all night and having had a mimosa recently. "I find it hard to conceive of being outed not ruining someone's life."

"Which is a shame, because I think there are plenty of people whose friends and family know and it's not a big deal, and so even though it's not a secret, no one cares."

"Like who?"

"I don't know. Speaking hypothetically: do you know the sexuality of Philip Glass?"

"The composer? No."

"That's what I mean. Who would care if Philip Glass was gay?"

"Is Philip Glass gay?"

"I have no idea, I'm just using him as an example. John Adams? Steve Reich? Pick the minimalist of your choice for comparison."

"But that doesn't prove anything, then. Because what if he was, and came out, and it changed everything?" That really made me wonder. "Or maybe it would be generally accepted as okay for an avant garde composer to be gay."

Sarah cleared her throat. "I guess the question might be what type of person does society find acceptably gay?"

"I don't give a fuck about society in general, you know, but I'm pretty sure neither of us is in that group of people. You said it yourself, Sarah: you're a sex symbol. Pretty sure that means hetero-sex symbol."

"Except maybe if I'm sexy enough I can get away with it. You know, lots of guys fantasize about two women together. It won't burst their bubble about me unless I suddenly quit shaving and start wearing Birkenstocks."

"Hm."

"You don't agree?"

"I don't know what to think, honestly. Am I crazy for thinking that coming out is a bad thing?"

"Well, Mills found out about you and your entire world imploded, but I don't think those two things were exactly related?"

"I don't know, Sar'. I've thought about it a lot. It's pretty clear Mills knew about me long before I knew that he knew. Maybe he didn't work as hard for Moondog Three because of homophobia. Or maybe it was when I started being seen with Jonathan that he decided to pull his support instead of trying to work with us."

"Or maybe he didn't do his job right in the first place and after low sales wanted to dump you, and blaming it on you being gay was the way he saved his own ego and got to pin it on you."

"I admit, that's the interpretation I find more likely." I got a sudden chill. Did Artie know? Should Artie know?

Maybe that was a good question to ask Remo. After a nap. Upstairs in Sarah's apartment, she was too tired to put sheets on the couch and she didn't have a spare blanket yet anyway. I would have happily crashed under a bathrobe, but she said no, the bed was more than big enough for both of us. It was huge, in fact, bigger than a regular king-size bed.

And the sheets were extra silky and smelled nice.

"I'm glad to have you for a friend," Sarah said when we were lying side by side.

My eyes wouldn't open, but I could still talk. "Does that mean you forgive me for being an ass about your rhinestone-studded bra?"

"Mostly," she said. "Mostly."

Tonight

That nap wasn't when the nightmares started. I think I was having them already, but I'm not sure exactly when they started. I think maybe I didn't remember the first couple of them. Pretty sure it was some time after I left LA and before I saw Ziggy again.

Maybe nightmare is too strong a word. The dreams were more annoying than terrifying, really. Have I told you the one where I'm a busboy? That one recurs in different configurations. I still have it once in a while. The really annoying versions of it feature Ziggy as either a waiter or host... I don't even want to think about them. Like that might make me dream that dream more often.

Another one that cropped up that week had me as a documentary cameraman, and I'm trying to follow Ziggy (of course) and the camera is insanely heavy, like a hundred pounds, and I'm running uphill with it on my shoulder, then in my arms, then it gets to the point I'm dragging it on the ground and praying I'm not destroying it in the process...

You get the idea. Thoroughly unpleasant dreams where I'm trying so hard at something and the situation keeps getting worse. Natural disasters get in the way, wars break out, you name it.

Ugh. I wondered if it was because I quit therapy when I left LA.

Anyway. I had a very long hot shower when I woke up. Sarah was still asleep.

In the shower I let my mind go around in circles. So Jordan Travers was gay. I was disturbed not by the fact that Jordan was gay, or by the fact that I'd missed it (well, okay, I was mildly perturbed about that), but mostly because I suddenly felt differently about him. I still liked him—heck, I probably like him more as a result of knowing?—but I felt like he was a different person now. And I knew he wasn't. I knew he was exactly the same. And yet because now I saw him in a whole new light, it was like he had changed, even though it was all my fault.

And I thought: shit, this is what happens when I come out to people like Christian. He acted really cool about it, but ultimately I think he felt like I'd pulled the rug out from under him. Things were good between me and him again, but maybe they'd never be "the same" because I was never the person he'd thought I was.

I hated the thought that someone who knew me could suddenly think they didn't know me because they found out I was gay. And I knew that part of it was because of the assumptions they'd put on what "being gay" supposedly meant. And I hated those assumptions.

And yet... here I was making those same assumptions about Jordan. What the fuck, Daron? How does that make sense? It didn't make sense, and I tried to unbend those wires. Did I still trust Jordan? Yes. Respect his opinion and his abilities? Yes. Had my relationship with him changed? Well, maybe only that we'd gotten to know each other better, which would have happened from hanging out even without me finding out he had a boyfriend.

A fleeting thought, one I couldn't stop myself from

having: would I do him? Date him? If we were both available and the time was right? Hm. Probably not. I wasn't particularly attracted to him, anyway. And I'd much rather maintain a solid working friendship since it seemed likely we might work together in the future.

Next fleeting thought I couldn't stop: did Ziggy know? And...?

That was the point where I smacked the wall with the flat of my hand so hard Sarah came and knocked on the door to find out if I was all right.

"I'm fine!" I yelled over the sound of the shower running, but I might have sounded kind of distressed. Because the thought that came to mind was that I knew perfectly well that Ziggy's m.o. was to sleep with anyone he wanted to influence. He'd told me, hadn't he, that the only thing that would keep him from doing it was that he didn't want to upset me?

But he didn't have much incentive not to upset me if I wasn't around.

And, well, if I wasn't around, then why did I care who he slept with? Why would I care whether he slept with Jordan or not?

I did care, though. That was the thing.

Dammit.

I shut off the water and toweled myself into a less water-logged state.

When I emerged from the shower, Sarah was on the phone. "Are you ready to take down this number? Here." She rattled off a phone number from a card. "Seriously. Best vocal coach I've ever had, and I've had a couple."

She was sitting on the side of the bed. The phone wasn't cordless: it ran to a base on her side table shaped like a small statue of Mickey Mouse.

"Uh huh," she said. "She's here in New York, but she travels a fair bit, too. I had tried to get hooked up with Joan Lader, but she wasn't available. I'm super happy with how it's turned out, though. Yeah, Speech Level Singing. I easily got another half-octave I didn't think I had."

She was clearly speaking to another singer. I stretched myself across my side of the bed again, only half-listening.

"Well, I'm supposed to see her tomorrow at two," she went on. "You want to come along and meet her? She said she only takes new clients on referral. Joan referred me, I'll refer you. If you like her, that is."

I started to drift back to sleep.

"Anyway, you want to talk to Daron? He's here."

I opened my eyes. "Who is it?"

She handed me the receiver. "Do you really need to ask? I'm getting in the shower."

It was warm from being pressed to her ear. "Hello?"

"Hey." Ziggy. "I'm in town."

My skin flashed hot and cold. "And meeting Sarah's vocal coach, it sounds like."

"Yeah."

We lapsed into silence while I groped around for something that was neither loaded nor pathetic to say. The feeling was... unsettlingly familiar. Dammit all to hell. I didn't just jump through the fiery hoops of therapy to find myself back to square one, did I? My throat felt dry.

"I didn't know you and Sarah knew each other," I finally said.

"We don't. I called there looking for you and she answered."

"Huh. How'd you get on the subject of vocal coaches?"

"I'm looking for one on this coast. I thought she might know someone."

And apparently she did. "Um. Cool." Dammit. Back to feeling awkward and stupid. "Looking for me, huh."

"Yeah. You, uh, you have plans for tonight?"

Only if the plans involve cornering you and burying my... nose... in your... hair. Was that me who thought that? I cleared my throat. "I'm not sure. Sarah's the one who plans. I'm just along for the ride. We did the VIP room at Limelight last night. She might want to stay in, order a pizza, and..." I steered myself away from saying *write a song* and instead said, "rent a movie. How about you?"

"I'm at the Carlyle. Why don't all three of us do dinner?"

"Is it all right if I ask her when she gets out?"

"Of course."

"Okay." I supposed that meant we had to stay on the phone until she came out. "How was St. Maarten?"

"Beautiful, except I got eaten alive by mosquitoes.

After the photoshoot, fortunately. Still. I'm all spotty with calamine lotion."

I could picture it. Ziggy's skin, tawny from sun, splotched with pink medicine.

A wave of longing for him swept through me. Sigh. I was caught up in it enough that I wasn't really absorbing what he was saying. Something about the food in St. Maarten, maybe.

He kept up the chatter until Sarah emerged from the shower, her hair in a towel atop her head and the rest of her in a robe so soft and fluffy it looked like it had been made from skinned stuffed animals.

I covered the receiver with my hand. "Zig wants to know if you have plans for tonight? For us, I mean? He's inviting us to dinner."

"Oh, we should totally do dinner with him," she said. "We can go dancing after."

Well, that settled it.

Everybody Dance Now

Sarah's driver dropped us off at what looked to me like a typical skyscraper-type office building, but through the lobby and up an escalator we came to a restaurant with styling so modern it bordered on futuristic. Which I suppose was the point. The doorman looked more like a Secret Service agent than a restaurant employee.

I swear I saw Tom Cruise while we walked through. Ziggy was already there, waiting for us in a private dining room in the back.

Is this going to happen every time I see him after we've been apart? I thought. Basically, I laid eyes on him and it was like taking a hit of some drug: my heart rate went up, my skin felt warm, my senses seemed to come alive...

This wasn't a new feeling. Remember that first, oh, six months or so after he'd joined the band? It was like that every time I saw him then, too. It didn't really stop until we did that tour... that tour where we slept together that first time. All those times.

The difference was that, back then, whenever I saw him my anxiety went up. Now, it went down. Like being in the same room with him calmed me, as if he gave off calming pheromones or something.

Not that I was completely chilled out. I wanted to rush over to him and slide my hands along the bare skin at the small of his back where the cute white denim jacket he was wearing rode up a little and pull him into a hug/kiss. But there was a waiter there, and there were introductions to be made.

"Ziggy, Sarah. Sarah, Ziggy," I said, gesturing between the two of them. Sarah reached out to shake his hand and he pulled her knuckles to his lips, kissed them, and bowed. "I figured I better put you two on a first name basis right away since neither of you uses your real last name."

"Charmed," Sarah said with an amused smile.

The three of us sat on the same side of a large oval table that looked like it could have come from the set of Star Trek. Indirect halogens made the edge of the ceiling glow like a horizon. On the theory that I was the one who knew both of them, they made me sit in the middle.

By the time we were done with the appetizer course, though, I made Ziggy switch places with me because my neck was getting sore from looking back and forth between them. The two of them did most of the talking, which probably surprised no one.

They had a lot to talk about. They were both at the same stage of their careers, really, as multi-talented solo artists with similar deals and similar aspirations. Sarah grilled Ziggy about movie stuff. Ziggy, meanwhile, grilled Sarah about her tour logistics, and they talked about things I'd never had to deal with before like choreographers and workout regimens.

Let me tell you, if I thought Ziggy had a perfect body before—which I did—I had a feeling that under his clothes it was only going to be even more perfect after working with a personal trainer and movement coach. That feeling would be intensified later on the dance floor.

But later. There was a reason Ziggy wanted to meet Sarah, besides trading stardom tips. He waited until we were about done with the main courses to bring it up.

"So, you know I fired Digger," he said.

"I know," she said. "We're getting ready to. Could be as early as next week."

"Can I ask you to do one thing first?" He twirled an unused fork slowly on the tablecloth with an outstretched finger, as if making the secondhand of a strange clock go.

"What would that be?" Sarah asked, pushing her plate back and leaning toward him.

"It's probably in your contract that you have a right to examine his books once a year, right?"

"Yeah, there's something about that."

"I should have looked at his books before I fired him. Now I need to subpoena them as part of a lawsuit, and that's going to be rough." His eyes were on the fork. "I'm sure he's going to doctor them before the court gets a chance to look at them. I'm wondering if you could get someone in there before he has that chance, though."

"Funny you should mention—I think we just had a guy go in and do that. He photocopied a ton of stuff. You want to have a look at it?"

"That would be great." Ziggy sat back in relief. "That would be really great. I don't know if you're interested in being party to this lawsuit, but—"

"Wait," I said. "I thought the lawsuit was about misuse of band funds from BNC. How would Sarah be part of that?"

Ziggy shrugged and played dumb. "Just asking."

"Seriously, what exactly is this suit going to be based on? Because I still haven't heard an explanation that makes me feel good about it."

Ziggy looked at me through kohl-rimmed eyes. "At the very least, there's something shady with tour support funds. One of the biggest elements of their whole 'the band wasn't financially successful' thing was that they supposedly paid out a huge sum to us for tour support. But do you recall getting a large sum for that?"

"I thought we went out on a shoestring because we turned BNC's tour support offer down." Was that what Carynne had actually said? I couldn't remember exactly.

"That's what I thought, too. BNC claims they made the payment, though." Ziggy's eyes wandered.

"Wait, but did they?"

"That remains to be seen."

"Does it? What did Mills say?"

Ziggy cleared his throat. "Does it matter? This puts everyone in the clear: Mills is absolved of making the property unrecoupable, the band saves face, and Digger gets nailed to the wall."

I put my hands on the table, like seeing them would help me think rationally. "But what if BNC didn't actually make a payment? Then we're nailing Digger to the wall on another one of Mills's lies?"

Ziggy looked at me with a slight frown. "Daron. You hate the guy. This fixes everything."

"It doesn't. Not if what it does is prop up a lie. For one thing, how do you plan to get that through court? Won't it become obvious if Mills is lying about the money?"

"Well, this is the thing, this is why we need a look at Digger's books. I feel it's really likely that Digger kept very shady accounting. And because we can prove his accounting's shady, the fact that the BNC payment mysteriously disappeared will be all the more incriminating. If Digger took the BNC payment for himself and never told us?"

"The BNC payment that might not have existed."

"But might have. Mills says it was paid."

"And you have to believe Mills because you're working with him and you can throw Digger under the bus because you fired him."

"You wanted me to fire him!"

"You fired him because of me?"

"Yes! Well, partly! Come on, Daron, you know he can't be trusted."

I did. I knew perfectly well. "Yeah..." But Mills couldn't be trusted either, so far as I was concerned. "So you're saying because Digger's been shady, he's getting what he deserves. He opened himself up to this kind of attack because he wasn't on the up and up, even if maybe this specific crime wasn't his fault."

"Exactly."

I still didn't like it. I knew it was supposed to be poetic justice, or maybe simply plain justice, but just because there was no honor among thieves didn't mean I needed to be a part of it.

"Let's go dancing," Ziggy said.

"No," Sarah said, and for a second I thought maybe she was going to take my side and argue against the whole lawsuit idea. But no. "Dessert first," she insisted with a conspiratorial grin.

The two of them had a lot in common, including whims, lots of whims, and a determination to have a good time that night. When you've got two master manipulators both working on you, it's hard to maintain a bad mood. I was happy enough to shed it and quit thinking about lawsuits anyway, I guess. Soon enough they had me hopped up on sugar and caffeine, and not long after that we were hitting the floor at Danceteria, under the watchful eye of Tony and his former crew.

The music and lights pumped, and we danced. I still wanted to slide my hands across the sweaty small of Ziggy's back. I didn't. We were on a dance floor that was all swirling color and lights, but we were in the middle of a couple hundred people and far too public to dare something like that. I did it to Sarah instead, who gave me a flirty look when I did, but I knew it was an act. We all knew it was an act. Just one step away from being choreography.

Can't Live Without Your...

We left the club in a stretch limo, Tony driving, and headed up the West Side Highway. No, maybe it was the East Side. I don't know. I was too busy kissing Ziggy.

I know. Sarah was sitting there, looking smug and watching. But I had reached some limit on my patience or my sanity or something. Do you think I had been able to keep my eyes off him while he was dancing? When every twitch of his hips and curve of his hands was so obviously aimed at driving me out of my mind?

So I was out of my mind, kissing him in front of someone he'd just met, in the back of a car with blackout windows, with no idea what I was thinking.

Well, I wasn't thinking.

I will tell you what I expected. Somehow I expected I was going to kiss him until we got wherever we were going and then he was going to leave and I was going to go and have a vicious wank in the shower.

He eventually freed his mouth from mine. "You could come upstairs, you know."

"Hm?" Words were not sinking in.

"At the hotel. Sarah, do you mind if I borrow him for tonight? I'll send him back in the morning."

"Bring him to the meeting at two o'clock," she suggested.

"Mm, that's a good idea. Earth to Daron, you all right with that?"

I absorbed that they had conspired to send me to Ziggy's bed. I made an affirmative noise against Ziggy's throat, where his sweat was salty. I'd try to remember to say thank you later.

When we got upstairs, I pressed him against the wall behind the door. Because the two minutes of acting nonchalant that the lobby and elevator had required had been almost impossible to get through. I shed my leather jacket. My palms found his hips; my lips found his ear.

"You need me," he whispered while I worked on his belt buckle with my hands.

I looked up sharply. "Don't make me regret it."

His eyes went round and he pulled my face close with an urgent hand. "That's not what I meant. It... it was just something to say. Not a threat." His thumb stroked my cheek, placating. "Don't be hard, Daron."

"Hard." My hands were in the small of his back now, against his bare skin, where they had wanted to be all night. "What do you mean?"

His voice was soft. "I can't take you angry right now."

I made myself take a breath. "I'm not angry. Just..." I didn't have a word for it. Needy, maybe, but that was what he said, and I didn't want to echo it when that was what might have made me border on angry in the first place.

"Come on." He pulled me by the hand into the room. It was different from the one he stayed in last time I was here. This one had French doors separating the bedroom from the parlor.

Don't be hard, he had said. I guess he meant except in one important sexual way. He laid me back on the bed and crawled over me. And gave himself to me like a gift.

Like a gift.

Cradle of Love

When I woke up, Ziggy was wearing me like a cape. We were nowhere near the pillows, curled in the center of the bed, with my arms around his neck/shoulders and the rest of me draped over his back. I freed one arm and pulled one edge of the duvet over us and then nudged him toward the head of the bed. I don't even think he woke, really, but he moved and then we settled into a more traditional spoon position.

The next time I woke up I figured out why I was hot and he was cold: I was still in all my clothes and he was buck naked. Right. I folded the duvet over him completely while I slipped out to take a piss and strip out of my jeans and sweaty shirt. When I got back in bed, I saw that Ziggy had magically transported himself under the covers. Good.

I slid in next to him and we settled in silence again. I could sense he was awake, but I don't think either of us felt talkative, or like talking was necessary right then.

I listened to the sounds of the city in the wee hours. Hotels always have a sound to them, a hiss or a hum or a murmur. Old buildings like that one especially. And cities have a sound, too, a root drone underneath everything else you can hear. The sound of New York was soothing, somehow. The hiss of taxi tires against the avenue was as calming as the wind through pines or ocean waves.

New York City is a strange, strange place. It didn't feel "like home" the way Allston did. But I felt "at home" there. Does that make sense?

Ziggy fell back to sleep and I enjoyed the simple pleasure of lying next to him, my mind humming quietly like the city around us.

I must have dozed off at some point because Ziggy's alarm woke him way too early. He said something to me about meeting a dance trainer at ten. I don't remember exactly because I was only half awake and I went back to sleep.

He was kind and put the "do not disturb" sign on the door. I slept through breakfast and woke up in time to think about lunch. He hadn't told me when he would be back, but I knew he had a meeting with Sarah's vocal coach at two. Would he be coming back before then? I assumed so. I assumed it was probably gauche to arrive at a vocal coach's while in one's sweaty dance-training outfit, so he'd come back to change. Then again, what the hell did I know?

I would have been happy with a granola bar if I could find one, but I didn't have any of my stuff with me and I didn't think it was a wise choice to dig through Ziggy's stuff. So I called room service and asked if they could bring me a granola bar and they convinced me I should have a spinach salad that had toasted nuts and oat clusters and dried cranberries on it, which would be kind of like having a granola bar crushed on top of a salad, right? Maybe if you threw some chocolate chips on there? I don't know. The Carlyle was fancier than I was used to.

They brought up the salad and a pot of coffee, and I was amused that the coffee came with chocolate-dipped coffee biscuits. I ate those first, drank half the coffee, and then picked at the salad, which was, admittedly, pretty tasty.

I had taken a shower and was wearing the bathrobe provided by the hotel when room service came. But after I got bored of eating the salad I figured next on my to-do list was get dressed, except I didn't much want to put the things I had been wearing yesterday on. The jeans, maybe, except they were somewhat suspiciously stained near the fly. Yeah, having sex with your clothes on is great, but be warned.

I was still trying to figure out what to do when Ziggy returned.

"You're coming with me to meet this vocal coach, right?" he asked me while he dug in the bottom of a suitcase.

"Yeah, wasn't that the plan? You hand me off to Sarah there?"

"If I end up staying in the city a couple more days, though," he said, piling a few things next to the suitcase on the bed, "would she mind if I borrow you?"

"I don't think Sarah has dibs on me exactly, if that's what you're asking."

Ziggy snickered at that. "Here, try these on." He handed me a pair of black jeans.

I pulled them on and they fit reasonably well. "It's not like I have much of an agenda. I mean, you know, the meeting I came to the city for is over. I'm just hanging out."

He pulled a T-shirt that wasn't too outrageous out of the pile and I put that on, too. "Are you going back to LA from here or home?"

"Home. I've got some stuff I want Bart to help me with, and, you know, see my sister and stuff."

"How's she doing?" He handed me a blousy blue flannel shirt, with shoulder pads in it (?) and long tails, but under my leather jacket it looked fine.

"Fine, as far as I can tell. She says Emerson is a piece of cake, but really good. She tells me I won't believe how many Emerson alums are in television and radio and film."

"Good." He fixed the collar of the shirt so it worked better with the jacket and then said, "So." It was one of those forced-casual "so"s, and I knew he was about to ask or say something pretty serious. He was standing right in front of me, looking into my face. "What meeting did you come to New York for, again?"

The way he asked made me think he already knew. Apparently he wanted to hear it from me and, I guessed, was miffed I hadn't told him yet.

I kept my cool. "Oh. It's kind of funny. You know that soundtrack stuff I've been working on?"

"Yeah."

"Bart and I made a demo tape of some of the songs when he was out west. He brought it home and played it for Carynne. Next thing I know, Carynne sent it to Wenco, to the A&R guy who signed Nomad back when. Boom. He tells me they want to put out a New Age album."

"Oh, really." He still looked and sounded a little miffed.

"Really. Kind of unexpected."

"How much does one get for a New Age album these days?"

"When you're essentially unknown like I am? Twenty thousand."

The miffed look turned to surprise. "That's all?"

"You can see why I'm not making a big deal out of it," I said. Well, that and Sarah had reamed me a new one the one time I'd gotten it into my head to brag. In fact, I said, "You know. People will listen to it while shopping for crystals and pyramids and shit."

"Hm." He seemed placated by the idea. He checked the time and gestured for me to follow him into the bathroom, where he dug out an eyeliner pencil and started working on one eye. "I guess it's a nice bonus, though. What do they call it? Found money."

"Pretty much. A feather in my cap." I tried to be cool about it, but I was probably blushing and I wasn't even sure why. "Bart and I need to lay down a little bit more when I go home, and then it'll be done."

Ziggy looked at me through his reflection. "I want to lay down a little bit more," he said, trying for seductive.

I knew we had to walk out the door any minute, though. "Of course you do," I said. "You had tap dance lessons at the crack of ten."

He chuckled. "Call Tony and let him know we're almost ready to go?"

"What's the number?"

"It's written on the pad by the bed. It's a car phone."

When I was done with that I returned to the bathroom to find that Ziggy had decided to touch up the black nail polish on his nails.

"What do you know about this vocal coach?" he asked.

"Nothing. This is totally outside my expertise."

"Hm."

I had one of those moments, then, watching him, while he was so absorbed in what he was doing it was like he forgot for a second I was there. One of those moments that made my heart ooze with affection. Do you know what I mean? I had a flash of the night before, of him crawling over me, and then I wondered when I was seeing him again. Tonight? Could we? What had he said, "if" he stayed in New York another couple of days?

I wondered if he'd want to spend Christmas with Remo and the guys. His mother was gone, and he didn't, as far as I knew, have any other romantic attachments at the moment.

The phone rang before I could think of how to ask. Tony, saying he was downstairs.

All right, I'd ask him later.

Promised You a Miracle

I learned something I didn't know from the vocal coach. I freely admit I knew only the rudiments of singing. You learn a little by osmosis in music school, even if you're not in voice. I sang in my junior high school choir one year, too, and learned a little bit there. You know how it goes.

I thought of Ziggy as a tenor. In my level of knowledge, stemming from chorus, the four voices were soprano, alto, tenor, and baritone. Very few guys are true basses, and most choral music is written with these four parts in mind. I knew that in opera there were more fine divisions, but in day-to-day modern music we really didn't worry about the difference between a countertenor and a tenor, say, or what "coloratura" was.

Sarah's vocal coach was an older woman with an impressive mane of salt-and-pepper hair, held back by large eyeglasses perched on the top of her head. She greeted us at the door of her Upper West Side apartment with a white cat twining around her ankles. The cat scampered off to hide as soon as we came in, though. The woman introduced herself as Doctor Priscilla Oates but then said we could call her Priss. We followed her into a sitting room where there were a couple of couches, many bookshelves, and a piano. I could see a copy of the *1989* CD sitting on top of the piano, next to a stack of sheet music.

The first thing Priss did once we'd all trooped into the room was tell Ziggy to hold still, and then she essentially grabbed his larynx with her fingers. Okay, *grabbed* is too strong a word. She felt around and pressed on either side, and while holding onto his throat like Darth Vader told him to move his head from side to side.

"Ow," he said. Sarah took a seat on the couch and I perched next to her, watching them closely.

"Hum," Priss told him, and kept poking around. Ziggy hummed. "You've got evidence of some strain here." She had almost no accent at all, but the way she spoke sounded like maybe English wasn't her first language. German, maybe?

"Eh," Ziggy said as she let go.

"Remember that cortisone shot when we were on tour?" I piped up.

Ziggy winced. "I almost forgot about that. Yeah, I was on painkillers and couldn't feel how ripped up I was getting. But I recovered."

"What did you do to recover?" Priss asked, looking skeptical.

"Sang kirtan in India for a couple of months...?" Ziggy offered.

"Hm." She took her cardigan sweater off and laid it over the back of a chair. "Well, if you were doing it right, that might have been beneficial. Sit."

She gestured for Ziggy to sit in a chair facing her while she took her place at the piano. She wore her glasses on a chain hanging from her neck, and she put them on as if she were about to read sheet music, then scolded herself and took them off again. No sheet music necessary.

"Here we go," she said, and she ran Ziggy through the familiar exercises I knew as warm-ups, the up-five-notes-and-down-again pattern, working him first down the piano and then up. I knew she hadn't reached the top of his range yet, but she paused and said, "Excellent. Good clarity."

"My falsetto gets higher," Ziggy said.

"Are you in your falsetto range now?"

"Yes."

"No." She tapped her hand on the wood of the piano for emphasis. "No. Who told you that's falsetto? That's no falsetto."

Ziggy and I exchanged a look. I think we both said, "It's not?"

"No. Do they no longer teach this at RIMCon?" She shot me a look and I found myself sitting up straighter, like I'd been scolded in class.

I tried to defend myself. "I wasn't—"

But she cut me off with a wave of her hand and the words: "A true falsetto is a voice quality. The octave jump is brought on by a variant movement of the vocal cords. Just because it is high does not make a note falsetto." She said this to me instead of to Ziggy, and I wondered how she knew I had gone to RIMCon. I guess she had done her homework on Ziggy, and by extension the rest of the band. "Your friend here has a true tenor; his so-called upper register is not a separate register at all but an extension of his true singing voice. Above *that* is a falsetto, where only the edges of the vocal cords come into play." She turned to Ziggy. "With me. Sing."

She played another set of the warm-up-style exercises, singing with him as they worked their way up and up. Ziggy was in fine voice despite partying late last night and everything. And now that I knew what I was listening for I could hear the difference, where the change came from full voice to falsetto.

Priss stopped again, and again spoke to me instead of to Ziggy. Which maybe was a bit weird, but I was caught up trying to absorb what she said more than how she said it. "In opera he would be called a *tenor leggero*. Interestingly enough, it's common for singers like this to be misclassified as baritones because of such excellent lower range. He has very good range, and the good news is that the strain he experienced was not likely from singing out of his range. At least if the songs on your CD are any indication."

Yes, Priss definitely did her homework. "I like his upper range and write for it a lot," I explained.

She patted Ziggy on the knee. "He is like the coloratura soprano. Flexible, expressive, able to jump pitches easily. A joy to write for, I am sure."

Then she turned to address Ziggy directly. "When you work with me I will adjust the placement of your tongue, the manner in which you employ your vocal cords, and so on. We will work on phonation, breathing, posture. You have a fine, fine instrument. I can strengthen it and make it so you will not need cortisone shots or anything like that."

"I got another half-octave I didn't used to have," Sarah reminded him.

Ziggy held up his hands. "Sign me up. I'm sold."

"And you?" Priss said to me. "Do you need voice work, too?"

I shook my head. "I'm pretty sure I'm a garden-variety tenor, and I only sing backup anyway."

She gave me a half-smile. "Fine. Go tend to your gardening. Sarah and I have a session to do now. You are welcome to stay in the kitchen...?"

"Was that a pizza shop I saw on the corner?" Ziggy asked.

"I could meet you guys there in an hour," Sarah said.

"Good." Priss clapped her hands and made shooing motions, and Ziggy and I beat a hasty retreat.

Touch and Go

I don't know what genius invented it, but let me say for the record that meatball pizza is awesome. Maybe it was a stroke of necessity: maybe one day a pizza guy was out of pepperoni and he thought, well, damn, maybe I should just slice up the meatballs I have for meatball subs, and put that on there? But I prefer to think it was a stroke of genius.

We got slices to go from the window on the street at the pizzeria and took a walk while eating them. The meatball was a little tricky to eat and walk with since it couldn't be folded in half as easily as plain cheese, but it was worth the extra work.

It was early December, and we were probably underdressed for walking around outside, but there was a little afternoon sun and no wind so we walked into a small park on the next block.

"I like her," Ziggy said. Priss, he meant.

I decided not to ask if he thought it was weird that she talked to me instead of him, because apparently he was fine with it. "So, personal trainer, dance instructor, vocal coach... all in New York?"

Ziggy shrugged. "And I'm supposed to start working with an acting coach, too. My new manager's based in Manhattan."

"You never told me who your new manager was."

Ziggy was down to crust only now, and he ripped a piece of it free with his teeth. "Man. It's night and day compared to Digger. Okay, maybe a lot of the difference is that now I have this deal, so maybe Digger would've been hiring all these people, too. But I dunno. I've got this entire agency behind me now, with a lot of professional services and expertise. It's not just Digger and Janessa."

"Janessa?" I'd never heard the name before.

"Digger's secretary? You probably talked to her on

the phone. Poor kid. He tells her he'll teach her the ropes, like she's some kind of protégé, but all he wants is for her to answer the phones and deal with the mail. And the thing is, she could be a fashion model, I swear. She's like Naomi Campbell, only actually pretty. But she kind of gave that up because she wasn't getting anywhere and needed steady income."

I wondered if the income with Digger was as steady as it should be. "Are you going to keep in touch with her?"

Ziggy gave me a sidelong look. "I hear that jealous tone in your voice."

"Oh, be serious, I am not jealous of Digger's office help. Even if I do feel sorry for her."

"She's a sweetheart and deserves better." Ziggy shrugged.

We came out the other side of the park and started walking around the block to circle back toward the pizza place. He still hadn't told me his manager's name. I decided to let it drop. After all, I'm sure I could just ask Carynne and she'd know the guy's name, phone number, and astrological sign.

So that left me wanting to bring up the thing I'd thought about bringing up earlier but hadn't.

"Hey, um," I said, like a dumbass.

Ziggy knew perfectly well that was my way of making a prelude to a statement that was possibly heavily laden with dumbassery.

"Um?" he prompted, when I didn't go on after a second.

Here goes. "Are you going to be here for Christmas?"

"Here?"

"New York, I mean."

"Um..."

I realized he had no idea why I would be asking. "Look. Remo's whole... clan, me included, are planning to do Christmas Big-Apple-style."

He looked down at his boots as we ambled. "You mean like skating at Rockefeller Center and shopping at Macy's?"

"Um, I think he just meant here instead of LA," I clarified. "Possibly because he's figured out I don't like LA much? I don't know. That thought only just occurred to me. Anyway, the guys in Nomad and their families. Matthew's here, too, and... you get the idea." I couldn't remember if he knew who Matthew was.

"Huh. Where are you staying?"

"I don't know. Some place he picked. It's Remo, so I'm sure it's not the Waldorf Astoria." I suddenly wondered if it would be the Penta. I hoped not.

"Remo and I really don't know each other," Ziggy said, steering us wide of a homeless man leaning against a building.

"I'm inviting you," I said. "Okay?"

"Will you be crushed if I don't?"

I blinked. This conversation had moved to a level I don't think Ziggy and I had communicated on before. Both of us were being so direct. "The point is if you come to Christmas, I won't spend the entire holiday wishing you were there. If you don't come, I will. That's not the same thing as *crushed*, though."

"You're serious about that."

"I'm apparently too sleep-deprived to filter today."

"You'd... take me to your family Christmas."

"Yes." Okay, maybe the filter was partly working, because I thought about telling him about bringing Jonathan to Thanksgiving last year, but before it could come spilling out I stopped myself. "If you have to be in St. Barts or the South of France or Hollywood, I understand," I said, leaving him an out if he felt he needed one. "But I had to ask."

"I'll check my schedule," he said. "And you won't freak out that your people are seeing us together?"

"Remo, the guys, they all know about me."

"And me?" Oh, the skeptical eyebrow.

"Remo knows. The rest have made guesses."

He came out and said it: "They wouldn't find the whole fucking-a-bandmate thing a taboo?"

I came right back. "We're not bandmates anymore, Ziggy."

He stopped dead in his tracks. His lips parted and his mouth opened slowly, and I realized that was his jaw going slack.

I wanted to reach up to caress that jaw. Instead I made my voice gentle. "We're not, remember?"

He frowned and started to walk again. "What... when did you do this processing? When did you...?" He shook his head.

I followed him, not sure if this was a fight or if it was a misunderstanding I could untangle before it escalated. "Was that not clear when I saw you in LA?"

He pulled his leather jacket down at the waist and then pulled his hands inside the sleeves. "LA proved we still work well together, I thought."

We wrote a song, I wanted to say. *You asked me to help you with a song and we wrote one and...* "I didn't think writing one song changed our... relationship status."

"Do we have a relationship status?"

"I could ask you the same thing."

He blew a breath out through his nostrils, not looking at me. "Hate to say it, but... I asked you first."

"Okay. Let's see." I stuck my hands into my pockets, taking a few moments to try to map the trajectory of my feelings and why I was going to answer yes. Getting the evidence together. I decided not to rehash the whole "helpless" time period, which included the end of the *1989* tour, the time he was in rehab, and most of while he'd been in India. Then there was the "try-to-forget" period, when I was in Japan and Australia and Spain, except I didn't come close to actually forgetting. Then I came back...

"Not to be overly dramatic, but I feel kind of like I took a pretty big risk trying to talk to you with Mills and Digger hanging over you." *On the other side of Central Park from here*, I thought, but didn't say. "I had no idea how that was going to turn out. And then, that time I showed up to help you at your apartment, and I stayed for a couple of days?"

"Yeah."

"I felt, or thought I felt, that we had something going." This wasn't the first time I'd said that.

"Uh huh. And then you felt I pulled the rug out from under you."

"By kicking me out of my own band, yeah."

"I did not kick—" He made a frustrated noise and stopped us from rehashing that argument. "So you've decided since we're not in a band together anymore, it's okay that we fuck."

"I don't recall kicking you out of bed any time recently."

"So you're saying what exactly?"

"That we've already got a relationship, don't we?" *Or was I just convenient to cry on, that time in LA, the warm body who happened to be nearest when you were missing your mother?* Was I just convenient *now?* When I imagined Ziggy was loving, was he merely placating?

"Hm." That wasn't exactly affirming.

I tried to backtrack to the bedmates-but-not-bandmates question. "Certainly everyone we know knows," I pressed.

"And you're okay with that."

"I don't have much choice at this point." We were wading into muddy waters, but I forged ahead with the kind of bluntness that I thought had been helpful in our recent conversations. "They all know I'm in love with you."

I didn't expect him to look at me with such intensity then. His eyes were narrow, focused. Bitter? "Say that again."

"They all know?"

His teeth were clenched. "The other half."

I was silent a moment, wondering why he felt the need to bully me into saying it. "Zig. I love you and I'm in love with you."

"Did your therapist tell you to say that?" He was angry.

So I was angry, too. "No, my therapist did not fucking tell me to say that." What the fuck? "It's not even the first time I've said it." I pointed toward Central Park as if I could remind him of it.

He looked sideways, considering. "Hm. True."

"Did you stop believing it or something?"

His jaw was set. "I need to think." His face closed like a storefront bringing down a chainlink gate.

Fuck. Fuck fuck fuck fuck fuck. I sighed. "About what?"

"Things." He shook himself like a dog, waved a hand, forced a smile. "It's all right. Don't let my being moody ruin a beautiful afternoon."

"Um, okay." What happened next was we walked back to the pizzeria, and met Sarah, and ended up having another night on the town that was perfectly fine, everything was sort of storybook-perfect on the surface.

But I felt like I was looking at a mask, not at Ziggy's face. Even when we went back to his suite at the Carlyle, just the two of us, even when he invited me into bed, even when we were lying there afterward, it was like he wasn't really there. He had retreated somewhere inside himself. I had the definite feeling it was my fault, but didn't know how to ask about it without pushing him to retreat even deeper.

By the time we fell asleep, he hadn't given me an answer about Christmas.

By the time I woke up, he had skipped town. Sudden meeting on the West Coast. Or so the note he left me read. He had checked out of the hotel and everything.

Maybe it was a sign of maturity that I didn't freak out. I took a shower. I thought about the fact that one time, when I had been really freaked out and overwhelmed, I got on a plane to Los Angeles, too.

Huh. Was it really emergency business? Or was there someone in LA Ziggy really needed to see? I found myself unable to muster any jealousy. It was too soon to know whether I should feel jealous, or angry, or maybe even optimistic. Not enough information.

I told myself I could be patient. He hadn't left the continent, right? I don't know why it never really sank in before then, but while I had always known I had to work on my own shit, I had really not grasped that Ziggy had shit of his own to deal with. Maybe because I had been so blinded by my own problems. And maybe because Ziggy didn't used to let me see so deeply into him.

I took the train back to Boston that afternoon. I slept most of the way. But while I was awake, I wrote a song about how vulnerability is scary as shit.

To Be Continued...

Want more of Daron's Guitar Chronicles?

Check out the DGC website at http://daron.ceciliatan.com to read the full serialized Chronicles for free online! In addition to many chapters beyond where this volume ends, readers will also find "liner notes" explaining background stuff and history, links to cool music and videos, bonus chapters, and more. Plus, Daron answers comments that are left for him on the website.

Acknowledgements

Thanks to the following folks who backed the Kickstarter that made this book possible. Their support paid the copyeditor, layout artist, cover designer, and the cost of the first print run of hardcopies. I'd also like to thank the fans of Daron and Ziggy for helping Daron's Guitar Chronicles to grow in other ways, too, in particular: Alan, Amanda, Bill, Chris K, Chris S, Lena, and Sanders, as well as the folks who have showed up at my house to pack Kickstarter orders the past two times, and whoever might turn up this time, too! YOU ROCK!

Alex
Alyse
Amanda Kay
Amanda Kelly
Amber Bell
Amber Goad
Amy Crook
Andrea G.
Andrew and Kate Barton
Andrew Hatchell
Ann-Kathrin N
Annabeth Leong
B. Cynic
Barbara Griffin
Beener
Beth
Beth K
Bill Campbell
Brian Cherry
cayra
Cheryl Trooskin-Zoller
Chris Cox
Chris DeKalb
Chris K.
Cris McIntyre
Dave Axler
David Thompson
Deb Atwood
Deborah Holzapfel
Dr.Chris Radio of Horror
G
Hanne Flatoey
JB Starre
Jeffrey Bledsoe
Joe Casadonte
Joel Ablett
John Bronston
John Frewin
Jonathan Woodward
Julie Cox
Kerri Smith
Kirasha Urqhart
Lenalena
M.C.A. Hogarth
Madeline Elayne
Maelia
Maggie
Mary M. Jones
Meghan Coyne
Melanie Campbell
Michael Cavallo
Nona Farris
Rebecca B.
Ronda D. Dennis
Sanders
Sheryl Dee
Stacey V
Stef
Steve
T. Horne
Trevor Beard
tzinnamon
Warren Lapine

Made in the USA
San Bernardino, CA
16 April 2017